Tony Warren is a former actor who turned into Britain's youngest scriptwriter. In 1960 he created *Coronation Street* and wrote all the early episodes. He also devised the film *Ferry 'Cross the Mersey*. At the end of the 60s he disappeared from the public eye, though the following decade of drink and drug addiction has been well chronicled by the tabloid newspapers. He abandoned these addictions over ten years ago. *The Lights of Manchester* represents his first piece of major creative writing since his recovery. Nowadays Tony Warren is consultant to *Coronation Street* and lives in Manchester.

THE LIGHTS OF MANCHESTER

Tony Warren

ARROW

Published by Arrow Books Limited
20 Vauxhall Bridge Road, London SW1V 2SA

An imprint of Random House UK Ltd

London Melbourne Sydney Auckland Johannesburg
and agencies throughout the world

First published in Great Britain by Century in 1991
Arrow edition 1992

3 5 7 9 10 8 6 4 2

Photoset by Delatype Ltd, Ellesmere Port
Printed and bound in Great Britain by
Cox & Wyman Ltd, Reading, Berks

ISBN 0 09 997190 9

For Mary Redman
with love

Author's note

Angel Dwellings is not *Coronation Street*. Sorrel Starkey is no actress I have ever known. I am not Mickey Grimshaw. Manchester *is*, I hope, Manchester.

Tony Warren

BOOK ONE

SHEILA INTO SORREL

Prologue

You're nowt a pound, in Manchester, if the flower seller in St Ann's Square doesn't nod as you pass. This morning he waved. Heads turned to look at the object of his interest just as people will bend and peer to see who is inside a passing Rolls-Royce.

Sorrel Starkey did not mind this attention. She had not gone into showbusiness to pass unnoticed. Manchester was welcome to stare as much as it liked, for Manchester had made her.

Sorrel paused and looked at her own reflection in Mappin and Webb, the jeweller's, window. Did it show? The happiness inside her was so new and so strong that she felt it should be shining out of her, like a searchlight. Once in a lifetime, everybody should be allowed to feel like this. She felt in tune with the entire world and her feet were on the pavements of the city she loved most on earth.

Sorrel's reflection shone back at her. It was very difficult to put an age on it: slim enough, elegant enough and she had been wise to let the hair go to ash blonde. The face was still all eyes but it didn't shout too loudly of plastic surgeons. She looked what she was, a queen of television soap opera.

With the sun still shining, light snow began to fall as she passed into King Street. Laura Ashley and Next, it could have been any prosperous shopping thoroughfare in England – except for the collapsible music stands on every corner. These are one of the hazards of Christmas shopping in Manchester and one of its delights. Students from three colleges of music fill the air with carols. Solitary oboists in doorholes, brass ensembles outside the Royal Exchange – the chances are that some of the voices raised in song will end up in the great opera houses of the world. This was not, it seemed, one of the years when the police were willing to tolerate the musicians.

'Now I'm not going to tell you lot again. Move on.'

'Don't be so mean,' said Sorrel, who had not always been a famous lady in a thousand-pound cashmere coat. She too had been ragged-arsed but merry. She thrust a fiver into a tin can and smiled at the four musicians who looked like intelligent Hell's Angels carrying silver trumpets.

Had been merry? *Had* been? As some unseen hand switched on the overhead Christmas illuminations and the snow sparkled past the coloured light bulbs, Sorrel stifled the urge to say: 'You don't know it but you are looking at the luckiest woman on earth.'

'I'm only doing my job, Lettie,' said the policeman anxiously to Sorrel as he pointed to the students of music.

'I am not Lettie,' the actress replied patiently. 'Lettie Bly is a character I have played, for twenty-eight long years, on television. This is real life.'

'I'm sorry, Miss Starkey,' said the policeman. Lettie Bly or Sorrel Starkey, the wrath of either was famous. Not for nothing did her enemies call her Madam Manchester.

'Look, you lads, I'm going once round the block, once mind you, and when I come back . . .' The policeman winked at Sorrel.

'What's going to happen in *Angel Dwellings*, Lettie?' asked the trumpet student with the shaved head.

'Keep watching every Tuesday and Thursday and please don't play the theme music.'

All grins, with one accord they raised their instruments and broke into 'Tenement Symphony'.

'Bastards,' said Sorrel. But she said it with love. Long experience also caused her to glance around. It would only take one person to ask for an autograph for half the street to come running.

A woman smiled at her, nodded across the road and said, 'I see our celebrities are out in force this morning.' She was beaming in the direction of a portly man tipping his suede trilby hat politely at Sorrel.

It was Bryan Mosley, Alf Roberts from *Coronation Street*. Sorrel waved back. These days there was little rivalry between the two shows. Both were institutions in their own right. But what was Bryan pointing at?

4

King Street is a paved walkway so it was easy to cross over and join him. Sorrel reminded herself that she must, for the moment, keep her new happiness and excitement to herself. The casts of television serials are like families. It wouldn't do for her news to get round the *Coronation Street* set before anybody knew in *Angel Dwellings*.

''Ow do,' said Bryan, still pointing significantly up the street and looking at her expectantly.

'Mornin', love,' replied Sorrel. In private life with one another, Manchester actors always overdo the Lancashire accent. Actually, Bryan was Yorkshire which was another reason why she didn't want to seem thick. So what the hell was she supposed to be noticing?

'He's spotted you now. He's putting on a turn of speed,' said Bryan Mosley, like some racing commentator.

Sorrel heard flying footsteps getting closer and her first thought was that a mugger was on the loose. Then she saw him. A tall man, with a very short haircut and a very large tweed overcoat, scattering indignant shoppers as he rushed towards her with arms outstretched. It was Mickey Grimshaw, the biggest single influence in Sorrel Starkey's whole life. Her best friend too and she hadn't seen him for a long time.

'Thought you'd be pleased,' said Bryan. 'Happy birthday. See you both at the jollifications.'

Now Mickey had his arms around her and they were in a great big tweed and cashmere hug. They were both laughing and Sorrel feared for her makeup because she was crying a bit too but these were happy tears. They were hugging in a way which makes being in the theatre different from being in any other business on earth. Though television had brought them both success they still thought of themselves as of the theatre. There was belonging in this reunion and shared striving and memories of younger years when mutual affection had been all they'd had. Yet they didn't hold one another like people who had been lovers. Whatever it was they shared was something way above physical attraction.

Sorrel loved Mickey and Mickey loved Sorrel and it infuriated people that these two parts of an obvious whole had never married. Sorrel would have viewed such a union as incestuous; besides, Mickey wasn't the marrying kind.

'You bought a ticket and came. Oh Mickey, you came.' It was Mickey who had originally dreamed up *Angel Dwellings* and given her the part of Lettie Bly but they had known one another far longer than that.

'All the way from America. Happy birthday to us. What's more, I've flown in with hot news . . .'

'It can't be as hot as my news,' said Sorrel a bit smugly.

'When I've come to change your life?'

Sorrel pulled away from him and looked worried. This was the one morning of a lifetime when she wanted things exactly as they were. No changes; none at all. Mickey could be loving and giving and he could also be totally disruptive. Newspapers were prone to describe him as 'Sorrel Starkey's personal Svengali'. She knew that look of old. As a boy, he had always reminded her of a young eagle. Mickey had come back to Manchester with his mind made up about something.

The snow was turning to sleet and whoever it was who switched on the overhead lights must have decided that the Christmas dress rehearsal had gone on for long enough, for now they went out. It was everyday King Street again and it was cold.

Sorrel put up her collar. 'Let me tell you my news . . .' She hadn't told a soul. She had meant this first announcement to be triumphant, not a defence measure.

'Me first. Have *you* spent a whole month convincing American Actors' Equity that a certain British actress is a big enough star to come out to LA and play the lead in my brand-new American series?' Mickey was ablaze with triumph.

'Let's go to Meng and Ecker and have a cup of coffee,' said Sorrel nervously.

'Dear God in heaven!' roared Mickey. 'I offer the woman Hollywood and all she can think about is morning coffee . . .'

'I don't know that I want to go to America,' said Sorrel in a wretched voice which gave little indication of the turmoil whirring within. 'Hollywood, and he means it. Hollywood at this late date.' Manchester was all of her belonging, now more

6

than ever. But Hollywood with Mickey . . . That would be another of their childhood dreams come true. She felt awful. It was like thinking with two heads.

'We're going to have an enormous success,' said Mickey, as if that was that. 'I need you. They're even prepared to buy out your *Angel Dwellings* contract. It's the best woman's part I've ever written and I need you. We go back, Sorrel . . .'

'I hate that expression,' Sorrel interrupted him. 'I don't know why but I hate it.'

In truth she feared it. In a minute he could be saying something he'd never said. In a minute 'We go back' could turn into 'You owe me'. And it would be no less than the truth.

'Tell me your own news.' His eyes were not unkind but Sorrel knew Mickey through and through. In this mood he would take anything she said and use it to shore up his own inexorable purpose. Even Mickey Grimshaw wasn't having her happiness for that.

'Not here, Mick. Not out in the wet.'

'Then let's go and have that coffee then. You'd better be warned though; I haven't come all this way to let you stamp on yet another opportunity. Not this time. And stop looking at me as though I was the enemy. You couldn't manage a flea circus, Sorrel – let alone your own life. And don't look magnificently hurt either. I know all your tricks. I taught you half of them myself. Come to think about it, I'm probably about the only one left who remembers you when you were still called *Sheila* Starkey.'

1

In 1944 Sheila Starkey was eight years old. She was
constantly assured, at Sunday school, that Jesus loved her.
The only proof she had of this was that he certainly seemed to
have spread out her treats, very considerately, over the year.
Sheila's birthday always came absolutely midway between
two Christmases. A month after her birthday, life took
another exciting leap when Sheila and her mother went away
on their annual holiday.

As the train chugged across Lancashire the wheels seemed
to be saying 'See you today, see you today, see you today.' It
was like that woman on the wireless who was always singing
that she was going to see somebody today and she was
treading on air and the people that she met, as she hurried
down the street, seemed to know she was on her way . . .
coming to you. It was exactly how Sheila felt about Blackpool.

The journey had its rituals. She never counted herself as
truly on holiday until she'd seen the two men, in the field,
carrying the ladder. This was a life-sized, painted plywood
cut-out. It advertised The Leyland Paint Co. To a whole
generation of Lancashire children that ladder was an arrow
pointing to a week of magic; or even a fortnight if you were a
little bit on the posh side, like the Starkeys.

Their compartment was in a carriage near to the front of
the train. It had faded blue moquette upholstery which
smelled of ancient cigarette smoke. The same smell which
sometimes hit you if you were first in at the pictures, before
the usherettes came round spraying everything with 'June'.
Sheila associated the smell of old cigarette smoke with
approaching excitements.

Above the seats were framed sepia photographs. This year
they were of Hunstanton and Gorleston-on-Sea. Why were
they always places in the opposite direction to which the train
was travelling? Always; still, they were confirmation that

everything was as it should be. Now Sheila was looking out of the window for the biggest landmark of all, Blackpool Tower.

People who didn't know better would point to some iron pylon, on the horizon, and think they'd succeeded in spotting it. Not Sheila; she knew exactly where the first glimpse came. It was between some hawthorn hedges, at the side of a five-barred gate. Only, this year, they were towards the front of the train and great clouds of steam kept passing the window and obscuring the view . . . and there, gloriously, it was; shining in the sunlight. Just as suddenly it was gone again.

'I claim the sixpence,' yelled Sheila triumphantly. 'Shh,' said her mother, out of the side of her mouth. 'We're in first class.'

The other passengers smiled and Sheila wasn't sure whether it was at herself or her mother. Privately, she considered her mother a woman capable of stopping birds from singing. But that didn't mean she wanted other people laughing at her. A man in an officer's uniform, topped off with a parson's dog collar, fished in his pocket and handed Sheila a silver sixpence.

'How you took me back,' he smiled. 'We always claimed sixpence, for being first to see the tower, when I was small.'

Sheila watched her mother relax. If posh parsons did it, it must be OK. They were only in first class because Sheila's father was also an officer and the travel warrant for their journey had allowed them to travel in these privileged seats for the same price as the third-class fare.

Mostly Sheila wished she wasn't an officer's daughter. It set her aside from other children at the council school. Everybody at school had a label and hers was 'Always in concerts. Her daddy's an officer.' There was a downright sneer in the choice of the title *Daddy*. The others had dads and warm, rounded mums who met them with hugs at the school gates. Honesty forced Sheila to admit that her own mother was outside the gates too. But thrust a lovingly painted picture at her and she would just fold it up like something that didn't matter – creases right down the middle. Gladys Starkey was also given to picking imaginary bits of fluff off Sheila's good reefer coat, a garment that drew sniggers in the school playground. Other children wore wartime reach-me-downs. Mrs Starkey hoarded clothing coupons in order to be able to send her daughter to school dressed like an imitation Princess Margaret Rose.

It seemed to Sheila that her mother was, hourly, expecting General Montgomery to turn up at their house and inspect them. Was she scared the General would discover that the wife and child of one of his officers were not quite the genuine article? Loudly as Mrs Starkey protested about the long enforced separation from her husband, Sheila knew his wife was relieved that he was being an officer at a distance. This meant that she didn't have to go to high-class do's where she might show Captain Starkey up. Quite what these do's were Sheila didn't know. She was, however, instinctive enough to realize that Gladys Starkey's fears were entirely groundless. With her looks and candour Sheila's mother could have held her own in Buckingham Palace.

Gladys Starkey looked a bit like Bette Davis but it would have taken Technicolor to do her real justice. The hair was dark red against white skin and her eyes were green. Not halfway green but genuine green, like a sucked Rowntree's wine gum, only beautiful.

The ten o'clock was a fast train. It sped past the windmills on The Fylde and Sheila's heart beat faster at the first glimpse, through sandhills, of the Big Dipper on the Pleasure Beach. She always felt that the approach to Blackpool North station was heralded by trumpets in words. These were painted onto the sooty brickwork of boarding houses backing onto the railway line.

Holmleigh – Friendly and Comfortable. 'Maybert' (Visitors from Oldham Especially Welcome) Mrs Tinsley – Boarding Establishment – Thirty Shillings per week: 'All Found'.

The train was grinding to a halt with an iron noise like twenty squealing dogs. Sheila and her mother were already on their feet and making for the corridor. First class not being chatty there were no goodbyes but Sheila managed to smile at the parson who understood about the sixpence.

The station's great span of glass archway had been blacked out with paint for the duration of the war. The only illumination came from dim gas mantles against sign boards and the occasional naked electric bulb, high up above. Sheila already had the door window down. Huge belches of steam, notorious for carrying blobs of soot and big bits of grit, were pumping back from the engine. Sheila found it all wonderfully exciting.

Slipping into a familiar routine, she held onto her mother's hand as they descended from the wooden running board onto the platform. Together they ran for the barrier. Their one passionate aim was to get to the top of the taxi queue before anybody else. That's why their luggage was always sent on ahead by Carter Paterson's van.

Getting through the ticket barrier was easy enough but the main booking hall was crammed solid with soldiers and airmen and snaking queues of families sitting on their own suitcases. The sight of returning holidaymakers always made Sheila feel temporarily sad. Their fun was over whilst hers was just beginning – and they were singing 'It's a Long Way to Tipperary', which somehow made things even worse.

Now they were through the crush and outside. The gloom of the station and its dank smell gave way to brilliant sunshine and giddy Blackpool air. There was a breeze coming in from the sea. Sheila filled her lungs with air that was newer than the air in Manchester but already, excitingly, mingled with the aromas of chip-shop vinegar and beerhouses with their doors open.

The tower was very near now and absolutely enormous. Only minutes ago it had been like a sharpened pencil on the horizon. Now its maroon-painted cast-iron rigging seemed to reach up into the air for miles. Getting to heaven must be a bit like this, thought Sheila. What's more they were right at the head of the taxi queue and there was one coming up from the seafront. This should surely put her mother in a good mood?

'When the papers fly round in Blackpool,' said Gladys Starkey, 'it's a sure sign it's going to rain.'

The taxi carried them up the back road, behind the big hotels which fronted onto the promenade, and on towards the Derby Baths. All the larger hotels had been requisitioned by government departments and turned into temporary offices.

11

'Funny to think of the income tax being in Blackpool, isn't it?' said Mrs Starkey conversationally to the driver.

The driver was plainly the kind who liked talking over his shoulder. 'We've had the lot here. Everything from cockney evacuees to Yanks. Polish airforce, they're the latest. Blackpool? Some afternoons that Tower Ballroom's more like the League of Nations.' Then he mentioned something puzzling about the birthrate. Mrs Starkey stiffened at this and plainly went off him.

The taxi was turning into Balsam Road and Sheila experienced that wonderfully complete feeling of being at the right time in the right place. Nothing had altered since last year. Balsam Road was terraced. But terraced in a lofty Edwardian, glazed red brick trimmed with sandstone, manner. Each house had a short front garden. The iron railings had of course been taken away, when Sheila was still a baby, to be turned into armaments.

French marigolds, white rock and blue lobelia – all the garden paths were edged with little clumps of these same flowers. Sheila was checking her landmarks; plumes of pampas grass in the garden of one house, a stained-glass window, decorated with a bunch of purple grapes, set into the front door of another. Many of the doors were covered with faded curtains of striped deckchair canvas. This was to prevent the paintwork from blistering. Gloss paint was as scarce as sugar. All of these houses were boarding establishments but there wasn't so much as a *No Vacancies* card, in a front window, to suggest it. This was, after all, North Shore. Why, it was almost Bispham. It went without saying that wet bathing costumes were never hung out of the window to dry in Balsam Road.

Not that Balsam Road swanked. Number 28 may have had *Juliana* chiselled into the stone gatepost but it was always known to paying guests as 'Mr Tuffin's'. And there he was on the front doorstep, big and bald with muscular arms folded over a generous belly. Seaside landladies' husbands were said to go down into the cellar at Whitsuntide, begin peeling potatoes, and never see the light of day again until October. Not Mr Tuffin. His wife only had one eye and she walked with a stick so her husband ran number 28 himself. And he ran it with a rod of iron.

As Sheila and Gladys emerged from the taxi Mr Tuffin already had one hand outstretched: 'Ration books please.'

Sheila flew up the garden path and flung herself at him with love. Mr Tuffin affected a very gloomy disposition but she knew that this was an act, designed to conceal a warm heart. His apron smelled of the same bleach he used to scrub down the kitchen. Sheila knew the kitchen well. Starkeys were privileged guests who were allowed behind the green baize door, to help with the washing-up. This was a signal honour at Mr Tuffin's.

'Have you got Polish airmen?' asked Sheila excitedly. 'We've just heard they're the latest.' All holiday landlords were expected to take their quota of billetees.

'Guinea pigs,' said Mr Tuffin. 'Morning, Mrs Starkey. Your luggage is upstairs. I'm just saying we've been landed with guinea pigs. Civil servants. The government pays me a guinea a week.'

'Aren't there any real visitors?' Sheila asked anxiously.

'Too many,' said Mr Tuffin dourly. 'One more season and I'm shutting shop.'

He always said that. It was all gloriously familiar. The same people tended to take the same rooms for the same weeks each year. The varnished paper sunshade was still in the hallstand, the garden chairs were stacked in the recess behind the door. Buckets and spades and paddling shoes had to be left there too.

'All the regulars here?' asked Mrs Starkey.

'Not Mrs Gash. She's gone to God. None too soon if you ask me. Mr Gash must have got nearly sick of waiting for her.'

'I put clean sheets in our luggage,' said Mrs Starkey. 'I know the war's put a great strain on your own.'

'Can I go and get Dinah?' asked Sheila.

Dinah had belonged to Mr Tuffin's married daughter. As Mrs Starkey never allowed Sheila to pack her teddybear, she always borrowed this black plush doll.

'Bit of a problem there. A boy's already got it.'

'A boy? What sort of boy?' Disbelief and jealousy were mixed in Sheila's question.

13

'Manners!' said her mother warningly.

'A rum sort of boy and no mistake. They're new people. Always went across the road to Mrs Mather but she's chock-a-block with landgirls. I'm only obliging. The mother's the size of a gasometer.'

Mrs Starkey handed over their ration books and asked, 'Are we in our usual rooms?'

'No. I've put her and the boy in there. Wasn't giving you the chance to go putting a towel over my good Jesus picture again.' This was said with narrowed eyes.

So he knew about the towel. Sheila's mother had said he would be bound to find out. The Tuffins were a bit High Church. The framed picture in question was of the face of Jesus. An inscription on the mount read *St Peter's Pocket Handkerchief: Gaze into the eyes of our Lord and they will follow you around the room.*

It even watched you while you got undressed. It terrified Sheila so her mother had covered it up with a little handtowel. It was all part of the holiday, though. Why should this new boy have the scary picture as well as having Dinah? It wasn't fair.

'I've put you in the first-floor front. And *you* can borrow a china pig,' he said to Sheila.

How could you cuddle a china pig? Mr Tuffin usually showed more imagination than that.

'Tell you what,' he said, 'I'll take your mother upstairs. Go in the front room and have a word with the little lad. Perhaps you can come to some sort of understanding. But don't hit him, Sheila. I won't have fisticuffs.'

Sheila felt better. It was nice when somebody understood you as well as Mr Tuffin did. She pushed open the door of the front room. A boy was sitting on the red Turkey hearthrug. He had the Dinah doll in one hand and a cast-iron doorstop, in the shape of Mr Punch, in the other.

'I'm thinking of having a puppet show,' he said. 'I'm Mick.'

And that is how Sheila Starkey met Mickey Grimshaw for the very first time. She was immediately fascinated by his eyes. They were the first thing everybody noticed about Mickey, for one was blue and the other eye green. It had the effect of making him seem to be brimming with excitement.

Once you got used to it, it was as though he could never, conceivably, have been designed any other way.

'Where are you from?' asked this very confident boy.

'Outside Manchester. You go through Salford and through Pendleton and just beyond Irlams o'th' Height . . .'

'But we live at The Height too.'

'Where?' Sheila was nearly shouting with excitement. This wonderfully odd-looking boy who could do puppet shows in Mr Tuffin's front room wasn't just going to be a friend for the holidays. He came from The Height. Sheila would always remember that, the moment she met Mickey, she *knew* him. It was almost as though some hidden part of her had been waiting for him to turn up. What is more she knew, beyond any shadow of doubt, that she would care for him enormously. Not like she loved Peter Bromiley, the best-looking and kindest boy in her school – more the way she felt about next door's dog Duke Tatton. She wasn't allowed to have a dog of her own so her feelings for Duke ran very deep and she always craved his approval. Only Mickey wasn't a dog, he was a catlike animal inside human skin. She knew that too.

'We live in Paloma Drive on the Dogdene Estate,' said Mickey.

'We live in Rookswood Avenue on Ravensdale Estate,' gasped Sheila. They were only divided by two main roads and a public park.

'I hate estates,' said Mickey. 'Why do they have to paint everything green and cream?'

'Except for the houses that are painted brown and cream,' said Sheila. 'And why do all the garden hedges have to be privet? Nothing but gloomy privet for miles and miles. It even tastes awful.'

'Have you tried it too?' asked Mickey. 'One day I'm going to get away. I'm not much struck on respectability.'

'Me neither,' said Sheila fervently. This boy was putting into words a lot of things she had always felt.

'When I grow up I'm going on the stage.' Mickey put Mr Punch by the door and handed Dinah to Sheila. 'You can have this if you want. Not for keeps. It's theirs.'

'I know.' What did a doll matter now? 'You mean you're going to be in concerts all the time for a living?'

'Plays, concerts, everything.'

'Could I do that too?' This was the most solemn question Sheila had ever asked. 'Could I? I'm the best in our school only I never say so because people call it swanking.'

'They call me precocious,' said Mickey glumly. 'Yes, you could do it too. I expect one day we'll both be famous together. Did you know that, if you get up early enough, you can see them taking camels from the Tower Circus for a walk along the beach?'

The sitting room door was pushed further open and one of the largest women Sheila had ever seen came into the room. Her great size was emphasized by the large blue and black printed design on her crepe-de-Chine frock. She had an air of confidence, even of power, about her.

'I'm Mickey's mummy,' she said.

Sheila marvelled. Somebody else in Irlams o'th' Height was forced to say 'Mummy' too.

'I expect you're thinking I'm a very big lady?'

'No,' said Sheila politely.

'Course you are,' said Mick. 'My eyes and her size – we should be in a sideshow on the Golden Mile.'

Mickey was plainly allowed to get away with far more than Sheila because all his mother said was 'It's glandular. I always think it better to mention it first.'

'Do they allow you extra clothing coupons?' asked Sheila, fascinated.

Gladys Starkey had slipped into the room quickly enough to hiss 'Manners!'

'I was just explaining my size.' Mickey's mother was quite unperturbed. 'It runs in the family but skips a generation. I expect Mickey's children will be enormous but maybe they will have found something by then. I'm Mrs Grimshaw, call me Beryl.'

Sheila held her breath. Under similar circumstances she had known her mother to say 'I'd rather wait, thank you.' Today she was plainly in holiday mood because she simply held out her hand and said: 'Gladys Starkey.'

16

'I shall call you Glad,' beamed Mrs Grimshaw.

'I'd rather you didn't. I take it hubby isn't with you?'

Sheila thought this was awful. For all her mother knew the man might be dead.

'Work of National Importance,' said Mrs Grimshaw.

'At the gas works,' piped up Mickey.

'Captain Starkey's with the Eighth Army.'

Sheila began to pray, inwardly, that her mother wouldn't start putting it on and ruin everything. The odd-eyed boy just grinned conspiratorially.

'I expect he rose up from the ranks,' said Mrs Grimshaw confidently. 'In the First World War they called them "temporary gentlemen".'

Gladys Starkey didn't answer back with words. Instead, she took a firm step towards Beryl Grimshaw's great bulk, raised her nose significantly, and gave a very cautious sniff.

It was below the belt, thought Sheila, but she had to admit that her mother was winning on points. Mrs Grimshaw did not appear discomfited except for her neck. It was mottling furiously.

'It's war,' said Mickey, under his breath.

'Gangway for a wounded soldier,' came a cry from the hall. The table in the bay window was already set for one o'clock dinner. Poor pale Mrs Tuffin limped in, on her stick, carrying a plate of ready buttered bread. Mrs Tuffin was famous for cutting bread. She could get it like wedding veils. Bread wasn't the only thing she dispensed. She also kept people abreast of the latest war news.

'Sound the gong, Sheila,' she said. 'Them as is late down will simply have to do without the headlines.' She cleared her throat and then announced in an important voice: 'Hitler has lost his trousers.

'I'm not being indelicate. It's not my style. Some German generals, it seems, tried to blow up the Führer but they made a pig's knee of it. They said on the wireless that reports are reaching them that the bomb blast blew off everybody's pants – Adolf's included. He is said to be rattled, angered and awaiting the arrival of Mussolini.'

17

'Shall we have a quick chorus of "There'll Always Be an England"?' asked Sheila.

'But is it just government propaganda to make us feel better?' cried Mrs Grimshaw.

'It was Stuart Hibbert reading the news,' said Mrs Tuffin reproachfully.

'And when it comes to inside information' – Gladys was very much the serving officer's wife – 'our fifth column is every bit as good as their fifth column.'

Beryl Grimshaw broke wind very delicately. 'I beg your pardon,' she said. But she didn't mean it.

A fortnight, of course, goes on much longer when you are eight. In that space of time Sheila absorbed most of Mickey's stage-struck attitudes and ambitions. It was as though she already owned one of those Pollock's cut-out theatre books and he was showing her how to use the scissors and glue it together and make it work. That summer holiday Mickey Grimshaw handed Sheila Starkey a licence to be herself.

She had always loved the golden glow that came from the audience at school plays and Sunday school concerts. Mickey found this entirely natural – it warmed him too. They were still young enough to try to put these thoughts into words without inhibition.

'Being on the stage is like paid showing-off,' said Mickey, 'so don't expect your mother to like it.'

Gladys Starkey did not like it. She didn't like it one little bit. She had already taken to referring to Mickey as 'that boy'.

'They're not his own ideas, Sheila.'

'They are!' said Sheila, already fierce in her loyalty.

'He gets them from his mother. She's already told me, but for her size, she'd have been the next Anna Pavlova. She even makes him go to tapdancing classes.'

'She doesn't make him. He wants to. Can I go too?'

'No you can't. Tap dancing's common. But don't you dare tell Mrs Grimshaw I said that. Tap dancing? Where d'you want to end up? In the Tower Children's Ballet?'

'I'd love it,' said Sheila.

Mr Tuffin, however, was not against the new friendship.

He was a man of firm likes and dislikes and he had decided that Mickey Grimshaw was all right. That was as enthusiastic as Mr Tuffin ever got but he ruled in his own kingdom, so Mrs Starkey could hardly refuse to let her daughter play with the boy. In 1944 children were allowed to roam very freely. Blackpool had eight theatres, a circus, and a skating show at the Icedrome. Mickey and Sheila examined all of these buildings closely, as though the very bricks and mortar might give off some of the theatrical magic hidden inside.

Sid Fields, the comedian, was at the Opera House in *Look Who's Here*. Sheila and Mickey knew every detail of the photographs outside the theatre. They were very glossy and retouched, with each eyelash painted on separately. The stage door was up a glass arcade leading into the Winter Gardens. A grumpy old commissionaire, in a blue uniform with gold braid, seemed to have been employed especially to chase the two children away.

Nothing daunted, they would bounce downhill to Feldman's Music Hall, an altogether lower class of establishment where standards were more lackadaisical. The photographs in their display cases were sometimes a bit battered and held in place by drawing pins. Unlike the other Blackpool theatres, shows at Feldman's only played for one week before moving on to another town. This music hall had one very definite lure. Go round to the back of the theatre and there was both a stage door entrance and another pair of doors – huge wooden ones. Scenery could be carried through these and down a ramp onto the stage. At just the right height for an eight-year-old, somebody had pushed in a knot in the grain of the wood. It had created a very generous peephole. Mickey and Sheila took it in turns to peer down onto performing xylophonists and crooners and even onto a lady taking her clothes off, to music, in a beautiful pink spotlight.

'I think we can see more of her titties than people who've paid,' said Mickey. 'Better not mention this at Mr Tuffin's.'

Sheila very much admired the way Mickey called a titty a titty. He didn't make it sound like talking rude. He was just matter-of-fact. Her own mother wouldn't so much as mention the word 'bust' without first clearing her throat.

19

From Feldman's they always went to the North Pier which was admission one penny. In their considered opinion, well worth it because the stars of *On With the Show* had to walk the full length of the pier, on open view, to get to their theatre. Happily copying Mickey, Sheila had used some of her holiday spends to buy an autograph album. They both had the leading comedian Dave Morris's signature, five times over. He was a jolly man in a straw boater, with thick glasses like the bottoms of pop bottles. He didn't seem to notice that they dogged his footsteps and tried to overhear what he was saying to his henchmen. Intriguing snippets like 'She's a disgrace to the bloody profession. One night I'm going to throw the gin bottle, onstage, after her.'

Today there would be no following anybody. It was nearly half past four by Woolworth's clock, over on the promenade. All the performers would be in the pier pavilion giving a matinée. It was a grey afternoon, of high tide and crying seagulls, circling the lead domes and minarets on top of the wind shelters of the North Pier. Sheila remembered to be afraid of the pier again. She had no qualms about the iron framework, that was sturdy enough. But you walked on planks, laid edge to edge, and between the planks were narrow gaps and through the gaps it was possible to see the sea, swelling and churning, a hundred feet below. Although there were always men repairing and replacing the planks, what if you put your foot on one they'd overlooked? What if you went *through*?

It was the Friday of the second week of the holidays. Last weekend it had seemed as though they would last for ever. By Wednesday the days were beginning to be tinged with a little 'going home' sadness. Come Friday afternoon everything had a last-time quality to it. This had been morbidly emphasized by Gladys Starkey who had instructed her daughter to go out and breathe in the ozone: 'It's the last you'll smell of it for another year.'

The pier was almost deserted as Sheila and Mickey clomped along it towards the fishing jetty. A pale old man with mad hair, pushing a bicycle, walked past them. He was better than nothing. This was Toni who ran the North Pier Alfresco

Orchestra. They didn't ask for his autograph, musicians didn't count. Anyway, they were deep in a discussion about the fancy costumes and would they get them?

One of Mr Tuffin's guinea pigs had a mother called Mrs Adair who was also staying in the boarding house but paying the full rate. The only thing Mickey and Sheila's mothers were united in was their dislike of this woman.

'She doesn't explain her complexion, to my satisfaction, by saying she's lived in Calcutta. There's a touch of the tar brush there,' said Mrs Grimshaw accusingly.

'Her stories of Dieppe are very far-fetched. I think the woman's a bit of a romancer,' charged Gladys Starkey. It was a polite way of calling her a liar.

Mrs Adair may have been vague and untidy and given to trimming her own hats whilst claiming they were Paris models – but had she fibbed about the costumes? She came from Putney Heath where, she maintained, she had mounted glorious dramatic pageants. All of this had been before the war. As a result, she now had a garage simply crammed with fancy-dress costumes. To Sheila and Mickey, the idea of these was infinitely more desirable than endless toffee coupons.

'It's like Aladdin's cave in that old garage of mine,' said Mrs Adair. 'You can't move for spangles. Tell you what, when I go back, I'll pick a couple out and forward them on to you.'

The two children had eagerly written their addresses down in her pocket diary. Their mothers were openly sceptical of their ever seeing the colour of Mrs Adair's sequins. Gladys Starkey sniggered and said, 'I wouldn't go giving her postage!'

'I'm only worried that she's got our address,' said Beryl Grimshaw. 'She's the kind who might turn up on the doorstep and want something.'

Mickey was of the opinion that Mrs Adair was a giver not a taker. After all, she'd bumped into them on the tram, one day, and insisted upon paying their fares.

'And she gave that photographer's monkey a bit of her chocolate ration,' said Sheila, who thought this spoke volumes for Mrs Adair's character. But would she send the costumes? As soon as they got back to Manchester they planned to put on concerts, in Mickey's back garden. With Mr Churchill's government telling everybody to *Make Do and Mend*, dressing-up boxes were fast becoming things of the past.

'Help . . .' Was it a seagull? Sometimes their cries sounded like real words.

'Help. Please somebody help me.' Even blown on the breeze, there was no mistaking that for anything but a real voice – a woman's voice.

'Cows! I'll murder you when I get hold of you . . .'

Sheila and Mickey quickened their steps. The voice was coming from somewhere beyond the pier pavilion. Hurrying past the stage door, they glanced up some wooden steps to the side of it. A railed walkway, overhanging the sea, ran round the whole building; and there was the woman in distress. A peroxide blonde, she was tied to the rail with a dressing gown cord. Yellow and white ostrich features, in her hair, were blowing furiously in the breeze. Her face was vividly painted. Her tight gold lamé evening dress was split to the thigh, revealing pure silk tights and white court shoes with elastic across the instep.

'She's got little red dots painted in the corners of her eyes,' whispered Sheila.

'It's one of the chorus girls,' said Mickey, awed. He knew this because his mother had taken him to see *On With the Show*.

'Don't just stand there. Bloody well untie me.'

'Who did it?' Mickey was struggling with the knots.

'The other girls, the bitches. Pardon the French but I've missed the finale. They've fixed it so he'll fine me. He'll definitely fine me.'

'Who will?' asked Mickey. 'And keep still or you'll only make the knots tighter. Who will fine you?'

'The stage manager.' The chorus girl was raging again: 'I never pinched her Yank. If I want GIs I can get GIs of my own. Like that!' She snapped her fingers, the knots were untied. 'You two are coming with me. Witnesses, that's what's called for . . .'

'Coming where?' asked Sheila. She was hoping against hope, and not quite daring to believe, that it would be through the stage door.

'Inside. I'm relying on you two to tell Mr Sonny Hinchcliffe just what state you found me in.'

Sheila and Mickey didn't walk through their first stage door, they were pushed. The young woman kicked the swing door inwards and bundled them down a corridor, through another swing door and up some steps. It was almost unbelievable. One minute they'd been walking down the pier and now they were in the wings of the stage. An orchestra was playing jaunty music in the distance. More people in gold and yellow costumes, with bright orange faces, were streaming towards them, undoing collars and removing jackets. On the stage itself, spotlights began to go out.

'It must be just over,' said Mickey in the kind of voice other people use in church.

An angry little man, like a gnat, buzzed up to them. He was in shirtsleeves with metal armbands and he was not wearing makeup. The only theatrical thing about him was a spotted bow tie.

'Who are these? And just what d'you think your bloody game is, Bernice? Where were you for the finale?'

'She was tied to the pier,' said Sheila who felt she ought to justify their presence before they got thrown out of heaven.

'This true?' said the man to Mickey. He plainly preferred dealing with men.

'Absolutely. I untied her.'

'It's worse than running a knocking shop,' sighed the stage manager. 'I wouldn't care, I used to be with the Carl Rosa Opera Company. I'm very much obliged to you. Both of you. Got kiddies of my own, back in Streatham. Missing them like hell. Don't suppose you'd like a bit of a conducted tour?'

It was too much for words; with shining eyes they just about managed to nod. He showed them the revolving stage and all the scenery stacked against the back wall. He explained how the trap door worked. It was used to shoot Dave Morris up from the bowels of the earth. Mr Hinchcliffe, he'd introduced himself by now, gave them mint imperials to suck and got somebody to make the lights go up and down and change colours. He even raised the curtain and let them try out a microphone. Sheila sang a chorus of 'Tell Me Lilac Domino' to the rows of empty seats and Mickey recited the last part of 'Where Are You Going to All You Big Steamers?'

'Very nicely spoken,' said Mr Hinchcliffe. 'Some nights I think this theatre's like a big steamer. One more blast of wind and we could all be heading for the Isle of Man. Very nicely spoken indeed.'

'I'm going on the stage,' said Mickey.

'Me too.' Sheila felt that Mickey should have included her as well.

'Then God 'elp you both.' Mr Hinchcliffe spoke fervently. 'Forget it, that is what I says – forget it. Get an education instead. Get letters after your name. They're the coming thing. Come on, I'll take you down to the chorus dressing room and you can say goodbye to Bernice.'

The noise from the dressing room was just like the juniors' cloakroom at school. Bernice had stopped being angry and was screaming with laughter. Sheila noticed one of the girls hastily dropping a towel over a bottle of Guinness as the stage manager led them into the room. No carpet, bare boards, wooden chairs, and the mirrors were just odds and ends propped up, against the wall, on a trestle table. There was a wonderful smell though – a cross between lemon verbena soap and good wax polish.

'Here come the heroes,' said Bernice to her friends. There must have been a dozen of them and they were all very nonchalant about being half dressed. Nobody hid behind a towel or ran for cover.

'What's that smell?' whispered Sheila.

'Greasepaint,' said Mickey who had been in more and better concerts than his friend.

'Sniff!' Bernice had picked up something like a big orange lipstick covered with gold paper. *Leichner* was the biggest word on the white label.

'Go on, have a good sniff.'

Twelve Tiller Girls watched as Sheila Starkey inhaled the scent of her future.

'Bernice gets Yanks to get it for her,' said one of them nastily.

Bernice looked annoyed again. 'Here,' she said, thrusting the stick of greasepaint at Sheila. 'You can have it if you want.'

The two children didn't walk back up the pier, they all but floated. Sheila's feet were so far off the ground that she quite forgot to worry about gaps between the planks.

'Didn't we look pale, in the mirrors next to the dancers?' She held out the greasepaint. 'Want a sniff?'

Mickey held the stick under his nose appreciatively. 'It's like being in the dressing room again. Let's not get the bus along the back road. Let's walk along the top promenade then we can see the pier pavilion, all the way.'

The cakestands should have warned them. Cakestands and sauce bottles had been appearing, on tables in the bay windows of boarding houses, all along their route. Five o'clock was the hour when Blackpool sat down to a big high tea. Sheila and Mickey felt as though they had been feeding on manna from heaven but this, and their walk, with its many backward glances at the pier pavilion, had made them late for tea at Balsam Road. There were several deadly sins at Mr Tuffin's but none graver than being late at table. Reproachful moon faces looked up at them from around the circle of white damask tablecloth.

'You're looking at two people who've been backstage at *On With the Show*,' said Mickey.

'We were even in the chorus girls' dressing room,' beamed Sheila.

Mrs Starkey, who had risen to her feet to reproach her daughter, swayed on her good cuban heels.

'The chorus girls' dressing room!' she cried in horror. 'Mrs Tuffin, would it be all right if I put Sheila straight in the bath after tea? It's an emergency.'

'Come along, Gladys, we mustn't fuss,' said Beryl Grimshaw.

'Anybody know what a knocking shop is?' asked Mickey.

2

The train from Blackpool groaned into Manchester Victoria Station and halted with a shudder.

The holiday was over. For the first time in her life, for a whole fortnight, Sheila had been part of a pair. She now considered herself luckier than girls who had a brother. Brothers came from the ready-made department. Mickey seemed, to her, to have been made-to-measure especially for her needs.

'What time will the Grimshaws' charabanc get back?' She asked this as they negotiated the wet slope at the side of Hunt's Bank.

'Trust me to go and pack the little umbrella.' Gladys's sigh turned to a snap as she added, 'And you can get those thoughts out of your head before you start. He lives across two big main roads and a park. Don't think you'll be going traipsing off to Grimshaws' whenever the fancy takes you.'

'You didn't bother about me going in traffic in Blackpool . . .'

'Blackpool's not the East Lancs Road. If I never see that Beryl Grimshaw again it'll be too soon.'

'You can't stop me seeing Mickey.'

'Can't I? Just you watch me. And don't dawdle, there's a 26 leaves at a quarter to.'

Not see Mickey again? Her mother couldn't mean it. Sheila froze in her tracks. 'I'll defy you.'

'Do that and you'll soon feel the buckle end of the strap,' snorted Gladys, as she seized her daughter's hand and jerked her like a rag doll. 'Now come *on*.'

Sheila knew better than to try tears. But that's what seemed to be trickling down the front window pane of the top deck of the bus. They passed Salford Royal Infirmary which always reminded Sheila that nurses had been bombed to death there. Mist was beginning to rise from the River Irwell, the mucky Irwell as it was known affectionately.

'That's the kind of mist that turns into fog,' said Gladys.

If there was a fog, thought Sheila, perhaps she could sneak out, under cover of it, and make her way across the East Lancs Road.

'Not that you get much fog in August,' said Gladys. Salford Hippodrome loomed up on the left-hand side. The posters outside advertised a show called *We've Nothing On Tonight*. Gladys shuddered. 'I've been thinking about your future, Sheila. I've got it nicely mapped out for you. All you have to do is pass your scholarship to the High School, and then you're going on to Greenwood's Commercial College to learn shorthand and typing.'

'But that's not what I want,' said Sheila.

'You're not old enough to know what you want. Anyway, it's what you're going to get. You're going to be a confidential secretary like your Auntie Phyllis.'

Auntie Phyllis? Sheila had a vision of herself, as an adult, in wire-rimmed glasses, droopy frock and flat heels. Auntie Phyllis worked in an office where everybody had their own individual cup and got very ratty if other people so much as touched it. Sheila knew, she'd been. Confidential secretary, my knickers! said Sheila's inner voice. When I grow up I'm going to be Ginger Rogers. Ever a creature of mercurial moods, she began to sing aloud:

> 'What do they do on a rainy night in Rio?
> What do they do when there is no . . .'

'Shh, don't show me up. People are looking at you.'

One day I'll show you up for money, thought Sheila. One day people will pay to see me sing and dance.

These earliest ambitions were inspired by films and inclined towards the variety stage. She wanted to be a lady wearing a crinoline gown, in a circle of toffee-pink light, bowing from behind the microphone and saying: 'Thank you very much, ladies and gentlemen. For my next song I would like to sing Gounod's *Faust*.'

All the while the bus had been climbing. Now it had reached Irlams o'th' Height. It was said that the front step of the Pack Horse Hotel was on a level with the golden ball on

27

top of the spire of Manchester Town Hall. Behind them were the cotton mills of Pendleton, further ahead pitheads would begin to loom on the horizon. Irlams o'th' Height was just a ribbon in between. Rows of shops were broken, on one side, by seven public houses and a turnstile factory. Across the street, the Methodist chapel had iron spikes on top of its turret. Were the Wesleyans afraid of the angels swooping down from heaven and breaking in? The parish church of St John the Evangelist was a preaching box of blackened stone set in a grimy graveyard.

The trees began at Irlams o'th' Height but their leaves were sooty, their trunks black. Even the white swan on the duck pond, in Light Oaks public park, was grey. People thought twice about sitting on the grass.

Before the war, there had been talk in Parliament of a Clean Air Act which would, one day, change all of this. When you got to The Height the slums of Salford were behind you and you were poised for the suburbs. Gladys and John Starkey belonged to that generation who had grown up and married between the two world wars. Their parents had lived in rented, back-to-back terraced dwellings. These newly-weds shocked their elders by taking out mortgages on semi-detached houses on newly created developments with grandiose names.

'Ravensdale Park,' called out the conductor. Gladys and Sheila were already halfway down the stairs.

Nothing had changed. The bus stop still said *Fare Stage*. The estate was still fronted by a row of shops. Everything was just as they had left it except for a big notice, whitewashed on the fish and chip shop window: *Closed Until Further Notice – No Fat*.

'Bang goes tonight's easy tea,' said Gladys. 'Sheila, I've been thinking on the bus. I might sent you for elocution lessons.'

Sheila flung her arms around Gladys. Love and gratitude burned fiercely within her. Her mother did understand her ambitions, after all. Now there was something to look forward to.

'Elocution should help you get a better class of secretarial position.'

Sheila slackened her affectionate grip. Something warned her not to protest aloud. Gladys could send her to elocution for one purpose, Sheila could put it to quite another. Now she wasn't going to be Ginger Rogers – she was going to be Greer Garson who was noted for talking lovely.

'When your daddy comes home, the chances are we'll be moving in different circles. Happen I could do with elocution meself.'

The child suddenly realized that her mother was also depressed that the holiday was over. She too was trying to look to a future. Sheila took her hand.

Gladys seemed to feel like talking. 'Did I tell you what your daddy said in his last letter? After the war we might move.'

'Away from here?'

'No. Still on the estate but into one of the bigger type.' Gladys sighed. 'Entertaining's a big problem with just the through room. I've always felt it's a bit like life in a goldfish bowl.'

'Is that why everybody has lace curtains?' asked her daughter.

Gladys was shocked. 'You surely wouldn't want a world without lace curtains? Where would you button up your blouse?'

'In the lav.'

'Toilet. How many times do I have to tell you, it's the toilet. Better still, don't bring the word into conversation at all. I want to tell you something. I'm going to tell you nicely but I want you to understand that I mean it. You're becoming very precocious, Sheila – very precocious indeed. And I won't have it. There's nothing worse than a child with an opinion on every subject on earth. Just look how people dislike Mickey . . .'

'I like him.'

'Well I don't. And I'm not having any more of this public stupidity about you going on the stage. One more word of it and you'll never be in a concert again. The holiday's over. I want my feelings understood before this key goes in our front door. Understood?'

Sheila said nothing but managed a nod. In that moment

Gladys Starkey had done more damage, to her own cause, than she would ever realize.

Let her have her lace curtains, thought Sheila. I can be secretive too. For a second she played with the idea of making a fibbing little speech about the thrill of learning Pitman's shorthand but decided that this would be disloyal to her real ambitions, now wonderfully burnished by Gladys Starkey's opposition.

Gladys let out a little scream.

For one terrible moment Sheila thought that her mother had turned into an even bigger mind-reader than usual. Then she saw the Servicemen's Aerograph letters, inside the hallway, on the doormat.

'Three of them, Sheila. Three in one go.' Gladys stopped to pick them up. 'And a picture postcard for you. Look, a camel and the pyramids. Run and show your Auntie Gander, you know how she loves animals.'

Sheila knew more than that. She knew her mother wanted to be left alone with her father's letters. Her father was simply somebody she couldn't remember so Sheila felt pushed aside and threatened. Were these letters sloppy love? Or were they something adult and mysterious like sanitary towels and Stewart's Surgical Stores with its separate entrances marked *Males* and *Females*?

'If Mrs Gander isn't in, play with June Monk for a bit.'

I'd rather sit in the coal hole, thought Sheila. It was June Monk who had filled Sheila's head with a load of garble and frightening information about monthly bleeding and Durex packets. She even claimed to know the places where the Yanks did *it* with good-time girls on Steadman's field. Mrs Starkey always referred to June as 'Sheila's best friend'. Sheila loathed her.

Any road, June Monk would still be away on holiday. Her real best friend was her Auntie Gander. Lily Gander wasn't a real aunt, she was a neighbour. Their side doors faced one another, across the driveway which led up to two more houses. As a baby, the first word Sheila spoke was 'more'; the second had been 'Gander'. The Starkeys tried to pretend it was Gran'ma but as soon as Sheila could toddle they saw where her real allegiances took her. It was to Mrs Gander's side door.

Tramps, stray dogs, people in distress, all the oddities of life found their way to Lily Gander's side door. Sheila knocked.

'Come in, you're better than nothing. I heard your voice a minute ago. Got a kiss for me?'

She was a dumpy little woman, all curves and clean pinafore. With black hair scraped back into a bun Auntie Gander always reminded Sheila of Mrs Noah from her toy Noah's Ark set. She flung her arms around the beaming woman and inhaled the familiar smells of Thermogene medicated wadding and good carbolic soap.

All her mother's strictures forgotten, Sheila burst out with: 'Gander, I've met a boy called Mickey and I'm going on the stage.'

'Course you are, duck.' The best thing about Gander was her eyes. They always understood. Mostly you only saw eyes as good as that on dogs. 'Course you're going on the stage, Sheila. I knew it the first time you ever sang a song.'

'They haven't brought our postman back out of retirement just to be pestered by you,' said Gladys.

'All I do is ask him whether he's got a parcel for me from Putney Heath.'

'Yes and every day for a week. Come away from the window, Sheila. I'm afraid you're going to whistle for your parcel. Mrs Adair had "romancer" written all over her.'

'There's still the second post to come.' If Sheila was possessed of one virtue it was Hope.

'Take your nose off my good window pane. I'll be glad when you're back at school. Can't you go and play out?'

'If I could just go to Mickey's . . .'

'Well you can't. So let that be an end to it. Trust Beryl Grimshaw to shop at Bloor's . . .'

Bloor's was the Fortnum and Mason of Irlams o'th' Height. Since returning from Blackpool, that's where they'd caught their sole glimpse of Mrs Grimshaw and Mickey. They'd seen them through the open doorway, having their ration books snipped by old Miss Bloor herself. Even from out on the pavement, Bloor's smelled deliciously of freshly ground coffee and eastern spices. It was doubtful whether these commodities were still available, even to privileged customers who thought nothing of paying a penny over the odds for everything else – but the rich pre-war aromas lingered on.

Mickey had dived out onto the step, eating a Nice biscuit and said, 'As soon as Mrs Adair sends my parcel, I'm coming over to your house to see you.'

It had seemed to Sheila that she was missing him more than he was missing her. If only the parcel arrived then so would Mickey. The school holidays had begun to seem endless and she was bored, bored, bored. Through the window she saw that a fat cat, called Paddy, was sitting on the Dolans' gatepost. So many Dolans seemed to live in the house opposite that Gladys Starkey said they must sleep in a chest of drawers. It was either that, she maintained, or they did it in shifts.

England ended at the Dolans' front door. The wireless was always tuned to Radio Athlone and, apart from *The Sacred Heart Messenger*, their only reading was *Ireland's Own* – until the war stopped it coming through. The war also took Mr Dolan off into the army. He was a big jolly man, in the building trade, generally known as Eddie Tarmacadam. All winks and muscles and a bit of something for the kiddies, hidden in his pocket. He wore his shirt a button too open for Rookswood Avenue's liking.

A battered pram now appeared through Dolans' front door. Monica and Delia were manoeuvring it down the steps.

'I'm going out in the avenue,' said Sheila. It wouldn't do to be more specific. She wasn't actually forbidden to play with the Dolans. But her mother had once gone mad when she heard that Sheila had drunk a glass of milk in their unhygienic kitchen.

Sheila hummed to herself as she skipped down the garden path. The Dolans could generally be relied upon to colour-in a blank morning. They clanked with holy medals which made them wonderfully exotic and different. Their priests didn't even let them say the last bit of Our Father. Her mother said it was a religion of fear. As making a glorious mess didn't seem to be any great crime to Catholics, Sheila was reserving judgement.

'How was Longsight?' she asked. There were too many Dolans to be able to afford to go on a proper holiday. They made do with days out at the seaside and the odd week with aunts on the other side of Manchester.

'Smashing,' said Delia. 'We had black-market ice cream.'

Delia looked like a gypsy in a picture book with tumbling black hair and rosy cheeks. The same age as Sheila, she already had her ears pierced and she wore little gold sleepers in them.

'I confessed the ice cream afterwards,' said Monica, a frailer, younger, more delicate version of her sister. She had a virtuous expression and the temper of a fiend.

'You shouldn't go telling other people about your confessions,' said Delia.

'It's the priest mustn't tell.' Monica was very well versed in these matters. She was going to be a nun.

'Would you believe what else she told?' The Dolan children spoke with Lancashire accents but thought with Irish heads. 'She told the owd priest all about June Monk teaching us to talk rude. She went in that box and give him the lot. Durex spunk-bags, ladies having to swallow Tampax with a glass of water, the whole flaming lot.'

'I just said "impure thoughts" and he wriggled the rest out of me.'

'I bet he asked you "How many times?" ' said Delia. 'You'd be hard pushed to answer that. Mention Brer Rabbit and June Monk could turn it into filth. Have you got a penny to help me buy a black baby, Sheila?'

Delia rummaged in Fingal's pram and produced a card marked out in forty little squares. 'I have to collect forty pennies – three shillings and fourpence. I put a pinhole in each space for each penny. When I've done, they sent it to Africa and baptize the baby anything I choose. Three and fourpence to save a little black boy from the gloom of limbo. Not bad, eh?'

'What are you going to call him?' asked Sheila.

'Hutch,' said Delia, naming a well-known negro music-hall entertainer. It was a well-established fact, amongst the juvenile society of Rookswood Avenue, that when Delia Dolan grew up, she was going to marry a black man. She thought they were absolutely lovely.

'What's a wide berth?' asked Monica.

'Search me,' said Delia. 'What d'you want one for anyway?'

'It's what Father Conklin said I'd got to give June Monk.'

'I shouldn't waste your time on presents for her. Not on a girl who's having a whole fortnight in Grange-over-Sands – may God and his Blessed Mother help the town. Sheila, look! The postman's carrying a parcel up your path.'

Sheila tore across Rookswood Avenue. The postman was talking to Gladys at the open front door. Yes. Gladys already had a battered brown paper parcel in her hand.

'. . . so if you let me have the linseed oil for Arthur's cricket bat,' the postman was saying, 'I'll oblige you with a bicycle pump.'

'Is it for me?' panted Sheila.

'You find yourself doing some funny swaps in wartime,' said Mrs Starkey.

'The parcel – is it for me?'

'Here,' said her mother, thrusting it at her. 'Perhaps we'll get a bit of peace now. Don't use scissors. Unknot it; we'll save the string.'

Sheila knelt down, with her treasure trove, at the bottom of the hall stairs. She hauled off the string and pushed it aside in an untidy heap – that could be unravelled later.

From outside in the avenue she heard loud jeers and catcalls. It sounded like that gang of rowdy boys on bikes from the bottom of Ravensway. What did they matter? The parcel was here. Gladys closed the door and stood over Sheila as she pulled the brown paper aside to reveal a layer of yellow crepe paper secured with blobs of red sealing wax.

'Doesn't Mrs Adair know how to make a present interesting?' Sheila broke the seals.

'I'm listening to that noise out in the avenue,' said her mother. 'Anybody would think this was a council estate.'

34

The yellow paper came off and the package got a bit smaller. Now it was covered with white tissue paper and tied with mauve embroidery thread.

'Don't use your teeth,' warned Mrs Starkey.

She didn't need to. The cotton pulled off quite easily.

Reverently, Sheila unfolded the tissue paper to reveal a lot of very squashed net frilling in dingy pink and mauve. It wasn't new, it was old. And there wasn't so much as one spangle. Disappointment hit the pit of her stomach.

'Whatever is it?' asked Sheila.

Gladys snatched up the puzzling garment and shook it briskly in the air. In places it was possible to see right through it. 'It's the oldest Bo-Peep outfit on earth,' she said. 'And it goes straight in the bin.'

The laughter, outside in the avenue, rose to a crescendo. At the same moment, they heard a sharp noise on their back door.

'Auntie Gander's throwing coal,' said Sheila. They always threw a little bit of coal at one another's back door when they needed to attract attention. Only a small piece. It was years since they'd been able to get new paint and the doors were already scarred by bomb-blast and shrapnel.

Looking at the tired net costume, Sheila felt as though she'd been through a war herself – and lost.

'Go and see what she wants, Sheila. Your legs are younger than mine.'

Sheila trudged across the through room and into the kitchen. All that waiting for what looked like the ghost of a Bo-Peep costume. She opened the back door. Gander was out on her step. The boys on bikes were by her garden gate.

'Can you come over for a minute, Sheila?' said Gander in a voice which usually betokened a pleasant surprise. 'I've got Little Ford Fauntleroy in our kitchen and he's come to the wrong house.'

Sheila and Gladys trooped into Mrs Gander's kitchenette. Mickey was standing by the table drinking a glass of pop and munching parkin.

Sheila's and her mother's mouths fell open. This was not

Mickey as they had known him in Blackpool. He was quite transformed. His parcel had also arrived from Putney Heath and he was wearing the contents.

'You're the most creased-looking person I've ever seen,' said Sheila. 'It's like a scarecrow that's been dipped in a flour bag.'

The white satin knee-breeches were going yellow with age. The ancient jacket was in the same hideously crumpled satin. It had a huge cavalier collar edged with moth-holed Nottingham lace. The most arresting detail was the white silk stockings. These were very much laddered and darned above Mickey's own Clark's sandals.

'It's not quite what I expected,' he said.

'You never walked all the way here in that get-up!' gasped Gladys.

'I've got a wig too,' said Mickey. He held up something matted and golden with ringlets. 'But it's a bit small.'

Gladys let out a shrill scream: 'Drop it in the sink this instant. Can wigs have biddies, Mrs Gander?'

'I'm Little Lord Fauntleroy,' said Mickey, turning around as though arrayed in cloth of gold. 'And I must say I always thought the book was awful too.'

There was a hesitant knock at the open back door. It was Delia Dolan with Monica.

'There's big boys at the bottom of your garden path, Mrs Gander,' said Monica in a tell-tale voice. 'And they keep singing "In My Sweet Little Alice Blue Gown" . . .'

'It's me they're singing about . . .' Mickey was blushing furiously but storming for the back door.

Lily Gander barred his way. 'Leave this to me.'

'I can fight my own battles, thank you. I often have to. I'm used to it.'

'And I respect you for that. But still leave this to me. You're on my territory now.' Lily Gander marched out of the kitchen, closing the door behing her. Monica Dolan pressed her ear against the wood.

'One word from Auntie Gander and they'll just salute and move on,' said Sheila.

Lily Gander marched back into the kitchen and straight up

to Mickey. 'Look me in the eye and answer me straight. Did you call that big boy a bastard?'

'Yes. He goes to our Sunday school.'

'Did you know that his mother's a lady who never married a husband?'

'Course I did. That's why I called him a bastard.'

'That was a very uncalled-for comment,' said Gander sternly.

'He'd already said I was a sissy,' said Mickey.

'Well he'd no right.'

'Course he had,' said Mickey reasonably. 'I am a sissy. I don't like games. I learn tap dancing. I like learning tap dancing. If that's being a sissy Fred Astaire's one too – and I'm on the same side as Fred Astaire.'

'Judge not that ye shall not yourself be judged,' said Mrs Gander to the ceiling. But she was definitely speaking sternly to herself. 'You and me will get on just fine, Mickey. I like your honesty, but less of the bastards if you don't mind.'

Sheila shone inside her heart. Because Mr Tuffin had liked Mick she had got away with being friends with him in Blackpool. Gander's approval was highly sought after in Rookswood Avenue. Even Gladys Starkey needed Gander's friendly support too much to argue with her. It was all going to be OK.

As the rest of the summer holiday passed by, Mickey took to spending more and more time in Rookswood Avenue. Gander, who was a heroine to half the rough boys in the neighbourhood, made Mickey's passage across Ravensdale Estate much easier. He became known as Mrs Gander's friend and the bullies, for the most part, laid off him.

'It's that wag in Mickey's walk,' said Sheila. 'That's what gets them going.'

Gander leapt swiftly to his defence: 'I was a tomboy and that was fine. Nobody saw anything wrong in that. If Mick wants to be a bit fanciful, why shouldn't he be? If he's going to be like that, for the rest of his life, he'll have to be tougher than the lot of them put together. Sometimes I think he already is – tons tougher.'

'And sometimes he's like Alice Faye,' said Sheila. 'He's not really girlish. He's a creature. If it said at school *Boys*, *Creatures* and *Girls* Mickey would go through the middle door.'

'Well there is no middle door,' said Gander. 'Mind you, he's the kind that'd have a go at knocking one through.'

Until now, Sheila had enjoyed a unique position in Gander's affections. Their side doors faced one another. Of all the children in the neighbourhood, this proximity had made her closest to Gander's heart.

Now there was Mickey. Was he draining off some of this affection for himself? Was this the price she was having to pay for the secondhand dancing lessons he was passing on to her in the Dolans' empty garage? Sheila tried these twinges of jealousy for size and found they didn't matter. Mickey only had to appear round the corner of Rookswood Avenue for colours to seem brighter and anything to be possible. Yet she still had a special place in her heart for handsome Peter Bromiley and knew that the pain of school starting again would be relieved by his presence. Mickey was more like having her own unicorn.

If Gander had once been head of a gang of boys, Mickey set about reversing the process in Rookswood Avenue. Within a week, he had organized a concert which was given in front of the Dolans' Anderson air-raid shelter, draped with Union Jacks, left over from the King's coronation. It goes without saying that Mickey and Sheila were the stars but he turned the Dolan girls into showgirls. He draped them in red, white and blue bunting and made them carry bouquets of rose willow bay herb (the children called it bomb weed) plucked from the garden of a derelict house. He even tried to get Mrs Tatton's dog, Duke, to be Winston Churchill with a pretend brown paper cigar in his mouth. Rose Dolan, the children's mother, called Mickey something which sounded like Twather-Da-Dan and meant the King of the Fairies – and she meant it as a compliment.

Sheila noticed that men did not warm to Mickey anything like so easily as women did. Gander may have been influential but the word sissy was never quite stilled. Sometimes people chalked things up on walls and Sheila would spit on her forefinger and carefully rub out Mickey's name. He said he didn't care what they wrote but she knew better.

Lily Gander's husband was all man; standard robust model. He wasn't in the army because he'd been gassed, in the Dardanelles, in the First World War. He had also suffered from shell shock. One pint too many was enough to cause him to relive incidents from the Battle of the Somme. His wife always described him as 'Dick Gander who needs a bit of studying'.

Apart from his pint, he liked a packet of Woodbines, an hour of shove ha'penny and a game of bowls. What he didn't like was his back doorstep cluttered up with other people's problems. Come five o'clock, when Mr Gander got home from work, beggars, stray dogs and even Sheila would scatter off Gander's doorstep – not Mickey.

He found Dick Gander's stories fascinating. He had only to smell a whiff of beer on the man's breath to get him going on the Battle of the Somme.

'I just don't see what people are scared of,' said Mickey. 'He's even worked out a better way of making metal joints for my marionettes.'

'Yes but he still calls them your dollies,' said Lily Gander sternly. She wasn't keen on little lads getting above themselves.

Auntie Gander dearly loved an outing. She came from the Pendleton district of Salford. At least twice a week she went back to her roots, to do her shopping, and to see her many relations. Sheila had accompanied Gander on these expeditions since she was a babe in arms. Now Mickey began to go along too.

'Why d'you want to go traipsing down there?' Dick Gander would ask them. 'That's what we've escaped from.'

'Because I'm interested in people. I'm not just going to be an actor,' Mickey would explain patiently. 'Somebody has to make up the words they say. I'm going to be a writer too.'

During the war people were always talking about the old days. Sheila got these mixed up with the olden days. Pendleton seemed what the olden days must have been like.

Nearer the river, it was mistier than Rookswood Avenue. Surrounded by industry, it was darker. There was still gaslight in the back streets and courtyards of Pendleton. Women were swathed in dark plaid shawls and clattered across cobblestones in clogs. There can have been few garments which became a face as well as the Lancashire shawl did. It framed beauty and softened the ravages of age. In Pendleton, men wore collars only on Sundays. Even then, some just settled for a brass collar stud or a white silk muffler, stabbed with a tie pin.

Huge dray horses still pulled wagons of raw cotton. The noise from the iron-rimmed wheels, as they ground over the paving setts, vied with a thousand rattles from the weaving sheds. Strangers couldn't hear themselves think and the residents of Pendleton mouthed their words rather than attempt to shout above the din. Pendleton smelled of coal gas and coke and sulphurous chemical works and new bread and stale beer.

The outings with Lily Gander always began at her mother's house. Both children were forbidden to accept money but Gander asked them, in the case of Mrs Stokes, to make a kindly exception.

'Just take it and be done with it. You see she's poor but proud. You needn't keep it. We'll nip into Boots Cash Chemists and you can put it in the blind box on the counter.'

'What's Lilian for Ladies and who is this Sister Drew you can write to for advice?' asked Mickey, pointing at a discreet display card on Boots's counter.

'June Monk would soon tell you,' laughed Sheila. You could always talk frankly in front of Gander just so long as it wasn't bawdy.

'June Monk? If you ask me there's a whiff of brimstone about that whole family,' said Gander. Guiltily, she clapped her hand over her mouth. Then she removed it, took a deep breath and added: 'I'm going to treat you as grown-ups and ask you to forget that I ever said that. It didn't happen. Right? Shall we get some Olde English Cough Candy? It's halfway to toffee and no coupons; I'm paying.'

'June Monk comes back from Grange-over-Sands tomorrow,' said Sheila.

'Whatever came over me, criticizing people like that. I'd no right. No right at all.'

'It's not like you,' said Sheila.

'Thank you,' said Lily Gander, 'but I'll have to show God I'm making amends.' Gander was not boringly holy. She was quite capable of mentioning the Almighty and saying 'bloody' in the same breath. She tended to reserve 'bloody' for Pendleton. That kind of talk went with the place.

'Tell you what,' she said, 'I've been putting it off for weeks. Let's go and see our poor Edie. Feel fit for a walk?'

Poor Edie lived through Pendleton and properly down into Salford. The trio walked as far as Eccles New Road and waited for a bus.

'Not that it's more than a cock's-stride,' said Gander. 'But the best thing to do with Eccles New Road is get along it, fast. Here you are. Get your hand out, Mickey. This one will do us. One and two halves to Stowell Memorial, please.'

Eccles New Road ran through districts called Seedley and Weaste which were no prettier than their names. It was dominated by a bus depot and haunted by a municipal cemetery. One funeral director's window featured a black tin urn marked *From the Neighbours*. Another was decorated with a white marble monument of an angel weeping over a harp with broken strings. The angel was holding up a little plaque labelled *Mam*.

Doleful was the only word for Eccles New Road. Halfway to the cemetery there was even a pub known as the Widow's Rest. Sheila viewed this stretch of road as straight out of the 23rd Psalm. To her it was the Valley of the Shadow of Death.

'We're not on the bus for long,' she said to Mickey. 'And when we get off something nice happens.'

'Are we getting nearer the docks?' he asked.

'Look!' said Lily Gander. 'You can see the liners, coming up the Ship Canal, towering over the houses at the end of that street. Come on. This stop's ours.'

The stop they descended at was by a herbalist's shop. The window was full of big glass jars of dried herbs. Each had a handwritten label: *Arnica, Damiana for Gentlemen, Sarsaparilla – Good for the Blood*. There was a white parrot in a

41

cage in the window and a tall glass cylinder, filled with clear liquid, and sealed with a cork. A long, dead, thin white snake floated inside.

'What's that?' asked Mickey.

'A human tapeworm,' said Sheila.

'The herbalist got it out of the innards of a sailor from Bengal,' said Lily Gander. 'It's his speciality. Known for miles around. He can get them out of anybody. Bugger off!' she said to the parrot.

'You bugger off too,' the bird replied.

Gander and Sheila laughed. 'There you are,' said Sheila. 'It always does that. I told you something nice would happen when we got off the bus.'

'Are we going nearer the ships?' asked Mickey. 'Abroad must be a bit like this.'

'Never been,' said Lily Gander. 'We go past the Seamen's Mission and not far from the dock gates. Before the war, it was nothing to meet somebody who'd try and sell you a tropical monkey. Lascars, Chinks with pigtails, all sorts used to come through them dock gates.'

Sheila could see Mickey drinking all of this in like the most wonderful pop on earth. 'It's coming on rain,' she said and wondered, guiltily, whether she sounded like her own mother.

'Not real rain,' said Gander, 'only a bit of mizzle. There you are, Mickey, that's where we're heading. Divine Dwellings. Not very heavenly is it?'

Divine Dwellings was on a corner. The shape of a tall black flat iron, it was a Victorian tenement block on five floors. The place looked like a prison. There were iron bars on all the windows at ground level. The landings on the higher floors were open to the street and people had hung caged wild birds, wrens and robins, above the sills. It seemed cruel to Sheila.

'Passing on their own misery,' said Lily Gander. 'I'd like five minutes with whoever built this shuddering heap. The bloody place is only held together by the wallpaper.'

'Do we have to go in there?' gulped Mickey. It made Sheila feel very worldly and experienced. For all Mickey's talk of not being keen on respectability, was Divine Dwellings too far a cry from safety for him?

A figure emerged from a doorhole at the bottom of one of the stairwells. It was a proud- and defiant-looking woman, in her early thirties. She was sporting a black eye, wearing an old raincoat but expensive shoes and leading a jaunty black and white collie dog on a piece of string.

'Bobby!' yelled Sheila and tore over to make a fuss of the dog. It immediately jumped up and began covering her in happy licks.

'Is that your poor Edie?' Mickey asked Lily Gander.

'Yes, and, from the look of that eye, Dobson's back from sea. Come on, nothing to be frightened of. Morning, Edie.'

'I'll swing for him, Lily.' There was a stunned hopelessness to the woman. 'So 'elp me, one of these days, I'll kill him in his sleep.'

'You two take Bobby for a walk round the block,' said Lily Gander.

'Don't even think of going upstairs, Lil. He's sleeping it off. Everything's smashed to smithereens – again.'

'Do as you're told and take the dog for a walk. Only round the Dwellings and don't talk to anybody.'

Sheila already had the dog's string in her hand. 'Come on,' she said to Mickey. 'Mick, stop turning back and staring. It's rude.'

'I need to remember it,' he stammered.

'You're all white and dithery. There's nothing to be scared of. Edie and Dobson don't hit other people. They only do it to one another. He's got tattoos.'

'I'm not scared. I'm excited. It's like a play. I have to remember it. How do you know they don't hit other people?'

'Because I've seen them at it,' said Sheila. 'Pans flying and the lot.'

'Tell me about it,' said Mickey. 'I want to hear every single detail.'

'I'm not sure that's nice. Bobby, don't tug!'

'I'm not talking about being nice,' said Mickey. 'Being nice doesn't come into it. I've got to remember all this. Every single bit of it. This place is like magic. One day I'm going to write about it. One day this moment will be in a play.'

3

'She says she's got a present for you,' announced Delia Dolan who was letting Sheila push Fingal round Rookswood Avenue. The word was out – June Monk was back.

'D'you think she's been shoplifting again?' asked Monica.

Sheila was not best pleased. 'Why a present for me?'

'She says you're her very best friend on earth,' piped up Monica.

'Well she's not mine.'

'She's trying to buy you,' said Delia.

'I'm not for sale.'

Fingal the baby suddenly sat bolt upright in his pram and began to scream.

Somebody cleared their throat and said, 'I expect he wants a suck on one of his mother's milkers.' The tones were strangely lewd for a young girl's voice. It belonged to June Monk.

Fingal redoubled his screams.

'So that was the trouble,' said Delia darkly.

Sheila suddenly wanted to do anything rather than talk to June. Absence had not made the heart grow fonder. It had acted in just the opposite way. She said quickly, 'Delia, how many pennies have you collected towards Hutch?'

'I've still got one and fourpence to find for the bloody little heathen, God bless him.'

Sheila was studying June covertly. What was it about her? Every class at school had its unfortunate fat girl; June missed being that by several candidates. But she was *blobby*. She had curly blonde hair and blue eyes and rosy cheeks. Her lips were a mite full for a child and, if you looked closely, her hands were a size too small for the rest of her body.

'I'll give you some money, Delia,' said June.

Sheila was a very fair girl and had to admit that old gentlemen would sit June Monk on their knee, seize hold of one of those podgy paws, and say in a voice of wonder, 'Her little hands.' Twice she'd seen that happen and twice she'd watched June glow.

'You can't give Delia any money, June Monk,' shrilled Monica, 'you're not a Catholic. When you die you're going to hell.'

'Am I going to hell too?' Sheila was distinctly worried. 'I'm not one either.'

'I shouldn't think so,' said Delia. 'You're lucky. Sheila's a Catholic name; I expect that'll just about scrape you into heaven.'

'June's not a Catholic name,' said Monica sternly.

'No,' agreed Delia. 'June's the name of that stuff they spray in the lavvies at the pictures.'

Any other child would have burst into tears. Not June Monk. She simply let out a little silvery laugh and waited for the next thing to happen. It was as though she'd paid for an orchestra stall. She knew she was doing this and it often threw people.

Mickey came round the corner of Rookswood Avenue.

'Here's Sheila's new friend,' said Monica, in like a flash.

From behind her back June produced a large stick of pink seaside rock. 'For you,' she said to Sheila.

'I don't eat rock,' said Sheila, 'it does your teeth in.'

'Never mind,' said June. 'Keep it anyway. Rock's a funny thing. There's always somebody who'll eat it. I've noticed that.'

Mickey bounded up to them. 'Can anybody have a bit of that?' he asked Sheila. He was indicating the pink rock.

June Monk smiled till her cheeks pudged. 'There you are, Sheila. What did I tell you? Now who are *you*?' June switched the fierce beam of her interest from Sheila to Mickey.

'I'm Mickey Grimshaw. I know who you are. And, no, you can't see my dick for sixpence.'

'One day I'll get to see it for nothing,' said June, with absolute certainty.

When it came to war news, June Monk was every bit as hot at dispensing it as Mrs Tuffin had been in Blackpool. 'The Yanks are nearly at Paris,' she announced, as though nobody else read the papers. 'My mother says that, any day now, there'll be plenty of ooh-la-la-oui-oui.'

Sheila couldn't imagine Mrs Monk saying anything of the kind. She was a thin woman. The whites of her eyes were a bit yellow and always brought opening medicine to mind. Mr Monk made up for this by being big and blond, almost pneumatic. He looked as though somebody had given him a couple of charges with a bicycle pump. It was from him that June had inherited her bursting rosiness. These parents were now coming down the driveway between Starkeys' and Ganders'. They lived in the right-hand house, at the top.

'Sorry, Sheila,' said Mr Monk, 'but I'm afraid we're going to have to rob you of June.' Like his daughter, Mr Monk viewed things exactly as he chose to view them, with scant regard for the finer points of the truth.

'I hope you don't need to go back and wash your hands, June,' Mrs Monk said. 'We're due at you-know-where in half an hour. Say goodbye to your little friends.'

'Toodle-pip,' said June, 'sorry I can't stop longer.'

'We're not,' said Delia Dolan, but under her breath. As the Monks moved away she mimicked the mother: ' "Due at you-know-where." They're just like that man on *Itma* on the wireless. The one who says, "Hush, keep it dark!" Why do they have to make a flaming mystery out of everything?'

'Because Rose says they're doing the devil's work up that pathway.' Monica was ostentatiously crossing herself.

Rose was the Dolan's mother they always called her by her first name.

'Will you stop that bloody crossing yourself in the street, Monica Dolan? Our Lord's not struck on swanky behaviour like that. Did Rose mention what sort of devil's work?'

Monica shook her head. 'She just told me to forget she'd said it.'

Sheila and Mickey exchanged a quick glance. Lily Gander had been equally adamant that they must forget she'd said there was 'a whiff of brimstone' about the Monk family.

It was cold for April but the hopeful news on the wireless was starting to match up with real life. The men were beginning to return to Rookswood Avenue. People were constantly asking Sheila how she felt about the idea of her daddy coming back from the war. Perplexed was not a word in her vocabulary so she just aimed for what would please and said, 'Excited.'

The war was not over yet but Paris had been relieved and the first American and British troops were across the Rhine, into Germany, and making daily advances on Berlin.

Half the fathers of children in Sheila's class had been home on a week's or a fortnight's leave; not Sheila's father. The classroom at school was full of captured Nazi flags and German shell cases. What, she wondered, would hers bring back from the Holy Land?

Sheila was out in the avenue when the postman came up it. He beckoned to her. 'I want you to come up the path with me to your mammy.' The old postman looked troubled. 'I think you might have to be a brave girl. I've brought a few of these before.'

Sheila peered at the small brown envelope in his hand. 'Shall I get Auntie Gander?' It was her standard response to any crisis.

'Good idea. I'll wait here.'

Sheila tore up the Ganders' path but not quickly enough. Her mother was already making her way down their own and the postman was looking agitated.

'Gander, come quick! It's a little brown envelope with His Majesty's Service and War Office on it.'

Sheila could see her mother opening the envelope and waited for the scream. Gladys screamed for anything. This time the noise would surely be very terrible – but no sound came.

Gander and Sheila rushed to join Gladys and the postman.

'Dear God, these are terrible times,' said Gander. 'Come on, Mrs Starkey love, what does it say?'

'It's the shoddiest little bit of flimsy paper that the War Office can bear to part with . . .'

Sheila had never heard her mother sound so grim and so bitter.

'It regrets to tell me that Captain John Baines Starkey is missing in action and presumed killed. A beautiful man like that . . .' Now she was crying. 'And he *was* beautiful. And all they can spare is this scruffy little piece of paper. Even the printing looks as though flies have done it. It's not good enough. It's just not good enough . . .'

'Sheila,' said Gander. 'Go and get the little brandy bottle from my medicine chest and bring a glass too.'

Sheila was glad of something to do. Apart from the swimming sensation in her head, which was already beginning to pass, she just felt blank. As she climbed on the stool, to get the brandy, this blankness was replaced by guilt. She remembered that, at the very moment that the postman had arrived, all she had been thinking about was what would her father bring back? Perhaps there was something wrong with her – why could she feel no strong emotion now? What was she meant to feel? Her father was just a man in snapshots. She couldn't remember the real him at all. At this moment a little gap inside her head opened and something came back.

When she was very small, before she went to bed, he used to hold her up to the window, in her nightgown, and let her see the lights of Manchester. Something hidden deep inside her had been waiting for him to come back and do that again. Now he wouldn't. Two tears found their way out of her eyes. There had once been somebody who had held her close and anticipated her need for bright lights.

But was John Starkey dead? That was the question which dominated the rest of the day. Was he actually dead? The letter only said 'presumed killed'. For really dead you generally got a telegram.

'I suppose they write that to stop you getting a widow's pension straight away,' sniffed Gladys. It wasn't a tearful sniff, just an angry one. The letter had affected her in a strange way. She had got out a tin of furniture polish and was attacking everything in sight.

'It does say that they'll be in touch with you at a future date,' said Gander.

'They'd better be,' snapped Gladys. 'They'd better be or I'll be down at that Whitehall wanting to know the reason why. I never wanted any part in this war. What did Poland have to do with us? And don't throw Mr Churchill at me because he's a bad bugger.'

Sheila could hardly believe her ears. Her mother was swearing and attacking Winnie, all in one startling breath.

'Before the war Churchill was considered very iffy. Very iffy indeed. It took this lot to turn him into Father Christmas. Well now we've seen the colour of his presents.' She picked up the letter again and slammed it down, wildly, on the dining room table. 'I'm not impressed. I'm not impressed at all. Get me the Brasso, Sheila. And please don't look at me pityingly, Mrs Gander. I can stand anything except pity.

'We'd got it all planned,' she continued. 'New house, holidays on the continent, a little car . . . What will I do?' All the fury in her voice was replaced by blind panic. 'Tell me, Mrs Gander, what will I do?'

Gladys sounded so afraid that Sheila began to cry. She could cope with her mother's rages and grim silences but Gladys Starkey afraid was something new and frightening.

'But we don't know he's dead for sure,' wailed Sheila.

'I'd rather face the worst,' said Gladys. 'It's how I'm built. Don't worry, Sheila. Come what may, you're having the education I planned for you. High school and commercial college – even if I have to scrub floors to pay for it.'

'There's no *need*,' said Sheila desperately.

'There's every need,' stormed Gladys, almost fanatically, 'and there'll be even more need for you to be grateful. And I'll trouble you to remember that.'

The day the letter came was the first day Sheila was ever allowed to cross the East Lancs Road on her own. It was an icy cold afternoon and the house in Rookswood Avenue was beginning to fill up with Gladys's female relations. It reminded Sheila of a Victorian engraving at her gran'ma's. The one of a seated woman, ripping a handkerchief to bits, surrounded by grieving handmaidens. Allowed to visit Mickey? She'd been sent out of the way. They'd even got the best tea service out of the display cabinet and some of her aunties were behaving like real visitors; they had kept their hats on.

'Did anybody think to ring the War Office?' asked Mickey. He had led her straight upstairs to his bedroom and they were looking along the bookshelves.

'We don't know anybody on the phone,' said Sheila. 'Who's E. Nesbit?' There was a whole row of titles by this author. They were in blue war economy bindings.

'The most magical writer on earth,' said Mickey. 'Start off with *Five Children and It.* You can have a lend. People ring the Red Cross too. Have you thought of ringing them? You could go to a phone box.'

'How can I ring anybody? I'm only a little girl.'

'I feel like taking that book back. "Only a little girl." That's the most weak-kneed thing I've ever heard you say.'

'Michael . . .' A voice floated up the stairs. 'My heart's angel . . .' These words were followed by creaking and panting. 'Who've you got in your bedroom?'

The door opened and Beryl Grimshaw appeared.

'It's only Sheila.'

'Not in bedrooms, Mickey, please.' Beryl Grimshaw had her reproachful voice on. 'Never girls in bedrooms.'

'Why?'

'Because Mummy says so. Why's that counterpane creased?'

'I suppose because we sat on the bed.'

'Never do anything, Mickey, that couldn't be photographed and put on the front page of the *Manchester Evening News.*'

'Will your father be in the paper?' Mickey asked Sheila. 'He's missing presumed dead,' he added to his mother.

'Oh my dear,' said Beryl, seizing Sheila and pulling her into her own great cushiony bulk. 'My poor girlie . . .'

Sheila's cheek was pressed uncomfortably into a buckle and she found herself breathing in a mixture of 4711 Eau de Cologne and camphorated oil. She only hoped there wasn't going to be a lot of this. Her aunts had already wept over her. People seemed to think it was expected of them.

'We must go and tell Mr Grimshaw,' Beryl announced importantly.

'He's on nights,' said Mickey.

'Does that mean he'll be in bed?' asked Sheila. Did death sweep away the bedroom rules and would she meet Mr Grimshaw in his pyjamas?

'No,' said Beryl, 'I'm just letting him have forty winks in an armchair.' Mickey's mother led the way downstairs. She took it very slowly so Sheila had plenty of time to look at all the reproductions of Old Masters framed in passe-partout. The Grimshaws' house was plainly more cultured than their own so she wasn't surprised to find that they had an upright piano in the through room.

'We've got a little armchair for Mr G. in the kitchen,' said Beryl.

The sleeping figure was tiny. A dapper little man in a blue blazer and grey flannels, he had Brilliantined hair and a neat golden moustache.

'Gently does it,' said Beryl, taking up a fly swatter and giving her husband a playful swipe.

'What's this then? And who's the young woman?' Sheila saw where Mickey's energy came from. The little man was awake and bounding around in seconds.

'This is the Captain's daughter,' said Beryl. 'Although we're very much afraid it may be the late Captain. Word's come through from the authorities.'

'And on the very day they're lifting the blackout,' said Mr Grimshaw. 'I call that tough luck. Very tough luck indeed. Take the child out, Mick, and cheer her up. Here's two shillings.'

Mickey and Sheila walked up to The Height with their collars up and had hot Oxo at the temperance bar.

'Your father's nice.'

'Until you mention the stage. He's another one who keeps going on about proper jobs and getting a cap and gown at college. He nearly went mad when he found the reply from *Children's Hour*. They said I couldn't have an audition to be in their plays till I was twelve. She shut him up though. She's on my side.'

'Do you have to be twelve to be on the wireless?'

'It's a good job you're not a boy.' Mickey was licking a bit of hard Oxo off the edge of the beaker. 'If you were a boy, I wouldn't tell you anything. You'd be competition. Come on, I want to show you something to cheer you up, before it gets dark.'

'What sort of something?'

'It's magic. We have to go through the back streets.'

There was already something different about this afternoon. Dusk was beginning to fall yet nobody was drawing the blackout curtains. Light was streaming out onto the pavements and whole lives were going on in the rooms inside.

'It's like plays on stages,' said Mickey. 'Aaaah . . .' he cried.

'Look!' yelled Sheila in the same moment. Everything had gone golden.

The street lights were back on for the first time in four years.

'It's not like dusk at all,' said Sheila, 'it's so friendly. Hold your hand out to it. Wouldn't you think it would be warm?'

'And this is the house,' said Mickey. 'This is what I wanted to show you.'

It must have begun life as a perfectly ordinary terraced dwelling but somebody had rebelled. From the carved Chinese front door, lacquered vivid red, to the bead curtains at the windows, this was a house transformed. Big pot dragons, vividly coloured and gilded, reared up on every window sill and a painted sign in oriental lettering, attached to the Irlams o'th' Height brickwork, announced that this was *Ali Baba House*. 'Even the dustbin's got silver stencil-work on it. It's the same at the back too,' said Mickey happily. 'I don't show this house to just anybody.'

Together they walked back towards the main road. Sheila knew she would catch it for being out after dark. Perhaps not today though. Anybody could see this was a very special sort of after dark. Just how special was revealed when they got out of the network of streets and onto the main Bolton Road. Below them, falling away into the valley and then rising up again on peaks and towers, were a thousand glittering orange and silver necklaces.

'Whatever are those?' she gasped.

'The lights of Manchester,' said Mickey. 'Sheila . . . why are you crying?'

When would the war be really over? It kept seeming to be but it wasn't. Mussolini was dead and his body had been dragged through the streets. The German forces in Italy had surrendered. Hitler committed suicide. And Nazi troops, in the north of Germany, were said to be surrendering to General Montgomery.

Sheila's father had been on General Montgomery's staff but the final postcard had been of a camel and some pyramids. Had he died in North Africa or gone on, with the General, to Europe? The same old question kept on coming back. Was John Starkey definitely dead?

Sheila got used to the sight of Gladys standing in front of the big wardrobe and taking out her husband's suits, on their hangers. Some days she would talk about sending them to the cleaners because you never knew . . . Other days, they were definitely going to be given away. Once Sheila walked into the room too quickly and caught Gladys sniffing a tweed sports jacket and weeping.

No further word had arrived from the War Office. Gladys simply wasn't equipped to make inquiries. She had no confidence in her own letter-writing abilities and she was afraid of telephones. She was even more afraid of the possible finality of the truth.

Gladys got a job. It wasn't a very glorious job. She was hired by a company who sent women round to offices in Manchester to clean and disinfect telephones. She had to fork out clothing coupons for a green gaberdine uniform with a forage cap. Gladys also had to pay a deposit on the company's official attaché case in which she carried her sterilizing equipment.

'I'm flaked out, Sheila,' she said. 'You'll have to wait for your tea and then we'll make do with Spam and a bit of salad.'

Gladys was sitting, in her underskirt, with her feet in an enamel bowl of steaming hot water. 'Nip up and get me the Radox,' she said.

Sheila was just crossing the hall when she heard a short, sharp ra-ta-tat on the knocker. The man to whom she opened the door was wearing an officer's uniform complete with peaked cap and white riding mac. He was tall, with a deep suntan.

'Good evening. You must be Sheila. May I see your mother?'

Gladys Starkey was already, frantically, scrambling into her skirt as Sheila led the man into the living room. Even Sheila could have wished that the battered enamel bowl was not steaming away in the middle of the floor. He had caught them at less than their best.

'I do beg your pardon,' said the man, who looked very large and alien and posh. 'I shouldn't have just barged in . . .'

'It's her fault. She shouldn't have let you.'

Sheila wondered why some ladies shaved under their arms and her mother didn't. Gladys quickly covered herself up with her uniform jacket and seemed very much rattled.

'Take a pew,' she said.

'My name is Guy Prothero.' The man extended a hand.

'Pleased to meet you,' said Gladys.

'Are you Colonel Prothero?' Sheila asked in wonder. Much had been made of this heroic name in John's letters. 'Are you the Old Man?'

'I expect I am.' The Colonel had a crinkly smile. Sheila decided she liked him and hoped she wouldn't be sent out of the room.

'Would you like a tot of whisky?' asked Gladys.

'We're saving that until me daddy comes back,' said Sheila accusingly. 'If he comes back,' she added lamely.

Gladys Starkey looked Colonel Prothero straight in the eye. 'He's dead, isn't he?'

Colonel Prothero looked stumped and then picked his words carefully. 'I presumed you knew.'

'Me? I know damn all.' Gladys sounded utterly defeated.

'I'm so sorry,' said the Colonel. 'I'd really no idea . . .'

'What brings you here then?' Gladys made it sound like an accusation.

'A friendly visit. My sister has a house out at Bowden.'

'She would have,' said Gladys bitterly. 'Where did it happen? Where was John killed? On the Rhine?'

'No. He was one of our chaps who stayed behind in the Middle East. It happened at Golgotha . . .'

'The place of the skull?' Sheila had done it in Scripture.

'I never read about any Battle of Golgotha.' Gladys sounded accusing again.

'He didn't actually die in battle.' Colonel Prothero looked embarrassed. 'He stepped out in front of a taxi.'

'Will that affect my widow's pension? It shouldn't. There was no way he'd have been in the Middle East except for the war.'

'I really wouldn't know about pensions. There's just a possibility it wasn't an accident. We had a lot of trouble with terrorists.'

'I'll settle for that version,' said Gladys. 'That explanation's much more likely. John would never have stepped off the pavement without looking.'

Sheila was watching Colonel Prothero. He was plainly very much out of his depth. 'I'll get that whisky,' she said, making for the sideboard.

'Your mother probably needs one too. Look, I brought some photographs . . .' He produced an envelope from an inner pocket. 'You're very welcome to keep them. I've got the negatives.'

'Ta.' Her mother didn't sound very grateful.

'I see you're doing your bit for England,' he said awkwardly. 'Wearing the WVS uniform and all that.'

'This is a uniform I wear to do a job of work. I clean other people's spit out of dirty phones. That's what your wonderful war's brought me down to, Colonel Prothero.'

Sheila held out a bottle of Haig and two glasses to her mother. 'D'you want it or shall I do it?'

'Put that back where it belongs.' Gladys treated Colonel Prothero to a cold look. 'Well, you've been, you've seen – though I don't expect John cracked on we were anything more special than we are. I suppose you meant well but you'll understand if I ask you to leave us to our grief. Scram off to Bowden. We'll just crawl back in the woodwork where we belong.'

Very carefully, she opened the envelope of photographs and took out a picture. Sheila knew what would happen. Gladys let out the terrible scream her daughter had been waiting for ever since the postman delivered the letter from the War Office. She didn't just let it out once – it was wrenched from her over and over again.

Colonel Prothero attempted to put one comforting arm around her shoulders.

'Out!' she screamed, shrugging him off. 'Out! I can't stand mauling men.'

Sheila led Colonel Prothero to the door.

'Tell your mother I'll write.' He looked down at Sheila with concern. 'I can't tell you how sorry I am. Such a nice chap, your father. Look, it may seem as though everything's over. But when the victory celebrations come, you'll have as much right as anybody else to celebrate; more in fact.'

'If I'm allowed,' said Sheila.

The Colonel fished inside his pocket, produced a pigskin wallet and extracted a white five-pound note.

'Buy yourself a National Savings Certificate. And that's an order.'

'I'm the kind who disobeys orders.'

'Good for you.' Surprisingly, the Colonel smiled. 'They're often the kind who make a name for themselves. P'raps we'll read about you, one day, in the papers.'

'You will,' said Sheila. 'I'm going on the stage.'

'Are you indeed? You'll probably become a big star. Doesn't surprise me in the least. Your father would have made a cat laugh. Nobody in our mess ever sang a comic song like Jolly Jack Starkey did.'

These were some of the most comfortable words that Sheila had ever heard. Her father had been a nice chap known as Jolly Jack Starkey. She wasn't just descended from misery.

The whole school was sitting in the hall on hard wooden chairs. On the wall behind them, in fading powder paint, was a huge graph showing how much they had collected during Wings for Victory week. Now Mr Crotty the Headmaster was on the platform, twiddling the knobs of the school's big radiogram, and extolling the virtues of peace.

'The war is over. The Nazi war criminals are being brought

56

to trial at Nuremberg. Some people may think you are too young to listen to these dreadful things. I think you should listen to them. The future of the world is in your hands. The horrors of the Nazi death camps must never be allowed to happen again.'

Mr Crotty was a man of many contradictions. Throughout the war, without actually being a conscientious objector, he had preached peace. This didn't stop him using the ping-pong bat on people's bottoms. Two afternoons a week, the children had joined the Dig for Victory campaign on the school allotments. When the war was won, Mr Crotty refused to allow them to put an effigy of Adolf Hitler on top of the victory bonfire.

He was a man who advocated a vegetarian diet and there were even rumours that Mr Crotty had once been to a nudist colony.

The children liked him because he had turned a perfectly ordinary county primary school into a learning adventure.

The school radio gave off a lot of crackles and rising and falling gurgling noises. 'Static,' said the Headmaster. 'The broadcast is coming directly from Germany. What we hear will be a translation.'

Evidence, relayed that day from the Nuremberg court-room, was to give Sheila nightmares which would recur for years. People had been ripped from their homes, crammed into goods trains, been unloaded in distant places and then gassed to death.

At the beginning, as in any school assembly, there had been a bit of muffled guffawing and the surreptitious passing of notes. After two hours, with no break for play-time, the entire school was stunned into horrified silence.

Mr Crotty switched off the wireless. 'You must never forget what you heard today. Any questions?'

Sheila's hand shot up, the words tumbling out of her. 'But who are these Jews? Are they like Bible Jews?'

'Some of them are perfectly ordinary people. Others are amongst the most gifted and talented people on earth. Painters, musicians . . .'

'Any actresses?'

'One of the most famous of all time, Sarah Bernhardt, was a Jewess. Let somebody else ask a question, Sheila, please.'

Sheila's head was spinning. There was a whole race of clever people who only wanted to be themselves and other people wouldn't let them. It was just like her and Mickey. She felt as though they'd finally found allies. Up shot her hand again.

'Yes?' By now Mr Crotty had his ping-pong-bat voice on.

'Are there any here in Manchester?'

'Certainly. Jews have long been some of the most important figures in the cultural life of Manchester.'

That was enough for her. There were allies. They were here. One day soon she would have to find them. Little could Mr Crotty have realized just how his peace-seeking efforts would colour the rest of Sheila Starkey's life.

The least likely things gave Sheila charges of energy and this was one of them. She had to talk to somebody.

The Dolans would be no use. Jews were in the Bible and, when it came to religion, Catholics always seemed to be spoiling for a fight. For one mad moment Sheila even considered the possibility of discussing the matter with June Monk. The thought died as quickly as it had been born. Anyway, Thursday was the evening when a gang of gloomy-looking people trudged up the drive to the Monks' house and June always stopped in.

If only Duke Tatton could talk. Duke was what Lily Gander called 'a Manchester mongrel'. You seemed to see them everywhere in the town. Fat and black, smooth-coated with amber eyes. Duke always seemed to be good at understanding but tonight Sheila needed responses.

She marched off to the bottom shops to get chips and broke one of the rules of Ravensdale Park by eating them out of newspaper as she walked back through the estate.

The restless surge of energy refused to go away. Food had fortified it. She wanted to *do* something – but what? Through the kitchen window, she watched the visitors trail up the path to the Monks'. It was getting dark. What did they do up there? The same people at the same time, every Thursday. A chink of red light was shining through a gap in the Monks' curtains. As red as a stop sign on traffic lights.

With sudden decision, Sheila grabbed her coat from behind the pantry door. There had been years of guarded talk about brimstone and the devil's work. She would use this buzzing energy for something. She would find out what went on at the Monks'.

Night was something Sheila generally glimpsed through windows. Either that or a grown-up took her hand. She was out on the pathway between their own house and the Ganders' and she was more than a little nervous. It was as though the blackout had not been lifted. There had never been a street lamp on the slope which led up to the Monks' house.

Drawn on by the mysterious red light, glowing through the gap in the Monks' curtains, Sheila continued uphill and towards their gate. A door creaked somewhere in the distance. Nearer, somebody cleared their throat and spat with a splat on concrete. Sheila could smell Michaelmas daisies and fish manure.

A dog barked somewhere. Duke Tatton, a friend. It barked again. Was it Duke? It sounded nearer this time and more like baying than barking. Tattons didn't let Duke wander at night. She felt a faint tug of fear but told herself that the Big Brown Dog, the wolf-like terror of Ravensway, never roamed as far as Rookswood Avenue. But that was during the day. What did the Big Brown Dog do at night?

It was said to belong to a black marketeer and trained to go for throats. Black market; could that be what the Monks were involved in? Black marketeers were like highwaymen and 'Watch the wall my darling while the gentlemen go by'. Whilst Gander and Rose Dolan might not have strictly approved, such people would not have given rise to comments about brimstone and the devil.

The moon came out from behind a cloud and put a highlight down the side of the Monks' house. Red light and white light. They didn't like you taking red and white flowers into hospital. They said it meant death. The dog bayed again. It was definitely getting nearer.

Sheila lifted the latch on the Monks' gate very carefully. The metal was so cold it almost burned and she could hear her own breathing. Was it imagination or could she also hear paws padding behind her? Her stomach crunched into a knot. Lily Gander always said, 'If you must run, run forward.' With quick and careful steps, Sheila headed for the Monks' window and edged towards the gap.

Somebody had put a red bulb in a table lamp. That explained the light. But what on earth were the people seated round the table doing?

Five grown-ups and June. They were all holding hands and June had her eyes closed and her head thrown back. Slobber was running down her chin. But it wasn't stopping her talking. The voice coming out of her was deep and booming and sounded like an old man.

'Churchill's lost this election and he'll never make it again.'

'What about Anthony Eden?' asked Mr Monk respectfully.

'Anthony Eden? He's going to wish he'd never been born.' It began to chuckle.

Sheila stifled a sudden urge to scream. However wobbly and swimmy she felt, she knew she mustn't. If she screamed, grown-ups would find out that she knew. Peeping through other people's windows was a much graver sin than eating chips in the street.

Sheila turned to run. A dog, with luminous amber eyes, barred her path.

It was Duke Tatton, trailing a piece of clothes-line with a ragged end and happily wagging his tail. Lily Gander was right. If there are angels amongst us unawares, some of them are probably dogs.

4

'You'll grow into it,' said Gladys Starkey.

They were in Henry Barrie's, the school uniform shop, in St Ann's Square. Sheila looked at herself dispiritedly in the long mirror. Was this her reward for passing the eleven-plus examination? A crested navy blue blazer, a size too big; and a gymslip with deeply pinned-up hem.

The woman assistant removed the pins from her mouth and got to her feet. 'She'll need a beret for next term and a panama straw hat for the spring and summer.'

Gladys consulted the official list which the High School had sent through the post. 'I've ticked off all the basics,' she said, handing it to the assistant. 'Just one summer frock to be going on with.' She turned to her daughter. 'I thought you could wear it on your holidays.'

Every item mentioned made Sheila feel more like the Man in the Iron Mask. She hated the idea of a minimum of five years in this awful outfit.

'Look! You can even get wooden plaques of the school crest,' said Gladys. She had on her special, falsely bright, shopping voice. As the assistant passed through an archway, into the stockroom, she reverted to normal tones. 'I've seen those school dresses out and about. They're not a bad little washing frock. It'll do for best at the seaside. We're giving Mr Tuffin a miss, this year, Sheila. I can't stand the idea of another fortnight of Beryl Grimshaw over the marmalade. We're going to Llandudno.'

'When?'

'Same weeks as usual. Last in July, first in August.'

Sheila improved the look of the sash on her gymslip and adjusted the sit of her blazer.

'You're finally wearing that uniform as though you mean it. What's got into you?'

'Grimshaws are having a change too.'

'Never Llandudno?' said Gladys in terrible wonder.

But it was Llandudno.

'We're going to Bettwsy Guest House,' said Sheila to Mickey.

'We'll be at the Emlyn Private Hotel. I've brought the brochure.' They were sitting on the swings in the park which lay between their two houses. 'Listen. "Dominated as it is by the two hilly promontories of the Great Orme and the Little Orme, the sweep of Llandudno's promenade has often been compared to the Bay of Naples. The Emlyn is a commodious home from home with electric lift and Vono spring interior beds in all rooms." It's not actually on the prom. It's just behind it. Look, there's a map.'

'Ours only sent a scrappy old postcard,' said Sheila. 'But it had the name rubber-stamped, in purple ink, at the top.'

Mickey and Sheila were as hot on clues for poshness as their mothers. It wasn't that they were snobbish. They just weren't much struck on the narrow lifestyle they had been born into. They wanted better. And better seemed to go with poshness. At Sunday school – they had now manoeuvred themselves into the same one – the vicar had preached a sermon saying that hymns were words dictated in heaven but written down by man.

When it came to

> The rich man in his castle
> The poor man at his gate
> God made them high or lowly
> And ordered their estate

Sheila and Mickey felt that the writer had heard God wrong. You were what you made of yourself. Sheila privately believed that she was a princess who had been delivered to the wrong doorstep. This was something else the stage was going to do for her – help her come into her true inheritance. She would earn her way there.

Llandudno did not do much for their ambitions. The town prided itself on not being Blackpool. Mickey's private hotel was all chintz and blue and white china on Welsh

62

dressers and open bowls of pot-pourri. This they found impressive. The curtains at Sheila's guest house were only cretonne and the teapots wore chromium- plated jackets. The Llandudno round of the snobbery stakes had definitely gone to Beryl Grimshaw.

If Blackpool was a coloured picture postcard Llandudno was a sepia one. Its gentle Edwardian charms took time to steal their way into the children's hearts. There was a shop on the pier which still sold model cottages and lighthouses made entirely from shells. Further down, in a little pavilion of his own, a man called Captain Bracegirdle would cut out your silhouette, in black paper, and mount it on a card for half a crown. There was also a fortune-teller's booth with a red and gold sign: *Madam Boswell – Romany Society Clair-voyant – Beware of Imitations.* She had a framed telegram outside, from the King, thanking her for loyal greetings on his ascension to the throne. She also had a signed photo-graph of George Formby, sitting on a motor car, holding a ukulele and grinning. There was a more puzzling picture of a racehorse.

Madam Boswell sat just inside the door, on a green Lloyd Loom chair, covered with a Spanish shawl. With hair that just had to be dyed and golden earrings, she looked as though somebody had painted her face with brown varnish which had cracked. Her eyes were all-seeing black boot-buttons.

Mickey spent the first week of the holiday trying to beat her prices down. He didn't actually have his fortune told and the lowest quotation he managed was five shillings. It reached the stage where they automatically paused to chat with her.

'I'll tell you something,' said Madam Boswell to Mickey. 'And I'll tell it you for nothing. You'll prosper. And that's not clairvoyance, it's common sense. Who's June? She's going to prosper too.'

'Do you ever sit round a table with a red light on and dribble coming down your chin?' asked Sheila. It was the first time she had ever mentioned it aloud.

'Indeed I do not,' said Madam Boswell. 'And you want to steer very clear of anybody who does.'

'June does,' said Sheila.

'Well I can't help that. All I know is she's going to prosper. It's not just a bit of dockering. It's very strong.'

'What's dockering?' asked Mickey.

'What I do for a living and I'd soon be bankrupt if they all held onto their money like you do.'

'You haven't told me anything about me.' Sheila sounded wistful.

'I haven't seen the colour of your cash. Keep following the lorry, my little love, that's what you'll have to do. Just keep following the lorry.'

'But what is the lorry?' cried Sheila.

'I'm not at all sure it isn't him.' Madam Boswell glowered at Mickey.

A potential real customer was hoving into view. 'You've got a lucky face, lady. And I've got the answer to that problem you shouldn't have brought on holiday. Come along, step inside. Both hands for a guinea or the deep crystal reading for thirty bob.' The woman entered the booth nervously. Madam Boswell, winking wickedly at Mickey and Sheila, drew a chenille curtain across the open doorway and was gone.

'What was all that about June?' asked Mickey.

'You promise you won't tell anybody else?' Out came the whole story. Sunlight reduced the horror of its proportions. Sheila actually felt lighter – physically lighter.

'Thank goodness I didn't part with my five shillings,' said Mickey. 'Now I can get June Monk to do it for nothing.'

'If I were you, Mrs Starkey, I would be very much inclined to put her on a course of Virol.'

Sheila disliked Mr Jepson, the dispensing chemist, from the moment she met him at the Bettwsy Guest House.

'Sheila could possibly be outgrowing her strength. And we have to remember that she is rapidly approaching *those* years.'

Sheila was sure that this last line would rapidly finish Mr Jepson with her mother. But no; she was hanging onto his every word as though they were coming from the mouth of Dr Moult who had brought Sheila into the world.

'There's nothing wrong with me,' she said.

'Did you hear that tone of voice, Mr Jepson? Just the way

you spoke to me then – that's what's wrong with you. You fly off the handle at the least little thing.'

'You're not alone,' said Mr Jepson. 'I get mothers bringing daughters into the shop all the time. Ask my sister.'

'She's just slipped to the front door to put her hand out to see whether it's stopped raining,' said Sheila. Louise Jepson was so faint and vague that it was surprising anybody noticed her comings and goings at all. He, of course, had a car. In 1947 men who had managed to get their cars back on the road considered themselves kings.

Mr Jepson looked like a wax dummy out of Burton's window. Tall with black hair and a pencil-line moustache, he did tricks with his brown eyes to make them look pleading. Sheila could just imagine him, in a starched white coat, saying, 'Your prescription's ready, Mrs Starkey.' He'd already let her have a tin of Nivea.

Louise Jepson drifted back into the guest-house lounge. 'The rain could be said to have stopped. But I'm not sure if there's enough blue in the sky to make a sailor a pair of trousers.'

How old was she? wondered Sheila. Miss Jepson's hair was not as blue-black as her brother's. She wore it untidily upswept. And considering the ease with which she should have been able to get hold of a good shampoo, it was a bit greasy. Slack-bodied, she looked halfway to artistic, in a dirndl skirt and those sandals which lace round the leg.

'Hang the petrol ration,' said Mr Jepson. 'Who's for a jaunt to Conway?'

'Could I go and find Mickey?'

'I'm afraid the Morris won't take five.' Mr Jepson looked up from checking the contents of his small leather purse.

'I meant I'd stay here.'

'I think Virol is the answer,' said Gladys. 'She's nothing but will-of-her-own.'

They went to Conway. When Mr Jepson suggested Gladys sat in the front passenger seat Louise looked distinctly huffy. Gladys demurred but that didn't suit Louise either.

'Don't worry about me,' she said. 'Norman's always putting stray females in the front.' There was nothing nasty in the way she said it. Louise Jepson just rattled on. All the way through West Shore and Deganwy she talked about the Hallé Orchestra and the need to sit in the circle, at the ballet, so you could really see the feet.

It was early closing day in Conway and the castle was, frankly, something of a disappointment. The outside was as promising as a toy fort but, once you got in, it was just an abandoned shell with no roof.

'And somebody's done a wee,' said Sheila. 'Sniff, you can smell it.'

'Just listen to her. This is the sort of thing I have to put up with all the time,' said Gladys.

'What's wrong with "done a wee"?' asked Sheila. 'We all have to go some time.'

Mr Jepson chose his words carefully: 'There's nothing wrong with actual urine. It's only that the mention of it brings to mind certain parts of the body.'

Just from the way he said the word *body* Sheila knew he was very keen on all that sort of thing. Mr Jepson was a male June Monk. Mr Jepson was rude. And her mother was too keen on him. These Jepsons were beginning to get in the way.

The evening meal at the Bettwsy Guest House was called late dinner but served at five forty-five. Mickey's hotel was slightly more sophisticated. They ate at six o'clock. Sheila only hoped he was doing better than they were. Spam – and for the second time in one week.

'I don't mind it as a scratch meal,' said Gladys indignantly. 'I can't pretend I don't know the flavour. But you do expect a bit of something fancier on holiday.'

'It's not even true Spam.' Mr Jepson was every bit as indignant as Gladys. 'It's that government stuff called Prem. Mrs Edwards can't be allowed to get away with this. We'll have to get up a petition. Louise, slip and get your writing pad.'

'Do the top part in your writing, Mr Jepson,' said Gladys. 'Then she'll know we've got a man behind us. I, for one, will definitely sign it.'

Sheila watched closely. The pair of them were joining forces and she didn't like it. There wasn't much belonging in her life but Gladys was at the centre of what there was. Mr Jepson somehow seemed to be after a share of her mother. For a wild moment she wondered whether to behave appallingly and throw the heavy cruet stand through the glass window so that he would see another, wilder, side to the Starkey family and be put off. No, he'd probably just prescribe something like castor oil. She rose to her feet and asked to be allowed to leave the table.

'How about a stroll and a sherry?' said Mr Jepson to Gladys.

'The trouble is there's Sheila. P'raps you could slip and see what Mickey's up to?'

'I'll stay with you.'

'You've had me all day. Be fair, Sheila. Give me a bit of a break. It's not often I get the chance.'

The chance, the chance, the chance for *what*? This was what kept thudding through Sheila's mind as she trudged round to The Emlyn.

'We caught a glimpse of your party, in Conway, this afternoon,' announced Beryl Grimshaw. She was spooning up the last of her jam roly-poly. 'Mummy put me in mind of that woman in the film *Love from a Stranger.*'

For that, thought Sheila, she can find out for herself that she's got custard on her chin. Beryl's little swipe had come a bit too near her own feelings on the subject.

'You kiddies run along and play. Daddy and I are going to a lecture on Druids at the public library.'

The evening sun was shining down on the white granite Cenotaph. Could the dead look down from heaven and watch you? Sheila wondered what her father was making of Mr Jepson and his blue chin.

'Let's go back to Happy Valley,' said Mickey. 'I've nearly got the littlest pierrot's monologue off by heart. Would you say he was just undersized or is he tall for a midget?'

Happy Valley was an open-air concert party. The troupe played on a wooden stage, in an arena, set in a hollow on the side of the Great Orme. There was no need to pay to go in. You could see everything from behind the railings. Real customers sat on deckchairs inside and the pierrots passed among the outer crowd collecting coppers in leather bottles with a slit in them.

'Don't forget the pierrots' was their cry.

Their heavy makeup looked strangely at variance with the daylight. It reminded Sheila of Bernice tied to the pier. She slipped a threepenny bit in the leather bottle and hoped that she would never have to beg like this when she became an actress. She would if she had to but she wasn't much struck on the idea. The thought was too near some of Gladys Starkey's prophecies for comfort. And what was Gladys up to, at this moment, with her blue-chinned stranger?

'Ladies and Gentlemen . . .' announced the man on the wooden stage. He was the one Mickey had referred to as tall for a midget. He always did a monologue about putting one red rose on the grave of his little daughter, Rosa. He also sang 'That Old-Fashioned Mother of Mine'. Where would they be having their sherry? Gladys didn't believe in public houses.

'Ladies and Gentlemen,' he repeated importantly. 'Tomorrow afternoon, at two o'clock, weather permitting, we will be having a Grand Kiddies' Talent Contest with first, second and third prizes. All comers will also be invited to take a dip in the bran tub . . .'

'At one time we'd have been thrilled,' said Mickey. 'But we're past all that now. Besides, the magic doesn't seem to work in daylight. Roll on our twelfth birthdays, that's what I say. I'm just living for the day we can audition for *Children's Hour*.'

'Do you ever think about stretching?' asked Sheila. 'I spend hours wondering how my body will ever pull out to be full size. Time seems to take for ever.'

'I bet it goes like a machine gun once we're on the wireless,' said Mickey. 'Come on. Let's clamber up and have two penn'orth of the camera obscura.'

The camera obscura was in an octagonal wooden hut, above Happy Valley, on a rocky promontory overlooking the bay.

The man who ran it could only let a few people in at a time. He grouped them round a circular table, painted white, and closed the door. In the darkness there came a creaking noise of ropes on pulleys. He was adjusting a set of mirrors in a little tower above the ceiling. The surface of the table suddenly lit up like a round cinema screen and you could see the Saint Tudno pleasure steamer crossing the bay. Successively, he showed them the Little Orme, the pavilion which housed *Catlin's Follies* and the whole sweep of the promenade.

'And now,' he said, 'let's have a bit of innocent fun. Let's see who we can catch spooning on the beach.' Once again the picture went blurred and then sharpened into focus, presenting a view of a couple sitting on the pebbles. They were gazing out to sea and decorously holding hands. It was Gladys Starkey and Mr Jepson.

5

At the new school Sheila encountered French and Latin. One end of the building, where the chemistry laboratory was, smelled of rotten-egg gas. Art was all right because they let you make a mess and so was English Literature – you got to act out Shakespeare in the classroom. Sheila was being Viola in *Twelfth Night*. It wasn't proper acting, it was just reading and you couldn't be in the school play until you were in the third form. It was the same at Mickey's new school but he said it didn't matter, school plays were for amateurs. They were going to be professionals.

The worst thing about the High School was the bus rides there and back. June Monk had also got a scholarship and insisted on sitting next to Sheila on the top deck.

'I mean I am your best friend, aren't I?' she would say.

'There is Mickey . . .' Sheila ventured.

June swept this aside with 'I don't count Mickey. You and I have known one another since we were in nappies.'

Sheila hadn't the heart to hurt June's feelings so she said nothing more. June Monk certainly was not her best friend, June was just around.

The day the letter arrived from the BBC, summoning Sheila to an audition, she was actually glad of an audience at the bus stop.

'I am the first to hear your news, aren't I?' asked June, almost greedily. 'I've had a letter too. More a parcel, really. From Arthur Mee's *Children's Newspaper*. I won first prize in the autumn poetry competition. "Happy Days" the poem was called. D'you want to hear it?'

'Not much.'

June looked hurt. 'You are mean. You come into it.'

'You don't actually mention my name?' Sheila was horror-stricken. Not at the idea of being in a newspaper; just at being put there by June Monk.

70

'I start off with dawn and the sunrise and then I list all the neighbours' names.'

Thank God I'm not on my own, thought Sheila fervently. She was praying a lot more these days. Oh God, let me get through the audition and I'm sorry I'm not nicer to Mr Jepson but he comes round too often and he's drunk my father's whisky. Amen.

'I wouldn't want you to think I was lagging behind in the competition, Sheila.'

'What competition? There is none.'

'There is as far as I'm concerned,' said June fervently. 'One way and another I'm going to be every bit as famous as you are. This prize is a sterling silver propelling pencil engraved "Well Done". They send you criticisms too. They were ever so stern about the poem I did in baby talk. It's a real thrill to be the first person you've told about the audition.'

Sheila marvelled at the speed with which June Monk had managed to turn her into a liar. It was too early in the morning to go into the complications of explaining that they were now on the telephone and that she had already spoken to Mickey. He'd had a letter too.

'Does yours say "two pieces of your own choice lasting no longer than two minutes each"?' he'd asked.

'I thought I'd do scenes from *Twelfth Night*.'

'Shakespeare? You must be off your trolley.' Mickey was at his most scathing. 'You want something to show them you can play children's parts. I'm going to do one posh and one scruffy.'

'But where will you get them?'

'Don't whine, Sheila. It won't sound good on the wireless. I'll look through plays at the library. If I can't find anything there, I'll just have to write something.'

'I suppose you wouldn't . . .'

'Find something for you? It's done. You can learn a scene from *Lace on Her Petticoat* to show you can do a Scots accent. And I'll write you a bit about the young Victoria being got out of bed and told she's going to be Queen. It's a good job you're not a boy, Sheila Starkey, or I'd probably be round at your house greasing the front step.'

'Mickey, you're the best person in the whole world. And the cleverest.'

'I know,' he said. 'I just hope those buggers at the BBC can see it too.'

The British Broadcasting Corporation being as respectable as the Archbishop of Canterbury, Gladys Starkey thoroughly approved of her daughter's latest ambition. Sheila had learned to thrive on opposition. When none came she felt thrown. In vain did she try to get Mickey to rehearse her in the pieces he had chosen.

'We've already been through them three times. It's radio. You only have to read it. If you practise it too often you'll sound all false, like people who go to elocution.'

It was one of those mornings which make you realize that the world starts again, brand new, every day. Sunlight shone on Market Street. They were much too early so they walked slowly, towards Piccadilly, looking in all the shop windows. They were particularly taken with one called Clifton's Film Star Fashions.

'I like that lemon Lana Turner model at six pounds nineteen and eleven,' said Sheila. 'I wonder if the film stars know the shop uses their names?'

'Look what they've done to poor Rita Hayworth.' Mickey was shocked. 'She's got "Reduced to Clear" pinned on her front.' Without pausing he added, 'My breakfast feels as though it's fallen to the bottom of my stomach.'

'So does mine. And it's going round and round.'

From the outside, the BBC looked like a white granite bank. Inside it resembled the pictures of ocean-going liners in the *Children's Encyclopaedia*; corridors with doors with portholes in them.

The commissionaire led them up to a woman with fuzzy hair and a list. She was surrounded by children who looked as though they were waiting to be executed. Some parents had plainly won the battle to come and now wished they hadn't. It was like the dentist's in a very big way. Yet there was excitement in the air too. The dentist's waiting room is not dappled with chance and opportunity.

'Mickey Grimshaw? Straight through that door. We're running early. We've nearly finished the boys. If you're Sheila Starkey, please sit down.'

The girl next to her was holding onto a piano accordion.

'Aren't you here to act?' asked Sheila.

'Yes, but you never know. I've brought a song just in case. It's a good one. It's won me five talent contests.'

Mention of talent contests unleashed a frenzied babble from the other children. They had all, it seemed, won something, somewhere. Sheila felt very out of it. Now they were talking about 'grades' in elocution. Some of them even produced certificates. It felt like being without fireworks on Bonfire Night. What chance did she stand against this lot with just a bit of a home-made speech of Mickey's?

Mickey reappeared through the studio door. He was almost as white in the face as the very new and important-looking script he was carrying.

'That boy's got odd eyes,' said the girl next to Sheila. 'One's blue and one's green.'

'Yes and they're very lucky,' Sheila replied fiercely.

'I've got to wait,' said Mickey. 'In a minute I've got to go back and sight-read this for them.'

Before Sheila could get a proper look at it, her own name was called and she went through the doors and into the studio. It was about the size of the living room at Rookswood Avenue with navy blue cloth instead of wallpaper and no windows.

'Good morning, Sheila . . .' The voice was disembodied and came out of a loudspeaker. 'I'm the man sitting behind the glass panel in the wall. The microphone is the thing on the stand, in front of you. Stand about a foot back and just talk to me, quite naturally, so we can check you for level. What are you going to do first?'

Sheila had planned to start with the extract from the proper, printed play. Suddenly she changed her mind. Mickey had obviously made a good impression so it wouldn't do any harm to mention him.

'I'm going to do a speech about the young Queen Victoria written by Mickey Grimshaw who you just asked to wait.'

'The young man who drank a phial of poison for us?' The voice sounded amused. 'OK, Sheila. In a moment that little green light, by the microphone, will wink. That's when you have to turn yourself into Queen Victoria.'

The light winked, Sheila became royalty. It winked again and her voice turned Scottish and wanted a petticoat with lace on it.

'Hang on, Sheila. I'm coming through.' A door in the wall opened and a man who looked like a younger version of Colonel Prothero, but wearing cavalry twill trousers and a beige cardigan, walked towards her, smiling. He was holding a very new white script.

Sheila prayed inwardly: Just let him hand it to me and ask me to stay. If he asks me to sight-read I'll even be nice to blue-chin Jepson.

Her prayer was answered. She was sent back into the corridor to study the script. It was a scene, between a boy and a girl, from an old *Children's Hour* serial. She had actually listened to it at home. When the moment came to do it Sheila and Mickey were called back in together.

'No fancy acting,' muttered Mickey. 'Just *be* it.'

When they'd finished, the man with the moustache said, over the loudspeaker, 'Thank you very much. Apart from the fact that you both sounded like railway trains, that was very good. Again please and take it nice and easily this time. Wait for your cue light . . .'

The pretending worked better the second time. It was as though the navy blue walls had melted away and they were really doing what the script said, which was sitting in a field and throwing stones into a pond, while they argued about somebody sinister called The Professor.

'That was very much better. You'll be hearing from us. And I think you'll like what you hear.'

They walked home, they were so excited. It was five miles but they walked it. That's not quite true; some of the way they danced.

Dear Sheila,
Thank you for coming along and auditioning for us. I am pleased to be able to tell you that this was successful.

We will be getting in touch with you again, shortly, concerning your first broadcast. Whenever possible rehearsals, recordings and live transmissions take place at weekends or in the holidays so as not to interfere with school work . . .

The phone rang. It was Mickey: 'What date's your first broadcast?' was his opening line. 'Mine's the week after next and it says the script will be following in due course. Does yours say that too?'

Sheila felt deflated. 'I haven't got an actual date.'

Gladys Starkey's reaction was 'I wouldn't build too much on it, Sheila. They probably send out hundreds of these letters. It stands to sense they can't use everybody. As a matter of fact, I've always thought Mickey was just that bit more nicely spoken than you.'

Beryl Grimshaw trumpeted the news to the local paper. The man who turned up to interview Mickey came on a bike and wore cycle clips. Sheila happened to be at the Grimshaws' at the time so her name ended up in the paper too.

'Nice to be listed as an also-ran.' Gladys didn't say this as bitterly as she would have done at one time. These days she was even wearing a suggestion of lipstick. Mr Jepson got her samples. She used to put it on and then rub most of it off, with her little finger. It was as though she was undecided about her true position in the matter.

The news affected June Monk in a very odd way. The morning the newspaper came out, she brought it from home and carried it onto the top deck of the bus. Sheila watched her reading and rereading the short article. June was very quiet but it was a frenzied sort of silence. She kept folding and unfolding the paper but all her attention was focused on the paragraphs about Mickey and Sheila.

In assembly that morning, just as the entire school sang 'Amen' to the hymn 'O Light Whose Beam Illumines All', June fainted dead away. Sheila was standing next to her as she keeled over. The rule was, if somebody fainted, you dragged them out.

Five hundred curious glances followed Sheila as she hauled June into the side aisle. Miss Saint, the physics mistress, was the nearest teacher and she flew towards them, in her academic gown, like a menacing raven.

Spittle began to run from one corner of June's mouth. The mouth didn't move beyond twitching but a loud voice was coming out of it.

'I am Navarna.' It was the same horrible old man's voice Sheila had heard on the night of the red light. 'Hear me for I am Navarna.'

'On the contrary, you're much more like Archie Andrews,' said Miss Saint, naming a well-known ventriloquist's dummy. 'Leave this attention-seeker to me, Sheila.'

The evil old voice continued to pour out of June: 'That lump you've got will be the end of you, Elizabeth.' Miss Saint looked startled and almost frightened. 'Don't worry, my dear, there's no such thing as death. There is no death . . .' The voice rose to a roar, June shuddered and then lay silent.

Suddenly, she sat bolt upright, as bright and as normal as somebody who had just enjoyed finishing a Mars Bar.

'Did anything happen?' she asked. Sheila was probably the only person to notice that June treated her to a tiny, sidelong glance of triumph.

Sheila was caught in a cleft stick and June must have known it. Miss Bolt, the Headmistress, had questioned her closely about June. The code of the school was definitely against ratting on friends so what was Miss Bolt expecting? Sheila maintained she knew nothing which could throw light on the trance performance. Miss Bolt, with no idea of what she was dealing with, wrote the whole scene down to 'changes in young bodies'.

Later that day the incident had an odd sequel. Everybody in the first and second forms was trooped into the science lecture room, shown a film about frogs breeding tadpoles, and asked whether they had any questions? The person who asked the most embarrassing ones was, of course, June Monk. She really made a meal of it. Outside, in the corridor, she claimed to be in correspondence with a girl who went to a school, in Grange-over-Sands, which showed biology films of actual human beings – in silhouette.

Nobody was interested. As it was, they'd already been kept behind long enough to miss two buses home. June's hour was over.

Should Sheila have said more? It really worried her. If she had told the whole story, would God have got onto the BBC and nudged them into asking her to do a broadcast? Mickey was already in a five-part serial. She took the problem, like all her problems, to Auntie Gander.

'You shouldn't have played Peeping Tom. God knows, I've often been tempted to nip up that path and have a good nosy meself. What they're doing is a religion with them. They call it Spiritualism. Mrs Monk's very big in it.

'But I most certainly draw the line at involving that kiddie. If they've got rules that must be against them. I might just have five minutes with Mrs Monk tonight.' Gander managed to make it sound as though the time would be spent in the boxing ring.

'You've done right, Sheila. You've told somebody. God's not annoyed with you. You've told me and got rid of it. Now let that be an end to it. Forget it. It's gone. Isn't that your phone I can hear ringing?'

A much-relieved Sheila dived down Gander's path, up their own, and in at the front door.

'Yes?' she said into the telephone. She was out of breath.

'Is that Sheila?' It was a woman's voice. 'We met at the BBC. Would you be free to do a broadcast on the twenty-seventh? I think you'll find it comes in the half-term holidays.'

'Yes please.'

The voice at the other end laughed and said, 'We'll be sending you a contract and a script.'

A contract and a script. Sheila sat down on the bottom stair. A script and a contract. Suddenly it was all happening. She was pegging level with Mickey again. And now she could admit something to herself. She'd hated lagging behind. She was finally going to be on the wireless. This new excitement turned her into a fizzing firework and she erupted from the stairs to the telephone. She had just started to dial Mickey's number when Gladys walked through the open front door. Sheila noticed that the lipstick was very definite today.

'What've I told you about using that phone without asking?'

'I've got some amazing news I've got to tell Mickey. I'm going . . .'

'Well I've got some news too. Put that phone down, Sheila. Put it down. I had me lunch out in town today. I'm getting married again. You can take your pick. It's Mr Jepson. You can either call him Daddy or you can call him Uncle Norman.'

6

The contract came before the script. It offered Sheila ten shillings and sixpence to play the part of Second Child Weaver in a children's documentary called *The Wreckers*. Gladys examined it suspiciously. 'There's no question of your signing it. Look at the date. It clashes with my wedding.'

Quickly, Sheila opened her pencil box and took out one of the new ballpoint pens.

'Don't you dare defy me,' said Gladys warningly.

She was too late. With one fast scrawl the contract was already signed.

'You little bitch. You downright little bitch. What will it look like? If you're not at your own mother's wedding, what will people say?'

'What they're saying already. "Those that cry loudest get over it soonest." '

Gladys seized hold of Sheila by the shoulders and began to shake her. 'Who said that? Even you couldn't have made that up for yourself. Somebody's been talking. Who? *Who?*'

Sheila was crying. She was afraid. 'My gran'ma for one.'

'That bloody woman.' Gladys let go of Sheila. 'She'd make a saint swear. The woman was born miserable. She's begrudged me every bit of happiness I've ever had.'

'Just like you do with me.'

The conversation was disrupted by a smack on the back door. Gander had obviously taken aim with a piece of coal. Now the houses had been painted again they'd taken to wrapping the coal in a twist of newspaper, so as not to mark the doors.

'Do your broadcast, Sheila,' said Gladys coldly. 'And I hope you enjoy it. But I'm going to have to think very hard about something. I'm going to have to decide whether I still love you.' She strode across to the back door and opened it.

'Yes, Mrs Gander?'

Gander, who already knew about the contract and was trying to see some good in the impending marriage, was beaming over her hedge. 'I've managed to find two bits of lucky heather. One for you and one for Sheila.'

'Sheila doesn't deserve lucky heather, Mrs Gander. Anyway, lucky heather doesn't do anything for little girls who were born bad.'

Studio One at the BBC was full of settees and smelled deliciously of Rexine artificial leather. There was a lot of sitting down whilst you waited for your own bit. Still, there was plenty to look at. Sheila was putting faces to voices she had previously heard on the wireless.

Fred Fairclough, the famous Northern actor, looked just like the old farmer she had expected. Violet Carson was more awe-inspiring in the flesh than on *Nursery Sing-Song*. She was wearing a man-tailored, black barathea costume with a marcasite brooch and a very expensive-looking hat. She was so impressive she could have passed for Winston Churchill's sister.

The Wreckers was a large-scale production which was why it was being done in the big studio with all the stalwarts out on parade. Mickey was in the production too. He had five lines. Sheila had four.

'The woman with the nice smile is Doris Gamble,' he said, 'and the one glowering is the famous Mamie Hamilton-Gerrard.'

'But she's old.' Sheila was astonished. 'She's about fifty.' Mamie Hamilton-Gerrard had been one of her personal heroines. She played all the best young girl's roles.

'And she hates real children,' said Mickey. 'You wait, you'll see. We call all the rest by their Christian names, even Wilfred Pickles. She insists on Miss Hamilton-Gerrard. She says youth is too good for the young. And she winces when we speak.'

Sheila stared at Mamie Hamilton-Gerrard in fascination. With darkly glittering coal-black eyes, she was like a tiny, chubby, powdered baby. Sheila moved a bit closer to get a better look. It was an antique baby. The pale ginger hair was very wispy. In some places you could almost see through it.

'She used to be in Variety,' said Mickey. 'She had a sister called Teddie. They were the most famous Babes in the Wood in pantomime. They were just the Hamilton Sisters then. She only went double-barrelled when she started broadcasting. Some of the others can be a bit snooty about Variety but she was a big star. She's got a mother worse than mine . . .'

A voice on the loudspeaker broke into these revelations. 'We'll do another run, straight through, good people. And would you please watch those pages for script rattle.'

Mickey had already instructed Sheila in this delicate art. You lifted the page by one corner and turned it very gently, so as to be absolutely silent. It wasn't as easy as it sounded.

One microphone was suspended from the ceiling and hung in the middle of the studio. This was for scenes which were meant to take place in the open air. Indoor scenes were done round a microphone in something called the tent. Sheila was saving details for Gander, who was a big fan of *Children's Hour*. She decided that the tent, which stood in front of the control room, looked like a garden shed made of olive-green eiderdown.

Sheila tiptoed through the doorhole. The microphone inside the tent was on a stand. They were all set to do the big opening scene where Mamie Hamilton-Gerrard cursed the machines which were causing the weavers to lose their jobs.

As Miss Hamilton-Gerrard tore into her first speech, Sheila marvelled. You forgot what a fright the actress looked. Everything was suddenly concentrated into the passionate voice. It was more young girl than any real young girl's voice, and Mamie knew how to break hearts with it.

Sheila was filled with admiration. She felt she wanted this brilliantly talented woman to be her friend, more than she'd ever wanted anything else. She was, of course, mistaking the performance for the person.

The old actress gave Sheila her first cue. Sheila answered with the correct line. Mamie's next speech was a short one and it cued Sheila to speak again.

Assuming the broad Lancashire accent required, Sheila said: 'And what's to 'appen if the overseer finds us in the . . .'

81

'Hold it for a moment.' It was the producer's voice over the talk-back. 'I'm getting a lot of rattle from those scripts.'

Sheila felt mortified. He'd stopped them right in the middle of one of her lines. Did he think it was her?

'It's most odd. It's more like creaking than your usual rattle.'

Relief flooded over Sheila. She knew what the noise was. It wasn't her fault at all. Anxious to exonerate herself she said, loudly, into the microphone, 'If it's creaking, it isn't scripts. It's Miss Hamilton-Gerrard's corsets.'

This unguarded remark was followed by a terrible silence. People seemed almost scared to breathe. Everybody tried not to stare at Mamie Hamilton-Gerrard but, even out of the corners of their eyes, they could not fail to see that she was turning the colour of a turkey's neck.

'All stay where you are. I'm coming out.' The producer had got his voice back. He sounded distinctly nervous.

'God help you,' whispered the girl next to Sheila. Suddenly the tent was absolutely full of script rattle and it was all very apprehensive.

The producer was the same one as at the audition. He marched bravely into the tent and said, 'Now then, I'm sure we can soon get to the bottom of this little mystery.'

If he sounded very falsely hopeful, Miss Hamilton-Gerrard had suddenly taken on the tones of the Wicked Queen in *Snow White*. 'Where do you find them, Barry? The slums of Salford? Or have you taken to holding auditions in girls' Borstals? I wouldn't care if the child could act . . .'

'You only heard me say one line,' said Sheila indignantly.

'Well, one and a half . . .'

'I don't wear corsets, Barry.'

'Of course you don't.'

'I wear a garment. What girl doesn't? It's just a wisp of a thing that keeps my stockings up. But it has got a few bones in it. That child must have the ears of an elkhound.' It was unfortunate that Mamie's garment chose this moment to creak with indignation.

'It's new,' she said defiantly. 'It's a very good one. It just needs breaking in.' She turned her glare onto Sheila.

'Perhaps you would like me to strip naked so you can give of your Art without any inconvenience . . .'

'But how would you keep your stockings up?' asked Sheila, genuinely concerned.

'Let's just step into the studio, Mamie,' said the producer quickly. 'I'm sure we can sort something out.'

It was Mickey who witnessed what followed: Violet Carson lent her a Marshall and Snelgrove's carrier bag and Mamie went off to the ladies' cloakroom with it. When she came back, she was looking much chubbier.

Once again, in the tent, they began to regroup around the microphone. Mamie's eyes glittered like black jet. 'Little girl, tell me your name,' she said to Sheila.

'Sheila Starkey.'

'I shall remember that. Well, Miss Sheila Starkey, I just hope you're pleased with yourself. It's not every girl who makes a deadly enemy on her first day in broadcasting. It could also be your last day.'

Sheila was still carrying the script as she came round the corner of Rookswood Avenue. There were far more cars than usual. Two men, strangers in best suits with carnations and fern in their buttonholes, were attacking Mr Jepson's bull-nosed Morris with a whitewash brush. A bucket stood on the pavement, near Tatton's grid. They had already painted *Just Married* on the bonnet. Now they were putting an exclamation mark to *Don't Worry – We've Killed the Stork* on the boot.

Sheila was momentarily stunned. These men were presumably friends of Mr Jepson's. If they too were chemists, then they were halfway to doctors – this meant they must know what they were talking about. 'Killed the stork?' Until now, Sheila had been of the opinion that the happy pair would be too old to make babies.

Rookswood Avenue suddenly stopped feeling like its safe self. Sounds of revelry were coming from the house which had, until that morning, been known as Starkeys'. Would it now be called Jepsons'? Even her gran'ma had said that the man wasn't bringing so much as a stick of furniture to the marriage.

'The bride certainly seems a hot 'un. Can't keep her hands off him,' said the man with the paintbrush. 'Raring to go, I'd say.'

The other one was standing back, admiring their handiwork. 'It could be all that Sauterne she's put back. Hope Norman's remembered to slip a few packets-of-three in his luggage. I shouldn't think there are many retail stockists in Llandudno.' He finally registered Sheila's presence. 'Excuse me, dear. Do you live round here?'

Sheila hated strange men calling her 'dear'.

'Could you nip and ask your mother whether she's got such a thing as a pair of old shoes that we could tie on the back of this car?'

'My mother's the hot 'un who's been putting back the Sauterne,' said Sheila in an icy voice she had learned, only that afternoon, from Mamie Hamilton-Gerrard.

The man dropped his paintbrush in horror.

Sheila marched up the garden path and into the house.

Louise Jepson and a lot of strangers were laughing and talking at the hall end of the through room. Down by the kitchen, on a hard wooden chair, sat Sheila's gran'ma, in deepest mourning, surrounded by her daughters. They could have been posing for an advertisement for disapproval.

Somebody had seen fit to hang three balloons from the centre light fitting. Underneath them stood Gladys in green georgette and a picture hat. The most noticeable thing about Mr Jepson's outfit was a blue blazer with brass buttons.

Sheila suddenly felt strangely shy. The figure in green georgette wasn't her mother. It was The Bride. The child went over to the dining table and helped herself to an Eccles cake. She didn't really want one. It was just something to do. Mr Jepson, she noticed, suddenly rapped on the mantelpiece with his knuckle, as if testing the quality of the wood.

Gran'ma Nuttall had noticed too. Her wicked old green eyes never missed a trick. 'Quite the auctioneer's clerk, isn't he?' She adjusted her stone marten fur tippet indignantly. 'Rum outfit for a bridegroom. Looks more like the Master of Ceremonies at a flannel dance.'

Gran'ma Nuttall's goitre, which had a black velvet ribbon

round it, was bobbing indignantly. 'You've missed nothing, Sheila. Nothing. It wasn't even a knife and fork tea – we've just been balancing bits on plates. Me stomach thinks me throat's been cut. In my day, it was only women who needed big bouquets, to hide their shame, who got married at Pendleton Town Hall. Wedding? It was more like going to pay your gas bill.'

Sheila pushed her way through the crowd and gave her mother a quick kiss. 'Hello,' she said nervously. 'Congratulations. What did you think of me?'

'Think of you? For not coming to your own mother's wedding? That's all over and done with. I can't pretend it's forgotten, though. I'm not *that* big.'

'On the wireless. What did you think of me on the wireless?'

'Now that I did forget. Oh dear. Louise . . .' She was calling down the room. 'Have you all got cake at that end?'

Was the 'oh dear' regret at missing her daughter's performance, or was it centred on the wedding cake? Sheila couldn't make up her mind and she suddenly felt very wretched.

In one day she had lost her mother and managed to make an enemy of an actress she'd idolized for years. And then there was Mr Jepson. Mickey had already taken to calling him Mr Murdstone, after the stepfather in *David Copperfield*. A joke was all very well but Mr Murdstone had really brought the Copperfields to grief. It was all too much. And the house was too full of people. Sheila wanted to be on her own.

She pushed her way towards the hall door and then clambered upstairs, edging past people sitting on the steps. Somebody had dropped a halfeaten tinned salmon sandwich on the landing carpet. It was definitely no longer Starkeys'.

Sheila had intended flinging herself straight down on her bed but it was covered in coats. She flung herself down anyway; and cried.

This was very jumbled-up crying because she felt pressed in at least three sore places. Tears over the loss of her mother – such as she was – gave way to regrets about having told the truth about the creaking noise at the BBC; these were pushed aside by fears for a future with a stepfather.

She would *never* call him Daddy. He was plain Mr Jepson. And she was going to practise turning this hateful name into a studied insult. 'Yes, Mr Jepson.' 'No, Mr Jepson.' 'I just hope you crash your car, Mr Jepson . . . only don't do it with my mummy in it.' It had been a long, pulled-out day and Sheila sobbed herself to sleep.

'Aren't you coming to wave them off?' Louise Jepson was shaking her. 'They're just about to leave for the honeymoon.'

'I'll only go downstairs if she comes looking for me.'

'I know how you feel,' sighed Louise. A loop of hair was coming adrift and her breath smelled of stale wine. 'Well, he's got what he wanted. He always said he'd wait for a widow with a nice bit of money.'

Sheila sat bolt upright. 'She thinks *he's* the one with money . . .'

'Norman? Don't make me laugh. All he's got is a hundred letters beginning "Dear Sir, Unless . . ." It's a wonder the bum-bailiffs haven't turned up at the reception.'

Distant cheers resounded round Rookswood Avenue as a motor car engine sputtered into life.

'There they blow,' said Louise bitterly. 'Sounds to me as though they deserve one another. Did you know they're spending the night, halfway, at Chester? I wouldn't be at all surprised if your mother doesn't end up running round the city walls, screaming.' Louise started to laugh.

'Why? Louise, stop that laughing. Why?'

'Because there's something about my dear brother she has yet to find out . . .'

The laughter became almost maniacal. What had her mother got herself into? Did something terrible run in the Jepson family? Louise wasn't just laughing, she was totally out of control.

Sheila raced quickly to the bathroom and ran a glass of water. Just as she got back to the bedroom, Louise flung herself on her back, on top of the visitors' coats, and started howling and screaming. It was impossible to tell whether this was with laughter or tears.

Sheila did something she'd only ever read about in books.

She flung the water full in Louise's face. This had a strange effect. Sheila was the one it made feel better.

'Your poor mother,' gasped Louise weakly. The water looked like dew drops on her wired corsage of dying anemones. 'The poor soul, what a time she's in for. I really ought to have told her.'

The muck cart is supposed to come straight after the wedding but Gander was never a slave to convention.

'Let's leave it a tip overnight. We'll lock the door on the debris. You can stop at our house and we'll tackle it in the morning. In fact we'll go one better than that. We'll take pot luck at the Jitty Cage, at The Height. And lash out on chips from Kidd's afterwards. Phone Mickey and see if he's at a loose end. We'll make a nice little night of it.'

The Jitty Cage was officially called the Olympia Cinema de Luxe. It showed nothing but very old films and changed its programmes five times a week. Mickey jumped at the chance of a Gander adventure.

'And we'll show her the Ali Baba House afterwards,' he said on the phone. Mickey had a very strongly developed sense of swap.

Suddenly everything seemed better. Sheila felt comfortable inside her own skin again. What's more, she could now see that this day had not been without its humorous side. She gave Gander a comical version of the whole story. Creaking corsets, Louise Jepson's revelations, the lot.

It was one of those evenings where everything goes right. The film was Carmen Miranda in *Way Down in Rio*. The chip shop was famous for miles around. It was nothing to see Rolls-Royces outside Kidd's. The recipe for their batter was a closely guarded secret.

They had four penn'orth of chips each and Gander asked Mrs Kidd for something the children would never have dared try to obtain.

'Any chance of a few scratchings, Mrs Kidd?'

Scratchings beat fish by a long chalk. Not that they cost anything – but they were only for the favoured few. Scratchings were the bits of batter which had floated off the fish, in the cooking process. In Irlams o'th' Height, Kidd's scratchings were the juvenile equivalent of John West Grade One tinned salmon.

Mickey, who had now read enough theatrical biographies to yearn to be a sophisticate, said, 'I expect lobster will taste like Kidd's scratchings.'

'Lobsters is lobsters,' said Gander firmly. She dearly loved her food and thought nothing of going all the way to town for Stilton cheese. 'Don't expect them to taste like something else and you won't get any disappointments.'

Sheila watched Mickey taking this in. She knew that it would soon be incorporated into their private language which was made out of odd things people had said.

'Lobsters is lobsters,' said Mickey, thoughtfully, with just a polite hint of Gander in his tones.

So that's the bit he's saving, thought Sheila happily. Oh it was good to have friends.

A tremendous truth had begun to dawn upon her. It was 'the rich man in his castle, the poor man at his gate' all over again. You weren't just stuck with what Fate handed you. You could make your own family of people who weren't even blood relations. It was possible to make your own belonging. And tonight she was sleeping at Ganders'.

'Here's a cup of tea. That house wasn't too bad in daylight.' It was morning. It was Gander. 'Me and the vacuum cleaner have broken the back of the cleaning up. The phone went. You've got to ring somebody called Barry at the BBC. I've put the number on the pad.'

Sheila didn't even bother to get dressed. She pulled an old coat of Gander's over her nightgown and ran home to use the telephone.

What could Barry want? Could Mamie Hamilton-Gerrard have lodged some sort of formal complaint; would this phone call be the equivalent of a trip to Miss Bolt's study? Oh well, he couldn't execute her down the telephone line. This didn't stop Sheila quaking in Gander's slippers as she dialled the number and asked to be put through to Barry Wrigley.

88

'Sheila? First of all, I thought you did very well yesterday. Thank you.'

'I'm sorry about Miss Hamilton-Gerrard.' She thought she'd better get straight in with it.

'We're all sorry about Miss Hamilton-Gerrard.' The tone of voice was wry. 'We just have to remember she's an exceedingly good actress. Watch her. Learn from her. There's plenty to be gained there including how *not* to behave in a studio. Sheila, can you do a Yorkshire accent?'

'Yes.'

'Do me a bit. Now.'

Sheila's voice flattened, and all the d's became t's, as she said, 'I had to get a hat from Bradford.' It was a direct imitation of Mrs Tatton from next door, who hailed from Bingley.

'Splendid. You've just landed yourself a six-episode serial. It's the part of a girl who's not afraid to speak up. No need for school permission. We're recording at weekends, beginning on the seventh.'

Gladys only sent one postcard from her honeymoon. It was of the Menai Bridge and the message read 'Dear Sheila, Weather shocking. Did I cancel newspapers? Feel as though I will need another holiday to get over this one.' No love, no nothing.

At one time, Sheila had worried that her body would never stretch to full size. That problem was over. She was beginning to be tall and slender with the beginnings of a bust. June Monk, of course, lived with a tape measure in her school-bag and was forever measuring people in the gym cloakroom.

Sheila was much more interested in the extent to which her mind could expand. Every day she seemed to be embracing some new and enormous thought. Mickey had been right. Now they were on the wireless life was indeed going like a machine gun.

When the bull-nosed Morris eventually drove back into Rookswood Avenue, it only paused long enough to disgorge Gladys and some luggage onto the pavement. Mr Jepson then drove off again without so much as giving his bride a hand with the cases.

'He's not left you, has he?' said Sheila, diving for the black patent-leather hatbox which her mother used for everything but hats. She noticed that Gladys was looking a little wild-eyed.

'Don't talk silly, Sheila. He's just slipped to the shop to get me something. Let's get in and put the kettle on. I'm gasping for a cuppa.'

'Did you have a nice time?' There had been no kiss but Gladys's kisses, even when she deigned to deliver them, were very hard and pursed-lipped.

'Nice time? Some honeymoon, it was purgatory. I've not so much as closed my eyes for a week. That's what he's gone to the shop for – sleeping tablets and some special French wax earplugs. Sheila, I've done something terrible. I've gone and married a man who snores like ripping calico. Honeymoon? Do you know who I spent the first night with? The hall porter at the Blossoms Hotel, Chester.

'Norman was in the bedroom, snoring like a pig in torment, and this good soul was calming me down, with cups of tea, in a little cubby hole under the hotel stairs. Wouldn't you think Louise Jepson would have mentioned it? The poor sweet-heart couldn't be expected to know himself. I could already be considering an annulment, if he wasn't so satisfactory in other ways.'

It was the first time Sheila had ever seen Gladys Starkey blush. Except now she was Gladys Jepson and the whole thing made Sheila feel very uncomfortable.

Even the smell of the house changed, with the advent of Mr Jepson. He brought with him the odour of masculinity and a lot of mysterious shaving tackle. He was also given to bringing home, from his shop in Chorltoncum-Hardy, free samples of beauty products. As Gladys hated waste, she took to using the eye shadows and mascara, and to dabbing herself with a whole range of perfumes. These love tokens arrived at Rookswood Avenue in little, testing-size bottles, so she rarely smelled of the same scent for more than a couple of days running. And their bathroom cabinet was now bursting with pills, sleeping potions and nerve tonics.

It seemed to Sheila that, when Mr Jepson wasn't administering something to knock Gladys out, he was beseeching her to try the tablets which had been developed to keep bomber pilots awake. These were now coming into vogue as a remedy for depression.

Gander would have tried to like Dr Crippen himself but she had difficulty in taking to Mr Jepson.

'Sheila love, I want you to forget that I used to call Chorlton-cum-Hardy "Debtor's Retreat". It was just an old music-hall joke.'

'Is selling the diamond engagement ring my father gave her a joke too?'

'That good diamond? She's never!'

'She has. Jepson says he's having something called "liquidity problems". And a man from Beecham's Powders came round at nine o'clock the other night, with a piece of paper in his hand.'

'Oh dear,' said Gander. 'Don't tell me. I mustn't ask. What happened?'

'It was a writ.' Her stepfather had brought a lot of new words into Sheila's life. 'But Jepson kept shouting it was only legal to serve them in the hours of daylight. *She* was scared to death the Tattons would hear, through the wall.'

'Poor thing, I can't blame her. This isn't a bit like Rookswood Avenue. That chemist might consider himself a cut above the rest of us but at least we pay our own way. Still, we mustn't judge. I've knocked some treacle toffee together. Take a handful and share it out at rehearsals.'

For a man who lived one jump ahead of his creditors, Mr Jepson was very keen on outward respectability. Clean shirt and handkerchief every morning, though Sheila noticed he wasn't so demanding of clean vest and underpants. It was the same with the parish church. He made a great show of going to Evensong but never managed to get up in time for Holy Communion. This did not stop him announcing that Sheila must be confirmed.

'What does it mean?' Sheila asked him suspiciously.

'It means you become a full member of the Church of England. Just like Princess Elizabeth.'

91

'I thought it meant you'd definitely settled for God,' said Sheila. 'And I'm not sure I have. Please don't tell Gander but I only half believe in it all.'

'I suppose it would take a bolt of lightning to convince you,' snapped Gladys. 'Why can't you be more like other children? You don't hear of all this fuss when the Dolans get confirmed.'

'No, because if they so much as put a foot out of line, the priest's round at their house wanting to know the reason why.'

It was a terrible thing to even think, but God would have to wait.

7

The menstrual cycle was no longer a mystery, it was merely a monthly nuisance.

'We started early so the chances are we'll finish late,' said June Monk, already looking towards the menopause from the top of the school bus.

To Sheila, it seemed that June automatically devalued anything which was happening in the now. Incapable of enjoying today, she had to have a peep into tomorrow. And she always wanted what somebody else had got. Correction, she always wanted what Sheila had got.

'You've got your name in the *Radio Times*, a Jaeger cardigan, you've even been in that Indian restaurant where prostitutes are supposed to go ... Oh well, I suppose my rewards will come later.'

'Rewards for what?' Sheila was surveying the set exercise, for Latin homework, in dismay. The subject was becoming too difficult for her; the result of days of truancy, spent reading plays, in the great echoing hall of the Central Reference Library in Manchester.

'Rewards for being me,' said June Monk. 'You're not the only one who's going to be well known. I've got the mark of fame on me too.'

'Who says?'

'My voices,' said June in an irritating tone which suggested she should have been standing against a stained-glass window.

'You want to watch out, with those voices, June. Look what happened to Joan of Arc.' Immediately she said it, Sheila wished she hadn't. But she was quite unprepared for what came next.

Tears began to roll down June's cheeks. 'You don't know what it's like,' she sobbed. 'How could you know? I'm set aside. I'm special. It's not just my poetry; there's the *other*. But

I daren't so much as mention it to anybody or they think I'm mental.

'Why can't you try and understand? One day we're going to be famous together. We'll have Norman Hartnell evening gowns and people will say, "There they go. They've been friends since childhood." '

Sheila found herself looking at June as a stranger would have looked at her. June's style was very chocolate box: all blonde curls and saucy curves and googly eyes, but there was no denying she was turning into a remarkably pretty young woman. Boys had already changed their attitude towards June. Even those who hadn't stopped disliking her hung around the pathway leading up to the Monks' house. It was as though they were awaiting some non-specific event. June Monk had turned into a sexual jam-pot.

This young woman now wiped away her tears with a handkerchief embroidered with a Mabel Lucie Atwell character. 'It's harder for me. You must see that. There's no *Children's Hour* for what I'm going to do. I've whole years to wait before I can get things moving.'

'But what things?' asked Sheila. It was very difficult to be sympathetic towards June. She wrapped herself in veils of mystery and then demanded to be understood. 'June, what things?'

'Don't ask. This is something I have to carry on my own. It's a very long and lonely road.' She gave her nose a loud blow, then dried it and said, 'Sheila, d'you think Mickey might be a homo?'

'He doesn't wear suede shoes or a corduroy jacket,' replied Sheila dubiously. At the High School, these were the acknowledged outward symbols of male homosexuality.

'Yet,' said June. 'He doesn't wear them yet. Oh, you are lucky. I wish I had your ankles and you even know art students in duffel coats.'

Mickey had wanted to get a duffel coat too but his father said he wouldn't countenance any son of his posing as a retired naval officer. Mickey was fourteen and a half at the time.

It was he who had first got to know the art students. Mickey

94

discovered there was a whole café life, centred round making one cup of coffee last for hours. Its headquarters were down in The Kardomah, on Deansgate; a subterranean coffee house with arched and vaulted recesses. Mosaics of Egyptian subjects were set into the walls, and the supports of the tables were in the shape of lyres.

The establishment was self-service, the menu very dainty. It featured items like creamed mushrooms on toast and croquette potatoes. Just the thing for a lady in a hat and gloves who had finished her morning's shopping at Kendal Milne and fancied the sort of light luncheon which has a nice cake to follow. Most of the customers fell into this category and sat up very straight.

Sprawled at the far end of the cafe, in a haze of blue cigarette smoke, were the art students. It was handy for the phone box and away from the gaze of the permanently outraged manageress. They had long hair and longer scarves, and sandals, and the girls didn't bother with stockings and nobody troubled to lower their voice – even when they were talking about free love and Picasso.

'However did you get to know them?' Sheila asked Mickey.

'I first saw them streaming out of Forsyth's, the music shop. I thought they must be some kind of very intelligent gypsies. They'd been buying a gramophone record and they were very excited. They kept yelling words like "erotic" and "orgasm". I wanted to know what it was all about so I followed them down the steps of The Kardomah and asked.'

The excitement, he discovered, had been induced by a recording of Ravel's *Bolero*. It was becoming all the rage in student circles and they had just heard it for the first time. Mickey soon had his own copy which he played over and over again. The year he and Sheila were fifteen, it was the accompaniment to the whole of one half-term holiday.

It made Beryl Grimshaw uncomfortable. 'As tunes go, that one's downright unnecessary. Give me something whole-some – give me "The Trumpet Voluntary". The pair of you are getting too old to be spending so much time crouched over a gramophone in our shed. It's about time you started playing with boys, Mickey.'

Sheila didn't know where to look. There was no denying that June Monk had set her thinking.

Mickey was no longer afraid of the bullies. He had grown as tall and as strong as the worst of them. It had taken one fight, in the Grammar School yard, to prove that his temper was as deadly as his tongue.

'I got a headmaster's caning for it,' he told Sheila. 'And it's a funny thing, that caning acted just like camouflage. They leave me alone now. I pass unnoticed. I do what I like.'

The fact of the matter was that Mickey hardly ever went to school. If Sheila had read a hundred plays in Manchester Central Reference Library, Mickey had read a thousand.

'The education they're handing out at school's no use to me. I'm grabbing my own. Next year I'll have to swot hard and get five of these new O level things. If I get into RADA, the Education Committee say five is the minimum they'll accept to give me a grant to live in London.'

The fact that they were child actors, with their sights set on the Royal Academy of Dramatic Art, just about made them acceptable to the art students. Being different was held in high esteem. And Mickey and Sheila were certainly that. The students tolerated them in The Kardomah but suddenly became lofty nineteen- and twenty-year-olds when the children demanded to be taken to meet Magda Schiffer.

Magda Schiffer was a Manchester bohemian legend. In fact, the word bohemian had gone out of fashion – and it was only outsiders who still called creative people 'arty'. Sheila and Mickey desperately longed to be insiders. Friendship with Magda Schiffer seemed to be a prime qualification. Jewish, a painter, born in Berlin, survivor of the Buchenwald concentration camp – Magda Schiffer nightly held court in the nearest thing Manchester had to a salon.

These gatherings took place in an attic flat, under the gothic eaves of some former cotton merchant's mansion, in the Victoria Park district. She was said not to have two ha'pennies for a penny, and to offer little more than a cushion on the floor and her famous cheese straws. Magda Schiffer nevertheless attracted the brightest young talents in

Manchester. Her dusty attics were reputed to throb with vitality and new ideas.

'And she's Jewish too,' said Sheila. 'I've been waiting for Jewish friends ever since Mr Crotty made us sit on those hard seats and listen to the Nuremberg trials.'

'We'll get there,' said Mickey confidently. 'Barney Shapiro will take us.'

'Who's he?'

'Another art student. He comes back from St Ives next week. Barney Shapiro is the most beautiful man I've ever seen.'

Sheila took a deep breath. 'June Monk thinks you're a homo.' There, it was out.

'A what?'

Sheila could see that Mickey was stalling for time. 'Queer. She thinks you're queer.'

'I don't like that word,' he said coldly. 'Americans at the air base, at Burtonwood, call it "gay".'

Sheila was astonished. 'I didn't know you knew American soldiers.'

'There's a lot about me you don't know; and never will. Plate-glass people are very boring.'

It wasn't an answer. Sheila decided to resort to wiles. 'Do you remember Diggory Mallet who came up from London to be in that thing we did about Lewis Carroll?'

'Donegal tweed sports jacket, looked like a goat.' Mickey was watching her carefully.

'I was talking to him about drama schools and he said I'd never make a real actress until I lost my virginity. The most important thing in my life is being a good actress so I was wondering whether . . .'

'You should jump into bed with Diggory Mallet?' Mickey was ahead of her; or thought he was. 'It's an old dodge. It's exactly what he intended you to wonder.'

'No, I thought you might oblige.' Sheila looked anxious. 'Just in a friendly way, in the cause of Art.'

'Oh I do love you . . .' Mickey was spluttering Kardomah coffee all over a mosaic mural of Cleopatra and howling with laughter.

'I didn't mean you to fall in love with me,' cried Sheila anxiously. 'That's not what I had in mind at all.'

'*Just in a friendly way*,' crowed Mickey. 'No, you meant to find out whether I was gay. And I'm not in love with you, I just love you. There's a big difference. You did mean to find out about me, didn't you?'

Sheila went back to being her usual honest self. 'Let's just say that, one way or another, I thought this could be a very useful conversation.'

'Of course I'm gay. So what? Would you really have gone the whole hog with me?'

Sheila nodded. 'Only because of being a better actress. You're nice and clean and I thought we could have approached the whole thing clinically. Mickey, do stop laughing, that manageress is hovering again. Let's go and get two more coffees. It would be awful to be barred from The Kardomah. I'll pay.'

'To prove how big you are about knowing a homo? You'd be buying coffee for half the theatrical profession. A cup for Noël Coward, another for John Gielgud . . .' They were now threading their way through tables full of Kendal Milne customers.

'I thought you said you didn't like the word homo,' said Sheila. 'Or queer. I thought you said you preferred to be called gay?'

A woman in a hat overheard some of this and bit into a meringue with such surprise that mock cream went all over her face.

'Mickey!' Sheila suddenly froze in her tracks. 'Something awful's just dawned on me. We should be keeping our voices down. You're against the law!'

On a night of subdued moonlight and driving rain, Mickey and Sheila first passed from Upper Brook Street into Victoria Park. This weather acted like a veil on some ravaged old beauty so that all the tall gables, the mysterious turrets and the inexplicable towers looked much as the Victorian cotton merchants must have intended, when they first raised their mansions on this solid estate of private roads.

The toll bars, at the entrances, were still in place but the uniformed attendants were now memories. Victoria Park had come down in the world. Many of the houses stood in ruins, the result of the blitz. Others, in equally dank and dishevelled gardens, had been converted into warrens of bed-sitting rooms. It was even whispered that Indian students, in turbans, lit joss sticks and bowed down to heathen gods, in Victoria Park, these days.

Yet it was still possible to catch glimpses of the past. A uniformed parlour maid was drawing the curtains on a firelit room which was all polished mahogany and silver and heavy picture frames and old brocade upholstery.

'It is magic,' said Mickey. 'Why did they build these huge houses on such little plots of land? Can't you just imagine them making their millions, in cotton, on George Street and then coming back here to be bossed by ambitious wives? All very Manchester.'

'Nobody loves Manchester like I love it,' said Sheila, 'but we're lost and I'm wet and how do we find Magda Schiffer's?'

'There's the street sign. Daisy Bank Road. Barney said to look for a tall terrace like a grey wedding cake. D'you really love Manchester, Sheila? I can't wait to get away from it.'

Sheila felt caught. Some of the Kardomah conversation had made it very plain that Manchester was dull, boring, provincial. It was an attitude she could never share.

'I love it like a friend. It may be black and battered and foggy but it's mine – it's part of my belonging.'

'No successful actress ever ran a career from this town,' said Mickey sternly. He sounded much more human and a little anxious as he added, 'I wonder where my city will be? Somewhere in America, I wouldn't mind betting. Then again, I might be like that boy in Dickens. "Always moving on, sir. Always moving on." Still that applies to everybody on the stage, doesn't it?'

It did. And Sheila found it very difficult to come to terms with the idea. The stage was the one thing which might fulfil her terrible need for belonging; yet it would, inevitably, tear her away from the one place where she truly belonged.

'Grown-up life, here we come!' yelled Mickey. 'Look,

there are the houses. It's just like Miss Havisham's in *Great Expectations*, but stretched out into a row. Isn't it ghostly? Come on, he said Magda's was the end one. She's at the top. I was told to ring and shout.'

At the side of the original iron bell pull was a panel of the cheapest electric bell pushes imaginable. Some of the names had been crossed out and altered. Others had no names. Against the top bell, secured by a rusty drawing pin, was a skewwhiff and yellowing visiting card: *Magda Schiffer, Pantherstrasse 19, Berlin.*

Mickey pressed the bell confidently. Sheila already felt very far from home.

Nothing happened. In the distance, a badly tuned radio was playing Deanna Durbin singing 'Harbour Lights'. Further up the terrace, somebody opened a door and pushed out a cat. The rain was coming down in stair-rods.

'There's definitely a light.' Mickey was gazing upwards at the gothic attic window. 'Hello,' he yelled. 'Open the door. Excitement's arrived.'

A curtain was pulled back and electric light streamed across the wet, leafless treetops. A small dark head poked out of the window.

'If you are carol singers, I am not a believer.' The voice was female and foreign.

'We're friends of Barney Shapiro's,' said Mickey.

'You don't look Jewish to me.' The woman aloft sounded almost accusing.

'No but we're very nice and clever.' Mickey was enjoying himself and completely unabashed. He had obviously come into his element. Sheila felt she was leaving hers. And her stomach was churning like it had done at the *Children's Hour* audition.

'I send Shapiro.' The head disappeared like a character on a puppet stage. The window closed with a rattling crash which made Sheila even more anxious. She feared the glass might come flying down on them.

'Are you supposed to be Jewish to get in?' she asked Mickey nervously.

'No. She's just trying to intimidate us. She's famous for it. I hope you're not making the mistake of expecting her to be nice.'

Deanna Durbin was still singing about the harbour lights leading her safely home. From inside the house, they could hear feet descending bare wooden stairboards. To Sheila, it sounded like the butler in *The Doom Family* on the radio. For the first time in her life, she took Mickey's hand.

Somebody was tugging at the door from inside. It seemed to be sticking in its frame. Suddenly it swung violently open.

Sheila saw Barney Shapiro for the first time and she would remember the moment for the rest of her life. The first thing she did was let go of Mickey's hand.

Barney Shapiro was tall and broad. His hair was as dark as any of the Dolans' but their eyes were sky blue whilst his were the colour of a sailor's collar. It was a face of great beauty yet it was a clown's face. Sad and comical at the same time. And this wonderful creature was laughing at her.

'You're scared,' he said.

'Never. It'd take more than you to scare me.'

'Who mentioned me?' Now he was *definitely* laughing at her. Oh he was beautiful. The house smelled of old hymn books but the man smelled like new bread.

For the first time in her life Sheila felt that Mickey was playing a smaller part than she was. A fizz of excitement was passing between her and Barney Shapiro. It was a living thing. It was almost tangible. It should have been a kind of zzz on the air.

'I've heard of people with stars in their eyes,' smiled Barney, 'but this is the first time I've actually seen it. Mickey, how old is this amazing creature?'

'I'm fifteen.' Sheila answered for herself.

'Jail-bait.' The current between them faltered but only for a moment. 'Purest jail-bait. Come upstairs, half Manchester's up there arguing about the Festival of Britain.'

As they clomped up the bare staircase, their footsteps echoed down shadowy green corridors which led off every landing. The three of them were making a noise like a team of cart horses but nobody so much as peeped out from behind one of the heavy oak doors, to see what was going on. It was all very unlike Rookswood Avenue. One door had a notice stabbed onto it with a carving knife. It was written in lipstick and read *Fuck Off Alistair – And I Mean It*.

Barney winked at Sheila and burst into mocking song:

> You thought you wanted Bohemia
> Amorous, glamorous Bohemia . . .'

Winking was supposed to be common so why was it making her feel as though they shared some wonderful secret? And why did she suddenly feel more alive than she'd ever felt in her whole life? Shadows seemed deeper, light more bright.

Now they were at the top landing. It had a zinc coal bunker on it. Standing next to this was a woman who looked like a marmoset in pain. Small and thin with a Dutch-doll haircut, sallow skin and singeing dark brown eyes. She was dressed in shapeless black with amber beads and holding onto a plate of palest golden cheese straws.

'You're very young.' The woman looked accusingly at Sheila and Mickey. 'Why you not in bed?' She sounded even more German than she had when she had called down from the window. 'I hope you not child prostitutes?'

Sheila didn't know whether to be shocked or thrilled.

'We are actors,' said Mickey, whose mother knew where he was going but had forced him to wear his school blazer. 'Is that painting by Max Ernst?'

'Is by me. I was doing such work when Ernst was sucking a dummy. You like?'

'No,' said Mickey. 'I love.'

Not for the first time, Sheila thanked God for Mickey whilst realizing why a lot of people wanted to kick him.

'Ho ho,' said Madga Schiffer, 'you have style. And you are one of the boys. Don't deny it – I can always tell. They can be very clever and very cruel. Your name?'

'Mickey.'

'Mikerl. The other is like that mouse in Hollywood. I prefer Mikerl. Come, I show you more work. Tell me about the girl? She looks a bit operette to me. All eyes and svelte waist and breasts like eager little apples.'

'I promise you she's very talented,' said Mickey easily. 'It's

102

just that she's clapped eyes on Barney Shapiro for the first time. She's stunned by all that sex appeal.'

Sheila could have killed him.

'Good job you're not child prostitute,' laughed Magda. 'Shapiro has no money. The mother and father they got pots of money. Money to burn. But only for nice, bourgeois Jewish girl.'

'Magda,' said Barney quietly. 'She's only a child. You go too far.'

'I go as far as I bloody well like. These are mein own floorboards. Mine. You want cheese straw? You, Miss Operette, I'm talking to you. You want a good cheese straw?'

What Sheila wanted, more than anything else, was to be alone with her thoughts for a few moments. She just wanted to go away and think about Barney Shapiro and the effect he was having upon her. Instead she took the proffered savoury biscuit and looked around the room which was a whitewashed attic.

The walls were covered in pictures, the floor had cushions on it, and Kardomah-looking people were sitting on them. Nobody seemed to worry that brilliantine might rub off on the wall. Not that these people were much given to beauty products. Sheila had never seen so much unchecked hair, on men and women, in her life. Nor so many folkweave skirts and drawstring peasant blouses (where could she get one?) and openwork leather sandals. If she was going to be absolutely honest, neither had she seen so many grubby ankles.

Barney was wearing a striped French fisherman's jersey and trousers like the bottom half of overalls. It was the first time Sheila had ever seen blue jeans and she found them disturbingly tight. Quickly, she looked down at his ankles and was reassured to see that they were nice and clean.

What was it about this man? She had known him three minutes yet she had already been through all the emotions of being engaged and married to him. A series of vivid pictures had flashed through her head which even included their first quarrel. It had centred round the opening of his important art exhibition which clashed with the premiere of her first starring role in a play at the Opera House in Quay Street.

Sheila was already well enough versed in things theatrical to know that, before plays reached Manchester, they had to be cast and rehearsed in London. In this moment she actually felt the pain of separation from Barney.

If this is love, she thought, it's like a rip-rap firecracker going haywire in my mind.

If this is love? The very idea of there being any question made her feel disloyal to her new passion.

The room had hardly any furniture but it was full of words. She caught a few from the babbling air. It would be as well to get used to Barney's world. What did ayonism mean? Well it sounded like ayonism and who was Salvador Darlee? They seemed to throw in the word 'sex' like other people used 'and' or 'but'. Barney had disappeared to answer the door again. Mickey was deep in a loud argument with Magda Schiffer which was punctuated with gales of laughter. Nobody seemed to mind that Sheila was wandering around and eavesdropping on different conversations.

Somebody with a name that sounded like fried pronounced with a cockney accent was obviously important to them all. Sigmund Fried.

A man with a big beard, which was so red it was rude, came up and put his arm around her waist. 'I am a painter and you are the model I have been looking for all my life.'

Magda Schiffer, spotting this, crossed the room swiftly and lifted the arm away.

'You mean she owns the little apples you have always wanted to fondle. Ignore him, Miss Operette. He couldn't paint a lavatory seat. And you, Mr Lonsdale, what you think I am? A brothel-mother for your jaded desires? Go! No arguments; just go. Not you, child. That clever Mikerl has just been telling me you have the divine creative spark. What a responsibility. Don't waste it on Barney Shapiro.'

Sheila went so red that the burning actually hurt. But not so much as the humiliation inside. Was her new state of mind so obvious that people could see it at a glance?'

Magda laughed and said, 'I am old woman. I miss nothing. Welcome to my house. Be happy here. Any trouble, you threaten them with me.

'Mr Lonsdale . . .' Now Magda raised her voice. 'Out into the night with you, you dirty old man. You shall not think you can come here and pop young virgins.'

Sheila noticed that Barney had returned and was watching all of this, anxiously. Perhaps he was wishing that he hadn't introduced them into this amazing place. Or was he just worried because his parents had pots of money and he didn't even own a pair of socks? In that moment Sheila wanted to be his mother as well as his wife. She wanted to hold him close and tell him that it didn't matter.

He began to move towards her. Maternal thoughts dissolved. She was a young woman again. What's more, Magda had given her an idea. This was quite definitely love. Lovers gave one another gifts. Sheila Starkey decided she would give Barney Shapiro the only thing she had to offer. She would give him her virginity.

Never was a present so difficult to give away as Sheila Starkey's maidenhead.

'You're like a jack-in-a-box,' said Mickey. 'Wherever Barney is, you pop up. It's beginning to be embarrassing. I think I should just concentrate on getting five O levels.' Mickey sounded firm. 'If you don't manage that, in your mock exams, they won't even consider you for a grant for theatre school.'

They were sitting on the huge sawn-off tree trunk in Oakwood Park, mid-way between their two houses. It was spring and everything was so full of the new life force that even this old stump was throwing out vigorous shoots. Mickey had abandoned truancy and was cramming furiously. He handed Sheila his history notebook.

'Test me on the Reformation.' He had learned his notes like a role in a play and began to recite. 'The Reformation. Causes. One: fat and lazy monks. Two: paying other people to pray for you . . .'

'Perhaps I could get the Dolans to light a candle for me,' said Sheila.

When it came to romance, the Dolans had marginally more sympathetic ears than Mickey. Sheila had taken to spending a lot of time with them in their old hen hut. The sepia postcards the children had tacked up, in the war years, of Bette Davis and Joan Crawford, were still on the walls. But pride of place today was given to a large and glossy photograph of a group of handsome negroes in gaberdine suits. It was captioned *The Deep River Boys* and lavishly signed 'To Delia, a sweet white sister'.

'Two hours in the bloody pouring rain, outside the stage door of Ardwick Empire, and all they want me to be is their sister.' Delia sounded disgruntled. At sixteen, she was beginning to look like a younger version of her mother with a fine Irish complexion and a great, gleaming cloud of black hair.

Monica was still lagging one indignant year behind. 'We're too young for everything. It's no joke wanting to be a nun. Reverend Mother at school's against me. She says she's known barnyard animals with more vocation than I've got. And Reverend Mother's got Father Conklin under her thumb. What chance do I stand? I'm thinking of taking a leaf out of St Theresa's book and getting straight on to the blasted Pope.'

'What d'you want to go and be a spiteful old nun for, anyway?' asked her sister. 'You've more the look of a beauty queen. If you didn't have that big bosom, you might make a mannequin.'

'If I can't be a nun, I'm going on the game,' declared Monica. 'I'm the kind of girl who needs a passionate occupation.'

'Can I talk about Barney again?' asked Sheila.

'Yes, but only for five minutes. And I'm timing you by my wristlet watch.' Delia Dolan was showing signs of joining the ranks of those who were bored by the name Barney Shapiro.

June Monk had finally come into her own. She had become a young woman who saw the sense of providing what people wanted. Sheila needed a listening ear – June listened. No detail was too trifling. If Barney so much as smiled at Sheila, June had to hear it told in lingering slow motion. And would immediately demand a repeat performance.

'I had a wonderful dream about you and Barney last night,

106

Sheila,' she said. 'You were under a bandstand together, in the rain, and he put his arm round you. Honestly, ripples started to go through me from here to Preston.'

Sheila knew she should be working for her examinations. The stage was still as important to her as Barney was. She knew she would have to leave Manchester to gain training. But she didn't want to go before some understanding had grown up between them.

She didn't just want to be with Barney, to touch him, to hold him – Sheila wanted a *deal* with him. Surely a Jew could understand that? She never actually told him any of this. She saw her own passion as such a bright and shining and tangible thing that she simply expected him to see it too.

He never told her to go away. He just smiled (oh that mouth and those teeth) and dodged. When they did speak, he always made it sound as though he was teasing. But that zzz was there between them; Barney might be trying to insulate the current, but that mysterious fizz was still there.

Sheila had entered into the year when nothing went according to plan. Too late, she began swotting for her O levels and the results were highly unsatisfactory. She only scraped through in two subjects, English Literature and Art.

Miss Bolt, her headmistress, was adamant; on this showing, there could be no question of a recommendation for a grant. Sheila would have to spend an extra year in the fifth form and do the examinations again.

Gladys Starkey renewed her dour rumblings about Pitman shorthand and typewriting. An unexpected ally emerged in the shape of Sheila's stepfather. Was it because the Academy of Dramatic Art had 'Royal' in its title? Mr Jepson was so passionately enamoured of the Royal Family that he even had his own copy of *The Little Princess* by 'Crawfie', their former governess. Mr Jepson simply treated Gladys to an extra phenobarbitone tablet and told his stepdaughter not to worry.

The year 1952 was when Sheila seemed to be marking time in leaden boots whilst Mickey soared ahead like a young eagle. She was obliged to sit back and watch while he scooped up six O levels and an open scholarship to the academy. The Education Committee were impressed enough to award him a grant. By early autumn he was packed up and poised to head south.

The steam and bustle of London Road Station never seemed the same when you were going to be the one left behind, waving to the departing train. Mickey was hanging out of the carriage window in a glow of anticipation. Sheila was standing disconsolately on the oily station platform.

'I'm lagging behind. You always said we were going to be the next Noël Coward and Gertrude Lawrence and now I've let you down.'

'You've let yourself down,' said Mickey. 'All you've done, for a year, is moon round after Beautiful Barney. It's about time you got one thing straight. I've read a thousand books about the theatre and I don't think you can have great love *and* the stage. They don't go together.'

'What about Laurence Olivier and Vivien Leigh?' asked Sheila indignantly.

'If you follow them home, I expect it's murder.' Mickey was totally unrepentant. 'Anyway, Barney's not an actor and he'll never marry you. He's a Jew. They don't marry out.'

'Who mentioned marriage? You're getting very conventional all of a sudden. And I don't want life secondhand, out of books. I want the genuine article. I want real life and I want to bite at it.'

'But what do you want to be? Happy in love or a successful actress?'

'Both.' Sheila glanced at the station clock. She was due at rehearsal at the BBC in exactly twelve minutes. 'I want both.'

'The cake and the ha'penny?'

'Just who the hell d'you think you are, Mickey? Why shouldn't I want the cake and the bloody ha'penny?' Sheila was shouting loudly enough to make a woman on the platform, with a heavy suitcase, decide to look for a seat a bit further down the train.

Mickey's steely look turned into a huge grin. 'You're wonderful, Sheila. There is nobody else quite like you. I was thinking in the bath this morning, I've known you exactly half my life. This is just a temporary setback. One day we'll still have a huge success together . . .'

Porters began slamming compartment doors. A billow of steam exploded and evaporated to reveal a large female figure bearing down the platform towards them. It was Beryl Grimshaw in a good belted raincoat with a small yellow teddybear held, accusingly, in front of her.

'We will overlook the fact that you refused to allow me to come and wave you off . . .' Beryl was glancing significant daggers at Sheila. 'You forgot to pack Teddy. Here.' She thrust the ageing toy at her son.

'For God's sake, Mother, I'm sixteen. I didn't *mean* to take him.'

'Pity you couldn't stuff me in the dirty linen box too. Poor old Teddy, I found him right down at the bottom, next to the perished hot-water bottle.'

The engine had continued to get up steam and now the guard's whistle blew.

'Grab hold of her, Sheila,' called Mickey desperately. 'She's capable of anything. She might try and jump on the train with me.'

'Lay one finger on me, young woman, and I'll belt you into the middle of next week. Mickey! I brought your sandwiches too . . .'

But the carriage had already pulled beyond her arm's reach and Mickey's was just one of many hands waving goodbye.

'Bye,' yelled Sheila. She was surprised to find that tears were rolling down her face. 'Don't get knocked down or anything.'

Mickey might not have heard her but God would and it was halfway to a prayer. With the train gone the tension went out of the platform like taut elastic gone slack.

'I suppose you recognize this moment for what it is.' Beryl sounded bitter. 'It's the end of both your childhoods.'

Sheila was itching to run to rehearsal. Did courtesy demand she should walk as far as the head of the platform with Beryl Grimshaw? The woman seemed as dazed as a widow at a funeral.

Once they were through the ticket barrier Mrs Grimshaw's legs suddenly gave way and she had to sit heavily on some mail bags.

'It's shock,' said Beryl. It was only now Sheila noticed that Mickey's mother was in her bedroom slippers. 'Perhaps you could get me into the station buffet? A small brandy might just pull me round.'

'I'm late,' said Sheila, propelling Beryl through the swing doors. The place was almost empty. It was all marble and mahogany, with a barmaid straight out of *Brief Encounter*.

'A small brandy,' said Sheila.

'Don't tell me you're eighteen because you're not.' The barmaid's tones were Manchester snappy.

'It's for me,' called out Beryl importantly. 'I've had a shock.' Sheila had unceremoniously wedged her into a wooden chair, with arms, designed for a less portly passenger.

Dear God, if she stands up, it'll come with her, thought Sheila in horror.

'Gone,' wept Beryl, not caring who heard. 'Gone without so much as giving his mother a kiss. And strong words had been exchanged on our front doorstep. I expect he told you that, Sheila, didn't he?' She called this out, right across the buffet.

'No he didn't.' If the clock above the bar was right, Sheila had exactly four minutes to get down the station slope and into the BBC.

'One and eleven,' said the barmaid. Sheila snapped down half a crown and, in the cause of speed, told the woman to keep the change. She'd often seen it done at the pictures.

'Never have sons,' sobbed Beryl. She took one painfully slow and refined sip of the brandy. 'All I wanted to do was make sure he'd got his sandwiches. Never have sons. They hurt your hand when they're little and your heart when they're big.'

How many of these dainty sips would it take to get the brandy down her neck?

'I'm sorry, Mrs Grimshaw, but I've got to go.'

'You can't leave me here!' said Beryl. 'Not with brandy on my breath. What if I was to fall over? They could take me in charge. At least see me to the taxi queue. If you won't do it for me, do it for Mickey. Ours is going to be a very silent house from now on.'

'I'm due at the BBC,' said Sheila. 'They go mad if you're late.'

Beryl downed the last of the brandy and rose to leave. The chair came with her.

'Mind my good furniture,' called out the barmaid.

Sheila was desperate. 'Sit down again and I'll put my weight on the arms. You force yourself upwards.' Desperation lent Sheila surprising strength and Beryl and the chair parted company with a light whoosh.

Once again Sheila manhandled the woman through the swing doors and out into the gloom of the booking hall.

'Look! You're in luck. There's a taxi waiting out in the daylight. Have you got enough money?' Sheila began pushing Beryl towards the vehicle.

'How much d'you think it would be?' gasped Beryl. 'Go easy, Sheila, I'm out of puff.'

In the distance, the Town Hall clock began to strike ten. Sheila panicked. She fished in her pocket, pulled out her last ten-shilling note, thrust it at the taxi driver and said, 'This woman isn't drunk, she's just peculiar. Please take her home.'

She began to run down the slope of the station approach. Sometimes rehearsals didn't start bang on the minute. Maybe they'd still be standing around chatting. She swerved past a couple of people and realized that her flying footsteps were taking her straight into the path of a man who was walking, unconcernedly, uphill. He was beautifully familiar. It was Barney Shapiro.

Sheila had no way of braking herself.

Realizing her predicament Barney held out his arms, opened wide. Instead of knocking him over she found herself held in a whirling embrace. He smelled wonderfully clean, and then came that faint, tantalizing, personal scent. New bread. His cheek felt rougher than it looked. If this was being late it was suddenly wonderfully luxurious. Yet she had been drilled in professionalism from her very first broadcast.

'I'll be in trouble,' she said desperately. 'I've got to go.'

'Come with me to Hayfield instead.'

'Don't tease.' He hadn't let go of her. Her hands were on

111

the muscles of his upper arms and she found herself tracing out their shape.

'I'm not teasing. Let's run away for the day.'

Sheila paused indecisively. She shook her head. All of this was too close to things Mickey had said, and now Mickey was gone.

'You're always teasing me,' was all she could think to say.

'Perhaps a bit.' Barney's eyes looked concerned. 'But a very loving bit.'

Sheila went gentle inside. And then her heart sang. 'A very loving bit' was a bold step in the right direction. Suddenly she felt valuable. And confident enough to put her lips against his cheek and give him the lightest of kisses.

'Now I've got to go and face the wrath of Barry. And Mamie Hamilton-Gerrard. Enjoy Hayfield.'

From the bottom of the incline, she turned to wave. He too had turned and was giving her his puzzled clown's smile.

Joy and panic were mixed as she covered the last hundred yards of pavement, pounded down the anonymous ground-floor corridor of Broadcasting House and into the iron cage of the lift.

It always astounded Sheila that all that stood between the world and Wilfred Pickles was a one-armed commissionaire. He swung the copper handle which closed the lift door and said, 'Morning, Sheila. Better late than never. Any minute now they'll be sending out the dogs. Mr Wrigley's secretary's already been to the front door, scanning Piccadilly for you.'

The lift groaned to a shuddering halt and Sheila's footsteps rang round yet another tiled corridor. Radio technique coming to the fore, she decided to pant a bit as she dived, guiltily, through the door of Studio One.

The cast were sitting silently, in a semicircle, on tubular steel chairs. Upstairs, alone on the balcony, Mamie Hamilton-Gerrard's old crone of a mother was knitting away, beneath the big studio clock. She had nothing to do with the production. She just refused to be separated from her daughter.

'What have you got to say for yourself?' said Barry.

'And do remember there's not an excuse on earth we

haven't heard before,' added Mamie Hamilton-Gerrard nastily. Her mother must have made the rainbow-wool jersey.

'I went to wave Mickey off and Mrs Grimshaw came over wobbly. She's a big woman.'

Barry suppressed a smile and opened his script. 'Well, it was only ten minutes . . .'

'That's not the point, Barry, if I may say so.' Nothing would have stopped Mamie. 'It's ten minutes of everybody's time. That amounts to whole hours. Of course, in the old days, she would have been made to go round and apologize to every single member of the cast.'

'I'm sorry I kept you waiting, Miss Hamilton-Gerrard,' said Sheila quietly.

'I forgive you. Or I will do, when you've been round to each of the others, individually, *and* to Mummy up on the balcony. Her good time's been wasted too. There's no point in looking at me like that, Barry darling. I'm only trying to drum some professional manners into the little madam.'

Sheila suddenly saw red and it coloured the tone of her voice. 'It was a stage mother who got me into this mess.'

'And she imitates me, Barry.' Mamie's voice was rising querulously. 'I listened to the transmission of last week's recording. You couldn't tell where I ended and she began. She beats Beryl Orde.' This was a reference to a variety artiste famed for her uncanny vocal imitations.

'Girls, girls . . .' Barry treated them to his best smile. It worked. The fact that it was a smile like the sun coming out left Mamie cold. Barry had called her a girl and this had made her morning. She stretched her little legs contentedly. Sheila noticed that Mamie was wearing two-tone court shoes, brown and white.

'Nice shoes,' she said. Sheila only wanted to get things back on a civilized level.

'Just don't buy a pair like them,' snapped Mamie. You couldn't win.

The rehearsal started. *Children's Hour* in the North Region was the wonder of the BBC network. It could produce an hour of top-quality radio in a day. The only break was for lunch.

In the BBC canteen, Sheila noticed that the Hamilton-Gerrards had got Barry, at a table, up against the wall. They were treating him to such intense conversation that other people steered clear of joining them.

Sheila had found a seat with two girls who worked in the offices. The pair of them were poring over a copy of *Stitchcraft*, discussing the possibility of pirating an embroidery transfer. Could a ballpoint tracing, they wondered, be ironed onto linen? Would it take? They wouldn't expect conversation and all Sheila wanted was an opportunity to think about what Barney had said.

Something like 'I may tease you a bit but it's a very *loving* bit'. That was the sense of it but she knew she was a couple of words out. She wanted the memory to be exactly accurate.

Was it Sheila's imagination or did she catch a worried glance, in her direction, from Barry? There was certainly a baleful one from Mamie but the old actress was always glowering at young ones. Could poor, dried-up old Mamie ever have been in love? She certainly wouldn't have been allowed to do anything about it. Her mother still went with her to the ladies'. And now that old tricoteuse was also glaring at Sheila across the canteen.

'Sheila?' It was Jean Wardle, Barry's secretary with the fuzzy hair. 'Sheila, I've got two letters for you in my folder downstairs. They look as though they're from listeners. Be sure I give them to you before you go.'

How would it be if she wrote Barney a letter, apologizing for not having been able to go to Hayfield? No. A letter would be laying it on a bit thick. Tomorrow she might ring him instead. For months she'd known the phone number by heart. Now she would have a valid excuse for using it.

The afternoon passed swiftly. The episode had already begun to take very definite shape; they were soon cutting one minute and forty seconds, to get it down to the exact, allocated length. Barry would instruct them to take out two words here, slice five there; sometimes he excised whole speeches. It was like elaborate patchwork and had been the most ordered and satisfying part of Sheila's adolescence.

A burst of pre-recorded closing theme music signalled the

end of the day's work. People began climbing into overcoats and looking for briefcases and making their goodbyes. Mamie's mother came down from the balcony. She wound her knitting wool into a tight ball and stabbed it with the needles. For the first time ever, she gave Sheila a cold, tight little smile.

'Thank you, good people.' Barry Wrigley's voice echoed out of the loudspeaker. 'Sheila, could you come into the box for a minute?'

The technicians were already leaving the control room. Jean Wardle paused in the doorway, took two unopened letters from a blue cardboard folder and handed them to Sheila. 'Yours,' she said.

'Come in, Sheila,' called out Barry. 'Mickey get off OK?'

They were alone together and he was looking awkward and almost nervous. Why didn't he say whatever it was he wanted to say? She wished he'd stop drumming his propelling pencil on the desk-top of the control panel. Sheila stuffed Jean's letters into her raincoat pocket.

Barry finally spoke: 'Look, Sheila, it's old Mamie . . .'

Sheila was glad of the chance to explain. 'I do imitate her, I think her work's marvellous. It was you who told me to – years ago, when I first started. "Watch her," you said. "Copy her." '

'I'm afraid you've made too good a job of it. I'm a bit worried about the poor old thing. There are limits and she nearly reached them today. Trouble is, she's now refusing to work with you.'

'Ever?'

'Ever's a long time. One thing's sure. I can't put the pair of you in the same production. Not for the moment.'

'But she's in practically everything.' Sheila was horrified.

'Not everything, but she's certainly very useful to me. Mamie's a tremendous asset to the Region. It's a good job all this has blown up at the end of a serial and not in the middle,' said Barry. 'She'll come round. I'll see to that. But I'm not going to rush things. I've also had a letter from Miss Bolt, your headmistress, asking me to bear in mind that you have examinations this coming year.'

' "For ever and for ever then farewell," ' said Sheila, misquoting from *Julius Caesar*, a play she'd never liked at school because it only had two women's parts, both of them rotten.

'If we do meet again then we may laugh.
If not this parting was well said.'

'It's not as bad as that,' laughed Barry. 'I'm sure the dust will have settled by the Christmas holidays. Cheery-bye and work hard at those exams.'

The Christmas holidays? It was like saying 'When the royal baby is king'.

Sheila walked gloomily down Market Street and glanced, as usual, into Clifton's Film Star Fashions. They had a passable, donkey-brown coat in the middle of the window. The label read *An Autumn Stroller – As Worn by Esther Williams*. Sheila felt like writing to the swimming star and telling her that another sticker added that the model was only available in Extra Outsize. Suddenly, she remembered the letters in her own pocket and fished them out.

One looked posh and interesting. It was on thick cream paper and written in fountain pen ink – only whoever had written it hadn't spelled Sheila properly. They'd put 'Shelagh'. She would save that one. She was already opening the other which was on lined paper in somebody very young's best handwriting.

> 27 Wilmer Grove
> Cheadle Hulme
> Cheshire
> September 24th 1952

Dear Sheila,
I think you are the best actress in children's hour. I am enclosing a 2½d. stamp. Could you please tell me how to get on childrens hour.

> Yours sincerely
> Heather Watts

P.S. It must be wonderful knowing them all. I am a big fan of Mamie Hamilton-Gerrard.

Sheila put the letter straight down a grid. Her conscience, of course, smote her immediately. But it was not wonderful knowing Mamie. Poor Heather Watts, she had no Mickey to push her to her first audition. Come to that, Sheila was minus Mickey too and it was all awful and who was this second letter from?

The address was somewhere she'd never heard of in Cornwall. The house had a name and no number or street. Definitely posh.

> Dear Shelagh,
> I am told that you were on *Children's Hour* last week, and that the programme came from the BBC North Region. I am writing to you, in their care, in the hope that this will reach you.
>
> All those years ago, long before the war, I was wrong and I was foolish. I should have accepted that engagement and come on the tour of *Dear Sinner* with you. My feelings for J. proved to be a tragic illusion. You and I could have had a whole life together though, by now, you would be looking after a comical old crock. My own partner is, alas, in an institution. They do their best to make her comfortable. I visit her every other Sunday and sometimes she recognizes me . . .

This is awful, thought Sheila. It's like eavesdropping, only worse. I shouldn't be reading it.

She looked at the envelope again. There was obviously another actress called Shelagh Starkey. Filled with guilty fascination, she read on.

> If what you and I did together in Hastings was wrong, then so be it. I have never ceased to glory in the memory. I can still remember how much it cost to replace the landlady's china ewer. Three shillings and fivepence ha'penny. Such an odd sum! And how did she arrive at it so promptly?
>
> Golden days and (may I venture to say it) nights too. Dear Shelagh, the best actress I ever saw as Cordelia, I hope that life has been kind to you. In my mind's eye, you

will always be bathed in the sunlight which is youth. Poignant to realize that, by now, you must have the same grey hairs and dread of the coming winter as does

Your affectionate and respectful
William Heythorpe

Sheila told herself that she hadn't really been reading someone else's letter; just trying to find a clue as to how to forward it to the right person.

'The sunlight which is youth' left her wondering whether age had addled Mr Heythorpe's grey head. Youth was more like picking your way through broken glass with the rain coming down the inside of your collar. Why did old people persist in remembering it like a picture on the front of a birthday card?

She put the letter in an inner pocket. Somewhere, there was a Shelagh Starkey who would be thrilled to have it. Funny to think that her own name could already have been up in lights. Would Barney ever send her a letter like this one?

No. This letter was the result of a sad separation. Sheila's one aim was to draw herself and Barney closer together. Tomorrow, she would ring him at home. Why wait until tomorrow? Youth didn't stand around in golden sunlight. She would ring him tonight.

'Barney?' Sheila was in the phone box down by the Rookswood Estate shops. It was generally held to be used by people having a bit on the side.

'Who's that?' He didn't half sound nervous.

'Sheila.'

'Oh hello, Monty.'

'What are you talking about, Barney? It's Sheila. Sheila from this morning.'

'Yes, Monty.' He didn't just sound nervous, he sounded haunted.

'Are you OK, Barney?'

'Fine, fine.'

'What's this Monty business then?' Down the line, in the background, Sheila could hear a woman's voice speaking indecipherably.

'Just a minute ... Monty? My mother says to tell your mother that Kendal's have taken stock of a new delivery of Italian shoes.' The female squawking continued. Sheila couldn't pick out actual words but even the inflections sounded determined.

Sheila could be determined too. 'Barney, I need to talk to you.'

'And Ruby says to be sure and tell her that the plain black patent ones are in now.'

'Can you meet me tonight?'

'No.'

'Just *no* like that? It's Sheila who kissed you this morning.'

'I'm waiting for some colour washes to dry. I've got to work over the top of them in Indian ink.'

'I see.' Sheila didn't see but it was the best she could manage.

'It would be a mistake. Do you understand? A mistake. I'm really sorry but that's how it is. Goodbye.' Click. He'd gone.

A bus was coming. Sheila pushed open the door and ran to the stop with her arm held out. She wanted to get as far as possible from that phone box where she'd made such a fool of herself.

'Where are you going, love?' said the conductor.

'I don't know. The terminus.'

'Are you full fare or are you still half?'

'I'm full fare,' said Sheila indignantly. 'I've been full fare for two years and much good it's done me!'

What had the telephone conversation meant? It was like trying to fathom Esperanto. It suddenly struck her that she'd chosen the right phone box. Somehow she was Barney's guilty secret.

Other boys aren't like this, she thought furiously. There's a whole queue willing to swank me out in broad daylight. The trouble was they were too available. She wasn't attracted to things which came easily. Should she march into The Kardomah with a boy on either arm, like an old Mae West picture at The Olympia? Would that make Barney jealous? She didn't want to make him jealous. She just wanted him.

As the bus groaned into Manchester, and stopped beyond

119

the Masonic Temple, Sheila decided to take another bus ride out to Magda Schiffer's. She was recalling Mickey's words of that morning: 'Jews don't marry out.' Something alien and exotic came into all of this and she needed help and advice.

At the side of the Town Hall it was nothing but number 42s going to Didsbury. 'Down the Palestine Road to Yidsbury' was how the comedians put it in the Palace pantomime. Sheila had reached the stage of finding Barney in everything.

Yet another 42. A walk might be a good idea. It was only a quarter past seven and it was well known that Magda Schiffer, who painted during the afternoons, did not care for visitors before sunset.

Princess Street went under a cast-iron railway bridge and emerged as Upper Brook Street. Now she was out of the warehouses and into an area potent with nostalgia for the stage-struck. In Victorian and Edwardian times, the streets running off the main road had housed the highest concentration of theatrical lodgings in England.

She paused at Ackers Street. Mickey had always maintained that it was the most famous street, of its kind, in the world. Touring actors still used it but, with theatres closing all the time, nothing like so many.

Oh how she missed her Mickey. In a moment he would have had her believing that the street was still full of hansom cabs and that Vesta Tilley was putting her feet up, at number 14, before the show. An autumn evening is a bad time to start missing somebody. Mickey had always said that they were going to be the next Noël Coward and Gertrude Lawrence. Those stars had stayed in these sooty terraces when they were beginning to make their names on tour. Sheila felt even more lagging behind than she had done on the station platform.

Gladys Starkey was fond of the horrible and puzzling expression 'A hiding to nowhere'. With Mickey's departure and Barney's defection, Sheila suddenly understood it. That's what she was on – a hiding to nowhere.

One of the dingy doors of Ackers Street opened. A woman with peroxided hair, in an old siren suit like pink flannel overalls, was holding it back to allow a small grey and white mongrel terrier to walk down the steps. Sheila stared in amazement. He was doing it on his back legs, like a dog in a circus.

'No show to go to, that's the trouble with him,' said the woman in a Birmingham accent. 'He's giving me gyp. My hubby's at Hulme Hippodrome this week, with the act. The vet said Tizer had to have a few nights off and the poor little animal doesn't know what to do with himself.'

The dog came down onto four paws and lifted a back leg against a lamp post.

'Good boy,' said Sheila.

Tizer came across and licked her hand enthusiastically.

'You've got to be in the business,' declared the woman. 'That dog won't go to outsiders and he's never wrong. Juvenile straight actress?'

Sheila nodded.

'Thought so. That dog can smell the greasepaint in your soul at a hundred yards. Come on, milord, let's have you back in the warm.'

Ever mercurial, Sheila felt warmed too. A dog who was a variety artiste had recognized her as an actress. She was the genuine item. She was the real thing. She even managed to enjoy the rest of the walk to Magda Schiffer's. It was as though the little dog had shaken her kaleidoscope and the colours of her life were suddenly brighter.

Magda was, as usual, dressed from head to foot in black. She was also in a mood to match.

'Too early,' she said as Sheila clattered after her, up the bare staircase, pouring out the story of the awful phone call.

'Still too early,' grunted Magda. 'I have not finished making the cheese straws. You can talk to me while I do it but you must turn your back. Recipe is secret. I have precious little of my own and what I have I bloody well hold onto. Prison camp teach you that. So, Shapiro would not admit you exist in front of the mother. What you expect?'

'I don't know. Tell me.'

'One day you might be artist, if actress can ever truly be called artist. Shapiro will never be more than art student.'

'That's an awful thing to say.' Sheila was tempted to turn

round and confront Magda but felt she might learn more by staying facing the wall.

'It is the truth. The family let him study textile design. No harm there. The family own a big textile firm, Shapiro, Son and Nephew, on George Street. Big money machine. And they do good things with their money. Good things for this town. They give a Matisse and a not bad Vlaminck to the art gallery. Some of their cash has helped John Barbirolli's orchestra. Shapiros have been here a long time. Bourgeois but rich bourgeois.

'They let Barney play at being an art student for a bit and then they say, "Toytime over. Bring what you learned to the money machine. You going to be businessman." They are not bad and they are not fools. If he had been good artist or good musician they would have known. He would have been sent to London or Europe and not to Salford School of Art.'

'But why did Barney keep pretending I was somebody called Monty? Why did he keep saying it was a mistake?'

'He spoke the truth. He knows all what I just told you.'

Magda Schiffer's broken English was so firm and decisive that, after a while, you began to wonder whether your own grammar was correct.

'Sooner or later they will send him to the barber and cover his beautiful body in a suit. Next he will need a wife. A good Jewish wife and not just any old Jewish girl. There could be problems there too.'

Sheila said the only thing she knew. 'But I love him.'

Sheila could hear Magda opening a tin canister and clearing her throat. Then Magda said carefully, 'He is not without feelings for you. Stay facing that wall. Oh, what the hell, you might as well turn round and see. Jews had better give you *something* today. The secret is in the cheese. It must be Parmigiano.'

'Does he really have feelings for me?'

'Yes. And if he was artist you could sweep the Jewish thing aside. He is a Shapiro and he will be a good and dutiful son. Anything he feels for you will be suppressed. He will do what is expected of him and shape another sort of life. You can't win, Sheila. You are up against antiquity.'

Magda hurriedly pulled down the sleeves of her black cardigan. Sheila looked guiltily out of the window. It was only now that she realized that she must have been gazing – without seeing – at the tattooed number on Magda's left wrist.

8

Opposition always turned Sheila Starkey's ambitions into obsessions. It was true that she was working at school but symptomatic of her state of mind that, in History, she found Disraeli easier to learn about than Pitt. Disraeli was Jewish.

For many months, Sheila's inner being had survived on glimpses of Barney. That autumn, search as she might, she never found him. The game of tantalizing hide-and-seek seemed to be suspended. Sheila refused to concede that it could be over.

She would never openly inquire as to his whereabouts. Instead, she would circle the tables of the reference library and watch the crowds coming down the steps of the Free Trade Hall after Hallé concerts. She spent a lot of time just sitting around The Kardomah.

It was a point of honour, when going up King Street, to walk through Duncan and Foster's, the bakers, and into their teashop at the back. It was becoming popular with students. Sheila never sat down, never ordered anything, just raked the customers' faces with her eyes. Failing to find Barney's amongst them, she would simply turn and leave.

He had to be somewhere. Sheila even penetrated the gloomy depths of The Hadassiah, a Kosher cafe, in the cellar of an office building. Pale green walls, dark green linoleum, bright green and white checked tablecloths and old men, in black hats, drinking lemon tea out of glasses.

In a corner she spotted Enid Rosenthal, a swarthy art student with thick pebble glasses and the faintest trace of a moustache. Sheila had often felt sorry for Enid, who specialized in pottery; when she came into The Kardomah she could never eat anything because her family kept strict Kosher. Enid was sitting beneath a framed sign which said *This Establishment Is Under the Direct Supervision of the Beth*

Din. With a fork, she was attacking something which looked like a little plump golden fishcake.

'What's that?' asked Sheila, sitting down.

'Chopped and fried. What on earth are you doing here?'

'I get about.' Sheila aimed to sound airy but it came out as nervous. 'I'll have one of those,' she said to the waitress, indicating Enid's plate.

'You get two in a portion.' The waitress looked more like Irlams o'th' Height than Tel Aviv. Perhaps she was a catering version of one of those Christian women whom Orthodox Jews get to light their fires on a Saturday morning. If they were on the same side, why was this waitress glaring at Sheila as though she was an interloper?

'Any beverage?' she asked, in tones lofty enough to suggest she was only used to serving the likes of King Nebuchadnezzar.

'White coffee.' The moment she said it, Sheila knew she'd dropped a clanger.

'Not 'ere,' said the woman, with satisfaction.

'Settle for black,' urged Enid.

'I'll bring you your chopped and fried, hot.' The waitress relented slightly. 'You'll find they've got a bit more taste that way.'

Sheila and Enid began talking about the craft exhibition at the Red Rose Gallery. Sheila had learned this kind of conversation at Magda Schiffer's and could have faked her way through it in her sleep.

The chopped and fried arrived. Two of them, on a little side plate. They tasted a cross between Kidd's fish and Gander's fishcakes.

'These are amazing,' said Sheila enthusiastically. 'They're enough to make anybody want to turn Jewish.'

'You can't.' Enid looked solemn. 'You can change your religion but you can't change your race. I sometimes wish I could tell that to all those poor shiksas, who sit round The Midland trying to hook a nice Jewish boy.'

'What's a shiksa?' asked Sheila.

Enid looked cautiously around and then, in a low voice, began to sing a parody of the popular song 'Walking My Baby Back Home'.

'Gee but it's great
After staying out late
Shlepping my shiksa back home . . .

'Non-Jewish girls. The boys never marry them. It's just romantic exercise.'

'Never?' asked Sheila, appalled. It was only now that she admitted to herself that her ambitions had extended to include a wedding. Herself and Barney under a canopy like one of those photographs in Guttenberg's window. 'Never?'

'Maybe the odd one. And the girls try to become more Jewish than Jews. And then they find out that their children don't count. Being Jewish descends down the female line.'

'Times are changing,' said Sheila firmly.

'Not our times.' Enid's voice was expressionless. She was just stating a bald fact. And then she stated an even balder one.

'Forget it, Sheila, and move on. You'll never catch him. Half Manchester's been watching and they're all laughing at you.'

Sheila rose to her feet and pushed the chair back. Its metal frame scraped across the linoleum like an animal in pain. The waitress rushed up.

'Don't say you've swallowed a bone? You're bright red in the face. That fish is meant to be chopped and chopped. Drink some water.'

'How much?' asked Sheila. 'How much to get out of this place?'

'Two and fourpence.'

Sheila opened her handbag, found her purse, savagely routed out half a crown, forced it into the waitress's hand and ran from The Hadassiah.

Outside, she found herself in a maze of old Manchester alleyways. A dark tunnel led to the daylight of Corporation Street where her angry footsteps took her through home-going crowds, making their way to Victoria Station.

People had been laughing at her. They'd watched and they had laughed. All she'd wanted to do was love somebody and it had turned her into a joke. Anger and hurt were inextricably mixed. The sound of her own blood was pounding in her ears and she could hear her little peg heels drumming out a similar rhythm on the pavement.

How far had she walked? She was long past Strangeway's jail. It was dusk but the street lights had yet to come on. She was in a poor district. The shop in front of her was illuminated by a naked light bulb, hanging on a flex from the ceiling. Silhouetted on the glass of the shop window Sheila saw a Star of David, the symbol the Nazis had forced the Jews to wear during the Holocaust. Had she gone mad and walked into a nightmare?

Common sense reasserted itself. Her steps had merely taken her up Cheetham Hill, the district used by the first Jewish refugees in Manchester. The symbol painted on the window simply advertised that this was a Kosher establishment.

Had Barney walked along these same streets when he was little? No. Shapiros were posh. They lived further uphill in another and more prosperous Jewish district, Broughton Park. Barney's grandparents might have started off round here. His father could have played here as a little boy. Barney must have been a beautiful child. There was a smell of yeast on the air from Boddington's Brewery at Strangeways. Barney, Barney, everything was Barney . . .

Sheila kissed the Star of David on the cold glass window. An old woman looked out from inside the shop in something close to disbelief. Did the woman think she was mad?

We are all of us a little insane at times. It is in those moments, when the barriers come crashing down, that we are distracted enough to be able to view ourselves honestly.

Ever since Mr Crotty had made his pupils listen to the Nuremberg trials, Sheila's heart had been singing one song. 'Someday He'll Come Along – the Jew I Love'. Enid Rosenthal wasn't the only person who could change the words of popular songs.

Barney had come along. He was the man she loved. If that meant people laughed at her, so what? She didn't like it but she could live with it. Nothing and nobody was going to stop her having Barney. Sheila only hoped she hadn't made people laugh at him too.

The letter from William Heythorpe to Shelagh Starkey began to weigh on the younger Sheila's conscience. She kept it in her handkerchief drawer. Occasionally she took it out, from underneath one of Gander's lavender bags, and reread it. She had become fond of the idea of these old lovers. By holding onto the letter, was she robbing the other Shelagh of a chance of happiness? Acting on the theory of 'Do as you would be done by' Sheila decided to try to see the letter safely home.

She wrote a note to Shelagh Starkey, enclosed the Heythorpe letter, sealed in an envelope so no outsider could snigger, and sent it to Equity, the actors' trade union. Sheila asked them to forward it on and to send her details of membership. Love was getting her nowhere so she had to do something, anything, to further her other ambition.

That autumn Sheila was glad when the first Christmas decorations started to appear in the shops. Older people might say they were there too early but she saw them as a tinsel arrow to a holiday which would bring back Mickey. How would it be if she was to send Barney a Christmas card? The Jews, of course, had killed Christ. But Jesus was a Jew himself. Thoughts of Barney never left her alone for long.

Like many of the desperate before her, Sheila thought of resorting to a fortune-teller. There was a woman called Madame Robina, at All Saints, who was said to be remarkable, but she charged two guineas. With no *Children's Hour* money coming in Sheila was beginning to feel the pinch. She had to content herself with reading her horoscope, every day, in Mr Jepson's *Daily Express*, and she got a book on astrology out of The Height library.

Sheila had never been much struck on the idea of being born under the sign of Cancer the crab. The book said she was a great homemaker and would hold onto things, people and ideas unto death. This sounded about accurate.

Both Barney and Mickey were Gemini. 'Two people with two sets of ideas in one body.'

What were Barney's ideas? '*It's a mistake.*' That certainly seemed to be one of them.

If Barney and Mickey were born under the same star just how alike were they? *'A mistake.'*

For the first time, she began to wonder just how well they knew one another? Nonsense. Or was it? Mickey always spoke of 'Beautiful Barney'. Was this just a nickname? Mickey had nicknames for practically everybody. Or could it be that Barney was too beautiful to love a woman in the way Sheila wanted?

She had given the idea legs and it started to march round her head. Was Mickey her friend or her rival?

By now she had a London phone number for him. That night, when her mother and Mr Jepson had gone to see Walter Pidgeon in *The Bad and the Beautiful*, Sheila rang Mickey.

'I want a straight answer to a straight question. Is Barney Shapiro one of those?' Would Mickey object to this expression? She wasn't sure if she cared if he did.

The only reply, down the telephone line, was a gale of laughter.

'He is!' stormed Sheila. 'I knew it. He's queer. And now you're laughing at me. That's what the pair of you have been doing all along, laughing.'

'Bollocks,' said Mickey. 'He's as normal as blueberry pie. What's more he's back from Israel. They came on a private ambulance plane.'

'Who's they? And what was he doing in Israel?'

'He's been there weeks. His cousin smashed up a jeep on a kibbutz. He nearly died. Barney went out to bring him back.'

Sheila was suddenly in love with the world again and Mickey was a rare and special friend. Like somebody who cannot believe toothache is over, she had to poke around at one lingering doubt.

'You promise me he's not queer?'

'I promise. Your department, not mine, more's the pity. Have you ever seen him with no clothes on? I have. I got him to give me a swimming lesson.'

'But Mickey, you can swim like a fish. You've been swimming since you were six. You are shameless. Do hurry up and come home. It's your kind of practical advice I need. I'm so glad he's normal.'

'Dead normal,' said Mickey ruefully. 'He knows all about me and it doesn't worry him a bit. It takes a man who's very confident of his own masculinity to be as casual as that about it. Term ends next week. This 'ere RADA aint all it's cracked up to be. I'm back on the nineteenth. I'll be coming on the six o'clock from Euston. Be sure to be on the platform.'

'I love you, Mickey.'

'Thank you, but no thank you.' He was irrepressible and he was gone.

The telephone call had left Sheila with something to look forward to, something with a specific date. Much more than that, it had lifted a great weight from her shoulders. Barney had not been avoiding her, he had been doing a good turn in Israel.

Suddenly Sheila felt part of the coming Christmas. She felt in it instead of nose pressed to everybody else's window pane. She opened the cupboard underneath the stairs and hauled out the dusty, artificial Christmas tree and the McVitie's biscuit tin in which they stored the decorations. It was as though Mickey had switched on the lights of her own tree. He deserved a present. What should she buy him for Christmas? She had a sudden inspiration. She would get him a new pair of swimming trunks. And on the card she would write 'For your cheek! With envy – Sheila.'

Most of the glass tree baubles were wrapped in old tissue paper but the whole of the inside of the box was packed around with old copies of the *Manchester Evening News*. Sheila unfolded one. It dated back to December 1939 and the women's hats were a hoot. As she turned the pages, trying to discover what had been on at the theatres, she caught sight of the headline 'Manchester Jewry'. The small article underneath said that whilst Jews would not be celebrating Christmas, their festival of Chanukah fell at practically the same time. Sheila was struck by a sudden thought. Were there such things as Chanukah cards?

Later that week, she took two buses to Cheetham Hill to find out. She got one in the same shop where she'd kissed the window. It sold everything and half the labels were foreign. The words of the greeting were in an indecipherable alphabet.

'What does it mean?' Sheila asked the old woman behind the counter.

'Not many people send them.' The woman put on tin-framed glasses and peered inside the card. ' "May all go well with you over the Festival of the Light".' The woman looked at Sheila curiously. 'Aren't you the meshuggeneh who kissed my window?'

Caught.

'That would be my twin sister.' Sheila crossed her fingers. Her imagination wouldn't let her leave it at that. She had to embroider. 'The poor thing is a most unhappy creature. I'm cheerful as anything.'

'The card's a shilling,' said the woman. 'You want to watch out. You can catch germs off people's window panes.'

Sheila had told no less than the truth about one thing. She was cheerful. Barney was here. He was in Manchester. He was breathing the same air she was breathing. Things just had to be made to work.

The pen in the General Post Office didn't want to write. Sheila had been thinking what to put on the card, all the way from Cheetham Hill. In the end she settled for just three words: 'Love from Monty'. Well, three words and a blot. Nobody develops style in one fell swoop.

A reunion with Mickey demanded special effort. She swept her hair back into a dancer's bun and, using a small paintbrush and mascara, painted a dark line on her eyelids, against the lashes. She had copied it slavishly from a photograph of Barbara Goalen, the *Daily Express* Model Girl of the Year. She felt wonderfully 1952. In fact she felt almost 1953.

'You look just like George Lacey as the dame in pantomime,' yelled Mickey. The train hadn't even stopped. He was calling through the open carriage window.

Sheila was blazing. All that trouble dismissed in one flippant line.

'Help me down with these bags, Sheila. What's the matter? You've turned into a great beauty. It's just that today you've overdone it.'

Sheila flung her arms around him. 'Have I really turned into a great beauty?'

'Did I ever waste time saying a word I didn't mean?' Mickey was regarding her critically, almost as though she was his own property. And, in a way, she was.

'You've cheered up that old coat with expensive buttons and you got one too few and hoped nobody would notice. There's nobody like you, Sheila. I *have* missed you. None of the girls at the academy light up, from inside, like you do. Let's go and get some coffee.'

The Royal Academy of Dramatic Art, it transpired, was by no means exempt from Mickey's criticism.

'Everybody warned me it was a sausage machine and it is. We're all meant to turn out the same. Half the girls are using the place as a finishing school, and the others are so intense they could only play St Joan. There are just a handful of people who are brilliant. But that's got nothing to do with the place. They'd shine wherever they were.'

'But you must have learned so much, Mick.' Sheila could hardly wait to learn secondhand. 'Swap suitcases. I've got the heavy one.'

'I've learned one thing. And I've just said it in that sentence. All our lives, we've been pronouncing the word "one" to rhyme with gone. It should rhyme with nun.' Mickey threw back his head and recited. 'One, none, Coventry . . . that new vowel sound's about all I've learned.

'It's all so solemn. God knows what it has to do with entertaining people. Hold this parcel whilst I fish for my ticket. It's a wildly expensive book. Your precious Barney sent me the cash, registered post, to get it for him.'

'You mean you've actually been in touch with him?' Sheila stopped herself from gasping but was, nonetheless, very much impressed. There were people who were in easy contact with Barney and Mickey was one of them. Under her breath she was repeating to herself, 'One, none, Coventry . . .'

Aloud, she said, 'I want a Christmas present off you, Mick. I want to be the one who takes this book to Barney.'

Mr Rolls first met Mr Royce in the Midland Hotel in Manchester and it always seemed, to Sheila, that they could not have chosen a more appropriately luxurious setting.

The forbidding exterior was like some great soot-blackened French chateau. The interior was said to have been designed to outstrip any of the other great hotels of Europe. The Midland was owned by the London, Midland and Scottish Railway. With nationalization, the hotel could be said to have been allowed to run a little downhill. But only a little. And there were customers who felt that touches of highly polished shabbiness added distinction.

The hotel understood celebrity. Visiting stage and film stars could think of staying nowhere else. The Midland was the place where Manchester merchants clinched overseas deals and displayed their wives and their wives' jewels. Upstairs, they hid their mistresses. All of the suites had marble bathrooms and two had white grand pianos. The Midland smelled of French scents and Havana cigars. Whiffs of rich roasts wafted from the Grill Room, brandy flames leaped and flickered in mirrors of the French Restaurant. The Midland was money.

As Sheila went round, in the revolving doors which led from doorstep to luxury, she clutched the parcel to her front. She could have wished that it had *Excuse for Being Here* printed on the wrapper, instead of *Collet's Russian Bookshop*. Not that she was remotely afraid of The Midland. She and Mickey had been sailing in, to use their lavatories, since they were ten years old. Mickey had called it 'Starting the way you mean to go on'.

The two hall porters nodded deferentially as Sheila headed towards the steps up to the main lounge. She could already hear the pianist playing last year's big hit song, 'Too Young'. It was as though the whole outing had been produced and directed by Mickey. It was he who had arranged a rendezvous with Barney, chosen Sheila's clothes, and forced her to go easy on the makeup.

133

Sheila's heart gave a little leap. He was there. Barney Shapiro was sitting in the middle of the room reading a newspaper. His only concession to the five-star hotel was a tie. The porters wouldn't let anybody without one through the doors. They could have had few other worries about Barney. He looked what he was, the very relaxed and confident son of a prominent Manchester family.

Sheila glanced, involuntarily, at her own reflection in a gilt-framed looking glass. Mickey had given her some words to remember as a talisman. She could hear his voice, saying them, in her head: 'You can't buy what you've got – you're special.'

Men were taking notice as Sheila walked across the lounge, but Barney was still deep in his paper.

'I brought the book,' she said.

Barney looked up. The smile he gave her was so lazy and relaxed that, for a moment, she felt as though they were in a great big feather bed together. She'd never been in bed with a man in her life. But in that flash she knew exactly how it would feel. Warm limbs casually touching –everything. This was disgraceful. And in the middle of The Midland too.

'Aren't you going to take your parcel?'

Barney rose to his feet. It was the first time a man had ever paid Sheila this courtesy.

'Did anybody follow you here?' The eyes, as always, were teasing. 'You do realize that this is a Communist book? Actually, it's a book on Russian design. Why don't we sit down? Where's Mick? I thought he was bringing it.'

The rehearsed excuse failed to emerge. Sheila was so pleased to be with Barney again that she was struggling to control a beaming grin which threatened to spread from ear to ear.

'Couldn't he come?'

'Birmingham. He had to spend the day in Birmingham.'

'That's funny, I could've sworn I saw him crossing John Dalton Street, not ten minutes ago.'

'I'm a rotten liar.' Sheila tried to sound miserable. But she didn't feel miserable. She felt wonderful.

'The pair of you always remind me of the Bisto Kids. So

what's he up to? Getting a bit grand, isn't he, demanding to meet people here?'

'It's more what I'm up to. I wanted the chance to talk to you.'

'Not tonight, I'm afraid. I'm in the middle of my thesis. That's what I needed this for.' Barney opened the book and studied a picture of a carpet.

'Will there never be a chance to talk to you, Barney?' All the happiness had emptied out of Sheila's voice.

'I'm really up to the eyes. I've got to pass this exam. It matters. I'm going home now and I'll have to work through until midnight. I don't expect you will be free at midnight?' he asked in his usual bantering tones.

'I might be.' Sheila said it levelly. 'I know where you live. We'll just have to see.'

'You will be very welcome,' said Barney serenely. And that was where he made his mistake. It never did to underestimate Sheila Starkey.

'I must go.' Sheila was on her feet again. 'I've got something to do.'

What she had to do was so shocking that it startled even Sheila. The plan had dropped into her mind, whole and complete, in the space of a second.

Barney rose too. 'Thank you for the Chanukah card. From now on I might start calling you Monty.'

Yes, thought Sheila. And from midnight you might start calling me shameless and outrageous.

All she said aloud was 'Au revoir'. In French, at school, she had been taught that this was what you said when you were definitely planning on seeing somebody again.

The pianist caressed the last notes out of 'Too Young', paused while he took a sip of his drink, and went into his next number. It was an upbeat version of 'Taking a Chance on Love'. Sheila sailed towards the door in perfect time with the music.

'I'm glad you're home at a respectable hour.' Gladys Starkey managed to make her pleasure sound like a grumble. 'I don't like the idea of you out, roaming, on these dark nights. Can you be trusted to make me a hot milky drink? I think I'll have Bournvita.'

'And while you're at it – ' Mr Jepson looked up from the armchair where he was reading *Fanny by Gaslight* – 'get your mother a couple of phenóbarbitone. They're in the kitchen cabinet, next to the gravy browning. I'll settle for Horlicks.'

You'll get more than that, thought Sheila grimly. For once, you're going to get a taste of your own medicine.

In the kitchen she poured the milk into a pan, lit the gas, and put the pan on the flames. Quickly, she lifted down two mugs from their cup-hooks above the sink. Opening the kitchen cabinet, Sheila took out the little poison-green glass bottle and unscrewed it. Very quietly, she shook out four tablets.

As Sheila began crushing two of them, under the handle of the bread knife, she covered the noise by singing 'There'll Always Be an England'. The crushed sleeping tablets blended unnoticeably into the Horlicks powder at the bottom of Mr Jepson's mug.

That's for turning my mother into a drug addict, thought Sheila. Honesty overtook this thought. Revenge didn't enter into it. Sheila was simply putting into action the plan she had conceived in The Midland. She didn't bother with a tray.

Gladys, who had an asbestos mouth, swilled down her sleeping tablets in a couple of boiling hot gulps and went upstairs to begin getting ready for bed.

As Sheila watched Mr Jepson sipping his doctored Horlicks, she wondered whether she had taken the first steps to becoming a wax model in Louis Tussaud's Blackpool basement. All she wanted to do was ensure Mr Jepson slept soundly, yet she couldn't rid herself of the idea that, one day, her effigy could be standing next to Mrs Merrifield, the bungalow murderess in the Chamber of Horrors.

Gladys returned clad in a stern winceyette nightgown with a man's cardigan over the top. Flimsy allurements had not lasted longer than the first year of her second marriage. These days, she even went to bed with her perm stowed away under a mauve sleeping net. As Gladys softened her wax earplugs by the fire, Mr Jepson was already snoring in his armchair.

'This is marriage you're looking at, Sheila,' she said grimly. 'Before you come up to bed, put the little fireguard up and be sure to check the locks on both doors. Come on, Romeo. Give him a shake, Sheila.'

Gladys was well aware that Sheila did not like touching Norman Jepson. 'Oh all right,' her mother grumbled. 'I'll do it. You'll have to get over this, Sheila. You really will. A time will come when you'll simply have to force yourself to touch men. That's what makes the world go round. My goodness me, your stepfather seems to be spark out.'

This would never do. This was not part of Sheila's plan. Forgetting all her scruples, she gave Mr Jepson a sharp poke in the ribs. He sat up abruptly.

'It's that tonic wine you brought home, Norman,' said Gladys crossly. 'I don't care if it is made by monks.'

Her husband yawned lavishly. 'I'm going to sleep well tonight.'

'Well just so long as it's not on your back,' snorted his wife. 'In that position I can even hear that through wax. Come on.'

Sheila often went upstairs later than this pair. She switched off the awful overhead light they were so fond of. In the firelight's glow, she counted off the familiar noises of the night. Water running, a cistern flushing, one set of protest from bedsprings followed by shoes dropping with a thud. A door closed, springs creaked again, and then there was silence.

Would Gladys get up and start roaming? This sometimes happened. She was even capable of sneaking down for an extra tablet. Sheila decided to give it five minutes by the mantelpiece clock.

Late at night, she often looked for pictures in the glowing embers of the fire. Sometimes she even tried to use them to tell her own fortune. Tonight she had decided to shape her own future. 'Barney, Barney, I'm coming to you at midnight.'

Sheila put up the fireguard for something to do. After a couple more agonized minutes she judged that phenobarbitone was ruling the room upstairs.

For a moment her conscience pricked her. Could good come out of doing this? She stifled the thought. She had yet another crime to commit. Theft. Well, it was borrowing, really.

Sheila slipped into her coat and, holding her breath, gently opened the front door and stepped out into the night. Inserting her key in the Yale lock, she closed the door behind her without so much as a betraying click. She was on her way. There was no moon but there were stars.

Looking across the avenue she was glad to see that somebody, with no regard for suburban niceties, had left the Dolans' gate conveniently open. Getting Delia's bike out of the old hen hut should be easy.

Within minutes, Sheila had already cycled down Dovesway and across the rest of Ravensdale Estate. She was soon by the Colliers' Memorial, at the top of Smithy Brow. Here the road dropped so steeply that even boys who understood three-speed gears were a bit afraid of it. Not Sheila; she allowed, nay encouraged, her bicycle to fly down the hill and soon she was crossing the bridge at the bottom over the inky black River Irwell. As she passed the soap works, the night air smelled of chemical roses.

Sheila found herself repeating lines from *The Merchant of Venice*:

> 'In such a night
> Stood Dido with a willow in her hand
> Upon the wild sea-banks, and waft her love
> To come again to Carthage.'

She had always loved those lines and now they helped her feet push harder on the pedals as the road began its climb to the Jewish heights of Broughton Park.

The first houses were like the ones near Magda Schiffer's. But, even on a winter's night, you could see that they stood in properly tended gardens and that the drawn curtains were all expensively lined.

Between these Victorian merchant mansions stood lavish houses straight from the pages of *Picturegoer*. Hollywood in Manchester. Riviera villas like cream-washed 1930s cinemas and mock-Tudor manor houses with yew trees fashioned into the shapes of birds and chessmen, in gardens that were trying to be grounds.

A notice board with a Star of David on it announced that she was passing the Cassel-Fox School. Some of the houses were like miniature versions of the completed ideal. It was as though their owners were announcing their future ambitions. It was almost impossible to believe that Rookswood Avenue was a mere three miles away, across the valley. Sheila turned her bicycle into Barney's road. She had been here once before on a covert spying expedition.

Juniper House was Edwardian; red brick with a black and white half-timbered tower. On the other side of the Irwell, it would only have been used as a private nursing home. All those windows with stained-glass tops, all those rooms inside – and just for one family. No lights were showing. Even the pruned rose bushes were covered in little sacking hoods.

Sheila got down from her bicycle. The white-painted five-barred gate opened with a gentle creak. She decided to park her bike in some rhododendron bushes.

A white gravel drive circled the entire house. Wasn't gravel supposed to crunch when you walked on it? Sheila settled for walking on the grass verge. She knew where she was with grass.

No lights, no lights, no lights. As she rounded a corner, her spirits suddenly soared. A beam of electric light was shining out of an attic. Art students and attics went together like paint and brushes.

A wooden fire escape, with landings on every floor, led all the way to the roof. Sheila thought of Rapunzel letting down her hair so that her lover could climb up it. And then she thought again. Romance and common sense were often at war inside Sheila's mind. Absolutely strictly speaking there could be no denying that she was here by invitation. Absolutely, strictly speaking. The only trouble was Barney had been teasing.

Suddenly, a figure appeared at the window and gazed over the treetops. It was Barney. As he stepped back into the light, she could see that he had no shirt on. Naked flesh in December. Were they so posh that they even had central heating in the attics? Now he was lighting a cigarette. Sheila didn't know he smoked. Come to that, he didn't know that she hung around other people's gardens at the dead of night.

He disappeared from sight. Terrified that he might leave the room and go to another, less accessible, part of the house, Sheila willed her feet to turn into swan's-down as she crossed the gravel and began to mount the wooden staircase.

There was frost on the hand-rail. That would mean frost on the steps. She had better be careful. At the first landing the wood beneath her creaked. Sheila kept stock-still. Nothing happened.

In the distance a clock began to strike the chimes of midnight. It sounded a very Church of England clock. The poor vicar, thought Sheila, must have a lonely time of it round here.

'Oh God, just get me safely to the top.' She continued her ascent. Nobody could have been sleeping on the second floor. The curtains weren't even drawn and she could see a black hat, fit for Ascot, lying on a bronze satin eiderdown. One flight to the attic.

When Sheila reached the top landing she realized that the light wasn't coming from a window. It was a door with a glass pane at the top. It suddenly swung open and Barney stepped out.

'Who the hell . . .'

'It's me,' said Sheila. 'I came. It's midnight.'

9

If Barney still seemed disbelieving, as Sheila followed him out of the night and into the attic, there was also admiration in his eyes. Admiration and a gleam of excitement.

Sheila was very aware of his naked torso, above the blue jeans. It was as classically defined as any of the illustrations of ancient Greek sculpture in her copy of *One Thousand Everlasting Things*. But this was better than cold marble. A deep suntan had faded to a warm shade of pale gold. Sheila tried hard not to stare at his nipples. They were in a secret-looking colour, which was neither red nor truly brown.

She looked instead around the room. It was disappointingly empty. The walls had been painted white, the floorboards sanded and waxed. Two things stopped it looking like a monk's cell – a designer's drawing board against one wall and a huge double bed against another. The headboard of the bed was straight out of a Hollywood gangster film. Inlaid walnut veneer in a design like the rising sun.

'Just like the Japanese flag, isn't it?' asked Barney. 'Guess what? I was conceived on that bed.'

'No books,' said Sheila. 'Somehow I'd always imagined there'd be lots of books.'

'You've thought about it then?' Barney could never resist the temptation to tease.

'I've thought about nothing else.' Let him make what he liked of that.

'Here.' Barney opened a door in the wall to reveal another, smaller, room. 'We used to keep trunks and suitcases in here but I cleared them out and lined it with shelves.'

These were not the usual student bookshelves, haphazardly constructed from planks and bricks. Barney's shelves were properly dovetailed and jointed. They had been made with patience and care and revealed him in a new light.

It was plain that no book had been thrown away since he

was a child. Sheila recognized many old friends. He had looked after his copy of *The Midnight Folk* much better than she had done. Mickey would have been envious of the complete set of *William* books. Next to a row of Rudyard Kiplings came a black, bound edition of James Joyce's *Ulysses*. It was well known, in Kardomah circles, that this banned book had to be smuggled in from the continent. Sheila was impressed.

Bookshelves can lead to shared intimacies but, with Barney standing disturbingly close to her, conversational exchanges were not what Sheila had in mind.

'It's not fair,' she said, moving back into the bedroom. 'You've hardly any clothes on and I'm covered in them.' She removed her coat and threw it across the end of the bed. 'Turn the big light off and put on a lamp.'

As Barney turned to do this Sheila took a deep breath, pulled her sweater over her head and quickly removed her bra. Now they were both naked from the waist upwards. She was already beginning to feel the familiar zzz on the air.

It had hit him too. The combination of excitement and panic caused his body to release some of that erotic personal scent. New bread. 'Sheila, I'm not sure we should be . . .'

Sheila silenced him with a finger over his lips. She could actually feel the blood thudding through the generous curve of the lower lip. He smelled of new bread and she wanted to taste it.

Barney's eyes were full of wonder. Silently, Sheila led him across the room until they were standing in front of a mirror.

'Don't we look beautiful?' she said to their reflection. 'Don't we look right?'

Her forefinger stretched out to the looking glass as she began to trace the outline of the reflection of his chest. Sheila turned towards Barney and ran her finger across the real thing.

Awed, she said, 'I never knew men's nipples swelled too.'

'Neither did I.' Barney's voice was husky with more than disbelief and his arms closed around her.

The whole atmosphere of the room had changed. It was as though they were in a different place. And yet we're suddenly part of the *now*, thought Sheila, as she pressed herself closely against him. Something's finally happening and it's happening to us now . . .

Something else happened. Footsteps began to climb a staircase; their sound was coming nearer and a woman's voice called out, 'Barney? Barney, are you still up, darling?'

'It's Ruby,' breathed that panic-stricken young man. 'It's my mother.'

Frantically grabbing together Sheila's clothes, he piled them into her naked arms and bundled her into the little book room.

Sheila could hear a knuckle rapping on the outer bedroom door. Fancy your own mother knocking! Gladys would have just barged in.

'Come in, Ruby,' called out Barney. 'I was on the fire escape.'

Sheila had to decide whether to close her door or spy through the narrow gap. Quickly, she told herself that closing the door might make a give-away noise. In fairness to Sheila, it has to be said that she thought about putting her fingers in her ears. But she only thought about it.

'Your father swore he heard something. The sweet love just said, "Oh well, everything's insured," rolled over and went back to sleep. I've been right round and nothing seems amiss.' There was silence for a moment. 'Are these the designs for your thesis?'

Ruby sounded very much a Kendal Milne account customer – posh with just a hint of a Manchester accent. If she was looking at designs, they must be facing the drawing board. Sheila risked peering through the gap.

Barney's mother was standing in profile, a sheet of paper held at arm's length. Straight and slim with a narrow waist, she looked like the ageless photographs of Helena Rubenstein in the beauty advertisements. A little Roman empress. Not quite ageless, there were two white wings in the black hair scraped back from a high forehead which gleamed with the sheen of night lotion. Ruby's eyes made Sheila think of a wise old parrot. She was wrapped in a severely tailored white garment which touched the floor. Sheila supposed this must be a housecoat and immediately wanted one.

143

'Do you like the design?' Barney sounded as though he really needed to know.

'It doesn't make me want to ring Miki Sekers and say I've found the next Oliver Messel.'

'Oliver Messel's a stage designer.' Barney rapped this out hotly.

'Yes. The best. And he's also done some very good fabric designs for Sekers. I like that Miki a lot. He came from Budapest with next to nothing and made his fortune by understanding excellence.'

'And my work isn't good enough.'

'Did I say that? Did I? I suppose I did. Midnight's a good hour for the truth.'

Ruby put her arms around Barney. Sheila was half jealous but impressed by the natural ease with which they touched. When she tried to embrace her own mother it was like hugging an ironing board.

'I don't want my son to be an unter-shlepper in a design studio. Is that wrong? Shapiros are bosses not slaves, thank God.'

'Look at this one.' Barney had broken away from Ruby and was holding up another sheet of paper. 'You must like this one.'

'I like. I like it.' Ruby stroked the top of Barney's head. 'It's to be hoped you hold onto this hair longer than your father did.'

'Barney, you're not bringing a picture home from kindergarten for Mother. I know what it's like, up at the top of the building, in our own studio. I'm trying to save you from getting hurt. Let me talk to you honestly. Just Ruby and Barney. It's not a dining room fight with your father. Nobody else is listening . . .'

'Not now.' Barney sounded desperate. 'Please not now.'

Sheila wished she could unmake the minute and start it again with her fingers in her ears. How much was her own presence adding to Barney's agony? This must have been the very last conversation he would have wanted anybody to hear.

'OK, Barney.' Ruby sounded weary. 'I can't start telling you what to believe. You have a good head and a good heart.

Somewhere you must know the truth of it all yourself. I don't want you to be a shilling man, I want you to be a pound man. No, a *guinea* man. You might not want to go into business but the ability's there. It was born in you. Your father and I saw to that.

'Don't stay up till all hours and, here, put a sweater on. So give me a kiss. I love you.'

'Love you, Ruby.'

'I'm shutting this fire escape door or we *will* have burglars.'

In the book room, Sheila, creature of instinct that she was, had already begun fastening her bra. It was as though Ruby Shapiro had hygienically vacuum-cleaned the room. The heady, sexually charged atmosphere was dispersed. As Sheila pulled the jersey back over her head, light shone through the wool. Barney had opened the door into the bedroom. Ruby was gone.

Barney said nothing. Instead he slouched back into the main room and flung himself, face down, on the bed. The back of his neck, above the jersey, looked young and defenceless.

Sheila felt as though she was aching with him. 'I can't pretend I didn't hear all that,' she said.

'Why didn't Ruby just cut my balls off and have done with it? Are you any good at that acting bit of yours? Very good? Special?'

'Yes.' There was no vanity in this. She viewed her talent as something that had been given to her. It had to be valued, it had to be guarded because it was her one ticket to wider horizons.

'Shall I come and just lie down with you, Barney?'

'No.'

'Why not?'

'Because I was conceived on this bed. It wouldn't be right.'

Sheila, who had been moving towards the bed, halted. Though what he'd just said was vaguely comical she also felt confronted by antique mysteries. Everything was turning Old Testament. She supposed that not lying on that particular bed was like not gazing on your own father's nakedness.

'There's always the floor' was the best she could think of suggesting.

'Have you no pride?'

He had misjudged her. Sheila had only wanted to hold him close, to comfort him.

'I've no pride where you're concerned. None at all. Didn't you know that?' She sounded about ten.

Barney stood up and put his arms protectively around her. 'I'm sorry. It's not you I'm angry with. I'm just swiping at anything.'

Even that small amount of closeness began to recharge the atmosphere.

'Let's stop this before we start.' But Barney didn't break away. 'It's not as though we could do anything. I've not got any of those sordid rubber things.'

'Have you ever had any?' It was halfway to the question she really wanted to ask.

'I once bought a packet at the barber's.'

'Did you use them?'

Barney grinned. 'I did a bit of experimenting in the bathroom. Played a solo, as you might say.'

'But you've never played a duet?'

Barney shook his head ruefully.

'I'm so glad.' Sheila held him very tightly. 'I want the first time to be with me.'

'Do you make a habit of this sort of thing?'

Now it was Sheila's turn to shake her head. 'I only want you.'

'Have you any idea how much I love you?' asked Barney.

Sheila couldn't believe her own ears. It wasn't an act. She could tell that. Barney was looking straight into her eyes.

'I've loved you since the first minute I opened that door, at Magda's, and saw you standing in the rain. Half the North of England knows I'm barmy about you.'

Now he had gone too far. Or had he? Hadn't Magda Schiffer said, 'He is not without feelings for you'? Hadn't she survived on this, hoping against hope, for months?

'But Sheila, you're only sixteen. Christ, you should hear the stick I've had to take.' He began to mimic unpleasant voices: ' "It's half past three, Barney, aren't you forgetting school's out?" "There's a public playground, Barney. Why don't you go and sniff the swings?" '

'Don't say Christ,' said Sheila, 'or I'll start saying Moses.'

'Sheila, you're not Jewish. You're only sixteen. It's wrong.'

'Keep your voice down or we'll have your mother up again. I like her.'

'And she'd like you. But not what you are.'

'A shiksa?'

'Where the hell did you learn that god-awful word?'

Sheila felt it only reasonable to point something out. 'My mother would call you a Jew-boy.'

Barney went a bit red and said, 'Would you laugh at me if I quoted a poem?'

'I'd never laugh at you. Unless you were being funny. Then I'd laugh like anything.' She wondered whether she dared slide her hand under the back of the jersey or was this meant to be a solemn moment? 'Go on. Quote it.'

Barney looked as though he wished he'd not begun this and then blurted out, ' "I could not love thee half as much loved I not honour more." That didn't come out right. I feel a shmo.'

He loved her, he loved her. He'd said so – twice. Only now it seemed to be wrapped in something menacing. What was this 'honour' he loved more?

'Just kiss me,' she said.

As their lips met, Sheila's mind went back to all the things she had heard about French kissing. It had always sounded a very nasty and complicated process. The reality proved to be the most natural thing on earth. This commingling was exactly what she had been needing. To taste, to suck, to tease, to twine. As Barney's tongue turned into a penetrating rod between her lips, Sheila gained her first glimmer of understanding of infinitely wider possibilities.

This is what I was born for, she thought. The thought seemed to have its own background music. She was brought back to earth by the fact that something hard was pressing against her. It was as though Barney had got a solid pipe in his pocket.

June Monk was the last person she wanted to think about but it was June's sniggering words which came to mind: 'Men's thingies swell.'

Sheila stifled the thought that it might be interesting to put her hand down there and touch it. No. At long last it was Barney who was making the running and she was well content.

Just for a moment they broke apart.

'Sorry,' said Sheila. 'My fault. I've not quite got the breathing right.'

'Beats all the talking, doesn't it?' said Barney happily. They nuzzled close for a moment and then they found one another's lips again. This time the inner exploration was more confident and more exciting. It was halfway to joining up into one person. Now she'd found this, she mustn't lose it. He might not want words but she had to speak. Whilst she had him on her side she had to hammer out a deal.

'I've got to tell you about me, Barney.' She knew she was talking too quickly but the words were flooding out. '*Really* about me. Not just what I let other people see. I think I'm like the swans. I mate for life. I've only ever wanted you. But I have to be an actress too. I need to pass my exams and then . . .'

Her inexperience let her down. Examinations were the last thing she should have mentioned.

Barney broke away from her arms and reached for one of his designs. 'Do you think this is any good?' he asked.

Was it a test? The swirls of poster colour reminded Sheila of a Goya perfume advertisement. Now she saw what Ruby had meant. She chose her reply carefully: 'The colours are very pretty.'

Not carefully enough. It was a test and she'd failed it. It was as though she'd put a hundred yards between them. A hundred yards on a cold day.

' "The colours are very pretty." ' The mimicry was savage. 'Sheila, I've got things I've got to sort out too. P'raps it would be better if we just stayed friends. I've really got to polish this thesis and then I've got to come to a lot of decisions.'

'Just friends? That ended when you let me walk through the door. You could have stopped me. I'd have taken "No" for an answer. Even now, I'd turn around and walk away if I thought it was the best thing for you. I would. I'd just go away for ever.'

Where were these words coming from? Sheila had the

uneasy feeling that she might have pinched them off Joan Fontaine, in *Rebecca*. Would she have to live with the consequences of what she had just said? If her statement had been dramatic, it wasn't far from the truth. She decided she might as well risk going the whole way and began to move towards the door.

'No.' Barney moved across the room and blocked any chance of Sheila reaching the fire escape.

'You're not going like this. I won't let you. You weren't to know you said the wrong thing about my design. I can't see how this thing can be made to work but it *has* to be made to work. To throw it away, just because it's difficult, would be like pissing on the face of God.'

In that moment, Sheila's admiration for Ruby Shapiro grew boundlessly. This was Barney the man. And he was something far more awesome than a textile designer.

'How strong are you, Sheila? How tough? I need at least six months to work my guts out and think like a razor. If I start snatching meetings with you, I know myself, all my energies will go into that. I need this time. I've a feeling I'm one of your swans too. But you've got to let me be one on my own terms.

'I'll make a date with you. August the first. Eight o'clock in The Midland. Until then we don't even try and see one another. No games. No hide-and-seek.'

'August the first is more than seven months away. You could meet somebody else . . .'

'So could you, Sheila. No letters. No phone calls. If what we have is any good it will last. It has to be tested. I don't even know what we do then. My instinct, everything I know, tells me there has to be breathing space.'

From the moment she met him, Sheila had wanted Barney to take control. 'It's not just a subtle way of getting rid of me?'

'That's not how I am. That isn't my style.'

This she believed to be true. She was looking at another of his drawings. It was that sorriest of things – not quite good enough. He would be a businessman.

'How did you get here?' Barney took the designs and closed them into a folio.

'By bike. It's in your bushes.'

'Let me get your coat. I'll walk you down.'

One half of Sheila's mind knew that everything had been said that could have been said. The other half wanted to ask Barney whether he'd got an alarm clock? Couldn't she stay the night? Even on the bed you were conceived on, it would surely be all right just to curl up and go to sleep?

Silently, she let Barney help her on with her coat.

'What are you thinking?' he asked.

Sheila's mind was so like quicksilver that she was able to answer, quite truthfully, 'I was wondering what I'd wear on August the first.'

'The time will soon pass.' Barney kissed her lightly on the cheek.

'Do you really believe that? It's more than half of three hundred and sixty-five days.'

'I'll be twenty-one then,' said Barney.

'P'raps you'll have the key to your own front door?'

Barney had quietly opened the one onto the fire escape. He put his arms around her and rubbed her shoulder. 'That coat's very thin for cycling through the night. Here. Take this.' Reaching over the back of a wooden chair, he unhooked his college scarf. The scarf she'd looked for so often in The Kardomah, the library and even in that awful Hadassiah.

'But when will I be able to give it you back?'

'August the first. Who knows, perhaps by then I won't need it.'

Yes, she thought, as she allowed him to lead her out onto the wooden landing. Yes, he is going to become part of the family firm.

Together they began their cautious descent of the icy steps. Once they reached the ground they both started going 'Shh' to one another. 'Shh!' at exactly the same moment, like drunks in a music-hall sketch.

Their breath made Eskimo clouds on the night air. It was deliciously light-hearted but also bitter-sweet. Once they reached the five-barred gate they would be arriving at a seven-months parting.

Sheila looked up at the sky. 'The stars seem brighter than when I arrived.' Had that been only twenty minutes ago? So much had changed. Suddenly they clung to one another and again they kissed. Now they weren't in a room with a bed in it, kissing seemed complete in itself.

'Do you know anything about astronomy?' asked Barney.

Sheila shook her head. She supposed there would be lots of things she would have to learn, to please him.

'Less than a mile from here, over three hundred years ago, a man looked through a telescope. He was the first human being to observe the transit of Venus.' Barney looked at Sheila with great love. 'Now I know how he must have felt. Venus in transit, that's who you are.'

'It's one up on being Monty,' said Sheila, and climbed on her bicycle. She didn't want to go but her sense of theatre was telling her she had just been handed a neat exit.

'Could I have another kiss?' she asked. 'And could we make it of the very best quality? After all, it's got to last till summer.'

10

It was a Saturday morning in February. Gladys Starkey had gone to take a bad egg back, in a cup, to the bottom shops. Sheila was using her mother's absence to sneak a quick telephone call, to Mickey, in London.

'Mick? My RADA prospectus and the entry form have arrived. They say I need to prepare two audition pieces. One Shakespeare, one modern; own choice.'

Mickey's voice came crackling back down the line. The long-distance trunk-call operator had given them a poor connection. 'Just so long as you don't do St Joan. Those auditions are full of girls pretending to be the Maid of Orleans and begging the examining board not to put out their eyes.'

' "Never again to see the light of day," ' quoted Sheila. 'It's strong stuff, Mickey. I can't absolutely promise not to rule it out.'

'What are you thinking of doing for the Shakespeare?' He sounded grumpy. 'Not that bloody hackneyed "willow cabin" speech from *Twelfth Night*?'

Sheila was beginning to get annoyed. 'You're only saying that because you know I love it.'

'It's got whiskers on it, Sheila,' he snorted. 'And don't do Juliet either or you'll risk being the fifth they hear that morning.'

'What does that leave me?' wailed Sheila.

She should have known better. It was a mistake to ask Mickey for a decision before noon. He was a man of midnight.

'It leaves you every other part in the world, you stupid cow. I should think you'll make a great success as an actress, Sheila. The one thing it doesn't require is great intelligence.'

'And what about you? I suppose it's different for actors.'

'Who said I was going to be an actor?' This was new. 'I'm

152

just here to learn all I can about the theatre. And that includes what not to do at auditions.' Sheila found herself left listening to the dialling tone.

She sat down on the bottom stair and began leafing through the prospectus. *The Meggie Albanesi Open Scholarship*, which offered free tuition, seemed to be her best bet.

The phone rang. She had been almost certain it would. Mickey would now be awake enough to have decided how to be more cutting with the last word.

She lifted up the receiver and said, 'Yes, Mr Pig?'

'Do something bold and stylish, even if it's too old for you. That's the kind of actress you'll eventually be. You might just as well make them sit up with it now.'

'I'll make my own arrangements, thank you.' Sheila said this loftily. Then she felt she'd better climb down a bit, but only a bit, as she added, 'I presume you will be kind enough to offer me some accommodation for that night? I could, of course, go to a small hotel.'

It was the 'small hotel' which started Mickey laughing.

'Don't worry, I'll have the red carpet ready. And Sheila, do what you like. You will anyway. I know you.'

What other people could never understand was that Mickey and Sheila had been thriving on these fierce spats since they were eight years old. Any misguided outsider who ventured to take sides soon found that the pair of them could instantly reunite, to turn on the unwanted ally.

The row had acted on Sheila like a tonic. Mickey, of course, would have to be shown that he did not rule her life. The only trouble was that without his creative guidance she was in something of a muddle. A procession of Shakespeare's heroines was stomping around her head in one direction, a long line of modern characters was trudging in the other. She could only choose two of them.

Sheila threw on her coat, grabbed the RADA prospectus and headed down the garden path. Mickey could scoff all he liked. She would take her problems to the public library.

'Sheila! Hang on a minute.'

It was Monica. The Dolans always had dilapidated wrecks of cars parked on their path and she was edging her way past

153

the running board of an old Armstrong-Siddeley and waving a letter.

'That eejit of a postman left this at our house instead of yours.'

Sheila took the envelope. Unknown handwriting and a London postmark. 'Thanks, Monica. My prospectus arrived ·this morning. Are you any nearer being a nun?'

Monica produced a tube of Spangles. 'Not one step, but our Delia's managed to click with an African engineering student from Salford Tech. He's got tribal tattoos on his cheekbones. She has to meet him on the sly. Me mother would go mad. You see, Sheila, he's not a Catholic.

'No bugger of a Mother Superior wants me for a nun,' she continued. 'So I keep going to town and having a look at how things stand in Lewis's Arcade. Only a look, mind you. They're a very dressy lot considering they take their clothes off for a living.'

Sheila was startled. It was well known that Lewis's Arcade was where the more blatant of the Manchester prostitutes plied their trade.

'You're serious, Monica, aren't you?'

'You bet your arse I am. If I can't have a life of chastity, poverty and obedience then I'm going in for hard cash. Listen, Sheila, hasn't that stepfather of yours turned into a chronic bust watcher? Undresses you, with his eyes, right in the middle of Rookswood Avenue.'

Before Sheila could answer, they were interrupted by Monica's mother calling from the front doorstep. 'Monica, come and get your black veil and your rosary. It's the Forty Hours Devotions for the Bishop's special intention. We're due, on our knees, in front of the Blessed Sacrament at eleven o'clock.'

The Dolans, like the Shapiros, represented religious mystery. A whole area of this Irish immigrant family's life was lit by wax tapers and heavy with the scent of incense. Sheila found it almost eerily fascinating. One day, she knew, she would have to explore these things for herself.

Whoever had written to her from London? The envelope

was safe Basildon Bond. As she walked down Ravensway, Sheila opened the letter.

It was from Shelagh Starkey. The handwriting was very like Miss Bolt's at school. You couldn't imagine it doing anything as flamboyant as signing autographs.

Miss Starkey – Sheila was already thinking of her as Miss Starkey – apologized for her delay in writing but she had been working in a production, in Paris, with Jean-Louis Barrault. This sounded more like it. 'A small part.' Oh well, you couldn't have everything.

She thanked Sheila for forwarding on the letter but poor old William Heythorpe came in for some criticism. 'Always over-imaginative and almost certainly confusing me with somebody else. I never played Cordelia in my life.'

Sheila's namesake went on to wish her great luck in the future, emphasized the importance of school work and suggested she might care to telephone '. . . if you are ever in town.' Goodness, but it all sounded wonderfully West End!

The train seemed to be putting on a final burst of speed. As Sheila gazed apprehensively through the third-class carriage window, the neon sign on the railside factory said *Ovaltine – Euston Station five minutes*.

There were so many dreams, connected with fame and fortune, invested in this journey to the audition at the Royal Academy of Dramatic Art. Financially, Sheila was already better off than she had begun the day. Gander had taken her on one side and handed her sixteen pounds.

'It's one pound for every year of your life,' Gander had said. 'It's just a little something to give you a nice push in the right direction. It doesn't mean you won't get a twenty-first present because, God willing, you will.'

The money was tucked inside Monica Dolan's best black handbag which had been offered, as a lend, for the occasion. Monica had placed an Evening in Paris bottle, filled with holy water, in one of the compartments.

Not all of Rookswood Avenue had been as open-hearted. It was true that Gladys had offered Sheila one of her iron kisses but she had spoiled the effect by adding: 'And if you don't get through you'll still be in plenty of time to enrol for Greenwood's Commercial College.'

Sheila had to get through. The last three years of her life had been geared to nothing else. Unless you counted Barney; and Sheila most definitely did. She wasn't actually wearing his scarf. It was in her mother's black patent hatbox which she was using as an overnight bag. People were already on their feet and getting luggage down from the racks. Sheila opened the hatbox and stowed two books inside it. They were the copies of the plays she had chosen. It wasn't that she was learning them at the last minute. They were, if anything, already over-rehearsed.

Now the backs of grey houses, like something out of a poem by John Betjeman, were banked up on the cutting, above either side of the train. Victorian bathroom extensions, like lead conservatories covered in drainpipes, all but overhung the railway line.

Through an open window, an old man with a towel round his neck waved to the train. Was he lonely? Or did he know all about people arriving in London, for the first time, with hope and excitement and a touch of fear all jockeying for position?

Steep walls, on both sides, suddenly rose up like a tiled Egyptian tomb. Was this a sign? Should she, after all, have learned one of Cleopatra's speeches?

A real sign said *Euston*. The train ground to a halt.

All the voices on the platform sounded like something out of an Ealing comedy. A porter, driving a clanking luggage trailer, was yelling 'Mind yer backs there.' He sounded like Jack Warner in *The Blue Lamp*.

Everybody was pushing and shoving in a much less considerate way than they did in Manchester. All stations are dirty but Euston was the filthiest and most smoke-filled Sheila had ever seen. Suddenly she felt like Ruth, in the Bible, when she first found herself amongst the alien corn.

Where was her ticket? In Monica's handbag. Sheila hardly dared to open it. She'd already caught sight of three teddy boys and a spiv.

She found herself being swept along by the other passengers towards the head of the platform. A dense crowd was waiting the other side of the ticket barrier; their faces were just pale blobs. Somebody in a white seaman's jersey seemed to be waving at her. A white slaver? June Monk had warned that they could be waiting anywhere with hypodermics.

No. It was lovely, familiar, safe Mickey. She hadn't recognized him immediately because he'd let his hair grow much longer and the dark glasses and the white jersey must be new acquisitions.

For the first time in her life she felt almost shy with him. He was established here. He knew the ropes. He was confident enough of this dark, echoing place to carry off sun glasses and a copy of *The Times*.

'How was your journey?' he asked.

'One and six for a sandwich. But it didn't matter, I'm rolling.'

'Good, because I'm skint.'

Everything was suddenly OK and they were just Sheila and Mick again.

'What d'you want to do first?' he asked.

'See RADA.'

'Fine. It's just round the corner. But we daren't go in. I've dodged off classes to meet you.'

Outside the station, all the buses were red and old and groaning. There was so much traffic that the air smelled like scruffy petrol stations.

'Give me the case and take my hand,' said Mick. 'Come on. What are you staring at?'

'Those Indian women in saris. They've got diamonds stuck in their noses.'

'Don't be so provincial, Sheila,' said Mickey loftily. 'They're probably maharanees or something.'

'I am provincial. I never intend to pretend to be anything else.'

'Poor you.' Mickey guided her expertly between a taxi and an ambulance. 'I aim to be international.'

'But not an actor?'

'We'll see.' He sounded evasive.

The sign on the wall proclaimed this to be Gower Street. It was awe-inspiring. Sheila had gazed on this name, a hundred

157

times, in her well-thumbed copy of the academy prospectus. On one side of the street were Georgian houses.

'It's like Salford Crescent but posh,' she said.

'We don't say posh in London any more. We say smart.'

'I'll smack your legs in a minute, Mickey. And I bet you've not read that paper, either.' Nevertheless she filed it away: 'Smart not posh.' Delia Dolan would have loved Gower Street. There seemed to be as many black faces as there were white ones.

'The big buildings belong to the university. That's Dillon's, over there. It's where we get some of our books.'

In Sheila's mind, a chilly-looking bookshop was suddenly bathed in theatrical glamour.

'Good afternoon, Sergeant.'

The man Mickey was addressing wore a dark commissionaire's uniform and a peaked hat. Around the hatband, in gold embroidered letters, was one word. RADA.

She'd arrived. The white Portland stone building was blank and anonymous except for the entrance. Two carved stone figures sat above the surprisingly small front door. Each had an uplifted hand; one removing the mask of Comedy, the other that of Tragedy.

'Bit like a smart skin hospital really,' said Mickey cheerfully. 'Keep moving,' he muttered. 'There's no black card against my name, on the board inside. I'm supposed to be in this afternoon. God help us if Nancy Brown looks out and sees me.'

'Who's she?'

'The Registrar. Draped turban hat and sticky-out teeth. I've already managed to make an enemy there.'

A woman in a white warehouse coat, with a brown paper parcel in her arms, walked towards them. A tag on the parcel read *The Holborn Hygienic Laundry*. This everyday detail made Sheila realize this wasn't a dream, she really was in London.

Mickey said 'Hello' to the woman. He added under his breath, to Sheila, 'That's the Warden.'

'The Warden? You make it sound like Dotheboys Hall.'

'It's worse than that. But don't let me put you off.' The odd eyes, as contradictorily blue and green as ever, flashed Sheila a defiant look.

She knew better than to say anything, but thought, He's changed. It's still as good as having a brother. And he's still exactly who I thought he was. Only now he's more so. And something's up!

Heraldic Mansions, Marchmont Street, London WC1, was a block of tenement flats. Sheila viewed the outside brickwork, in shades of purple bruise, with horror. It was just starting to rain. Was she meant to unpack her things and spend the night in this place?

'Mickey, it's just like Divine Dwellings where Gander's poor Edie came out with the dog on a piece of string and a black eye.'

'In London a good address is everything.' Mickey led the way nonchalantly up a stone staircase which could have come out of the ballet *Miracle in the Gorbals*. 'Heraldic Mansions looks most impressive at the top of a letter. Bet you were kidded.'

The flat, it transpired, belonged to an actress who had gone to Australia in a musical. Temporarily, the place was turned into four single bed-sitting rooms. The student tenants all shared the kitchen and the bathroom.

Mickey's room looked down onto a dank courtyard where overflow pipes dripped onto old zinc milk bottle crates – standing amidst bomb weeds.

'This is a slum,' said Sheila, in hushed wonder.

'This is thirty bob a week, which aint 'alf bad for rahnd 'ere.' Mickey seemed to talk a lot in mock cockney these days. Sheila felt very far from home and reflected that Gladys would die if she knew where her hatbox had landed up.

'Are there bugs?' she asked respectfully. 'What a very unusual lamp.' She added this hastily; the last thing she wanted to do was hurt Mickey's feelings.

'It's not unusual at all, it's a converted Chianti bottle. Half the bed-sits in London have got them. And flimsy Indian cotton bedspreads like this one. And posters begged off travel agents on the walls. No, there aren't bugs, not unless you've brought any with you.

'This place is only a springboard, Sheila. I've no intention

159

of staying here for ever. We can make two beds by splitting the base and the mattress. D'you need coat hangers or anything? Did you really convince your mother you were going to a saintly YWCA hostel?'

It had all turned back into an adventure again. Sheila began to unpack. Mickey gazed in horror on the first items to come out of her suitcase.

'What in God's name are those?'

'Flowers. They're cloth flowers.'

'I only hope you don't propose going out with me wearing them.'

'I don't wear them. I throw them around!'

As Mickey was looking at her in something approaching total disbelief, Sheila felt she'd better explain further.

'At the audition I'm going to do Ophelia's mad scene from *Hamlet*. I sling these flowers around a bit. It's all properly rehearsed.'

'I see.' Mickey said this in such blank tones that Sheila knew he was being supremely careful. 'And what are you planning to give them for your modern extract?'

'*Peg o' My Heart*.'

Mickey's face was such a study in self-control that Sheila immediately went on the defensive. 'It's a very moving little scene. I talk to a dog in it.'

'Don't tell me you've got a stuffed animal in your luggage too?'

Sheila threw her Bakelite soap box at Mickey. There was a brand-new tablet of French Fern inside. He ducked and the box smashed right through the window and dropped, with a lot of broken glass, into the courtyard.

'I'll pay. I'll pay.' Sheila was all contrition.

Mickey didn't appear remotely concerned. Instead, he was studying her closely.

'A thought's just struck me,' he said. 'And it's sent shivers down my spine. If I ever make a character out of Gander's poor Edie, you would be absolutely sensational. Come on. Hurry up. All of London's waiting for us.'

'Can we go where RADA students go?'

'If we must.' Mickey made a face. 'I have to warn you that

they talk balls. It's all Stanislavsky and third-hand West End gossip. Wouldn't you rather see the theatres on Shaftesbury Avenue?'

'Those too, but I want the other first.'

Mickey groaned. 'I thought I'd brought you up better than this.'

As they walked towards Tottenham Court Road, under a big black umbrella, Sheila reflected that this was – in many ways – precisely what Mickey had done. He had brought her up. It troubled her to think that he was already disenchanted with RADA and questioning his vocation as an actor. She was also wishing she'd let him choose her audition pieces. But it was too late for that now or he would certainly have suggested changing them.

Olivelli's was exactly what Sheila had hoped for.

'RADA people use this coffee bar on the ground floor,' explained Mickey. 'But there's a restaurant in the basement and upstairs is lodgings for variety artists.'

The walls were covered in framed, signed photographs and hung with strings of onions. More of the pretty Chianti bottles were tied amongst them, as decorations.

'Two cappuccinos, Bridget,' said Mick and added, as the waitress moved away: 'She's got religious mania so she always adds up the bills very charitably, which is handy. Well, this is it. *La Bohème* 1950s style. Feast your eyes.'

Sheila was already doing that. It made her want to send a postcard to Barney, but a deal was a deal so she couldn't. Minnehaha hairstyles were much in evidence in Olivelli's. And big skirts made out of curtain material clasped in, at the waist, with elasticated belts. Most of the boys looked as though they'd raided government-surplus shops though Sheila considered a couple of them to be a bit on the 'dressy' side. One had kept a big trilby hat on indoors and had a paisley cravat tucked into his sweater.

'Kenneth Halliwell,' said Mickey, noticing where Sheila's gaze had rested. 'Got money of his own. Hi, Joe! He's over there.'

Mickey obviously knew everybody and was popular enough for people to pause at the table and chat and be introduced to

Sheila. Yet he was somehow caged and anxious to move on. Not just from this place, here, tonight. He was poised to make a change in his whole life. By the third cup of coffee it all came out.

'My scholarship comes up for review at the end of next term. They won't renew it. I know it.'

'But you're so good.' Sheila had already taken on the earnest tones of the drama students around her. 'I don't know of anybody else quite like you.'

'That's half the trouble. Wonderful as Ariel, less good at anything more butch.'

'You're not effeminate.' Sheila was hot to his defence.

Mickey remained coldly analytical. 'No. But there's just something about me that troubles the teachers.'

'Is it that wag in your walk?' asked Sheila. 'Couldn't you put bits of lead in your boots?'

'Sheila, I don't want to go through life with lead in my boots. Anyway, RADA just isn't what I expected. They're forever going on about the theatre as Art. I'm interested in Entertainment. As far as I'm concerned the music hall's as big a shrine as the Old Vic. Shall we go and see Max Miller at The Met on Edgware Road? It's only one and nine, up in the gods. I'll pay.'

'I can see variety acts at home,' said Sheila. 'What I really want to do is taste what goes inside those raffia bottles.'

'Chianti? They only serve it with meals. This isn't an off-licence. There's one round the corner, in Goodge Street.'

'Let's take some back to Heraldic Mansions,' wheedled Sheila. 'You're fed up and my stomach turns over every time I think about tomorrow. A drop of Chianti wine might buck us up a treat.'

Gladys Starkey would have said that Gander's money was burning a hole in Sheila's pocket. She tried to tempt Mickey into first a Greek restaurant and then an Indian one but he refused to let her spend money on anything other than the wine. She bought two bottles.

'I already got German sausage and sauerkraut, from Schmidt's, for us,' he explained. 'They're waiting at home.'

Fancy calling Heraldic Mansions home! Then Sheila felt

162

awful. Mickey was doing his very best to entertain her and she wasn't being properly grateful.

She wished they were still under the companionable umbrella but the rain had almost stopped. Instead, to be close, she linked his arm. As they crossed the shining, lamplit streets of Bloomsbury, Mickey dutifully pointed out the blue and white plaques on the houses where famous people had once lived.

'You'll get one, Mick,' she said. 'You know that.'

'Oh I know that.'

'You once said you had to find your town. Is it London?'

'No. London is not my town.'

There was nothing beaten about him. Sheila knew Mickey well enough to realize that he must be marching around the idea of his future career, sizing it up, determining how to attack matters from another angle.

Sheila suddenly squeezed his arm and gave him a quick peck on the cheek. 'I often think I should write to Mr Tuffin, at Blackpool, and thank him for you.'

'Are you suggesting that I'm the result of my lady mother having a quick romp with a boarding-house keeper?'

Everything was back to normal. They laughed and joked all the way to Heraldic Mansions which Mickey was now openly calling the House of Horror.

Once they got upstairs, the first thing they had to do was mend the broken window with cardboard and Sellotape. Mickey then disappeared into the kitchen and returned with a corkscrew.

'Somebody else is using the gas cooker but I managed to grab one burner. He won't be long. He's only frying Sainsbury's bacon scraps. Did you know they sell cracked eggs too? I borrowed glasses. Hand me that bottle.'

Mickey went to work with the corkscrew. 'Do you want to meet the others? They refuse to believe we're splitting the bed in two. They suddenly see me in a daring new light.'

'Don't they know about you and sex?' Sheila was astonished.

'Are you mad? It doesn't pay to advertise. I don't want the police coming knocking. Besides, I'm going to need to do the

163

rounds of the agents. The funny thing is, once you're established, it seems perfectly OK to be gay. Here. Cheers! Let's drink to getting established.'

'One day the law will change,' said Sheila earnestly. 'It must.'

'Don't be so solemn and drink your Chianti.'

It tasted how you would expect red ink to taste. A bit like distilled suede. Sheila couldn't pretend she was much struck. Only that was at first.

After the second glass, she started to think about the aching, lonely place which had always been inside her. Her not-belonging place. Miraculously, this wine seemed to be healing that up. What's more, in some indefinable way, it had also brought Barney closer. This was really extraordinary. Perhaps she should have another glass and see whether it brought him closer still.

'Go easy.' Mick looked anxious. 'You can't have eaten anything for hours.'

'The sandwiches on the train were an elegant sufficiency.' She was surprised to find that her voice seemed to have a lot of extra s's in it.

'Oh my God!' said Mickey. 'I'll go and see how the food's coming on.'

What a spoilsport he was, she mused. A sweetheart but a spoilsport. The s's in her mind were perfectly under control. Perhaps the effect of the Chianti was wearing off. The only other drink she'd ever had was lemonade shandy. But if the effect was wearing off, would this feeling of closeness with Barney evaporate too? P'raps she'd better have another glass and hold him captive.

Once you got used to the flavour it wasn't all that bad. Why were the glasses so small? You should be able to drink this stuff like pop.

This time, as she tilted the bottle, some of the wine sloshed onto the carpet At that moment, Mickey returned with a steaming pan and some plates.

'Fancy boiling sausages,' said Sheila, grandly.

'Say that last word again.'

'Sausages.' There was no denying it was suddenly the most

164

difficult thing she'd ever had to say. It was also the funniest. She began to laugh.

'You're pissed.'

'I'm not,' said Sheila. 'I'm Ophelia. Lend me a sheet to dress up in and hand me my flowers. I think I'll just do the mad scene for you.'

When Sheila woke up, the next morning, for the first time in her life she understood the meaning of the phrase 'a sick headache'.

'I think I must be starting with flu.' She shuddered at the sight of the steaming mug of black coffee which Mickey was trying to hand her.

'No you're not. You've got a hangover. And I'm afraid I've not got much patience with them. Would you like a full account of last night's antics? I shouldn't, for one moment, think you can remember them.

'Not only did we see Ophelia; by the way, you insisted I get everyone else in as an audience. You also recited every fucking poem you've learned since you were six. Even including "Three little kittens have lost their mittens and they began to cry . . ." That's when *you* began to cry.

'And then you had to tell us all about your great passion for Barney Shapiro. Stolen bike, fire escape, the lot. You should see the looks I've just got in the kitchen. They think I've spent the night with Nana of the Boulevards.'

Sheila felt like one of those conjuring tricks where the illusionist asks people to stick swords into a basket that has somebody crouched inside.

'Get up!' snapped Mickey. 'I'm late and you've got an audition to do. What train are you getting back, Peg o' My Heart?'

'Don't call me that.'

'I may never call you anything else. Do you realize that you made poor little Oliver Jenkins, from Bangor, kneel down and be the dog?'

It was almost beyond bearing. 'Who undressed me?'

'Who d'you think? There's mouthwash, with my name on it, in the bathroom cabinet. Use it.'

Mickey stormed out of the room. A moment later she heard a rattling slam which could only be the front door.

Sheila reached for her sponge bag and towel and limped to the bathroom. When she turned on the hot tap, an enamel geyser, above the sink, blew out blue flames and made her jump. The hot water quickly ran to stone cold. Mickey had mentioned a penny in the slot meter but neglected to tell her where it was. How could she have a bath? She did as best she could with a sponge and cold water. The soap refused to lather.

If I cry, she thought, I'll look even worse. The mirror had already shown her a head of hair like a wig that had been slept in. She brushed it back from her forehead savagely. Every tug was agony. A black velvet ribbon would hide the elastic band. Why wouldn't her makeup go on properly?

She had just twenty minutes to get to RADA. Back in the bed-sitting room, Sheila flung on the dark green tartan dress which Gander had pressed, so carefully, in Manchester. She piled the rest of her belongings back into the hatbox. It could come with her. RADA was halfway to Euston Station.

Her whole adolescence had been geared to this one morning. Now Sheila couldn't get it over quickly enough. She had never felt so ill in her life. Last night, the alcohol had seemed to close up the lonely, unhappy place inside her. This morning that place had grown to twice its usual size. Perhaps fresh air would make her feel better.

As she carried her hatbox towards Russell Square, a taxi slowed down beside her. No. A London taxi might shake her up and down and that was the last thing she needed. It was only Sheila's streak of dogged perseverance that got her feet to Gower Street.

In her imagination, Sheila had always expected the RADA entrance hall to be like the crimson and gold foyer of the Palace Theatre in Manchester. In a restrained way it was much more posh. She corrected herself – smart.

Pretty was actually a better word. Cream paintwork, a crystal chandelier, gilt-framed portraits and a comfortable smell of good wax polish.

A woman with a list took Sheila's name and told her to join

the other candidates who were already sitting waiting, in ascending order, on the stairs.

The girl on the step above Sheila was wearing a full stage makeup and complained that she had been expecting the audition to take place in the academy theatre. 'But they're seeing us in Room Two,' she said.

Room Two? It sounded like something out of a Gestapo film.

'What are you doing?' Sheila asked her.

'Juliet and St Joan.' The girl was gazing into the middle distance and frantically mouthing silent lines. She paused and said, 'Could I ask you not to talk to me?'

Nothing could have suited Sheila better. Even the slightest noise was going through her head like the drill at the dentist's. What's more, she was suddenly feeling very nervous.

Succeeding candidates passed into Room Two and emerged looking either relieved or shattered. Sheila moved places, step by step, up the staircase. Next she was on the landing. Now it was her turn.

The woman with the list led Sheila, who was wishing she wasn't still carrying her dratted hatbox, into the room. Now she was announcing her.

'Miss Sheila Starkey.'

Sheila hadn't been expecting 'Miss'. Six people were grouped on a row of chairs at the end of the room. They brought highly polished antiques to mind. They must all, at some time, have been on the stage because their limbs were so well arranged. Four men, two women. One fur coat, good quality but old-fashioned square shoulders. The man in the middle, she decided, must be Sir Kenneth Barnes, the Principal.

It was one of the other men who spoke. 'May we have your Shakespeare first? Just tell us what you're going to do and then go ahead in your own good time.'

Sheila put down the hatbox. This was no place for home-made cloth flowers. She would mime them instead.

Sheila had taken Shakespeare's original text and run parts of it together. It was bit of a botch and cobble job and began with Ophelia's crazy little song. She got through this without any problems but when she came to the spoken line 'There's rosemary, that's for remembrance', the oddest thing happened. Scenes from the previous evening began to flash through her mind. With each succeeding line, she remembered what had happened when she'd said it the night before. Even to the point where she'd tripped over the fender. These memories might have added to the general air of madness but they meant, for the first time in her life, that Sheila's performance was out of control. The insanity felt almost real.

'Thank you, Miss Starkey. And for your modern?'

'Peg from *Peg o' My Heart*.' Why hadn't Mickey made the effort to find her on the stairs and wish her luck? Sheila took a deep breath and went into the speech.

For any actress an audience – even six people sitting at the end of a room – turns into a single animal. Its confidence must be gained, it has to be wooed, won over. At first, Sheila felt she was getting nowhere and then it began to build. That warm golden glow came rolling towards her. She had them. They were hers. This was belonging.

At the end of the speech Sir Kenneth Barnes got to his feet and moved towards Sheila. For the first time, she noticed that an old brown dog had, all the time, been sitting underneath his chair. Dogs were generally on her side. For a wild moment she found herself wondering whether this animal held the casting vote?

'That was most simple and touching, Miss Starkey. Nothing like the original production but none the worse for that. I have to ask you a very direct question. If we don't award you a scholarship, can you afford to come here?'

'No.'

'Thank you very much. You will be hearing from us.'

11

The letter from RADA took two weeks to arrive. Was there anybody on Ravensdale Estate who hadn't heard that Sheila was awaiting the result of a London audition? Word had spread as far as Irlams o'th' Height. Virtual strangers had taken to giving 'the girl who's been on the wireless' smiles of encouragement. It was almost as though they hoped to be the first person to hear the good news.

This attitude is one of the most heart-warming things about the North of England. But what if it all went wrong? What if she hadn't passed? As Sheila started to open the envelope her mind was filled with a morbid vision of faces filled with kindly, unbearable pity.

The vision froze like a cinema still.

The letter from London regretted to tell Sheila that she had failed to reach the required scholarship standard.

Would every single person who had wished her luck have to be told the shoddy truth? Who were RADA anyway? Their letter went straight on the back of the fire. And the envelope.

The bad news had arrived by the second post. Sheila was only at home because she'd been excused hockey so as to be able to revise for her O levels. No reason now why she shouldn't burn her textbooks too. Strictly speaking they belonged to the Education Committee. Anyway, it might set fire to the chimney. The last thing she wanted to do was draw attention to herself.

What was wrong with failing to get into a sausage factory? That's what Mickey had called it. They were back on speaking terms. He had rung her to say that he was going off to St Ives 'to think'.

Queen Elizabeth was being crowned next Wednesday. The first thing she should do, after her Coronation, was look into her Royal Academy of Dramatic Art. There was something very wrong with an establishment which didn't want Sheila

Starkey and was all set to get rid of Mickey Grimshaw. If he could launch himself, on London, without a full training so could Sheila.

She dialled DIR and got the number of the Theatre Girls' Club. She didn't dare write it down on the pad. Sheila was all set to run away from home. Gladys must be left no clues.

Quickly, she rang the club. The Matron of this residential establishment, in Soho, asked her a few pointed questions. Sheila assured the Matron she had just finished working in a radio serial, that she had money and that she would only need the room for two weeks, whilst looking for more work.

The reference to the radio serial was truthful enough. Barry Wrigley had relented and given her a job in the half-term holidays. Sheila crossed her fingers as she added two years to her age and claimed to be eighteen.

'I don't know where you got the idea we have rooms, dear,' said the Matron. 'We only run to cubicles.'

Precious money wasn't going to be wasted on train fares. The Kardomah crowd were forever talking about hitchhiking. They claimed that if you wanted to head south, all you had to do was get to Mere Corner in Cheshire, and stick out your thumb.

There could be no question of borrowing Gladys's hatbox this time. That would be stealing. Equally, she couldn't run away packed in brown paper parcels. Sheila suddenly remembered the fibre suitcase that the War Office had sent back from the Middle East. Nobody could accuse you of robbing your dead father.

She knelt down and opened the little cupboard under the stairs. The case was stencilled *Capt. Jack Starkey, His Majesty's Transport Ship Panattia.* Was he having to hide his face in shame, at her failure, in heaven?

The front door opened suddenly and Gander walked in with the spare key in her hand. She took in the scene at one worried glance.

Sheila looked up from the floor. 'I failed. I've got to go back to London and do it another way.'

'Think twice. There's a wind getting up. I slipped over to close your mother's front bedroom window. Sheila, love, don't go, please.'

'I've got to.'

'Don't.'

Sheila shook her head sadly.

'Hold out your hand then.' Gander fished in her apron pocket and produced her worn leather purse. Opening it quickly, she tried to tip the contents into Sheila's palm.

'No, Gander. You can't. You already gave me my luck money. I don't want to turn my good luck round by grabbing extra cash just because you're upset.'

'Rum sort of good luck!' Gander almost managed a smile. Then she looked serious. 'Promise me one thing. Don't go like a thief in the night. Write your mother a proper letter. That much she does deserve. I'm sure I should be doing more to stop you . . . You weren't just the nearest child, Sheila. You were always the best – you rum bugger.'

Gander held Sheila close. 'It's not as if I'm on the phone. You can't even ring me. Blow your nose and listen. If it all goes wrong, you can always come back and live with me and Mr Gander. Even if it does mean we have to move house.'

'D'you think she'll be finished with me?' asked Sheila.

'At one time I could have told you. These days it all depends on how many tablets Jepson's fed her. I don't know, and that's the truth.

'Listen, you're taking this white five-pound note whether you like it or not. Either you take it or I'll be joining your mother in his queue for sleeping pills. There, I've spit on it! You can't turn that down – my spit's the best good luck for miles around.'

In later life, whenever she heard a high wind on a black night Sheila Starkey would restrain a shudder and say, 'Good weather for running away.'

The first lorry got her as far as Burton-upon-Trent. Rows of terraced houses were already packing up for the night. The last of the curtains were being drawn on enviably safe living rooms where there were plates of biscuits and warm fires. The handle of the suitcase had began to cut into Sheila's hand and rain was adding teeth to the bite of the wind.

It took two hours of standing thumbing, by a road sign, to

get her next lift. This was from a commercial traveller who only wanted an audience for his theories on a vegetarian diet. As he droned on about the merits of the lentil, Sheila found herself longing for oxtail done Gander's way. It didn't do to think too hard about Gander. By now Sheila was beginning to miss sleep and miserable tears, behind her eyes, were seeking an excuse to start rolling.

The vegetarian dropped her off at a transport cafe standing in the middle of a big, dark car park, outside Rugeley. The headlights of lorries revealed the cafe as a ramshackle building, like a wood and asbestos cricket pavilion.

Some of the parked lorry loads were covered with tarpaulin sheets. When the wind got under them, their corners whipped with protesting cracks. Sheila picked her way through oily rain puddles. The voices coming from the cafe were masculine and rough and arguing.

At least it was warm inside but the bacon and egg had been cooked in lard and tasted reasty. The wind had risen to a high whine and the rain was now back again, throwing itself against the steamed-up windows. Sheila sat it out for three more cups of tea. Apart from a few stares in her direction, and an overheard comment about 'The little mystery', the girl passed unremarked.

The man behind the counter was replaced by a woman in a collar and tie with a Tony Curtis haircut. Eventually she came across and wiped Sheila's table.

'Evening, duck.' Her voice sounded like Beryl Reid doing Birmingham on the wireless. 'We don't get many girls so just shout out if you want a wee or anything.'

'I'm desperate for one. That and a lift to London.' Sheila uncrossed her legs gratefully. As she got to her feet, her spirits were already beginning to rise again.

The woman beamed. 'Through the plain green door and leave the rest to Billie. That's me. I'll find you a driver guaranteed to keep his hands to 'imself. A nice girl like you shouldn't be doing this. Men are bastards. It's not safe.'

When Sheila returned from the lavatory, the helpful woman already had a lorry driver, called Jeff, waiting by the car park door.

'An Arsenal supporter,' she said. 'But you could trust him with Betty Grable.'

Somebody called out, 'And what about you, Billie?' The woman flushed angrily and all but pushed Sheila and Jeff out into the night.

Billie had chosen well. Jeff had 'family man' written all over him. The step of the cab of his lorry was so high up that he had to reach down and haul Sheila up through the rain.

'London?' he asked. 'Right. Why don't you get your head down for a bit. We've a few drops to make on the way.'

Sheila couldn't, for one moment, imagine herself falling asleep in the cab of a roaring lorry but that's what happened and she didn't even dream. When she opened her eyes again, dawn was breaking over streets of peeling grey houses with pillared front doors and railings and empty milk bottles at the top of tall steps. Cats seemed to be the only things moving.

'Good old London,' said Jeff. 'Just dropping down into Camden Town. I've been thinking things over, sweetheart. I'm sorry, but I'm going to have to take you to Harrow Road police station.'

'Why?' Though only half awake, Sheila was already sizing up her chances of jumping out of the moving lorry. 'Why?'

'Stands to sense. You've escaped from a girls' Borstal. Must have done. Everything points to it.'

'I'm an actress,' said Sheila desperately.

'Anybody could say that.'

'But I am. And I can prove it. Listen!'

Without hesitation she went into the scene from *Peg o' My Heart*. It might not have got her into RADA but it would surely keep her out of the police station? In dawn's thin light all of Peg's yearning and heartache was easy. Sheila was ten times better for this lorry driver than she had ever been for Sir Kenneth Barnes.

'Strewth!' said Jeff in wonder. 'You're as good as Jean Kent. Where would you like me to drop you?'

'The West End.'

Jeff dropped Sheila off at Cambridge Circus. He even got out of the cab to help her down with her suitcase.

'There's Shaftesbury Avenue,' he said. 'Now think on, I'm

expecting to read in my *Daily Mirror* that you've made London your own. Me and the wife will be expecting orchestra stalls.'

As she waved him goodbye Sheila hoped that friendliness was not disappearing with the tail lights of the lorry. The overhead street lamps suddenly went out. It was a pale grey morning but the sun was already trying to break through. There was hope in the air and the theatres were draped with bunting. Would next week's Coronation hold things up? Would all the theatrical agents' offices be closed for the period of the festivities?

The Palace Theatre was presenting Anna Neagle in *The Glorious Days*. It looked as though the show had been produced to cash in on the royal event. The blown-up pictures outside the theatre were decked with Union Jacks and showed the film star dressed as both Nell Gwynne and an ATS sergeant.

Miss Neagle had no greater fan than Gladys Starkey. Sheila wondered what her mother had made of the note she had left on the mantelpiece. The runaway had got as far as the corner of Rookswood Avenue when she decided to rush back and add a PS: 'Please don't stop loving me.'

Shaftesbury Avenue was almost deserted. Sheila began to carry her suitcase towards Piccadilly Circus. She didn't know that was where she was going. She was just heading in the direction of more theatres.

Up a side street, for the very first time, she saw a star's name in lights. Manchester didn't have them. The neon sign read *Vic Oliver in Three Cheers*. The Casino Theatre was also decorated with painted cut-outs of Britannia. Vic Oliver was a Viennese Jew who had married Winston Churchill's daughter. Come what may, Sheila had to make something of her life before August the first and her meeting with Barney.

Piccadilly Circus was well known to be the centre of the world so Sheila was a little disappointed to find herself sharing it with just two people. And one of these was made of wax – a dummy of an Edwardian woman in a red frock who sat on a chair, in a dry cleaner's shop window, perpetually demonstrating invisible mending. Even Sheila recognized the other woman, standing under the canopy of the cinema, as a lady of the night.

She was old and past it and though her ensemble was topped off with orange fox furs, the prostitute was also wearing white woollen ankle socks, inside her court shoes, for a bit of extra warmth.

'I trust you're not looking for business, young lady?' The voice was daintily threatening.

'Oh no.' Sheila was shocked. Not wishing to seem suburban – this was after all Piccadilly Circus with Eros statue boarded up against revellers – she added hastily, 'But a friend of mine's thinking, very seriously, about taking up your profession.'

'Bottom's dropped out of it, dear.' The woman had a cold and wiped her nose neatly. 'Too many people paid monthly these days. Gets cruel hard towards month end. Makes you lose heart. I didn't even bother bringing out the poodle. Watch yourself, darlin'. This bastard coming up's not a client, he's a ponce.' The woman blew her nose loudly, gave the man in question a black look and clacked off, round the corner, on her high heels.

He was as good-looking as a man on a knitting pattern and very well dressed – until you looked closely. Then you saw that the edges of the camel overcoat were a bit scuffed and that his tie was rayon, masquerading as pure silk.

'Good morning, my little mystery.'

This was the second time that phrase had been used about her. In the transport cafe it had been said in rough tones. This man seemed to have modelled himself on Michael Wilding in *Spring in Park Lane.*

'Has anybody ever told you that you're quite amazingly pretty? I'm not going to ask any questions, I'm going to guess.' His smile came very easily and he had good teeth. 'You left home on a whim and now you're wondering what you're going to do about breakfast. May I be permitted to offer to buy it for you at the Regent Palace Hotel? It's just across the way.'

'What's a ponce?' asked Sheila coldly. She wasn't Gladys Starkey's daughter for nothing.

'My card,' said the man, completely unabashed. His wallet

was of better quality than his shoes and the engraved visiting card read:

Mr Matthew Gillespie
103, Half Moon Street
Mayfair, London W1

'I flatter myself I am something of a West End figure,' he announced cheerfully. 'Always say hello when you see me. You're sure I can't treat you to a delicious breakfast? Don't you find yourself tempted by the idea of sizzling grilled ham?'

'I'd rather starve,' said Sheila.

'The funny thing is they all say that. All the good ones . . . to begin with.'

The Theatre Girls' Club cured Sheila, once and for all, of wearing her hair in a pony tail. The place was full of them. All on dancers. There can be few more excluding cliques on earth than young girls who have trained for the dance.

Sheila's cubicle was quite tolerable; a large dormitory had been partitioned into individual sections. The girls through the dividing walls were less hospitable. They seemed to walk around with their noses stuck in the air and their feet turned out at a quarter to three. They only talked amongst themselves and their conversation was larded with bits of secret-sounding, ballet classroom French.

Sheila found herself overwhelmed by a sudden rush of homesickness. If anybody had told her, she would never have believed that the first person she wanted to speak to would be Mother.

Sheila asked the operator whether she could reverse the charges and gave her the necessary details. During the ensuing dialling sounds Sheila felt distinctly nervous. How would her mother have received the note?

'Hello, caller? The subscriber in Manchester refuses to accept the charge. Will you pay?'

'How much?'

'Please insert one shilling and ninepence . . . Thank you. You have three minutes.'

'It won't take that long.' Gladys's voice was like a bucket of cold water. 'You've made your bed and you must lie on it. And don't think you can get pregnant and bring the brat back here because you can't.' Gladys didn't even say goodbye. Sheila emerged from the phone box, in the hall of the club, with tears rolling down her face.

'Are you homesick?' One of the dancers had actually paused and spoken. Sheila nodded. The call had added to her sense of desolation. Even Gladys's swipes and reproofs were better than not belonging at all.

'Everybody is at first. We heard you talking to Miss Bell. We all think you've got a fabulous speaking voice. Sort of smoky. Do you do drama?'

It was a start. In truth it never got much beyond that but at least it proved the dancers were human. They were just young girls who had finished their training too late for summer season and too early for pantomime. What's more, they already knew some of the ropes. Contacts, they assured Sheila, were everything.

For six months she had been carrying around, in her handbag, Shelagh Starkey's letter with its invitation to telephone '. . . if you are ever in town'.

First, Sheila decided to give the older actress's house the once-over, from outside. Bedman's Row proved to be a narrow alleyway off St Martin's Lane. Sheila passed down a dingy tunnel and stepped straight into the eighteenth century.

The houses were like bow-fronted dolls' cottages with bay trees, in tubs, either side of white front doors. All the window boxes had been planted out in loyal colours for the Coronation. Red geraniums, white rock and blue lobelia.

'Mind your feet.' A woman was hosing down the courtyard. Definitely a lady for all she was wearing rubber wellingtons. 'Are you looking for anybody in particular?'

'Miss Starkey.'

'Guilty. And who, may I ask, are you?'

'I'm the other one – the Manchester Sheila Starkey.'

'Not a trace of an accent. How do you do.'

And that, thought Sheila shaking hands, is what she could be. A teacher of elocution. That or a senior librarian. Miss

Starkey was in her forties, wore very little makeup and had kind eyes.

She's a bit on the prim side, thought Sheila. And she's finding all this running away business rather shocking.

By now they were in the basement kitchen of one of the houses. It had a beamed ceiling and a red tiled floor and was so like something out of a pantomime that Sheila felt as though Widow Twankey should be putting her son through the mangle.

'Good morning, my darling,' called a wonderfully throaty woman's voice from upstairs. Sheila couldn't believe her ears. It was a very famous voice. She and Gander had often listened to it on the wireless.

'Very silly, to leave your front door open. London's full of peeking tourists.' Slim ankles in alligator shoes appeared at the top of the stairs. These were followed by a mink hemline. And then there was a lot more mink coat and above it, *yes*, the amused and laughing face of Lily Bear.

Best known to Sheila's generation for a hugely successful radio comedy series, this entertainer had been a pre-war revue star and was now carving out a whole new career, as a leading character actress, in British films. The hair was scarlet, the pale blue eyes enormous, the mouth wide and beautifully painted. However old was she? Lily Bear exuded an aura of defiant glamour and smelled deliciously of Guerlain's Mitsouko.

'My dear, this Coronation makes you proud to be British. I've just met a contingent of Canadian Mounties on Garrick Street in full uniform. Boy scout hats and leather legs like tree trunks. It seems I am *not* unknown in Canada. They were kind enough to give me three rousing cheers.'

'Stop throwing stardust about, Lil.' Miss Starkey sounded fondly severe. 'I need some help with a problem. Sheila, tell Miss Bear your story. Do you want coffee, Lil, or have you just called to use me as a parcel room?'

'Coffee.' Lily Bear listened carefully to Sheila's story. As Sheila felt she was telling it better, this second time round, the ageing star's response was all the more disappointing.

'Go home, go home, go home!'

'Exactly what I said.' Miss Starkey produced a tin of very good shortbread biscuits.

'Mind you . . .' Lily Bear was walking around Sheila as though she was a display figure in a shop '. . . if she still decides to see it through, despite the pair of us, perhaps that's what she's meant to do.'

'Lil, you're impossible. You're as stage-struck as the child is.'

'The day that stops is the day I give up. Neat waist and wears her clothes well. No, better than well, beautifully. Can you act? *Don't* start reciting!'

'I was good enough for Mamie Hamilton-Gerrard to get me the sack.'

'Poor Mamie,' said Lily Bear. 'The other sister was a darling. Of course it was always said, when they were kiddies, that the mother fed them gin to keep them small. It doesn't work.'

'Mamie's mother doesn't like me much.'

'Then the chances are your work might have a bit of something about it. Stop frowning, Shelagh. She's got looks. And nerve – you've got to grant her nerve. Of course the name would have to be changed if there isn't to be confusion. Equity would insist on it anyway. Let's try your mother's maiden name.'

'Gladys Nuttall.'

'Poor woman. You'd better stick to Starkey. Susan Starkey? No, it sounds like a brand of cotton frock. Siobhan? They'd never be able to pronounce it in the provinces. Still I like the two S's. Sally? Fine now but you'd regret it at thirty. I've got it. Are you ready? One, two three . . . Sorrel Starkey.'

Lily Bear beamed. 'I've always been good at this. I pride myself on being the one person who begged Peggy Ashcroft to leave well alone. Do you like it, *Sorrel*?'

'I love it.' Impulsively, Sheila threw her arms around the actress and gave her a whacking great kiss.

'Whoops, dearie, mind the paint job! So much to learn. If you must kiss another actress, always do it above the cheekbone and *lightly*. Almost kiss the air.'

Sheila felt as though she had finally arrived at her own,

personal academy of dramatic art. 'Sorrel, Sorrel, I must remember that I am now Sorrel.' She kept saying this to herself as Shelagh Starkey began to lecture her on the necessity of gaining stage experience. *I am Sorrel Starkey.*

'You can't do anything about starting to find work on a Saturday. I think you'd better stay to lunch.' Miss Starkey began to rattle pans.

'You've struck lucky,' said Lily Bear. 'Shelagh's my best friend. Not only is she a beautiful actress – performance like fine needlework – she is also an excellent cook. What's more, she's right about repertory experience. You need the chance to go away and make a fool of yourself. And as far out of London as possible. Nothing knocks the edges off an actress like weekly rep. I'll give old Esther Mooney a ring, on Monday, and see if she'll have a look at you.'

'Esther Mooney?' Shelagh Starkey sounded horrified. 'Is she still going?'

'She may be the wickedest old woman in London. I even knew a man who tried to stab her. Mind you, that was when she was still trying to be a performer. Two of her wouldn't have made a good actress. That's why she became an agent. When it comes to weekly rep, there isn't another theatrical agent to touch her.'

Lily Bear transferred the blaze of her attention to Sorrel. 'Are you very brave, dear? You'll need to be with Esther Mooney. I shall make a point of ringing her on Monday, Shelagh. It will make a nice little baptism, by fire, for the child.'

The office seemed to be up hundreds of dusty stairs in a building off the Charing Cross Road. Painted notices on closed doors advertised circus representatives, variety managements and even an agency specializing in midgets. Sorrel finally reached the door marked *Winslow and Mooney – Dramatic Artists' Representatives.*

Sorrel knocked.

'Come.' It was a man's voice. She opened the door and saw that he was small and clerkly with spectacles and a washable celluloid collar, sitting at a roll-top desk and adding up columns of figures in a ledger. The framed photographs on the wall were yellowing. All the women in them seemed to favour the pre-war marcel wave hairstyle.

'Lily Bear made an appointment for me to see Miss Mooney.'

'Send her in.' It was a female voice streaked with nastiness.

Only now did Sorrel realize that she was being sized up by a pair of beady eyes, set in a podgy old face, peering through a hatch in the wall. Just as Sorrel was thinking that the creature looked exactly how she imagined women who were supposed to do terrible things with knitting needles, the hatch slammed shut.

'The door marked Private,' said the man. 'I'd knock if I were you.'

'Come in, come in. Sweet sixteen and never been kissed, kicked or run over.' This was said in a snarl.

'I'm eighteen, actually.'

'Oh, it's "ectually" is it? Who d'you think you are? Jessie bleeding Matthews? You're sixteen or my name's not Esther Mooney. And I'm never wrong.' The voice should have been selling whelks. Its owner was dressed in black, spattered with cigarette ash.

'Get one thing straight, dear. I'm far more use to you than you are to me. Got that?' Miss Mooney opened a greasy paper bag and began to eat a cream doughnut. 'Radio does not count as experience. Not round 'ere.'

'I'll do anything,' said Sorrel.

'You'll have to. And tonight you should go down on your bended knees and thank your God that I owe Lily Bear a favour.' The woman chewed and swallowed. 'Do you know what an assistant stage manager is? It's the lowest form of theatrical life.' Miss Mooney scooped some cream off her chin with her little finger and licked it clean. She had pudgy paws like June Monk but June Monk's knuckles weren't ringed round with grubby diamonds.

'Are you prepared to be called boy, prompter and scene shifter, and then stagger on, as the maid, in the opening scene? That's what an ASM does, Miss Sorrel Starkey. Walk towards the door. Let's have a look at you. Not that it would matter if you were shaped like a dustbin.

'It just so happens that I have such a job within my giving. Been asked to look for a likely girl and dispatch her, pronto, to a new season. Or had you come to London to hang about and see the Coronation? Open the hatch and ask the gentleman, in the office outside, to nip down and get me some bismuth powder.'

Sorrel opened the little window. 'She wants bismuth powder.'

'She wants hanging,' muttered the man and scuttled from his ledger.

'You're a very lucky girl.' Miss Mooney burped gently. 'You know that, don't you? There's hundreds out there, knocking at my door, begging for a first chance. So when people tell you that Esther Mooney's every breed of old cow, I want you to answer *"But she gave me my chance"*. Got that?'

'Cream's dripped on your blouse,' said Sorrel. 'Yes. I've got it.'

'The money's four pounds ten a week. The theatre's in some hole outside Manchester. You should really have been there yesterday. Beggars can't be choosers. You can come back and sign the contract at four o'clock. OK. Let's try it. "Esther Mooney's every breed of cow on earth." And you say?'

'But she gave me my chance. What theatre in Manchester?'

It suddenly struck Sorrel, with terrible clarity, that Esther Mooney must also have come into this business simply because she too wanted to be loved.

'What theatre? Does it matter, dear? You'll soon find that one second-rate blood-tub is very like another.'

12

'Salford Hippodrome?' Gladys Starkey's face was a study in horror. 'Of all the theatres in England why did you have to go and choose that dump?'

It was Shelagh who had maintained that, when Sorrel got back to Manchester, her first task should be to make peace with her mother.

Gladys was keener on making war.

'It's been nothing but nude shows for years. They've had Phyllis Dixie there. Not long ago it was those *Soldiers in Skirts*. Nice to think that you'll be doing dramatic art on the same stage that was used by a broken-down circus with a drugged tiger. No, Sheila, think again!'

'I can't think again. I've signed a contract. And I keep telling you, I'm not Sheila any more. I'm Sorrel.'

'Yes and a nasty, bitter-sounding name it is too. Salford Hippodrome. If you wanted to break my heart you've certainly gone the right way about it. And don't think you're showing me up by going in flea-bitten theatrical lodgings at the back of Cross Lane, 'cos you're not. You can pay me your keep and come back here every night to sleep. Let's at least keep up the pretence of respectability.'

All things considered, this was a rather warmer welcome home than Sorrel had expected. Salford Hippodrome was no better and no worse than the rest of the number-three touring theatres of Britain. By now, many of them had tried every breed of touring attraction, failed, and gone into bankruptcy.

The Hippodrome was made of sterner stuff. Instead of calling in the Official Receiver, they invited the Charles Courtney Repertory Players to present a resident season. A different play every week, performances twice nightly with the addition of a matinée on Saturday afternoons.

For the performers, this was the theatrical equivalent of being galley slaves. When giving performances of one play at night, they would already have spent the day rehearsing the following week's production.

An assistant stage manager is every kind of dogsbody but the part Sorrel hated most about the job was the constant borrowing. She was forever being sent to local shops to see whether they would lend furniture, china, silver, anything and everything needed for the following week's production. All she was allowed to offer in return was a pair of complimentary tickets or an acknowledgement in the programme. Some days she found herself wondering whether she'd gone on the stage simply to be confronted by shopkeepers reaching for their *Closed* signs.

At night, when Sorrel wasn't summoning actors from their dressing rooms to the stage, she was to be found in the wings, holding the prompt copy of the play.

For several weeks, she made no friends in the company and no enemies either. She had one fan who turned up at the stage door, every Monday night, after the show. It was June Monk. Sorrel should have been clearing the set, ready for the next morning's rehearsal, but June always wanted to hang around and talk. Mostly it was about somebody called Martyn Gee, a commercial traveller with a greetings card company.

'Did I tell you that he goes in for body-building contests, Sheila? I promise to try and call you Sorrel. Or would it be nice if I was just the one person left calling you Sheila?

'Did you see Victor Mature in *Samson and Delilah*? Not a patch on Martyn. And he's not just mindless muscle – he's doing a correspondence course in positive thinking. I wish you could feel his biceps. In fact I'll *let* you feel his biceps when I introduce you. They're like hard melons.'

'I think I can live without that,' said Sorrel. 'If you want to talk you'll have to come and help me clear the stage. I want to get home before midnight. I've got lines to learn.'

On the stage, the curtain was raised and Salford Hippodrome was revealed in all its battered red plush and gilt splendour.

'Look at those naughty carvings of women holding up the boxes,' gurgled June. 'Wouldn't you think the sculptor would have covered up their knockers? I must admit, I don't stop

Martyn having a feel of mine. I always put up a token fight because I feel you should. Of course we've not gone the whole hog. I'm not daft. I want a wedding ring.

'It's very awkward though,' she giggled. 'I keep fainting. Doctor Moult says it's sexual tension and intercourse will regulate it.'

In the hope of shutting her up, Sorrel handed June a pile of cushions. She took them, moved to the centre of the stage, and gazed out into the auditorium.

'One day,' said June with sudden authority, 'I'll be on bigger and better stages than this.'

'You?' Sheila almost dropped a tray of crystal glasses in surprise.

'Yes. I'm really working at my psychic mediumship. I go all the way to Crewe on Saturdays. It takes me three buses to get there. I'm in Phoebe Slater's clairvoyant development class. Mrs Slater's the absolute tops. She's getting me ready for platform work. I always told you I was a girl who was going places.'

The passing weeks were not marked, in Sorrel's mind, by their calendar dates. Instead, she remembered them by the titles of plays in performance. *Gaslight* gave way to *A Yank in Lancs* which was succeeded by *Honeymoon Beds*.

Only one calendar date mattered. August the first. On that night, at eight o'clock, she had to keep her long-standing date with Barney at The Midland.

Unfortunately, it fell on a Saturday, a day when the Charles Courtney Players always gave a matinée at two o'clock and two more performances in the evening. The play scheduled for that week was *Love's a Luxury*. When the cast list went up, on the theatre call board, Sorrel approached it with a prayer in her heart and crossed fingers.

Her luck was in. Her name was not on the list. Staging a fainting fit would not be half so grave a sin when she would only be excusing herself from the duties of a general dogsbody.

When Saturday morning arrived The Hippodrome was bathed in sunshine but gloom pervaded backstage. Mr Courtney himself, an awesome figure who presented five repertory companies, in different provincial towns, was rumoured to be likely to descend on Salford that very evening. Sorrel wondered whether she would still have the nerve to play truant? She had already found the impresario to be a dyspeptic elf of a man, who wore a golden toupee and delivered stern criticism, of everything and everybody, in a voice like a cornered snake.

When he chose to make his pounce at the Saturday matinée, adding himself to the twenty other cheerless souls in the stalls, Sorrel was the only member of the company who was pleased to see him. The evening was safe. It would still be hers to steal.

With Mr Courtney's departure, the atmosphere backstage was almost heady with relief. When Sorrel went into her faint, in the wings, during the interval of the first evening performance, the stage manager didn't even need prompting to send her home.

In the underground ladies' lavatory, in Albert Square in Manchester, Sorrel washed off the white face powder which had added veracity to her fake collapse and changed out of slacks and jumper into her prettiest cotton dress. She had brought it with her in a carrier bag. She decided against more makeup than a bit of base and a quick dab of lipstick. A comb through her hair, some Lenthéric Tweed cologne behind her ears and she was ready for Barney and The Midland.

The hall porter received her carrier bag as though it was Bond Street luggage. The Midland was like that. She noticed that they'd introduced some new display cases. White fox furs were draped across a gilt chair in one. Diamonds sparkled, on blue velvet pads, in the other. It all seemed a million miles from the tarnished sequins of Salford Hippodrome.

The same pianist was at the same piano. Sorrel didn't know the tune he was playing and she didn't care because the right man was sitting, smiling, in a big armchair. As Barney rose to his feet and their arms went around one another, Sorrel breathed him in and said, 'I never doubted, for one moment, you'd be here.'

'Me neither. Swans, that's us. I'm afraid we're stuck with the fact that we're like the swans.'

If there was one moment in Sorrel Starkey's life which sealed her absolute commitment to Barney Shapiro, it was this one. He had remembered their conversation in the attic. He knew that swans mated for life.

'Have you eaten?' asked Barney.

'Let's not bother about food, yet. There's so much to catch up on.' Sorrel had rehearsed what she would say, on this evening, a thousand times. Faced with Barney as a reality, she found herself tongue-tied. All they could do was gaze at one another and beam and then both of them started talking at the same time.

'Could you get used to the idea of calling me Sorrel?'

'I may be going to leave Salford Art School and do a year's concentrated diploma course at Manchester.'

Out it all came. RADA and Salford Hippodrome, Barney's good examination results and the photographs taken on a fortnight's holiday in Florence.

'Good evening, Barnet.' The speaker was a Junoesque woman in her late forties, wonderfully well corseted and lightly upholstered in coffee lace.

'Hello, Mrs Dintenfass.'

Sorrel was admiring the bronze kid shoes and handbag. If the pearls were real they must be worth a mint. Pearls for tears, she thought, and wished she hadn't.

'Is this the Solomons girl?' The big lace woman was one of those confident people who enjoy being a discomfiter.

'No, this is Sheila, er Sorrel Starkey.'

'You don't seem very sure, Barnet.'

'I changed it,' said Sorrel.

The woman was adding up Sorrel's clothes, penny by penny, and said: 'I know dozens who've changed the surname, the country club's full of them. But changing the first name is a bit unusual, isn't it?'

'I had to change my Christian name,' said Sorrel blithely. 'I'm on the stage. There was another Sheila.'

'This is Doris Dintenfass.' Barney's words seemed to be falling over one another. 'My mother's best friend.'

'Christian name, eh?' said Doris. 'Love the little dress. Horrocks? I didn't bother ordering dinner at home tonight,

187

Barnet. Not with going away tomorrow. We're eating here. Remind Ruby that we're picking them up at a quarter to seven sharp, in the morning.'

Doris Dintenfass nodded at Sorrel, in a way that suggested she was trying to memorize every detail, and started to move towards the door.

'Why did she call you Barnet?'

'It's my name. They're all off to Monte Carlo in the morning. Doris is a tremendous gambler.' Barney suddenly started to laugh. 'She certainly needed her poker face when you said *Christian*. I wonder if she'll keep her mouth shut? Of course Doris is a sport. But how much of a sport?'

'So what does that make me? A bit of fun?'

'No.' Barney was fierce. 'You know better than that. We're here, aren't we? I wouldn't have told a bit of fun to wait six months and more.'

'I'm sorry.' Sorrel reached for his hand. 'She threw me. What's this country club?'

'A tennis place in Fallowfield. They wouldn't let Jews into The Northern so we built one of our own, across the road.' Barney looked around the room. 'I suddenly realize just how like the country club this place is on a Saturday night.'

He nodded politely to a middle-aged couple sitting under a standard lamp. 'Kaplans,' he said. 'Rag trade. They've just moved up the ladder to a house in Hale Barns. Ghetto-minded people follow very formal patterns.'

'Tell me about it.'

'I've been meaning to tell you about the most extraordinary little man who was weighing me up, before you came in. Don't start staring round. I'll tell you where and when to look in a minute. His hair's glued on and I can't decide whether he's very carefully painted or not. Now! Over there, by the door, with the woman who looks a bit theatrical.'

It was Charles Courtney. He nodded gravely at Sorrel.

'Paging Miss Sorrel Starkey . . .' A uniformed page boy, so small he could have been a dressed-up doll, was striding around the lounge carrying a salver. Amazing to think that his voice had already broken. 'Paging Miss Starkey.'

Barney held up an authoritative hand. 'Over here.'

Dropping a shilling on the salver, he took the proffered note and handed it to Sorrel with a grin. 'I bet you put somebody up to doing this.'

Sorrel shook her head and opened the folded sheet of headed hotel paper. The handwriting was large and dramatic. The pen seemed to have almost stabbed the page. The message read: 'Miss Starkey – you will find that love is *indeed* a luxury.' The note was signed 'C.C.'

Sorrel and Barney appreciated the romance of the great Victorian warehouses of Manchester long before critics of architecture rediscovered them.

'Fancy them building something fit for Venice, just to store cotton,' said Sorrel. 'When I was little, I used to see mill girls, walking home, with bits of raw cotton waste in their hair. My friend Gander worked in a mill. She looked after five looms. Can you imagine the clatter? She taught me how the weavers used to speak without making any noise. Watch!' Silently Sorrel mouthed and finger mimed, 'I love you.'

Barney took her hand and said, 'Now I'll show you something. Come on, we go left and round this corner.'

Gas lighting took over from electricity in these side streets. Palest green with an incandescent hiss to it. They walked a couple of blocks and then Barney drew Sorrel up some steps, under the canopy of an impressive portico, and held her close.

'Do you know where we are?' he asked her. 'Look!' In the eerie green light, he pointed to a sign painted on one of the pillars. *Jacob Shapiro, Son & Nephew Ltd.* 'All ours.'

'Do you have a key?' asked Sorrel.

Barney shook his head ruefully. 'I'd always heard that was the trouble with being in love. Nowhere to go.'

'I've got a key to somewhere,' said Sorrel triumphantly. 'Salford Hippodrome. I have to have one because I often open up. If we waited till they'd all gone, we could use it tonight.'

Barney's eyes shone with delight. 'Shall we?'

'I've had it planned for weeks.'

'What exactly have you got in mind?' Now the eyes were teasing.

'The same thing as you've got in mind. I bet you remembered to buy something.'

'Would you feel cheap if I said I had?'

'I'd feel cheaper if you hadn't. I'd march you round to Boots all-night chemists.'

'It's OK. I got some.'

'There's no need to sound so nervous.' Was Sorrel talking to Barney or to herself? 'We've still got two hours to kill.'

First they had a Chinese meal at the Ping Hong, under the Continental Cinema, on Market Street. Sorrel dipped into Barney's steamed oriental vegetables but he seemed wary of her chicken chow mein. The film showing upstairs was *Les Enfants du Paradis*.

'The Children of Paradise,' translated Sorrel. 'That could be us.'

Barney knew better. 'Colloquially, it's "Children of the Gods". Not the gods in heaven – it means the gallery in a theatre.'

'You and me in a theatre, Barney. Tonight is going to be like everything I care about rolled up in one.'

As they began to walk over Blackfriars Bridge, where Manchester leads into Salford, Barney pointed across the street. 'That island round the church used to be called the Flat Iron Market. Jake's grandfather began with a stall there.'

'Who's Jake?'

'My dad. He's a lovely, funny man at home but a demon when it comes to business. Shall we grab that taxi?'

'We'd be there too soon. Anyway, it's a beautiful evening for a walk.'

'I'm really too hot in this jacket.' Barney removed it. 'I only put it on for The Midland.' He began to roll up his sleeves. The sun in Italy had turned his forearms dark gold.

Sorrel was imagining what it would be like when he took off his shirt. Would he let her take it off for him? She wanted to uncover him, part by part. In the same way, she needed him to discover her. She suddenly envied Eastern women their veils. That's what she wanted – to be unveiled.

If these were wild and abandoned thoughts then this was a special night. This was the night she was going to lose her virginity on an antique bed, in the property room, under the stage of Salford Royal Hippodrome.

The theatre was already in inviting darkness. Sorrel led Barney down a narrow side street, took a big iron key from her handbag and unlocked the stage door. Once inside she only threw on a minimum of lights on the flaking whitewashed corridors. They smelled of scene-painter's size and grease-paint. Sorrel thought back to the North Pier Pavilion at Blackpool where she had smelled greasepaint for the very first time.

Down in the darkness of the property room she put her hand in Barney's pocket, took out a box of matches and lit some stubs of candle, in a tarnished silver candelabra, left over from *Streetcar Named Desire*. Flickering light danced across a huge brass bedstead with a Persian shawl thrown over the bare mattress.

Barney's arms were suddenly tightly around her. All her plans of undressing him flew out of Sorrel's head and were replaced with just one thought.

Would it hurt?

It did hurt. They went at it too quickly. There was a piercing feeling like bright burning light and, eleven painful rubs later – Sorrel actually counted them – it was all over. Was that it? She could stand the pain but the desolation and disappointment were much harder to take.

Was this what all the fuss was about?

'Sorry.' Barney was still out of breath. 'I couldn't hold back. It's amazing. I'd no idea. You're so intricate down there. All those tiny folds going on for ever. Phew. Just give me two minutes and then we have to put some love into it, some care.

'Don't worry, we'll get it right. Wow!' he yelled at the top of his voice. '*Wowee!*'

'I thought men had to wait ages in between.'

'Not this man. Look for yourself. Ready, willing and able.'

'I'm sore, Barney. I hurt.'

'Where? Let me see.' He was breathing normally now. 'Let me kiss it better. A whole new place to kiss. There. Mmm . . .'

New bread and greasepaint and she was on the North Pier at Blackpool and the waves were lapping underneath her.

And now they were rolling and turning. Suddenly she *was* those waves and they were going as far as the Isle of Man. Only there was no island to get in the way. The waves were riding higher and crashing onwards, with white foam on their edges, for ever and ever and ever.

Nobody seemed to notice any difference in her changed physical status. Gladys Starkey accepted that Sorrel had been late home on account of having to help dismantle a particularly elaborate stage setting. Charles Courtney failed to follow the note, sent across in The Midland, with any disciplinary action.

Whilst wondering whether there was any truth in the expression 'the calm before the storm', Sorrel just got on with her job of playing Edith, the maid in the comedy *Blithe Spirit*. She was also required to get together all the furnishings and trimmings for a dramatic tragedy advertised for the following week.

One thing was different. With his parents in Monte Carlo Barney took to turning up at the stage door, after the show.

On the Monday evening, June Monk, in regular weekly attendance as usual, took one look at Barney and said, 'Yum-yum, lovely grub! Let nobody say I don't know when to scram.'

June's uncanny ability to size up a scene, at a glance, was growing. What's more she vanished almost too quickly. This geisha-like desire to please had something weird about it.

'That's my oldest friend,' said Sorrel as they watched her go. 'She believed she would be, when we were little, and she's made it come true. There's much more to June than I ever realized, but she still gives me the creeps.'

'And she's your best friend?'

'Oldest friend. Mickey's my best. I don't even like June. I love Mickey. Does that make you jealous?' Sorrel put her arms around Barney.

'When he was clever enough to produce you, like a rabbit out of a hat? No.' Barney kissed Sorrel on the ear. 'Besides, you and Mickey need one another. I saw that from the word go.'

Being understood was wonderfully luxurious. And Barney saw the point of going for chips every bit as much as he enjoyed the splendours of The Midland.

As they walked along The Height, eating Kidd's fish, he said, 'These are a feast but I'm in the mood for a banquet. Let's give a party. I haven't had a party since I was seven.'

'I've never had one.'

Barney had that likeable ability of being able to outline plans as though he was unrolling a magic carpet. His parents would be in Monte Carlo for another fortnight. This coming Saturday, their housekeeper would be going off to stay with her sister in Fleetwood. Sorrel would have no show on the Sunday evening. How about rapture in his attic on Saturday night and a bottle party, on the ground floor, on Sunday?

Sorrel decided against asking anybody from the theatre. Let them continue to view her as just a fetcher and carrier. It was none of their business if she chose to have a private life in her own right.

What did a bottle party entail? Barney assured her that all they would have to provide was food, space and background music. The guests would furnish the rest.

There and then they started to make a guest list on the back of his cheque book. Art students, friends from The Kardomah; Magda Schiffer could never be persuaded to stir from her crow's nest but wouldn't resent Barney poaching a few regulars from her Sunday salon.

'Anyway they can go to both. Carloads of talent whizzing both ways along Bury New Road.' Barney was full of enthusiasm. 'Are you sure you don't want to ask June? OK. Don't glower. It was only an idea. It's a great mistake to compartmentalize your life. I'm certainly beginning to find that out.'

If Barney had turned against life in separate compartments, did this mean that he would eventually present her to Ruby and Jake Shapiro? Sorrel didn't dare dwell on this thought though, at the back of her mind, she had already decided she would wear white for the occasion. Or would virginal white turn her into a walking lie?

She was much too occupied to give it more than a passing

thought. Besides, she was well loved and that was plenty to be going on with. The only time she could steal off for shopping for the party was the hour before the Saturday matinée.

Barney had provided a wad of money and given her strict instructions to buy all the things she liked best. Sorrel dived into Cross Lane Market and began to unpeel pound notes in exchange for good bread and best butter and roast ham and Morecambe Bay shrimps.

To keep the food cool, she put it in the prop room. She found the theatre cat and locked him into an empty dressing room with a tub of prawns all of his own. Sorrel was guarding against accidents. The biggest accident was, of course, her choice of party food.

Barney rolled up at the theatre, after the scenery was struck and the stage cleared, with his friend Monty Klein who had a car, no looks, thick glasses and a lively sense of fun.

'Ham!' he said. 'Your mother would drop dead at the roulette wheel, if she knew. I'm going to try a bit. I've always wanted to. Uuugh. I thought it would be like wonderful quality roast beef. It tastes just like fleshy salt.'

'Have a shrimp,' Sorrel urged Barney. Suddenly she noticed that he was looking distinctly nervous. 'Don't tell me these are forbidden too?'

'There are lots of non-Jewish people coming. Not all Jews keep Kosher.' But he did. And how cleverly he'd always managed to disguise it. Black coffee in cafes must be as far as he departed from ritual rules. No. He'd eaten Kidd's fish. She'd seen him do that.

Barney was obviously looking for somewhere to dump the inoffensive little shrimp.

'Sorrel, we can pick up more stuff from a delicatessen tomorrow. Don't be upset. I'm not. It's my fault. I should have said something. Maybe you'll convert everybody. I'm not all that frum. Who cares what's trayf and what isn't?'

He gazed, fascinated, as Sorrel took it from him and ate it with defiant enjoyment.

That Saturday night they made love in Barney's attic. Afterwards he took her home in a taxi.

As Sorrel crept up the garden path in Rookswood Avenue,

the light suddenly snapped on behind the curtains of the through room. She opened the front door. Gladys was waiting, in her nightdress, in the hall.

'You look like a girl who's just been well and truly kissed.'

'Me?'

'You. And don't deny it. I know beard-burn when I see it.'

'He hasn't got a beard.'

'So there *is* a he.' Gladys was triumphant. 'I've known all week. You must think I've just come over.'

Sorrel seized on this last line, hopefully. 'Just come over, that's an immigrant expression. Were our family once immigrants?'

'No they were not. I've come down for another pill and no wonder. It's all the worry over you. Why the sudden interest in immigrants? You've never gone and fallen for an Irish Catholic? Like should go with like, Sheila. Anything else only leads to trouble. Just tell me one thing. He is white, isn't he?'

'Yes.'

'And he's not married already?'

'No.'

'Unusual of you to be so accommodating. Thank God I don't have to ask you whether he's a Yid. Even you've got more sense than that. I wouldn't say this to just anybody, Sheila, but when you're on the pavement, in Market Street, and they're trying to drag you into one of their shops, well . . .'

'Well, what?'

'You can't help wondering whether Hitler didn't have a point. Your legs are younger than mine, slip and get me a cup of water. The one without a handle will do to take upstairs.'

Ruby Shapiro must have owned as much crystal and china as the Midland Hotel. Waterford, Coalport and Spode. And complete sets of everything.

'Use what you like,' Barney had said.

The trouble was the ham sandwiches. Sorrel had cut enough for the feast of the five thousand. If she was going to rock Broughton Park convention, she wanted to do it on a really big plate. In the end she unearthed one, covered in Hebrew writing, from the back of a cupboard. Piling this high with sandwiches, Sorrel used the little matching dishes for loose prawns on cocktail sticks.

'I should think that's about as trayf as you can get,' said Monty Klein in tones that were approaching awe.

'Have I done something even more wrong?'

'There can be no guilt without intention.' Monty Klein was studying Law. 'What you've done is just a bit comical.'

'I'll change it.'

'Forget it, Sorrel. It's a party!'

The drive was full of cars. The big drawing room was lit with candles set in bottles. All the chairs had been moved into the dining room and replaced by cushions propped up against the walls. Dozens of heads were now resting against hand-blocked French wallpaper. Other guests, and some very odd gate-crashers, were attempting to dance to the loud zither music blaring from the polished walnut radiogram. The tune was the Harry Lime theme from the film *The Third Man*.

Barney was drawing corks at a table by the door which led into the hall. The air was beginning to get thick with cigarette smoke. French windows were open onto the garden. Two very suntanned women stepped in from the night, and surveyed the scene in amazement. They were Ruby Shapiro and Doris Dintenfass.

'Barney,' called Sorrel, urgently. She paused helplessly from circulating with plates of food.

'Who are you?' asked Ruby Shapiro in horror.

'I'm Sorrel. Have a sandwich.'

'Isn't that ham?' Doris Dintenfass was speaking in a voice of total disbelief.

'And isn't that my dead mother's Seder plate?' breathed Ruby. Now she was yelling. 'Barney? Barnet . . . where the hell is he?' She grabbed the plate from Sorrel.

Doris Dintenfass said, 'I don't worry about these things, Ruby, but I'm sure if you bury the plate in the ground, for three days, it'll make it Kosher again.'

'That's a legend,' snorted Ruby. 'You can't do it with china. And what about the shiksa? Can I bury her in the ground for three days? I'd certainly like to.

'Here he is. Are you ashamed of yourself, Barnet Shapiro?

Because you should be. D'you know why we're back? We've flown home to see a specialist. Your father's outside in the car with a male nurse. He's had a heart attack.'

Ruby turned to Sorrel. 'If you don't want a death on your hands, young woman, you'd better get straight out of this house. And from now on steer clear of my son. I chose to believe you were just a rumour. You're not, you're very beautiful but you'll never get him. I'll see to that.'

13

Nothing good had ever happened to Sorrel Starkey on a Sunday and Barney's defiant party had been no exception. Now it was hopeful Monday. Contrary to popular opinion, Sorrel thought of Mondays as the most exciting day of the week. A day when one got the chance to begin again. It was like having a big, blank sheet of cartridge paper to draw on.

The sun was shining on brand-new posters outside Salford Hippodrome. *Love Isn't Everything* was the play they advertised. As Sorrel pushed open the stage door she decided that she could not quite endorse the sentiments of this title. Love was enormously important to her. With the romantic side of her life in chaos, there was also a great deal to be said for a career which allowed her to hide in a world of paid make-believe.

'Just a minute, love . . .' It was the stage doorkeeper, a frail old man with blue eyes and a thin neck. He always wore a brass collar stud but no collar. 'There's a letter for you.'

Could it be from Barney? Not that she would recognize his handwriting because she'd never really seen it. Her own name stared at her from the envelope in angry mauve typewriting. The cream envelope was heavy and chinked as though it contained cash. Why was the stage doorkeeper looking so anxious?

Sorrel ripped open the envelope and pulled out a folded cream page, some very new ten-shilling notes and a few grubby-looking silver coins. The kind that made you wonder why coins were called 'silver' when they were really the colour of a nasty old zinc scrubbing board.

Dear Miss Starkey,
My first thought was to sack you on the spot, in the Midland Hotel, on August 1st. On reflection, I decided to wait until your replacement was installed in Salford

198

Hippodrome. This has now taken place and you have fifteen minutes to gather together your belongings and get off the premises.

Enclosed please find, as per contract, one third-class rail fare to London. I am not obliged to give you seven days' notice, nor salary in lieu of same, as you absented yourself from a performance without permission. Not that such permission would ever have been granted. I would have thought that even an amateur like yourself would have known that.

I am reliably informed that your deceit on August 1st far outweighed any traditional acting ability you have shown during your engagement with us.

I would most seriously suggest that you give up all further thoughts of a life in the Theatre. You have neither the talent, the temperament, nor the dedication needed for our profession.

Cordially yours,
Charles Courtney

For the first time in her life, Sorrel knew what it was to feel faint. The stage doorkeeper's hatch began to swim in front of her eyes and she had to reach for his counter for support.

'Has he give you the push?'

Sorrel nodded. 'And look . . . he's typed the letter so furiously that all the o's are holes in the paper.'

'Probably wishes he was still a young girl himself.' The old man did not say this unpleasantly. 'Look, love, this is a bit awkward but I've got to make sure you're out of the building toot sweet. Those were the little bastard's actual words – toot sweet.'

He looked at her with genuine concern. 'Sorrel, I wouldn't say this to just anybody but you're a nice kiddie and you're local. Get out of this pig-swill while you still can. It's not a natural life. I know. I've seen. They get hooked on it like drug addicts. They're always going to be better than Gracie Fields. I've seen women of forty reduced to sitting, waiting, in that cobbler's round the corner. One pair of shoes to their name and still hanging on to the idea that, some day, they're going to be better known than Gracie Fields.'

'But that's *here*,' said Sorrel desperately. 'Salford Hippodrome's tatty.'

'Yes, and you've just managed to get yourself the sack from it. What chance d'you think you stand further up the ladder?' Realizing he was getting nowhere, the old man's voice took on huffy tones. 'If you won't be told, you won't be told. You'd better go and get your things. Profession? It's more like a serious illness.'

Guilt, that was the emotion Charles Courtney's letter had set whirring round Sorrel's head. And what would she tell her mother? Deep down, Sorrel had always known that something would come to get her for missing that show on August the first.

She had broken one of the sternest rules of her own religion. The only trouble was Sorrel had two religions – her career and Barney. All her life she had wanted both the cake and the ha'penny. Now her cravings seemed to have left her with nothing. Her tin makeup box chose this moment to slide from her unsteady grasp and clatter to the ground, disgorging sticks of greasepaint across the pavement.

As Sorrel bent to pick them up, the silver spokes of the wheels of a red MG sports car flashed past her, roared up the road and round the corner of Rookswood Avenue. If the car was unusual for this housing estate, a woman driver was practically unheard of. Especially one wearing a savagely elegant scarlet turban and a pair of huge dark glasses.

Sorrel had not been expecting to hurry to the corner of the avenue but curiosity lent her speed. The brand-new car was parked outside their own house. Ruby Shapiro was marching up the crazy-paving path in black slacks and a cashmere windjammer in the same determined shade of red as the turban.

Gladys Starkey must have already been having a good nosy through the lace curtains because the door opened, almost immediately, to reveal her slipping a comb into her apron pocket, on the top step.

Sorrel was now close enough to hear her mother ask: 'Have I won something? Is it the Bullets competition in *John Bull* magazine?'

'I'm afraid you've won yourself a heap of trouble,' said Ruby. 'Can I come in?'

Both mothers disappeared into the house. Sorrel, who had gone unnoticed, hurried up the path and headed for the side door. Already she could hear the muffled exchange of angry female voices, but it was just fury; Sorrel couldn't pick out actual words. She burst through the side door and dropped what she was carrying onto the kitchen table with a clatter whereupon Gladys appeared from the living room.

'What d'you think you're doing home at this hour and why have you brought a jumble sale with you? Never mind about that, Sheila. *Jew-boys*, that's what I want to know about. Have you been deliberately going with Jew-boys?'

'What a way to talk about love,' said Sorrel indignantly.

'*Love?*' Ruby Shapiro had exploded into the kitchenette. 'Love? I've got quite another name for it. You only went and left one of your hair-grips in my son's bed, you little slut.'

'Don't you go calling my daughter names,' said Gladys dangerously. 'I can do plenty of that without your help, thank you. And how did she get into the bedroom, in the first place? Go and ask your dirty pig of a son that.'

'He's not a dirty pig,' cried Sorrel indignantly. 'He's beautiful.'

'He won't stay beautiful for long,' stormed Gladys. 'Not when I've finished with him. Anyway, it's a well-known fact that Jew-boys go off faster than milk.'

'Insults will get us nowhere.' Ruby removed her dark glasses. She looked tired beneath her suntan.

'Insults?' Gladys looked astonished. 'I've not even started yet. She switched her attention to her daughter. 'Are you pregnant?' she asked.

'Not that I know of,' said Sorrel.

'You mean you've actually gone and let a Yid do it to you? You little fool . . .'

'There can be no question of marriage,' Ruby chipped in hastily. 'Nothing personal. It's just on grounds of religion.'

'And does your religion permit him to go putting it wherever he wants?' Gladys all but spat out the question. 'There certainly can't be any question of marriage because it

201

would be over my dead body. Some people think Hitler was right about the Jews. I happen to be one of them.'

There was a terrible pause.

'I never thought to hear that said again in England.' Ruby was speaking very quietly. 'I only came here because I thought the pair of them were young and misguided and two mothers might make more sense of the situation than two children.'

'We're not children. My mother doesn't know what she's saying. She's upset. How's Barney?'

'Don't you go making excuses for me, milady. And you *are* a slut.'

'Barney's very upset,' said Ruby. 'They took his father into hospital last night. I'm tempted to pretend it's your fault but it wouldn't be true. Not that you helped any.'

'I do love Barney' was all Sorrel could think of to say.

Ruby looked weary. 'I'm afraid I've heard too much of that kind of talk in the last twelve hours.'

'Does Barney still love me?'

'Have you no bloody pride?' shouted Gladys. 'Love counts for damn all, with them, if you haven't got the right-shaped nose. I know that. I didn't work in town for all those years for nothing. They're out looking for it straight after breakfast. But it doesn't come with a wedding ring attached.'

'She's not far off the truth,' said Ruby sadly. 'It's not how I would've put it myself but, crudely speaking, your mother's right.' The Jewess began to head for the back door. With her hand on the knob she turned and said, 'I've been trying to think who you reminded me of, Mrs Starkey, and now it's come to me. You have a very definite look of Mussolini. Good morning.'

Gladys reached threateningly for an empty milk bottle but Ruby was already through the door and gone. Would her mother dive after Ruby and scrag her on the way to the gate? No, judged Sorrel, she wouldn't. Even when passions were at their highest, thoughts of what the neighbours would say always came first with Gladys.

'You dirty little melt. I never thought to say it to a child of mine but that's what you are – nothing but a dirty little melt.'

'And I've got the sack,' said Sorrel, thinking she might as well be hung for a sheep as for a lamb.

'It's no good, I'll have to sit down.' Gladys walked back into the through room. 'If you think I'm dipping in my pocket to keep you, you've got another think coming.'

'I'll get a job.'

'Yes, and a proper one this time.' Gladys sank down into one of the cold Rexine armchairs. 'When are your monthlies due? P'raps Norman can fetch something home from the dispensary to bring them on. You can go to Kendal Milne's and train as a junior saleslady. They're crying out for girls with high-school qualifications.'

'No. Nothing and nobody's going to get me to work in a shop. I've never wanted anything but the stage. It's like a terrible itch that I can't get rid of.'

'Strikes me you've got more than one itch you can't get rid of,' snapped Gladys. 'Either you phone Kendal's for an interview this minute or I'm finished with you and out you go for good. Men, the stage . . . whatever did I do to deserve a daughter like this?'

'I only want to be loved,' said Sorrel. It wasn't easy to say but she said it.

'We *all* only want to be loved,' snarled her mother. 'I only wanted to be loved and look what I got. A walking Brylcreem advert with creditors coming out of his earholes. Love's not all it's trumped up to be and neither is the stage. Go and get the phone book and look up Kendal's number.'

'No. I want more.'

'Then you'll have to go and look elsewhere for it!' Gladys assumed a painful expression. 'I only hope you know you're making me poorly. Go and get me a pill.'

'Get your own bloody pill.'

'Don't you swear at your own mother. And shh . . . We don't want Mrs Tatton hearing our private business.'

'Who doesn't?' Sorrel dived for the hearth, grabbed the poker and rapped, with the knob-head, on the dividing wall. 'Can you hear me, Mrs Tatton?

'I want *more*,' yelled Sorrel. 'I don't want to be a mean mind peeping out from behind lace curtains. I want to be famous and I want rounds of applause. Last Saturday I had an orgasm and I want another.'

'You're bad,' said Gladys in a voice of total disbelief.

Sorrel leaned her head against the wall. Tears rolled down her face. She was beginning to wonder whether Gladys was right. She hoped she hadn't brought on one of their next-door neighbour's asthma attacks.

The raised oatmeal splodges of the wallpaper pressed into Sorrel's forehead. Tears rolled down her face as she sobbed, 'I'm sorry if I've offended you, Mrs Tatton. I only do things because I want to belong.'

Sorrel wiped the tears from her face with the back of her hand and said to her mother, 'It's all right, I'm going. I'm going and I'm not coming back until I'm famous.'

'You seem to be presuming one thing,' muttered Gladys, giving the dividing wall an anxious glance. 'You seem to be presuming you'll be welcome back.' Suddenly her face crumpled. 'Eeh Sheila, whatever are we going to do with you?'

In that moment she sounded just like everybody else's mothers. She sounded what Sorrel had always wanted. The girl moved eagerly towards Gladys, who fended her off with a coldly dismissive hand.

'Just answer me one question, Sheila. Has my husband ever tried anything on with you?'

'No.' Sorrel was still eager to be friends. Once again her appalling honesty took over. 'He once rubbed up against me in a funny way but it could easily have been an accident.'

'What sort of funny way? No, I can do without your lies. It *is* time you went. Just be sure and go a long way off. And Sheila . . . don't rush to come back.'

The mid-day August sun was beating down so hard that tar bubbles were forming on the road in Deansgate. Once again the handle of a heavy suitcase was cutting into Sorrel's fingers.

As she began to descend the Kardomah stair-well, light gave way to gloom, and the smell of tar to that of new linoleum. The new lino saddened her. A new Kardomah crowd, in search of adventure, would soon be treading on it. Sorrel was already thinking of The Kardomah as part of her past.

Two thirds of the way down the staircase you could peer

through an iron lattice-work grille and see who was sitting below, in the cafeteria. Sorrel was looking for any face familiar enough to be trusted to hand a note to Barney.

The first person she saw was Enid Rosenthal, the swarthy pottery student who had not hesitated to speak her mind in The Hadassiah. Enid was in earnest conversation with a man in a white tee shirt, his elbows on the table, his head hidden in his hands.

I've had those arms around me, thought Sorrel, and her heart leaped hard enough to make a thud in her chest.

Sorrel had been thinking of Barney as locked away from her, unattainable. And here he was drinking black coffee in The Kardomah. Her first thought was to leave the suitcase where it was and to run to him. Then she recalled that this suitcase contained all she owned in the world so she heaved it down the rest of the stairs and used it to push open the 1930s Egyptian doors.

Barney hadn't seen her but Enid was glowering like an official inspector from the Beth Din, confronted by meat and milk in the same pan.

Sorrel parked the case where she would be able to see it and ran for the table with a joy that was the more glorious for being so unexpected.

'Don't you think you've done enough?' asked Enid Rosenthal coldly. 'I thought we'd seen the last of you.'

Only now did Barney register Sorrel's presence. 'D'you want a coffee?' he said, rising to his feet.

'I want you.' Sorrel threw her arms around him. For the first time ever, his body felt reserved and unyielding.

'You can't have him,' said Enid. 'I tried to tell you once before.'

'What's it got to do with her?' asked Sorrel dangerously.

Enid ignored the danger. 'Mrs Dintenfass is my aunt. I know the whole story.'

'Keep out of this, Enid,' said Barney.

'No, Barnet. I won't. And d'you know why I won't? Because you're too kind-hearted. It's always been your trouble. Ever since you were a little boy at the Cassel-Fox School. Too kind, too good . . .'

'You fancy him rotten,' said Sorrel.

Enid bit her lower lip.

Sorrel thought of mentioning electrolysis, but didn't. It would have been cruel, and beauty treatment might make Enid attractive. Sorrel had suddenly realized with blinding clarity that, in the long run, even the plainest Jewish girl stood more chance with Barney than she did.

'Go away, Enid,' he said. 'I need to talk to Sorrel. Don't argue, just go.'

The way Enid just got up and went reminded Sorrel of an Arab wife. 'Don't ever think you can talk to *me* like that,' Sorrel threw at Barney, 'because you can't.'

'I'm not supposed to be talking to you at all. You're forbidden territory.' Barney was trying to smile but it came out perplexed. He had dark shadows underneath his eyes. 'Why the suitcase?'

'I'm going to London. I phoned Mickey. I'm getting the one o'clock coach from Lower Mosley Street bus station. Come with me.'

'I can't. I want to but I can't. You wouldn't understand.'

'I think I do, I think I've always understood. Magda Schiffer said it could only come to this. I didn't want her to be right but she was. Goodbye, Barney.'

'You can't just go like that. Who's going to carry your bag?'

'I am. It's just going to be me and me from now on.' Sorrel began to move towards her suitcase and the door.

'I'm not letting you shlep that all the way to Lower Mosley Street.'

His hand was already on the handle. As he lifted the case, Sorrel smelled the faintest and most tantalizing whiff of the scent of new bread. To her own amazement she found herself wondering whether there was anywhere on God's earth where they could make love for one last time?

Gladys's voice rang in her ears: '*Have you no pride? You little melt.*'

If the morning had taught her anything, it had given her the first glimmerings of a dangerous new understanding. Sorrel Starkey was beginning to learn how to hate herself.

When they got out onto the street the sunlight seemed to

have nothing to do with her. People were walking along laughing and talking and eating strawberries out of punnets, as though it was just a normal summer's day. They struck Sorrel as cruel. Surely the fact that her whole life was ruined must be visibly streaming out of her?

'Sheila, Sheila . . .'

'Not June Monk. Please God not June.' But it was, accompanied by a man with a toothpaste advertisement smile and too many muscles for a tailored suit. This could only be the famous Martyn, the positive thinker.

He has kind eyes, thought Sorrel. In fact, if he was a puppy, you'd choose him from the litter as the friendly-looking one.

'Of course there are no coincidences,' said June firmly. 'We were taught that, last Saturday, at Development.'

Then the introduction started. 'This is my oldest friend, meet my fiancé. And here . . .' she announced like a lady conjurer, 'here is the ring.' A single diamond glittered on the appropriate podgy finger.

'We've just this minute come from choosing it at Bravington's. We got a single solitaire so we can fill it out, with more stones, as we prosper. Have you two started saving up yet?'

Dreading that tears might begin to fall, Sorrel said, 'I should keep on with that clairvoyance, June. In a hundred years you might just get it right.'

'I'm going to forget you said that.' June was all controlled reproach. 'It wasn't worthy of you. In fact I don't think it was you speaking at all. A bad entity must have slipped in and taken over. Are you going somewhere, Sorrel?'

'Away.' June was too ludicrous for tears. 'And I'm not coming back until I'm famous.'

'Which you will be.' Now she was engaged June sounded fully forty-five. 'We'll stroll along with you. Martyn can give you a hand with the luggage.'

'I've got somebody to give me a hand, thank you.'

'Have you?' asked June. She was suddenly looking as though she could see further than other people. 'Have you really, Sorrel? Don't forget it's *me* you're talking to.' June treated Barney to a cold look.

Sorrel marvelled. How did June do it? Somehow she had managed to turn criticism of her clairvoyance into a spotlight on this dubious claim to fame. All Sorrel wanted to do was break up the unfortunate gathering and get down to the bus station.

'You want to get moving,' said June. 'I quite understand.'

Sorrel recoiled from June's slobbery kiss.

'Keep in touch.' June's diamond was flashing as she waved her hand. 'Don't think I'm letting you go as easily as that.'

The sun was relentless. One of the Lord Mayor's attendants emerged from the Town Hall in cockaded top hat and rolled-up shirtsleeves. Courting couples were sucking ice lollies on the steps of the Albert Memorial.

The notice on the board outside the Friends' Meeting House said *A Good Road and a Wise Traveller Are Two Different Things*. Sorrel said a mental goodbye to the Central Reference Library. Sunlight was turning the turrets of The Midland into a sooty, enchanted palace.

Suddenly filled with blind, unreasoning anger, Sorrel rounded on Barney. 'It's not fair,' she stormed. 'You get to keep Manchester too.'

Barney looked mystified. 'What's so important about Manchester? Nobody can own it.'

'I can. I do. It's mine.'

'That's the difference between us,' said Barney. 'I don't even feel a safe tenant. That's a Jewish upbringing for you. D'you know what my mother keeps in a little suitcase under her bed?'

'Her heart I should think.'

Barney ignored this. 'This case has got all our passports in it and about ten thousand quid in dollar bills.'

'Bully for her!' Sorrel had barely ten pounds in the world. 'Why?'

'Against the day. She lives in fear of having to take flight.'

'What's she done?' She looked at her watch. 'Can you hurry?'

'Ruby's done nothing. She's just Jewish.'

'Your mother wants to watch out. After this morning, I might be the one to put the first brick through her window.'

Sorrel was saying this aloud and thinking, Goodbye Central Station. Perhaps June Monk was right about bad entities. Some demon, not herself, seemed determined to continue to abuse Barney. 'I'm sick of all this talk about Jewishness. It strikes me you ought to keep yourselves to yourselves.'

'Perhaps we try.' Barney put down the suitcase. Sweat was running down his face. Sorrel tried hard to see him as unattractive, and failed.

She had thrown herself at him. There was no denying it. Barney had done everything possible to keep her at arm's length and she had refused to take 'No' for an answer.

Sorrel looked at the buildings around her. Was there anywhere else she ought to bid farewell? Only every stick and every stone, that was all. It was like the last night of the holidays in Blackpool. When she was little, she had always believed that if you remembered to say goodbye to the tower you would be bound to see it again.

She took a deep breath. 'I'm not saying goodbye to you, Barney. Leave the bag where it is. I'll manage on my own from here.'

Barney looked hesitant and profoundly unhappy as he said, 'I'll never love anybody else.'

'No, but you'll marry them. And when you do, you might have the courtesy to let me know. I like knowing where I stand. That's all I want from you. I've taken enough, Barney. Just turn round and go back to your mother and her bag of money!'

An instinct of self-preservation had finally taken over. Without so much as a backward glance Sorrel picked up her own bag and carried it down the slope which led past the Adult Education Institute. Her eyes were blurred with tears. A hundred unbearable thoughts were pressing in on her and she couldn't bear the idea of even one of them coming into sharp focus. What had begun in moonlight, outside Magda Schiffer's front door, had ended in the light of common day on the road to a broken-down bus station.

The stench of petrol fumes was almost overpowering. Sorrel felt very thirsty. The cafe opposite, known as the

Snake Pit, was the haunt of furtive-looking boys in mascara and women who weren't quite whores. Good-time girls they were known as. They used the cafe to take the weight off their stiletto heels whilst they killed time until the next train brought GIs into Central Station from the American air base at Burtonwood. Monica Dolan was standing in the doorhole drinking Tizer from the neck of the bottle. Goodbye Monica, for the thought of any sort of conversation was unbearable. Goodbye 'Tizer the Appetizer'. It was well known, to Northerners, that this fizzy nectar was unobtainable in London.

Surely there was a drinks-dispensing machine within the coach terminus? And she needed an inspector to tell her which was the bay for the London bus.

Sorrel went in search of both and, instead, found Barney.

He was leaning against an advertisement for the Norfolk Broads. Lily Gander would have said that he looked as though he'd dropped half a crown and found sixpence.

'Are you speaking to me?' he asked.

'What's there to say?'

'Have you got your ticket?'

'You pay on the coach.' This was agony. 'What d'you want?'

The expression on his face made Sorrel think back to the night in the attic when Ruby had talked about little boys bringing home paintings for Mother. There was no way she could really hate Ruby Shapiro, Ruby loved Barney too.

'I couldn't just go like that, Sorrel. I couldn't do it. Nothing's changed. I've still got nothing to offer you. It's just that I want to say one word – and I've no right to say it.'

'What's the word?'

'Swans. You're right, Sorrel. We're swans. We've always been like swans; and there's nothing we can do about it.'

'You *bastard*!' Sorrel screamed it so loudly they must have heard her in the Snake Pit.

'What did I say?' Barney backed away from her in alarm.

'The one word you shouldn't have said. I'd given you your freedom. I've not got a job and I've not got a mother and I'm leaving the place I love. How much more do you want? You couldn't leave it alone, could you? You had to come back and have the luxury of rubbing your salt in. Well you've done it. And I just hope you know it leaves me in torment. Write and tell me when they marry you off. That's when I might just get a bit of peace.'

'Will passengers for London please move across to Bay Thirteen.' A fussy little uniformed inspector was shouting this out as he consulted a silver turnip watch. 'Bay Thirteen for London. You never know, it might prove to be lucky.'

Sorrel looked around for Bay 13 and then turned to Barney. He had gone.

14

The ancient long-distance coach seemed to be drawing on its last teaspoon of petrol as it shuddered into the London terminus at Victoria.

Above the anxious blobs of faces awaiting arriving passengers a placard flapped wildly on a stick. *BROKEN HEARTS MENDED* it said. The man waving the placard was also wearing a top hat crazily labelled *CAREERS RESTORED*. It was Mickey.

'Welcome to the city of opportunities!' he cried as Sorrel climbed down the steps of the bus.

'The luggage comes out at the back,' she replied. 'Hearts mended? What if somebody had read that and taken you at your word?'

'Somebody did. I'm having dinner with him next Thursday. You'll find I have dinner with quite a lot of people these days. If we're going to live together, you'd better get that straight from the start.'

'Men?'

'Well I've not gone peculiar. Of course men. I'll carry that. We can walk, it's not far. There's one man I don't want to hear about. Beautiful Barney. Just accept that it's over and cut your losses.'

'He saw me off. He said . . .'

'It's over, Sorrel. I wouldn't like his mother's phone bill. He's been pouring his heart out for three quarters of an hour. And no, I'm not telling you what he said. You were just an interruption in one another's lives.'

'Please . . .' begged Sorrel. 'Just tell me a bit.'

'He's riddled with guilt but stuck in the mould. Nothing will ever get him out. That's what you fancied in the first place. Was he any good at the other? I gather you've been testing the bedsprings.'

'Amazing.'

'Of course I have very high standards these days. This is Eaton Square. The next one over's Belgrave. We live just beyond that, in a glamorous slum.'

'Who's we?'

'Just you and me. By the way, the landlord's been told we're brother and sister. We'll soon find you another man. Better still, we ought to get your career off the ground. You might have blotted your copy-book with Esther Mooney but I know dozens of other agents.

'Take notice, Sorrel, I never want to hear you droning on about Barney again. He was just an interruption.' Mickey threw his top hat up in the air and caught it, exclaiming, 'Isn't Belgravia beautiful?'

Looking around her Sorrel decided that, though this was an obviously expensive area, there was something monumental and anaemic about it. The tall terraces of stucco-fronted houses looked as though they had been carved out of Co-op margarine. Creamy-yellow with uniformly black front doors. Marge and coal – what had happened to Mickey's love of colour?

They turned a corner. A street sign, high up on a pub wall, said *Cornucopia Mews SW1*. Sorrel let out a cry of joy. This cobbled mews, at the back of an anonymous square, was as colourful and friendly and bustling as the opening scene in a pantomime.

Old stables had been turned into houses. It was all colour-washed brickwork and white shutters and stone tubs of unexpected country flowers. People with drinks in their hands were spilling out onto the pavement from two pubs which couldn't have changed since Queen Victoria was on the throne. The pubs looked welcoming and wonderfully battered and full of exciting possibilities.

'It's getting smart,' said Mickey. 'People are beginning to spend fortunes on these little houses. Some of the others are just done up with a million pounds' worth of imagination.'

Sorrel was marvelling. Foxgloves in the middle of London and front doors in every shade of a Reeve's paint box. It was like finally walking into something she'd always hoped might exist.

'It's a street that cries out for Christmas,' she said in wonder.

'When it comes, we'll have a tree.' Mickey smiled. 'The people are pretty colourful too. See that woman with a bulldog? She's a sculptress. Used to paint herself silver from head to foot and dive off bridges, in Venice, for coins. Evening, Honoria. I'm just telling my friend Sorrel how you came to burst one of your eardrums.'

They continued up the mews. 'The people here are either rich or clever. Some are both. Jack Mungo, the comedian, lives in the house with the drawn blinds – they're always drawn. Hermione Gingold holds court around the corner. People arrive in this street on handcarts and leave in Rolls-Royces.'

For the first time in her life, Sorrel felt as though she'd stopped swimming against the tide.

'And we're here,' she said. 'We're in on it.'

'It's only rooms above a shop. Still, it's ten times better than Heraldic Mansions. Come on – through this white door and up the stairs.'

The staircase was dark and creaked asthmatically. Sorrel pushed aside guilty thoughts of poor Mrs Tatton. Mickey turned a key in a lock and flicked on a light.

Sorrel had never before seen a room like it.

The walls were the red of a guardsman's tunic and topped off with a bold gold and white Grecian key border. The centre light had been replaced with two theatrical spotlights. One of these shone down on a huge white plaster bust of Queen Victoria wearing a false moustache. The other beam of light illuminated an alcove solid with books interspersed with Pollock's toy theatres.

'Why are the curtains drawn?'

'Why not?' replied Mickey. 'This is a place for doing just what you like!'

Sorrel looked around. 'Where did all the amazing furniture come from?'

'It's Victorian bamboo. Junk shops practically pay you to take it away. I just repainted it to look like Chinese Chippendale. The seats and the curtains are good old

214

unbleached calico from Salford. The marble fireplace was already here, underneath about ten coats of paint. It's not really a room. It's a stage setting.'

'Aren't you worried about clashing with it?' asked Sorrel nervously. 'It's very red.'

'I wear a lot of black and white,' Mickey replied defensively. 'Here's the bedroom and, look, it leads to a kitchen-bathroom combined. That lid lifts up and the bath's underneath. I generally light a joss stick about this time of day. We're over a greengrocer's and the pong can get a bit niffy.

'Put the kettle on, Sorrel. I'm very glad you're here. We're going to do what we always said we would. We're going to be famous. You've seen the setting. Now it's up to us to make the play.'

Mickey was already living in a play. That fact soon struck Sorrel. The plot was dictated by the telephone which never stopped ringing.

Mickey had stencilled the standard black GPO instrument with white question marks. It was as though he was athirst for excitement. Calls came asking him to pose for knitting patterns and attend auditions for intimate revues which all seemed to be at club theatres in Notting Hill Gate. Sorrel also got used to making a note of pressing invitations for him to dine at everywhere from La Popote to The Ritz. More calls were from other would-be writers. They were always asking for things like 'two snappy rhymes for Lady Docker' and could Mickey stand in for somebody, for one night's cabaret, at the Stork Room?

'Straight acting doesn't seem to come into it, Mick,' she said reproachfully. 'And it's not quite decent to have all these men queuing up to pay for your dinner.'

'Why? I'll pay for somebody else's, one day, when I've got money. If they want to support my talent, I see no harm in letting them pick up the tab.'

'It's not just your talent they're after. Some of the noises I hear in the middle of the night are very exotic.' Sorrel wasn't really sitting in judgement. She was having too much fun for that.

'I'm a great believer in everybody getting exercise in their own way,' laughed Mick. 'You don't complain when they ask you along to dinner too.'

Mickey and Sorrel either lived high on the hog as guests in expensive restaurants or dined on food bought at a shop, specializing in bent tins, in Victoria. Unlabelled cans, from Victor Value, were a bigger adventure. They had also begun to teach themselves to cook.

'I could write a book on a thousand things to do with half a pound of mince.' Mickey was frying onions and pungent spices in a cast-iron skillet. 'I wish I was as clever at drumming up the rent. Modelling's all very well but you don't get paid till months afterwards. I hate owing money. I suppose that's the Paloma Drive in me coming out.'

'I could take that temporary job in the coffee bar starting next week,' said Sorrel, getting out of the bath.

She wondered which would have alarmed her mother most. The smell of curry powder or the sight of her daughter naked, in front of a young man. Sorrel and Mickey were blithely unconcerned about nudity. Sometimes they had companionable baths together to save money. Sorrel conceded that Mickey had a good body. But, for all the effect it had on her, she might just as well have been sharing the bathwater with Michelangelo's marble statue of David.

'We need cash this week, Sorrel. I've never let the admirers pay actual bills. Would it count as whoring?'

'I wouldn't care if you loved them!' Sorrel was drying herself on a towel with *Property of Westminster Swimming Baths* woven into one of its stripes.

'I can't have love.' Mickey stirred in the meat. 'Love gets in the way. I want a career.'

Yet he's not hard, thought Sorrel, grabbing Mick's dressing gown and beginning to make her way down the stairs for the post. She picked her way carefully, trying not to make a revealing creak. The greengrocer –below – was their landlord and they were now two weeks behind with the rent. If Mick was hard, he wouldn't have me here cramping his style.

Stairs, she reflected, seemed to be a very London thing. She must have climbed thousands, in the last month, in her search for theatrical employment. And shoe leather was so expensive. No wonder many aspiring actresses resorted to metal Dinkie tips on the soles of their shoes. You could hear them coming from a whole landing below and there was a desperate sound to their tread.

'I'm beginning to shock you, aren't I? Answer me, Sorrel.'

'I worry about you. That's all.' What had she said? Mickey was as mercurial as herself and the least likely thing could get him raging.

'Well, don't worry about me! Life handed me a peculiar deal. All I'm doing is making the best of it – with the help of a few people in the same situation. You may be driven on by love, Sorrel; that desperate need to have an audience to care about you. I'm not. D'you know what fires me? Anger. And it's potent fuel.

'Every time someone yells "Queer" or "Poof" I think, You wait! You'll still be mouthing obscenities from the gutter when I'm driving past you in a Bentley.'

Anybody going into showbusiness needs to be good at taking rejection. Sorrel had been trained for this, from the cradle, by an expert. There wasn't a theatrical agent or management who could say 'No' half so cuttingly as Gladys Starkey.

They might maintain that Sorrel was short on experience but she was well versed in the art of picking herself up, dusting herself off and starting all over again. Sorrel never had the slightest doubt about her own abilities. She knew she was good. She knew that talent, like cork, will eventually bob to the surface. Her day would come.

In the meantime the rent had to be paid. She didn't want to be a drain on Mickey. Nipping out early to pinch their morning milk was not, she felt, enough. So Sorrel took the temporary job at La Bamba coffee bar in the King's Road in Chelsea.

Coffee bars, suddenly opening everywhere, tended to be run by slap-happy amateurs with no previous catering experience. They put a down payment on an Italian coffee machine which metered the number of cups served. Each month, the manufacturers collected a levy, on every cup. Eventually, the machine was paid for.

Decor was everything and La Bamba's was typical of the whole explosion. Darkness, with pools of candlelight, even in daytime, rattling bead curtains and potted rubber plants. A talking mynah bird, in an elaborate bamboo cage, had been taught to screech '*Vive la révolution!*' This was meant to add atmosphere.

To the same end, on Friday and Saturday evenings, a boy called Simon Cunliffe-Owen sang rather tentative flamenco songs to his own guitar accompaniments. He only knew a few chords but he also knew Princess Margaret. This got La Bamba mentioned in the *William Hickey* column as 'The place where Society meets the Stage'. The waitresses did not wear uniforms. Some had theatrical ambitions, others were ex-debutantes.

Judy Weatherall was both. She looked like Snow White and she could have wrung a tip out of Ebenezer Scrooge. The best waitress in La Bamba, Judy always managed to look dazed and helpless. This was because she was very short-sighted but too vain to wear glasses. Every farthing was being saved up for a pair of the new American contact lenses. Her grandfather was Field Marshall Weatherall but she hated people knowing this.

'They'll think I'm just playing at the theatre. They should cocoa! I've got one pair of ladder-free nylons to my name. You've no idea how lucky you are, Sorrel. You sound as grand manner as anything but you can talk broad Lancashire too. So useful for work – like having a second language. Come on, teach me "Albert and the Lion".'

'Just put your glasses on for a second,' said Sorrel. 'I want you to look at somebody.'

'Certainly not. For all I know, J. Arthur Rank could be in. I'll never get discovered in specs!'

'It's nobody important.' Sorrel was peering through the cigarette smoke. 'Just a man who once talked to me, first thing in the morning in Piccadilly Circus. He gave me his card. Matthew Gillespie.'

'Mucky Matt!' exclaimed Judy who, more or less, spoke in exclamations the whole time. 'I'm certainly not putting on my specs for him. It might give him ideas. D'you know who that

218

man is? He's only the biggest procurer in London. Whose table is he at?'

'One of mine.'

'D'you want me to come with you, while you take his order?' Judy was one of those people who, friendship given, was there through thick and thin. Broke to the wide, with nothing to give but her time and her considerable enthusiasm, Judy would have *expected* to be got out of bed at three in the morning. Would have been disappointed if you had taken your problem elsewhere.

'What can he do with everybody looking?' said Sorrel. Matthew Gillespie had plainly recognized her and was already beaming in her direction. Mr Gillespie was obviously prospering. Today his clothes were as good as his excellent teeth.

'Watch yourself,' said Judy firmly. 'That man would try and put Dame Sybil Thorndike on the game.'

Sorrel crossed the room, her waitress's pad at the ready.

'We meet again,' smiled Matthew Gillespie. 'A cappuccino and a brioche, please.'

Sorrel returned to the counter feeling distinctly disappointed. 'He only wants a cappuccino and a brioche.'

'That's for openers,' said Judy darkly. She pulled the handle on the coffee machine so that it hissed like warning geese. 'He's got to begin somewhere. Don't let your guard down for so much as a moment. I know a girl who let him buy her a gin and tonic, in South Kensington. She ended up, tied to a chair, with a high court judge stuffing twenty-five pounds down the front of her bra. One cappuccino and one brioche!'

Sorrel carried them over to the table.

'Are you allowed to sit down with customers? No, of course you're not. What time does this afternoon shift finish? Perhaps I could buy you a drink?'

'Yes and perhaps you couldn't,' said Sorrel firmly. 'Don't think you can tie *me* up with your clothes-line.'

Gillespie spluttered coffee all over the tiled table top and howled with delighted laughter. 'Don't say that old chestnut's still doing the rounds? How much was she supposed to have earned? Twenty-five quid, or has it gone up? Still stage-struck, my little mystery?'

'I never mentioned the stage.' Sorrel was busy with her pad and pencil.

'You didn't have to. It's written all over you. I know a lot of important people in your business . . .'

'*Aux barricades!*' screeched the mynah bird.

'Important people? Good for you!' Sorrel slammed his bill down in a wet patch.

Gillespie looked her straight in the eyes. 'It could be good for you. It could be very good for you.'

He had the thickest eyelashes she'd ever seen on a man and was still talking. 'I know people who would really appreciate that imperious manner of yours,' he said. 'What's more they'd show their appreciation. I'm a fixer, darling, that's all, a fixer. You want to hire a Daimler for the day? Matt can find you one. Tickets for Wimbledon? No sooner said than done. Bit of company in the evening . . .'

'You can rake up a prostitute.'

'Nothing so crude. Mine's a class service. I can produce pretty girls who want film contracts. I've even been known to fix film contracts too. The best parts aren't cast at auditions. There are more ways of breaking an egg than hitting it with a big stick.'

It was one of Gladys Starkey's favourite expressions. He's clever, thought Sorrel. He's managed to turn it all into something perfectly natural. In a minute he'll have me feeling a spoilsport.

'I presume you go on dates?' Matthew Gillespie had, somehow, transformed himself into a disinterested but professional man behind the desk of an office employment agency. Sorrel felt she could have been at the Alfred Marks Bureau.

'You go out on dates anyway. So what's wrong with *paid* dates?'

No. They wouldn't have said that at Alfred Marks.

'Mr Gillespie?' Field Marshal Weatherall's granddaughter had now materialized like somebody coming over the top of the trenches.

'Mr Gillespie, I wonder if you could be kind enough to do me a very great favour? Please piss up your leg and slide down the steam.'

'I could send for the manager,' said Matthew Gillespie, rising to his feet.

'Yes and I could send for Scotland Yard,' retorted Judy Weatherall. 'You will find the cash desk to the left of the door.'

It worked. He went.

Sorrel was impressed. Never, for one moment, had Judy sounded less than a lady. She filed the performance away for future reference. As theirs was a relationship of fair swaps, Sorrel also vowed to teach Judy 'Albert and the Lion' so well that the Field Marshal's granddaughter would pass for true Lancashire – even in Irlams o'th' Height.

It was the first time that Sorrel had ever had a female friend of anything like her own age. June Monk didn't count. June had been thrust upon her. And the Dolans were a group rather than individual units. She was friends with all of the Dolans but no one child in particular. A bit like knowing the Children of Mary or the League of St Agnes.

Gladys Starkey, who was of the opinion that all Catholics were common, would have been startled to find that the posh Weatheralls paid Peter's Pence and bowed to Rome.

Judy Weatherall came into Sorrel Starkey's life at exactly the right moment. Sorrel, suffering from a bad case of homesickness, had been viewing London as a place of exile. Judy forced her to turn around and open her eyes to the magic of the great capital city.

'If you'd had my terrible upbringing,' Judy said firmly, 'you'd be thrilled to have got here.' She always spoke of her childhood as a wasteland of desolation. Her father had not followed the military traditions of their family. He was a career diplomat.

'How would you like to have been born in Shanghai?' asked Judy. 'And then dumped in that awful boarding school, outside Brighton, for years and years. At least your father did his duty for King and Country. Mine spent the war years being high ranking in the British Council and got an OBE at the end of it. What kind of military medal's that?

'Good evening.' Judy was now beaming at a Chelsea

Pensioner. As a Weatherall, she tended to be very proprietorial about anything, or anybody, military. The afternoon shift was over and she and Sorrel were walking along the King's Road. The pubs had just opened and the shops were pulling down their blinds.

'Your mother was practically an admiral in the Wrens,' said Sorrel. 'The most mine did was wave an old Red Cross box around.' Both girls were in permanent competition as to who had been hardest done by.

'I think Ma had to do that,' said Judy. 'She was bitterly ashamed of the fact that Daddy forced people to watch Shakespeare under gunfire. She was so busy imitating Nelson that I always had to stay at school for the holidays. Nothing to look at but the mournful sea. I didn't have a bed of roses, like you, in lovely, cosy suburbia. No Mickey and certainly no Gander to make me treacle toffee. Even my headmistress had a spooky name. Miss Horobin!'

'Roedean's a very famous school.' Sorrel was amazed to think that anybody would have swapped such an elevated, fee-paying existence for her own.

'All I thought about, watching the waves, was getting to London. Well now I'm here. And who do I land for a best friend? Somebody who views the place like a penance. Snap out of it, Sorrel. Have a good look around you!' Once again Judy was filling the air with exclamation marks.

'London's magic! It's full of energy. The cleverest and the prettiest have found their way here. They're going places. They're doing things. Look at the flowers, look at the hats, look at that woman with a spotted cardboard hatbox. It's all as crisp as a song by Noël Coward. I love it.'

And Judy wasn't just in love with the London of today. Blue London County Council plaques, on the walls of old houses, threw her into transports of delight.

'Just think, Ellen Terry, the greatest English actress ever, once lived over there. Bernard Shaw could have called on her for a nut cutlet. See that plaque, on the big house, set behind the gates? Princess Astafieza fled the Russian Revolution to teach ballet behind those doors. And now it's a night club. What more excitement could you bloody well ask for?'

Judy swore like a sailor, and sang like a choirboy. The voice was clear and bold and defiant. Heads turned as she treated the King's Road to a chorus of 'London Pride'.

'Grey city, stubbornly implanted
Taken so for granted for a thousand years
Stay city, smokily enchanted
Cradle of our memories, our hopes and fears . . .'

One day, thought Sorrel, Mickey will write something like that about Manchester. Only it will be a play. And I'll be in it. It is thoughts like this which, against all odds, keep young actresses clinging to the frail raft of their ambitions.

As they trooped up Sloane Street, Judy insisted on pausing outside the Cadogan Hotel and reciting the historically appropriate 'Arrest of Oscar Wilde'.

The poems of John Betjeman had been childhood friends to Sorrel. '*No*,' she said. 'Judy, no. You're murdering it. Listen . . .'

When Sorrel finished reciting the poem, and came back from Betjeman's dream world of lace curtains and portmanteaux and pain, she realized that Judy was watching her intently.

'You're good, Miss Manchester,' said Judy. 'You're not just good, you're bloody amazing. You make it sound as though the poet had just whispered it to you, in the next room – and you were passing it on. It's a good job my ambition's to do musicals or I'd murder you on the spot. Isn't it wonderful to be young and talented and to be in London?'

As they crossed Lowndes Square the evening sunlight was filtering through the trees and a uniformed butler was parading a mongrel, on a leash, behind the railings of the private garden in the square.

'I bet that dog's going to get a better dinner than we are,' said Judy. 'Come on, let's see what your own Oscar Wilde has cooked up for us.'

As they turned the corner into Cornucopia Mews, a taxi was pulling away from Sorrel's front door. The window wound down and Mickey's head poked out.

'Guess what?' he said. 'I'm off to do a cinema commercial. Twelve guineas and two more for providing my own dinner jacket. It's night-shooting on the docks at Tilbury. There's a note for you, by the phone, Sorrel.'

Sorrel and Judy pushed past a crate of Fyffe's bananas, and made their way into the hall.

'Judy.' Sorrel spoke sternly. 'Put that fruit back. It belongs to the landlord. We don't steal from people we like.'

The two girls creaked their way up the stairs. Sorrel opened the door with a bit of deft pressure from her shoulder. It was easier than fiddling for the key.

'I love this flat,' said Judy. 'It's like a sophisticated nursery. Sorrel? Are you OK?'

Sorrel was standing by the telephone, her face as white as the sheet of paper quivering in her hand. Mickey had printed the message in blue crayon. It read: 'Urgent. Please ring Jacob Shapiro at the Savoy Hotel.'

On the telephone, Barney's father had made 'a quarter to eight in the downstairs bar of the hotel' sound very natural and matter-of-fact. 'We can have a nice, quiet dinner.'

Why? That was the question Sorrel wanted to ask but it was pushed aside, in her own mind, by thoughts of what, in God's name, would she wear?

She told herself that she was only going because she'd never seen the inside of The Savoy and it would be an interesting experience. Interesting? It would be a *Shapiro* experience; even if it was father rather than son. Months of trying to dismiss thoughts of Barney had proved that this was as futile a cause as trying to hold back tides and seasons. Her love for Barney was a force of nature.

'I've nothing fit for The Savoy,' wailed Sorrel at Judy. 'Nothing at all.'

'Then we must improvise.' It was in the blood. Judy's great-greatgrandfather had once ordered his troops to throw empty wine bottles at Napoleon's advancing army. 'Did you never see *Gone with the Wind*? Scarlett O'Hara took down the curtains and went out in them.'

'I'd look well, in The Savoy, trailing Rufflette hooks behind me.' Sorrel felt the least she needed was the confidence offered by a good label.

Judy's eyes flashed around the room, seeking inspiration. They lighted on an olive-green, watered-silk divan cover.

'The very thing,' she said. 'All we need is a strapless bra, my elasticated belt and a lot of imagination. Go and throw yourself into the bath. I'm going to turn myself into Christian Dior. And I'm going to turn you into Cinderella.'

The result was eventually achieved in less than five minutes. Judy, afire with the creative urge, draped and pinned and tucked the olive-green silk into a strapless bodice. Next she nipped it in, with the belt, at the waist. Ripping a huge, shocking-pink silk rose off a hat Sorrel had bought second-hand, Judy arranged it to rise out of the bodice and onto one shoulder. She secured this piece of panache with a couple of almost invisible stitches.

'Now go and have a look at yourself.'

Judy had made magic. As Sorrel gazed at her reflection, in the faded silver mirror, somebody shimmeringly expensive stared back. It wasn't just the old mirror playing flattering tricks. Sorrel was finally able to believe what Mickey had so often said. She had become a beauty. If only it was Barney who was going to see her like this and not just his father.

'Should it be full length?' she asked anxiously. 'It's almost like a ball dress.'

'For The Savoy, it can be any length.' Judy had all the authority of a debutante season behind her. 'Besides, he might offer to take you on somewhere afterwards. Plump for the Café de Paris and remember to bring some nuts home in your handbag.'

'But what does he want?' Sorrel sat down, on the denuded divan, with a thud.

'Stand up! Don't crease my creation before you make your entrance. Let's take a few empty bottles back to the pub to raise a bit of cash. Then we can walk as far as Piccadilly Circus. That way, you'll only need a taxi for the last bit. It will help your performance if you arrive in style.' Judy suddenly looked worried. 'You don't think the old boy fancies you himself?'

'P'raps you've saved me from one paid date and dressed me up for another,' laughed Sorrel. But she wasn't laughing inside. She was seriously perturbed. What *could* Jacob Shapiro, merchant of Manchester, want from her?

15

As the taxi turned off the Strand, Sorrel saw that it was hard to tell where the Savoy Theatre ended and the hotel began. She found something reassuring about the idea of a hotel in a deep embrace with a theatre. The place might just prove to be on her side. If Judy's creation had turned Sorrel into a *Vogue* cover, in her heart she was still the child who had picked her way, superstitiously, across the paving stones of Rookswood Avenue reciting:

> 'Tread on a nick
> And you'll marry a stick
> And a beetle will come to your wedding.'

The uniformed flunkey who stepped forward to open the cab door was in deep conversation with a bald-headed man in a dinner jacket. This hotel guest, smoking a cigar in a gold and amber holder, looked so correctly prosperous that The Savoy might have paid him to stand outside, to set the tone of the establishment and to warn off interlopers.

Sorrel, familiar with The Midland, Manchester, since childhood, was not over-awed by the great London hotel. What's more, she had seen the cigar smoker's eyes in The Midland too. They were blue and perplexed – they were Barney's eyes. Beyond any shadow of doubt this monument to prosperity could only be Jacob Shapiro.

'Miss Starkey?' His voice was not quite English, it just missed. 'How d'you do? I must say that you're even prettier than your photograph.'

Sorrel remembered that Barney had said that Jake was a lovely man but a fiend when it came to business. What kind of meeting was this meant to be?

'I just stepped outside to finish this cigar and take the evening air. Did you know that this quadrangle is the one place in London where you can drive on the wrong side of the street?'

Sorrel resisted a nervous impulse to say that all of her life seemed to have been spent travelling on the wrong side of the street, and allowed Mr Shapiro to usher her into the hotel. It was like The Midland with an extra coat of glossy varnish and thicker, more silky, carpets.

'Being on the stage, I expect you're a great reader?' He was smiling Barney's smile. 'Arnold Bennett used this establishment as the inspiration for his novel *The Grand Babylon Hotel*. Or would that be before your time?'

'Oh, I don't care how old books are . . .' Sorrel was sniffing her host appreciatively. He was the first man she had ever met who smelled of heady, continental eau de cologne. On him, it wasn't at all sissified. It went with the cigar. It was rich and right.

'I'll read anything,' continued Sorrel. 'If there's nothing else going, I'll even read the label on a sauce bottle.'

' "Cette sauce, appétisante et piquante . . ." ' quoted Mr Shapiro. 'Which bottle?' His wonderfully blue eyes were now narrowed, teasingly. 'Which label does that come from?'

'HP,' replied Sorrel, in delight. 'I would have expected you to be too grand to know about sauce bottles.'

'What goes better with chops?' He was smiling. 'I thought we'd have a drink here, on the tier. And then, perhaps the grill room? I'm told actresses like the Savoy Grill. How would a champagne cocktail strike you?'

It struck Sorrel that she was being treated more than a bit like a Gaiety Girl, at the turn of the century. It was time to get down to business.

She took a deep breath. 'Mr Shapiro. You are, no doubt, aware that I had an affair with your son.' Sorrel was very pleased with the way the word 'affair' came out. She'd never said it aloud before.

Sorrel's next line, delivered in her very grandest voice, could have been written by Gladys Starkey: 'I just hope you're not looking for a slice off a cut loaf.'

The blue eyes rounded in astonishment. 'Nothing was further from my mind.'

'Good.' If she'd shocked him, so what? She owed the Shapiro family nothing. 'How's Barney?'

'Coming into his own.' Mr Shapiro spoke carefully. 'Yes, coming into his own. He's left the art school and joined the firm. The train could be said to be on the track again and heading in the right direction.'

'Is he happy?' A waiter had inserted the largest menu Sorrel had ever seen under her nose, and whipped it open.

'We're not in this part,' she said to the waiter. 'We're eating in the grill.'

'I am from the grill, Madame.'

'Goodness me' – this was to her host – 'you are well organized.' Sorrel's admiration for him was growing by the minute. The waiter bowed and glided away. 'Mr Shapiro, why is your menu so much smaller than mine?'

'I always stay here because they can cope with a Kosher diet. That's why mine's smaller.'

'Being Kosher seems to limit everything.' Sorrel could have wished she hadn't said this. What the hell! Perhaps it would get the conversation going in the right direction. 'I asked you whether Barney was happy.'

'He needs to put down roots.' His father looked troubled. 'It's time he started thinking about a household of his own.'

Even at this serious moment, Sorrel couldn't help noticing that there were no peanuts on the table. She could hardly swoop little green olives into her handbag. Now she admitted to herself that she was just playing for time. The next question could land her with an unpleasant answer. She asked it anyway.

'D'you mean it's time he got married?'

'Precisely.'

Another waiter arrived with two pale golden champagne cocktails. Jacob gestured towards her glass. Sorrel took a sip. It tasted like cider and autumn, mixed.

Mr Shapiro looked anxious. 'I hope this is to your liking.'

'I like the drink very much. I can't pretend that I'm all that keen on the idea of Barney getting married. Not unless you're auditioning me for the part of his wife.'

'You have your menu, we have ours.' Jacob spoke gently. 'Sometimes we go a little way off it. I'm not even sure whether HP sauce is Kosher.'

'So that's what I am? Like the sauce label. "Appetizing and piquant". You've got a bloody nerve!'

The fun went out of Jacob Shapiro's eyes and his mouth set like a rat-trap. Sorrel was now seeing the 'fiend when it comes to business'. A sudden and terrible thought came into her mind.

'Are you going to offer me money to fade into the background?'

'I was assured you'd already done that. Do you want money?'

'No I do not.' Sorrel realized that her voice was rising above a suitable level. She lowered it without removing the steel. 'But I want to know what *you* want? What's your game, Jacob Shapiro?'

He sighed sadly. 'I can certainly see what Barney saw in you. You've got real chutzpa. That's a compliment,' Jacob added hastily.

He is so nice, thought Sorrel. Under any other circumstances, she and Jacob Shapiro would have been having great fun. He was like the best sort of uncle. A man designed for high jinks. Somebody you could enjoy pulling a Christmas cracker with. Only Christmas didn't come into his calendar.

Jacob Shapiro tried again: 'On the train today, as Barney and I were coming down to London . . .'

Beautiful fireworks went off in Sorrel's mind and they were accompanied by angel trumpets. These had nothing to do with the champagne cocktails. Barney was here – he was in London. All her resolutions of forgetting him dissolved in a golden mist. Now The Savoy was indeed a five-star hotel!

'Is he here in this building? Where is he?' Sorrel suddenly looked like an advertisement for energy and happiness.

Jacob refused to be dazzled. He had plainly rehearsed this conversation and was only going to deliver the information in his own way, at his own pace.

'Barnet needs a wife. He's going to be married. It seems he gave you some promise; said he would tell you about it. Shapiros always keep their promises.'

'And you're here to do his dirty work for him.'

'Barnet can get very emotional,' sighed Jacob. 'I thought I would bring a little calm to the proceedings.'

'Well you can stuff your dinner. I'd rather starve.' Sorrel slammed the menu so firmly on the table that the waiter came out of his docile trance, by the wall, and hurried across.

'Is everything to Madame's satisfaction?' he inquired anxiously.

'Everything is *not* to Madame's satisfaction. But it's not your fault. Please go away.'

'Thank you, at least, for that,' said Jacob. 'We don't want a scene.'

'Who doesn't? Speak for yourself. If you don't take me straight to Barney, I'm going to make the most enormous scene anybody's ever made here.'

'I should think they're well used to scenes at The Savoy,' said Jacob easily. And that was where he made his mistake.

Sorrel rose to her feet. 'Are they used to dresses which are just one piece of material held together by two stitches and an elastic belt? Either you take me to Barney or you'll find yourself next to a girl in her bra and pants, screaming blue murder for British justice.'

'This is blackmail,' gasped Jacob Shapiro.

'Precisely,' said Sorrel. And she enjoyed saying it.

'Stay clothed, stay clothed.' Jacob was also on his feet. 'Barney's upstairs in the suite.'

'And don't tell me women aren't allowed upstairs. I've read about big hotels. Just so long as you book a private sitting room you can get away with murder.'

'You would have been such an asset,' said Jacob in wonder. 'Such an asset to the family.' He sounded really sorry. 'Come with me.'

As they got to the lift, he paused. 'You were just joking, about the dress?'

'Either you press that lift button or I'll give you a full demonstration.' Sorrel's hand went threateningly to the belt at her waist.

'More style than one of the French Rothschilds,' said Jacob. The lift door opened. 'Second floor,' he sighed to the attendant.

The lift was the kind with an expensively muted shudder. As they got out, and the panelled doors closed behind them,

Jacob said, 'My brain must be softening. What's to stop you screaming "Rape"?'

'Your brain isn't softening and you know it. I won't scream anything like that. You and I got the measure of one another downstairs. We're two of a kind, Mr Shapiro. We both take chances. What's this girl – the one he's going to marry – like?'

'She's not like you and that's for certain.' Jacob was shaking his head in wonder. 'Are you sure your grandfather wasn't called Cohen?'

'Would it help if he had been?' Sorrel already knew the answer.

'No. With us, there's no such thing as being a little bit Jewish.'

The rest of the walk, down long corridors which seemed to have Dunlopillo for underfelt, was achieved in silence. The corridors had a smell which always seemed to go with expensive places. Sorrel thought of it as 'newness'.

Taking a key, on a Bakelite disc, out of his pocket, Jacob paused at a door and opened it. He motioned Sorrel into a small entrance hall lined with mirrored cupboards. Sorrel could hear her own heart beating. Jacob flung open another door. It led into the sitting room.

Barney leaped out of an armchair. But this was a new Barney, a neat and tidy one. He looked so transformed as to be almost alien.

'You,' snapped his father coldly, 'are a bad lot. This young woman has the makings of a great lady. Sorrel, you are welcome here. Please sit down.'

She could hardly believe her eyes. Barney looked so conventional. Clipped hair, charcoal-grey suit, white shirt, black tie with white spots on it . . . whatever had become of Barney of The Kardomah? There are, however, no clothes conventional enough to kill sex appeal. If anything – by contrast – they made that magnetic zzz even more compelling.

'Hello,' said Sorrel. 'I think you've got something to tell me.'

The young man looked awkwardly at his father, who offered help of no kind. Now Barney looked at Sorrel. 'I'm engaged. It will be in the *Telegraph* tomorrow. We didn't want you to read it there and find out that way.'

'Why the *Daily Telegraph*?' Sorrel was ready with a dozen questions but, feeling suddenly concussed, this was the first one that came out. 'Why not the *Jewish Chronicle*? Why mix your world with ours? It only leads to trouble. What's she called?'

'Mandy.'

'Can't say it's a name I've ever been struck on.' This was generous of Sorrel. She actually thought the name was awful. 'Do you love her?'

Barney didn't answer. Sorrel walked over to the window and looked out. Dusk was beginning to fall over the Thames. A lone coal barge, with angry seagulls crying around it, was heading upriver towards the Battersea Pleasure Gardens. On the wall of a dingy warehouse, on the South Bank, a red neon advertisement for Oxo began to flash on and off.

'Even The Savoy can't posh up the view,' said Sorrel. Suddenly she rounded furiously on Barney. 'You sent that nice old man to do your dirty work for you.'

'He wanted to do it,' Barney replied, so hotly that Sorrel felt forced to believe him. 'They've got me on their railway line now. Everything has to run on oiled wheels.'

'Barney . . .' Jacob spoke in a voice which made Sorrel realize how nice he must have been with his son when Barney had been a child. 'I only want you should be a mench.'

'What's a mench?' asked Sorrel.

'*Somebody*,' replied Jacob. 'A man.'

'Him?' Sorrel was now swiping out with words. 'All I can say is, he's got a long way to go. Some man! I was the one who had to do the seducing. 'And if it's against your religion, to mention that in front of your father, all I can say is *screw* Leviticus! Are you in love with this Mandy whatever-her-name-is?'

'Mandy Poyser.' Barney was ashen in the face. 'She's very suitable. She's very nice. No, I don't love her.'

'You still love me.' It was a statement not a question. One minute in the room, one glance at him, and she'd known that.

'Don't make things worse.' Barney was all but begging. Sorrel's heart could only go out to him.

She hardened it. 'You're pathetic! You don't love her but you'll go through with this wicked farce in the name of religion. Come into the twentieth century, Barney – that's where I am. I'm here. I love you. I'm waiting for you.'

Barney looked helplessly at Jacob, who said, 'We are not your enemies, Sorrel. You are just hammering against religious tradition.'

'Your tradition stinks. When does this horror film of a wedding take place?'

'May the first.' Barney was very close to tears.

'Where?' Sorrel was determined to hear every last, grisly detail.

Again Barney darted a glance at his father. 'She can read it in the papers, Jake,' he said helplessly. 'The Great Synagogue, in Manchester.'

Jacob was watching Sorrel like a tricky board meeting. 'Sorrel, you wouldn't be thinking of making a scene?' In this mood, he had the same wise parrot's eyes she had noticed in his wife. 'You wouldn't spoil their day?'

'Spoil their day? You have the nerve to ask me that when you've wrecked my whole life. I don't know what I'd do. I'll have to think. It's suddenly struck me that there's one of your traditions I *can* join in.'

Now it was Barney who fixed her with an unblinking gaze. 'Meaning?'

'An eye for an eye and a tooth for a tooth. Isn't that what you lot believe in? Well, Mandy Poyser's got what's mine so she'd better watch out. One day I might just come and collect my pound of flesh.'

Sorrel walked out of the room, crossed the little hall and slammed the second door behind her.

Out in the corridor, she felt one of Judy's pins prick her viciously in the hip. Sorrel was glad of that pain. It gave her a bearable reason for crying.

As November gave way to December, Sorrel could not decide whether Mickey Grimshaw was her comforter or her scourge. She was spending a lot of time moping. Under the circumstances, she felt this to be normal, to be only natural.

Mickey had other ideas: 'You're crying over spilt milk and nothing stinks faster. All that lolling in bed, with the blankets pulled up, is not going to get you anywhere. Activity creates energy and lifts depression.'

June Monk's fiancé was not the only devotee of positive thinking. It was, currently, hugely fashionable and Mickey had invested in a course of lectures, at the Caxton Hall, entitled *Self-Mastery for the 1950s*.

Queen Victoria now had a home-made placard hanging around her neck which read *Negativity is the Only Real Enemy*. Over the bathroom mirror, a pinned-up postcard proclaimed *I Like Me – I Like Today*.

It was all very wearing. And oh how it jars and jangles, thought Sorrel. I don't like me and I hate today. It had been one thing to part company with Barney in Manchester. It was quite another to learn that he was about to be served up on a plate, for somebody else's pleasure.

Out-of-work actresses are always low on self-esteem. Finally confronted by the reality of Barney's engagement in cold newsprint, Sorrel was left feeling totally valueless. Can nothing plummet to less? She was pondering on thoughts like this as the first of the December fogs rolled against the window panes of Cornucopia Mews.

'Come on,' said Mickey. 'I've run you a bath. Then we're going out to choose a Christmas tree. Of course, if you ask me, what you really need is a great big roll in the hay with somebody else. I must keep my eyes skinned for some nice, normal young man.'

Sorrel turned her face to the wall.

'Out of bed, Sorrel, and into that bath. I have to give you a lecture about something else. I don't think you should be spending so much time hanging around with my gay friends. God forbid that you should turn into a queens' moll!'

As Sorrel climbed into the bath she examined this unsavoury thought. Queens' molls were women who hung around with homosexual men. They had exclusively gay friends. The word 'gay' had now definitely started to take over from 'queer' in Mickey's circles. These women went only to gay places, laughed solely at gay jokes. They were often very elegant but always ended up in bed on their own. Sorrel shuddered. No, she did not want to turn into a queens' moll.

'There's always Neil Fairweather,' she called out, through the steam. 'May I use some of your bath essence?'

Not all of Mickey's friends were homosexuals. Sorrel was referring to a film designer who had shown very definite interest in her. Neil Fairweather had already begun to make a name for himself with several interesting, low-budget British films. The biggest point in his favour was that he was brawny and blond and curly. He would not stir up memories of Barney.

'No.' Mickey materialized through the steam wearing his firmest expression. 'Not Neil Fairweather. Sorry, Sorrel, but *no*.'

Mickey should have known better. 'No' was always the wrong word to use with Sorrel Starkey.

'Do you fancy him yourself, Michael? You've always said he's not gay.'

'I've only just learned that he's something much more complicated.' Mickey was definitely in a lecturing mood. 'Let me explain . . .'

'I can do without your explanations. I think Neil Fairweather's perfectly lovely. He's kind and safe and who do you think you are – my mother? He's always asking me out. And if I want to ring him up I will.'

Opposition was the one stimulant guaranteed never to fail her. In Sorrel's quicksilver mind, Neil Fairweather had turned from a bit-part player into Prince Charming.

Mickey and Sorrel muffled themselves up in overcoats and put scarves over their noses, to walk to Strutton Ground street market. Sorrel was still very lofty with Mickey. She actually forbade him to mention Neil Fairweather's name.

The fog was getting thicker and the market, off Victoria Street, was illuminated by naphtha flares and paraffin Kelly lamps. As they walked down the line of Christmas trees Mickey suddenly rounded on her, pulled down his scarf and said, 'Right, Miss Obstinate! If you won't let me tell you – and don't stuff your fingers in your ears – I'll demonstrate.'

'What d'you mean by that?'

'You'll see.' Mickey held up a small Douglas pine and half closed his eyes.

Sorrel knew him well enough to guess that he was, mentally, covering the tree with tinsel and baubles and putting a star on top.

'OK, Mickey, tell me.'

'This tree's a bit too small,' he said. 'We need a bigger one.'

'I like Neil Fairweather.' Sorrel hoped she sounded reasonable rather than plaintive. 'He'd take me out of myself. You were the one who said that's what I needed.'

'I wonder which stall sells Lametta?' mused Mick. 'I always think it shimmers better than tinsel.'

Now Sorrel ripped her scarf aside. 'Mickey Grimshaw!' she roared. 'Will you please tell me about Neil Fairweather.'

'What's the point? You won't listen. I'm going to stage a demonstration.'

Sorrel knew that there would be no point in trying to do anything with him in this mood. If Mickey was twice as nice as a brother, he was also three times as dictatorial and stubborn.

The little market was all 'Mind yer backs' and 'Get your festive nuts'. The theory that action produces energy certainly seemed to be working on Mick. The purchase of a tree led to that of a box of silvered glass baubles and then he handed over more cash for some trembling, silver wire icicles. He bought little white candles and tin holders and his joyful enthusiasm for the task suddenly reminded Sorrel of how he'd looked, when they first met, in Blackpool.

'Mick, tell me . . .'

He shook his head in a preoccupied way and began to recite: 'Desire, belief and affirmation. Desire, belief and affirmation.' This mantra was all part of his new positive-living regime.

'You've got to want something, believe it's going to happen, keep saying it's going to happen – and then you must sit back and await the results with pleasure. I'm not buying one star to go on top of the tree, I'm getting two.

'*Desire, belief and affirmation . . .*' Now he was whispering it like a spell. He continued to speak in this all but hypnotic drone as he added, 'Those stars are going to be us. *Us* right on top of the tree.'

Sorrel and Judy would never have dreamed of eating at La Bamba, even if the management had been giving food away. The girls had seen too much of what went on in the kitchens. They'd even been a party to it themselves. Never insult the waitress, she is perfectly capable of spitting in your soup.

'If Mickey's eating out, why don't you come and have supper at my club?' asked Judy.

'Don't you have to be a Catholic?' Recent events had left Sorrel understandably nervous of anything which smacked of religious segregation.

Judy could never hear enough about Sorrel's childhood. In her turn, the Manchester girl longed to see the inside of the Safety-Curtain Club. Though the place was supposed to be on its last legs, it was still something of a theatrical legend. Nobody used the club's proper name. It was always spoken of as the Old Fire-Iron.

The club was residential and had been founded to meet the needs of Roman Catholic members of the theatrical profession resting between engagements. It was housed in a battered Queen Anne dwelling, tucked between two restaurants, in Soho.

As Sorrel and Judy passed under its peeling portico, an old man on a stick emerged, purposefully, from the front door. He nodded at Judy and began to toddle towards the pub opposite.

The club door burst open again to reveal a middle-aged woman, with an Eton crop and glasses, holding a pair of dentures in her hand.

'Come back and put your teeth in, Mr Costigan,' she yelled after the figure disappearing on his stick. 'You're a lovely old gentleman with your teeth in.'

Too late. The saloon bar door had swung shut on him. The woman sighed. She looked like the kind of maiden aunt who was used to holding her own in an argument. 'I don't like our oldest member going out looking less than his best,' she said. 'My mother always maintained that he was once the most handsome leading man in the whole of the West End.'

'This is Bertha,' said Judy by way of introduction. 'It was Bertha's mother who started the Fire-Iron. May Sorrel come to supper, as my guest? I've got the one and sixpence.'

'Then of course she may. Are you a Catholic, dear?'

Winking covertly at Sorrel, Judy replied for her. 'No. But she could be ripe for conversion. Bertha believes we get a bonus in heaven, for converting lost souls,' she explained to her guest.

'Are you ripe for mackerel stuffed with gooseberries?' asked Bertha. 'Because that's all you'll get.' She sounded a kind woman but one who would stand no nonsense.

Inside the house, they clattered up a bare staircase like an illustration from *Country Life*. All that was old in the house was solid and of museum quality. Newer items seemed to be gimcrack and shabby. Bertha disappeared into a room where a group of women, clutching rosary beads, were reciting Hail Marys under a painted plaster statue of the Holy Virgin.

'A lot of that goes on,' said Judy casually. 'But it can get very dramatic and argumentative as well. I always think of the Old Fire-Iron as a cross between a boarding school and a ramshackle Dublin hotel.'

The club sitting room led into the dining room. The walls were covered in pictures. Those with glass looked as though they had not seen a window-leather in ages. A lurid oleograph of the Sacred Heart beat anything owned by the Dolans. Jesus Christ with his own heart, dripping blood, in his hand. Next to it hung a huge Edwardian portrait, in oils, of a very pretty girl with fuzzy hair, labelled *Miss Ellaline Terris in Bluebell in Fairyland*.

The whole place struck Sorrel as being wonderfully haphazard. Some of the dining chairs could have been Chippendale, others were tubular steel with chipped paint-work. And the club understood the fact that all actors eat like gannets. The promised mackerel was followed by large portions of sultana sponge pudding with custard. The coffee, alas, was weak and watery.

'I think it's blended with acorns,' explained Judy. 'Bertha bought huge quantities of it, cheap. They have to save money somewhere. You and I need to earn more. Let's have a look in *The Stage* and see what's going.'

The *Artistes Wanted* column of that theatrical newspaper was worse than useless, unless you happened to be a pretty female impersonator or a dwarf with acrobatic experience. It was a bold panel advertisement which caught Judy's attention.

'Listen to this. "Night club hostesses wanted. Ed Shotter's Attaché Club, in the heart of Mayfair, are always looking for beautiful girls with outgoing personalities." That's us.' Judy lowered her voice. 'I suspect I'd have to keep a bit quiet about a night club, round here. They say they offer "excellent emoluments". We'd still be free for auditions in the daytime. I'm sick of La Bamba. Change, that's what's called for in our dull lives. Change!'

One of the great advantages of the Old Fire-Iron was that it was in the middle of all things theatrical. The two young actresses took leave of the club and wandered through Soho to Shaftesbury Avenue and theatreland. The front-of-house photographs, outside The Globe, were by Angus McBean. For some time now Sorrel had been thinking that new photographs might help her get proper theatrical employment.

'Angus McBean, that's who I want to go to,' she said. 'I wonder how much he charges for a sitting?'

'Ten guineas.' Judy had been seeking fame longer than her friend and was well versed in such matters.

'Where am I going to find that sort of money?'

'How about Ed Shotter's Attaché Club?' asked Judy. 'I'm more than half thinking about it myself.'

Sorrel was less open-minded. 'Working as a hostess sounds precious close to tarting.'

'Not at that club.' Judy was very definite. 'I've been. I've seen. I used to get taken there when I was doing the season. I once saw one of the hostesses get very hoity-toity with a customer who was trying to get fresh. What's more, Ed Shotter took her side. We could change our names for it.'

'Again? I can't see Lily Bear dreaming up another name for me so I can go and whisper sweet nothings to tired businessmen. Dear God, whatever would Shelagh Starkey have to say about it?' Sorrel had remained in contact with her namesake and come to know her as a thoroughly good woman who was a bit strait-laced.

'At least we'd be sitting down.' Judy was never less than realistic. 'You must admit La Bamba's murder on the feet.'

Just then a number 19 bus stopped for the traffic lights.

'That's mine,' said Sorrel. 'Thank you for the mackerel,' she called over her shoulder. Diving through the traffic, she just managed to clamber onto the deck before the bus started moving towards Piccadilly Circus.

She descended at Knightsbridge. As she turned the corner, into Cornucopia Mews, Sorrel reflected that there were no two ways about it – her feet were killing her. Would hostessing be like a paid date?

Dates; oh dear, when she got home she must be careful to steer clear of the subject of Neil Fairweather. But she did like him and she would go out with him. Some of the houses in the mews already had Christmas wreaths tied to their knockers. Yes, it would be nice to have some sort of boyfriend to go to parties with.

The greengrocer's cat jumped from a crate onto the window sill of the shop and tried to lick Sorrel's fingers. His tongue was like a tiny emery board. The attraction must be the mackerel, thought Sorrel. All in all, she had enjoyed a thoroughly pleasant girls' night out.

Her legs ached again as she toiled up the stairs. La Bamba's days were definitely numbered. Sorrel opened the door and let out a cry of delight.

The room was illuminated by countless little candle flames on a Christmas tree which was all silver shimmer and sparkle. Her cry of pleasure came to an abrupt halt. Two men were lying on cushions, in front of the gas fire. They were holding hands. One man was Mickey. The other came as more of a surprise. It was Neil Fairweather.

Sorrel could hear Neil going down the stairs. Not one word

240

had been spoken since she walked through the door. Neil had got to his feet, climbed into his overcoat and tied a scarf round his neck with all the blushing concentration of somebody attempting a complicated ballroom dance for the first time.

He hadn't even attempted to say 'Goodnight'. He'd just gone. Sorrel waited until she heard the street door shut before she felt she could trust herself to speak to Mickey.

'It was so *cosy*.' She was very angry. 'If you'd been at it like knives, I wouldn't have minded so much. I know about you and sex. You have it instead of exercise. This was different. It was almost romantic. You've got all of London to go at but you couldn't keep your hands off the one man who was interested in me.'

Mickey was totally unrepentant. 'I promised you a demonstration and you got one.'

'Demonstration?' snorted Sorrel. 'Seduction more like!'

'He's bisexual,' said Mickey. 'He likes both men and women.'

'You're in a fine position to judge anybody, Mickey Grimshaw.'

Mickey kept his temper. 'I'm not judging. I'm just trying to save you from getting hurt. It would take another bisexual to understand Neil properly.

'He's a man with a weathercock mind. I know you, you're looking for total commitment. Neil was born with an inbuilt excuse to be unfaithful. I've had some – I've been around one. They will always tell you, if they could just meet the right person, man or woman, it wouldn't matter. And then they look the other side of the fence and find that it does matter.'

'I'm sick of you,' said Sorrel. She was very near to tears. 'If it's not positive thinking, it's psychology. You've only to read a pamphlet on something and you're a world expert.'

Mickey went bright red in the face. 'If you must know, the one person I ever loved was a wavering bisexual. In the month of May, we were David and Jonathan. Come June the first, he had the nerve to ask me to be best man at his wedding.'

Sorrel was unconvinced. 'It's the first I've ever heard of a great, lost love.'

'Perhaps I didn't want to talk about it.' Mickey spoke

quietly. Adopting a dismissive tone he added, 'Anyway, that's why I staged tonight's little tableau for you.'

If Sorrel had been angry before, she was now maddened into fury. 'Just who d'you think you are? Mickey the puppetmaster? I liked Neil Fairweather. I was looking forward to just going out with him. I'm sick of tagging along in your wake. I enjoyed the idea of being invited out to dinner in my own right. You lecture me about queens' molls and then you do everything in your power to turn me into one. Perhaps I should be allowed to make my own mistakes.'

Now Mickey was shouting even more loudly than Sorrel: 'Perhaps I'm sick of watching you make them. Perhaps I'm trying to guide you in the right direction.'

'There you are!' Sorrel was triumphant. 'What did I tell you? You *do* see yourself as the puppetmaster. You've designed a flat like a tatty grand opera and now you're staging living tableaux. Well don't think you can pull my strings because you can't.'

Sorrel's eyes alighted on one of the Pollock's model theatres on the bookshelves. It suddenly seemed to contain an awful explanation. Never one to think before she spoke, Sorrel decided to hurl the thought at Mickey.

'Adults are just children's toys to you.'

Mickey dived under the divan, pulled out Sorrel's suitcase and kicked it across the room.

'*Out!*' he yelled. 'On yer bike, Sheila Starkey. I don't have to take this crap from you. Let's see what sort of success you can make on your own.'

Sorrel ripped open the cupboard door and a lot of rattling dry-cleaner's coat hangers fell out. Blindly, she began to pull out clothes from the wooden hangers on the rail.

'And don't think you can take that blue dressing gown,' said Mickey, snatching. 'It's all I've got left to remind me of a love affair with a bisexual.'

It took a lot to make Sorrel Starkey cry but she started now. She cried helplessly and hopelessly and she wept for tonight and for things long past. She was weeping now for events in the past which had been starved of their fair share of tears. She wept till it hurt. And the fact that she was crying over a suitcase made it worse. Suitcases that cut into your hand and endless staircases with nobody wanting you at the top of them ... these seemed to be the only rewards her ambitions had brought her.

She had been less than fair to Mickey. She would have to explain that shouting at him was really railing at a world which didn't care. She would certainly have to apologize. He had never been less than good and kind. Where was he?

Quickly, Sorrel looked around the flat. No Mickey. She darted to the window and pulled back the net. He was stomping across the street towards the pub.

This hadn't been one of their firework displays. This row was the real thing. Slowly, and much more carefully than usual, she began to pack the hated suitcase.

Sorrel spent the night in Judy's room at the Old Fire-Iron. The next morning, Judy marched her friend into Bertha's office and pleaded the homeless girl's case for her.

'I know she's not a Catholic, Bertha, but we're always praying for the conversion of England, so wouldn't it be a good idea to start with Sorrel Starkey?'

As Bertha pondered this in silence, Sorrel looked round the office. It struck her as the distilled essence of the place. The walls were hung with framed and faded playbills and, high on a plinth, a statue of the Infant of Prague gazed down on the proceedings like a holy referee.

'I'm just wondering what St Genesius would want me to do,' said Bertha.

'Who's he?' asked Sorrel.

'The patron saint of actors,' explained Judy. 'Bertha's practically got him cornered, for her own uses.'

Sorrel was allowed to stay. Bertha said she could share Judy's bedroom which was in the annexe, over a wholesale trouser-maker's, across the street. This meant that they were not overly supervised and could come and go as they pleased.

'All to the good when you consider what these cocktail dresses are in aid of.' Judy's mouth was full of pins. She was down on her knees adjusting the hem of Sorrel's taffeta frock. It was a Butterick Easy-to-Make model.

Judy rose to her feet. 'I'm leaving well alone. It's definitely one of my better efforts. It may be just a little bit short. The extra flash of leg will be just the job for what we've got in mind. How does mine look?'

'A million dollars.' Sorrel spoke with genuine admiration. 'We look smashers.'

Judy's dress was in midnight blue with a full skirt. Sorrel's was black and fitted to show off her waist. Nobody would have guessed that Judy had run them up out of two and eleven-penny taffeta from John Lewis's.

'Right.' Judy slung a coat around her shoulders. 'I'm off to Benediction at St Pat's.'

'Can I come?' asked Sorrel.

'Feel free, but nobody's making you.'

Sorrel didn't need any making. All her life she had been fascinated by mystery. Anything hidden intrigued her. It was this which had drawn her to stage doors – the public weren't meant to pass behind them. It was this that had attracted her to Barney – he belonged not just to a foreign religion but to a race which tried to keep itself mysteriously separate. Throw a veil over something and Sorrel Starkey had to try and lift it. What was Benediction?

'Just copy me,' said Judy, as they walked across the darkness of Soho Square, towards the lighted doorway of St Patrick's Church. Judy whipped a black lace veil out of her pocket and plonked it, mantilla-fashion, over her head. Sorrel immediately felt excluded and almost shy. Inside the porch Judy dipped her fingers in a holy water stoup which made Sorrel feel even more of an outsider.

'Have some,' said Judy, touching Sorrel's fingers and wetting them from her own. Sorrel felt grateful but she didn't copy her friend as Judy made the sign of the cross. She was scared of getting it the wrong way round. People could think she did black magic.

They passed through some swing doors and into darkness filled with the smell of incense. It brought the Dolans to mind. There'd been incense when they took her to their May procession. Gander too; if Gander wanted to pray she didn't mind what church she went in. She and Sorrel had even lit Catholic candles at the Hidden Gem Church in Manchester.

All the candles in this church seemed to be banked on the high altar. The service was just starting and this concentration of wax light surrounded something, like gilded metal sunrays, on a stand. It looked to Sorrel as though it had a glass eye in the middle. Gander owned a vase with an eye on it with the inscription *Thou Lord Seest Me*.

The sung service was in puzzling Latin.

> 'Genitore, genitoque
> Laus et jubilatio . . .'

Sorrel had done Latin for O levels so she just about managed to pull the words 'praise' and 'jubilation' from this. Goodness, but you were on your knees for a long time.

At one point the priest held up the golden object and everybody fell forward and Sorrel was the only one left kneeling bolt upright. As she didn't know why they were prostrating themselves, she felt that joining in might be tantamount to telling a lie to God. The priest took something out of the middle of the gold thing, put it into a cupboard on the middle of the altar, closed the doors, twitched a lace veil over the gleaming sunburst and that seemed to be that. It was all very puzzling. For a while, there had seemed to be more than people in the place.

Outside, in the street, Judy removed her own veil and crammed it, matter-of-factly, into her pocket.

'Explain it, Judy. What was that gold thing?'

'A monstrance. The Blessed Sacrament was in it but now it's been put to bed.'

'What's the Blessed Sacrament?'

'Our Lord. Jesus Christ to a proddy-dog like you.'

Sorrel was frankly incredulous. 'You must think I'm barmy.'

Judy shook her head. 'There was one Communion wafer behind the glass in the middle.'

'And that's meant to be Jesus? But *how*?'

'It isn't a wafer any more. It's been consecrated. It's his body and his blood.'

'You can't really believe that? Nothing on earth would get me to believe in that.'

Judy started to laugh. It was happy laughter. 'Oh, what a topple there'll be when you do come crashing down. The ones who protest loudest always make the best converts.'

'Not me,' said Sorrel staunchly.

'I'm praying for it.' Judy said this as though her prayers guaranteed the certainty of Sorrel's conversion. They were all on very easy terms with the Almighty at the Old Fire-Iron.

'Mickey would have adored it,' ventured Sorrel. 'Banks of candles and all that incense.'

'I'm afraid the Church is a bit down on people like Old Mick,' sighed Judy. 'They can *be* homos but they're not supposed to do anything about it.'

'No sex?' Sorrel was genuinely shocked. She could not, she felt, have anything to do with a religion which would not allow Mickey to be himself. She might have quarrelled with him, they might be at outs – in fact it was entirely possible they would never speak again. But he was still her great friend. She'd been talking to God about this during the more puzzling parts of the service. Mickey was still in her heart even if she was no longer in his.

She'd mentioned Barney to God too and she didn't care if he went and told Moses. Sorrel was suddenly struck by a very Protestant thought. 'Judy, have we just been bowing down in front of idols?'

'Have we buggery. We've been saying "Goodnight" to Our Lord. He's given us his blessing.'

Sorrel felt more than a bit perturbed. Was this the right thing to do on the very evening they were going to be interviewed for jobs as night club hostesses?

Judy must have had somewhat similar thoughts but she expressed them in Catholic jargon. 'I prayed very hard that the Attaché Club would not present us with the occasion of Sin.'

Mayfair, on a Saturday evening, is a place of stray cats and caretakers. All that seemed to be roaming loose, at the bottom end of Bond Street, were a couple of jaded French prostitutes. They were cackling to one another, from corner to corner, in their native tongue.

'That accent's Marseilles,' said Judy, who was having a night of seeming to know everything.

Cartier's windows were lit up but stripped bare of jewels. It was as though they expected nobody of any real consequence to be in London at the weekend.

'Is it down this courtyard? It is.' Sorrel was more nervous than she was admit. 'There's a neon arrow with his name on it.'

Judy nodded but did not budge from the safety of New Bond Street.

'Come on, Judy. Where's your fighting spirit? Try and remember that your grandfather was a Field Marshal.'

'Yes, and my Aunt Veronica's a Mother Superior,' said Judy. Nevertheless she followed Sorrel under a winking sign which said *Ed Shotter's Ooh La-La Follies at 11.30 & 2 A.M.* The two girls passed through a nail-studded door.

The door was quilted with mauve satin on the other side and the entrance hall was lined with dozens of photographs of groups of celebrities. In each and every one of them, the most famous person was shaking hands with a man who looked like Billy Bunter, in a velvet smoking jacket.

A uniformed cloakroom woman switched off her vacuum cleaner, so as to hear what the girls wanted, and went to fetch Ed Shotter.

He turned out to be the Billy Bunter look-alike. His clothes were the same as in the photograph but Sorrel noticed that he had tried to add extra inches to his height by wearing built-up shoes. They made him walk a bit stiff-legged as he came towards them, already talking.

'Right, girls. You be straight with me and I'll be straight with you. Common and proud of it, that's me! Nobody's going to tell that Ed Shotter rose from the ranks, and became a Captain in the Catering Corps, because he'll tell you himself. I earned that title, so the monicker's Captain Shotter. Coats off, please. I want to view the merchandise.

'Very nice, very trim. Follow the Captain's rules and you'll end up at the Captain's table. Why, there's girls from the

Attaché Club who've walked down the aisle 'ung in diamonds. But you keep your legs crossed. Understood? You're hostesses not whores. No pancake makeup and no four-letter words. Get pissed-unpleasant and you're out on yer arses.'

Sorrel couldn't think of an appropriate expression to put on her face so she just nodded like one of those dolls, with its head on a spring, trapped in a cage with a self-important budgerigar.

'At some clubs the girls might make their own after-hours arrangements with the customers. Not 'ere!'

'How did the girls get the diamonds then?' asked Sorrel, interested.

'They collected a lot of cocktail sticks.' Captain Shotter spoke with satisfaction. He went on to explain that each cocktail, paid for by a guest and served to a girl, carried a commission. All she had to do was save the sticks and turn them in at the end of the evening.

'Champagne carries the best commission,' he said. 'Keep the corks in your handbags. And before you think of it, we do know our own corks. The aim is to go through as much champagne in a night as possible.'

'And keep sober?' asked Judy. 'I know men. They're bound to make sure our glasses are filled.'

'But that's not to say it has to go down your necks.' Captain Shotter spoke reprovingly. 'What the hell d'you think the potted palms are for? You point out a visiting film star with one hand and unload your drink with the other. You *never* point at royalty.'

'We know that. We are post-debutantes.' Judy was being lofty. It was a mistake.

'Sorrel might be,' said Captain Shotter. 'But not you, darling. Not unless my name's Douglas Fairbanks Junior. He comes here. And half the officers in the Brigade of Guards. And Jack Spot and the Paddington Mob.'

Gangsters? Sorrel was beginning to wonder what she had let herself in for.

'Remember, girls, the customer is always right. First time he gropes you, you remind him he's a gentleman. If he goes for another quick feel, you get to your feet and come for either me or Mr Bonicello. That's the head waiter. We replace you with a girl who can handle herself.

'Saturday's mostly tourists and provincials. The clientele won't start falling in for another half hour. Put your coats in the staff room and have a wander round.'

The Attaché Club was a series of red velvet-lined boxes. These culminated in the big cabaret room where the crimson plush was tented from the centre of the ceiling to the skirting boards. It was ruched into folds, like cinema curtains. The crystal chandeliers were lavish and spectacular – what you could see of them. Sorrel judged that none of the bulbs could have been stronger than fifteen watts.

'It's just like the foreign royalty section at Madam Tussaud's,' said Judy.

'Sorrel and Judith?' The man who asked the question was haggard, with liquid spaniel eyes. The effect of well-tailored evening clothes was spoiled by striking tufts of black hair sticking out of his ears. His voice sounded a mixture of cockney and Italian.

'Actually, my name is Judy,' said that young woman.

'You'll be Judith while you're here. Captain's orders. He doesn't like anything suburban.'

Considering that Judy's father had just handed his Adam mansion over to the National Trust, Sorrel thought that her friend took this slur on her origins with considerable dignity.

Bonicello hadn't finished. 'Has the Captain told you about chocolates? If they buy you a box, and you don't break the cellophane, you can flog them back to us at half price. Same goes for the can-can dolls. The dancers come round selling them after the cabaret.'

'Don't forget me, Mr Bonicello.' An elderly woman with swoops of feathers in her hair came up and joined them. Her evening dress was solid with grey bugle beads. One of the black feathers in her hair curved upwards and the other one went down.

'Lady Boswell, Society clairvoyant,' said the head waiter, by way of introduction.

Something about the stove-black hair and the glittering

eyes was familiar to Sorrel. Where had she seen Lady Boswell before?

'Llandudno!' She'd got it. 'You used to be Gypsy Boswell and you were on the pier.'

'Have they smartened your name up too?' Judy asked this with only the faintest hint of bitterness.

'Oh no. The handle's genuine enough. I married a nice little baronet with a house overlooking Chester racecourse.' She turned to Sorrel. 'You might remember. I always had a picture of one of his geldings, outside the booth.'

It was a wonderful moment. That picture of a racehorse had always puzzled Sorrel and here was the explanation.

'The little sweetheart went and died on me. The baronet, not the gelding. I gave up the house. I think you're all very brave to live in them. The place used to creak out messages to me in the night. I've got the varda – my caravan – parked up behind King's Cross. Lady Higgins is the genuine title but Boswell's better for "The only titled gypsy seer in Mayfair". If you girls can get your gentlemen to invite me to the table, for a reading, there's good commission in it for you.'

'Just tell me something now,' said Sorrel urgently. 'I'm not sure I'm going to be any good at this place. I need a peep into the future.'

Lady Boswell's eyes narrowed. 'You'll just have to keep following the lorry, m'dear. Who's June? She'll prosper.'

Sorrel was amazed. 'That's exactly what you said all those years ago.'

'Proves I'm genuine. Twenty-five per cent. That's what I'm offering you. I ask five guineas for the palm and ten for the crystal.'

'My goodness, you have gone up in the world!' gasped Sorrel. Even a hand-reading cost more than a week's full board at the Old Fire-Iron.

'You'll go up in the world too.' Lady Boswell now switched her attention to Judy. 'What's a genuine blue-blood like you doing posing as a little taxi-dancer? Your family would go spare. Be sure and get me business, dear. Emphasize to the gentlemen that I'm shit-hot when it comes to the Stock Exchange!' Lady Boswell's cackle of laughter caused her feathers to tremble. 'After all, us aristocrats must stick together.'

Some night clubs kept their hostesses tucked away, behind the scenes, until they were needed. Ed Shotter sat them in pairs, at tables against the wall, to dress out the cabaret room.

Sorrel found herself systematically split from Judy and paired up with a dark redhead named Imogen.

'I'm from Putney,' she said. 'The better end, near the towpath. D'you think I look like Fiona Campbell-Walters? Everybody's always remarking on it. I'd go in for modelling myself but it's so chancy.'

Waiters were finishing setting the tables. The band arrived and then the first of the customers. Most of the men seemed to have brought their own women. Imogen proceeded to give Sorrel a long lecture on the rival merits of National Savings certificates and various building societies. Sorrel found it every bit as puzzling and marginally less interesting than compound fractions. If this was nightlife, it was about as wicked as grey flannel.

'Sorrel?' Mr Bonicello, now very much the forbidding head waiter, was clicking his fingers in her direction. 'A gentleman on his own would like your company.'

The band was playing 'Magic Moments' as Sorrel followed Bonicello across the dance floor. Trying to pretend to herself that she was simply a mannequin modelling a cocktail dress, Sorrel couldn't help thinking that 'Ten Cents a Dance' would have been more appropriate. She suppressed a nervous desire to head for the ladies'.

'May I be permitted to introduce Sorrel to you, sir? I don't have to tell you who this gentleman is.' Bonicello spoke with pride and nodded down gravely at the untidily seated figure who had made no attempt to get to his feet or even extend a hand.

He's just a boy, thought Sorrel. Was her mind playing tricks? Could it be the low lights or did he really look like a younger version of Barney? The Shapiros certainly had a daughter. Was there a younger brother who'd never been mentioned?

'What's your name?' she asked urgently.

'You must be joking!' The boy had a most engaging grin and a thick Liverpool accent. 'I'm Kenny Shorrocks.'

'Oh,' said Sorrel. She was none the wiser.

He seemed to find this amusing, attractive even. 'Don't you follow soccer?'

The head waiter pushed Sorrel down into a chair and said hastily, 'Mr Shorrocks has played for both Manchester United and City and now he's been transferred to . . .'

'Kenny,' said the youth expansively to the waiter. 'Call me Kenny. Everybody does. You can call me Kenny too.' He grinned at Sorrel again.

'I'll remember that,' she replied. It sounded very prim. Dear God, this was awful; she would have to do better than this. Did geisha girls feel as stupid as this when they were first called upon to perform the tea ceremony?

Bonicello, his liquid eyes darting daggers at her, asked, 'Champagne, Sorrel?'

'Why not?' she assented weakly.

'Why not!' roared Kenny. 'I've already drunk two bottles of the stuff in Fulham.'

Sorrel looked helplessly across the room. Judy, she noted, had been paired off with a huge man who looked like King Farouk without the fez. Her friend had not been wasting time. Judy was already clutching a large box of chocolates but she looked a little dazed and wild-eyed.

'Double portion of scampi for me and a few chips,' called Kenny after the departing waiter.

Bonicello turned and bowed. 'Of course, sir.'

'Crawler,' muttered the footballer and lit a cigarette. 'Where you from?' he asked.

'Manchester.'

'I've given that dump two separate chances.'

Sorrel controlled herself but it was with great difficulty. How dare this drunken little oik knock her city? And how could she have thought he looked like Barney? If there was any resemblance, it was a coarse one. And one of Kenny Shorrocks's front teeth was chipped.

Noticing where she was looking, he ran his tongue over the tooth. 'Wants fixing,' he said. 'But the rest of me's in good nick.'

All Sorrel's conversational abilities seemed to have abandoned her. She needn't have worried. The young footballer was taking her, goal by goal, through that afternoon's match.

'Am I boring you?' he asked suddenly.

'A bit.' Sorrel was damned if she was abandoning the truth in the cause of Ed Shotter's night club.

'You're wonderful.' The champagne arrived. 'Just pour it out,' he said to the wine waiter. 'All that testing and tasting routine is for poofters. You're something very special, Sorrel. There are girls who would have queued up for that conversation about the match. You like me for myself. I like you too. Tell me your hopes and your dreams and your telephone number.'

Reminding herself that she was simply doing a job of work, Sorrel took a swig of champagne and embarked on a comedy version of her life to date. Two glasses of wine later, she found she was actually beginning to enjoy herself. Kenny had laughed in all the right places and now he was gazing at her in frank adoration.

'I've never met anybody like you,' he said. 'Would you like scampi and chips too? Or a rump steak? Have a rump steak. Have what you want. I've never heard a life story like it. You're a girl who's turning herself into who she wants to be.

'Bring this lady the menu,' he called out. 'I'm nothing really. I'm just a lad who started kicking tin cans early enough. I've got lucky feet. You're something special, Sorrel. Your dad was an officer and I'm still on National Service deferments.' Kenny snatched the menu proffered by Bonicello and waved him away.

'I'm not just shooting a line, Sorrel. You've got class and style. I never came here expecting to meet a lady.' He looked young and shy and more than a little drunk. 'Unattainable. My beautiful lady. I suppose there wouldn't be any chance of a fuck?'

Sorrel rose to her feet and headed towards the cloakroom. Would Ed Shotter agree that Kenny Shorrocks had gone too far? She didn't know. She needed to think. She looked across to Judy's table and collided with a man in a dark lounge suit.

'Our worlds are getting closer and closer, my little

mystery.' It was Matthew Gillespie. Mucky Matt. 'So now you're selling company. Don't deny it. I've been watching you with the Liverpool Wonder.'

'It's only talking to people.' Sorrel spoke indignantly but there was guilt there as well.

Mucky Matt treated her to a cold look. 'I can respect a woman who sells her body – that's honest.' He sounded as though he really meant this. 'What I can't stand is girls who sell fake friendship. You're in a dirty job. It half promises and never delivers.'

'For once I'm in complete agreement with you,' said Sorrel. 'Thank you for putting me right.' She shook him firmly by the hand then stalked through the tables to Judy and her Egyptian.

'Judy, we're going. This place definitely represents your occasion of Sin.'

'You're telling me.' Judy rose to her feet with relief. 'This Turk doesn't speak a word of English but he's just tried to put my hand on a very international place indeed.'

'Never mind that. You can always wash your fingers.' Sorrel looked round the place in horror. 'To think we came straight here from church. I've a terrible feeling we'll pay for that. Gander always used to say, "Be sure your sins will find you out." I don't think I'm going to get away with tonight. I think it's going to bide its time and then come back to haunt me.'

17

The saying only covers fish and actors, thought Sorrel. Actors and fish travel on Sundays. It doesn't mention people with broken hearts, on cheap day returns, to Jewish weddings where they're not wanted.

The train for Manchester was already an hour late when it reached Stockport. For the last fifteen minutes it had been stationary, on a high bank, back or beyond of nowhere. Surely it could only be within a couple of miles of its final destination?

With growing impatience, Sorrel went out into the corridor, let down the carriage window and poked out her head.

In the far distance, she could see Manchester Town Hall tower. That meant the Town Hall clock could also see her. Sorrel did not like this. She was breaking a promise. She was returning to Manchester before she was famous. But it was Barney's wedding day and one promise to herself had come into conflict with another. In The Savoy, Sorrel had vowed to be present at the marriage. According to the Town Hall clock, she would never make it on time.

She felt a bit like the Wicked Fairy in *The Sleeping Beauty* – another woman who had not received an invitation. Come to think of it, the Wicked Fairy hadn't got there until the end, either. More impatient passengers were coming out into the corridor and a uniformed guard was pushing his way through them.

'What's up?' asked Sorrel. The sight of the Manchester skyline had released this Northern-sounding query.

'We're at the mercy of a signal fault.' The guard must have gone down on the early morning train and returned on this one because he too sounded Manchester.

'I'm in a rush. D'you think I could scramble down?'

'We're miles off the station and you're hardly dressed for clambering down a steep gravel banking.'

Being as there is no correct attire for a wedding to which you are not invited, Sorrel had settled for the proverbial little black suit. She only meant to stand outside the synagogue. Whilst she did not want to pass for a guest, neither did she wish to be taken for the Shapiros' fire-goy. The black suit had seemed to be the answer.

'I can't let you off this train, madam.' The guard was enjoying his moment of power. 'It would be against company regulations.'

'Good afternoon,' said Sorrel as, opening the door, she stepped down from the train. It was a deeper drop than she'd expected. It left her up to the ankles in wooden railway sleepers and still a good hundred feet above the ground below. In the distance, she could hear lions roaring. That meant she must be somewhere near Belle Vue Zoo.

'I took you for a nice girl.' The guard was shouting down from above her head. 'You're in direct contravention of the company rules.'

'First thing I've enjoyed today,' called back Sorrel as she began to climb down the gradient. The gravel was already playing havoc with her black patent stilettos. At one point she was forced to sit down on her bottom. Sorrel didn't care. The train remained stock-still on the line. Sorrel Starkey was back in charge of her own destiny.

The nearer she got to the ground, the more momentum she seemed to gather. A man, walking a muzzled greyhound, was watching in alarm as Sorrel finally stumbled up against a makeshift corrugated-iron fence.

'Where do I get a bus into town?' she asked him.

'One's just gone,' he replied in that infuriating tone of satisfaction which is one of the less endearing characteristics of the citizens of Manchester. 'It's Sunday service. They're every hour.'

'Where's the main road?'

'Take the plank over the ditch and cut across the cinder track.'

It was a gloomy afternoon with puddles from earlier rain. As Sorrel headed towards the main road she had to pass the back of a row of terraced houses. Through an upstairs bedroom window she could see a woman slowly changing a bolster case. The woman looked down at Sorrel with casual interest.

Sorrel wanted to cry out, 'Don't look down at me yet. I'm not really back. This isn't me. One day I'll turn into myself and I'll be somebody worth looking at. You'll go to the top of your stairs and yell, "Come quick! Sorrel Starkey's in our back entry." '

Any thoughts were better than thoughts of Barney's wedding. But Sorrel had to think about it. She needed to get a move on. The marriage was due to take place, at three o'clock, at the Great Synagogue on Cheetham Hill. Her watch was already showing five to three and God alone knew where she was. How long did Jewish weddings last?

'Mrs?' It was a small girl dressed for Sunday school. 'You've got all chalk on your skirt.'

It must have happened as she stumbled down the railway banking. Sorrel gave the skirt a frantic bat with the palm of her hand and asked, 'Which way's town?'

'Which way's town?' mimicked the child. 'Don't you talk posh?'

'You're playing wag,' said Sorrel, who'd been a Sunday truant herself, 'and I bet you've already spent your collection.'

'Town's that way.' The child pointed and looked at Sorrel in awe.

Sorrel began walking. The streets of back-to-back houses were deserted. People were alleged to send their children to Sunday school so as to snatch a precious hour of privacy. Was it possible that hundreds of men and women could be making love behind these rows of lace curtains? Sorrel skirted a pool of vomit. Some people spend Sunday lunchtime getting drunk and the afternoon sleeping it off. Her shoes seemed to be making mocking, clacking noises as she continued to march through the empty streets.

Suddenly she heard a car engine. A small van came into view and pulled up beside her. It was marked *Excelsior Boot & Shoe Co.*

'Am I right for Salford?' asked the driver through the open window.

'Give me a lift and I'll show you the way.' Sorrel, who already had her fingers on the handle, opened the door, got in and sat down. 'Straight ahead,' she said. Though she spoke confidently Sorrel was praying that she would eventually recognize some landmark.

'Where are you going yourself?' He was all smiles, in his forties, in a boiler suit.

'The Great Synagogue on Cheetham Hill Road.'

His beaming smile vanished. 'I'll drop you when we get to Manchester,' he said. 'If you think I'm going to chauffeur you up to the front door of that place, you've got another think coming to you.'

Sorrel was in no position to argue. She needed a lift. Without so much as another vehicle in sight, this driver was still a cautious dawdler. Were they even going in the right direction? Sorrel had no idea. Anonymous estates of council houses offered no clue. Suddenly, she recognized the public washhouse on the corner of Hyde Road.

'We turn left here.' Yes this was the high wall of Belle Vue Pleasure Gardens with the skeleton outline of the Big Dipper rearing up behind flags on tall poles. Despite the gloom of her mission Sorrel could not suppress a glimmer of the glorious feeling of coming home.

The tortoise of a driver must still have been thinking about his aversion to synagogues. 'Hitler went too far,' he said. 'But Oswald Mosley was one of the finest speakers who ever came to the Free Trade Hall.'

Under any other circumstances Sorrel would have hit him. Instead, she sat in silence until the car reached Piccadilly.

'Drop me here,' Sorrel said. 'Salford's down at the bottom.'

'Yes I will drop you here.' The driver couldn't even stop his van decisively. 'And I've got a suggestion to make to you. You lot have got your own country now. Why don't you go there? Why don't you all just bugger off to Israel?'

'Did you know that you spit when you talk?' asked Sorrel, and then she got out.

On the taxi rank, in front of Queen Victoria's statue, two cabs were mercifully waiting. Sorrel tried to get in the first one she came to but the driver made her take the one in front.

'Cheetham Hill Road,' she said and left it at that. She wasn't sure how good she would be at coping with any further anti-semitism. Come to that, today, which side was she meant to be on? There was no real doubt about this. Even when it didn't suit her purpose, Sorrel was always on the side of people being themselves.

As the taxi sped down Market Street, the sun broke through the clouds and brightened the glazed cream brickwork of the Continental Cinema. Underneath the cinema, in the basement, lay the Ping Hong Chinese Restaurant. It was where Barney and Sorrel had eaten before they went to Salford Hippodrome and made love for the very first time.

The memory was too painful. Sorrel turned her head and looked across the street. Clifton's Film Star Fashions. Would Mickey be at the wedding as a properly invited guest? Since their quarrel he had turned into handwriting on punctiliously forwarded letters. He and Sorrel had not so much as spoken on the telephone. The taxi seemed to be waiting, interminably, for the lights to change at Corporation Street.

'They've been like this all day,' explained the driver. 'Sod it! Let's take a chance.'

As they swung round the corner, Sorrel suddenly wished he hadn't. It would get them there faster and she still didn't know what she was going to do.

According to the two clocks, like spectacles, over an optician's door, the service should have been going on for thirty-four minutes. How long did Orthodox Jews take to get married? Would they have got to the part where anybody who knows anything is supposed to speak up or for ever hold their peace? Sorrel had no rights in the matter and the chances were the question would be asked in Hebrew. Why was she here?

Because she had to be. Gander had once said that the only way to be sure, in your heart, that a dog had really been put to sleep, was to watch the vet give it the needle. It left you with no illusions. You couldn't get to the surgery door and change your mind.

'I want the Great Synagogue,' she said to the driver.

'I came past not quarter of an hour ago,' he replied. 'Money must be getting married. I never saw so many Rolls-Royces in my life.'

Sorrel noticed there was still some chalk on her skirt and gave her hip a few vigorous smacks. The mark had worked itself into the weave and refused to budge.

The driver was friendly. 'I thought black was supposed to be unlucky at weddings. I'm sorry, love. That was very ignorant of me. For all I know you could be in deep mourning.'

He shouldn't have called me *love*, thought Sorrel. It was that which had brought tears to her eyes. There is a special Manchester way of saying it which implies that you are OK. That the speaker likes you. The taxi driver himself would probably have denied that it had any meaning at all. But it had and it went straight to Sorrel's heart. Blindly, she thrust a ten-shilling note at him and got out of the cab.

He was right about the cars. Empty limousines, some with chauffeurs leaning against them, were parked halfway to the Jewish Hospital. It was like Hollywood meets all the foreign embassies.

The Great Synagogue itself revived thoughts of *The Sleeping Beauty*. It was as though somebody had held a design, for an enchanted palace, at the back of a fire, until it was liberally kippered with soot. Even the sunlight overhead was breaking its way through foggy clouds. There was something Moorish about the iron railings, in front of the building, which brought The Kardomah to mind.

But The Kardomah was the past. The present was a huge door bursting open to disgorge a crowd, revolving like sequins in a kaleidoscope. These were the women guests. Sorrel had not expected them to be in evening clothes. Their husbands, struggling with fluttering prayer shawls, came streaming out in a separate procession. Everybody was chattering like jackdaws. The men were even dressed like jackdaws. Were top hats, and soft black Homburgs, usual with dinner jackets?

It was all diamonds in daylight, more scent than Kendal Milne's ground floor, bare powdered shoulders and Arctic fox furs and Russian sables and old women in ermine. And the dresses! Full length and the new ballerina length – the beading and sequining were enough to blind you. These weren't dresses, they were *gowns*. Descendants of black-clad immigrants who'd arrived in the town with all that they owned tied up in a bundle, these wedding guests were rich and successful and they wore what they were on their backs.

Even today, despite the pain wrought in her by religious division, Sorrel loved this jostling crowd for its lack of restraint, for bringing hot excitement to a dim bit of the city that nobody had ever much wanted. These people might not want her but they were as definitely a part of Manchester as she was.

At the top of the synagogue steps, a photographer was fussing around a group of bridesmaids, in sweet-pea shades. This must be the bridal party. Sorrel's stomach lurched. She couldn't see Barney. The bridesmaids fluttered aside and there he was.

Sorrel closed her eyes but the lids might just as well have been made of glass. They had dressed Barney up, in white tie and tails, to marry a kewpie doll in a halo of virginal tulle veiling and a spangled net crinoline.

Some people pushed past Sorrel. A woman in gold brocade was saying, 'Put Enid in the Rosenthals' Daimler. She's having one of her asthma attacks.'

Sorrel opened her eyes again. Somebody called out: 'Smile, Barnet, say cheese!'

But he wasn't smiling. He was looking deadly serious. He had seen Sorrel; and there was nothing he could do about it. He was no longer her own Barney. He was just part of a Jewish wedding group. Even the children were in little dinner jackets and miniature cocktail frocks. Barney was part of a whole and Sorrel was one person, on her own, got up to look like that widow in the poster which said *Keep Death off the Road*.

'People have come from as far as Philadelphia.' It was the woman in the gold again. 'Somebody get the car keys off Danny Rosenthal. His daughter needs to lie down.'

Poor Enid only had a crush on him, thought Sorrel, and everybody's running for the smelling salts. I loved him. I still love him and he loves me; his eyes say so. He's my lover and they've turned him into ritual bloodstock.

Her thoughts were now becoming wilder and more fragmented and abrasive. Sorrel was suppressing a desire to scream and to claw her way through the happy crowd and start tearing at that fairground prize of a bride.

Barney wasn't the only person who had noticed the uninvited girl in black. Ruby Shapiro had seen her too. Whispering something in her husband's ear, Ruby descended the steps and began pushing her way towards Sorrel who was now weeping openly.

Barney's mother looked more than ever like a tiny Jewish empress in bronze and black. Sorrel remembered the night she'd climbed the fire escape, to be with Barney, and seen the black Ascot hat on the bronze satin eiderdown.

In the watery sunlight Ruby looked carefully painted and infinitely worried. She spoke quietly: 'You've not come here to make a scene?'

Sorrel shook her head. 'No scene,' she said. 'I just had to see it for myself.'

'Come here.' Ruby put her arms around Sorrel. 'Whatever have we done to you?' She was holding Sorrel close and rocking her like a child. 'Whatever have we done?'

Sorrel tried to speak but all that came out was sobs, not sense.

Ruby's voice took on assertive tones: 'One day I'll be a good friend to you, Sorrel – the best. And that's a promise. But now you have to do something for me. Go. It's the only stylish way out of this mess.'

Sorrel Starkey, who was always clay in the hands of anyone who was kind to her, did as she was asked. She'd seen what she came to see, what she needed to see. Now she knew exactly where she stood. She didn't look into any of the limousines, full of guests, that sailed triumphantly past her as she stumbled down Cheetham Hill. At that afternoon's wedding reception, the Midland Hotel would be theirs. One day she would make it her own. From now on everything had to go into her work. One day Barney and the doll creature would walk into The Midland and the head waiter would say:

'I know you can see a table left but we're keeping it for Miss Sorrel Starkey.'

The thought was only a smokescreen around pain. Tonight, that girl would be stealing what Sorrel considered to be hers. The new Mrs Shapiro would be breaking up a pair of swans who had mated for life. And how would their God of Abraham and Isaac square that with his conscience?

There was no train back to London for a good two hours. Brief thoughts of a visit to Rookswood Avenue were quickly dismissed. There would be nothing triumphant in this return and it would be impossible to call on Gander without her mother finding out. Gladys Starkey had become a ten-shilling note inside a Christmas card signed 'Yours sincerely, Mummy'.

Sorrel wondered whether she should go for a wander round Manchester. There wouldn't be a street she hadn't walked along with Barney. No, she decided that an aimless wander would be tantamount to picking sores. She would head for somewhere specific. She would go to the City Art Gallery. The pictures inside the heavily gilded Pre-Raphaelite frames, *Ophelia* and *The Last Watch of Hero*, had been friends to Sorrel long before love came into her life.

She could look at Mr Lowry's paintings too. Mickey knew the artist better than she did but, whenever he saw her, the gruff painter always tipped his trilby and said, 'And how is my little thespian?'

Would they have any of the new pictures? These days he wasn't just painting the street scenes with all his skinny-legged people in boots. Pictures of tramps and grotesques were beginning to emerge from his studio too. Even this thought was painful. Barney had been the first person to tell her of the artist's change of direction.

As Sorrel turned into Albert Square, she saw a figure who could have been one of these paintings come to life. A woman in an ankle-length black coat, with a black cloche hat pulled down over a greyish-yellow face, was walking slowly along the edge of the pavement. Cruising behind her, at the pace of a hearse, came a taxi with his *For Hire* sign switched off.

It was Magda Schiffer, the painter who was supposed never to leave her attic in Victoria Park.

'Miss Operette,' she said, recognizing Sorrel. 'You have fulfilled early promise and become very svelte.' More than ever, Magda sounded like Dennis the dachshund in *Toytown* on the wireless.

'This is the first time I've ever seen you in broad daylight,' said Sorrel.

'It is the first time, in England, I have ever taken a taxi,' replied Magda loftily. 'I have been a servant in England when I first came. Oh yes, I have emptied my fair share of chamber pots. But I have never *had* a servant in your country. The German government have finally settled my compensation for the years in Dachau so I am splashing out.'

'Where are you living?' asked Sorrel.

'Christie's Hospital.'

The significance of this did not take one second to sink in. Throughout Sorrel's Manchester childhood Christie's Hospital had only meant one thing – cancer.

'Yes. I have krebs. Sounds even nastier and more invasive in German, doesn't it?'

'They work miracles at Christie's,' said Sorrel.

'In this case they can do nothing.' Magda spoke with little short of pride. 'I have become a fiend to their morphine. I insisted on this taxi ride. Oh how I shouted. They were glad to let me go out for the afternoon, I can tell you that. I have a very short time to live. You are too young for black, Sorrel. You should experiment with a prettier palette.'

'Barney got married this afternoon.' Sorrel thought this would be enough for her old friend to understand.

Magda did. 'I tried to save you from this day, Miss Operette. What you want now?'

'I don't know. I'm going to the Art Gallery and then I thought of going into the Hidden Gem, St Mary's Mulberry Street, to pray.

'Pray?' snorted Magda. '*Pray?* There is no God. And I have a professional's word for it. The rabbi in the camp gathered us together and told us that. There is no God. Prayers don't work. You must *wish* instead. That works. Mr Walt Disney had it right. "If your heart is in your dream, no request is too extreme." '

Sorrel couldn't imagine herself abandoning the Almighty for a song from *Snow White and the Seven Dwarfs*.

'Affirmations!' said Magda.

Sorrel pricked up her ears. Perhaps there was something in it after all. Wicked Mickey was forever talking about affirmations and he always seemed to get what he wanted.

'Those Shapiros asked me to the wedding,' said Magda, 'but nobody could ever accuse me of selling out to the Bourgeoisie for a plate of smoked salmon. I never gave you a present, Sorrel. The recipe for the cheese straws hardly counts. You must decide what you want and we will wish for it together. I have no use for my dying wish. I give it to you. Don't tell me what you want. Just think it. And then we will both say *I wish . . .*'

Sorrel thought about fame and success and about everybody in Manchester knowing who she was. The thought was framed by the idea of Barney and Mickey back in her life. She tried to rub this border away but it wouldn't vanish.

'You have thought?'

Sorrel nodded.

'Together we will say it. *I wish . . .*'

'I wish.' And in that moment Sorrel knew, beyond any shadow of doubt, that every last corner of her affirmation would come true. She wanted it. She believed in it. It was going to happen.

'So much for my dying wish,' said Magda. 'It is only to be hoped that we have not made a great wickedness.' She pronounced this word with a V. 'Perhaps I should add a little homily. I am very fond of an old proverb that says: "Take what you want. Take it and pay for it." Goodbye, Miss Operette.' Magda opened the taxi door. Waving away Sorrel's offer of assistance, she began to climb, stiffly, inside it. 'Remember me kindly, some time.'

The door slammed shut. The taxi moved away from the kerb. It gathered up speed, turned down Princess Street and disappeared.

There wasn't another soul in sight. Sorrel held out her

265

arms in Albert Square, to the Town Hall, to the Gas Showrooms, to the outline of The Midland in the distance. To all of these she cried out, 'You're going to be mine.'

BOOK TWO

SORREL INTO LETTIE

1

In later life, at the height of her fame, journalists would beg Sorrel Starkey for stories of her first ten years on the stage.

'I simply learned my job,' she would say. And they had to be content with that. Sorrel was telling no less than the truth. A written account of her apprenticeship would have failed to keep even the most avid of her fans away from their ironing boards for any appreciable length of time.

For the record: late in the spring of the year Barney got married, Sorrel went back into weekly repertory. It took two years for her to become experienced enough to graduate to fortnightly. Chesterfield gave way to Colchester which was followed by a season in Perth. Eventually, she worked her way as far south as Liverpool. There they did a play every three weeks and an actress from the Playhouse had roughly the same standing, in the town, as a Liberal councillor.

During the gaps between these far-flung jobs Sorrel always returned to the Old Fire-Iron and signed on at the actresses' labour exchange in Great Marlborough Street. Judy Weatherall got married to a Guards officer at St James's, Spanish Place, and Sorrel was a bridesmaid. June Monk asked Sorrel to perform the same function for her. Fortunately that wedding clashed with a matinée so Sorrel sent a set of Pyrex ovenware instead.

The actress had little interest in real life. Everything was going into her work. When Princess Margaret renounced Group Captain Townsend, Sorrel felt like writing her a letter saying she knew how she must feel. When the princess eventually settled for Tony Armstrong-Jones, Sorrel was glad she'd kept the top on her fountain pen. The royal bride was not, after all, like herself. The princess wasn't a swan. She hadn't mated for life.

Actors often commented that whilst Sorrel was charged with sex appeal on the stage, this inner light switched off the moment the curtain fell. Sorrel viewed her inborn ability to fascinate men as simply another attribute that had to be weighed and measured and woven into performances.

During one of her spells of unemployment, only one historical event kept her awake, the crisis in Cyprus. A Turkish support group set itself up in a basement opposite the Old Fire-Iron. The mob beneath Sorrel's bedroom window was forever chanting the letters EOKA and shouting things about somebody called Makarios.

The day they hanged Ruth Ellis, Sorrel felt like shouting aloud herself. These were some of the few headlines which penetrated her cocoon of rehearsal and performance. Here was something she understood. Ruth Ellis, who shot the love of her life in a fit of blind, baffled rage, could easily have been Sorrel.

The memories which remained, from that period, were a rag-bag of oddities. When the Russians put a little dog up into space Sorrel got very worked up indeed. Dogs like company. For her, they could keep the moon if getting there involved making one small dog unhappy. Come to that, what would be the point in landing on the cold, inconstant moon?

One star, a woman she had never met, came back to haunt Sorrel. It was Gertrude Lawrence. During one of Sorrel's periods of unemployment, Shelagh Starkey and Lily Bear took her to the theatre to see *Nude with Violin* 'on paper', which meant they'd got complimentary tickets. Shelagh Starkey was just explaining that, in her view, any professional who accepted such tickets was duty-bound to dress as well and behave as appreciatively as the paying public when Lily Bear suddenly paused and said, 'God bless Gertie!

'I was standing on just this spot the night Gertie Lawrence died,' explained Lily. 'And they dimmed the lights of Shaftesbury Avenue for her. They dimmed them on Broadway too. It's never happened for anybody else.'

At that moment a neon sign, above Sorrel's head, began to make a spluttering noise. Two words had gone on the blink. They were *Noël* and *Coward*. For a moment Sorrel's heart stood still. When they were little, Mickey had always said that he was going to turn himself and Sorrel into the next Noël

Coward and Gertrude Lawrence. The quarrel in Cornucopia Mews had never been mended. She hadn't seen Mickey in many months.

Months of silence turned into years. Where could Mickey be? It was hard to believe that such a definite person had vanished without trace. At a trade showing of *Room at the Top* Sorrel bumped into the original cause of their ancient quarrel, Neil Fairweather. It was from Neil that she learned that Mickey had persuaded somebody to pay for him to go and study television production in America. Mickey was in New York.

English acting was going through great changes. When Sorrel began on the stage, young actresses wore twin-sets and pearls and hoped to be taken for ladies. Suddenly, it was as though somebody had rung a bell and yelled, 'All change to bleedin' common.'

With plays like *A Taste of Honey* and films like *Saturday Night and Sunday Morning* Sorrel should have been coming into her own. The times had moved on to match her provincial origins. The trouble was that Sorrel had already changed herself to fit in with a previous period.

'I went to an audition at Granada's offices in Golden Square,' she said to Lily Bear. 'The producer of *Coronation Street* was down from Manchester. They got me to read. I gave them my best Salford accent but they said I looked too upper class for them.'

'A red rinse.' The technicoloured old actress was studying Sorrel through narrowed eyes. 'Henna, that's what's called for. Funny I never noticed it before. By rights you should have been a redhead. The answer's perfectly simple. Dye your hair and you'll match the times.'

Lily Bear was childlike in her enthusiasm. 'Come on, let's go to the chemists in Cranbourne Street and buy a potion. I'm sure Shelagh will let us do the deed in her bathroom.'

Sorrel could not have had a better theatrical godmother. Lily Bear had not become a star by accident. She knew every trick in the book. Pennies twirled into the tops of silk stockings removed the wrinkles which suspenders had missed. False eyelashes were always stored, to curl, around a pencil. If Lily Bear chose to wear scent onstage, she always lavished it on the hem of her dress so that the aroma would sweep out into the audience. Old Lily was the perfect person to turn Sorrel Starkey into a redhead.

In Frizell's, the theatrical chemists, they greeted Miss Bear like royalty. The old Italian behind the glass display counter with its thousand sticks of Leichner greasepaint, joined in their adventure with continental pleasure. Sorrel had, he explained, two choices. A tentative water rinse or a bold dye.

'Let's go the whole hog,' said Sorrel. 'Let's have the dye.'

'And we will need a pair of rubber gloves and a bristle toothbrush,' added Lily Bear, liberally spraying herself with Frizell's sample atomizer of Mitsouko. 'You will, of course, be giving Miss Starkey professional discount. It won't be long before you'll be very proud to have her as a customer.'

Thrilled was the only word for the two actresses as, buzzing with excitement, they made their way to Shelagh Starkey's house in Bedman's Row.

'Red hair will make her look common.' Miss Starkey sounded more than ever like a senior librarian. 'Do let us think about this. Lily, you could be wrecking her whole career.'

'I could be making it too.' Lily was already swopping her suede gloves for the rubber ones. 'It won't be pantomime-dame red. It will be dark titian. She will simply look a little outrageous. Outrageous can play common; and common's the order of the day.'

Lily Bear was in full flood: 'We can't all be like you, Shelagh. We can't all be bishops' daughters. Some of us have to invent our own style. We are now going into your bathroom to weave a spell. Years ago I gave Sorrel a name. She's a good girl, she's been away, she's got experience. So now I'm handing her a look to go with the name. What Sorrel needs next is a nice showy part in the West End or the lead in a television play. All we're doing is giving Fate a bit of a nudge.'

The hair dyeing took hours and the bathroom began to reek of pungent chemical. Lily refused to be rushed. Even when the washing and the soaking and the saturating were over, she would only use the hair dryer on the lowest of heats.

'The hair's had a shock,' she explained. 'It needs wooing back into shape.'

Would it turn green? Haunted by memories of what happened in *Anne of Green Gables*, this was Sorrel's only real worry. It was plainly groundless because Shelagh Starkey kept coming in with cups of tea and a plate of biscuits and then another of little Gentleman's Relish sandwiches. Though she tutted a bit, she never actually cried out in horror.

Lily had hung a towel over the mirror. She was a woman who believed in saving everything for the grand-finale.

'Greasepaint,' said Lily suddenly. 'Shelagh, get me your makeup box. Others might worry about the effect in real life. We are creatures of the theatre. Let us see how the whole thing will look on the stage.'

Old Lil closed the bathroom curtains with a rattle and switched on the overhead light.

'Don't even think of going near that mirror, Sorrel. I never had a daughter so I'm going to pass on my own stage makeup to you. I'll only ever do it for you once. It's all a matter of tricks, little illusions. It's conjuring, really. Grace de la Motte gave the basics to me in nineteen-hundred-and-frozen-to-death but it's still as good as anything you'll meet on a stage today. Poor Grace was a martyr to gin but her makeup was a triumph of art over ruin. Shelagh, hand me a stick of Leichner number five . . .'

With all the glorious confidence of somebody who knows exactly what they're doing, Lily Bear began to apply the theatrical makeup. As she daubed and smoothed the grease-paint, the scent unlocked doors in Sorrel's mind.

The first time she had ever smelled it was on the North Pier at Blackpool when the chorus girl gave her a stick as a present. She'd thought of that, the night she'd smelled greasepaint with Barney, at Salford Hippodrome. Where was he these days? How was he? Sorrel didn't know. She had never set foot in Manchester since the day of his wedding. She had even turned down the offer of a long tour of *Goodbye Mr Chips* because it would have meant playing a week at the Manchester Palace. That kind of touring return, to her native city, had not seemed spectacular enough to feed her old promise to the Town Hall clock.

Manchester was as much in Sorrel's blood and bones as ever. When the Munich Air Disaster killed half United's football team, it was all she could do to stop herself getting on a train and going North. Sorrel knew nothing about football and cared less but she did care when newspaper reports described her Manchester as 'A town in mourning'.

'You're all eyes, child.' Lily Bear recalled her to today. 'All magnificent eyes. I'm done. Go to the mirror and look at yourself.'

Sorrel got to her feet, crossed the room, pulled back the towel and gazed at her own reflection. It was a miracle. Lily Bear had made her look how she had always felt inside.

'I match with me,' she said in wonder.

'Gypsy aristocracy.' Lily Bear spoke with great satisfaction. 'You look like gypsy aristocracy. And if that doesn't get you a big break nothing will.'

The new look brought its own problems. Photographs are vitally important to a young actress. Producers scan pictures before asking to see the performer. Sorrel was so transformed as to render her present photographs useless.

Instead of going to one of the grand old theatrical photographers, Sorrel booked a sitting with Keith Wrigley. He was one of the first of a new breed who made much of having come from the East End and of having abandoned formal studio backdrops in favour of tough, realistic locations. For the sitter, it was the difference between enduring a permanent wave and having the wind blow freely through your hair.

Keith Wrigley was young and arrogant and confidently sexy. His photographs made Sorrel look the same. He hauled her off to an amusement arcade near Oxford Street and positioned her against a slot-machine labelled *Allwin de Luxe*. The results were grainy and almost mockingly bold. Sorrel felt that, even caught off her guard, she could live up to them.

Keith Wrigley's photographs got her the audition at the Theatre Royal in Windsor. But it was her own reading of the part, for a new play, which landed Sorrel the job.

Windsor had a unique reputation in the English theatre. They didn't maintain a resident company. Being so close to London they could afford to pick and choose, and even established stars were delighted to be asked to travel down daily to rehearse a production for a fortnight and to play it for a week.

Preparing a new play at Windsor meant getting the early train from Paddington, it meant lunch by the river – their productions were hard work tricked out as a theatrical picnic. Everybody wanted to go down to Windsor because West End managements kept a close eye on what the guidebooks called 'This historic gem of a playhouse'.

'Windsor's one on its own,' enthused Lily Bear. 'It's a theatre like a maroon velvet hug. It's just to be hoped you're ready for it. It can be a springboard to much bigger things. With a new play, everybody who's anybody will be down to see whether the old goose of Windsor has laid another golden egg.'

Nine years in the best provincial repertory companies had left Sorrel well prepared for this opportunity. She had been in new plays before so she was used to the director and author changing whole pages of script as they went along. If they had asked her to learn a page of the local telephone directory, Sorrel would have been dead-letter-perfect in three quarters of an hour.

By now, she was also accustomed to standing up for herself. Another, older, actress, accustomed to longer re-hearsals and struggling with a difficult scene, pleaded for cuts. These would have deleted Sorrel's finest moment in the play.

Firmly but professionally, Sorrel dug in her heels. The scene stayed as it was. Being a successful actress has little to do with winning popularity awards from fellow members of the cast. Those scales had long since fallen from Sorrel's eyes. Vanity didn't come into it either. These days she simply saw herself as a set of professional accomplishments. They had to be honed and polished to ensure that she would give the finest possible performance. All the hard work had to look effortless, seamless – as natural as pure silk.

One worry daunted Sorrel. Would she be good enough for Shelagh Starkey and Lily Bear? This was going to be the first time they would see her on any stage. They had been endlessly kind to Sorrel over the years but they were dyed-in-the-wool professionals. Any actress who gave a performance that was merely adequate would be dismissed as *competent*.

To the outside world, this may be a perfectly respectable word. In the theatre it is a polite sneer of dismissal. Sorrel desperately craved the two older actresses' approval. She knew it was now or never. She had either got it or she hadn't. They would know at a glance.

The new play was already being spoken of, in the press, as controversial. Pinned to the theatre call board, by the stage door, was a letter from Windsor Castle. Her Majesty the Queen's private secretary regretted to say that the royal party would not be visiting the Theatre Royal that week. Older members of the cast said that, in her theatre-going days, Queen Mary would have come. Private London club theatres were full of photographs of the old martinet attending plays which had been banned for public performance by her own son's Lord Chamberlain.

Sorrel had a first-night telegram from Judy Weatherall who had left the stage and was being a wife and mother in Aberdeenshire. She also had a Medici Society greetings card from Shelagh Starkey. Nothing from Lily Bear, but Sorrel's stomach churned as she realized that Lily's must be one of the voices she could hear laughing and chattering, in anticipation, on the other side of the curtain.

'Beginners please. Beginners on stage.'

Sorrel's stage fright was so terrible that, at this moment, she would willingly have changed places with the assistant stage manager. Nine years since Salford Hippodrome. Nine years of simply learning her job. No life, no love, everything had gone into the work.

Sorrel moved from the wings onto the stage and took up her opening position by the telephone. The mirror, above the phone, was partially sprayed over so as not to dazzle the audience. Sorrel could nevertheless catch enough of her own reflection to see that the stage makeup, passed on by Lily Bear, had turned her into a semblance of a real leading lady in false eyelashes. But were the eyelashes the only thing that was false? Was Sorrel herself the real thing, the genuine item?

She could hear the musical trio, in the orchestra pit, bringing their selection from *Annie Get Your Gun* to a close. The Old Fire-Iron hadn't turned Sorrel into a Catholic but it had given her a solemn respect for St Genesius, the patron saint of actors. She offered up a quick prayer to him: Ask God to show me what to do and give me the strength to do it.

The first-night audience applauded the trio. There was a hushed pause broken by a few nervous coughs from somebody in the stalls. The curtain went up.

The first act was too slow. The second went better. When Sorrel made her exit, in Act III, it was to a vigorous round of solid applause. At the end of the play Sorrel returned to the stage to line up with the rest of the cast and they took five curtain calls.

Good, but was it good enough? People were singing on corridors as they made their way back to their dressing rooms. Sorrel was charged with adrenalin but that was always the case after a performance. These days the golden glow of an audience was her substitute for physical passion.

Sorrel sat down in front of the dressing room mirror, dabbed her face with Crowe's Cremine and began to remove her stage makeup.

From out in the corridor she could hear Lily Bear exchanging theatrical noises with somebody. No point in trying to read signs there. These backstage banalities were as automatic as bowing to an audience. Sorrel was steeling herself for something more than that. She was awaiting a considered judgement. There was a knock at the dressing room door.

'Come in.'

'My dear!' Lily Bear threw her arms around Sorrel. 'I haven't cried so much in years.'

'But it wasn't meant to be sad.'

'The play left me cold. It was you. I'd always had an instinct about you but I was still terrified you were going to be awful. Oh my little love . . .'

Happy tears were rolling down Lily's painted face. 'You weren't just good, you've got *star quality*. I never, ever, say it but you have. Wasn't she wonderful, Shelagh?'

'Excellent. And the more remarkable for having done it in a fortnight. You've picked up a couple of rather mannered tricks in the provinces. But those can soon be ironed out. You're a fine actress, Sorrel. Lily's right: you've got that little extra something. I'm very, very proud of you.'

Sorrel couldn't speak. All the years and all the stairs and all the rejection and all the suitcases cutting into her hand had been worth it. If only her mother could have seen her tonight.

'Oh, let's *all* cry,' exclaimed Lily Bear joyfully. 'What a night! I'm wrung out. Get your clothes on. I'm superstitious about champagne too soon but I do remember, from when I played here, that there's a splendid fish and chip shop in Slough. I've got my little car by the stage door.'

These plans were interrupted by another knock on the dressing room door. It was Bertha, the organizer of the Old Fire-Iron. Sorrel had not been expecting her and found herself much touched that the old woman had trailed all the way down to Windsor to support one of her members who wasn't even a Catholic.

'I didn't send you a wire, Sorrel dear.' The old woman was blinking through her thick spectacles. 'But a candle has been burning for you in St Patrick's since six o'clock. I think it can be said to have done its work. I must go back tomorrow and say thank you.'

Nobody could have looked less theatrical than Bertha. Against her, even Shelagh Starkey was very much the actress; even if it was in a self-contained, low-heeled way. Bertha wore men's shoes because they were the only ones she could get that were broad enough to fit. She looked as though she should have been running a white elephant stall or emptying tea urns, yet the news she proceeded to impart was positively dazzling.

Bertha took her time about it. 'That was a very peculiar play, Sorrel. Left one wondering whether the author wouldn't have done far better to have gone to confession. He doesn't like women, either. No, dear, nobody's going to buy this one for the West End.'

'And so say all of us,' agreed Lily Bear. Introductions had been unnecessary. Bertha might look like an owl that had fallen out of a straw nest but she knew everybody who was anybody in the theatre. This she proceeded to demonstrate.

'Somebody who used to stay at the club, as a young man, was in the bar in the interval. Dominic Savage.'

'Dominic Savage!' cried Lily Bear. 'He was going to be a great big film star until Jack Hawkins came along and did the whole thing much better. They even looked alike so there wasn't room for both of them. Dominic went in for marrying after that. Is he still with that girl with the magazine column?'

'Yes,' said Bertha. 'He was with her tonight. A worrying kind of woman. It was most odd, her face is about ten years younger than her neck.'

'He's become a television producer,' put in Shelagh Starkey who was trying to tidy the top of Sorrel's chaotic dressing table.

'ITV, the new ones with the advertisements in between.' Bertha had reached the stage of wittering on. Members of the Old Fire-Iron could all do imitations of her doing this. Three times round the houses before she got to the point.

'He was a little bit embarrassed about seeing me. It's twenty years since his rent cheque bounced. But club funds are club funds so when he offered to pay it back, tonight, I said I would only settle for cash. The wife gave me the money. They were most impressed by your performance, Sorrel, most impressed. Wanted me to bring them round to your dressing room but I wouldn't. I said you'd be bound to be seeing friends. I did tell him he could ring you, at the club, tomorrow morning.

'I hope I haven't done wrong?' Bertha began to stuff her theatre programme into an overflowing handbag which, most noticeably, contained a glass bottle of holy water in the shape of the Virgin Mary with a gold plastic halo round the stopper. 'He wants you for a television play. I know, from past experience, that some people can be very funny about lending their name to ITV. It's the leading part,' she added guile-lessly.

None of this was an act. Though Bertha knew as much as anybody else in the room about showbusiness, some divine force had kept her a Holy Innocent. Bertha simply saw actors and actresses as children and, whenever she could, she tried to do them a bit of good.

Sorrel was exploding round the room like the steel ball-bearing in the *Allwin de Luxe* machine on her new photographs. Bertha got the first hug. Only Bertha could have announced this kind of sensational news as though she was trying to push raffle tickets.

This was it! This was the magic moment. Sorrel knew she would be telling the story for the rest of her life. Why were people not being more forthcoming with their congratulations?

'Fancy you knowing Dominic too,' Bertha said to Lily Bear.

'I know him,' replied Lily in a voice which left Sorrel wondering what the old actress had just decided to keep to herself. 'Him and his wife. I used to know the pair of them quite well.'

'Congratulations, Sorrel.' Shelagh Starkey didn't smile often but when she did her smile was genuine. 'This is a wonderful opportunity.'

'It's no use,' declaimed Lily Bear, 'I cannot let opportunity be the indiarubber of conscience.' In a much more natural voice she added, 'That was a line from a pig of a play about pacifism. Oh dear, I so hate bad-mouthing people. Let me pick my words carefully. When it comes to Dominic Savage, there is one thing you must be absolutely certain to wear to rehearsals.'

'What's that?' asked Sorrel.

'It's an undergarment that's not very easy to get hold of. With Dominic around, you'll need to wear a pair of tin drawers.'

The television play was called *Beware Beryl Jones*. Set in an unspecified Black Country town, it was the story of a drab and neurotic woman who was capable of exercising great fascination over men.

Sorrel's was the title role. Actresses are notoriously bad judges of plays. They can rarely see beyond what's in it for themselves. It didn't need a tape measure to show Sorrel that Beryl's was, by far, the longest part. It offered spectacular opportunities. The character had to withstand a battery of poison pen letters. And in the last scene she had to dodge a flying brick. Rehearsals were scheduled to begin, two weeks from the day Sorrel got her script, at a boys' club in Hammersmith.

She decided to learn her part beforehand. Shelagh Starkey heard her through her lines. Shelagh was not blinded by the thrill of a first television appearance. She had often appeared on the screen herself.

'The play's a mish-mash,' she said. 'It's one of the older school of writers trying to be modern. And Dominic's hardly an angry young man.' Shelagh looked troubled. 'Old Lil can be a bit sweeping in her judgement but even I've heard tales about Dominic. Darling, do watch out for yourself.'

The biggest shock that rehearsals brought was that Sorrel found herself working with famous television faces. It felt a bit like meeting Mickey Mouse and family, in person. She would have expected these actors to be enormously secure but this was not the case. They fussed and fidgeted around their new roles as though they were searching them for leaks. With their already established reputations, every television performance had to be at least as good as their last appearance. Television had closed a lot of theatres. It could make your name overnight and break it a month later.

'Out of an audience of millions, you really only have to please about three hundred and fifty people,' said Dominic Savage. 'They're the ones who are in a position to give you your next job. The trouble is, they're constantly changing. Then there's the future to be thought about. The ten-year-old boy who's watching your performance closely today could grow up to be the dynamic young producer of the 1970s. They're getting younger every day,' he sighed.

Dominic Savage was large and muscular but he should not

have worn denim jeans. His face was handsome if rubicund and the thick black hair was streaked with silver. Sorrel couldn't take her eyes off it. She had the feeling that it was *all* silver but some of it had been dyed back to black. She felt sorry for him. He was always making self-deprecating jokes about his advancing years. It made her sad to think that women had once needed tin drawers in his presence.

He was very patient with her in rehearsals: 'Don't panic,' he would say, 'we've got time. We can get it right. But you do have to get it right, Sorrel. It's too spectacular a part for you to be able to afford to come unstuck. You won't. Don't worry. I'll see to that.'

Sorrel had one advantage over the television director – Dominic knew nothing about her. Long before he had come into her life, Sorrel had read articles about him. His wife was Nona Yates who wrote a column in a women's magazine and another one in a Sunday newspaper. She never referred to Dominic by name. Her readers simply knew him as 'The Head of the Household'.

Nona Yates's columns were a light-hearted and entertaining view of a glossy existence set in and around their house in the country. Though they were full of pen portraits of their glittering friends, Nona was a dab hand at 'the common touch'. Her readers might not entertain the Duke of Bedford to lunch but, every quarter day, she joined in their agony as her own pile of bills arrived. To hear Nona tell it, she and the Head of the Household were never further than one step away from the poorhouse. But they were always clutching a glass of champagne. Even their housekeeper had been turned into a character, with a heart of gold, who had not hesitated to offer a few words of comfort to Mrs John Profumo.

Dominic Savage was full of comically indiscreet stories about his wife's grand friends. With himself painted as very much a bit-part player, his own versions of Nona's column enlivened many a lunch break. Some days the cast ate at a Hammersmith pub called The Dove. Sorrel found this as exciting as meeting the famous faces. The Dove had been the setting for one of her favourite books, *The Water Gypsies*.

Unlike some members of the cast, Sorrel never had a drink

at lunchtime. Drink and Sorrel Starkey were a bad combination. The provinces had taught her a couple of unpleasant lessons. Glass in hand, in Chesterfield, she had screamed and shouted at an untalented actor. At a party in Perth, Sorrel had told a member of the Playgoers' Club to put her criticisms where the monkey put the nuts. Two drinks and Sorrel could not guarantee her subsequent behaviour. For years now, she had steered clear of alcohol.

On the days when they didn't eat at The Dove, the cast descended upon a workman's cafe. It was there that Dominic Savage persuaded Sorrel to try boiled eels and mashed potatoes served with a spectacular green gravy called 'liquor'.

Diarrhoea; by four o'clock that afternoon Sorrel was in the throes of the worst bout she had ever experienced. For an hour, she couldn't so much as come out of the lavatory. The doctor had to come in and minister to her on the throne. He spooned out a dose of potent opium mixture, handed Sorrel a small bottle of this same medicine and sent her home with instructions both to rest and to continue to dose herself at regular intervals.

Dominic Savage insisted on giving Sorrel the next day off. They would, he said, rehearse around her. They could tidy up other people's scenes. Having once lived at the Old Fire-Iron, he was worried that Sorrel wouldn't get a proper chance to rest.

Seeing the sense of this, Sorrel phoned Shelagh Starkey who immediately offered her the use of her spare bedroom. A car was summoned, at the television company's expense, and Sorrel was dispatched to Bedman's Row.

In the early days of ITV, television companies were making money fast and throwing it around with considerable style. The car was from Daimler Hire. Long and black, the sleek limousine was lined with pale beige wool, like the most expensive Jaeger camel coats. Sorrel felt more than a little woolly herself; the effects, no doubt, of the doctor's white poppy prescription. She felt like a jewel in a padded beige box marked *Daimler*.

Words seemed to have taken on a strange significance. As the car sped through Kensington she wondered who Ken had been? Similarly, when they got to Harrods, she felt guided to slide back the glass partition and ask the chauffeur whether he had any idea where the bridge was? The one the knight had crossed. Sorrel was well and truly zonked in Knightsbridge SW1.

It struck her that the chauffeur had taken a roundabout route but curves were suddenly nicer than straight lines and a signpost had said *Diversions*, which meant pleasant pastimes, and Sorrel was certainly enjoying herself. Unscrewing the top from the medicine bottle, she took a good deep swig – at least an hour sooner than she was meant to do.

The sweet mixture blasted her halfway to Xanadu. She remembered that Thomas de Quincey was said to have eaten opium in a basement off John Dalton Street in Manchester. London street signs began to take on a curious fascination. At Hyde Park Corner, the SW1 district gave way to London W1. Sorrel found herself wondering what had happened to all the departed S's.

Before she could weep for them, Sorrel found herself raised to a new plateau of consciousness where she could suddenly see herself as others saw her. As the car passed Green Park underground she leaned forward and again slid back the dividing partition.

'Guess what?' she said to the driver. 'I'm a bloody lucky woman.'

'Of course you are, miss.' He sounded paid to say it.

'And I didn't know it,' said Sorrel. 'I just thought I'd tell you.'

She looked at the doctor's little bottle with respect. It contained a magic mixture. She wondered whether – when this was finished – she could get hold of some more. Just occasionally, it might be interesting to take a swig and have a look at herself.

Yes, she was a bloody lucky woman, there was no denying it. The lonely, aching place inside had vanished. Was that the prospect of success or was it the doctor's mixture? The night before her RADA audition – the time she got drunk at Mickey's flat in Heraldic Mansions – alcohol had seemed to offer the same solution.

Was this bottle her friend or her enemy? There was only one way to find out. Sorrel took another swig.

'I'm sure you must have drunk too much of it.' Shelagh Starkey was struggling into her raincoat. 'You came through that front door like Brenda Dean Paul.'

'Who's she?' Sorrel had just awoken from a very troubled sleep where she had dreamed the television cameras were ready to roll when all of the words of her script went marching out of her head like toy soldiers. 'Who was Brenda Dean Paul?'

'They said she wasn't even popular in Holloway,' grunted Shelagh as she pulled on one of her Clark's fur-lined bootees. She was getting ready to walk round the corner and give her performance at the Arts Theatre Club. 'Brenda began as the most beautiful girl in London and ended up scrounging fivers at stage doors. That's what drugs do for you,' she added with grim satisfaction.

'This was prescribed,' said Sorrel indignantly. 'I've got to take some more.'

'You'd be better off with a raw egg beaten up in milk.'

'Oh no.' Sorrel was shocked. 'I have to have *nil by mouth*, he said so. Nothing but my mixture. Later on, I can have boiled water. Where's my little bottle?'

'I was tempted to put it down the lavatory pan. It's on the kitchen draining board. I have to dash or I'll be late for the half. Promise me you won't overdo that stuff. How's your stomach now?'

'It feels as though it's churning behind a curtain.'

'I'll come straight home just as soon as our curtain is down.' Grabbing a stubby umbrella, Shelagh treated Sorrel to a quick kiss and a worried glance, and headed for the front door.

Sorrel drifted into the kitchen. Her hostess might disapprove of the doctor's prescription but this had not stopped her taking the trouble to leave a spoon by the green glass bottle on the draining board.

This kindness acted as a brake on reckless Sorrel and she only took a very little more than the prescribed amount. Once again she felt herself suffused by a warm, loving glow. This stuff was like good audiences inside a bottle. Sorrel floated back upstairs and turned on the bathwater.

The sitting room was opposite the bathroom. She wanted something to read. Nothing heavy; perhaps a big book with pictures. Her eyes lighted on a volume called *Bitter-Sweet Decade*. She pulled the book down and opened it. It was just the sort of thing she had in mind.

Page after page of amazingly retouched photographs of pre-war stars of revue and musical comedy. She decided against taking the book into the bathroom. She was feeling a bit woozy, she wouldn't want to drop it in the water. Anyway, steam might play havoc with the glossy pages. The book would be a treat for afterwards.

The bathwater felt wonderful. It felt like somebody she loved putting their arms around her. No, several people she loved. Not lovers, friends. There was a great deal to be said for good friends.

As Sorrel got out of the bath and began to dry herself she was feeling very-nicely-thank-you. She fastened a large white Turkish towelling sheet around herself. There would be no need for a dressing gown. Shelagh had left the central heating on. Come to that, it was a bit too hot.

Sorrel went downstairs to fathom the workings of the radiators. As she reached the hall somebody began to ring the doorbell.

'Who is it?' she called out.

'Delivery man. Flowers,' came the muffled reply.

Flowers? At this hour? Cautiously, Sorrel opened the door onto the gaslit alleyway. The scent of roses was overpowering. There must have been dozens of them. Red roses in yards of shining cellophane.

The bouquet was lowered to reveal the delivery man's face. It was Dominic Savage.

Sorrel crossed her hands, involuntarily, over her bare shoulders.

'You'll get your death,' he said. 'Aren't you going to invite me in?'

'Yes of course . . .' Sorrel replied hastily. She wasn't

feeling 'of course'. Her head might be poppy-hazed but that couldn't quite dim out a small alarm bell. Tin drawers? She was wearing none at all. What would her heroine, Gertrude Lawrence, have done?

'You will have to take me as you find me,' she said airily. It didn't sound very Mayfair but, at least, it would get him through the door and give her the chance to reach for an old coat.

As she turned, she caught sight of herself in the hall mirror. The bath had left her glowing. The white towelling showed off her skin very well. Where it cut across the curve of her breasts they looked high and firm. Leading ladies did not wear old coats and Sorrel was supposed to be a leading lady. She decided to brazen it out.

'Come up to the sitting room,' she said. 'I'll fix you a drink. Thank you very much for these, they're beautiful. Wherever did you manage to get flowers so late?'

'The Ritz.' The stairs were steep and Dominic Savage was panting a little. 'I love The Ritz. They treat you as though you are five years old and an only child. The porter can generally manage to find anything at a price.'

At a price? Was that ominous? No, of course it wasn't. The stairs had nearly finished the poor old thing off.

'Whisky?' asked Sorrel. Under these circumstances, she had no qualms about raiding Shelagh's decanters. Her namesake would understand and the whisky could be replaced.

'Whisky, straight, no ice, would be lovely.'

Sometimes Dominic's theatrical air reminded Sorrel of a homosexual. The resemblance became even more striking as he began to turn the pages of *Bitter-Sweet Decade* and sing the praises of forgotten stars.

'Nobody could come down a staircase like Alice Delysia,' he said. 'And she had another amazing ability. Alice could look out into the audience and you would be absolutely convinced she was only seeing you. Dietrich can do the same thing. It's as though they know what's in your heart and want to sympathize.

'Sometimes I think you've got that quality, Sorrel.' His

287

arms went around her waist. 'Forget that drink of mine. I want to speak to you very truthfully. Some actresses have it and some haven't. It's that little extra something which seems to make the lights shine more brightly, when nobody's turned them up. It doesn't matter what they're wearing . . .' Slowly, skilfully, he was unfastening her towel.

Sorrel smacked him hard across the face. The towel was really slipping and she turned away to adjust it. As she turned back he was grinning like a schoolboy.

'At least I got a glimpse.' Dominic held up his hand authoritatively. 'You have great style, Sorrel. Very considerable poise. Don't say anything either of us would find hard to live with. I apologize. I'm sorry. And I'll let you in on a shabby secret. I very much doubt whether I could have risen to the occasion.' He sighed and looked tired. 'At one time that sort of thing was almost expected of me. I was just trying to live up to a faded reputation. Shall we try and see the funny side of it?'

Sorrel handed him the whisky and said, 'I suppose we'd better.'

Beware Beryl Jones was her big opportunity and the poor old thing had only seen slightly less than the Lord Chamberlain would have allowed Phyllis Dixie to unveil in *Peek-a-Boo* at the Chelsea Palace. Nevertheless, she took a brown travelling rug off the back of Shelagh's sofa and draped it around herself. Better to look like Gander in the middle of an air raid than have the warning bell ring for round two.

Dominic Savage downed the whisky in one straight gulp. 'You mustn't blame me for trying,' he said as he headed for the door. 'It was meant as a compliment. Get some sleep. Get well and we'll see you the day after tomorrow.'

'No,' said Sorrel. 'I'll be back in the morning.' Twenty-four hours would be plenty of time for him to replace her. She was taking no chances.

At the front door Dominic turned and said, 'Tomorrow then, but don't come in until twelve. You're a good little thing, Sorrel. And I meant what I said about your work. Goodnight.'

After he'd gone, Sorrel went back upstairs. *Bitter-Sweet Decade* was where Dominic had left it, on the sofa. Sorrel began to turn the pages. Should she be feeling more than anger mixed with amusement? If she should she didn't care. She knew one thing, she was rattled enough to feel like a drink. And that, for Sorrel, was unusual. She reached for the whisky bottle and a clean glass.

As the alcohol glugged into the tumbler, Sorrel's attention was caught by an illustration of a strikingly beautiful, half-naked girl who was wrapped defiantly in the stars and stripes of the American flag. The caption underneath read: *Brenda Dean Paul: Society beauty whose brief stage career was wrecked by drink and drugs.*

Who did the girl remind her of? Sorrel looked again and closed the book. Swap the stars and stripes for a bath towel and she could have been looking at herself.

'Let's see how well *I* can walk down a staircase,' she said aloud.

She carried her whisky with her. When she got to the kitchen she poured it down the sink. Taking the bottle of medicine from the draining board, Sorrel emptied it after the whisky. Bottled audience was too dangerous a potion.

Again Sorrel spoke aloud. 'Thank you, Brenda Dean Paul,' she said.

'These flowers are fresh enough –' Shelagh Starkey was wrinkling up her nose – 'but they have a stale odour about them. It's as though somebody went mad and sprayed them with scent, for extra effect.'

It was the following morning. Though Sorrel had explained the arrival of the bouquet, she had made no mention of the favours Dominic Savage had expected in return. It took all of Sorrel's self-control to stop herself from moaning, out loud when she remembered how guilelessly she had opened the front door, in an artfully draped bath towel and a drug-induced glow.

The doctor's mixture had worked but Shelagh was insisting that Sorrel stay on, with her, until the play was safely tele-recorded.

'You only get one of these chances in a career,' she said. 'This is no time to be sleeping on a truckle iron bedstead. If you make a success, you'll need a better address than the Old Fire-Iron. It's nothing to do with snobbery, it's common sense. You haven't got an agent so you'll need every dodge going to beat up your own price. There comes a point in a career when the Old Fire-Iron smacks of failure.'

Whilst Sorrel saw the sense of this, it also saddened her. Where else in the world but the Old Fire-Iron would she have learned intricate scandals about Yeats and Lady Gregory? Where else would she have met old Miss Cathcart who hadn't worked since the last tour of *Ladies' Night in a Turkish Bath*, yet – brushing aside the complication of a wooden leg – had not given up hopes of facing another audience? How could you just leave behind people who were actually praying for you to have a success in *Beware Beryl Jones*?

When Sorrel got to rehearsal everybody seemed to be uniting to help her. The moment she arrived Dominic stopped work on the sequence they were running through and went straight into the big scene with Beryl Jones and the psychiatrist in the mental hospital.

Dominic's behaviour was at its most impeccably professional. Instead of forcing his view on Sorrel, he encouraged the actress to dig within herself and find the right notes for the character out of experiences from her own past. Dominic made Sorrel better at being herself.

By the end of the day, when the scene was three times the thing they had begun with, Sorrel felt like throwing her arms around the director. Common sense prevailed. 'Thank you, Dominic,' she said. 'You did that, not me.'

He was smiling at her. 'We both did it. I hope you put those wretched flowers where they belong, in the dustbin. Coming for a drink?'

They walked down to The Dove, where they carried their drinks out onto the little stone wharf of a terrace which overlooked the river. Sorrel was sticking to tonic water. As usual, she automatically read every word on the label of the bottle.

'What's Indian quinine?' she asked.

'Something bitter and nasty,' said Dominic. 'I told my wife

about last night's little nonsense. I hoped you wouldn't mind, but it was on my conscience.'

Sorrel was watching some sparrows on the wall. 'All I hope is she doesn't go putting it in one of her columns.'

'But she *should* be writing about you.' Dominic was all advising eagerness. 'That's why she wants to meet you. It would be good for you and good for the play too.'

'Didn't she mind about your making a pass?' Sorrel was startled.

'We're not like that.' Dominic had found a bit of old pie crust on a stone shelf. He was crumbling it up and throwing it to the sparrows. 'She just reminded me that I was a red-rose cutie, half as old as time, and suggested I bring you down for dinner, tomorrow night.'

'How would I get back?' Sorrel knew that their famous house was somewhere beyond Dorking.

'You'd stay the night. Nobody ever complained, not even Gertie Lawrence; though, God knows, she could be a Grand Duchess when she wanted to be.'

'Would it be the same bed she slept in?' Sorrel didn't care if she did sound gauche.

'If you wanted it to be. That could certainly be arranged.'

'Then I'd love to come.' If only Mickey was around to tell. The bed Gertie Lawrence slept in, and without his help!

'That's settled then.'

Dominic flung down the largest crumb of all. A huge seagull which had been all the while waiting, cold-eyed on the wall, swooped down and seized it.

2

Surrey struck Sorrel as the countryside in a panty-girdle. It was so controlled. All the fences looked as though they'd had at least two coats of gloss paint and every blade of grass seemed counted. They were in Dominic's blue Jaguar on the road between Dorking and Whelper Green. Even farm labourers' cottages had been fancied up to look like something on a cross-stitch sampler. They were obviously in the hands of commuters. Where were the real farm labourers? Had they been shunted onto some hidden council estate?

'Diana Dors was looking at a house down here last week.' The sun had nearly set and Dominic was turning down a side road dense with dark green rhododendrons.

'I think Diana Dors's work is vastly underrated.' Sorrel was wondering whether she had brought the right clothes for an overnight visit.

'She called in to see Nona.' Dominic slowed the car and then swung, sharp right, into a tarmacadam drive.

No lodge but this was definitely a proper drive. Oh dear, say they changed for dinner? Would the reduced-price Susan Small dress be up to it?

As if reading her mind Dominic said, 'It's not Blenheim, you know.'

Sorrel did know. All Nona Yates's readers knew. In her column, the journalist had described the house as 'Not Blenheim' so often that her public had come to take this for modesty. The car rounded a bend. Nona had spoken no less than the truth. The house was not Blenheim. It was a Victorian rectory tricked out to look Georgian. It was still a very far cry from Rookswood Avenue. Sorrel knew posh when she saw it. With its white-porticoed front door, with gloomy lead urns either side of it, this was definitely posh.

'Can you let yourself out?' Dominic reached over and grabbed Sorrel's bag from the back seat. 'We don't change for dinner. I hope you don't mind being one of the family? We generally have our baths and then come down in dressing gowns.'

Sorrel's heart sank. She had borrowed Shelagh Starkey's housecoat for the occasion. It was pale blue with a long zip fastener and very sensible.

Oh well, she thought, I'll scrub the face to shining and then pile on a load of mascara. Sorrel noticed that the house was surrounded by morbid elm trees. The autumn wind was rattling the empty nests of magpies who had fled to more salubrious places.

'Soon be dark,' said Dominic. 'Let's go in.'

Before they reached the front door, it was opened by a plump housekeeper in a short white cotton coat, like Dr Kildare's, and a black skirt. She had thick pebble glasses and an unkind expression.

'This is Miss Starkey,' said Dominic.

The woman took Sorrel's overnight case from him and the actress thanked God that she had washed her hairbrush. This was definitely the kind of household where somebody would unpack your bag. Being in plays was socially useful. Plays taught you what to expect.

'You'll be the *Daily Express*,' said the woman, nastily.

Sorrel, at sea, detected a whiff of gin on the housekeeper's breath.

'In the morning,' said the housekeeper almost accusingly. 'You will want the *Daily Express*.'

'Yes, please.' It had been a perceptive guess. The newspaper was going through a period of carrying the best theatrical and fashion news and was indeed Sorrel's current favourite.

'I'm never wrong,' said the woman with unpleasant satisfaction. 'We only give MPs and editors the full selection. She's burning scent again,' she added, darkly, to her master.

The pickled-pine panelled doors, in the hall, must have been a decorator's addition. They were older than the house. Dominic flung one of them open to reveal a haggard woman, in a lemon and gold kimono, holding a night-light in one hand and a china Buddha in the other.

'I can't get this fucking thing to work,' she said.

In that first glimpse of Nona Yates, Sorrel experienced true understanding of the expression 'a faded blonde'.

'It's perfectly simple,' said Dominic, 'you rub the essence on his stomach, light the candle, put him on top and the room gets flooded with the scent of roses.'

'You do it,' said Nona, thrusting the items at him. 'You must be Sorrel.'

'How d'you do,' said Sorrel. It was as though Nona Yates was trying to prove who was boss in the house. But Nona was frightened of her husband, Sorrel could tell that.

'There you are.' Dominic placed the china figure over the flame. 'Why you want to stink the house out like a Cairo brothel is beyond me.'

'It was you who brought the Attar of Roses home.' Nona sniffled appreciatively. 'Lovely. Don't you agree it's too lovely, Sorrel?'

Sorrel was actually thinking that Nona must have had a couple already and that the columnist had decided to act a bit famous but unspoiled for her. She filed her hostess's performance away in her mind. One day she might revive it on a stage. The smell of roses, which drifted across the room, was exactly the same as the nightmare bouquet. So he *had* scented them.

'Porrit's delivered the gin,' announced Nona.

'Sorrel doesn't touch the hard stuff.' Dominic was already at the drinks tray, clanking bottles around.

'How sensible,' said his wife. 'Of course, I shouldn't drink. Not if I want the lift to last.'

Sorrel remembered that Bertha, at Windsor, had described Nona as a woman whose face was younger than her neck. As Nona moved towards a table lamp, Sorrel saw that the skin had been stretched tightly, over the cheekbones, and that Nona's eyes were unnaturally wide open. She resembled a pale watercolour of a pantomime horse.

'Have a look at your future, Sorrel.' Nona spoke defiantly. 'We all submit to the surgeon's knife in the end. God knows I always said I wouldn't. Then the morning dawned when I couldn't stand the mirror any longer and off I trotted to Harley Street. Would you like to see my scars?'

'Yes please.' Sorrel was a bit ashamed to find she was so fascinated by the idea of a face lift.

'Will you for fuck's sake stop it!' Dominic was shouting at his wife. 'What's the point of creating an illusion and then handing everybody a map? It turns my stomach.'

'Dominic is not beyond a few little artifices of his own,' smiled Nona. 'I'll show you to your room. Bring your drink with you. After all that rehearsing, I'm sure you'd love a bath.'

The guest room was very well thought out. 'I'll give you a tip.' Nona was proving to be a much nicer woman when her husband wasn't around. 'When you get a house of your own, and you come to do a guest room, spend a night in it yourself. That way, you can be absolutely certain that nothing is missing.'

Nothing was missing; from the choice between an extra lambswool blanket and an electric one to Floris essence in the adjoining bathroom.

Sorrel lay in the water chewing on an almond biscuit from a tin she had found by her bedside. What if she did spoil her dinner? This was living. This was luxury – though she could have wished her hosts were a little less fractious. Was it steam in the pipes she could hear or were their voices really raised, in rumbling argument, somewhere along the corridor? Shelagh Starkey's dressing gown was going to look a bit prim in the middle of this living page from *House and Garden*. There was even a carved blackamoor in the bathroom with a spotted mother-of-pearl waistcoat.

Sorrel suddenly remembered the navy and white spotted foulard scarf at the bottom of her own overnight bag. With that tied in the neck of the dressing gown she wouldn't look prim, she would look *tailored*. This caused her to lavish the scented bathwater over her skin with contentment. Sorrel was one of those actresses to whom clothes are the best mood-changing drug in the world.

Dinner was clear soup followed by roast saddle of lamb. Everything went without a hitch until they came to the new potatoes. These appeared over Sorrel's left shoulder, proffered by the housekeeper, in a china dish which was wrapped in a napkin. Sorrel had never done a dining room scene in a play so she was unfamiliar with the routine. Instead of reaching for the silver spoon she grabbed for the whole tureen. It was boiling hot. Sorrel let out a squawk.

'You'll find the spoon easier,' said Nona and added, in a surprisingly human voice, 'I once did exactly the same thing, at Lady Cunard's, when I was still in the chorus.'

'You were on the stage?' asked Sorrel in amazement and immediately stopped caring what the housekeeper thought of her.

'I was one of The Exquisite Eight in a revue at The Apollo. You're so lucky to have it all in front of you.'

It seemed to be accepted that Sorrel was a girl with a future. And the dining room was soon ringing with laughter at the kind of wicked stories of the famous that Nona would never have dared turn into print.

'Coffee should be through in the other room, by now,' announced the columnist. 'If you'd excuse me for a moment, I have to give Mrs Bidders her orders for tomorrow.'

In the drawing room, Sorrel walked across to look at a Dutch flower painting. Nona was always writing about it. Sheila had recently come across a piece by her hostess at the hairdresser's, where she said that she gazed at the picture instead of taking tranquillizers. Nona had claimed that she could hardly wait for the right time of year for all the flowers to be out so that she could make a living reproduction, in a vase.

Sorrel was just thinking, She'd wait a long time for poppies to be in bloom with chrysanthemums, when Dominic pounced.

'Your cravat exactly matches my dressing gown,' he said. As he pressed Sorrel closely to him, she became aware that he had not been totally truthful with her. Dominic Savage was more than capable of rising to the occasion. This was awful. And in Shelagh Starkey's dressing gown too!

'No, Dominic,' she said.

'No, Dominic,' he mimicked. 'Why don't you slap my face again? I quite enjoyed that. I'll always take my pleasure with a bit of pain if I have to.' His arms were round her like a vice. 'Is that what you like? Biting? Scratching? Want me to beg for it?'

Sorrel was panicked. This boozy creature was speaking matter-of-factly about deeper waters than she had ever fathomed. There had been no man in Sorrel's life since Barney. Nothing that had gone beyond holding hands and the odd kiss on the front doorstep. In her own mind Sorrel was spoken for. When male friends had shown signs of turning into ardent admirers she had always sent them packing.

'You're on my territory now.' There were little whiskers in a crack where Dominic had neglected to shave the corner of his mouth closely enough. 'You can't get rid of me this time.'

'I could tell your wife.' Why was he looking in the mirror? Sorrel was almost sure Dominic Savage was wearing something, under the dressing gown, to flatten his stomach. It didn't extend to lower down. She already knew that. Dear God, if he got what he wanted, would he keep this garment on or would he remove it?

'*No*,' she said and ran to the other side of the room.

'You like playing at rape, do you?'

'It wouldn't be playing. It would be the real thing.'

The drawing room door opened and Nona came in. She was ripping cellophane off a box of crystallized fruits.

'Dom? Could you be a love and go back and talk to her about logs?'

Nona reached over and put a friendly arm around Sorrel. 'Everything all right?'

'No,' said Sorrel. 'I mean . . .' It had all been too much. Least said soonest mended. Only she didn't say anything. Tears took over.

'There,' said Nona comfortingly. 'Everything's fine. I know. It's all right. I know.'

'How could you know?' sobbed Sorrel.

'Because I saw. That's a most unusual mirror. It's two-way. I saw everything from the dining room. It's Dominic's turn now. He's in there watching.'

Nona's hand went to the zipper on Sorrel's dressing gown. Before the girl realized what was happening the older woman had slid it down and was sliding her fingers against one of Sorrel's breasts.

'No. No, no, no, no, no . . .' Sorrel was handing Nona the

297

sort of clawing and kicking which Dominic had craved. 'A lesbian's the last thing I'd have taken you for.'

'I'm not a lesbian.' It was a cry of terrible desperation. 'I just love him. And I'd do anything to keep him. Anything at all.' Now it was Nona sobbing. Sorrel had drawn blood at the side of her mouth. 'If you're what he wants, then you're what he gets.'

'Oh does he? See this?' Sorrel was making stabbing motions towards her own lips. 'That's my tongue. And it talks. Get in here, you dirty bastard,' she yelled at the mirror.

'I'm not a lesbian,' repeated Nona brokenly. 'I'm just the kind of woman who gets them a bad name. It's not me, it's Dominic. He likes watching things like that.'

The door opened and in he walked.

'Lay one finger on me,' said Sorrel. 'Just one. And this story will be round the West End quicker than you can say *News of the World*.'

'You wouldn't.' There was still calculation in the way the man was watching her.

'Try me.' Sorrel's iron inflection left neither Dominic nor his wife in any doubt.

'It's two reputations, Dominic,' said Nona quietly. 'Yours and mine.'

'OK.' Dominic spoke with decision. 'It was a mistake. I regret it. It's over.' He took a cigarette from a silver box and lit it. 'Just as a matter of interest, why wouldn't you? Am I all that unattractive?'

'Take a look at yourself in your own mucky mirror, Dominic.' Sorrel knew that the balance of power had shifted in her favour. 'Take a good long look. You are *old*.'

'*I'm* allowed to say that.' His voice was deadly quiet. 'You aren't. I presume you'll be wanting a taxi to the station? If one word of this gets out I'll have you labelled the biggest prick-teaser in England. *Old*, eh? It's too late to fire you, but that's the word you'll pay for.'

Sorrel did not want to watch herself in *Beware Beryl Jones*. She did not want to be reminded of the last ten days of rehearsal. They had been painful.

As the recording date had grown daily nearer, Dominic Savage had developed the habit of talking to himself under his breath.

'Good,' he would mutter, as a performer did a scene to his liking. 'Splendid, but save the energy for the end.' 'Exactly what I was after.' All of these were for the benefit of the supporting cast.

When it came to Sorrel it was a muttered case of 'She did it better yesterday' and 'Where's her timing gone?' And '*Oh my God!*' If he was trying to throw her he was succeeding.

This method of kicking Sorrel's confidence from underneath her was as subtle as it was invidious. Dominic blamed only himself. In mutters and sighs he let the whole rehearsal room know that if Sorrel was wrong for the part, if she wasn't experienced enough, it was he who should have seen it sooner. This left Sorrel feeling about as valuable as a pile of spare change.

Whenever he had to give her direction, Dominic had stopped looking Sorrel in the eye. She was only treated to his direct gaze when he used one word.

That word was *old*.

Three times a day he would contrive to work it into the conversation like a dagger. He also took to humming the Maurice Chevalier song 'I'm Glad I'm Not Young Any More'.

This had been going on for several days when the author turned up, at rehearsals, looking worried.

'These camera changes are not my idea,' he said to Sorrel.

'What camera changes?'

The author looked guiltily towards the director and replied, 'I shouldn't have mentioned them. Don't you worry your head about it. Just get on with the acting.'

It wasn't as easy as that. An actress deals in make-believe. Dominic made it only too clear that he had stopped believing in the reality that Sorrel was attempting to create. It would have been much harder to do this to her in the theatre. She knew where she was on a stage. In television Sorrel needed help. You don't get much assistance from a man who is looking for opportunities to stab you with one of your own unguarded words.

They moved from the rehearsal room into the television studios, which weren't far from Wembley Stadium. Sorrel began to have nightmares about Christians and lions and booing crowds and a thumb being held downwards.

At this juncture, the play ceased to belong to the actors. It had now become the property of studio technicians whose job it was to get *Beware Beryl Jones* onto the screen. Some of the effects they were attempting struck Sorrel as distinctly odd. One afternoon they spent two hours lining up a tracking-shot of her *feet*.

On the day of the dress rehearsal the makeup girl said to Sorrel, 'We'll do your face but it doesn't really matter.'

Doesn't really matter? Sorrel had taken this to be in the cause of the new style of television 'reality'. But if this was the case, why were other members of the cast being given the full treatment? Her insecurities grew and these added nothing to the finished performance.

As she watched the transmission, with Lily Bear, she saw that reality had nothing to do with it. She had been a victim of something infinitely more old-fashioned – revenge.

Beryl Jones may have been the leading character but you never really got to see her face. Dominic had used the luxury of five television cameras to get reaction shots of everybody else. It was no longer a play about Beryl Jones. Sorrel did all the talking, all the hard work, while other people got the big close-ups. Devious camera-work had turned it into the story of Beryl's effect on everybody else.

They were watching the play in Lily Bear's flat. At the first advertising break Lily let out a low whistle and poured herself a stiff gin and tonic. By this time Sorrel was marching up and down the room and weeping with rage.

'I'm awful, terrible. Why didn't Dominic tell me what he was doing? I should have been giving something like a radio performance. He was the one who encouraged me to rant and rave. With five cameras rolling around, how could I be expected to know what was happening?'

The television screen was now filled with a shot of a girl coyly revealing her armpit. A heavenly choir was singing:

'Mum Rollette rolls on
You easily apply it.
Mum Rollette . . .'

Sorrel switched off the television set and stormed, 'I'm the one who stinks.'

'We don't do that,' said Lily Bear, rising to her feet and moving across the room to switch the set back on. 'We sit and we watch and we learn from our own mistakes. And when it's over Aunt Lil's going to ask you a few questions and give you a penny-lecture you'll never forget.'

The next hour was one of the longest of Sorrel's life. She watched and she winced and shuddered and turned her head away from the screen, only to be drawn back in awful fascination. To think she'd gone to the trouble of learning this mile-long part. For all you saw of Beryl, she might just as well have carried the script in her hand. The final credits began to roll. Sorrel hoped against hope that Dominic would have gone the whole hog and erased her name. No. There it was. Just like a name on a gravestone.

Where did she go from here? This was the performance which had been meant to get her a good agent. She couldn't imagine anyone wanting to touch her with a barge pole. This had been the point in her career where she had intended to put her photograph in *Spotlight*, the actors' casting directory. Any advertisement which drew attention to tonight's showing would be tantamount to professional suicide.

She remembered what Dominic had said about actors only having to impress three hundred and fifty people. Dear God, how many of these would have watched her performance?

'Now you can switch it off,' said Lily. 'You don't have to tell me what happened. I can guess. You went down to Dorking and didn't fancy what that pretty pair had got in mind.'

'I promised I wouldn't tell anybody,' said Sorrel. She was as panicked as she'd been on the day Charles Courtney ordered her out of Salford Hippodrome. On that occasion she'd wondered whether she'd ever work again. But this was worse. It was so public that Sorrel actually felt naked and exposed.

'May I have a drink?' she asked.

'No, Sorrel. I don't like you when you've had a drink, and that's the truth.' Lily Bear looked thoughtful. 'It must be all of thirty years since the Savages invited me away for the weekend and tried to pull the same stunt. Go on, Sorrel, have a glass of sherry if you must. But some people in this business shouldn't and you're one of them. It alters you.'

Sorrel poured a minute quantity of sherry, very carefully, into a glass. 'I didn't drink when I went to Dorking. And I didn't *do* anything, Lil.'

'I can tell that by what we've just seen on the screen. Do they still insinuate themselves through the steam whilst you're trying to have a bath? I didn't do anything either but your old auntie contrived to leave a pleasant taste behind.

'Listen to me, Sorrel. If somebody makes a pass – and you don't want to do anything about it – you must summon up all of your acting skills. First of all, you must assure them that they've made your day. Treat it as a huge compliment. Then you have to say that you'll probably regret it to your dying moment but you simply cannot respond. Say you're working hard at being faithful, claim you're having a period, claim you're having the clap if you must; but be firm. I'm talking about people who could be important to your career. Ever afterwards, you must make it seem to them that you've missed out on one of life's great joys.'

'Then they'd start again,' said Sorrel.

'That's when you tell them that they have turned into one of your great fantasies. And that you don't want to spoil it with reality.'

Sorrel looked at Lily Bear with new admiration. As the old actress had been talking, Sorrel had caught glimpses of what must once have been great beauty. Whilst old Lil was still in this mood, and she had the chance, Sorrel felt the need to question her further.

'Lil? What if they don't make a pass and you *do* want to do something about it?'

'Oh, my little love.' Lil's voice tinkled with affectionate laughter. 'That one's very easy. You just tell them it's your *birthday*.'

Sorrel looked gloomy. 'Today's the day my career went down the Swanee.'

Lil assumed a practical face. 'We simply have to turn your luck around. Where's my blue address book? Whilst I was up in Manchester, doing my own television thing, I met a most remarkable young man. He's written a new soap opera called *Angel Dwellings*. They wanted me for it but I've already promised to go to Stratford East for that clever Miss Littlewood. Thank you, dear.' Sorrel had handed Lily the address book.

She continued, 'There are bound to be lots of parts in this new thing. I can't think why I didn't mention you to Mickey before.'

Sorrel, who had been slumping in her chair, sat bolt upright.

'Mickey *who*?'

'Grimshaw. Odd eyes and more energy than a benzedrine tablet. We became instant friends. He's a young man who's going places. I've got his home number here . . .'

'You mustn't ring it,' said Sorrel. Her head was in a whirl. In her own mind Mickey was filed under 'America'. Lily Bear had now revealed him as one of those three hundred and fifty people who mattered. Sorrel and Mickey were still at outs. This needed thought.

'Mick, my little love?' Lily Bear was already breathing glamour down the telephone. It is an ageless commodity and she had it by the yard.

'No I haven't changed my mind but I've had an interesting thought. Do you, by any chance, know of a clever young actress called Sorrel Starkey?' Lily looked surprised and then delighted and said, 'Well there's a turn-up for the book!'

Lily turned importantly to Sorrel. 'According to young Mr Grimshaw, this telephone call is an Act of God.'

'He doesn't believe in God.' Sorrel spoke indignantly. But the excitement that Mickey had always been able to conjure up was fizzing back into her life.

'He does now,' said Lily, holding out a receiver that was quacking like the soundtrack of a cartoon. 'He wants to know why the hell you aren't in *Spotlight*? You're the one person on earth he needs to find. Here . . .' She handed Sorrel the telephone.

'Hello,' said Sorrel in a blank voice which was giving nothing away.

'Hello yourself. I've just seen your left elbow in the world's worst television play.' Mick's voice was brimming with mischief and energy. 'Even those awful camera tricks couldn't quite wipe you out. I've been searching everywhere for you. I was just going to try your mother again. Come home, Sorrel Starkey. Manchester has need of you.'

3

For nine years Sorrel had been planning her return to Manchester. She had thought about it in draughty provincial dressing rooms and on interminable Sunday train calls. She had dreamed about it in uncomfortable beds in frowsy theatrical digs. She had the whole itinerary off pat, in her head, like a highly polished tap-dancing routine.

She would buy a first-class ticket which would entitle her to sit in the Blue Bar under one of the arches of the Great Hall at Euston Station. As she strolled down Platform 5, a porter would carry her luggage onto the train. As the engine pulled the carriages to the North she intended to count off the halts: Watford, Rugby Midland, Stoke-on-Trent . . . like a personal version of the Stations of the Cross.

This wasn't what happened at all. The line between Euston and London Road was in the process of being electrified. Trains were going instead from St Pancras to Manchester Central. Only two details of the production in Sorrel's mind were fulfilled. The waiter, in the dining car, ladled soup from a big silver tureen and when she got to Manchester there was a lot of smoke and steam.

As she passed through the barrier, grit kept winking in and out of one eye so that her first glimpse of a dear, infuriating, familiar figure was like one of those music-hall dance routines – where everything gets speeded up by a flickering light. Mickey was sitting, unconcernedly, in a very white raincoat on a very grubby porter's trailer. He was replete with an American crew cut and at least three yards of electric-blue woollen scarf wound impatiently round his neck. More than ever, in a world where men were still dressed in sombre peahen shades, he resembled a daytripper from another planet. A folded blue television script was jutting, tantalizingly, from one of his coat pockets.

'My God, it's Nell Gwynne!' he said. 'Black and white television didn't warn us to expect a redhead.'

'Considering you look like a coconut you've not got much room to talk.' They could have been picking up the conversation from where they left off, eight and a half years ago.

'Sit down.' Mickey spoke peremptorily. 'We have to get this right, in one go, and we're short on time.'

Sorrel sat next to him on the trolley. It might turn her good grey skirt black, but in their years apart Sorrel had come to recognize and value creative energy. Mickey was thrumming with it. Out came the script from his pocket and she knew that if he told her to jump, the only question would be 'How high?'

'Have a look at this,' he said. 'Start there.'

It was a section of stage direction which read *Studio Exterior: Angel Dwellings: Day. Lettie Bly emerges from the tenement block. She is a battered-looking woman, in her late thirties, wearing an old raincoat. Lettie sports a black eye. She is leading a white border collie dog, with a black patch over one eye, on a piece of string.*

Sorrel found herself wanting to cry. This was both of their childhoods. Lettie Bly, dog and all, could only be based on Gander's 'poor Edie'. The tenement where she'd lived, Divine Dwellings, had been translated into Angel Dwellings. Mickey had done what he had always said he would do. He had remembered.

'The trouble is, I'm the only one who wants you for the part.' Mickey had grabbed back the script and was flicking through the pages, in search of a scene.

'The producer thinks you're too young. The director watched you lurking in the shadows of *Beware Beryl Jones*, last night. He doesn't know what to think. I know what you can do. They don't. Read me that speech there. Play it like your mother. I want all that suppressed fury and those terrifying flashes of honesty.'

Sorrel hadn't grown up in radio without being able to sight-read. There and then, with people carrying luggage around her and the station announcer clacking away about the next train for Warrington Central, Sorrel Starkey turned herself into Lettie Bly.

The speech was bitter and explosive. The character

maintained that there were many routes into Salford but no road out of it. The dialogue carried Sorrel along effortlessly until she came to a line which caught on real emotions of her own. As the speech rose to a climax the tears which rolled down her face were entirely spontaneous. But these days Sorrel was a highly experienced actress so she used technique, to control the tears' descent, to the best possible effect.

Mickey had been watching Sorrel like a hawk. At the end of the speech, he flung his arms around her. His eyes were shining as he said, 'Thank you, Sorrel. At long last I've seen Lettie Bly. You read it exactly as I heard it, in my head, when I was writing it. Can you learn that speech in ten minutes? Go and sit in the refreshment room.'

'Mickey. Promise me that nobody else will play this part. What other actress knew the real woman? I'd kill to play the part of Lettie Bly.'

'Just learn the lines and trust me,' he replied. 'Learn the preceding page – the long speech – and then the page after it. I'm off to Boots. I'm going to buy a cheap red Tangee lipstick. We'll get the makeup girl to paint it slightly over the outline of your own mouth. On the screen, the red will come out as almost black. That should age you up. They may not want you but we'll make them have you.' He glanced at his watch. 'Just get those lines into your head. Your camera-test is in three quarters of an hour.'

To hear Mick tell it, Manchester had turned into television city. 'It's all go! The BBC are in the old Manchester Film Studios. Granada are building off Deansgate. ABC have been transmitting, at the weekends, from the Capitol Theatre, Didsbury. There's even a man trying to make independent comedy productions, in a photographer's studio, near Weaste Cemetery.'

Sorrel was sitting, nervously, in the makeup chair, being transformed by a girl in a white overall. Mickey had brought in another, older woman from the wardrobe department.

Mickey was in full flood: 'Her blouse and skirt are fine but she needs a beaten-up white raincoat. One like Humphrey Bogart's with a different belt tied round the waist.'

'We'd have to send out,' said the wardrobe woman dubiously. 'There just isn't time. D'you mean a coat like your own, Mickey, but ancient?'

Mickey ripped off his raincoat. 'Take it. Break it down. Walk over the thing and drag it round the floor. But make it look as though it's taken years to happen.'

'You're daft, Mick,' laughed the wardrobe mistress, carrying the coat towards the door, 'but you're the kind of daft I understand.'

Sorrel found it most odd that these dedicated technicians had Manchester accents. She always thought of television as an essentially London thing. The cotton trade had thrived on attention to detail and modern Manchester was devoting the same pains to its newest industry.

Sorrel loved that television studio from the moment she passed through the front door. Excitement was in the air and so was creative energy. Everybody was young and on first-name terms. In the theatre Sorrel had fought her way to being 'Miss Starkey'. She had been addressed equally formally throughout *Beware Beryl Jones*. Here she was 'Sorrel' and Mickey was making sure that everybody knew she was Sorrel-Who-Has-Come-Home.

It was as though a whole generation had been waiting for television to hit the city.

'I used to see you standing at that bus stop before The Height,' said the makeup girl. 'I remember it because we both had the same Horrocks cotton frock. White with kites on it and its own built-in petticoat.'

It was the dress Sorrel had worn to meet Barney at The Midland.

'She still looks too young,' said Mickey. 'Shade in by the sides of her nose. Do it with a very soft drawing pencil.'

'I'll report you to my union for interference,' said the girl good-naturedly. Picking up an ordinary 4B pencil she began to emphasize one of the ageing hollows. 'Like this? Listen, Mick, do we have to put a face on Red Biddy too?'

'No. We know what she can look like. She's already cast. They're doing her contract today. She's just going to stand there and feed Sorrel the cues.'

'Who is it?' asked Sorrel. 'Anybody I know?'

'I hope you believe in Method acting, Sorrel?' Mickey was trying to take the pencil from the makeup girl and do a bit himself.

The girl slapped his hand away and said, 'Ever since Mickey got this show of his own, he's been like a child with a toy theatre. Wants to do everything himself.'

'He always did.' The love which welled in Sorrel's heart was overtaken by curiosity. 'Why Method acting?'

'The scene you've got to do is all hatred and fury. When you see who you've got to do it with, I'm hoping you'll give us the real thing.'

Before Sorrel could ask any more questions the wardrobe woman burst back into the room. 'This coat of yours is too new to break down in five minutes. Look what I just found on a rack in the corridor. It's marmot.'

From behind her back she produced a little fur jacket which looked as though it was made of dead rat.

'Yes,' said Sorrel and Mickey in one triumphant voice. The coat was exactly the right brand of tragically awful.

'Poppit beads?' asked the wardrobe mistress, fishing a length of them from out of her pocket.

Mickey grabbed the beads and kissed the wardrobe mistress.

'Get away with your bother,' she said. 'It's *you* landing in that's put him in this unusual mood,' she told Sorrel. 'We're beginning to think he's normal.'

Mickey went bright red with embarrassment. 'Sorrel has to get this part,' he said. 'It was written for her. I'm keeping a promise I made when we were eight. Can we leave the face at that?' This was to the makeup girl. 'That black eye is wonderful. Thanks. Sorrel, try the coat.'

The actress struggled into the old jacket and fastened the necklace around her neck.

'No,' said Mick. 'Forget the beads. They make you look like Dave Morris in a landlady sketch.'

'Mick, tell me who's playing Red Biddy?'

'Nothing on earth would persuade me to tell you. It's going to be a ghastly surprise.'

309

'What a cow!' The wardrobe woman spoke with feeling. 'She's already turned down five different cloth caps. Props are nearly in despair. She refuses, point blank, to settle for any of their clay pipes.'

'Who is it?' asked Sorrel.

'You'll see.' Mickey took her hand and began to lead her down a maze of corridors. 'Stop for a minute, Sorrel, I've got to tell you something.' They were outside a door labelled *Central Control.*

'You're not just the best young actress I know. You're my actress. That's why you have to get this part. There are people here who are fond of me but some of them loathe my guts. You've got to go in and stun them. Do it for both of us. This is the best part I've ever written.' He looked awkward. 'They're saying it's unplayable. They want me to tone her down.'

'Unplayable?' Sorrel was blazing in her contempt for anybody misguided enough to think this. 'It's got passion and it's got heart and it just needs playing with tremendous control.'

'Show them, Sorrel.' Mickey spoke quietly. 'This is the first time I've ever asked you to do anything for me. Get in there and show them.'

Beckoning Sorrel to follow him, he crossed the corridor and pushed against a door marked *Silence.* It opened onto a square black space leading to another door with a pane of glass in it. Sorrel looked through this window.

'There's your Red Biddy,' whispered Mickey.

Sorrel could only see the rear view of the little woman leaning against a sound boom and talking to a technician. The first things that caught her eye were pink, thigh-length, high-heeled Russian boots leading up to a very short mini-skirt in shades of the rainbow. The hair, which could only have been false pieces, cascaded down the woman's back in a tumble of gingerish-blonde ringlets.

And then the diminutive figure turned round. If Sorrel had ever had an enemy this was she. Their feud dated back to *Children's Hour.* It was Mamie Hamilton-Gerrard.

'Jesus!' Sorrel's exclamation was more a cry for help than a piece of blasphemy. 'I thought you said she wasn't going to be in costume.'

310

'She isn't,' said Mickey. 'That's just Mamie's new image for the 1960s. And cop a load of what's sitting in the far corner.'

It was Mamie's mother and she was still knitting.

'Age hasn't mellowed Mamie,' Mickey continued grimly. 'We've already crossed swords twice. Hasn't she got scrawny? She's going to be wonderful as Red Biddy but for God's sake stand up to her or you're lost.'

Pushing open the door and again taking Sorrel by the hand, Mickey led her into the studio.

'Hello, Sheila,' said Mamie warily. 'I always swore I'd never work with you again.'

'My name's Sorrel these days.'

'I can't guarantee to remember that,' smiled Mamie.

Sorrel smiled back and said, 'Well you'd better try or I'll get onto Equity. Or are you still in the Variety Artistes' Federation?'

If this was below the belt, Mamie had asked for it. As a matter of fact, Sorrel had come to have high regard for variety performers but the division between them and legitimate actors had only narrowed a very little. Mamie had always been self-conscious about her music-hall roots and her neck began to mottle angrily.

Far from looking disturbed, Mickey seemed delighted. It was almost as though everything was going according to some preconceived plan.

Striding across to the floor manager, who was wearing a set of earphones, Mickey said, 'Would you tell them in the box that we've got Sorrel Starkey here? She's ready and dressed and she's already learned it.'

Turning to Mamie he smiled and asked, 'I presume you know your big scene with Lettie Bly?'

'I'll *read* it,' snarled Mamie. 'Mother,' she called out, 'bring me the script. Mickey, that bit of a kid's much too young for the part. Even you must be able to see that.'

Old Mrs Hamilton-Gerrard tottered across the studio. The years had added a walking stick and did not appear to have sweetened her.

'Hello, Sheila,' she said to Sorrel. 'How you've managed to spoil yourself!'

Mamie, obviously preferring not to be seen in ageing but necessary spectacles, held the script out at arm's length and peered. It made her look like a trombone player.

'Ready?' she snarled at Sorrel.

The floor manager regained control of the situation by reciting an official-sounding litany of 'Absolute quiet please. We're going for a take. Stand by. Sorrel Starkey, camera-test, take one. And *action*!'

There was a clash of a clapper board and Sorrel went into her opening speech. Her last television experience had taught her more than she had realized. She took hold of the fury which Mamie had engendered and began to channel it into her own performance. She knew exactly where she was with these lines. Mickey had been an actor himself so he had provided her with dialogue which darted easily from the tongue.

As a child, Sorrel had only ever wanted to be Mamie Hamilton-Gerrard's friend. The old cow had thwarted her at every turn. All of this went into Sorrel's interpretation of Lettie Bly – and it exactly matched the scene which Mickey had written.

If anything, Mamie Hamilton-Gerrard's work had grown in stature. She was countering Sorrel's raw energy with tightly controlled technique. This brought Sorrel's own skills into play. The two actresses might detest one another but they were creating something which was making even jaded stagehands move away from the studio wall and take notice. The scene rose to a clashing, shouting climax. A last spectacular curse from Lettie Bly and it was over.

'Cut and thank you,' said the floor manager. 'That was quite something.' Pointing to his headphones he said, 'Upstairs in the box, they were actually cheering the pair of you. Yes, that really was something.'

Sorrel turned to Mamie with respect. 'You were so good,' she said. 'I'd forgotten just how good an actress you are. You're amazing.'

'I know.' Mamie didn't even sound interested.

Mickey came flying across the studio floor and joined them. 'I was watching on the monitor. It was breathtaking. I'd better dive up to the box.'

The floor manager nudged Mickey and tapped his head-phones significantly. 'Want to know something?' he asked. 'They sound as though they're going to open the champagne up there. Sorrel's got the part.'

Angel Dwellings was not like the other soap operas which erupted in the 1960s, the ones that held up a mirror to everyday life. In his serial, Mickey had dipped back, systematically, into the day before yesterday and retrieved a world which was all tram-cars and fogs and muffled ships' sirens hooting, as they came up the great canal from the sea. It was the story of an inland port.

The majority of the action took place in and around a tenement block on the dock road. The other important backgrounds were a seamen's mission and a ramshackle pub – the haunt of sailors of all nations, petty criminals and women of questionable virtue.

Mickey had drawn bold characters to hold his show together. The best women's parts were undoubtedly Lettie Bly, forever waiting for a series of men to come home from sea, and Red Biddy. As Biddy just sat and watched and hated, the uncharitable maintained that Mamie was a perfect piece of type-casting. The old actress made no secret of the fact that, given half a chance, she would have far preferred the role of Lettie Bly.

In the show, Red Biddy was greatly given to talking to a parrot whilst Lettie Bly was always supposed to be accompanied by a border collie on a piece of string. This animal character was named Spud. An appeal in the *Mr Manchester* column of the *Evening News*, followed by several auditions, had failed to find a dog with all the characteristics detailed in the scripts.

When Sorrel asked, 'Why can't I just buy a pup and train him myself?' the television company were, at first, hesitant. Mickey was inclined to think that they saw such a move as relinquishing control. After a third morning of yapping camera-tests they changed their minds.

As stagehands mopped and disinfected the studio, Mickey and Sorrel were handed a five-pound note and put in a taxi for

313

Tib Street. It was a gloomy November lunchtime so all the electric light bulbs were lit in this narrow street of pet shops. It wasn't raining enough to quell the frantic chorus of a thousand caged birds. Most of the shop windows had been converted into barred animal cages. Sorrel was torn between excitement and pity. As an actress she understood, only too well, the look in the monkeys' and puppies' eyes. It was as though all the animals of Tib Street were permanently auditioning for every single passer-by. 'Take me – Love me' they seemed to be saying.

Mickey knew exactly the animal he wanted. There was nothing in the windows on the left-hand side so they crossed over and began to work their way back.

'Everybody's supposed to love this street,' said Sorrel, 'but the tanks of fish are about the only things that don't upset me.'

A fierce-looking man in striped shirtsleeves, standing on the steps of one of the shops, said, 'Could I interest you in a pair of nice chinchillas?'

'We're looking for a puppy,' said Sorrel. She couldn't resist adding proudly, 'We're going to make him into a star.'

'And we're very poor people on a limited budget.' Mickey threw this in firmly. 'Come on, Sorrel, dogs seem to be thicker on the ground at the bottom end.'

'Hang on,' said the man. 'What sort of dog?'

'Border collie pup.' Mick seemed more interested in his own watch. 'Must be white with a black patch over one eye.'

'It seems to me you're talking about Horace,' said the man. 'Step inside.'

The shop smelled of damp straw and new leather and linseed oil.

'I call the animal Horace,' said the proprietor, 'but to be quite honest he's had a few names. Patch, Tinker, Horace – he's a spirited little bastard. That's why people keep bringing him back.'

Ever afterwards, Sorrel was to swear that those were the words which caused her to love the dog before she had so much as set eyes upon him.

'What were his crimes?' asked Mickey sternly.

'He's just, well . . . spirited.'

314

'Oh, me too,' said Sorrel eagerly, 'every time! Could we see him?'

'Stay where you are.' The man headed past a bin of corn and pushed aside a frayed chenille curtain. 'I've got him tied up.'

'The very idea!' As the shopkeeper disappeared Sorrel was all whispering indignation. 'Let's just pinch the dog and leave the man tied up instead.'

A muffled oath came from behind the curtain followed by a loud cry of 'Come back, you little sod!'

The next noise was claws tearing frantically across linoleum. Strictly speaking it was not a puppy but a young dog which burst under the curtain and began to look eagerly around the shop.

'It's him,' said Mick in a voice of total disbelief. 'That's not just any old dog. That's Spud himself.'

Ignoring Mick, the young collie, tail wagging, made straight for Sorrel.

'Sit,' she said, stroking his head.

The dog sat.

Sorrel held out a hand. 'Give me your paw.'

The dog obeyed.

'Thank you. That was a rehearsal. This is the real thing. Here's my hand. Try again. Give me your paw.' Right on cue, the dog obliged.

The pet-shop owner, perspiring profusely, lumbered back into the shop. The animal backed away from him. It was only a couple of steps but they were two paces closer to Sorrel's heart.

'How much?' she asked.

'Thirty bob and I'll throw in the collar.'

'I'll pay for him out of my own money.' Sorrel said this firmly to Mick. 'He'll feel safer knowing he really belongs to me.' In truth it was Sorrel who wanted to feel safer. 'Can you sell us a lead?' she asked the man.

'I'd like to buy him a present,' said Mickey. 'Do you engrave those discs for dog collars?'

'Certainly, sir. What shall I put on it?'

'Just put Spud of Angel Dwellings.'

315

The man looked puzzled. 'With respect, sir, I don't think that's a complete enough address.'

'It will be,' said Mickey confidently. 'Just give us a couple of weeks and it most certainly will be.'

4

The time had come for Sorrel to go home and see her mother. She telephoned first.

'I'm in Manchester. I've got a big part in a new television show. Do you want to see me?'

The fractional silence at the other end of the line lasted just long enough to revive all of Sorrel's old feelings of rejection. Then Gladys cleared her throat and said, 'You do think of your mother sometimes then? It's a nice thing when I have to get news of my own daughter, secondhand, from Mickey's mother. Beryl Grimshaw was swanking her head off in the pork butcher's. Don't come between half past seven and eight, Sheila. I'll be watching *Coronation Street*.'

Sorrel took a taxi from the studio. Spud came with her, on her knee. He was proving to be a most adaptable young animal. It was as though he had simply been waiting for Sorrel to turn up in his life. It was impossible to believe that this was a dog who had been so badly behaved that people had returned him to the pet shop. Or was it? One glance at Mamie Hamilton-Gerrard had been enough for Spud to pretend to have mistaken her long Russian boot for a leather lamp post.

The taxi threw up spray from the puddles on the curve of the Crescent and the River Irwell gleamed in the moonlight. As they passed Salford Hippodrome Sorrel held Spud close. The theatre, abandoned and boarded up, was now called The Windsor. Somebody else had tried another repertory season there, and failed.

Rehearsals for *Angel Dwellings* were going well. For the first two episodes the cast were enjoying the luxury of a fortnight's preparation. Thereafter, they would have to rehearse and record each pair of episodes in a week.

More attention was, if anything, being lavished on Spud than on Sorrel. The RSPCA were insisting upon inspecting his dressing room. And there was even talk of the animal-actor being obliged to have an official minder.

The cab reached Irlams o'th' Height. There had been a time when Sorrel would have known every changing item in every shop window display. She and Mickey had been children who yearned for wider horizons yet their search for fame had brought them right back to where they started. Sorrel turned round and looked out of the rear window of the cab.

'There you are, Spud,' she said. 'Have a good look. Those are the lights of Manchester.'

Tonight she would be sleeping on the other side of the city in a furnished cottage which Mickey had rented in Didsbury. With the aid of half the blooms from Dingley's flower shop and a constantly changing cast of clever visitors, he had managed to re-create the highly charged theatrical atmosphere of Cornucopia Mews.

The cab swung into the respectable sobriety of Ravensdale Estate. Sorrel had always imagined that, in her absence, time would have stood still – that on her return everything would be exactly as it had always been. This was not the case. Even in the dim street lighting, Sorrel could see that many of the lace curtains had disappeared. Halfway up Ravensway, somebody had added a decidedly ambitious extension to one of the houses. And where were the sunray gates which had always marked the home of the district nurse?

'Stop here,' she said to the driver.

The landmarks of Sorrel's childhood might have diminished but the old fears were still intact. It would never do to sail round the corner in a cab. Rookswood Avenue viewed women who travelled in taxis with dark suspicion.

The old strictures were closing round her like the scent from the wet privet hedges. Dear God, now she remembered just why she'd had to get away. An anxious Spud started to lick her hand. He must have noticed that she was actually trembling. Sorrel made a conscious effort to pull herself together. She refused to be ruled by the past.

'Keep the change,' she said to the driver. 'But do me a favour. I'm getting back in. Drive me right up to the front gate of my mother's. It's up there, on the left, the one with the concrete bird-bath.'

If Sorrel had still been Sheila, returning from a trip as a child, her first port of call would have been the Ganders'. Strangers, with an ugly asbestos garage, lived there now. Gander had moved to Blackpool.

It was all very unsettling. And what had happened to her own mother's green and cream paintwork? The front door, which was already opening, had been painted maroon and grey.

'You do get here some time then?' said her mother. 'And mind that rambler rose. It should have been pruned but I can't be expected to do everything for myself. Wipe your feet. That hair's awful. And Sheila, I don't want to hear your stepfather's name mentioned in this house. Is that understood? I want no mention of him and none of Monica Dolan either.'

Gladys darted a baleful glance at the Dolans' house opposite and slammed the front door.

The hall smelled of new carpets. Sorrel felt almost like a bona-fide visitor. Gladys led the way into the through room.

'Sit down,' she said. 'I suppose you're better than nothing.'

Gladys sat down herself. Spud immediately positioned himself in front of her and offered the woman a paw.

Don't bother, thought Sorrel. All my life I've tried to do the same thing and it just doesn't work.

She was wrong. That most remarkable animal was succeeding where she had always failed.

'It's nice to see somebody likes me.' Gladys was stroking his head. 'Wait a minute and your gran'ma'll get you a biscuit.' Looking up at her daughter she said, 'I suppose you're here about the money.'

'What money?'

Gladys was all bristling indignation. 'Don't think I'm after more than my fair share, because I'm not. The solicitor's letter was forwarded on to you at the Safety-Curtain Club.' The Old Fire-Iron's proper name sounded doubly alien on Gladys's lips.

'What money?' asked Sorrel again. 'The letter must be following me around.'

'I'm sure I never expected anything.' Gladys could still turn the simplest statement into an accusation. 'I called her an old bag when she was living. As far as I'm concerned, a funeral makes no difference. Your Gran'ma Starkey took pneumonia and died. All I can say is, she must have made that will a long time ago and never got round to changing it. We've copped for the lot.'

Gladys Starkey had managed to quarrel with her mother-in-law when Sorrel was still carrying a school-bag around. All she could remember about the old woman was the smell of camphor and parting gifts of half-crown pieces carefully wrapped in tissue paper.

Gladys sighed. 'It's going to be nothing but trouble. Who wants a hardware shop? And what good are stocks and shares? Trust that ten-bob-toff not to leave real money.'

'But they *are* real money,' protested Sorrel, who was struggling to come to terms with all of this. It was unbelievable. She was an heiress. First she'd got the biggest break of a lifetime and now she'd come into money. Sorrel flung her arms around her mother. 'It's wonderful, wonderful . . .'

'Get off, Sheila.' Gladys pushed her daughter impatiently aside. 'I can't stand cupboard-love. Never could. Let me find this young man a biscuit.'

Sorrel followed her mother into the kitchenette.

'You're wearing well,' she said. It was no less than the truth. Gladys had a back-combed hairstyle and the family waist was well displayed in a simple black dress. But where was her mother's husband? Sorrel decided to take the plunge.

'What happened to Jepson?'

'He hopped it,' snapped Gladys. 'And please let that be the last time you mention him. I thought that was understood.'

'If he's gone, surely the money will come in handy?'

'I can look after myself, thank you.'

It certainly looked like it. Gladys was breaking up a sugared Nice biscuit for Spud. In Sorrel's childhood they'd never got beyond plain digestives.

'I'm in Ladies' Gowns at Kendal's,' announced Gladys. 'And while I think about it, I don't want you marching in there and showing me up.'

Sorrel was mortified. 'How could I do that?'

'To be quite honest I've played you down. They don't actually know I've got a daughter.'

There were no two ways about it, Spud must have been brushed with the wings of genius. In the space of three minutes he had contrived to get himself hand-fed by a woman who thought nothing of denying her only child's existence.

'They're bound to find out about me.' Sorrel was immediately annoyed with herself for sounding so guilty. 'It's a new show. The studio have already sent out the press releases. Everything about me is in them. It'll be in all the papers.'

'Am I mentioned in these press releases?' asked Gladys dangerously.

'Not by name but they say where I come from.'

'You always were one for drawing attention to yourself.' Gladys put the top back on the biscuit tin. 'Do me a favour, steer clear of Kendal's. I'll break it to them gently. Mind you, I don't think there's room for another soap opera. And why you had to dye that hair red I do not know. People will only say you've copied Pat Phoenix. Now there *is* an actress. I couldn't enjoy my programme properly tonight for wondering what you wanted.'

Sorrel was hurt. It was as uncomplicated as that. Experience should have taught her not to expect more than this, but love and common sense don't often go hand in hand. Things were the same as they always had been. Sorrel wanted to be loved. Gladys couldn't or wouldn't do it.

Only Spud kept the conversation on an even keel. Whilst making it perfectly obvious that his heart belonged to Sorrel, he paid enough attention to Gladys for her to be charmed into suggesting another visit at some future, unspecified, date. It wasn't much but that household had never offered a lot for Sorrel's comfort.

She left her mother sitting sucking nougat. Gladys didn't see her to the front door. As Sorrel let herself out she saw that a light had gone on in the Dolans' house.

Crossing the avenue, she opened their gate and began to make her way up the path. The ancient cars had vanished but

321

you still had to pick your way between old jerry cans and rusting bicycle wheels.

They'd got a front doorbell with an emerald-green glow to the push. That was new; Sorrel pressed it.

In the distance she could hear an Irish tenor singing. 'The Rising of the Moon' to an orchestral accompaniment. Had the wireless been kept at the same Irish radio station for all these years?

The door was opened by Rose, the Dolans' mother.

'Well isn't this a grand surprise,' she said with such genuine pleasure that Sorrel could have wept.

'Come in. Bend down and pick up me evening paper, would you, love? Move that cat and get yourself sat down on the old settee. Your hair's beautiful, Sheila. Going red was an inspiration. You look good enough for a Dublin girl.'

Sorrel looked around. The room was as untidy as ever but the washing, waiting to be ironed, was beautifully clean and the milk bottle – always a feature of the Dolans' dining table – had been replaced by a green pot jug.

Rose looked bigger, slacker, but she was still gently beautiful. She sighed as she said, 'I know, awful quiet isn't it with all the childer gone. Fingal's still with me but he's out playing snooker.'

The framed oleograph of the Sacred Heart had once seemed the outward exotic symbol of the religious divide between the Dolans and the rest of the avenue. After her years at the Old Fire-Iron, it was now as usual and familiar to Sorrel as a framed photograph of the Queen.

Rose Dolan plainly understood collies. Her fingers had found just the right spot behind Spud's ear and she was scratching gently. Sorrel suddenly realized what a natural actor he was. Over the road Spud had been giving the required performance. Here he was just his happy self.

'Did your mother tell you we buried Eddie? The drink got him in the end but it never made him nasty, Sheila.'

Sorrel didn't mind being 'Sheila' in this house. Poor Eddie Tarmacadam who'd always had toffees in his pockets for the children.

Aloud she said, 'He was a lovely man.'

'Wasn't he?'

There was such sad gratitude in Rose's voice, for this most meagre of compliments, that Sorrel wanted to reach out and touch her. Why shouldn't she? People not touching one another enough was half the trouble. She stretched out a hand and stroked Rose's old arm.

'Mick's going to make Eddie Tarmacadam famous.' Sorrel wondered whether she was doing the right thing in telling Rose this. 'Years ago I told him the story of Eddie squaring up to Father Conklin with the gun and he's put it in a script.'

Rose roared with laughter and quoted her late husband's words: ' "Are you after an arse full of buckshot, Father?" Will it be on the television?'

Sorrel nodded. 'I'm going to be in it too.'

'And who will represent Eddie? Jack Warner?'

'They've brought a man over from Ireland.'

'I suppose it's work for somebody,' sighed Rose. 'I'm sure I've no objection. Let me get the kettle on.'

'Not for me. I've got to get back.' Sorrel was wondering how she could ask Rose about Monica Dolan and Mr Jepson.

'I've just found out that my stepfather's gone. Rose, was he a particular friend of Monica's?'

The Irishwoman sighed again. 'Monica has an awful lot of gentlemen friends. Too many, it's a regular occupation with her . . . if you get my meaning.'

'How's Delia?'

'Her!' snorted Rose. 'That's the girl who broke her father's heart. Upped and ran off with a black man. I blame myself. I was the one who bought her the black doll. Now she's got two piccaninnies of her own. They're twice as nice as white childer. We're back on speaking terms.'

Sorrel laughed. 'And what happened to Rory?'

'Mrs Gander always used to say that Rory would end up as one of two things. They'd either hang him at Strangeways or make him the Pope. I'm pleased to be able to tell you that Rory's in a parish outside Warrington. On the phone, mini-car, the lot. Should you ever need a Mass saying for anybody, Father Rory's your man.'

Sorrel got to her feet. 'I must go,' she explained. 'I'm

meeting Mick in town.' Sorrel's stay at the Old Fire-Iron had changed her views. Sheila, the child, would have been shocked to think that her grown-up self would calmly say to a Catholic, 'I've got a great big opportunity coming up, Rose. I could do with a few prayers. Would you say some for me?'

Rose laughed. 'Every night, when I get to "All wanderers and travellers" I go through a list of people in my head. You've been on it for years. Now I'll have to thank God for your safe return and put up some special prayers for your intention.'

And the funny thing was, this was the first moment that Sorrel felt she'd actually come home.

The cast of *Angel Dwellings* had moved from the rehearsal room into the studio. Now it was the first night of transmission.

Out on the dressing room corridor, Mamie Hamilton-Gerrard as Red Biddy was a sight to behold in her cloth cap and ragged little shawl, fastened with a variety of safety pins. A large mole, affixed to the side of her nose, had a coarse whisker coming out of it and genuine smoke emitted from her stubby clay pipe.

'They're brilliant in that makeup department,' she enthused to Sorrel in a rare fit of apparent friendliness. 'They've built this mole out of a Rice Crispie.'

The last word caused her to cough. Taking the pipe from her mouth Mamie explained, 'I'm not quite used to this tobacco yet. It's coarse shag. The things we do for Art! How did they manage to make your bust droop like that?'

Nothing had been done to Sorrel's bosom. But Mamie had asked the question with such conviction that Sorrel quickly found an excuse to rush for her dressing room and the mirror.

Her bust was where it had always been. Why hadn't she had the sense to realize that Mamie's mind was also where it had always been? And still leaking poison.

The call boy does not come round, announcing how long there is to go, in television. There is no Tannoy. In drama productions, no audience. There is blank, terrifying nothing. Any performer foolhardy enough to think of the size of the television viewing audience runs the risk of throwing themselves into something much more fearful than ordinary stage fright.

Not for the first time, Sorrel wondered why actors hold this brand of nervous tension in such high regard and say, 'The time to worry is when you don't get it.'

The show was going out live. Sorrel's stomach lurched and the shaking started. This would be as good a moment as any to remove her own good watch and slide on Lettie Bly's wedding ring. Strictly speaking, this Woolworth's ring didn't just belong to the new character. Sorrel had used it for every married part she'd played since Salford Hippodrome. It had cost her three and eleven and it wasn't true they turned your finger green.

There was an urgent rap on the dressing room door.

'Come in.'

It was Mick. For the fortnight of rehearsals he had stayed, superstitiously, in the same blue jeans and polo-necked jersey. Now, unaccountably, he was in a suit.

'Why so glamorous?' Sorrel asked. She was hugging her own stomach. As Mick had been an actor there was no need to explain what she was going through.

He looked very white as he replied, 'There was absolutely nothing more I could do about the show so I went home and changed, for something to do. I thought we might go out afterwards. There's a piece about us in *Mr Manchester's Diary*. It's the whole Noël and Gertie routine. I'm supposed to have given you a sacred promise in Mr Tuffin's boarding house, when we were both in ankle socks.'

'You did.'

'I must have been out of my mind.' Mick put his arms around her. He was shaking as hard as she was.

'To think we *chose* to do this,' she said in horrified wonder. 'We could have done any other job on earth . . .'

'No we couldn't,' he snapped. 'And you know it. We've waited all our lives for this moment. I just wish I didn't feel so ill.'

'At least you've not got to give a performance.'

'I'd give two if I thought it would make the show a success.'

Sorrel sighed. 'I always knew tonight would happen but I always thought, when it came, it would be in a theatre.'

'God preserve me from actresses,' stormed Mickey. 'What theatre? The theatre's in the doldrums. You've got to grab your chances where you can. D'you know what opportunity is? It's an old woman, riding on a bicycle, whose hair grows only on the front of her head. You've got to get out there, Sorrel, and snatch her bald.'

'What a nasty thing to say. Do my tits droop?'

'We're not in a nice business. Ten years should have taught you that it only pretends to be nice. The truth is, scratch and claw and climb over dead bodies if you have to. I've cleared a path for you, Sorrel. All you've got to do is breathe life into Lettie Bly.'

All? thought Sorrel indignantly *All?*

There was a rap on the door and it opened an inch. An unseen woman said, 'Spud's been round the car park and he's done a big job and a little job. Could we have you in the studio in one minute, Sorrel, please.'

'Christ, even the dog's shitting himself!' Mickey's reflection looked haunted as he gazed back at her from the glass.

'Don't say Christ like that. You'd be better off saying a quick prayer.' This was precisely what Sorrel was trying to do herself, under her breath.

Mick was still looking at their reflections. It was as though he was trying to memorize the moment.

'We'll never be the same again,' he said. 'I'm going upstairs to watch it in the office. Next time I see you, we'll both have started to be famous.'

It's bad luck to wish somebody good luck in a dressing room so he said nothing. Mickey had done his part. Now it was up to Sorrel.

How had it gone? Sorrel flopped down in the dressing room chair and began to reward Spud with chocolate drops. She wished somebody would hurry up and reward her. With no immediate audience feedback, television can be a frustrating medium. Actors, tensions released, singing outside on the corridor, was the only thing which was like the theatre.

She had remembered her lines. She hadn't walked into the furniture or fallen over any of the camera cables. The difficult scene with Red Biddy had gone like clockwork but with no audience there had been no reaction.

'It's like radio in fancy dress,' she said to Spud.

The makeup girl came casually through the open door with a small waxed paper cup of remover and some Kleenex.

'Did you get to see any of it?' asked Sorrel eagerly. 'What did you think?'

'I couldn't stand it. But one of the other girls, who was ready for home, got really involved and watched it to the end.'

They were joined by the wardrobe woman. By now she had a name. It was Mabel.

'Can I just have the fur coat, love? I've got to lock it up.'

'What did you think?'

'You've got a winner. There's a special atmosphere to a winner and the place is buzzing with it. Pity, really.'

'A pity?' Sorrel couldn't believe her ears.

'I'll take the blouse and skirt while I'm here. Yes, a pity. You and Mickey are a couple of nice kids. A success will be the end of that.'

'Never!'

'It's the truth.' Mabel reached down and picked up Lettie's ankle-strap shoes.

'Mabel.' Sorrel spoke urgently. 'If you ever find me getting big-headed will you promise faithfully to slap me down?'

'I could promise till the cows come home but it wouldn't make a scrap of difference. It's nothing personal, love. I was in films before television swamped everything. Fame's a funny thing. It's like putting a pan on a high flame. Sooner or later there's bound to be a smell of burning.'

'But I've asked you to tell me if I start showing the wrong signs.'

Mabel gave Sorrel a kindly smile as she said, 'They *all* ask me to tell them that. Don't take too much notice of me. I sometimes think I've been at this game too long. You've got a winner and that's what matters. Congratulations – and congratulations to you too.' This was to Mickey who had burst into the room like a windmill gone berserk.

His arms went round Sorrel. He kissed her, he kissed Mabel, he even kissed his own reflection in the mirror and said, 'Are we clever or are we clever?'

'Mabel says we'll change.' Sorrel was still worried.

'Too bloody right,' said Mickey. 'Come on, Starkey, get your clothes on. Let's go and kill some time at the Marshall Arms, until we can get our hands on the early editions of the papers. I *want* to change. I want to be very rich and very famous and beautifully unspoiled. The last part will be a terrible act but that's what I want. What do you want, Sorrel?'

'I want you to say I was good.' Something else struck her. 'Do they have a phone book at the Marshall Arms?'

'You were amazing. You should hear what they said upstairs. They're taking up the option on your contract for twelve months.'

'Goodnight,' said Mabel.

'I'll prove you wrong,' called Sorrel.

Mabel turned. 'That's just possible. I know a good girl when I see one. And you're *that*, Sorrel, if you're nothing else.'

This faint praise was so Manchester it made Sorrel cry, which got Spud agitated.

Mickey had to lend her a handkerchief. As he handed it to her he said, 'Nobody else on earth could have played Lettie like you did. You brought magic to the part. Thank you.'

This made Sorrel weep all the more. She was so red-eyed when she'd finished that she had to go to makeup and borrow some Optrex.

The Marshall Arms had always boasted theatrical connections. It was just across the road from one of the few stage doors left in Manchester. Conversation, these days, tended to be about programmes overrunning and audience ratings but the past clung to The Marshall's walls in the shape of framed, yellowing signed photographs of stage stars of the last seventy years.

'Look how all their handwriting is enormous,' said Mick. 'Just like actors' signatures today.'

The pub did a brisk evening trade – not only with television people but also with those of the citizens of Manchester who

328

enjoyed rubbing shoulders with this new injection of energy. The Marshall Arms also offered bed and breakfast. The fact that theatrical residents had signed the register was used as a licence for a lot of boisterous after-hours drinking on the premises.

As yet, it was only ten minutes to nine.

'Two of the newspaper printworks are just up the road.' Mick still sounded nervous. 'In a couple of hours' time we should be able to get the first editions, wet off the presses. What d'you want to drink?'

'Anything. You choose. Will you excuse me for a minute?'

She had just seen a sign on the wall: *Public Phone through Arch – No Change Given.*

Sorrel pushed her way through a crowd of noisy technicians. A cameraman halted the actress and congratulated her on the show. This pleased her but it was a professional reaction. Sorrel still wanted to know how the show had struck ordinary members of the viewing public.

The directory was hanging by the phone on a piece of string. Should she or shouldn't she? The phone book had represented a temptation ever since she returned to Manchester. With the first performance safely out of the way, there would be no harm in just looking.

Sorrel lifted up the book and began to skim through the S's.

Shapiro, Jacob still lived at Juniper House and there were two more listings under the same surname. Neither of them belonged to Barney. Thinking, regretfully, that this was probably just as well, Sorrel decided to telephone her mother. The phone rang a long time before Gladys answered.

'You caught me on the toilet, Sheila,' she said severely.

'I just wanted to know what you thought of it?'

'Of what? Or am I supposed to be a mind-reader?'

'The show. What did you think of me in the show?'

'Was it tonight? It clean slipped my mind. Oh well, it'll be on again. You'll have had more practice by the time I do see it.'

'I suppose so. Sorry for dragging you downstairs. Goodbye.'

329

Wearily, Sorrel replaced the receiver. Had her mother *meant* to reduce her back to Sheila Starkey who couldn't do right for doing wrong? Strangely enough, it had been the accusing tone of 'caught me on the toilet' which had done the most damage.

Sorrel pushed her way back to Mickey. In her absence he had lashed out on a bottle of champagne. The Marshall Arms was well used to coping with sudden flights of celebration. Everything in showbusiness had changed yet everything was still the same. Mick was handing out glasses to Mamie Hamilton-Gerrard and her mother.

Mamie was in her Russian boots and mini-skirt but she had added a jockey's silk shirt which, with her ringlets, made her look like Lester Piggott in drag. She also looked very pleased with herself.

'Wasn't my little girl compelling tonight?' asked Mrs Hamilton-Gerrard in tones which dared anybody to deny it.

Sheila Starkey turned back into Sorrel and purely professional appraisal took over. Yes, Mamie had been special. The parts of Lettie Bly and Red Biddy were of equal weight. Sorrel eyed Mamie's racing colours. If tonight had been a race, Sorrel had been given an advantage. She was Mickey's own actress and he had handed her everything he knew to give her the chance to shine. Mamie was just a vile old cow playing a vile old cow. But how would the public see it? Lettie Bly was the sort of loser they could take to their hearts. Red Biddy could easily prove to be the woman they loved to hate.

God, but that wicked Mickey was clever. On the screen and off he had realized that she and Mamie would be at one another's throat. Around the studio, people were already saying that *Angel Dwellings* had an energy of its own. Released from the tension of rehearsals Sorrel could suddenly see that Mickey had always known that it was the sparks flying between Mamie and herself which would generate the volatile entertainment.

Sorrel wasn't a fool. She had understood the theory of this intellectually. Now she was having to face it emotionally. Her old loathing of Mamie had been set to the tune of ringing cash registers. And now the studio wanted to take up an option on

Sorrel hating Mamie – professionally – for another year. If this meant fame, it wasn't going to taste how she'd expected.

Mick had his glass raised. 'Let's drink to something. I know, whatever we want in our own hearts.'

What did Sorrel want? Barney wasn't in the phone book, her mother had come no closer. Success seemed almost at hand so she just raised her glass and said, 'All I want is to hear what some ordinary viewer, watching at home, thought of *Angel Dwellings*.'

'Sorrel Starkey. Telephone for Miss Sorrel Starkey . . .'

The young man calling this out was the landlord's son. Catching sight of Sorrel he pointed towards the arch from where she'd just come.

As she made her apologizing way back to the telephone he came across and said, 'It's some madwoman who's just seen you on television and says she knows you. Gave me a lot of flannel about having a psychic vision that you'd be in the pub. Here . . .' He handed Sorrel the receiver.

'Hello?'

'Sheila? You were wonderful.'

'Who's that?'

'It's June.'

June Monk, of all people. Only nowadays she was June Gee. Yet was it so extraordinary? Sorrel wanted a reaction and June had always been a great one for providing people with what they wanted.

'Sheila, you and that old woman were amazing. It was just like watching a battle. You won, of course. You're my oldest friend and now you're going to be the most enormous star.'

'Thank you,' was all Sorrel could get in before June was off again.

'I want you to have dinner with us one night next week. I've not been letting the grass grow under my own feet. I've got a business proposition to put to you. I think we can do one another a bit of good. Have you got your diary? Why don't we make it Tuesday? And Sorrel . . . I am trying, I did remember your new name that time, I want you to do me a favour.'

'What?' Sorrel felt as though fleshy tendrils were trying to suck her down the phone.

'Bring Mickey.'

When in doubt tell the truth. 'Come on, June, you're not exactly his favourite person. You never have been.'

'Nonsense. That's just his little game.' June had developed a silvery giggle. 'He's mad about me really. Always was. We'll have an absolutely super time. We are all going to be wonderfully famous.'

We? That was the bit which puzzled Sorrel. Why *we*? How did June Gee come into it?

5

'Success is like a new love affair,' observed Mickey. 'It seems to unleash tremendous vitality.'

Angel Dwellings had been running for a month. Television critics had either loved or despised the show but they had not ignored it. The same was true of the public who were watching in their multi-millions. The breakfast table, at the rented cottage in Didsbury, was piled high with viewers' mail which had been forwarded on by the studio.

'It's wonderful.' Sorrel was opening her tenth envelope of the morning. 'But everybody seems to want something. And the letters aren't really to me. They're to Lettie Bly. Would you believe that this woman wants the diamanté earrings Lettie wore in Thursday's episode?'

Mickey was deep in letters of his own. 'I'd believe anything. I'm looking at one from a woman who says I show such understanding of the North of England that she's sure I won't mind paying her gas bill. I wouldn't care but I've just put another down which calls me a disgrace and says I've turned Lancashire into a laughing stock for cockneys.'

The telephone rang.

'*June.*' Sorrel and Mickey spoke simultaneously. This telepathy, which had been passing between them since childhood, was proving daily more useful in a new world of success, where all doors were suddenly wide open to them. A world where the crawlers had come running.

Sorrel had managed to cancel the original dinner appointment thrust upon her by June Gee by claiming that she had to give a magazine interview on the same evening. June had been suitably gracious and understanding but had never ceased bombarding Sorrel with telephone calls and letters. The previous day's effort had been ten pounds' worth of bronze chrysanthemums, delivered to the studio with a card which read: 'Dinner: when? June.'

Mickey answered the phone.

'Didsbury brothel,' he said into the receiver. 'All tastes catered for . . . Hang on.' He handed the receiver to Sorrel. 'It's your mother.'

'I suppose he thinks he's funny.' Gladys's voice came down the line like carbolic. 'I want to know what you think your game is, Miss High-and-Mighty? I've just had June Monk on this phone in a flood of tears. I suppose you realize you're breaking that poor girl's heart? It's a bit much when you consider yourself too important to speak to your oldest friend.'

'She was never really a friend of mine.'

'Never a friend of yours?' Gladys's tone could have been snitched from the soundtrack of an *Old Mother Riley* film. 'She was your friend the day they took you to Rhyl.'

Memories of that North Wales afternoon of lukewarm lemonade, and sand in banana sandwiches, came back to Sorrel with awful clarity. Forced on the outing against her will, she had been quite convinced that she would come back to find her mother dead.

'She was your friend then so you can damn well go and see her now. And if that's swearing, a snob like you would make a saint swear.'

'I'm not a snob.'

'Prove it. Phone June and make a proper appointment. If you don't, I'll do it for you. Today makes twice she's pestered me. Next thing you know she'll be grabbing me in Kendal's. How's Mickey?'

Gladys interested in Mickey? This was something new. Sorrel was, to say the least of it, startled.

'He's fine.'

'I suppose *his* mother's out at Didsbury all the time?'

So that was it.

'Not really. Look, why don't you come to supper one night?' Everybody could be told not to say 'fuck'.

'Or come for the day on Sunday?'

'On two buses?' snorted Gladys.

'I could send a cab.'

'A fool and his money are soon parted. If you want to splash

334

your wealth around, send a taxi for June. Ring her, Sheila. Ring her right now. I've given her instructions to stay by the phone.'

A click and the dialling tone announced that Gladys had gone. She had never been one for elaborate farewells.

'She's jealous of your mother.' Sorrel found herself strangely encouraged by this. Was Gladys, at last, showing some maternal emotion? Sorrel pushed aside the most insistent thought that Gladys was more interested in contact with the newly fashionable *Angel Dwellings*. Perhaps she'd finally owned up to having a daughter and the girls at Kendal's were pressing her for juicy details.

Mickey was looking solemn. 'My swamping mother is one of the reasons why I'll soon be leaving Manchester.'

Sorrel didn't take this seriously. Where would Oedipus be without his mother? And why should he walk out on the town which had handed him fame? Her own trouble was that *Angel Dwellings* had given her too much fame. She was now immediately recognizable in the street. 'I'm going to have to dream up some kind of disguise.'

Mickey dropped three letters into the waste-paper basket, saying, 'Those are from very unpleasant people who forgot to sign their names. The cleverest disguises are arrived at by *subtraction*. No makeup, dull colours . . .'

Sorrel pulled a face.

'If that doesn't suit, you'd better go the whole hog and become a real old-fashioned star. I'm surprised you need telling. I'd do it automatically.'

'Teach me.' Sorrel was all attention. 'I'm serious.'

Sorrel had no doubt of her own acting abilities but it often seemed to her that Mickey had been born with other theatrical instincts which she had to learn. She was never too proud to ask him for help because, time and again, he had pointed her in the right direction.

'Give me a lesson, Mick. Here and now.'

'Real stars go out and about, wherever they please, because they're in control of the situation.' Mickey paced the room as he talked. 'It's a matter of being friendly with the public but knowing how to distance yourself. Nobody's better than you at coping with men you don't fancy.'

'That's years of experience.' Sorrel couldn't see the connection. 'I put out signals saying "thank you but no thank you".' The connection began to dawn on her. 'You mean I have to let the public know they can look but they can't touch?'

'Yes, but you must do it subtly. You have to be one iota better dressed than they are and twice as well groomed. The idea is to dazzle them into keeping their distance. When you sign an autograph always use the American expression "There you go", and they *will* go. It never fails.'

Mickey looked unashamedly pleased with himself. 'Anything else you'd like me to tell you while we're at it?'

'Yes. How do I cope with that monster of a June? She and the body-builder are determined we're going to dinner.'

'Body-builder eh? I'd forgotten that bit.' Mick's odd eyes were dancing with mischief. 'What does he look like? Give me your address book.'

'Mick.' Sorrel spoke sternly. It was her turn to be in charge. 'You're not to get June's husband to teach you to swim.'

'Would I?' Mickey was already dialling the number.

'You would. She'd let him. We'd be forever in her power.'

'This is Mickey Grimshaw calling. I would like to speak to the last of the Lancashire witches.'

Sorrel could hear a flurry of excited babble coming from the other end of the phone.

Mickey stemmed this with 'Of *course* you knew it was me, June, the very moment the phone rang. That's the kind of irrefutable statement which earns you fortune-tellers a mint of money.' Protesting gurgles flew out of the receiver followed by some silvery questioning noises.

Mickey raised an eyebrow at Sorrel. 'Tomorrow night OK with you?'

She glowered but nodded.

'Tomorrow will be splendid, June. Eight o'clock? I particularly need some advice from your husband. I'm thinking of taking up body-building. Goodbye.' He replaced the receiver. 'You didn't tell me she tries to talk posh these days. She called me *darling* twice. I expect she thinks theatricals like it.'

'Mickey.' Sorrel was giving her sternest elder sister performance. 'That husband is a very nice man.'

'Good. I'm a bit too willowy. It's going out of fashion on the sex scene. Perhaps he can help me bring my body up to date.'

'Oh dear,' sighed Sorrel.

Was he being serious or was this some elaborate tease? You never knew with Mickey. It suddenly dawned on Sorrel that Mick used precisely the technique he'd prescribed, to keep autograph-hunters at bay, on even his closest friends. Was there a heart inside all that glossy self-confidence or had he turned into a set of calculations?

'Mick? You're not really thinking of leaving Manchester?'

He was a great deal to do with her happiness here. Indeed he could be said to have given her that happiness. These days Sorrel Starkey could look the Town Hall clock squarely in the face. She had kept her promise. She was back. She was famous. Everybody knew who she was.

'Yes,' said Mick, 'I'll soon be moving on. I have to find my city.'

Sorrel suddenly felt depressed. 'I thought it might have been New York.'

'Spud!' called out Mick. 'Where are you, Spud the pirate?'

The dog immediately came in through the French windows and laid a dead rat at their feet.

'No,' said Mickey, picking up the rat by its tail and throwing it back into the garden, 'New York was not my city.'

'Now wash your hands.' Sorrel knew that there would be no point in asking further questions. Mickey had raised the invisible wall between them.

Spud was gently chewing Mickey's wrist, the collie's fondest sign of affection. It was as though Spud understood Mickey better than she did. The dog was through the wall and on the other side. Sorrel felt ashamed. Mickey had never been less than loyal and steadfast. He had even crossed an ocean to look for somewhere to belong. How could she have doubted he had a heart?

Mickey got to his feet. 'If you want a lift into Manchester you'd better get a move on. We need to ring for a taxi and we must remember to get rat poison. Perhaps a rat-catcher would be better. God forbid that anything should happen to Spud.'

At this moment Sorrel actually debated confessing to disloyal thoughts about heartlessness.

Then Mickey, stroking the dog's head, added, 'It would never do if he dropped dead. We've just outlined sixteen consecutive episodes for him.'

The taxi dropped Sorrel off at the bottom end of King Street.

'Got your cheque book?' yelled Mickey who was staying on, in the cab, with Spud.

You needed money on this shopping thoroughfare. Manchester claimed it as 'The Bond Street of the North'. In the mid-1960s Jaeger was the only Mayfair name over a shop window. The rest of the businesses were owned by Manchester people who understood how to serve the most luxurious of Manchester needs. King Street stood as much for solid quality as it did for expensive frivolity.

Sorrel liked the old-fashioned shops best. Ever since she could remember, Marsh's the saddlers had featured a stuffed racehorse in the middle of their cluttered window display. Louis et Bernard, the court hairdressers, could hardly have altered since Queen Alexandra visited Manchester. It was all polished mahogany and much-washed chintz and faded gilt signs which mentioned *Wig-Work* and *Postiches*. They still had cubicles at Louis et Bernard.

Clothes, that's what she was here for. The kind of glamorous clothes which Mickey had maintained would mark her out as a star. Automatically, Sorrel began to study what other women were wearing. Time and again she found her attention straying to their extravagant hairstyles. Bouffant was still the order of the day. Some of the styles were back-combed as high as two feet. However did people manage to sleep in these lacquered creations?

It was a cold morning. You could see your own breath. Christmas shoppers were out in force. Out of the corner of her eye Sorrel registered that a woman had noticed her. The woman nudged a friend, beamed at the actress and began delving in her handbag.

'Excuse me,' said the woman. 'But could I trouble you. . . ?'

'Of course.' Sorrel began to write her name with the

woman's leaking ballpoint pen. It wasn't an autograph book. It was a small memo-pad with a picture of Laurence Harvey on the cover. 'I hope you're enjoying the show?'

'Is Red Biddy going to manage to get you evicted?'

'I'm afraid you're as wise as I am,' smiled Sorrel. 'We don't know anything about the story until we get the new scripts. They seem to enjoy keeping us in the dark.'

This was no less than the truth. The woman didn't seem to believe her. They never did. What's more, she was looking at Sorrel's signature with some disappointment.

'Something wrong?'

The autograph-collector hesitated for a moment and then said, 'You've only put your own name. I wanted Lettie Bly.'

This had started to happen more and more often. Sorrel took back the pad and added the fictitious name. Requests for this addition always made her feel as though her fans were attacking her true identity with an indiarubber.

Now the woman's friend moved in. 'I once had a coat in that material,' she said, stroking Sorrel's sleeve.

This might or might not have been true. What Sorrel did know was that the woman had felt the need to *touch* her.

None of this had gone unnoticed by yet another female, sitting at the back of a shop window, on the edge of a display rostrum and looking out onto King Street.

Sorrel handed back the pad.

'There you go.' It worked. They went. Ten marks for Mick.

The woman looking out of the shop window smiled at Sorrel conspiratorially. The actress was impressed. This wasn't just any old shopkeeper. Rita Salmon was the uncrowned Queen of King Street. She and her sister Etta owned the best dress shop in the town. The Salmon sisters were Manchester legends.

'They have no price tags' was the usual awe-struck comment. That and 'They never put the best dresses in the window because they're so exclusive they're scared of them getting copied.'

Salmon's had twŏ windows. The premises had begun life as two separate shops. Stories were told of wives being served in one and mistresses in the other. People were also said to have gone in for a cotton frock and emerged with a ball gown.

Sorrel was weighing all of this up against the fact that she was finally earning real money on a twelve-month contract. What's more, there were options for two further years at an increased salary. She took a deep breath, mounted the marble step and pushed open the door.

Inside, there wasn't so much as a dress in sight. Just dove-grey carpets and dove-grey velvet hangings (did these, she wondered, conceal fitting rooms?) plus a crystal chandelier and some little gilt chairs.

Rita Salmon rose from her seat at the back of the window and greeted Sorrel with delight.

'I'm so glad you came in,' she said. 'The temptation to come out and grab you was very strong. I'm afraid I can't keep out of the window. It's in the blood.'

I'll be all right here, thought Sorrel. She's the best kind of Jewish.

Rita Salmon was well past fifty, short and dumpy in a black dress cut with almost surgical precision. The diamonds in a triangular brooch, high on her shoulder, were real.

'We'll call you Miss Starkey if you like, but I'm afraid I already think of you as Sorrel. My sister and I are big fans. Etta!' she called out. 'Look who's come to see us.'

More grey velvet was pushed aside, revealing lights in the shop next door, and a thinner version of Rita Salmon appeared. Etta, also in black, had escaping hair and glasses and looked a worrier. Sorrel found herself wondering whether it was Etta who did the books.

Etta Salmon smiled with every bit as much charm as her sister and said, 'If you want somebody to murder Red Biddy, we're the girls to do the job.'

'Come to that,' Rita threw in, 'should you want somebody to murder Mamie Hamilton-Gerrard, we'd still be happy to bring along a gun.'

'I can't stop.' The bespectacled sister was looking over her shoulder. 'I've got Ruby Shapiro on the other side. We're fitting the bronze cocktail dress. I think you might have to reassure her, Rita. It's a Balenciaga copy and Ruby says it puts her in mind of a cheap Bar Mitzvah in Crumpsall.'

'Are you taking my name in vain, Etta Salmon?' A laughing voice, from the other shop, was coming closer. If Sorrel had frozen at the mention of Ruby's name, the thought of a confrontation made her want to turn and run.

A familiar small Jewish empress, in bronze satin and black bugle beads, strode through the gap in the drapes. She was attended by a pretty blonde shop assistant with a mouth full of pins.

'Rita,' roared the empress, 'I look like Sophie Tucker in this shmatte. It's not a copy, it's a caricature. Jesus, I could have done better in Henry's basement.'

'Don't say Jesus,' said Sorrel severely, 'or I'll say Moses.'

The Salmon sisters actually laughed out loud.

Ruby was not one whit abashed. 'Sorrel!' she exclaimed in a tone that sounded suspiciously like joy. 'Clever Sorrel, and I've found you! I've been glued to your show. I was going to write but I thought everybody would be driving you crazy with attention.'

Ruby's arms went impulsively around the girl. 'I've been so *proud* of you. Wait till you come to see us, Jacob will tell you. At the end of that first episode I was so proud that I sat down and cried. We didn't eat that night till half past eight.'

Ruby rounded on the Salmon sisters. 'Now listen, girls, just you look after this young lady properly. No tickling up the prices because she's famous. No leaving her wondering whether you've added the date in. We have great respect in our family for Sorrel Starkey.'

The dress-shop owners were obviously as impressed as they were puzzled. For Sorrel it was a strangely heady moment. If there was any quarrel it had been with tradition; never with Barney's mother.

Ruby's eyes twinkled as she said to the sisters, 'I bet you're dying to find out how I know her, aren't you?'

'Yes.'

They both said it so boldly that Sorrel liked them even more.

'Perfectly simple.' Ruby spoke airily. 'Sorrel is Barney's old shiksa. It's a terrible word and I apologize for using it. There was nearly a mixed madness in our family and Sorrel behaved with great distinction. All that's water under the bridge. That's past. Now we can be friends.'

And Sorrel *wanted* to be friends. She had always admired Ruby Shapiro's style and attack and she knew, instinctively, that Ruby would not give her friendship lightly. It had been promised years ago, on Barney's wedding day. Ruby's words came back to Sorrel: 'One day I'll be a good friend to you – the best. And that's a promise.'

Good enough to answer the question which had to be asked?

'How is he?'

'Well enough.' Ruby's vitality seemed, for a moment, dimmed.

'Yes, you could say he was well enough. No children. We're all friends here so I don't mind saying it's a sorry marriage. Clothes! This famous young lady's not come here to reminisce. She wants clothes. What are you after, Sorrel? Two heads are always better than one in these matters.'

That morning Ruby Shapiro began the slow process of teaching Sorrel Starkey the bold rules of high style.

'Line,' she declared imperiously. 'That's the first thing to look for. Be sure the shape's right. In a place like this they can always change the fabric or copy a garment in another colour. The one thing that has to be right is the line.'

An establishment like Salmon's was a new experience for Sorrel. She was allowed to try on a few ready-made coats and dresses but evening clothes were paraded before her on the back of a haughty mannequin called Miss Clegg. The Salmon sisters were in neither, precisely, the ready-to-wear nor the haute-couture business. Their method of trading was one which had evolved over the years. Their one aim in life was to please rich Manchester.

An hour and a half later, after Ruby left, Sorrel realized that she had been mesmerized into ordering no less than five separate outfits. All the Salmons would allow her to carry away was a cream cashmere coat and dress. Some of the other items, they predicted, would take at least two fittings.

Whenever money had been mentioned there had been much reassuring talk of 'But we'll make a special price for you' and Rita had said, 'You will, of course, tell people that you shop here.'

Sorrel felt that the time had come to be firm. Etta Salmon definitely seemed to be the money one so she asked her, 'How much does all of this come to?'

'Nothing. Not a penny. It's all to go on Mrs Shapiro's account.'

'I couldn't possibly allow that.'

'Let her in, Sorrel.' It was Rita Salmon who said this. Her bright old eyes looked full of friendly concern as she continued, 'Ruby Shapiro wants to be your friend. Accept her peace offering and let her into your life. You won't regret it.'

At first glance, Worsley, eight miles to the north of Manchester, appears to be a spectacular example of the perfectly preserved Tudor village. Closer examination reveals that the picturesque half-timbered cottages set around a village green are, in fact, a Victorian catalogue of English and European building styles. But the passing years have added moss and twisted the beams. Roses have rambled riotously and the hollyhocks have seeded themselves so many times over that the place has developed a genuine charm of its own.

'Fake as a glass eye,' said Mickey as the taxi bounced along the track which bounded The Green. 'The place is phoney and low-lying. In short, the perfect setting for June Gee. What did you say the house was called?'

'Evening Whispers,' said Sorrel. 'And you leave Worsley alone. I like it. She must have prospered. Property prices on The Green have always been shocking.'

'Stop here!' Mickey was addressing the driver. 'Oh look, June's got a plastic Christmas arrangement in the garden, in a dear little cement wheelbarrow.'

'Behave yourself!'

'I was only saying.' Mick was all innocence. As he jumped out and began to pay off the taxi Sorrel followed him more gingerly. The cab was ancient and grimy and she was wearing the cream cashmere outfit for the first time.

343

'You look as great a star as Garbo,' said Mickey with approval.

'It's got a matching dress underneath.'

Mickey made a hmph noise. 'Unless June's changed very considerably, the chances are she'll soon be inviting us to take all our clothes off and play rude.'

The short front garden was dark and the December damp had summoned back the scent on long-dried tufts of lavender. As Mickey pushed open the gate, light suddenly shone forth from a multicoloured glass hanging lantern, on an iron bracket, over the front door. Now the front door opened to reveal, arms outstretched, June.

'You've found us,' she said dramatically. 'Welcome to Evening Whispers. I've waited a long time for this moment.'

There were no two ways about it, thought Sorrel, as she submitted to a scented embrace, June had certainly got her act together. Everything about her was overstated but meant. The hair was a bouffant blaze of shining blonde. The eye makeup brought pandas to mind. The dress was white lace over pink silk and the mini-skirt could have been mistaken for a deep belt. It showed off June's jaunty legs, which had always been one of her better assets, to defiant advantage.

June noticed where Sorrel's gaze had landed and gurgled, 'I can't take to tights. I still wear silk stockings and a frilly suspender belt. Martyn says my one aim in life is to drive men mad.'

She led the way into the cottage. 'He's mixing blue cocktails. We first had them at Brian Epstein's. Have you met the Beatles?'

Mickey started making not very covert motions of somebody laying it on with a trowel. Sorrel kicked his leg.

'Come into the lounge. My hairdresser calls it "The Flowery Bower".'

In the lounge June had taken the rose for her motif. And she'd taken it just about as far as it could go. The curtains and covers were in rose-patterned chintz. You sat on roses and walked on roses. Vases embellished with rose designs were full of china roses on plastic stems.

'Roses, roses, all the way,' said Mickey. 'I see you even

feature their ghosts.' He was pointing at a pink bowl of potpourri.

'Naughty.' June slapped his wrist. 'I'm used to cracks about my psychic work. It's when they don't talk about me I'll worry. *Woman's Own* calls me Mrs Mystic. I'm never out of the magazines. What I'd really like is a column of my own. Of course my platform-demonstration tours are doing a bundle. You've caught me right on the brink of the Big Time.'

Caught? thought Sorrel indignantly. Caught? The truth is we've been dragooned here to be impressed.

At that moment Martyn came through the door bearing a silver tray with four cocktail glasses on it. They were brimming with a vivid blue liquid. An equally blue flower floated in each drink. Sorrel recognized it as borage. She felt cheated. Surely it should have been a rose-bud?

Or did the borage indicate that Martyn was also allowed to have a say in this vivid household? As the tray came closer she realized that the blue flowers were plastic.

He looks like the male equivalent of a Bunny Girl, she thought. Everything had been done, to improve him, that could be done. Muscles exercised, teeth capped, hair blow-waved; this was a man who had just got off the sun-bed. Yet there was still something appealing about him, thought Sorrel. He always brought dogs to mind. He was like a friendly labrador crossed with some more decisive breed.

'Introduce me,' muttered Mickey.

Oh dear, thought Sorrel, does that mean he's Mickey's type? June ought to be doing the introducing.

'What am I thinking of?' said June. 'You two don't know one another. This is Mickey who would never let me see his dick for sixpence. Meet my sexy husband. Would you like to see some physique photos of him?'

'How d'you do.' Mickey was completely unperturbed.

'Martyn's best friend at school is a head window-dresser these days so he's grown up very broadminded in these matters.'

Mickey smiled easily and proceeded to be the perfect guest. His charm, when he chose to exert it, was considerable. And Sorrel watched fascinated as Mickey sent their host a

345

series of skilful social signals which made it perfectly clear that his interest was in no way predatory. What's more, Mick's interest in exercise was proving to be genuine. Martyn was soon offering good advice about gyms which was exchanged for suggestions for a press release for June's forthcoming tour.

The medium and her husband excused themselves. The meal, it seemed, had to be got from the kitchen into the dining room.

'You're coming on a bit strong aren't you?' Sorrel was feeling a bit left out of things. Everybody seemed to be starring except herself.

'I like him.' Mick was at his firmest. 'I like straight men very much. Martyn's extremely attractive and he knows I think so. He's also confident enough not to care. He's another Barney. We could be good friends. Confident straight men are the nicest animals on this earth.'

Sorrel dismissed lurid memories of Cornucopia Mews. Why oh why had Mick gone and mentioned Barney? The skin over that wound had always been tender. And Sorrel's meeting with Ruby Shapiro had already stirred up feelings that refused to be stilled again.

The dining room was very D'You-Ken-John-Peel with hunting-scene wallpaper and fake antique horns, in brass and copper, on the plate rack. Everything was brand new except for a stuffed fox which was beginning to fall apart.

The guests had already tackled huge prawn cocktails. Martyn began to carve the roast saddle of lamb.

'Of course I could easily be a vegetarian,' said June cosily.

Blood spurted from the joint.

Dear God, thought Sorrel, underdone lamb. And what's supposed to be luxurious about central heating turned up to boiling point?

Mickey, who had been encouraged to unscrew a catering-sized jar of red currant jelly, remarked, 'You two seem to live very high off the hog. I suppose I should say sheep. Where does the money come from?'

There was still enough of Rookswood Avenue, in Sorrel, for her to find this question just a bit too direct. Not June and

Martyn; it seemed to be the very conversational opening they were looking for.

'Anybody can make money,' announced Martyn. 'We're living proof of that. Study any situation closely and you'll soon find the gap that will lead you to a crock of gold.'

He began to pile lamb onto plates decorated with a design of Highland stags. June was pouring champagne into glaringly silver-plated stirrup cups.

'When I met June,' continued Martyn, 'I was a traveller in greetings cards. D'you know what she asked me? You tell them, June. It was your moment, you take over.'

'I said, "Who writes the verses?" And that's how we began. I wrote a few for Christmas and birthdays and then Martyn began to study the market. Help yourselves to braised chicory.'

Martyn was passing the gravy. 'At that time, bereavement cards were very thin on the ground. There was a big gap at the condolence end of the market. Have you any idea how many people die each day?'

'Not that there *is* any death,' said June automatically. 'That's how I came to write *Death? Don't Make Me Smile.*'

'We put that inspirational verse on a first-quality card –' Martyn was remembering with something approaching awe – 'and it's sold in its millions. June's on a farthing royalty.'

'One farthing for each one sold,' smiled June. 'It was those little coins which bought this house. It's still a good earner today.'

'My goodness me,' said Mickey. 'How your heart must sing at the news of a killer-epidemic.'

Martyn smiled a confident sexy smile. 'I think we're going to make your heart sing tonight, Mickey. Yours and Sorrel's. I'm presuming you own the copyright of *Angel Dwellings*?'

Sorrel noticed that Mickey was suddenly wearing his unforthcoming face. The one he saved for people who were after bites from his cake.

'Get the prototype, June. It's in the knife drawer. Before you look at it –' Martyn turned back to his guests – 'I want you to realize that June is becoming famous in her own right. She's leaping to the fore with her mediumship and these hearts-comfort verses have brought her a specialized public of her own.'

'You know what he said to me yesterday?' Their hostess rosied prettily. ' "June," he said, "June, you're like a rocket in a bottle. You're all set to go off." '

Sorrel didn't dare look at Mickey. Suppressed laughter was already building in the pit of her stomach and she was terrified that her shoulders would begin to heave. If that happened she knew she would be lost.

'I know you think I'm highly comical.' June sounded remarkably unworried by this. 'And you wouldn't be the first to say that this house is a monument to bad taste. But just you wait until you see the prototype.'

Martyn was already at the sideboard drawer and he returned to the table carrying a white envelope.

'Yes, have a look at that,' he said, passing the envelope to Sorrel.

She opened it and pulled out a greetings card. On the front was a photograph of herself, as Lettie Bly, hugging Spud. The picture was overprinted with a message in gilt lettering: *Old Friends Are Best.*

Sorrel opened the card and said, 'Is it meant to be blank inside?'

'Oh no, there'll be yards of text,' said June. 'But I thought I'd *recite* the poem for you.' She cleared her throat and began. The voice she had assumed was that of an infants' school teacher telling a nursery story.

> 'When I think back to childhood days
> And how we used to wander
> Along the path through summer haze
> To visit Auntie Gander . . .'

'You never called her Auntie Gander,' Sorrel interrupted indignantly. 'She was always Mrs Gander to you. Anyway, who'll know what you're talking about?'

June sighed patiently. 'I've turned her into a symbolic figure. Like Old Nokomis in *Hiawatha.*'

Martyn now transferred his businesslike attentions to Mickey. 'Whilst the ladies are brawling perhaps you'd like to

348

glance through the words of the whole poem?' From an inner pocket he had already produced a slip of typescript.

'I wouldn't care but it's an awful picture of me,' muttered Sorrel. She was beginning to feel a bit like a butterfly on a pin and gazed anxiously at Mickey for help.

He looked up from the poem and said, 'That photograph belongs to the studio. So does the character of Lettie Bly and all the subsidiary rights that go with it.' His attention reverted to the typescript.

'But Sheila, you still own your own face.' June was being so reasonable that Sorrel could have smacked her. 'And the dog's your own. You already said so.'

Mickey let out a howl of joy. 'Listen to this bit . . .

> 'Though Fate has smiled on both of us
> We've stood the acid test
> Through thick and thin
> We'll lend a pin
> Old friends are still the best
>
> June Gee Copyright 1964

'It's bloody rubbish!' gasped Sorrel.

'It'll sell,' smiled June. 'You see, it's not just about you and me. It applies to everybody.'

Sorrel would have expected Mickey to rip the ersatz verses to pieces. Not a bit of it. Instead, he gave her a lecture about not losing the common touch, granted that the idea might have possibilities and even went so far as to question Martyn about royalties. How much were they proposing to pass on to Sorrel? Mickey was now in a world he enjoyed.

'While the men are talking, would you like to see the wee folk?' asked June.

Was this some euphemism for the lavatory? Sorrel was beginning to feel the need of one.

'A pause before dessert will do none of us any harm.' June was already on her feet. 'Come upstairs. We can be girls together.'

The well of the staircase was decorated with framed greetings cards displayed to show both illustration and verse.

'If you did but know it, Sorrel, I'm trying to do you a favour.' June pushed open one of the doors off the landing.

'Shh,' she said. 'Whisper who dares.'

Why was June quoting from *Christopher Robin?* wondered Sorrel. And then she saw the two small beds. How on earth had she managed to forget the twins?

'Jason and Junelle.' Their mother said it reverently.

They were beautiful children. There could be no scoffing here. It suddenly struck Sorrel just how well June had got it made. Children, husband, house. You might not care for the style but June had got everything a woman could want.

'I'd give anything to be as famous as you, Sorrel.' The longing in June's voice was almost vicious. 'But I'll make it. You'll see. Let's go next door. I want to put a bit of Creme Puff on my snout.'

The master bedroom was a tribute, in lilac, to the frill and the flounce. As June dabbed at her nose and caught up a stray curl with a squirt of lacquer, she seemed to have put all thoughts of business aside.

'I tried to get up a little surprise to go with the coffee. I invited the mummies. Want a toothpick?'

The mummies? Was this something occult? Surely not. Sorrel tried for a more likely explanation: 'Your mother and Martyn's?'

'Martyn's hasn't spoken to me for years. And mine's away, in Cromer, doing a course on Karma. No, I rang your mummy and Mickey's. I thought it would make a nice novelty. Want a drop of Chanel? It's Number Five.'

'Novelty?' Sorrel waved away the offer of scent. 'It might be more like a third world war. The pair of them are age-old enemies.'

'Aaah . . .' June was doing some complicated probing in a back molar with an orange stick. 'That might be the explanation. They both seemed to want to leave it a bit open. Listen! Isn't that an owl?'

It was indeed an owl and just as Sorrel was reflecting that Worsley was still wonderfully peaceful the night air was rent with a horrendous crash.

Both women rushed for the window. Below them, on the

track in front of the cottage, two cars had come into a head-on collision.

Two men in overcoats had leapt from the vehicles and were already arguing fiercely. A white-faced Gladys Starkey emerged from the back of one car. Beryl Grimshaw all but rolled out of the other.

By the time Sorrel and June got downstairs people were beginning to flood into the lounge. One driver was already phoning for a breakdown van and Martyn was dispensing brandies all round.

'Gracious living?' exclaimed Gladys Starkey. 'It's more like Muldoon's picnic! And aren't these houses poky?'

Seeing her mother in these strange circumstances, Sorrel was forcibly struck by the fact that Gladys carried herself wonderfully well. June began to help Beryl Grimshaw out of a squirrel coat. Sorrel thought that somebody must have had to trap a lot of animals, to cover Mickey's mother.

'Well, Beryl, the years haven't made you any more petite,' observed Gladys dispassionately.

'I've always been glandular,' glowered Mickey's mother. 'But in the past few months, I confess it, I've been eating for comfort.' The glower, like a rolling fog, had shifted to her son.

Something had to be done about changing the course of the conversation, decided Sorrel. 'It's not like you to take a taxi, Mother.'

'June sent them. She wouldn't take no for an answer.'

'Over to you, June,' said Sorrel, giving up.

June was staring fixedly at the taxi driver who was now accepting a cigarette, from Martyn, to go with the brandy.

'Mother's in spirit, isn't she?' asked June.

'Eh?' The driver had a flaming Zippo lighter halfway to the end of the cigarette.

'Is your mother dead?' asked Gladys as though she was talking to somebody deaf. 'It's hardly a tactful question, June. Not everybody holds your views. People could take exception.'

June, who had been watching the driver closely, began to clutch her chest. 'Why do I feel short of breath? Was mother's passing-condition bronchial?'

351

'They had to give her oxygen,' said the driver gruffly.

'Course they did. She's showing me the cylinder. Who's Nell?'

'She was my gran'ma.' The driver was beginning to look as though he'd come through more than a car crash.

'She's here. She's with us. Bit of a character. Says she used to clout you one but your mother didn't like it.'

'My God!' exclaimed the driver in amazement. 'You do well to pass round the brandy. You're sending shivers down my spine.'

'It's nothing to be afraid of.' June was all cosy reassurance. 'You go to her grave, don't you? Mother says you took daffs. She's not there, George. That's not where she is.'

'How the hell did you know my name?'

Mickey treated Sorrel to a significant look. It directed her eyes to the telephone, where the driver had left a pair of woollen gloves. Next to them was a used envelope with a phone number scrawled on it. The envelope was addressed to Mr George Binns.

June smiled enigmatically at Mr Binns. 'Mother knows all about the trouble you're having getting ITV. There is no death. They're watching everything we do.'

'Don't tell me they can see us getting undressed?' snorted Gladys.

'And are they telling you anything about a mother who might just as well have lost her son, for all she sees of him?' This was from Beryl Grimshaw.

'For God's sake!' groaned Mickey.

There was no stopping Beryl. 'His bedroom's just as he left it. Nobody's been allowed to sleep there. I just go in to dust and talk to his teddy.'

Mickey was plainly rattled. 'You make me sound like a Victorian child who died of consumption.'

'You might just as well be dead for all I see of you. Two visits a week! And you've no sooner arrived than you're chomping at the bit for off. Who put you on the stage in the first place? Who had you trained?' Beryl's voice was rising wildly as she turned to Gladys and said, 'I suppose you know that your daughter and my son are living in sin?'

'Mother, I have explained to you till I am sick of explaining . . .'

'I refuse to accept that filthy nonsense.' Beryl had lost all control and was shouting. 'You could go to prison for it. I prefer to think of you as living in sin.'

Gladys shook her head in overstudied pity. 'Very sad,' she said, 'very sad indeed.'

June suddenly started to tremble and sat down with a thump.

'I think she's going to give direct voice,' announced Martyn excitedly. 'Her spirit guide takes over her larynx and – if we're in luck – you'll hear him speak.'

Martyn sounded, to Sorrel, exactly like a barker, outside a freak show, on Blackpool's Golden Mile.

'Peace,' boomed June, in that horrible voice which Sorrel had first heard through a window as a child, 'I am Navarna.'

Her mouth wasn't moving but, from one corner, an almost luminous stream of spittle had begun trailing towards her chin. The ventriloquial voice droned on: 'Sorrel, my child, you have come back to all of heart's desire. One ingredient alone is missing. He will return and then you will find yourself at the gateway of choice. But remember this – everything comes at a price.'

The impromptu séance continued for a further five minutes. There were many cryptic references to storm clouds and rainbows and some much more brazen talk about old friends being best. Navarna, it seemed, couldn't rest contented until he'd stated this fact in three different ways. Then, June gave a few epileptic convulsions, shuddered violently and came to, bright as a button.

'What happened?' she asked. 'Did I transfigure?'

'You've just treated us to a performance which beat Madam Arcati in *Blithe Spirit*,' Gladys said drily. 'Did you ever see that film, Beryl? I've heard it said that Noël Coward is "one of those" too.'

The strange man had definitely followed them in from outside the Midland Hotel.

Sorrel and Mickey were with Bernard Conroy, the

replacement producer of *Angel Dwellings*. Neither of them felt quite comfortable with this ginger-haired nonentity. He had begun his working life as a schoolmaster. Perhaps unreasonably, they found it hard to view him as a fully paid-up professional.

The Midland lounge was like a club. Night after night you saw the same faces in the same armchairs. Bernard was meeting somebody from *The Guardian*. Sorrel and Mickey had booked a table for supper. The lounge was more comfortable, for a drink beforehand, than the American Bar.

The man, who had trailed them right across St Peter's Square, had not taken a seat. Still studying them closely, he looked distinctly out of place.

Sorrel was covertly sizing him up. Accounts clerk in a warehouse? His suit looked as though it had once belonged to somebody else and had been altered to fit him. What did he want? In his mid-thirties, he looked a male spinster. There was something menacing about the way he slid his hand into an inner pocket. And then he produced it – an autograph album.

Sorrel should have relaxed but she didn't. The man seemed to carry an aura of prim nastiness around him. Was it self-hatred which had caused him to knot the brown Tootal tie so viciously?

'Excuse me, Miss Starkey –' he pushed the book under her nose – 'would you mind?'

Angel Dwellings had been running for long enough for Sorrel to simply sign her name and scrawl 'Lettie Bly' in brackets, after it. Gone were the days when she used to dream up individual messages for each album.

Suddenly her conscience struck her. The poor little man had trailed them like a patient bloodhound. Four measly words wasn't much in return. He should, she felt, be offered something more. She inserted the word 'Love' before her own name and said, 'This is Mickey Grimshaw. You must have seen his credit on the screen. I'm sure you'd like his autograph too.'

'No I wouldn't,' said the man, 'I don't collect queers' autographs.'

Oh God, thought Sorrel and wished she could take back the suggestion or that she could simply melt into thin air.

Mickey was already on his feet. 'I'm not queer, I'm gay. G-a-y,' he spelled it out. 'Know what that stands for? Good as you.'

Why, why, why, must he do it? thought Sorrel. Heads were turning. She tried to pull Mickey down into his chair and hissed at the man, 'Scram or he'll scrag you, I'm not kidding.'

Mickey's sense of the ridiculous had plainly risen to the surface because he suddenly started to laugh. At that moment the head waiter hurried across the lounge, raising a questioning eyebrow at the autographcollector. The man with the autograph book treated the actress, the author and the producer to a sweeping dirty look, turned on his heel and made for the exit.

'Scram or I'll scrag you.' Mickey was still laughing. 'I can't imagine Dame Edith Evans saying that.'

'It's not funny, Mick.' Bernard Conroy was plainly smarting at having been included in the dirty look. 'You shouldn't have said what you did. If that story gets around it could seriously harm the show.'

'And am I supposed to take all they throw at me in the cause of *Angel* fucking *Dwellings*?' Mick's voice was now a series of whip cracks. 'If that's the case, *Angel Dwellings* has just turned itself into Frankenstein's monster.'

'At least sit down.' Bernard Conroy was looking uneasily at all the interested faces which were turning towards them. Lowering his voice he added, 'You really can't go round telling people your sexual preferences. The only ones who'd be interested are the police.'

Mick did not sit down. Neither did he lower his voice.

'I don't have to tell people. They take great pleasure in telling me. You just saw that. What's more, it's time I stated my case.' He looked round the audience who had not been expecting a free cabaret and said, 'I'm Mickey Grimshaw. I'm gay. I invented *Angel Dwellings*. I don't just take from this life, I'm a contributor.' Now he did sit down but he hadn't finished with Bernard Conroy, who looked as though he wished he were back in the safety of the grammar school common room.

'If people don't have the courage to stand up and be counted your vile law against us will never be changed.'

'It's not my law,' protested Bernard Conroy weakly.

Sorrel watched in horror as several husbands, shaking their heads, led their wives from the room. The looks Mickey was getting varied from hostile to puzzled to pitying.

One man began to walk towards them, his hand held out as though he intended shaking Mickey's. Sorrel's heart gave a jump. Why on earth hadn't she noticed him before?

It was Barney Shapiro.

'Congratulations on *Angel Dwellings*, Mickey. You've made it. You're a man.'

The bright blue eyes were still as full of concern and understanding as they'd always been. The years, thought Sorrel, had made Barney even more attractive. All the expensive tailoring on earth could not hide the easy, animal arrogance of the body underneath the clothes.

'Hello, Sorrel.'

He spoke so quietly that Sorrel felt as though they were in a big double bed. This would never do. What if Bernard Conroy noticed? He was known to have religious peculiarities.

'I love you in the show.'

But the eyes just said, 'I love you.'

Sorrel hoped he could read her own. They were saying, 'I love you. I've always loved you. There'll never be anybody else.'

For the benefit of the rest of the world she managed, 'Thanks. Your mother's become quite a friend of mine.'

'We don't see enough of her.' Barney glanced over to the woman he had left at a table, across the room. 'We live in Southport these days.'

The bride hasn't worn as well as he has, thought Sorrel, trying not to stare. The kewpie doll of yesteryear was as expensively dressed as her husband but the gleam of youth had gone and she needed the glitter of real diamonds, in her earrings, to draw attention away from the beginnings of a double chin.

Did convention demand that Sorrel invite him to bring his

wife over? What had she and Barney ever had to do with convention?

Her gaze rested on his hands. Those lean, tanned fingers had once had the freedom of her whole body. Below the knuckles blood was throbbing inside a pale turquoise vein.

'We tried to get a table in The French,' said Barney, 'but he says he's got nothing for an hour.'

'Have ours,' said Mickey. 'We've got one booked for ten. Suddenly I don't feel like eating. These days, Sorrel only ever picks.'

She could have wished that Mickey's glance had not gone quite so accusingly to her glass of gin and tonic. Everybody drank in Manchester, why pick on her?

'I'd better get back to Mandy.' Barney looked reluctant to go. 'Excuse me if I don't introduce you, she's not a very sociable animal.'

'I'd better get the hell out of here too.' Mickey was on his feet again.

'Where are you going?' Sorrel was alarmed. She knew that tone. It could lead to airports.

'Somewhere, anywhere that isn't Manchester. I've given you your show, Sorrel, and that's given you your town. Now I've got to go and find somewhere of my own. Thanks for your support, Barney.'

With a tight nod at Sorrel and the producer, Mickey began to head for the door.

'He really can't be allowed to carry on like this.' Bernard Conroy was plainly very much put out.

'Shut your face,' snapped Sorrel. 'Without him, neither of us would be in work.'

At this, surprisingly, Barney put his arms around Sorrel and gave her a little loving kiss.

'You've not changed at all.' He said it with uncomplicated delight. 'Loyalty was always your middle name.'

Sorrel tried hard to remember that he had a wife sitting not ten yards away. She tried hard not to think that this belonging moment would be over in seconds. Even as she was wondering what had happened to his once potent smell of new bread, Barney eased himself away from her.

'Goodbye,' he said.

Sorrel couldn't, wouldn't, reply. Lights seemed to be going out of her life. Mickey had gone – she knew that. He would be out of the town long before midnight. Barney's reappearance had been as brief and spectacular as a stage illusion done with mirrors. He was already on the way back to his wife's table.

'Suddenly it's just us,' said Bernard Conroy.

Yes, Bernard, she thought wearily, it's just us. Rehearsals five days a week, personal appearances in bingo halls on Saturday. The two most exciting men in my life have left me and you've not got the sensitivity to realize that I'm dying inside. It's just us, stuck on the treadmill. Except I'm not even me any more. I'm Lettie bloody Bly. Barney's retreating jacket had a centre vent. Suddenly he turned and hurried back.

Why – why was he coming back? And how old would he be now? Thirty-three or thirty-four? Oh God, she could still see the eager youth he used to be. Now Barney was looking down at her with unconcealed love.

'I'll find you again,' was all he said. And then he really hurried away.

As if on cue, the hotel pianist began to play some sophisticated tune which Sorrel could not quite recognize. It was tantalizingly familiar yet she couldn't catch hold of the title. Who cared what the tune was called when Barney was going to find her again and the lounge of the Midland Hotel had suddenly turned into one of the inner fields of heaven?

6

Whatever possessed Sorrel to make her move to Buxton? By the early 1970s the place was only the melancholy ghost of a Northern spa town. A deserted pump room still dispensed Buxton waters at tuppence a glass. The few devotees left had no need to pay; fifty yards away they could get all they wanted for nothing, in a tin cup on a chain, where the waters flowed out of a bronze mouth on St Anne's Well.

The well was opposite the crescent. Behind its noble colonnade, elegant as anything at Bath, were hidden antique hotels and an assembly room and all the hydro apparatus of a once-fashionable nineteenth-century watering place. By the time Sorrel got there, all that seemed left of these glories was an elderly woman who directed a hosepipe of cold Buxton water onto bathers, before they were allowed to enter the municipal swimming bath.

The town was twenty-eight miles from the studios. Depressed people settle on depressing aspects of their surroundings. Others, who moved there from Manchester at this time, were attracted by solid stone buildings and the glories of the surrounding Peak District. Not Sorrel; houses might be being restored, new restaurants could open, she only dwelt on the deserted conservatories of the Winter Gardens and the fact that Buxton's dusty little Opera House was hardly ever open.

When the sun shone Sorrel hid behind dark glasses. When the rains, which had gathered over the peaks and tors, descended on Buxton, Sorrel relaxed. Those were the days when the weather matched her melancholy. Famous, successful, richer than she had ever expected to be, the star of *Angel Dwellings* was living on four words.

'*I'll find you again.*'

Four words and as many years since Barney had said them in The Midland. Not so much as a message had come from him. A lesser woman would, long since, have relinquished the idea; not Sorrel Starkey. That chance meeting had brought a chink of light into a darkness which she had thought of as hers for this lifetime. In her own mind she was mated to Barney for ever. What were four years against Eternity? He had said that he would find her again and sooner or later he would. She had to hold onto that. She had to believe it.

Mickey had yet to find his own city but he was busy being hugely successful in Los Angeles. The American television quiz show he had invented, *Take Your Dime*, was bringing him in an even larger income than the one he was still getting as creator of *Angel Dwellings*. He had by no means gone out of Sorrel's life. Their feuding, loving relationship was kept alive by letters, telegrams and the Bell Telephone Company. Still a creature of midnight, Mickey often chose that hour to call Sorrel. Translated across the Atlantic this was breakfast time in Buxton.

'Good morning, Shirley Temple. How are you?' The transatlantic connection was remarkably clear today.

'I've got a hangover.' Sorrel was barely awake. What was this fear of doom impending?'

'Go to Alcoholics Anonymous.'

'I'm not *that* overhung, Mickey.' Now she'd remembered. Last night Bernard Conroy, the producer, had sent her a terse note demanding her presence, in his office, after rehearsal, today.

'Why do you punish yourself with all this booze?'

These long-distance phone calls were somehow safe as a diary. Propping herself up in bed, Sorrel had no hesitation in answering the question completely honestly.

'I do it to forget.'

'To forget what?'

'Things. And sometimes I do it to live in the past.'

'You need a good shrink.' Mick's voice had not become American but it was no longer absolutely English. 'I don't have to ask whether you've still got a candle in the window for Prince Yid. Does Ruby Shapiro ever offer any clues?'

'He's the one subject we don't discuss.'

'Where do you do all this unhappy drinking, Sorrel? I have

awful visions of you sitting alone, in a corner of Yates's Wine Lodge.'

'Manchester's changed. You can't move for clubs. There's one on every corner. Last night I went out to the Golden Garden at Wythenshawe.' Sorrel reached for a glass of water. Her mouth felt as though it was lined with suede.

'Whythenshawe's nothing but council estates,' said Mickey.

'I don't care, it's got its own night club. Shirley Bassey was on last night. There was a fight afterwards. Wythenshawe must be the last stronghold of Mods and Rockers.'

The bedroom door was pushed open and Spud came in wagging his tail. The dog treated Sorrel to a cautious look. She patted the bed and he jumped up onto the eiderdown.

'I expect I'll read all about it in the English tabloids. They cost me about a pound each and I wouldn't care, but they're a day old when we get them.'

'Don't talk to me about the tabloids,' grumbled Sorrel. 'They never leave us alone. I bet you, if I looked out of the window, I'd find the *News of the World* hidden in the rhododendrons.'

'You must simply view it as part of the job.' Mickey could still hand out stern lectures. 'And what's all this I read about Sorrel Starkey being surrounded by homosexuals? At this late date, they surely can't mean me?'

'I've got a housekeeper. He's a man. Well . . . He doesn't say he's a man. He maintains he's a queen. He says that, in his heart, he's Ginger Rogers.'

'Oh my God,' groaned Mickey. 'I can just imagine!'

'No you can't.' Sorrel was looking round the bedroom. It needed decorating.

'Does he drive for you as well?'

'Nope. I'm still taking taxis.'

This unleashed a barrage of: 'Rented accommodation, hired cars, you'll never have a farthing. Where did you find this monster?'

Sorrel decided to ignore the last word. 'He used to write me fan letters,' she continued. 'I thought it was a woman. And then he waited outside the studio and I met him. He's had a most unusual life. He's run a shooting gallery and been a chorus girl in a drag show. His walnut cake's better than Fuller's. Spud thinks he's lovely. Hang on . . .'

Holding the receiver to Spud's ear, she said, 'It's Mick.'

Sorrel made an encouraging growling noise to the dog who made just such another into the telephone. The over-indulgent could have taken this sound for 'Hello'.

Sorrel put the receiver back to her own ear to hear Mick saying, 'We must be barmy. Telephone calls at two dollars a minute and she wants me to talk to a performing dog! Now hear me, Sorrel, and hear me well – this boozing over Barney Shapiro can't go on. Either get yourself a husband or a good psychiatrist.'

'Ray Fossett says that what I really need is a good fuck.'

'Who's Ray Fossett?'

'The new housekeeper.'

'And watch yourself there too' was all Mick managed before some international static rose to a howling crescendo and somebody, somewhere, cut them off.

The bedroom door was pushed open again and Sorrel's breakfast was brought in, on a tray, by the man they'd been talking about.

For once, thought Sorrel, Mickey was wide of the mark. She certainly didn't have to watch herself where Ray Fossett was concerned. In many ways he was the mother Gladys had never been. Of indeterminate age, small, stocky yet dainty, this maid-of-all-work had even dyed his hair red, in tribute to Lettie Bly. Sorrel had no greater fan.

Over-respectful he wasn't: 'It's time you got your fanny washed and your trolleys on.'

Gladys Starkey maintained that Ray Fossett's conversation needed the services of the censor. A chance meeting with Mamie Hamilton-Gerrard had led her to gaze at him and wonder, aloud, why burning at the stake had gone out of fashion. It only took Ruby Shapiro five minutes to say that if Sorrel didn't hire Ray she would employ him herself.

'Our friend June is in the morning papers, dear,' he said, plonking the tray on an invalid table and sliding it across the bed. 'I didn't bring them up. I thought the rattling might go through your head.'

'Mick's already done that.'

'Some people would be thrilled to hear from Hollywood. Eat your egg. How is he?'

Sorrel foresaw tragedies. When it came to *Angel Dwellings* Ray Fossett was the fan to end super-fans. Mickey Grimshaw was high on the list of his icons. Or rather the *idea* of Mickey. Sorrel shuddered to think what would happen when he was eventually confronted by his hero. Mickey had plainly taken against the idea of her new helper.

Ray was in full flood again? 'According to the *Daily Mirror*, June brought Errol Flynn back to the grieving members of his British fan club. Women fainted, St John's Ambulance rushed off their feet, the lot! You've got to hand it to Mrs June, she certainly knows how to hit the headlines.'

Ray assumed a cherubic expression which alerted Sorrel to the fact that the worst was coming next.

'I wonder whether all those people who think of her as St Bernadette realize that she's slept with everybody but the Accrington and Stanley Brass Band.'

'Ray, you really mustn't say things like that.' Sorrel pushed away the boiled egg. He'd done it just the way she liked them, but these hangovers were getting beyond a joke.

'Wife-swapping,' said Ray as he swept the tray onto the dressing table. 'Want more coffee? I'll leave the pot. June and her hubby advertise in adult contact magazines. I'm told they even put photos of themselves in.'

'They'd never dare. She's too well known.' Sorrel couldn't help but be fascinated. 'What if the press came across them?'

'Masks,' said Ray enigmatically.

Understanding that Sorrel needed introducing gently to daylight, he only pulled the curtains back halfway. 'In the photo they both wore black masks. But who could mistake June's big jugs and his pectorals? I suppose it's the danger that appeals to them. I was the same myself, in the blitz, behind Queen Victoria's statue. Half the fun's gone out of life since they made us queers legal.'

No, thought Sorrel, he and militant Mickey, who publicly campaigned for these changes, will not get on.

She didn't have to wonder why she had homosexual

friends. Where would female stars be without them? They made perfect escorts. They were safe – they wouldn't pounce. They were often handsome and usually entertaining. Ray Fossett may not have been particularly good-looking, he might have been blessed with a viper's tongue, but he had also come to this earth with a heart the size of Manchester's Free Trade Hall.

'Why shouldn't Mrs June have her bit of umpty?' he asked. 'All that tangling with the dead probably leaves her very hungry for warm flesh. What do you propose putting on your back today?'

'Red.' Sorrel spoke with decision. 'It's got to be red.'

'Oh dear.' Ray's understanding of Sorrel had matured quickly. She only wore red when she was planning to take the centre of the stage in a fury.

'Are you proposing to give somebody gyp?'

'Bernard Conroy wants to see me in his office after rehearsal.' Sorrel was now out of bed and on her feet. 'He's the bastard who tried to get Mickey to moderate his behaviour. Just let him try it with me!'

'Definitely red.' Ray Fossett moved towards the wall of wardrobes. 'And to go with it, might I suggest a nice Bren gun?'

The general public had some strange ideas about *Angel Dwellings*. Some people believed that the whole thing was real. Let a flat in the tenement block fall empty and the studio would find itself bombarded with letters from would-be tenants. Other viewers understood that the show was a fiction but the performances struck them as so effortless that they thought that the cast were only required to attend, twice a week, for half an hour.

Readers of high-circulation newspapers and magazines had been deceived into believing that the residents of *Angel Dwellings* were 'one big happy family'. The people who wrote these articles had, in their turn, had the wool pulled over their eyes by the cast of the soap opera.

'Strike one and we all bleed' was true enough. The cast could be guaranteed to close ranks against outside interference. Amongst themselves they were equally capable of making angry waves. These storms were never allowed to last. Life in a continuing serial is too claustrophobic for that. The ability to rub along in rehearsals is almost as important as the on-screen performance.

The third-floor rehearsal room was the size of a school gymnasium with an oppressively low ceiling. Off it was the green room – the cast's retiring room. Many actors being superstitious about the colour green (Sorrel wouldn't so much as own a thread in it) the room was painted cream. Cigarette smoke had kippered the woodwork to a pale shade of amber.

Sorrel often wondered what the invisible cleaners, who did their work early in the mornings, made of the notice board. It was covered in a selection of the most abusive of the letters sent in by viewers and with hand-drawn caricatures and cartoons. Actors doodle and draw endlessly in rehearsals and the results can come close to gallows humour.

That's because we know how cold it can be in the great big world outside, thought Sorrel. We have to remind ourselves that there's still the dole queue and tatty agents' staircases.

And this was the trouble with her relationship with Bernard Conroy, the producer. He'd not come in from the cold. He had always basked in central heating. He was an erstwhile amateur actor who had first moved into television as a programme presenter, in the religious broadcasts department. Giant career leaps had not been unusual in those early prospecting days of television. Sorrel still found it hard to believe that this passionless creature had ended up as producer of *Angel Dwellings*. He was about as theatrical as washed jam jars.

Sorrel smoothed the red dress over her hips. What did Conroy want to see her about? It was three weeks since he had called her a rabble-rouser. That had been on the boiling hot day when she had gone to his office, on behalf of the whole cast, and asked for an electric fan.

The card players had got the fan, down at the far end of the green room, and they were welcome to it. The bloody thing *whirred*. Sorrel's headache was marginally better. A hair of the dog that bit her, in the Marshall Arms at lunchtime, had partially restored her equilibrium.

Tomorrow, she thought, I shall give up drinking.

Diggory Mallet and Nadine Taylor were playing bridge with the two young black kids who had brains like computers. They would only consent to sit down and play if it was for proper stakes.

'Sorrel,' called out old Diggory, 'have you got change for a fiver?'

Was that the same egg mark, on his tie, which had been there when Sorrel was in *Children's Hour*? He was the man who had once tried telling her that she would never make an actress until she lost her virginity.

Nadine Taylor came across with Diggory's five-pound note. She was a nice enough girl but sometimes she struck Sorrel as almost too obliging. They were often the kind who sit waiting, patiently, for somebody to slip up – then in they slide and grab the opportunity for themselves. Not nice to have in the next dressing room.

Mentally, Sorrel slapped herself. That kind of thinking was unworthy and destructive. All it did was make your mouth droop at the corners. She handed Nadine four pound notes and some silver.

The pale young brunette said, 'She must have got him to run that scene ten times over.' Nadine was nodding in the direction of the rehearsal room.

'*She*', pronounced in this significant tone, meant only one person: Mamie Hamilton-Gerrard. Young directors dreaded working with her. Probably the most experienced person in the building, the ageing actress was a stickler for detail. Everything had to be done the right way. This usually meant Mamie's way.

The door burst open and in she came looking like Bo-Peep in a tiny, black and white gingham dress. The false ringlets looked as though they'd been pulled through a thorn hedge backwards. Her red court shoes could have been on loan from Minnie Mouse.

'What's this boy-director's name?' demanded Mamie. 'I'm thinking of going straight upstairs about him. Anybody would think this was a Sunday school concert. First he had the temerity to give me inflections and then he tried to send Mother to the coffee machine. She was so shocked she dropped a stitch. Anybody got a safety pin?'

Nobody had. Mamie was a notorious borrower.

The stage manager had followed the actress into the room. 'Thank you, everybody. That's it for today,' he said. 'Ten o'clock in the morning, please, and no scripts in the hand.'

The torpid activity in the green room suddenly quickened. Sorrel moved across to the window sill to collect some bits of shopping in Kendal's pretty, violet-decorated, paper carrier bags. Mamie followed her, grabbed a sturdy cardboard box of her own, opened it and began examining a brand-new rubber enema syringe. She even sniffed it.

Sorrel said nothing but filed the moment away for Mickey. He could never hear enough of Mamie's latest atrocities.

'Three guineas,' she said, 'and they're nothing like the quality they used to be. They don't seem to shoot as far these days.'

Sorrel found herself left alone with Mamie as the rest of the cast departed with alacrity. Mamie was looking angrily out of the window at the wide, sunlit panorama of Manchester.

'The sun shines too brightly,' she said. 'It shows up all the cracks and mending. How would Red Biddy look with a face lift?' Mamie's voice was bitter. 'I might want one but she's standing in the way of it. The only thing that's as good as it used to be is *success*.' She slapped the window sill viciously with the red rubber appliance.

'They love me,' she said more quietly. 'The public and I go back a long way. It's not you who's everybody's favourite, it's me. I don't just get the piles of letters you see here. People are writing to me, privately, at home; fans of mine since I had the biggest panto contract in England. Prince Littler used to say he could book me five years ahead and still be sure of filling every seat. I hate this bloody sunlight.'

'You're going to bring on one of her asthma attacks, Sorrel.' Old Mother Hamilton-Gerrard had sidled, unnoticed, into the green room.

'Me?' Sorrel couldn't believe her ears. 'What've I done?'

'You're just *here*,' screamed Mamie. 'You're here, you're here, you're here! And I don't want you. You don't know what it's like to have been idolized and forgotten. I've got it all back. And neither you nor anybody else is going to grab my spotlight.'

The *Daily Mail*, thought Sorrel, light dawning. This morning, that paper had called Lettie Bly 'Queen of Angel Dwellings'.

'Mamie, there's room for both of us.'

'Sez you!' snarled the old wraith. 'In five years' time will you be as gracious to Nadine Taylor? I've watched, I've noticed.'

And anything you've missed your mother's registered. Sorrel only thought this, she didn't say it aloud.

'Mamie is a Star,' said Mrs Hamilton-Gerrard in a voice of hallowed reverence.

'She's a has-been who got lucky.' Sorrel had taken enough.

Mamie swayed dramatically and reached for the back of a chair.

'Now you've done it,' she said, closing her eyes. 'You've hurt me very deeply. Very deeply indeed. It will almost certainly bring on one of my attacks. I may not be able to make tomorrow's recording.'

'You'd make tomorrow's recording if they had to prop you up in a plaster cast.' Though Sorrel was blazing she felt obliged to add: 'It's the one thing about you I admire. That and your unquenchable talent.'

'She won't be satisfied till she's finished me off,' gasped Mamie. 'And I've not got my asthma pump.'

'Have an enema instead,' stormed Sorrel. 'It might get rid of some of the poison inside you.'

Before Sorrel's horrified eyes, Mamie Hamilton-Gerrard turned into a tiny, pathetic old woman who was holding out helpless hands in supplication.

More chastened than she would ever have believed possible, Sorrel wished with all her heart that she could unsay the things that had just been said.

'I'm sorry, Mamie. I'm so sorry . . .' Sorrel tried to put her arms around the fragile heap of skin and bone and false hair.

A stinging blow sent her flying across the room. Tragic antiquity had been nothing but a performance. Sorrel was now facing a spitting, venomous ten-year-old, who was made of energy.

'I wish you were *dead*, Sorrel Starkey. Dead and in your coffin. I'd gladly spend a hundred pounds on lilies.'

Somebody had to call a halt to this madness. Even though a startling red welt was already coming up on her arm, Sorrel decided it had better be herself. Trying to behave as though nothing untoward had happened, she offered Mamie the opportunity to leave, with 'Weren't you going upstairs to complain about the new director?'

Never one to be outdone, Mamie had collected herself equally quickly and she replied, 'I won't bother Bernard Conroy now. I expect he'll have his time cut out this afternoon, talking to you.'

Sorrel picked up her carrier bags and walked out of the rehearsal room. So Mamie knew about her summons to Bernard Conroy's office? That didn't bode well. Was the old bag at the bottom of whatever it was?

As Sorrel headed for the lift she thought about herself and Nadine Taylor. In her own turn, would she eventually begrudge Nadine a share of the limelight? No. And that was the truth.

If the character of Lettie Bly began to wear thin and Nadine's role grew in prominence, so what? Sorrel had no intention of boring the public to death. When Lettie outlived her period of usefulness, Sorrel could always return to the theatre. These days she sometimes ached for the warm embrace of a live audience.

The cast of *Angel Dwellings* had recently taken part in a Royal Variety Performance. It had shown Sorrel that an audience is just an audience, be it at the London Palladium or Salford Hippodrome. They are simply a lover to be wooed and won. Come to that, fifty people facing an illuminated platform are exactly the same thing – an opportunity for a public love affair. Yes, eventually she would go back to the stage. Only not yet because there was still last year's income tax to be paid.

As Sorrel got out of the lift, on the executive floor, she wondered whether the thick carpets were designed to tone down angry footsteps and prove who was in charge. Her arm was already beginning to swell alarmingly. Would there be ice in Bernard Conroy's office?

There was ice all right in the shape of Conroy's secretary, Sandra. Reproach was written all over her face. Of course the girl was more than a little in love with her boss. This probably explained why she behaved like a thermometer.

'Go straight in,' said Sandra. 'You've been holding him up. He wants to get away.'

Sorrel pushed open the door. Bernard Conroy was wearing a new pair of glasses. Tortoiseshell, in a most unattractive shade of pubic ginger. They made him look like somebody who had been invited to a fancy-dress party but had not really bothered changing and was having a tentative stab at impersonating the late Buddy Holly. Above his head was a framed picture of himself shaking hands with a Greek Orthodox priest. It wasn't showbusiness as Sorrel understood it.

'I'll come straight to the point.' Conroy's stare was unblinking. 'There've been complaints about secondhand gin.'

Sorrel was completely nonplussed. What on earth was the cold soul talking about? The glasses must be meant to bring out the hint of ginger in his mousy hair. What was all this about secondhand gin?

Conroy elucidated: 'People don't like rehearsing in the afternoons with other people who've been drinking.'

'Half the cast does it. Why pick on me?'

'Because the complaint was very specific.'

'She's a bad bitch.'

'I don't think I heard that.' Conroy spoke so primly that Sorrel was left wondering what on earth his secretary saw in him.

'If you won't believe your ears,' she said, 'let's see how good those new glasses are.' Holding out her arm, Sorrel announced indignantly, 'Mamie Hamilton-Gerrard just wanged me one.'

'I think you mean *winged*, Sorrel.' The schoolmaster in him was never far from the surface.

'I know what I mean and I mean wanged. She belted me one.'

'I don't believe you.'

And he didn't. Sorrel could see that.

He hadn't finished either: 'All this lunchtime drinking's very bad for the whites of your eyes.'

'They're my eyes. I'll do the worrying about that.'

'You seem to forget you have a contract with us. Strictly speaking they're our eyes too.'

Sorrel felt like a rat in a trap. The best answer would have been 'Stuff your contract'. But she wasn't free to say it. The Commissioners of Inland Revenue were already writing her threatening letters. Her only chance of earning the sort of money they wanted would be in *Angel Dwellings*.

Giving her a look that he must have perfected when people were late with their homework, Conroy said, 'I'm very well aware that you don't like me, Sorrel.'

'You shouldn't have got shut of Mickey' was all she could manage in reply.

'Mickey got rid of himself. And you're going the right way to do the same thing.'

The secretary burst effusively into the room carrying a framed picture. It was an old theatrical photograph labelled *Mamie Hamilton-Gerrard as Humpty Dumpty. London Coliseum 1929.*

'A messenger's just brought it back, Bernie,' said the girl. 'I think you were right to settle for the better-quality frame.'

'We'll put her next to Archbishop Xouthou.' Conroy smiled for the first time. 'I just wish her mother was on it too.'

So the rumours, that they went out to steakhouses together, were true. I don't stand a cat in hell's chance here, thought Sorrel.

Aloud she said, 'I'll buy a bottle of stronger mouthwash,' and walked out.

'Give me a vodka.'

Sorrel was in the American Bar of The Midland. Had she

371

been a bit too clever? Was it the dress which had acted like a red rag to a bull? No, Conroy might sneak off for meat dinners with that elderly midget but he was too bloodless to be described as a bull.

'Make that a large vodka.'

The American Bar was a remnant from the 1930s. It was full of chromium touches. Sitting on a high stool, at the swooping curve of the counter, Sorrel was full of unresolved anger. The change to vodka was meant to be a positive step. She'd read somewhere that it smelled less than gin.

'Ice and tonic?' asked the barman.

Sorrel nodded tersely.

Two men came into the bar from the reception corridor and quickly cased the room. CID men from Bootle Street? The size of sides of beef, they wore Italian suits that looked as though they might have come from George Best's boutique. One had a broken nose. Were they coppers or well-groomed thugs?

'He'll be all right in here,' said the barman. 'We've got nothing but another celebrity and a lot of empty tables. How are his legs?'

'Plaster's due to come off tomorrow.'

'A great tragedy.' The barman had assumed a funereal expression.

Sorrel transferred her irritation to this present situation. What was it all about? And this new masculine fashion for sideburns was awful. Why were they behaving like lofty men in a man's world when this was supposed to be a mixed bar?

'He'll be all right in here,' repeated the barman. 'Just so long as he doesn't get legless.'

'The poor bastard's legless already.'

And why was the barman allowing swearing in front of a woman? Sorrel felt distinctly trivialized.

'He smashed a glass table last time.' The barman actually smiled at the memory.

'Stands to sense. He's upset. He'll never play again.'

The two men had half registered Lettie Bly but, as they disappeared, it was obvious that they had more important matters on their minds.

'Stand by for action.' The hotel servant breathed on a glass and polished it. 'They're bringing in Kenny Shorrocks.' He filled the glass with ice and jiggered three shots of spirit across the shining peaks. 'Kenny likes his vodka too. Wouldn't do to keep him waiting.'

Kenny Shorrocks? Sorrel's mind went back to the night when she'd tried to be a night-club hostess at Ed Shotter's Attaché Club. The footballer might recognize Lettie Bly but would he associate her with the paid company he'd once tried to buy in Mayfair? Sorrel suddenly remembered the dress she'd worn that night. Black taffeta at two and eleven a yard from John Lewis's.

The henchmen returned. One held open the door, the other went up to the counter.

'That his drink? How much?'

Sorrel had to grip the counter to steady herself. One drink hadn't done this to her. It was the man swinging through the doorway on crutches. The fashion for long hair in men had not changed Kenny Shorrocks's resemblance to Barney Shapiro. If anything it had increased it. It was like a conjuring trick. Now you saw it, now you didn't.

'Same again,' she said across the counter.

'On me,' called out Kenny. 'Come on, Lettie, you'd never refuse a wounded soldier.' The years had added polish and authority. He had learned how to use the Liverpool accent to winning advantage.

'Scat!' he said to the henchmen.

Less winning, thought Sorrel.

'If you want us, Kenny, we'll only be in the lounge.'

Sorrel suddenly found the fact that these hulking men were so full of concern for their injured friend curiously endearing. It was like watching a documentary about lions.

'These fixed stools are a godsend to a man on crutches.' Kenny had settled on the one next to Sorrel. He gave her a slow, confident smile. She knew that kind of smile. She often got it. He'd only recognized Lettie Bly. Kenny Shorrocks didn't remember the night-club hostess. Last time he'd smiled at her there had been a chipped front tooth. Somebody must have mended it very skilfully.

'Who's your dentist?' she asked. A craftsman as good as that would be worth knowing about.

'Never need one,' he said, 'I'm in perfect nick. All except for these; and the bloody judge did me five hundred pounds for dangerous driving.'

The bitterness was corrosive. Then he smiled again and, unaccountably, he reminded Sorrel of a sailor. She tried to rationalize this. Was it the blue eyes and the suntan or was it his absolute confidence in his own sexual magnetism?

There is an indefinable sheen to stardom, and Kenny had it. Put him in a country where nobody had ever heard of him and the public would still have turned round to stare. On holidays abroad, Sorrel had found herself signing autographs for people who immediately puzzled over the signature, in an attempt to discover her identity. That's the sheen of stardom.

We're two of a kind, thought Sorrel. And how *dare* he wink at me.

'I love women in red.' Kenny spoke lazily, confidently. 'They're generally as dangerous as I am.'

7

It did not take five vodka and tonics for Sorrel to discover that she had found a new playmate, but she had them anyway.

Kenny Shorrocks matched her drink for drink. Not that they got her drunk. Far from it. They were so busy finding out about one another that their own intensity burned away the effects of alcohol.

Kenny was, she discovered, a strange mixture. Just as she thought she had him pinned down as a sweet dope, he began to let fly with conversational arrows of considerable brilliance. He was Liverpool-Irish – that cunning, exciting mixture. It was impossible for the actress in Sorrel to tell whether his effects were planned or spontaneous.

'The career's over,' he said. 'There's no way I can limp back on these legs. Ten years ago maybe, but I'm thirty-two now. Even before the accident, it was getting tougher every game. All I'm scared of is ending up like Freddie Mills.'

Freddie Mills was a famous ex-boxer who had been found shot dead, in a car, outside a seedy London night club.

'Is somebody out to get you?' asked Sorrel, secretly impressed.

'Plenty,' grinned Kenny. 'But that's not what I'm talking about. Freddie was everybody's favourite too. And when the career was finished, all the punters did was get him to relive his fights, over and over again. I watched, I saw. I even assisted. Moments of glory done to death in saloon bars. It can be just the same for footballers. I want a future, not a past. I don't want to be some bore in a railway compartment, remembering winning goals.'

'Won't you miss the audience?' Sorrel could only try to understand his situation in the terms of her own world.

'Yes, I'll miss the crowd.' Kenny's eyes were seeing something far beyond the American Bar. 'I'll even miss "Kenny, Kenny, not worth a penny". That's what they used to sing when I lost the ball. They just had a big benefit for me at Maine Road. When I hobbled out onto the pitch, you could've heard the cheers at Old Trafford. Now I need tomorrow.'

'What will you do – become a manager?'

'Team manager? I've been too bad a lad.' The grin had no repentance in it. 'I want to manage players. Promotions, that's the coming thing. Advertising endorsements, personal appearances, that's where the new money's coming from.'

'I could do with a manager myself.' Sorrel spoke ruefully, she was still smarting from Bernard Conroy's attack. 'Sticking up for yourself's tough work.'

One of the henchmen reappeared with a tentatively inquiring expression on his face.

'Let's go to the Cromford Club,' said Kenny. 'You'll be quite safe, Lettie. My lads'll see to that.'

For a moment he looked unhappy. In that moment Sorrel realized, with absolute certainty, that he was wishing he was physically fit enough to look after her himself. So she went.

The car was a big white Jaguar. Both the henchmen answered to nicknames. The one with the squashed nose was called Eeek. The even larger one was introduced as Little Dabs. Sorrel presumed that this must have something to do with the fact that he had very small hands. Taking their cue from Kenny, both they and the driver were behaving very respectfully towards the star of *Angel Dwellings*.

Surrounded by all this muscle, Sorrel felt like Mae West in a Hollywood production number. There were no two ways about it, she was enjoying herself.

They parked the car off Corporation Street and continued, on foot, through a maze of old alleyways. Sorrel was so busy taking care not to go too quickly for Kenny that she didn't really take in where they were. It was only when they passed a surgical store, and began to descend a grimy marble staircase, that she suddenly realized where she was.

She had been here before. The premises of the Cromford Club had once been the Hadassiah Kosher cafe. Memories came flooding back of little fishcakes and Enid Rosenthal saying that half Manchester was laughing at Sorrel's passion for Barney. The whirligig of time had brought about its revenges. Tonight, Manchester would see what she was really made of. They were already down on the level and being bowed in by a doorman.

'I'm taking your arm, Kenny,' she said.

His reply was gleeful: 'This should knock their eyes out.'

Oh he was so *nice*. The henchmen and the driver fell two respectful paces behind them.

'Ladies and Gentlemen, it's cabaret time at the Cromford Club and, once again, we present a very, very lovely cabaret for your entertainment . . .' The compere was already behind the microphone, in full flood, when he caught sight of them. A beam immediately spread across his face.

'Two legends!' he boomed. 'Two legends have just walked into this club at one and the same moment. Ladies and Gentlemen, let's have a round of applause for the King of Football and the Queen of Television.'

And up yours Enid Rosenthal, wherever you are, thought Sorrel contentedly as solid applause turned into cheers. They're not laughing now. Tonight I've knocked Manchester sideways.

'Are you there, Buxton?' asked the international operator. 'Your Los Angeles call should be coming on the line in a moment. It *is* Mr Grimshaw you want?'

'Yes.' And how she wanted him! In times of excitement or despair, Sorrel always reached for Mick. She picked up the beer-mat from the bedside table and studied Kenny's handwriting. He had written down his name and telephone number in a secretive, childlike fist. Tight, wary little numbers.

'Mick . . . can you hear me? Why are you hiding behind servants?'

'It's one black maid. She's protecting me from the world while I pack.'

'Never mind that . . .' Sorrel spoke impatiently.

'I do mind.'

Oh dear. He'd got the rattlesnake tone on.

'I'm due at the airport in half an hour,' he continued. 'I'm off to find my city.'

Not that again, thought Sorrel, who was bursting with news of her own.

'I've been all these years in Southern California and it looks as though it might have been there, waiting, just the other side of the desert.'

'Lovely.' She even sounded unconvincing to herself.

'I've a terrible feeling you're going to tell me you just got laid.'

'When we've only shaken hands?' Sorrel was all but squawking with indignation. 'It was the height of respectability. Three other men watched us. Listen, Mick, I've got a manager. He says nobody can go out and sell themselves in the marketplace so he's going to do it for me.'

'Then I just hope it's one of the international offices. I might have plans for us, in the future. Who is it?'

'Kenny Shorrocks.' Even Mickey, with his minimal interest in sport, must have heard of him.

He had. 'Are you out of your mind? It's breakfast time in England. You surely can't have started drinking already?'

Sorrel slammed down the receiver in a fury. She wouldn't have cared but Ray Fossett had been no more enthusiastic. He'd said Kenny Shorrocks belonged in the tabloids, with his shirt off, surrounded by bathing beauties.

Let them scoff. They'd soon see. All right, it was unusual, but when had Sorrel Starkey ever claimed to be usual?

She'd borrowed that line from Mickey. It was one he always used about himself. Exasperation took over. Their lives were inextricably tied together but he was an ocean and a continent away. She needed help, in negotiating her new contract, here and now.

In fairness to Kenny it must be said that he handled that first contract very well. He went to the studio bosses, at a time when Sorrel's standing with them was at a low ebb, and by emphasizing her continuing popularity with the general public, emerged with an excellent new deal. The people he had to negotiate with were men. They were impressed by his fame and much surprised by his business acumen. Kenny took his own experience of poor contracts and used it to secure Sorrel's future for a further two years.

He was her new hero. He never made the slightest pass at her. Sorrel was only too pleased to turn herself into one of the boys, a good sport. Kenny was uncomfortable in the company of just one person; he was only happy in a gang. Restaurants were always having to put two tables together for the footballer and his lieutenants. At the head of the table, Sorrel sometimes felt like Snow White with the seven dwarfs.

Which of those cartoon characters was most like Kenny? Grumpy, Bashful, Doc? The answer was *all* of them and Pinocchio too. Kenny Shorrocks was a whole wagonload of monkeys. If he and Sorrel had one thing in common, it was the fact that neither of them was quite tamed.

There were definitely sexual sparks in the air but that's where they remained. Their whole relationship was based on denying this attraction. The performance they were giving for one another was that of 'good mates'.

This was not how the newspapers viewed it. For years Sorrel had been something of a disappointment to them. Lettie Bly was all come hither but Sorrel Starkey had studiously avoided romantic attachments. Suddenly she was being seen everywhere – from dog-tracks to gambling casinos –with a beauty chorus of handsome sportsmen.

At first Sorrel claimed that there was safety in numbers. Early press stories hinted at the emergence of a Manchester version of the Hollywood Rat Pack with Sorrel in the role of Shirley Maclaine. The participants were being watched too closely to get away with this for long. One of Sorrel's constant companions was significantly more famous than the rest. Sorrel always sat next to him. It was a romance made for the tabloids. Or was it a romance made *by* the tabloids? The keen wind of press attention seemed determined to fan small sexual sparks into a blazing reality.

Everybody Sorrel knew seemed to feel obliged to put in their tuppenny worth.

'He might be handsome but he's a messy bastard,' grumbled Ray Fossett. 'He needs house-training. There's ash everywhere. And I hope you don't think it's me that's emptied the drinks cabinet. Sportsmen? They're just greedy leeches, the lot of them.'

June Gee was in ecstasies. Without abandoning her clairvoyance, she had lately embraced astrology because it was much in vogue and an easier subject for her to write about. These days she had a column in one of the more gaudy women's magazines.

June burst into print with: 'My best friend Sorrel Starkey is a Cancer subject. Kenny Shorrocks was born under the sign of Scorpio. Their astrological combination could make for dynamic sexual encounters. Unleashed, theirs will be the kind of passion which breaks beds . . .'

Whilst June was already well into the new sexual revolution, Sorrel and Kenny had yet to hold hands.

Gladys Starkey, unpredictable as ever, took to Kenny in a big way. The footballer had insisted upon being taken to Rookswood Avenue to meet her. Himself an orphan, he had an almost religious devotion to the idea of mothers. This went down very well with Gladys.

'I won't call upstairs, after him, to lift the seat,' she said. 'I can always go in there afterwards with a cloth. There's not much you can tell me about men. Grab this one, Sheila, while you can; you're not getting any younger.'

From Mickey, surprisingly, there was silence. All she'd had from him was a postcard of a rainbow over Golden Gate Bridge in San Francisco. On the back of the card he had written: 'I have found my city.'

When Sorrel tried to telephone Mickey, she got an answering machine. It was the first one she had ever encountered and she found the experience unnerving. At the very time she needed Mick he was hiding behind a metallic recording. She left a message on the machine but it took several more days of newspaper headlines before he returned the call.

'Good morning, Lola Montez. Are you alone in bed? Can you speak?'

'Don't you start that too,' sighed Sorrel. 'How was San Francisco?'

'Home. I'm moving there this week. People try to tell you that it's beautiful but it's not. It's just very, very pretty. What's more, a million of my kind have moved there. It's Mansworld

USA. So there I was, cruising down Castro Street, and what do I see on a newsstand? You and Mr Bollocks on the front page of the English *Daily Mirror*.'

'There's nothing in it, Mick.'

'I sincerely hope not. I've had him checked out.'

'Sometimes you go too far.' Sorrel was immediately spoiling for a fight.

Infuriatingly, Mick refused to rise to the bait. He just said, 'What's the point in having all this money if I can't use some of it to save my friends from themselves?'

'And what if I don't want to be saved from myself?' snapped Sorrel.

'I thought you said there was nothing in it?'

'Well . . .' It was Mick. It was safe: 'Kenny and I have said there's nothing in it so often that I'm beginning to wonder who's kidding who.' Intrigued fascination took over. 'Did you really have him checked out?'

'And at American rates too, you costly trollop. I got a Californian investigation agency to send somebody from London up to Manchester. I'm afraid your Mr Bollocks sails very close to the wind.'

'Don't call him that. In what way does he sail close to the wind? Not that I believe it.'

'Some of the company he keeps is very questionable indeed.'

'Of course it is.' Sorrel spoke blithely. 'He knows all the top gangsters.'

'He's got no money, Sorrel.'

'*Wrong!* His benefit match raised a small fortune.'

'And I'm told he's already spending it like a drunken sailor. You'll end up keeping him.'

This was not what Sorrel wanted to hear. She had finally met a man who understood her status but wasn't over-impressed by it. Kenny's fame matched her own. He wasn't short of money and he was full of ideas for making more. She certainly didn't want Mick to take against the idea of Kenny so she decided to try a peaceful approach.

'It's funny you should mention sailors, Mick. He always reminds me of one.'

'Oh God,' groaned Mickey. 'Not blue eyes again. I can't bear it. Look, I'm not going to make the mistake of arguing with you. You'd probably go straight out and propose to him. Answer me one question and I'll leave it at that. Does Spud like him?'

Sorrel cursed the day she was born honest. Her only reply was a silent pause.

'Oh dear,' said Mickey. And Sorrel heard him put down the receiver.

Now there'll be a stern letter, thought Sorrel. And I wouldn't care, but there's nothing in it.

The only trouble was, Mick's razor-sharp mind had cleared the windows of her own. There was plenty in her friendship with Kenny Shorrocks. In recent weeks, a life which had been drab had grown unaccountably vivid.

The bedroom door was pushed open and Spud walked in and flopped down in a way which was, endearingly, all his own. It was as though the dog was a marionette and somebody had suddenly cut the strings.

'You can come up on the bed if you want,' coaxed Sorrel.

It didn't work. She had known it wouldn't. It had been a whole week since Spud had looked her directly in the eye.

'Well *I* like him,' said Sorrel defiantly. 'And bugger the lot of you.'

Sorrel checked her luggage on the back seat of the taxi. She was getting famous for leaving things in cabs. Gucci handbag, Revelation overnight case and an old Tesco carrier containing a big brownstone pot of home-made meat and potato pie. Yes, they were all there. Sorrel had been spending the weekend in Blackpool with Gander.

That great friend of her childhood had given Sorrel a lovely time. Kenny was away in Germany, where he had gone to watch an international match. Sorrel had been treated to real fires and a feather bed and all her favourite childhood foods including pea soup, in a basin, made with pig's trotter. The idea might make other people heave, she and Gander had always loved it.

Gander's bungalow was to the north of Blackpool, in

Cleveleys, a place which has a gentle lifestyle of its own. They had fed the seagulls and watched old men playing bowls. On Saturday evening they'd taken front deckchair seats, for the pierrots, at the open-air Arena. No telephone, port wine bought specially, Gander lived such a relaxed life that she didn't even bother having the newspaper delivered. A weekend of autumn on the Fylde coast had done Sorrel a power of good.

Now it was mid-day and she was back in Manchester. Her rehearsal call was for two o'clock. First she would have to endure lunch with June. The clairvoyant and her husband still maintained their cottage at Worsley. Nowadays, they also had a London flat in a block named Chelsea Cloisters. June was beginning to be famous.

They had arranged to meet in the restaurant of Kendal Milne's department store. Gladys Starkey no longer worked there. These days Gladys was busy weighing nails in the hardware shop which she and Sorrel had inherited.

Was it Sorrel's imagination or were the public taking more interest in her than usual, today? These things went in fits and starts. It all depended on her prominence in the story-line of *Angel Dwellings*. As the lift rose, floor by floor, to the top of the department store, there was certainly a lot of nudge-nudge going on. And the women shoppers seemed to be smiling at her more brightly than usual.

As Sorrel emerged from the lift, she almost collided with a mannequin carrying a piece of cardboard with a number on it. Kendal's restaurant featured fashion parades at lunchtime.

Across the room she caught sight of June who was a one-woman fashion show in herself. The supremacy of the mini-skirt was finally being challenged by maxi-dresses. June Gee had embraced the new style with fervour. She looked like Anna Karenina gone mad. Black velvet all the way. Sorrel supposed it could be called a suit. The skirt touched the ground, there was a lot of frogging across June's front and she had set a huge, circular white fox hat, at a crazy angle, on her buttercup curls.

'What's the perfume?' asked Sorrel.

'Joy by Jean Patou. I wore it specially. Sweetheart, I'm so thrilled for you,' breathed June. 'Give us a kiss.'

Even the combination of June's hat and the sight of Lettie Bly, in the flesh, could not be drumming up all the interest which was throbbing round the restaurant.

Ignoring the request for a kiss, Sorrel said, 'Is it my imagination or are we stopping the traffic? And why are you thrilled?'

'Come off it,' guffawed June. 'You must have spent the morning surrounded by reporters.'

'I've only just got back from Blackpool.' Sorrel sat down, arranging the carrier and the overnight bag on the floor.

June rose to her feet and, like a showgirl with a placard, held up a copy of Sorrel's least-favourite tabloid. The bold, front-page headline read *WILL YOU MARRY ME LETTIE?* Underneath this was a picture of Kenny wearing a beseeching expression.

'Hasn't he got style?' murmured June.

'He's got a bloody cheek,' retorted Sorrel, snatching for the paper and kicking over the carrier bag in the process. The lid came off Gander's brownstone pot, and meat and potato pie began to ooze across Kendal's discreet beige carpet. Gander always believed in plenty of gravy.

'Kenny must be out of his mind.' Sorrel spoke in a voice of total disbelief.

'With love, darling, with love. It's all there. You can read it for yourself. He told a reporter, in Munich last night, that you are his one obsession.'

'I'll murder him.' Sorrel was trying to read the article but her head was swimming. If this was meant to be a serious proposal, how did she feel about it?

'Waitress,' she called out, 'could you get a cloth? We've had a bit of an accident.'

'I think I'd better be quite honest.' June was looking a mite uncomfortable. 'My own editor's already been on. He wants me to do a big piece about you.'

'That hat's bloody ridiculous, June,' snorted Sorrel. 'Have you got any pennies on you? I need four for the phone. This little lot wants sorting out. I'll try and get Kenny at his landlady's. That's if he's dared come back.'

'I'll come to the phone with you.' June was already reaching for her Russian muff.

'To write down everything I say? No thank you.' Sorrel noticed that somebody had left a pile of coppers under a saucer, as a tip. Unhesitatingly she stole them.

'Put a shilling in their place,' she instructed June. 'I'll pay you back.' Clutching the change, Sorrel stomped across the restaurant towards the public phone by the ladies' cloakroom. Let them stare. Let them all stare. Proposals should be on bended knees, not in cold print.

Quickly she dialled the number. Kenny answered the telephone himself.

'Well?' she said.

'I'd had a couple,' was the mumbled reply. 'They offered me five hundred quid. You can have half if you want it.'

It was a little boy talking and Sorrel's heart melted. 'You daft bat,' she said.

'I meant it, though.' He sounded hopeful. 'I meant the proposal.'

'That's not good enough.'

'What d'you want me to say? Just a minute . . . Ouch. I've gone down on me bended knees.'

'Kenny, get up! Your legs won't stand that yet.'

'Will you marry me?'

'Just for the cheek – yes. I will. I can't stop and talk. I've just knocked a pot of potato pie over.'

The moment she put down the phone Sorrel began to hear Barney Shapiro's voice inside her head.

'*I'll find you again* . . .'

She had been in bondage to her own past for too many years. It wasn't letting her go without a struggle.

'Shut up, Barney.' Sorrel actually said it aloud.

Barney Shapiro had done nothing but haunt her head. Kenny Shorrocks was the man who had shown her that success and enjoyment can go hand in hand. You can live for just so long cooped up with a promise. After that comes madness or a decisive change of heart. If Sorrel had chosen freedom, why did she still feel constrained – still frozen to the spot? She found herself wishing she was having lunch with anybody on earth but June Gee.

Yes, she rationalized, that's what's wrong, it's June. She'll want me to work myself up into a lather of Brussels lace before I've so much as got used to the idea.

Sorrel had never really thought much about her own wedding. As a child, of course, she had wanted it to be as much like the grand finale of a pantomime as possible. Once Barney came into her life, Sorrel had stopped thinking of weddings and herself in the same breath.

'Go away, Barney! I mean it.'

This talking to herself would have to stop. A woman waiting to use the phone booth was looking at her through the glass, as though she was mad. The door was a sliding effort which opened with a nasty rattle. As Sorrel retraced her steps across the restaurant floor, she made up her mind not to tell June.

Dear God, I'm engaged, she thought wildly. Sorrel Shorrocks, what a mouthful. June Gee's certainly not going to be the first one to find out.

At their table a cleaner was already at work, down on her hands and knees with a floor-cloth and a steaming bucket, cleaning up Gander's potato pie.

'Hello, Lettie,' she said. 'You're a careless bugger, aren't you?'

Sorrel was glad of the old woman's presence. It would give her a chance to divert the conversation and knock June off the scent.

She should have known better.

June gazed up at her, through false eyelashes like chickens' claws, and said, 'He went down on his bended knees at the other end and proposed, didn't he?'

'Did you accept?' asked the cleaner interestedly.

What could Sorrel do? Strictly speaking it wasn't telling June first; it was telling a member of the public. For a long time the public had been all she'd had.

'Yes, I accepted.'

The ancient cleaner let out a wild whoop. Drying her hands on her coarse hessian apron, she rose creakily to her feet and flung her arms around the actress. 'Let's give you a kiss,' she said.

It was a whiskery kiss and June followed with one that was more blubbery.

'She's accepted,' yelled the cleaner to everybody in the restaurant. 'Lettie Bly's going to marry Kenny Bollocks.'

The pandemonium which was to characterize the forth-coming wedding was already under way.

'May I have your daughter's hand in marriage, Mrs Starkey?' He had changed into a new suit for the visit to Rookswood Avenue.

'Nobody else seems to want it so you might as well.' But Sorrel noticed that Gladys seemed pleased to have been asked.

'Mind you,' Gladys went on, 'I can't be expected to run a hardware shop with one hand and stage-manage a wedding with the other. I've been expecting this visit. You'll find a thick brown envelope in the bureau.'

Sorrel moved across to the little desk where she had so often been forced to sit and do her homework. There should still be some marks inside the lid where she'd once stabbed it with a pen-nib.

Gladys hadn't finished: 'I'm not having people saying I didn't do the right thing by you. I went to see Mr Monk. June had a lovely wedding with no expense spared. Have you found that envelope, Sheila? There's cash inside to the tune of what June's cost. And a tidy bit to cover inflation. Fancy a date, Kenneth?'

For a mad moment Sorrel thought that her mother was offering her fiancé a social engagement. But Gladys was only holding out a box of preserved fruits. They must have been left over from last Christmas. Sorrel opened the brown envelope. It was full of white five-pound notes.

'Mother, there must be hundreds in here.'

'Nearer a thousand,' said Gladys complacently. 'And Sheila, should anything ever happen to me, all your profits from you-know-what are in the thingy under the doings.'

Kenny might have been elevated to 'Kenneth' in the cause

of becoming her future son-in-law but she wasn't letting him know where Sorrel's share of the rewards from the hardware shop were secreted. Gladys trusted neither banks nor men.

'There'll be no need for this money.' Kenny had his important voice on. 'I've already started doing a deal.'

'Who with? What for?' asked Sorrel.

'One of the papers has offered to pay for the reception in return for exclusive coverage.'

'No.' Sorrel was horrified. 'I draw the line at that.'

'Don't be so daft,' scoffed her mother. 'It's about time you had something back from them. They've certainly made enough out of you. I've had reporters knocking here, trying to stir up trouble. I just said to them, "I'd be more worried if she was marrying a man who *hadn't* sown a few wild oats."'

Gladys was studying Kenny with interest: 'They didn't half try to credit you with some antics. You're sure you're not going to find married life tame?'

Kenny winked at Gladys, who now burst into a vulgar laugh. Sorrel hadn't seen her mother like this since the days of Mr Jepson.

'We're not taking this cash,' said Kenny. 'We're not short.'

'Neither am I,' answered Gladys roguishly. 'I'm five feet six inches tall. If you don't take it I'll be very much offended. Sheila's always had what's right. When she was little, all her clothes came from Henry Barrie's. I've been putting money aside for years. I was beginning to think I'd never get her off my hands. There was once a Jew-boy but that was doomed to failure from the start.'

Thank you, Mother, thought Sorrel. Kenny, it seemed, was being offered more intimacy, in one night, than her mother had offered her in a lifetime. She had watched Kenny file 'Jew-boy' away, presumably for future questioning.

Their own relationship was still very chaste and proper. They had yet to get beyond a goodnight kiss on the doorstep at Buxton. Kenny's reputation with women may have been lurid but he plainly kept fiancées on the same sacred shelf as mothers.

Sorrel was glad that Gander no longer lived across the gap from the side door. Gander would have been bound to have asked about love. And love was a word that had never been mentioned.

'Keep the money and buy a good bed,' said Gladys. 'Where are you going to live?'

'I've got big plans.' Kenny opened Sorrel's handbag and slid the brown envelope inside it. 'It's going to be my surprise for Sheila.'

'Don't call me by that name.'

'See what I've had to put up with?' said Gladys. 'Years, I've had, of this.'

Sorrel didn't care whether she was presenting herself in a bad light. *Sheila* was somebody other people told what to do. Sorrel Starkey wasn't just a name, it was a creature of her own creation. And that creature was blazing. Kenny had gone into her handbag without so much as a by-your-leave and she'd learned, quite by chance, that the wedding pictures were on offer to a newspaper before they'd so much as decided when the marriage would take place.

'I'd like one of those dates too,' she said huffily.

'I didn't think you liked dates.' Her mother offered the box again to Kenny.

'I'd just like to be asked.'

'Bridal nerves.' Gladys spoke with irritating complacency. 'And doesn't Mum get to kiss her future son-in-law?'

Kiss his face off while you're at it! thought Sorrel bitterly. I notice you're not offering to kiss me. It must be donkey's years since you so much as put an arm round me.

Something suddenly dawned on her, something she should have seen a long time ago. Everything would have been all right with Gladys if only she'd been a son instead of a daughter. And why on earth had her mother never got rid of this glaring overhead light?

Though the paintwork was no longer green and cream and even Gladys had discarded her lace curtains, Rookswood Avenue could still weave its cold, unmagical spell. The one which left Sorrel on the outside looking in.

'Have you been to see your own mother and father yet?' Gladys asked Kenny.

'They're dead.' He was all big blue eyes. 'I was brought up in homes.'

'How awful,' said Gladys. 'Never mind. We'll just have to show you what real family life is all about.'

Sorrel had been doing some mental arithmetic. It was twenty-one years since Gladys had last kissed her.

'Do you love Kenny, really love him?' asked Ruby Shapiro.

The pair of them were alone, in Ruby's sitting room in Broughton Park, going through the wedding-guest list for the umpteenth time. In recent years, Sorrel had grown very fond of this plain, dark room which was often as brilliantly coloured, with conversation, as the Matisse painting over the fireplace. This morning the conversation was of that privileged kind which only strong friendship allows.

'I'm fond of him.' Sorrel was weighing her words carefully. 'The other might grow. Who knows? Anyway, I thought Jewish people believed in arranged marriages.'

'And who arranged this one?'

'Fate.' The answer came back quickly because it was the one which Sorrel had already settled upon for herself. 'Fate was the marriage broker.'

'Fine words.' Ruby didn't sound impressed.

Sorrel sought to explain: 'Everybody's part of a pair. The world seems designed for twos. I'm sick of being one on my own.'

'And that's enough?' Ruby donned a huge pair of spectacles and gazed again at the list.

'I asked you whether that was enough?' Her magnified eyes looked straight into the actress.

'Famous people are better off married to other famous people.'

'With this I could argue. Is it wrong of me to want happiness for you?'

God, but we're on dangerous ground, thought Sorrel, and we both know it. You're the woman who once stood like an iron door between me and the only man I truly wanted. No. It wasn't you. It was tradition.

Ruby must have been going through similar thought processes because she said, 'I sometimes wish . . .'

'What? What do you sometimes wish?' Sorrel was startled to see a suspicion of tears magnified behind Ruby's thick lenses.

Ruby shook her head. 'I won't say it. I can't. But we both know. All I can do is help. I just hope I'm not helping you to a piece of madness. Where had we got to? We were trying to get the guests down to two hundred and fifty.' Without pausing she added, 'He's feckless, that Shorrocks. Keep your business affairs separate from his. Have you got a good accountant?'

'Stop worrying, Ruby!'

'I do worry. He's not a bad man. He's just a very ordinary boy who's had too much too easily. Don't let him get his hands on what's yours.'

'I'm shocked,' said Sorrel, who wasn't. 'Is that how good Jewish wives talk?'

'He's not a Jew, more's the pity. Except that's where we came in. Oh dear . . .' She went back to the list: 'Who are Mr and Mrs Tuffin with Blackpool, in brackets, in your mother's writing? Are they two we could think of striking off?'

Ruby was being a tower of strength in the middle of mayhem. Public interest in the forthcoming marriage was proving so intense that Sorrel had decided to get the wedding over as quickly as possible. Kenny had won the day in the matter of the reception. It was being funded by a Sunday newspaper. The representative they assigned to the task was called Libby Taylor. It took only two minutes to realize that Libby needed firm handling. Sorrel assigned the task to Ruby.

'Taylor?' scoffed the Jewess. 'They were called Schneider when they first came to Manchester.' Ruby hated any suggestion of her own kind trying to pass as non-Jewish. 'Miss Libby Schneider will need watching. They're one of those families that taste forgot.'

Sorrel, as usual, felt obliged to defend the oppressed. 'They were probably called something different again, before they got to Middle Europe and were landed with that name.'

'Don't tell me about my own race,' said Ruby. 'That woman's a vulgarian in any language. She should stick to reporting murders. The way she went on about The Midland was plain mishegoss.'

Libby Taylor had wanted the reception at The Midland simply because it was The Midland. At such short notice, all the hotel had been able to offer was a suite, like a night club in the daytime, down in the bowels of the earth. Libby Taylor had proposed installing a sound and light system and hiring a disc jockey from Radio Luxembourg.

Ruby was opposed to any such idea: 'Nobody's fonder of the hotel than I am, but not that suite. Let's look elsewhere.'

She dismissed The Piccadilly-Plaza as too modern, The Grand got nervous about the idea of screaming fans outside, Ruby decided to go to the other extreme.

The Marshall Arms was a charming Victorian pub with both theatrical and sporting associations. Ruby persuaded the landlord that it would be possible, for a single Saturday lunchtime, to close everything but one bar to the general public. She would transform the rest.

Next, Ruby enlisted the services of a clever young florist. And she and this girl dreamed-up a fairy-tale scheme involving banks of fresh flowers and false ceilings of tented ribbon.

'It's wonderful,' said Sorrel, who had abandoned the guest list for the moment, and was looking at the designs for the proposed transformation. 'It's like a Gala Night at Covent Garden.'

'If money's no object, we might as well have a proper show.' Ruby smiled at Sorrel. 'Will you do something for me? Will you at least *think* about being married in another outfit?'

'What's wrong with a white lace trouser suit? It's only for a register office.'

'Fashionable these trouser suits may be. But in ten years' time the wedding photographs will look a joke. Was that a car I heard drawing up?'

Sorrel nodded 'Yes' to the car. Kenny was a lapsed Catholic. The best she could be described as herself was 'nominally Church of England'. The register office, on All

Saints' Green, had seemed a sensible compromise. Sorrel certainly had no intention of turning up in a wreath and veil. She wouldn't see thirty again and she wanted no part in any wedding outfit which would suggest mutton dressed as lamb. She had regarded the trouser suit as little short of divine inspiration. Such suits were everywhere these days. But not in white lace.

'Your mother has natural chic,' sighed Ruby. 'And what a woman for a bargain!'

In the cause of this wedding, Gladys Starkey and Ruby Shapiro had become unlikely allies.

'I bumped into Gladys on Deansgate,' continued Ruby. 'She was going to the Model Room at Kendal's to look for her outfit. That woman is a perfect size twelve. She chose what she wanted: dove grey, beautiful. And then she and the assistant exchanged what I can only describe as *a very significant look*. Do you know where the money changed hands? At half past five, outside the staff exit. Your mother exchanged cash for a wrapped parcel.'

'They were never shoplifting?' asked Sorrel in horror.

'Staff discount,' said Ruby with reverence. 'Such a pity Gladys is a Fascist, otherwise she'd be a woman after my own heart. Do think again about those lace pyjamas. Who's this?'

Ruby turned. The door of the sitting room had opened and in walked her son. Barney was carrying himself wearily and his handsome face looked creased with worry. Sorrel learned, for the first time in her life, that it was truly possible for a room to begin to spin around. She steadied herself with a deep breath and heard Barney saying, 'Ruby, would you for God's sake go out to the car and talk to my wife?'

Only now did he register Sorrel's presence.

'Hello,' he said in a startled voice, then anxiety turned him back to his mother: 'Mandy's got an appointment with Doctor Urban in St John Street. I've taken the morning off to drive her there. Gynaecologist? I sometimes think she needs a psychiatrist. We were halfway up the East Lancashire Road when she suddenly started to scream and shout. Arms flying everywhere. Just see whether you can calm her down. She certainly can't keep her appointment in this state.'

Ruby began to hurry towards the open door. For a moment she paused on the threshold, giving Barney and Sorrel a worried glance. Then, shrugging her shoulders, she left the room.

'Is your wife having a baby?' asked Sorrel.

'We're not having one. That's the problem. I know your news. Congratulations.'

'I'm not sure that's the right word. It would have been if I hadn't seen you . . .' Emotion overcame better judgement and Sorrel burst into confused tears.

'Sorrel, don't.' His arms were around her. 'Don't do that. You're brave Sorrel who never cries.'

'You said you'd find me again . . .' Sobs drowned out further attempts at words.

'I tried. I kept my promise. Didn't that woman give you the message?'

'What woman? Nobody ever gave me any message. What woman are you talking about?' She broke away from him. The sobs were tugging like pincers inside her.

'Mamie Hamilton-Gerrard. I rang the rehearsal room. Didn't she tell you? It was a Friday night when I saw you and I rang the following Monday. I left my office number.'

'She never gave it to me.' Sorrel's voice was dazed and blank.

'I thought you'd decided not to see me.'

Now Sorrel was almost shouting: 'I'd never decide that, never. You should know that. But why did God have to send you this morning? Why couldn't he leave me in peace? I'm trying. I was really trying.'

'Don't you want to get married?' asked Barney anxiously.

'I only want you.'

His arms were around her again and he was stroking her hair. 'Not a day goes by,' he said. 'Not one single day . . .'

He didn't finish the sentence. He didn't have to.

'Why can't we be together?' Sorrel had dared to say it. '*Why?*'

Yet what was the point of stumbling over that old ground again? It was useless and she knew it. Sorrel felt for her handkerchief. If she gave her nose a loud and prosaic blow perhaps that would reintroduce reality. But she didn't want reality. Sorrel blew her nose anyway.

'Bridal nerves,' she said. She'd always hated it when other people said that. It sounded just as trite coming from herself.

'Kenny Shorrocks was a great player.' Barney suddenly seemed very solemn and formal. 'I used to watch him when I followed City.'

Barney at football matches? That was a surprise. There was so much about him she didn't know. Yet she knew his *core*; she knew his inner-being.

'D'you think you can make a go of this marriage?' he asked.

He had not asked her whether she loved Kenny. Sorrel sensed that Barney knew there was no need.

'I can try,' she replied. 'I'm good at trying.'

'I know. I remember. You're my good times, Sorrel. You were the best bits. Do you remember the party, here in this house, when you used the Seder plate for ham sandwiches?'

'And the night I came up the fire escape.'

'When I called you Venus in transit.'

The eagerness of these memories was drowned out by the sound of a car horn honking peremptorily.

'Mandy,' said Barney. He was shifting indecisively, from one foot to the other. 'I don't know how to go, but I must. I daren't say what I want to. It wouldn't be fair on other people.'

'And who's been fair on us?' asked Sorrel. 'I just hope that marriages are only for this lifetime. I just hope that, when this lot's over, there's somewhere we can be together.'

'Me too.' Barney spoke with absolute conviction. 'Yes, me too.'

And with this he turned and walked out of the room, as more noise on a motor-hooter summoned him back to being somebody else's husband.

Sorrel's eyes were gazing, unseeing, at the picture over Ruby's fireplace. Gradually they registered the familiar fact that it was of indoor shutters pulled back to reveal a very blue river. For the very first time she noticed something else. On the river, far into the distance, was a pair of swans. And these were swans who were floating contented and free.

8

'Is that you, Kenny?' The public telephone box smelled of somebody else's cheap scent.

'What d'you want?' asked her fiancé. Before she could reply he continued, 'I'm whacked. I've just got back from the physio.'

'Kenny . . .' Sorrel had nothing prepared. Once out of Ruby's front gate she had simply dived into the first box she came to. 'Kenny . . . we've never talked about love.'

'Course we haven't.' She could hear him yawning. 'I'm marrying you because you're the one woman who *doesn't* want to talk sloppy-love.'

'How can we think of getting married without it?'

'For God's sake, Sorrel!' Kenny sounded horrified. 'The whole of Britain's watching us. You're never going to make a cunt of me by backing out now? We get on, don't we?'

'It's not enough.'

A green and yellow Salford bus was going past. For the first time since she got famous Sorrel wished she could just climb up onto the top deck and be nobody in particular. Perhaps it was the many windows of the phone box which were heightening the feeling of life in a goldfish bowl.

'It's not enough.' She didn't care if she was repeating herself.

'We'll make it enough. You do like me, don't you?'

'Very much.'

She could hear Kenny breathing a sigh of relief. 'There you are then, that's all right.' Now a puzzled note entered his voice as he asked, 'Is all this because you didn't like the engagement ring?'

'I'm funny about anything green.' Sorrel looked down at the emerald in its fancily chased gold setting. 'It's supposed to be unlucky.'

'I already offered to change it. It was just that I managed to get it wholesale.'

Wholesale? This was news. Sorrel found herself wondering whether the ring was stolen goods. She hadn't let him change it because she had found the idea of his going off alone, to choose it, somehow touching. These thoughts were getting her nowhere.

Her momentary silence had obviously panicked her fiancé: 'If you don't marry me I'll be a laughing stock. Is that what you want?'

'No.' Why wouldn't the right words come?

Kenny wasn't about to give her the chance: 'Just shut up, we're very well suited. The physio's receptionist showed me an article that says so. It was by your friend June Gee. I'm doing everything I can to get my legs right for your big day. You'd never walk out on a wounded soldier, would you?'

'No,' said Sorrel unhappily, 'I don't suppose I would.'

In the back of the hired wedding car, Sorrel's bouquet was making Lady Inver-Ross sneeze. When Sorrel first knew her titled bridesmaid, she had been plain Judy Weatherall – actress, resident of the Old Fire-Iron, failed night-club hostess. Good old Judy who had once made a dress out of a divan cover.

Today Judy was dressed by Hardy Amies in discreet hyacinth blue. Even though Sorrel's white lace trouser suit was lined with silk, it still itched. What with her scratching and Judy's sneezing they hardly presented a picture from *The Tatler*.

'I hate this suit,' said Sorrel with sudden decision. 'D'you think we've time to stop and get something else, ready-made?'

'Your dressmaker would never forgive you.'

This was true enough. The Salmon sisters would already be on their way to the reception. Invitations to the register office were strictly limited but half of fashionable Manchester had been issued with special passes to get them into the Marshall Arms.

'You look fine,' said Judy. 'But I think you were wise to rip up that awful hat. Just the flowers, on top, look much better. I must say I'm loving all this public attention.'

A gang of women had surged to the edge of the pavement

and were calling out: 'God bless you, Lettie!' 'God bless you, love.'

Sorrel's mind went back to the day when she had been Judy's bridesmaid at St James's, Spanish Place: 'This is all very different from the way things were at yours in London.'

'Of course it's different.' Judy could still be a lecturing Catholic. 'My marriage was a sacrament. God was there. This is nothing but a civil disgrace.'

'You mean it doesn't count?'

'Not in the eyes of heaven. Oh dear, what am I saying? I'm awfully sorry . . .'

'No, don't be. Don't be sorry at all.' Relief was flooding through Sorrel like sunlight. A great, guilty weight had been lifted from her shoulders. She had no compunction in taking part in 'a civil disgrace' just so long as it didn't count with the Almighty.

'Oh I do love you, Judy,' she said. 'Thank God for people who are uncompromising.'

'And I'll never understand you, Sorrel Starkey. Not in a million years!'

'You might in eternity. In fact you will. You'll see me and you'll see Barney and then you'll understand. Promise me one thing, Judy. There is going to *be* eternity, isn't there?'

'You-bet-your-bippy there is,' replied Lady Inver-Ross with holy fervour.

The car paused for a moment. A woman's head came through the open window.

'Tonight's the night, eh?' she said and narrowly missed decapitation as the chauffeur chose that moment to move off again.

'At the risk of sounding like the Pope, I'd say you were going in for legalized sex,' said Judy. And then she sneezed again.

'I don't think this is going to be a very sexy marriage,' Sorrel assured her earnestly.

'Then why? Why are you going through with it?'

'I was lonely.'

This was the only time Sorrel had told anybody the plain truth of her sorry engagement. 'It's as simple as that. I was very, very lonely.'

'Doesn't look a lonely life to me,' said Judy excitedly, 'not with crash barriers and mounted police.'

'Horses? Where?' For the first time that day Sorrel was thrilled. 'They're beautiful. But all the fuss is for *her*, for Lettie Bly. Kenny's not marrying Lettie, he's marrying me.'

In the past, Manchester had known big showbusiness weddings and big football weddings. Today both forces were combined and the public turn-out was phenomenal. The crowds were milling across the road, in front of the register office, and onto All Saints' Green. People were up lamp posts and on top of parked cars and hanging out of office windows. The sun was beating down and it took the combined efforts of a dozen sweating policemen to get Sorrel and Judy through the crowd and up the steps of the soot-blackened building.

Kenny was waiting just inside the Victorian stained-glass doors with his longest-serving henchman, Eeek.

They might both date back to an orphanage, thought Sorrel. But they're so scrubbed and shining that a whole army of mothers could have got them ready.

'You look dead young,' said Kenny. 'As good as Sandie Shaw. Did you see all my girl fans got up in black mourning? One of them swallowed tablets. They had to take her to the infirmary. Your mother's in the bog.'

Gladys now appeared, at the end of a corridor, straightening the skirt of a dove grey dress. Sorrel recognized the white hat as one of Ruby's.

'Somebody keeps that toilet beautifully,' said Gladys with approval. 'And the paper's Bronco. Where's Ray Fossett gone?'

Eeek had the answer: 'Trying to find Sellotape to hold his glasses together.' To Sorrel and Judy he explained, 'They got knocked off his nose when we was fighting our way in.'

A door opened and Ray Fossett flew out. It was the first time Sorrel had ever seen him without spectacles. He looked much more innocent.

'Now the bleeders have snapped in two,' he said. 'I'll just have to go through the ceremony like Bette Davis in *Dark Victory*. Anybody spare a clean hanky? I'm bound to weep.'

From outside the building a huge roar started to go up: '*Ken, Ken, Ken, Ken, Kenny*.'

'They always did that when he scored.' Squashed-nosed Eeek was visibly moved.

The registrar appeared in a black jacket and striped trousers. 'Would you all like to come this way?'

Did they usually have this amount of flowers? wondered Sorrel. The registrar's office looked like Dingley's window. Perhaps the flower arrangements were to compensate for a ceremony which was, to say the least of it, basic.

The first words Sorrel spoke, as a married woman, were to her friend Judy: 'Not much of a script, eh?'

Yet, strangely enough, it was this flippant reference to scripts which brought tears to her eyes. Where was Mickey? It wasn't right without Mick. They had always shared all the big adventures. He might not approve of her choice of husband but it wouldn't have killed him to have bought an air ticket and come.

'Buck up, love.' Kenny looked concerned. 'Your crying days are supposed to be over now.'

'Or just starting,' said Gladys, with whom old habits died hard. 'Where's the Chief Inspector? I suggested he might smuggle us out the back way.'

'Never!' said Sorrel.

Her new husband was quick to agree: 'You couldn't do that to the fans. They'd never forgive us.'

He understands, thought Sorrel. And how many men would? He belongs to the public too. He's the one man in Manchester who could cope with being saddled with me.

Kenny put his arm around her. 'The police will get us through at this end and I've got bouncers on the door of the Marshall Arms. Everybody ready? Let's go into combat.'

As Sorrel and Kenny appeared at the top of the steps, in the sunlight, the cheering was deafening. It was like the sound of rival roller-coasters. Sorrel knew audiences, and this vast crowd was the most loving she had ever encountered. The District of All Saints seemed to have turned into a sea of smiles. Clouds of confetti filled the air and women and girls ducked under policemen's arms to thrust out silver cardboard horseshoes and sprigs of lucky heather. When Sorrel's own hands were full she was forced to hand some over to Judy.

'The pair of you are like royalty,' said Lady Inver-Ross in awe.

'Lettie?' It was an old woman, at the front, with blackened teeth. 'I hope you'll be changing those lace pyjamas for a nightie!' Manchester never lets anybody get too much above themselves.

Finally, regretfully, the crowd let Sorrel and Kenny get into the first car. Looking out through the window on the way to the reception, it was smiles and waves for the whole of the route.

'Have you noticed, they've kept the lights at green for us, all the way.' Kenny spoke with awe. 'This beats bringing back the cup.'

Another huge crowd had gathered around the Marshall Arms and somebody tried to get Kenny to sign an autograph. Gladys Starkey, who was just emerging from the second car, shouted out: 'I forbid that and I'm his mother-in-law.' The crowd burst out laughing but Gladys wasn't hanging around to bask in their favour.

'Come on, you two,' she said. 'Let's get in and see what Ruby Shapiro's managed to do to a four-ale bar.'

Roses, ribbons, gypsophila – everything was in place. Sorrel had privately worried that Ruby's scheme, in white and cream, might be just a bit anaemic. Trust Ruby to have known what she was doing! These subtle shades made a perfect backdrop for the paint-box colours of the wedding guests.

For the first time in her life, everybody Sorrel knew and loved was together in one room. Everybody except Barney and Mick; and they would just have to take care of themselves. Old Mrs Tatton from next door was talking to Gander and Lily Bear. Mrs Gillibrand the hairdresser, who had cashed Sorrel's first *Children's Hour* cheques, was introducing Diggory Mallet to Mrs Monk. Where was June? Sorrel moved across the room to speak to Bertha from the Old Fire-Iron. On the receiving line she'd hardly managed to say more than 'Hello' to anybody.

Gladys, champagne glass in hand, blocked her way. 'Have you ever seen such a sight as Beryl Grimshaw? I think she's come as a striped refreshment tent.'

Sorrel suddenly realized that her mother was more than a bit squiffy.

'I've kissed Russell Harty,' said Gladys. 'And I've kissed Matt Busby. But the handsomest man in this room has got to be Jacob Shapiro. Are you sure Kenny's not a Hebrew? There's a very definite resemblance there.'

Sorrel suddenly saw a lace picture hat, of mammoth proportions, bobbing its way towards her. Only one person could be underneath that low brim – June Gee. The crowd parted for a moment and revealed the clairvoyant in all her glory. Sorrel could hardly believe her eyes. June was done up, from head to foot, in a white lace trouser suit.

'Snap!' said June. 'That will teach you to abandon your oldest friend for Lady Muck. If I'd been matron of honour this could never have happened.'

Libby Taylor, the representative of the newspaper which had set all the champagne corks popping, rushed up and joined them. Her unaccustomed wedding finery did nothing to stop *Planet of the Apes* springing to mind. She looked just like one of the intelligent monkeys.

'Mrs Gee,' she said. 'Am I right in thinking that you've brought a professional photographer?'

'Naturally!' bridled June. 'I am a fully accredited columnist.'

'He'll have to go,' protested Libby. 'We have an exclusive contract here.'

'Kenny,' shouted Sorrel. 'Can you come over?' There seemed little point in having a husband and barking herself. 'Sort this lot out, will you?'

As June began to raise her voice in protest, Sorrel pushed her way through the gang of Lucie Clayton's Manchester model girls who were draped round footballers, and joined Ray Fossett. He had a waitress's lace apron tied around his waist and was pushing a dinner-wagon, piled high with gift-wrapped wedding presents.

'There's no need to bother feeling them, to see what's inside,' he said. 'People keep coming up and confiding in me. You should have had a list. By my calculation, you've now got enough electric hotplates to start a small Chinese restaurant.

D'you know what's missing from this do? There are no kids sliding across the parquet.'

At that moment two did and almost ended on their eyelashes. Martyn Gee dived through the throng and hauled Jason and Junelle to their feet.

'June's a bit upset,' he said, confidentially, to Sorrel.

'June can speak for herself.' His wife had come up from behind them and she was snarling. 'They've had the nerve to send my photographer downstairs. I'm speaking now as a member of the press. Sorrel, would you just answer me one question? Where's Mamie Hamilton-Gerrard?'

'Not here,' said Sorrel icily. An invitation had been extended and refused.

'Sheila . . .' June's cow-like eyes went limpid behind the false eyelashes. 'Why are we being like this with one another? I only want what's best for you . . .'

She's copied him and had her teeth capped, thought Sorrel.

'And I truly hope you're going to be very happy. Wouldn't you just let my man take one little piccy?'

'You'll have to talk to Kenny.'

'I already did. Of course he's beautiful, Kenny's scrumptious. And we both know he's a dead ringer for somebody else.' June batted her false eyelashes. 'It may be terrible of me but I can't help wondering whether you'll be pretending it's Barney Shapiro, when you open your legs tonight.'

The first blow, which Sorrel landed in June's right eye, was for brazen cheek. The second was for more complicated reasons. Sorrel had been horrified to find herself momentarily considering whether there mightn't be just a grain of truth in the idea. *Would* she be thinking of Barney?

'Even if you blinded me, I'd still be able to see further than other people.' June was speaking through gritted teeth.

'Then you'll have no difficulty in finding your way to the door.'

June wasn't leaving it at that. 'One of my eyelashes is now stuck to your knuckles,' she said. 'They're French. They cost me ten guineas.'

Sorrel repressed a shudder as she peeled back the spidery object which was adhering to her skin with rubber solution.

June smiled sweetly as she took it and said, 'You'll be more than shuddering on that bed tonight. And that's not clairvoyance, it's common Manchester gossip.'

9

It is not every wedding reception which ends with a honeymoon procession. Dusk was falling fast as they came into Flintshire. In the back of the leading car, the bride turned round to look through the rear window.

'They're still behind us,' she said. 'All of them. I should have had stickers printed saying *Sorrel's Circus*.'

'You mean Shorrocks' Circus.'

Sorrel looked down at her wedding ring. Such new-looking gold had an almost false lustre to it. The ring had been specially shaped to fit underneath the fancy curves and bevelling of her engagement band. Sorrel's finger felt significantly heavier than it had done when the day began.

'Where have the pavements gone?' blurted out Kenny nervously.

'We're in the country. They don't have them. You must have noticed that on the way to football matches.'

'On the way to matches, the coach is full of the lads.'

To Sorrel, he sounded like a wartime evacuee who had got separated from the rest. God knows they weren't far behind. The procession was in strict order of precedence. Behind the bridal limousine came just such another containing Libby Taylor and her photographer. This was followed by Kenny's white Jaguar driven, as usual, by Irish Dez and carrying Eeek and Little Dabs as passengers. Officially, they had come along as 'minders'. This was the new word for bodyguards. Privately, Sorrel considered that Kenny was incapable of being separated from either a crowd or a card game. The car following this one was full of chancers of a different breed. Were the pubs of Fleet Street deserted? Half the journalists and photographers in England seemed to be bringing up the rear of this procession through North Wales.

For weeks, the honeymoon destination had been a secret, supposedly known to only the bride, the groom and Libby

Taylor. Sand had been thrown in everybody else's eyes in the form of vague references to the wonders of the Greek islands. Though Sorrel refused to lie, she had seen little harm in dissembling in the cause of eventual privacy.

The original plan had been for a car to take Sorrel and Kenny to Manchester Airport. En route, they would transfer to another for North Wales. Halfway through the reception, a man from the *Daily Mail* had poked his head through a first-floor window of the Marshall Arms (he had come up a ladder) and said to the bride, 'Congratulations, love. What time are we all leaving for Portmeirion?'

As word of the honeymoon location was plainly out, there had seemed little to be gained from further subterfuge. Gladys Starkey said of the line of cars, outside the pub: 'Honeymoon? This is more like the feast of the five thousand. Whatever happened to reticence?'

Pulling her daughter into a doorway, she added: 'I don't know how much you know about the intimate things, Sheila – and I don't want to know. I took to that side of marriage like a duck to water. Should you find you don't like it, you'd be well advised to claim that your monthlies go on for three weeks. That's a bit of motherly advice which has kept many a woman sane.'

Though the night had grown black as the car began to pass through Glen Conway, a small quayside was suddenly illuminated by a violent flash of lightning. Sorrel could actually see to read a name on a boat; it was *Endeavour*.

Kenny was looking ashen. 'People who live in places like this deserve a medal. No overhead street lights, no nothing. I never thought I'd be relieved to see a chip shop. I don't want to stop,' he added hastily. 'It's just that it's a sign of human life. Anything could happen in a godforsaken hole like this.'

The lightning was followed by a dramatic clap of thunder. The car swerved to avoid a stray dog and then lurched as it turned onto a narrower mountain road. Kenny, a footballer with a gaudy reputation for rough-housing, reached hastily for the hanging loop of cord, provided by Rolls-Royce for nervous passengers who needed to steady themselves. Another flash of forked lightning illuminated the bleached outlines of crazily twisted, dead trees on the edge of a sheer drop into a ravine.

'If you opened that window,' he said in awed respect, 'I bet you could smell the sulphur in the air. Sorrel, *don't!*'

He was too late. A blast of stinging rain came flying into the safe, beige interior of the limousine and Sorrel thrilled with excitement. She loved storms. And then, pressing the button which closed the window, she suddenly remembered something.

It hadn't always been like this. Once, she too had been as afraid of thunder and lightning as Kenny was tonight. It was Gander who had put a chair and a little stool in the open kitchen doorway and encouraged her to sit and view a storm as a concert. At the time, Sorrel couldn't have been more than six. She remembered Gander's words and repeated them to Kenny.

'It's just God moving the furniture about in heaven.'

He reached for her hand and squeezed it and she saw that it might be possible to love him.

By Blaenau Ffestiniog the devil himself seemed to be stage-managing the weather. The pyrotechnics were more haphazardly dramatic than any firework display. Flash, crash, night, day – the lightning was dancing above the peaks of great piles of broken slate rising, like giant slag-heaps, at either side of the streaming road. The rain was now torrential. Kenny had his eyes shut and Sorrel tried hard not to think of the Aberfan disaster. Could one loose slate bring the whole hillside crashing down?

Just as these threats were behind them, a flooded road brought the whole procession to a halt. The chauffeur got out of the car and disappeared, bravely, into the night to size up the situation.

Sorrel and Kenny were suddenly startled by a tap on one of the car windows. Sorrel could hardly believe her eyes. Under a striped golfing umbrella she saw a man from the *News of the World* proffering a silver hip flask.

Just as Sorrel had opened the window and gratefully accepted his offer, the flask was snatched from her hand by a soaking-wet Libby Taylor.

'Your contract is with *us*.' Miss Taylor was another furious storm in herself.

'Shut your gob, Libby,' said Sorrel wearily. 'Either do that or have a swig of his brandy. Correction, let me have one first.' The golden warmth revived Sorrel's fighting spirit. 'Contract? All's fair in love and war and I'm not sure which one this is.'

The man from the *News of the World* had his pad out in a second.

'Thank you for handing our rivals a headline.' Libby was icy with fury. 'If you wanted brandy, there's a cocktail bar inside the car. It's right opposite your feet.'

Everything suddenly cheered up. The bar of the limousine contained not only generous decanters and Waterford crystal glasses but also smoked salmon and caviar sandwiches, thoughtfully covered with a damp table napkin. In a matter of moments a nightmare had turned into a picnic. The driver returned, the car started up again. As they passed across the private toll bridge to Portmeirion, Sorrel and Kenny were raising glasses to one another and munching merrily.

Man seemed to have reclaimed the landscape. There were even signposts. As the car swept up a wooded drive, the headlights picked out banks of hydrangeas in highly theatrical shades of scorched pink and peacock blue.

'Whoever put those colours together knew what he was doing.' Sorrel spoke with approval. And then she let out a gasp of glorious disbelief.

Below her, tucked into a Welsh hillside and curving down to the sea, was a village which looked as though it belonged in Italy. The moon had come out from behind the clouds to reveal domes and fountains and castellated buildings and colonnaded walks.

Portmeirion had just been the name of a place they were going to. Libby Taylor had merely said, 'It's a safe hideaway.'

Sorrel had known nothing of the history of the village. She hadn't known that Portmeirion was one man's dream turned into bricks and mortar; that old stone buildings, from all over the country, had been dramatically rescued to be brought here in numbered pieces. Some were still lying hidden in the undergrowth of the surrounding woods. The best had risen up again amidst gardens like new Babylon. Sorrel, who had expected dank fir trees in North Wales, had been handed flowering bougainvillaea.

Their car halted and the driver slid back the glass partition. 'They're not keen on traffic in the village,' he said. 'I understand a shooting brake will take you down to the hotel and they'll show you to your cottage.'

If Sorrel had a favourite bit in the Bible it was 'For, lo, the rain is over and gone; the flowers appear on the earth; the time of the singing of birds is come, and the voice of the turtle is heard in our land.'

She had no idea what the voice of the turtle would sound like but, if she was ever going to hear it anywhere, it would surely be possible at Portmeirion. As they got out and stretched their legs, Sorrel saw that the boundary of the woods was marked by a cast-iron pillar, painted yellow and surmounted by a yellow star.

'All this place needs is a Fascist dictator,' shuddered Kenny. 'Oh my God! Now I know why I felt as though I'd been here before. It's where they did that television serial. It's where they made *The Prisoner*.

'Hey lads . . .' he called out to his emerging entourage. 'Watch out for a big red balloon coming bouncing towards you. You might spot Patrick McGoohan and a dwarf too.'

Couldn't he see the weathervanes? Couldn't he see the stars? Sorrel found herself wishing that she was here, in this magical place, on her own. That feeling was to intensify as the evening went on.

She and Kenny were taken straight to their cottage. The rest of the circus, it transpired, had reservations in the main hotel building. Libby Taylor was not at all keen on the idea of Sorrel and Kenny going over to the bar.

'All our rivals are heavily represented,' she explained. 'We need to keep some sort of exclusivity on this honeymoon. I'll just nip and get the photographer.'

At that moment a knotted condom, filled with water, came flying through the open window and bounced, sloppily, under the bed.

'The lads,' said Kenny, pleased.

'You leave your lads to me.' Libby Taylor stalked grimly from the cottage and Sorrel repaired her makeup for the photographs.

The bride and groom unpacked for the camera and fended off Libby's suggestion that they should pose, decorously, under the eiderdown.

Left to themselves, they ate an excellent dinner, examined the antique furnishings of the cottage until they could have described them accurately to an auctioneer and then, with nothing else to do, they settled for an early night. Nervousness was in the air.

Kenny had the bathroom first and came back with a towel wrapped round his waist. Sorrel tried hard not to stare at his body, which she had never seen before. It was remarkably similar to Barney's (Curse you, June!) but Kenny had a hairy chest.

Sorrel spent a long time soaking in the bath. It had suddenly dawned upon her that this wedding, which she had viewed as just another production, was for real. That hairy chest had come as a surprise. It must start low down. It had never shown in an open-necked shirt. In a minute, by all the rules, that hairy flesh was meant to be touching her own body. What would happen if she got out of the bath, got dressed and cut and ran?

One thing was certain. Sorrel began to laugh almost hysterically. If she ran she wouldn't be alone. Libby Taylor would be certain to insist that she'd bought the right to accompany her. Privately, Sorrel had begun to admire the woman's sheer professionalism. Libby had a job of work to do and nothing was allowed to get in the way of it.

In marrying Kenny, Sorrel considered that she had signed a contract. Now it was up to her to deliver the performance. She got out of the bath, dried herself and applied liberal quantities of talcum powder. Bodies which have soaked for too long in bathwater feel like crepe de Chine. The talc would add polish and allow fingers to slide.

Oh my God . . . What had she let herself in for?

Sorrel suppressed revulsion. She had signed a contract.

She was obliged to give a performance. The white lace negligée could have been supplied by a theatrical costumier.

'I'm sorry, Barney,' she said softly. 'But you did it too.'

Opening the door she passed into the bedroom where Kenny had reduced the lights to one bedside lamp. Moonlight was streaming into the room from a high uncurtained window. Somebody must have furnished him with a pair of cream silk pyjamas. The jacket was partly buttoned but the gap in the silk trousers was hanging ajar. She was allowed to look. She was a married woman. He wasn't the same shape down there as Barney. It didn't have a dome, it had a hood. Only the whole thing was growing and the hood seemed to be retracting.

Kenny looked down guiltily. 'Sorry about that,' he said. 'Natural excitement. This is a big moment for me. Ever since I first saw you on the screen I've wanted to fuck Lettie Bly.'

Sorrel thought she'd married a man who knew who she really was. And he didn't.

Rape. Could a man rape his own wife? Sorrel didn't know but last night, by her reckoning, that's what had happened. It had been rape.

She remembered lovemaking with Barney as abandoned curves and getting lost together. Kenny's invasion of her body had been a jagged experience with Sorrel only too conscious, throughout, of where she was and what she was allowing to happen. Halfway, she had begged him to stop but Kenny Shorrocks had cared nothing for protests of pain and had only continued with his heedless thrusting and that vile, panting running commentary on what he was doing to Lettie Bly. The only way he'd seemed capable of reaching a climax was by suiting every action to the spoken word. Sorrel Starkey had learned by moonlight, in Portmeirion, the true meaning of the word *lewd*.

Now it was morning. Kenny, it transpired, had to have background noise to everything. He was whistling tunelessly as he carried a transistor radio around the cottage. This was blaring out 'For All We Know'. Not the song which says 'For all we know we may never meet again' – Sorrel would have found that idea entirely tolerable. This was the one about love looking at the two of us and being strangers in many ways and having a lifetime to say 'I knew you well'.

A lifetime? One night had been enough. The light of common day had not cut Sorrel's problems down to size. She was full of guilt. Marriage was meant to be a serious business. They'd turned it into an excuse for grabbing a large cheque. And if Kenny didn't turn his wretched radio down, she'd wrest it from him and throw it into the sea. Now Sorrel could even admit something else to herself. Secretly, all along the way, she had been hoping for a miracle. She had tried to believe that a wedding ceremony and a honeymoon might transmute cheerful companionship into some frail species of love. She had simply been trying to belong.

'Something up? Sorrel, I'm asking you, is there something wrong?'

Sorrel turned down his radio before she spoke. 'We're going to have to talk about last night.'

'Sex is for doing –' Kenny had blushed bright red – 'not for talking about.'

'You raped me.'

'I like rough stuff.'

'Well I don't.'

Kenny looked perplexed. 'The trouble is I've only ever been with scrubbers.' He also looked very young. 'I don't know how to shag a lady.'

'You don't use that word for a start.'

'OK.' Young? It was a guilty little boy. 'I don't know how to sexual intercourse a lady.'

Under any other circumstances Sorrel would have found this reply laughable. It was the sort of line actors quoted to one another in boring rehearsal waits. But this wasn't a rehearsal. This was life. This was the show.

Kenny turned the radio up again and lit a match. He was now adding the first of this morning's cigarette smoke to the remains of last night's. Sorrel needed fresh air. Opening another window wouldn't be enough. She needed to open a door, to step outside, to run a hundred miles from this place. Only she couldn't because there would be a ready-made band of pursuers in the shape of the assembled press corps.

As she stepped out into the sunlight, Sorrel's enchantment with Portmeirion had grown understandably jaded. Gazing round at the colour-washed buildings, with their glittering leaded windows, she found herself thinking that all the place needed was Little Noddy, coming round the corner in his car. No, cars were banned. But Libby Taylor wasn't banned, more's the pity. The monkey-lady was sitting outside another cottage, on a fan-shaped cast-iron chair, reading *The Secret Garden*.

'Good morning,' she said brightly. 'I found this book in my room. It's a book I've always loved. It was like finding an old friend.'

Sorrel tried to keep the wonder out of her voice as she replied, 'I've read it so often I can nearly recite it.' So Libby was human after all. She must be to care for a book which was about believing that all good things are possible. 'Mickey Grimshaw practically ranks *The Secret Garden* with the New Testament.'

'Pity he couldn't come yesterday,' said Libby. 'I love Mick. I was once commissioned to write a piece about him and we ended up feeding the monkeys at Belle Vue Zoo. You're lucky in your friends.'

She talks too much for early in the morning, thought Sorrel. But if she's like a monkey, it's quite a beautiful one. Fancy Mick taking her to feed them!

'Your friend Ruby's been a tower of strength throughout all of this,' Libby rattled on. 'She and my mother don't see eye to eye. Of course the Shapiros are tremendous Zionists. They must have given a small fortune to Israeli causes. Years ago, I was once going to go off and live on a kibbutz with Barney Shapiro.'

'*What?*' Sorrel couldn't believe she was hearing properly.

'Just a friendly arrangement. We'd have been travelling companions. He was madly in love with some non-Jewish girl and Ruby and Jake had split them up.'

Did Libby know what she was saying? Sorrel didn't think she did.

Libby continued with 'Poor Barney was in a terrible state. Before we could pack our rucksacks they produced Mandy Poyser. What do you make of her?'

No, Libby didn't know. 'I don't think I've ever met her.'

'She gives him a hard time,' sighed the reporter. Her tones became businesslike again: 'Are you OK, Sorrel?'

'Of course.' Sorrel had turned back into a guarded actress talking to a journalist. 'I'm fine.'

'I wouldn't want you to think I'd been snooping but I had to make sure that the opposition weren't sneaking round your cottage last night.' Libby had the grace to look awkward. 'I heard a lot of noise.'

'Me and Kenny?'

Libby nodded.

'Did you hear actual words?'

'I'm going against every professional instinct in my body,' said Libby, 'but don't leave him. If you were to walk out now, we could keep the story going for weeks. But it would finish you off with the public. They'd see that bastard of a husband of yours as a jilted fallen hero. The man who's still limping. Kenny loves the smell of a cheque book. He'd sing like a bird for the first paper who offered him the right money.'

Libby looked genuinely anxious: 'It's not the sort of story the public wants to read, Sorrel. You're meant to be Mr and Mrs Moonlight-and-Roses. Trust me, I know what I'm talking about. It could ruin your career. It would wreck everything you've ever worked for. Do you think you can fake it?'

'I can try,' sighed Sorrel. How many more times would life force her to utter this dutiful phrase? Her eyes suddenly filled with tears but they were not of self-pity. These were tears of gratitude.

'I was quite wrong about you, Libby. And I've got to say it. I just thought of you as a nuisance and you're really my friend.'

'Get yourself into a bikini,' smiled Libby. 'Force him into a pair of bathing trunks. While we've got this sunlight we might just as well snatch a few shots down by the sea.'

'I owe you, Libby.'

Sorrel had been around enough Jewish people to understand the significance of what she'd just said. She owed Libby Taylor a favour and, if the journalist ever chose to ask for one back, Sorrel would be honour-bound to deliver.

414

For the moment, posing for pictures would be something to do. Something that she understood. What's more, other people would be present which meant she wouldn't be faced with the prospect of being left alone with Kenny. Yes, she would hurry him into bathing trunks and get him down to the beach.

Sorrel walked back into the cottage and pushed open the bedroom door. Kenny was lying naked, face down, on top of the bed. He wasn't asleep, she could tell that by the breathing. But his shoulders were going up and down. Was he laughing? And then a strangled noise escaped him. Kenny wasn't laughing, he was crying.

He had plainly registered Sorrel's presence because the inarticulate sob turned into strangled words: 'You'll go away. They all do. They never come back for more.'

'Who?' Her natural impulse was to put her arms around him. Yet this was the same man who had triumphed over her with words straight from the soundtrack of a pornographic movie. Only it hadn't been her he'd triumphed over. It had been Lettie Bly.

'Kenny, what are you talking about? Who goes away?'

'Girls, anybody . . .' The sobs took over again. Then, attempting to control himself, he babbled inarticulately, 'Just girls. It's only women. At least I'm not a poof.'

'And what is it they don't come back for?' Sorrel knew only too well but she also knew that Kenny's guilt needed ripping from night's protective shadows.

'The other. Sex.'

'Don't blow your nose on the sheet. Wherever were you brought up?' Sorrel could have bitten her own tongue. She already knew the sad answer to that question. Kenny had been raised in Catholic orphanages.

'Take this.' She handed him her own handkerchief.

He blew his nose loudly, wiped it and then said wearily, 'I crack on it's me. I tell the lads I'm always after a bit of fresh. It's not true. It's the girls who can't take it twice. If I don't talk dirty, I can't do anything. And they don't like it, Sorrel.'

He was telling her all this as though she was his good friend who would be bound to try and understand. There was actually puzzled hurt in his blue eyes.

Now he'd started, it was all spilling out: 'They think they want me but when they've had a taste, they all run. God knows how it's never got in the papers. I know there's talk about me. I'm surprised you never heard.'

'June Gee tried to tell me.'

'Her,' he said contemptuously. 'She'd *like* a bit.'

'If you ever make her dreams come true, that's it. I leave you.'

He sat upright. Joy was shining out of him.

'You mean you're staying? I don't believe it. I don't deserve it.' Now he was even more eager to try to explain. 'You see I thought it would be all right with you, I thought something magic would happen and I'd be different.'

'We've got to talk about this.' Sorrel was seizing her advantage. 'Why do you do it?'

'They always said it was dirty.'

'Who's they?'

'First the nuns and then the man behind the iron grille. Priests. They used to cart us off to confession and you had to tell everything. Even if you just *thought* things, it counted. They give you little codewords to make it easier. The one for that's "impure thoughts".'

'But what's that got to do with the way you carry on in bed?'

'I don't know,' said Kenny.

Sorrel could see that he was telling the truth.

'I wish I did know,' he stammered. 'But it *has* got to do with it.'

He was still telling the truth and it left Sorrel's head spinning. In that brief instant her new husband had lifted the cover from a brutal mind to reveal a cowering child.

'If I explained, I'd have to use some of the things I said last night. When I go, "You like that, don't you? You like it, you dirty mare," that way it's *you*. If I think it's me, it becomes a sin and I'm wrecked.'

'Then why weren't we married in church?'

'I wouldn't give the Pope the satisfaction. I finished with that lot years ago.'

'It strikes me they've not finished with you.'

'You've not heard the lot.' Kenny had plainly been trained

416

to make a very full confession. 'I used to pay a brass, a prostitute in Moss Side, to tie me up. That way I wasn't to blame for what happened after. Whips, everything.' The blush, which began in his cheeks, spread to his neck and then continued right across his naked chest. 'You could say it was the pleasure and the punishment in one go.'

'You don't need punishment. You need help.'

'Then help me. And I want to tell you something else. I couldn't play mucky games with you. I like you too much for that. I could only do them with Lettie Bly. You won't tell your mother, will you?'

Kenny was weeping again. Automatically Sorrel put her arms around him and began to rock him like a child. Good sunlight had reduced Kenny to a human being in need. She was trying to adjust to the idea of him as victim instead of monster. Something fell from his hand and hit the floorboards with a clatter.

Her husband started guiltily.

What was it? These recent revelations had made Sorrel wary. Was it something from a sex shop? He wasn't reaching for whatever he'd dropped. She couldn't look. 'What did you drop?'

'Keys. It was meant to be a surprise.' Kenny reached down and picked them up. It was a sizeable bunch varying from Yale and Chubb to the sort of big old iron key they'd had to the coalshed in Rookswood Avenue.

'I've bought us a house,' he said. 'It's just like the swimming baths at New Brighton. It's at Mere,' he added proudly.

Their sketchy residential plans had been for the pair for them to move, temporarily, into Sorrel's house at Buxton and then look around for somewhere more suitable.

'I don't want to live at Mere. Why didn't you let me choose it with you?'

'Oh no,' said Kenny reproachfully. 'The man goes and chooses the house and then the woman goes in after, with her mother, and settles on what curtains they're having.'

Were all his visions of life as primitive as a child's drawing?

'I want to talk to you about the house.' Kenny was all eagerness. 'I've bought it for cash. It's your full luxury home and it's paid for. The way I look at it is this . . .' The next bit was plainly well rehearsed.

'It needs a bit doing to it. You and me, we're a partnership. By buying the house, I've provided the bread and butter. If you want jam on it, your job will be to go out and earn it. We'll decide about things like the gas bill later.'

If I'm not putting my head in the gas oven, thought Sorrel. And she wasn't altogether joking. Childlike simplicity? The man was mentally retarded.

'Kenny. I'm sorry. There's no future in any of this. Let's put an end to it before we get ourselves too deeply in. If there's any sin, it's this whole farce of a marriage. I want out. It's too complicated on too many fronts.'

'They always walk away.' He said it matter-of-factly. 'For a minute there, you had me kidded you were different. Don't think I'm giving you the pleasure of waving at me from the opposite pavement, because I'm not. Girls? They're just a trap. When I do it, Eeek's the only one who'll be really sorry. Eeek knows what I'm like. He's always known but he doesn't go away.'

'When you do what?' Surely he was never going to pull that stunt on her?

'Take an overdose.'

He was. 'And where will that leave me, Kenny? I've never been one to worry about what people say but they'll certainly say plenty if you do yourself in.' He might too. He might think he'd told her too much. He might be scared that she too would sing like a bird.

Kenny was watching Sorrel closely. She suddenly saw why Spud didn't like him. She'd seen the same calculating expression in the eyes of an unreliable rogue-collie.

'There you are then,' he said. 'You've got a choice, haven't you? Stick with me or give evidence at the inquest.'

From outside, in the grounds, Sorrel could hear Libby Taylor talking to somebody about getting shots down by the water. Her words had that bright echo you only hear at the seaside. The world beyond the confines of this room was, unbelievably, still the same place and life was going on as usual.

Sorrel picked up the bunch of keys. It said on the label: *Bellaire – Mere.*

10

Mere never stood a chance with Sorrel Starkey. It had once been a very ordinary village, set by watery lagoons, half an hour's drive from Manchester. When the Duke of Windsor was still Prince of Wales, rich city businessmen had moved out there and built huge villas. Beverly Hills on the monotonously flat ground of the plain of Cheshire.

When the sun shone, the rich disported themselves on a golf course which was well kept to the point of fanaticism. The course was built around a nineteenth-century mansion which served as a country club. When it rained, which was often, it is possible that the members gossiped, over their pink gins, about the likes of Sorrel Starkey and Kenny Shorrocks. But it would only have been to congratulate themselves that such nouveau riff-raff was unlikely to pass under the sacred Regency arch which divided the rich from the road.

Sorrel's first sight of Bellaire was not inspiring. Ruby Shapiro had abandoned her red MG in favour of a Morgan sports car in British racing green. Sorrel and Ruby left Manchester in sunshine. By the time they got to Altrincham, they had to stop and raise the canvas hood. The rain wasn't coming down in buckets, it was just that fine, chilling drizzle which perfectly heightens depression. As they swept beyond The Swan at Bucklow Hill, Sorrel's spirits lowered to greet the dripping Lombardy poplars and box hedges which fronted the mansions of Mere.

'Look!' she said. 'Somebody's tried to grow palm trees in the garden of that one. What a sorry sight!'

'Those trees are yours.' Ruby turned the car up a tarmac drive and just managed to stop before the potholes got too deep.

The house – a huge cream cube – looked as though it had been built to celebrate the Age of Jazz. It was a building like a geometry lesson. Some of the windows were triangular, others were steel-framed circles. Had somebody placed a neon sign, on its cream tiled front, saying *Lido*, you would have been hard-pressed to tell whether you were facing a cinema or the entrance to a seaside swimming pool.

'Oh dear,' said Ruby darkly. 'I've seen houses like that before. And so has the Official Receiver. How the neighbours must loathe it. The place has been allowed to go to rack and ruin.'

'Of course giant cow-parsley always looks awful in the rain.' Sorrel was trying to be cheerful. She gave up. 'There's so *much* of it. Is that other stuff hemlock?'

'Deadly nightshade.' Ruby was a good gardener. 'Don't even think of touching it without gloves. Every part is poisonous. Let's get out and go in.'

After ages spent fiddling with keys, they discovered that the front door was merely on the latch. Ruby pushed it open.

'No wonder he didn't offer to carry you over the threshold. *Jesus!*'

For once, Sorrel did not admonish her. All she could say was, 'If Joan Crawford came down that wrought-iron staircase, at this moment, and announced she was going mad, I wouldn't be one little bit surprised. The whole place is a Hollywood nightmare. You know he's bought the contents too?'

'Whoever sold this pig in a poke got out at just the right moment.' Ruby was examining curtains with an expert eye. 'Look, these linings won't stand another trip to the cleaner's. And, if I'm any judge, you'll have to recarpet throughout within a year. Oh look, they've left you a bent chromium-plated cocktail shaker. How thoughtful! Let's find out where that tap's dripping.'

The house smelled of camphorated damp. The sitting room featured huge, rusting French windows and a Medieval-Moderne fireplace with white stone seats inside it. The dining room furniture was a nightmare in red lacquer with a design of little Chinamen, in raised gold, running all over the vermilion surfaces.

The place seemed to go on for echoing miles. Upstairs in the master bedroom, the bedhead was made of huge sunrays of tinted mirror which was peeling under the glass.

'Yet the whole thing has great possibilities,' announced Ruby.

'Are you mad?' breathed Sorrel. 'How on earth do I disguise all this?'

'You don't disguise it. You emphasize it. Art Deco's just coming back into fashion. You should still be able to get big pieces quite cheaply. We'll make it a thirties paradise. We'll throw out all these musty velvet curtains and replace them with great swags of silver lamé.'

'It will cost the earth,' groaned Sorrel.

Ruby brushed this aside with 'I can get it wholesale.' She was suddenly all businesslike common sense. 'Running two careers from the house, you should be able to claim some back as tax expenses. That's Kenny's worry.'

'Yes, and I suspect mine will be finding the money to pay for it all.'

It was.

That house, Bellaire, ate money. Clearing the garden cost over a thousand pounds. The builder's accounts came to many more. At the end of their expensive labours, Sorrel found herself confronted by an empty shell, in urgent need of painting and decorating.

Kenny came into his own as Sorrel's personal manager. To earn extra cash she presented prizes in bingo halls, opened launderettes and made personal appearances at holiday camps. The fitted carpets came courtesy of a football pools company. Sorrel accepted them in lieu of two fees for presenting winners with their cheques. She would smile for the cameras and wish, with all her heart, that it was Kenny's winning line which had scooped a record-breaking dividend.

The cost of curtaining the vast house, even at wholesale prices, came to another small fortune. Sorrel earned this by selling her memoirs to a women's magazine.

The really big money, Kenny maintained, was lying waiting for them in the shape of endorsements. He talked a mail-order company into producing a Sorrel Starkey range of fashions. Her contract with *Angel Dwellings* precluded any such a deal. The money the catalogue people were offering was more than a year's earnings from the television show. But they made it clear that they would not be interested in Sorrel unless she continued to play Lettie Bly. A determined Kenny set out to tackle Bernard Conroy.

He got nowhere. Endorsements were contractually forbidden and that was that. Kenny refused to accept this and raised so many backs, amongst the television executives, that a day dawned when he was escorted from the studios and asked not to return. It was also pointed out to Sorrel that her husband was not an accredited agent. The television company told her that – in the future – they would prefer not to be asked to deal with him.

Husband? Sorrel always found the word startling. Theirs wasn't a marriage. It was a pose. Attempts to mend matters in the bedroom always ended in dismal failure.

'Couldn't we go and see a marriage counsellor?' Sorrel would ask. 'Not all Catholics are in this guilt-ridden mess. Judy and her husband have a whale of a time in bed. Wouldn't you go and see somebody? I'd come with you.'

'And how long before that found its way into the papers? We've got an image to protect.'

This kept them in a double bed. Kenny, who was putting on weight, began to snore. In this quarter at least, Sorrel sought advice from her mother. How had Gladys coped when Mr Jepson snored?

'I regarded it as the price I had to pay,' was the sanctimonious reply. 'And I thought I told you never to mention that filthy pig's name again. You could try wax earplugs.'

One day Sorrel actually met Mr Jepson in the street. He was leading a little girl by the hand.

'This is your famous sister,' he said to the child.

'No I'm not,' Sorrel countered. 'There's no blood in common at all. Did you get married again?'

'Shh!' Mr Jepson raised a guilty finger to his lips and hurried the child into a Wimpy Bar.

The little girl waved at the actress through the glass. And it was such a nice, bright wave that it left Sorrel feeling mean.

Mostly, these days, she felt worried. It reached the point when any letter that began 'Dear Madam, Unless . . .' was consigned, unread, to a pile under a heavy paperweight labelled *Bellaire*.

Eventually, somehow, the house she'd never wanted got finished, and the last of the bills was paid. The morning she wrote the final cheque, Sorrel vowed never again to shake hands – for money – with anyone on earth. Now, at least, she would be free of commercial personal appearances. That evening she returned home to find a mechanical digger in the back garden and the beginnings of a sizeable hole.

'What's that?'

'Every star should have a swimming pool. It's as good as paid for. I've got you a contract with a new chain of butchers. All you've got to do is turn up and be photographed handing out meat-vouchers on Saturday mornings.'

Kenny was unstoppable. Ray Fossett called him Bess of Hardwick: 'She thinks she'll die if she doesn't stop building.' Very much the major-domo of Bellaire, Ray always referred to his master in the feminine gender. You had to be a real man to rate 'he' from Ray.

Kenny had worked his way through irritation with the male housekeeper to a point where he had come to regard him with wary respect. Ray Fossett was more than capable of looking after himself. A champion jockey, a close friend of Kenny's, who had attempted to insult Ray, had found himself pitched headlong through the hall window. The glazier was forever making emergency visits to Bellaire.

Some of the company Kenny kept was highly disreputable. Let a boozy boxing heavyweight find his way to Manchester and the road could only lead to Bellaire. Snooker players, bookies, owners of seedy drinking clubs, they all raised glasses in the house that Sorrel's money rebuilt. On her way to rehearsal, in the mornings, she was forever picking her way over sleeping bodies.

The girls they brought along were a tawdry bunch who were not above helping themselves to makeup. It was April Fool's Day when Sorrel had to force her way backstage, in a night club, and wrest one of her own evening dresses from the back of a stripper. She threw it away immediately afterwards but it proved who was boss of Bellaire. Or did it? The car which drove her away from the seedy club was a Mercedes. It had been bought in Kenny's name with Sorrel's money.

The mornings were worst. These days she always woke up with a hangover.

'Take your earplugs out, sweetheart. It's me.' Ray Fossett was admitting the light of yet another Mere morning. Breakfast had recently reduced itself to a slimming pill and black coffee. They were already waiting on a tray on the bedside table. Ray had taken the trouble to add some daisies in a little vase. This small kindness, which presupposed she was still a human being, made Sorrel want to weep.

'Where's Kenny?'

'Well you might ask! Still out on the tiles. Swallow your pill – you're going to need it.'

These pills worried Sorrel. They certainly suppressed her appetite but they also filled her with fiendish, unnatural confidence and too much energy. She got them on private prescription.

'It is Monday, isn't it?'

'Yes and the Robb drawing of you, in the Frank Usher ball gown, has got half a page in the *Express*.'

'But that's not what's going to bother me.' Sorrel voiced the thought aloud. Something was up. She could read Ray Fossett like a book. Something untoward was in the wind. Though he was mildly titillated by whatever it was, he was also concerned for her.

Ray confirmed this with a heavy sigh as he said, 'I thought of burning the thing. But some dear, kind friend would be bound to show it to you. Kenny's made the front page.'

Ray Fossett held up a copy of Britain's most lurid tabloid. The long, bold headline read: *WHO WAS HE WITH LAST NIGHT, LETTIE?* Underneath was a picture of Kenny, looking sheepish, in the company of a blonde Ursula Andress look-alike.

'Full story pages four and five,' quoted Ray as he rattled the newspaper open. 'There's a photo for every night of the week. Different girl each time.'

'Do we know any of them?' asked Sorrel wearily.

'No, though I couldn't swear for Wednesday's. She's got a handbag held across her face.'

'I'm past caring.'

This wasn't a brave front, it was a statement of fact. Sorrel had never loved Kenny. She had long ago stopped liking him. Part of her was sorry for the man but she was beginning to see this as foolish. All they had in common, these days, was massive tax debts. Sorrel had been in the process of settling her own when Bellaire had opened its demanding jaws. Now she also owed tax on money the house had eaten up.

Ray Fossett had been studying the row of newspaper photographs. 'Tuesday looks as though she's been drugged into submission. And if it wasn't for the bouncing knockers, you could take Thursday for a man in drag. It says he takes them to hotels in Ardwick. I'd rather do without sex than have it in Ardwick.'

Ray's musings were interrupted by a scrabbling sound at the bedroom door.

'Let Spud in or he'll have the paint off again.' Sorrel took the newspaper from Ray.

'I'm afraid you're going to have to cope with a lot of public sympathy.' Ray headed for the door – a long Bellaire walk – and Sorrel looked at the photographs for herself.

They didn't look like bad girls. They didn't look wicked; just primped up and empty-headed. The kind who embark on the sort of dubious modelling course which never leads to a fashion show. Whatever must their poor mothers be thinking this morning? And then Sorrel saw who had written the piece. Strictly speaking it had been assembled by a team but the name in the largest letters was Libby Taylor. She must have changed newspapers. The woman who had persuaded Sorrel to stay with Kenny had now handed her grounds for divorce.

The slimming pill was beginning to clear Sorrel's head and sharpen up her wits. 'Separate rooms,' she said decisively. 'It's going to be separate rooms from now on.'

'If he's been putting it anywhere and everywhere,' Ray called back over his shoulder, 'I think you'd better go to the clinic for a blood test.'

He opened the door and Spud bounded through, headed

for the bed, jumped up onto the peach satin eiderdown, gave Sorrel some wild licks, dived off the bed and took up a guard-dog position by the door. He was now growling warningly and throwing Sorrel anxious glances.

'OK, Spud, I get you. He's back. Enough, Spud! You've made your point.'

It was odd that this dog, who had grown into a comically jaunty animal, shed all charm at the approach of the man he had never considered to be his master.

Kenny ambled into the room with a stupid smile on his face. He was still dressed in the blazer and cavalry twill trousers in which he had left the house, the previous day. Why were there grass stains on the knee of the pants? Kenny didn't look as though he'd had any sleep and he wasn't quite sober. His eyes were raking the room for something. They found it – the morning papers.

'Yes you dirty stop-out,' said Ray Fossett. 'You might at least have had the sense to cover your tracks and save her feelings.'

'*Mea culpa*.' Kenny's hand struck his left breast. '*Mea maxima culpa*.'

'And don't think you can blind me with bits of German.' Ray Fossett's tones had turned dangerous.

'It's Latin.' Sorrel really did not feel up to a big scene. 'It's part of the Catholic Mass. I did it once when I played Schiller's *Marie Stuart*.'

'Mine the blame,' repeated Kenny in the same penitential tones but this time in English. 'Mine the blame. Mine the most maximum blame.'

Sorrel staged a yawn in an attempt to stop the story which she knew was coming.

It came: 'The Mass was all Latin gibberish to us lads. One Saturday morning, a priest came to the orphanage and explained that *mea culpa* meant my fault. After that, if we bumped into anybody, we always said, "Sorry mate, *mea culpa*." '

Sorrel treated Kenny to a glare. 'If you're going to blame your church for your own failings – yet again – forget it! It won't wash.'

'I was just saying . . .' Kenny's voice trailed off weakly and his hands fell to his sides. Uncomfortably, he began to whistle 'Barefoot Days'.

'You've got a whistle like chalk on a blackboard,' snapped Ray Fossett. 'She *is* a star, you know. She *is* loved by millions. What's it going to look like when she has to go and queue up, with the dregs of Moss Side, at the clap clinic?'

Kenny, cornered, was snarling: 'One thing's certain. You'll know the way there, you fucking arse-bandit. One day – so help me – I'll knock you into the middle of next week.'

'Try it! Go on, give it a whirl. Hit me. I may be a flaming queen but I'm ten times faster on my feet than a wreck like you. You're just the ghost of a footballer, Kenny. And if that hurt, it was meant to. You're the forgotten man. You'd be nothing these days without Sorrel. All you do is use her name to keep your own in the headlines . . .'

'Are you going to let him talk to me like that, Sorrel?'

Ray Fossett hadn't finished: 'You're not even a good fuck. And I have that on the authority of somebody you paid ten quid. At least hookers are clean.' Ray picked up the newspaper and slapped it savagely. 'These amateurs could have been anywhere.'

And now Kenny will go into his wounded, little-boy routine, thought Sorrel wearily.

He did. Surrounded as they were by red rims, the bloodshot eyes were labouring under a disadvantage.

'I never did nothing till you called a halt, Lettie.'

The conversation was about sex, so suddenly she had to be 'Lettie' again. Sorrel felt physically sick. 'I called a halt when you put a cane in my hand and begged me to use it on you.'

Tears began to roll out of her husband's bleary eyes.

'You're a very great lady, Sorrel. I've always thought that. You're the tops. You're a big star. You're my lady. If you want to humiliate me, in front of this nancy-boy, then I'll just have to take my lashes.'

'He's getting off on this!' cried Ray Fossett in near disbelief. 'He's managing to turn his own disgrace into some kind of kinky jolly.'

The weird atmosphere which Kenny, in this mood, could always generate, was suddenly broken.

Now he spoke matter-of-factly: 'Don't crack on she never told you about my tastes.'

It was Sorrel who answered: 'I didn't tell him. I wouldn't. And Ray, you forget you heard any of this. You hear me?'

Ray wasn't leaving it at that. He addressed his reply to Kenny: 'You didn't go in for any of this fancy stuff with the girl I know. I got every detail. She said you were just boring vanilla with a bit of talking dirty. You certainly didn't ask her to whip you.'

'She wasn't worthy,' said Kenny. His eyes went imploringly to Sorrel.

'It's no use, Kenny.' She got out of bed briskly. 'You're too bizarre for me to understand. If we weren't in such a financial mess, I'd walk straight out on you this morning.'

'Lettie, I couldn't have given you a dose. I've not got one myself. I'd know. And I didn't start shopping outside till you drew the line. I promise you that.'

'I believe you.' And she did. 'But that doesn't mean I have to sleep in the same room. You can have this one. I'll try the spare bedroom for size.'

As a matter of fact, she had already tried it. All those years ago, when she was rehearsing *Beware Beryl Jones* and had gone down to Surrey to stay with Dominic Savage, his wife had said, 'When you come to do a guest room, spend a night in it yourself.'

Sorrel had always remembered that woman with revulsion. Not now. The poor soul had done what she did in an attempt to keep her husband satisfied. Sorrel had failed a similar strange test. Nona Yates, yes that was her name (you never saw her column nowadays), had been an early recruit to the sexual revolution. She had joined it in the cause of love. The best Sorrel could be said to have married for was companionship. And companionship could certainly stand the test of separate bedrooms.

All this bland common sense was systematic wrapping around a marriage from which she saw no escape. Speeding thoughts began to race through Sorrel's head: His bills, my bills, our bills. Oh God, *please* let some light in.

Later that morning, as Sorrel crossed St Ann's Square, she found herself reminded of the day after they got the news of her father's death. She and her mother had gone to The Height to do some shopping and everybody had been embarrassed to see them.

People hadn't actually crossed to the other side of the road, but neither had they lingered. It had just been polite nods and a lot of amateur face-acting, meant to suggest that these shoppers had suddenly thought of something else, which was desperately urgent, and must be done immediately.

It was the same this morning. The sight of Sorrel seemed to disconcert people. Her marital dilemma must already be common knowledge. A less sophisticated soul might have thought that the newspaper in question would not be read by the elegant habitués of St Ann's Square. Not Sorrel. Dirt spreads fast and she knew it. She also knew that the first person to openly mention Libby Taylor's article would preface their inquiries with 'Of course I never take that newspaper but . . .'

She was wrong. Her friend, the handsome flower-seller, greeted her with 'Morning, love, I make a point of never believing anything I read in that paper.' No messing there, he said it straight out and added, 'Have this extra bunch on me and keep smiling.'

She had to hurry away because her eyes were smarting with tears of gratitude. Now she was worried that he might have thought that she had walked off in a huff.

As her steps took her towards Market Street, she caught sight of a paper-stand outside the newsagent's. The headline hadn't shrunk any in this later edition: *WHO WAS HE WITH LAST NIGHT, LETTIE?*

A well-dressed man was bending down and taking a copy from the rack. He opened the paper, obviously intending to turn to the full dirt inside.

'You might at least buy the thing,' she said sternly. 'That shop's got a living to earn.'

The man looked up. It was Barney Shapiro. His dark hair was still as thick but it was winged with silver at the sides. The seasons of life were beginning to change. Sorrel found herself wondering how much grey there was beneath her own red tint. Barney Shapiro was standing right in front of her yet – ridiculously – her thoughts could have come from the soundtrack of a L'Oréal commercial.

His smile was full of concern for her. Nodding down at the newspaper, he said, 'You've copped me red-handed. What can I say?'

'Say you'll come and have a drink with me; this minute, right now. Put that rubbish back in the rack and let's go and make some happiness.' And then Sorrel remembered a tip that Lily Bear had given her many years ago. A romantic tip that was supposed never to fail.

'You can't say no, Barney. It's my birthday.'

11

Whatever had happened to the Sawyer's Arms? Sorrel had always remembered the Deansgate pub as being half deserted. A Victorian gin palace, full of polished mahogany and etched glass. Its ground-floor rooms had been a series of discreet hidey-holes with cast-iron Britannia tables and linoleum in the public bar and red Turkey rugs in the parts where drinks were a penny and tuppence extra. She and Barney had thought they would be able to sit in the comparative privacy of the billiard room which was generally empty of customers in the daytime.

The billiard room was now part of a whole. The Sawyer's Arms had gone open-plan with Tyrolean overtones. There were fitted carpets in glaring purple and green and a jukebox was announcing that it begged your pardon but it had never promised you a rose garden.

'Don't look now but it's Lettie Bly' was also to be heard on the air. The Sawyer's was packed. They decided to stay. At that hour, anywhere else would also be full of office workers on their lunch-break.

Barney got the drinks whilst Sorrel went in search of a table.

A woman pushed up to let her past and said eagerly, 'We can make a bit of space here. You don't have to worry about us, we'll respect your privacy.'

Sorrel knew better. 'I think there's more room over in that corner.' Seventy sets of eyes swivelled with her as she moved across the room and she heard the name Kenny Shorrocks mentioned twice.

'Vodka and tonic for you?' Barney had returned and was registering the fact that they had an audience. 'Is it always like this?'

'Always. And I can't complain because it's what I thought I wanted.'

'What *do* you want?'

'You.' The reply was unhesitating. 'You asked me so I'm telling you. I want you. If you head straight for the door and run, I'll quite understand.'

Barney looked right into her eyes. 'If you knew how much I love you . . .'

'Don't say that. I'm practically sitting on my hands as it is. I want to touch you. I'm having to stop myself. I just want to put my arms around you, Barney, and breathe you in.'

'I'm not sure you could,' said Barney. 'Because, in my mind, my own arms are already round you.'

'Excuse me, Lettie, would you mind just signing this?' It was an elderly potman, in a white jacket, holding out a beer-mat and a stub of indelible pencil.

Sorrel signed.

'Ta, love. And thank you for many happy hours.'

Sorrel smiled as gracefully as she could and the man moved away looking red and pleased.

'You're theirs, aren't you?' Barney seemed almost awed. 'They really love you.'

'Can I bring you some happy hours?' Sorrel had to lower her voice in the cause of secrecy. 'Did you hear me, Barney?'

'I hear you. How's marriage?'

'A fake. How's yours?'

'We both make sure we're out a lot.'

'And you and I are meant to be miserable in the cause of respectable fronts?' There was nothing wistful about Sorrel's question. It was fiercely delivered.

'Sorry to bother you again.' The potman was back. 'Would you sign another for the girl behind the bar? Could you put "To Helen"?'

Sorrel felt like putting 'Go to hell', but she didn't.

'Thanks. Is that a vodka and the gentleman's a tomato juice?'

'What?'

'We'd like you to have a drink with us.'

Just as you were ready to kill them they always made your heart bleed.

'Come here,' said Sorrel to the potman. And she gave him a smacking kiss on the cheek.

'I'll never wash me face again,' he beamed, and headed for the bar.

As Sorrel finished signing this second beer-mat, she said to Barney: 'The first time you and I went to bed, I didn't want to get in the bath afterwards. I can remember standing there, in that cold bathroom in Rookswood Avenue, sniffing my own arm. There was just a faint trace of your body-scent and I didn't want to wash it away. If that sounds wanton and abandoned, I don't care. When it comes to you, I've always slung all the rules away. I want you, Barney. Sitting here, now, with rehearsal due to start in ten minutes – I want you. I'd even keep the rehearsal waiting. I wouldn't care. And that's theatrical blasphemy. You're the only man on earth who could make me even think of it. I've had years to learn what yearning means. I yearn for you . . .'

Openly, on top of the table, he took her hand.

'They'll never think I'm your lawyer now,' he grinned.

'Is that what you've been kidding yourself?' Sorrel laughed aloud with joy. Oh, it was wonderful to be inside Barney's head again. Only she needed more than that.

Barney knew it. 'Where? Where and how?'

'I don't want to take my hand away, but I'd better. Those girls by the fruit machine have already got eyes out on stalks. Give me your office number.'

As he opened a black leather wallet she found herself wondering whether his wife had given it to him as a present.

'There.' He slid across a visiting card. 'My direct line is the bottom number.'

For Sorrel, the words 'direct line' were suddenly charged with infinite romantic possibilities.

'I don't know how I'll make it work.' She slipped the card into her handbag. 'But I *will* make it work. I promise you.'

The potman returned with their drinks.

'Good luck,' he said. 'Good luck to both of you.'

In that moment Sorrel felt more genuinely married than she had ever done, to Kenny Shorrocks, in the register office on All Saints' Green.

*

It should have been one of the greatest nights of Sorrel's life. It was not that she had arranged her romantic rendezvous with Barney. Anticipation being half the pleasure, that was a matter which was taking time and thought and planning. No, tonight Sorrel was due to switch on the Blackpool illuminations.

Half a million light bulbs, and Blackpool only ever invited a very famous name to press the button which would signal the opening of *The Greatest Free Show in the World.* Sorrel had wanted this honour since she was a little girl when she and Mickey had stood, in Talbot Square, and watched Anna Neagle perform the first opening ceremony after the war.

Tonight was the night, but as yet it was still morning. In the downstairs hallway of Bellaire, Sorrel stepped aside to allow Ray Fossett to pass. He was carrying the dress, specially designed for the occasion by the Salmon sisters, out to the car. Scarlet and spangled, it was nearly a light-show in itself.

'Skirt big enough for *Come Dancing*,' he cried as he swished it past her. 'You'll look like Cinderella-gone-wicked in this.'

There was less excitement about Kenny who was roaming around, unshaven, in a white towelling dressing gown that had seen better days. He took a swig from a large earthenware breakfast cup and muttered, 'I've decided about tonight. If they won't pay me a separate fee, you're on your own.'

'Dear Lord,' groaned Sorrel, 'I've told you, I keep on telling you; there's no fee. It's an honour. They've asked me what I'd like as a present. I'm having something for the house. Nobody could ask for a fairer deal than that.'

Kenny was still muttering. 'They've not offered me a present. Everybody seems to take it for granted, these days, that I'll just turn up. Well I won't.'

Ray Fossett had said it all earlier in the week. Sorrel's star was shining as brightly as ever – Kenny's was on the wane. It was true that, at a major personal appearance, people expected the actress to be on her husband's arm. But it was Sorrel the public turned out to see, not Kenny Shorrocks.

'Suit yourself, Kenny. After all those pictures in the paper, on Monday, I should think everybody will have a pretty good idea of how you prefer to spend your time.' If Sorrel felt any twinge of conscience, as a result of her own amorous designs, this was quickly suppressed when Kenny stopped muttering and started snarling.

'You think you're it, and you're not. Queen of *Angel Dwellings*? So what! What's so special about being queen of a heap of fucking cardboard?'

'I shan't need you tonight, Kenny.' And if that sounded imperious, she didn't care. Sorrel had suddenly thought of a much more original escort.

'May I wish you bad luck?' Kenny attempted an aggravating smile.

'You can, but I wouldn't if I were you. Bad luck might turn round and bite you.' She sniffed. That was stale beer in his earthenware coffee cup.

Irish Dez, the alleged chauffeur, was still sleeping off a hangover in the flat he shared with Eeek, over the garage. Rousing him was too much like hard work for Kenny so it was Ray Fossett who finally drove Sorrel into Manchester. Spud sat next to him in the front passenger seat. The dog had to be kept away from the dress which was erupting like Vesuvius, next to Sorrel, in the back.

Ray, who was an eccentric driver, wound down the window and yelled, 'Get off and milk it!' at a cyclist who had dared to wobble into the car's path.

'Sweetheart,' he said to Sorrel, 'I've got some bad news for you. I can't come tonight. You'll be all right for a driver, Blackpool are sending a limo. It's Mother; they've carted her into Stepping Hill. She's in a side ward. My sister rang at sparrow-fart and she says they don't give much for her chances. I've called the old bat every name in the book but I always promised myself I'd be there, at the end, to hold her hand.'

'Ray, I'm sorry . . .'

'Don't be. Just get out there and dazzle them with your smile. You *have* had your teeth scaled specially. I'm just bothered about you being on your own.'

'I won't be. I've got an escort and he's one the crowd will love.'

'Who?' Ray swerved again to avoid a woman pushing a pram full of washing. 'Who will you swank out with?'

'Spud. After all, he gets nearly as much fan mail as I do. I'll bring him out in my arms. The crowd will love it.'

'It's inspired,' said Ray. 'And black and white always looks lovely with red. Shall Spud have a dickie-bow? I think he should.'

Sorrel passed the journey, as far as Stretford, reading the morning papers. She saved one till last. These days June always had a Friday column entitled *Mystically Yours . . . June Gee.*

It was sad to think that nobody of her own would be in Blackpool to cheer her on tonight. She had tried ringing Gladys, to suggest she might enjoy a trip to the coast, in a Rolls, but her mother's response had been: 'When you've seen the illuminations once, you've seen them.'

As they passed the Old Cock, at eighty miles an hour, Ray Fossett asked, 'What's Mrs June got to say for herself today?'

'I'm saving her.'

'Don't be mean. Spoil me, I'm nearly an orphan. Mind you, June can keep her astrology. The part I like best is when she answers readers' problems, psychically.'

Sorrel knew she would get no peace until she read it to him so she searched through the pages until she came to the column which featured a heavily retouched photograph of June sniffing an orchid. Inset, in the middle of the article, was another photograph. It was of Sorrel, looking poorly, outside Angel Dwellings.

'I don't believe it,' she gasped. 'I refuse to speak to her so now she's using her newspaper space to address an open letter to me. Listen . . .

' "Darling Sorrel, like half the wives in Britain, I was staggered by those photographs of Kenny – out on the town – with a string of girls. And, let's be brutal – they were noticeably younger than you are . . ." Nice of her to be the first one to be brutal!

'Slow down, Ray. Where was I?' Sorrel continued reading aloud: ' ". . . but as I write this, a record is spinning on my turntable and our American cousin, Bob Dylan, is reminding me that 'The Times They Are A-Changing'.

' "You have been too busy with your career, Sorrel, to notice that the Swinging Sixties have turned into the Sexy Seventies. Monogamy is no longer at a premium. Sex has become exercise, even in the suburbs. The birth pill has changed the meaning of fidelity. Never mind what your husband does with his body. Who holds the key to his heart?

' "*You* do, Sorrel. My psychic gifts qualify me to tell you that ..." ' Sorrel put her lips together and made a loud raspberry.

'She's good, y'know,' exclaimed Ray Fossett, driving straight through a red traffic light. 'You've got to hand it to her.'

'I'm handing her nothing,' stormed Sorrel. 'Offer June Gee five bob and she'd give a psychic interpretation of your own stomach rumbling.' She returned to her reading but not aloud. This was meant to punish Ray for taking June's side.

She couldn't keep the silence up. 'Dear God, listen to this bit: "I want you to cast your mind back to the day you got engaged. As readers of this column will remember, I was the first to be privileged to know your news. There we sat, in that intimate little bistro ..." That's Kendal's restaurant she's talking about and I didn't tell her at all. I told a woman who was mopping up potato pie.'

'Artistic licence,' pronounced Ray airily. He was a born fan. His major preoccupations were Edith Piaf and Sorrel Starkey. But the latter could tell that he was starting to build a small shrine to June Gee.

That settled it. She definitely wasn't reading more aloud. He would just have to wait and see for himself that she was alleged to have described Kenny as 'football's answer to Richard Burton'.

Ray drove painfully carefully for half a mile before he said, 'Don't be mean, sweetheart. What's the rest like?'

Sorrel let out a little scream. 'Put your hands back on the wheel! Thank you. It's all psychic rubbish after that. I'm to remember that Kenny is still the same person. She has a strong feeling that he won't be at Blackpool tonight. She claims to have watched the illuminations with me as a little girl. Absolutely untrue, they always went to Grange-over-

Sands. Mick's the only person I ever watched them with. The hottest news gets its own little headline: *BLASTS FROM THE PAST*. Apparently I'm to expect them today.'

'And that's all?'

Sorrel looked back at the paper. 'Frantic of Godalming is asked to send her name and address so that June can write to her in confidence. That's a joke! And there's a message for Bewildered of Elstree. Apparently, June's been in contact with the former owner of the woman's house and there are no objections, from the Other Side, to her moving the lilac bush.'

'Oh sweet Dorothy Squires!' cried Ray. 'I knew I'd forgotten something.'

'What?'

'Petrol.'

The car made some choking noises and rolled to a halt.

'Hmmph,' said Sorrel with contrary satisfaction. 'Your wonderful Mrs June didn't see fit to warn us about this.'

But the trouble with June Gee, either in person or on the printed page, was that her words always left Sorrel with uncomfortable doubts. Was it possible that June really could see further than other people? Sorrel wasn't sure she felt up to coping with blasts from the past.

Sorrel's arrival in the green room coincided with that of a wicker basket containing two dozen red roses.

'For me!' cried Mamie Hamilton-Gerrard, thrilled. 'Mother, get the boy a toffee.'

It was well known, amongst the cast of *Angel Dwellings*, that Mamie sometimes sent flowers to herself. She was now fluttering round the gilded basket of roses with a pretty simper on her face. She was also drowning out the studio messenger's attempts at explanation with a snatch of song.

> 'Roses for the girl from Daly's
> Posies brighten up The Strand . . .'

Mamie was singing this as she opened the envelope. Not for the first time, Sorrel forgot all harsh feelings towards the ancient star and marvelled that even here, in a sterile rehearsal room, Mamie could sing a snatch of a forgotten number and manage to make magic. Years seemed to have fallen away from her embittered face and Mamie was giving a totally convincing performance of the eagerness that comes from a light and happy heart.

Just as quickly, it turned to darkness. 'They're for you,' she snorted, and thrust the card at Sorrel.

Mamie rounded on the messenger boy. 'Have you unwrapped that toffee yet?'

'No.'

'Well give it back to Mother.'

Sorrel smoothed out the card which was now angrily bent. The handwriting on it was serene and the message wonderfully welcome:

> Sorrel – wherever you like,
> whenever you like. Great good
> luck for Blackpool. Love as ever

Barney had not signed it. Instead, there was a cunningly economical line-drawing of a pair of swans. Here too was talent enough to cancel out the urbane image of the Barney of today. The drawing brought back memories of the art student who had looked like a gypsy boy.

Rehearsals were due to start in just four minutes. Pam, from the upstairs office, came into the green room with the big black box-file which she used to carry round incoming letters from viewers. Sorrel prayed that it had already been sorted into individual stacks. When these letters were dealt out on a 'One for you and one for you' basis, Mamie's eyes were always too hungry for comfort. It wasn't decent to watch.

The small prayer was answered. Pam had already ringed them with elastic bands and Mamie had a nice thick pile to get her teeth into. At that moment, the stage manager put his head around the door: 'Everybody on the floor who's required for the first dock-office scene.'

Most of the men began reaching for scripts. The room began to empty until just Sorrel, Mamie, Nadine Taylor and a new girl, called Nancy Varndell, were left. Nancy had brought a breath of fresh air into *Angel Dwellings*. Young and pretty, with her enthusiasm still intact, she played a dizzy office cleaner. The scripts were always calling for her to flash her excellent legs. Male viewers wrote to her in droves.

'The one from Lewisham's had another dream about me,' she said excitedly. 'We went to Pegwell Bay and we took a canoe. He's enclosed a photo of himself this time. He looks a bit like Ken Dodd. Are any of yours funny, Sorrel?'

Sorrel hadn't got beyond the first. It took her right back into her past and needed a bit of digesting. The writing paper was almost ridiculously thick. The die-stamped heading boasted an address in Mayfair. The letter came from the managing director of a company called Intimacy Assured. The writer's name was Matthew Gillespie.

> Dear Sorrel,
> May I be permitted to refresh your memory? Cast your mind back, if you will, to the little mystery with a suitcase who refused breakfast, from a total stranger, early one morning in Piccadilly Circus. More recently we met when you were offering your services, as a hostess, in Ed Shotter's Attaché Club.

Sorrel's blood ran cold. Mucky Matt hadn't so much as marked the letter 'Personal'. She read on.

> You have gone up in the world, my dear, and so have I. These days I own and operate an escort agency at jet-set level. I also undertake to arrange 'intimate meetings' for people who are too well known to risk rebuttal.
> A very well-known gentleman indeed is most interested in the idea of 'passing time' with Lettie Bly. He is of advancing years and respected as high up as Downing Street. The fee would be negotiable but quite frankly, Sorrel, the sky is the limit here.
> Would you examine the idea in principle and let me have your reactions? This would be a cash transaction and discretion would be expected and assured.

Sorrel fished in her handbag and took out her purse. Heading straight for the green room telephone – a coin-box on the wall – she picked up the receiver and dialled Telegrams.

'Operator? I've got a lot of change ready . . .' Sorrel began by dictating Mucky Matt's name and address.

'And the message?' asked the operator.

'Very simple. Just "Get stuffed" and please sign it Sorrel Starkey.'

The operator let out a little gasp. 'I don't think we could undertake to send a message like that.'

'Why not?'

Interest crept into the operator's voice. 'Are you *the* Sorrel Starkey?'

'I most certainly am. You only have to check where this phone is situated.'

'You are,' babbled the operator excitedly. 'In our job we're very hot on voices. Tell you what, Sorrel, seeing as it's you, I'll have a go. I mean it *is* going to London W1 and they're meant to be very sophisticated down there.'

'I don't know about sophisticated but this man's got the morals of a tomcat,' said Sorrel grimly.

'Get away!' The girl was plainly fascinated. Recollecting herself and reverting to more professional tones, she added, 'Please insert forty new pence.'

As Sorrel returned to her handbag the messenger boy came back into the room with more red roses. There might have been the same number of flowers as in the earlier delivery, but they didn't look as many because they were only done up in cellophane.

Mamie snatched them from him. 'About time too!' She glared at the roses. No song this time. 'I see I don't rate a basket. Perhaps that's because I'm not switching on the illuminations.'

'Did you pay for one?' asked Sorrel, interested. This slipped out before she realized what she was saying.

Mamie's eyes narrowed. 'You're not the only girl with admirers. What's more, I've got a whole pile of letters over there saying it ought to be me in Blackpool tonight. When you press that switch, I just hope the bloody thing *fuses*.'

Nadine Taylor, always the peacemaker, looked up from a newspaper. 'June Monk says here that you're going to get blasts from the past tonight.'

'I think I've already had them.' Sorrel closed her handbag on Mucky Matt's letter and sniffed her roses.

'I wouldn't be too sure, love.' Nadine was checking with the paper. 'Yes, it says "blasts from the past both day and evening". Old Mother June is never less than specific.'

12

It was almost nine o'clock. In the red dress, her shoulders bare, Sorrel shivered slightly as she stood hidden in the shadows of the doorway of Blackpool Town Hall.

Beyond her, in the spotlight, the Master of Ceremonies was coming to the end of the warm-up. He had already gone through the whole 'Are we happy?' routine with the vast crowd out in Talbot Square. Now he changed to solemn drama.

'Blackpool delivers what Blackpool promises,' he announced. 'In just thirty seconds' time, Lancashire's own favourite lady will be coming out to a tune you will all be very familiar with . . .'

It was a gusty night. Even in the doorhole Sorrel could taste the salt on the air. She had meant to wear her white fox furs with the dress but an animal rights group had sent a message saying that they would take the sight of Sorrel, in furs, as an invitation to throw paint at her.

She had always felt guilty about the foxes, so more than half her sympathies were with the agitators. It was colder than Christmas. Sorrel bent down and picked up Spud.

'When I press the button there'll be a bang,' she said to him. Not that he had ever been the kind of dog who needed tranquillizers on Bonfire Night. Spud was as full of suppressed excitement as Sorrel. He dearly loved a storm and the wind was lashing in from the Irish Sea. Out in the light – in front of Sorrel – was a raised open-air stage with an aisle up to the microphone. On either side of the aisle sat the Mayor and Corporation and sundry civic wives whose hair was already taking a battering from the elements.

Strangers. Nothing but strangers. Why was there nobody of her own here? There should have been just somebody in the audience who knew that she had been waiting for this moment since she was in ankle socks.

Now the wind had got under the canvas awning, which was

creaking in protest. The scalloped pelmet was making slapping noises against the iron frame. What if a gust got under her frock and blew it over her head? Sorrel reassured herself that this was good old Blackpool where they would simply cheer at the unexpected sight of her legs.

'Ladies and Gentlemen, to the world she's Lettie Bly. To us she's our own Sorrel. Let's hear a big Blackpool roar for the one and only Sorrel Starkey.'

Three spotlights conjoined into one, a brass band began to play the *Angel Dwellings* theme music, Sorrel stepped out from the shadows, into the limelight, with Spud in her arms and the crowd roared its loving approval.

For a moment it was almost too much. One tear and she'd be lost. Spud chose that moment to give her a friendly lick and that nearly finished her off too. The roars redoubled at the dog's spontaneous gesture and this gave Sorrel a chance to control herself and carry Spud down to the microphone.

'What a night!' she exclaimed. 'I feel as though I should be singing "Stormy Weather".'

For safety's sake, Sorrel had her speech written out, in block capitals, on two postcards. As she glanced down at them, another spotlight – which was raking the crowd – picked out a tall, familiar figure. Could it be? Only he'd grown a moustache. It was. It was Mickey.

'What the hell are you doing here?' she said in joyful astonishment, straight into the microphone.

The crowd couldn't have known what she was talking about but they loved it. They were ready to love anything. On a sudden impulse, Sorrel threw the two postcards to the wind.

'Ladies and Gentlemen, I had a neat little speech ready but I feel as though I've come home so please will you let me tell you a story instead?

'Years ago, when I was a little girl, the very first stage door I ever went through was over there, on the North Pier. I wasn't on my own. I was with a boy called Mickey Grimshaw. He promised to make me a star. And he did. I wasn't expecting him here tonight but the good little love's come all the way from Hollywood. Come on, Mick, we've always shared the big moments. You come up here where you belong.'

444

She could see that he hadn't bargained for this and didn't look best pleased, so she added, 'If you don't come, I won't switch on the illuminations.'

Even Mick's stubbornness was not proof against a crowd which –encouraged by Sorrel – practically manhandled him onto the stage.

'You came! Oh Mick, I might have known you'd come.' Pushing him towards the microphone, Sorrel said, 'Say something.'

'Good evening, Mrs Shorrocks.'

'Shorrocks?' The microphone crackled and Sorrel's adrenalin was running high. 'Don't mention that name to me. Kenny's probably over in Yates's Wine Lodge – chatting up blondes.'

In any other town, in the light of recent newspaper revelations, this comment would have prompted a gasp. Not in Blackpool. Unfaithful husbands are the stuff of Bamworth comic postcards and the crowd bellowed its approval of Sorrel's fighting spirit.

The Master of Ceremonies seized this moment to regain control of the proceedings by beginning the count-down to the switch-on. 'Here we go, folks. Ten, nine, eight . . .'

Sorrel joined in with him and nudged Mickey, who was saying hello to Spud, to do the same.

As they got to '. . . three, two, one' Sorrel took Mickey's finger and used it to press the button. He hadn't been warned about the explosion which would follow, so he nearly shot up into the sky with the rockets. It was Mickey's agitation, not the bangs, which caused Spud to bark violently into the microphone.

In a moment, outer darkness had turned into miles of twinkling electric light. The Town Hall was suddenly lined in dancing bulbs. The whole of Blackpool Tower was a moving zig-zag. From its top, a searchlight was sweeping across the wind-lashed waves of the sea. Awaiting the official party, on the promenade, was a tram ablaze with more bulbs. The tram had been cunningly disguised to represent a ship coming up the canal with the *Angel Dwellings* tenement building rising out of the top deck.

'I wouldn't like to be up there in this gale.' Mickey put up the collar of his leather jacket.

'That's where we've got to sit. We have to do the grand tour.'

The tram swept them along the promenade. Up aloft, they felt dangerously close to the festoons of coloured electric bulbs, swaying above them, in the wind. Sorrel borrowed a councillor's overcoat. It would be even breezier when they got out on the cliffs towards Bispham; but it would also be more exciting. These cliffs were used for the spectacular climax of *The Greatest Free Show in the World*, the giant illuminated tableaux.

Some of these set-pieces, towering over the man-made rocks, were as old as Sorrel. These were the ones she loved the best. Every year something new was added. This season it was a cut-out of the *Angel Dwellings* tenement with Red Biddy looking out of a window at Lettie standing on the step. You could see Red Biddy's painted outline but, unaccountably, her lights had failed.

'That's what comes of ill-wishing people,' said Sorrel, but before she could explain, she saw something else. They had come to her all-time favourite. They had got to the nursery-rhyme section. It was 'Hi Diddle Diddle'.

'Mick!' she exclaimed in awe. 'D'you know what we did tonight? We made the cow jump over the moon.'

Mick began to quote:

> 'The little dog laughed
> To see such fun
> And the dish ran away with the spoon.

'Let's run away,' he continued. 'Just us. Let's get off the tram at Bispham and go and see Gander.'

Sorrel sighed. 'We can't. There's a civic reception afterwards. The Mayor's invited you, too.'

'Fine. We'll have our nuts and wine with the aldermen, then we'll go and see her. It would be a crime to be in Blackpool without seeing Gander.'

'I knew you'd come. I stopped up specially.' Gander had

aged. She was wearing a red flannel dressing gown and the plait of her bun was hanging down over one shoulder.

'Were you there? Did you see us do it?' asked Sorrel eagerly.

Gander shook her head. 'I can't get out these days.' Any sadness was erased by a fast smile. 'But I made sure *he* got there.' She was nodding triumphantly at Mickey.

'How?'

'Phoned him, didn't I? All the way to America. Went next door to do it. You'd have thought he was in the next room. The operator tells you how much it costs, afterwards.' It had plainly been a big moment.

'I'm dying to wee,' said Sorrel.

'You'll have to be careful in that frock.' Gander was respectfully stroking the beading.

'That's why I didn't go at the Town Hall.'

'You know the way,' smiled Gander. 'You look as good as Rita Hayworth. No, better.'

Sorrel gave Gander a hug and made for the door. She did indeed know the way. She knew everything about this little dormer bungalow. All the furniture had come from Rookswood Avenue. In the bathroom she even spotted the rainbow-shaded glass bottle with the smelling salts inside. The same one she'd sniffed as a child, and blacked out.

The lavatory was in a corner so the skirt presented some problems. Really, the most sensible thing to do was unzip the dress and step out of it. One way and another, making herself comfortable took several minutes. By the time she was dressed again and out on the corridor Gander and Mickey were already deep in urgent conversation.

Breaking one of her own rules, Sorrel paused outside the door and listened. It was Gander who was talking.

'. . . and the doctor gives me six months. I couldn't go to my grave without trying to help her. That's why I phoned you. I don't object to anybody taking a drink, Mick, but it's the hole and corner way she does it. Last time she came to see me, she was just in a blur.'

Sorrel could take no more. She opened the door and walked into the room.

447

'I was listening.' Then her arms went round Gander. 'Don't die. Please don't die.' Sorrel began to sob uncontrollably.

'Believe you me, that part's nothing.' Gander was all reassurance. 'It's just going home. What bothers me is leaving you behind in this boozy mess.'

'It's not that bad,' snuffled Sorrel. Part of her was even glad that somebody cared.

'I come from Salford.' Gander had turned fierce. 'You can't kid me. I know bad, and it's bad. Don't take on, love. Gander's not cross with you. She just wants to help.'

'I thought nobody'd noticed,' wept Sorrel.

'They all think that.' Gander was stern again. 'Our poor Edie thought that. You had a flat bottle in your handbag last time you came. Oh, it did make me feel mean. There was I thinking I'd got in everything you wanted and ...'

'You *had* got in everything. It was beautiful. It was the best time I'd had in ages.'

'Then why do you do it? I'm not scolding. I want to know.'

'I'll stop. I promise. I'll stop tomorrow.'

'They always say that.' Gander wasn't accepting easy promises. 'It's always tomorrow. They used to say that strong drink was the fastest road out of Salford. What are you trying to run away from?'

'Me. Her, Lettie Bly. I'm trying to run away from myself. It's all such a mess.'

Now Gander's arms were making her feel safe.

'I know, love,' she said soothingly, 'I know. You're still Pandora, aren't you?'

'I never heard you called Pandora.' Mick spoke quietly.

Sorrel registered that he was looking as concerned as the old woman. If only she could let them inside her head for a minute, perhaps they would understand. Hailstones were now rattling against the windows.

'It was in her story book when she was little.' Gander bent down and poked the fire. 'There was this girl called Pandora whose mammy had a box. "Whatever you do," she said, "don't open that." Only Pandora wouldn't be told. She lifted up the lid and the room was filled with things like mucky dusters, floating about. You can laugh, Mickey. Them dusters was all the troubles of the world.'

'I'm not really laughing. I'm remembering. Wasn't there something left at the bottom of the box?'

'One little scrap of silk, very scrumpled up.' Gander was dispensing the story as though they were still children in her kitchen in Rookswood Avenue. 'This bit of silk straightened itself out and it could talk.

' "I am Hope," it said. "If you've got the sense you were born with you'll hold onto me." It was a nice book but June Monk went and crayoned all over it. I'm afraid June was always very destructive as a child.'

'I won't give up hope,' vowed Sorrel aloud. 'That much I *can* promise you.'

'You'd better not or I'll come back and haunt you,' laughed Gander. 'Now don't start all that weeping again. I want 'All Things Bright and Beautiful" at my funeral and nobody in black. You'll only be waving me off. I'm only going home. Eeeh . . .' Suddenly she sounded much more contented. 'I'm glad I've got the chance to really talk to you. I've done me best and angels can't do more. Did you just break wind, Mickey?'

He started guiltily. 'It's jet lag.'

'It's putrid. Sheila, you're not too big a star to go and get the Airwick from the pantry. Anybody fancy a basin of home-made pea soup?'

And the funny thing was, even after a civic banquet, they found they did.

The Blackpool Corporation limousine carried Sorrel and Mickey through the night, back to Bellaire. Originally, Sorrel had been meant to stay in Blackpool but the Imperial Hotel had been unable to find a room for Mickey. Both the actress and the author were now too well known to think of sharing a bedroom without expecting reporters for breakfast.

'In the beginning, you welcome the press with open arms.' Sorrel kicked off her red satin evening shoes. 'You have to. You need them. And then you suddenly realize that it's a tap you can't turn off. Since I married Shorrocks, they've been behind me like an extra shadow.'

The car was passing through the windmills of The Fylde. In Sorrel's childhood, these had stood amidst lettuce patches. Nowadays, housing developments were creeping up around them and their sails were immobilized. The driver chose this moment to slide back his partition.

'I'm sorry there was no vodka on the way out from Manchester, Lettie. I got the Catering Superintendent to put some in, for the return journey.'

'Be sure your sins will find you out!' Sorrel opened the drinks cabinet. 'Want one, Mick?'

'Why not? And don't think I'm about to police you, because I'm not. I know you, you'll stop drinking when you want to stop and not a moment before. What about that impromptu speech you made tonight?' Mick began to laugh gleefully. 'There you were, emoting into the microphone, like Sarah Bernhardt. I don't suppose you realize that it came quacking out of the loudspeakers like Donald Duck?'

Mickey began to imitate her. 'No but seriously folks, when I was just a stage-struck little girl . . .'

Sorrel clocked him one.

'It's OK, Spud!' she yelled above a furious chorus of barking. 'It's not for real. I'm just glad to see him back. Mick . . . I'm going to admit something and if you say "I told you so" you can get out and walk. Kenny Shorrocks was the biggest mistake of my life.'

Mick's reply was guarded: 'Your career seems to be booming.'

'Oh yes, it's all limos and civic banquets and cash in his back pocket for my personal appearances. Do you know how much I've got in my current account? Seventeen pounds. And that's not really mine to call my own. Every morning my waking thought is "Will the taxman choose today to swoop?"'

'When I do personal appearances, I find myself looking for the taxman in the crowd. I always imagine he'll be in a bowler hat and that he'll pull the writ out of a black briefcase stamped with a gold crown. Regina versus Starkey. Or will it be Mrs Shorrocks?'

As Sorrel handed Mickey his drink, it seemed that the limousine was moving too quickly for anything to catch them.

The wind was still bending the trees on the far horizon but the interior of the car was womblike and safe and she was with the nearest thing she had to a brother. If ever she was going to dig up her troubles, the ones she·normally kept buried, it would be now.

'You earned your way into this mess.' Mickey added much more tonic to the drink she had poured. 'You can earn your way out of it.'

'When Kenny handles all the cash? Personal manager? He doesn't even open anything labelled *On Her Majesty's Service.* They just get slung into a drawer. When the tax people send somebody to call, he makes one of his henchmen say he's out.'

'Sorrel, I want to ask you a deadly serious question. Are you afraid of him?'

'No.' This answer was unhesitating.

'Good, because that means I won't be either. Is he a bully? I do hope so. I learned bullies at school.'

'He's more of a blackmailer. His ace card is always the suicide threat.'

'I presume you want out of this marriage?'

A week ago she would have agreed. Now she wasn't so certain. Sorrel was planning a peccadillo of her own. Unsure of the divorce laws, the last thing she wanted to do was drag Barney Shapiro into any sort of public scandal.

'Divorce is something I'd have to think about.'

'You're up to something, Starkey.' Mick was watching her closely.

'Yes, but don't ask me. Anything else, anything on earth, but not that.'

'I don't have to. That face, that tone, it's only ever meant one person. And what will your friend Ruby have to say about these plans?'

As usual, Mickey had gone straight to the heart of the matter. Whenever Sorrel tried to give practical shape to the idea of an affair with Barney, visions of good little Ruby rose up to haunt her.

'It's all going to be very discreet.'

'I expect Christine Keeler said the same thing. Oh well, it's your business. I'm going to make Kenny mine. Nobody is

451

allowed to crap on you and get away with it. I never gave you a wedding present. I'll take all your papers to my English accountant instead. His offices are in Manchester. The bill can come to me. Just one other thing: how inescapable is Lettie Bly?'

'Totally inescapable. She dominates everything.'

'That one's my fault.' Mickey suddenly looked tired. 'I wasn't experienced enough to know what I was handing you. I should have let it go to somebody else, somebody I didn't love. Here's a promise: one day I'll write you another part which will be so strong that it will cancel Lettie Bly off the face of the earth. How would you feel about coming to the States?'

'The States?' Sorrel, who was already pouring herself a second drink, slopped it in alarm.

'I sometimes think you were born on a chain to Manchester Town Hall,' sighed Mickey. 'One day you'll put the glass down and be hungry for new opportunities. That's when I'll ask you again.'

'Would you tell *me* something, Mick? Why the moustache? It's big enough to paste wallpaper.'

'Badge of office. All the gay men in San Francisco have moustaches. And check shirts or Lacoste shirts and Levis with one button undone.'

'Why?'

'What good would it do you to know?' But he enlivened the rest of the journey with stories of a lifestyle which Sorrel found totally inexplicable. Her many months in Cornucopia Mews had left her thinking she was an expert on gay men. She was, it seemed, hopelessly out of date. Pretty boys being taken for candlelit dinners by elegant older men had given way to raunch and black leather. The gossipy parties that she remembered had been stamped out by homosexuals in workboots. Social preamble had been abandoned. They simply took their sexual expertise to back rooms and bathhouses.

'You mean you don't even know their names?' she gasped.

'I mean I don't need to know their names,' laughed Mickey.

'It sounds so loveless.'

'Oddly enough –' and he stopped laughing – 'that's the one thing the whole city lives in hope of. We might deny it but we're always looking for love.'

'I hope you find it, Mick.' The moment the words were out she knew that the inflection had been too solemn for the moment.

'I've learned to love myself.' It was like a book snapping shut. 'And the sooner you do the same, the happier you'll be. You could start by just *liking* yourself. My God! Does Lana Turner live here?'

'No, I do.'

They had reached gleaming Bellaire.

It was no longer the abandoned shell which Sorrel and Ruby had first happened upon. The weeds had been cleared, the drive gravelled, the box hedges shaped into stylized pyramids, the cream tiling washed to a high lustre. These days the place looked like a house. It didn't look exactly homely. Bellaire was too floodlit for that.

'I'm impressed,' said Mickey. 'Is the yellow Rolls-Royce yours too?'

'It wasn't when I left this morning.' Sorrel was looking at the line of cars. Two were their own but the rest belonged to as low a selection of Kenny's associates as she had ever seen mustered, in one place, at the same time. The house on which she had lavished so much time and taste must be full of incipient beer bellies and flared trousers and kipper ties.

Yet everything was curiously silent. All she could hear was the artificial waterfall splashing in the rear garden. Sorrel looked again at the empty cars and counted off two club owners, the proprietor of a Cheshire gymnasium, one stuntman and a couple of ex-footballers. What's more, it was unlikely that they would all have arrived alone. Some must surely have brought passengers? What was going on and why was it all happening so silently?

Sorrel slipped her key into the front door and led the way into the house.

'Welcome to Bellaire,' she said to Mickey. Whatever was that whirring noise, coming from somewhere in the depths of the house?

'It's magic.' Mickey was gazing around the white entrance hall in delight.

His gratifying reaction made Sorrel forget about the puzzling whirr. For a moment she was able to appreciate the entrance hall through Mickey's eyes. Ruby had said that the great thing about 1930s design was its gleaming newness. Sorrel had restored that feeling. The white marble treads of the wrought-iron staircase had been repolished to a high sheen. The Berlin night-club drawings by Magda Schiffer, on the staircase wall, were in huge chromium-plated frames. On the glass telephone table, white lilies were arranged in a clear crystal cylinder with tiny silver fish, darting through the water, between their stems.

'It's ten miles over the top,' said Mickey, 'and if I'd done it I'd be very proud of myself.'

Sorrel pressed another switch. It illuminated a row of Erté costume designs, for *The Ziegfeld Follies*, in mirrored frames.

'They're fakes,' she felt forced to admit. 'A man from the graphics department did them for me.'

'I like them better for being fakes,' said Mick loyally. 'It's not just lavish, it's clever.'

Now, Sorrel could finally admit to herself that – all the time she had been doing up the house – she had been waiting for this moment. If there was one person on earth whose approval she sought, it was Mickey Grimshaw.

He was still looking around in gratifying wonder. 'We really *are* Noël Coward and Gertrude Lawrence in this setting.'

It was so exactly what she'd hoped he would say that, for a moment, all the agony that had gone into Bellaire seemed worthwhile.

A door opened and Ray Fossett emerged looking startled. Sorrel noticed that he was wearing that silly maid's apron again. She also registered Mick's critical glance at it.

'Oh,' said Ray.

'Just "*Oh*"? This is Mickey Grimshaw.'

Ray looked uncomfortable. 'It's a difficult moment. We thought you were away for the night . . .' His voice trailed off and he looked nervously over his shoulder.

'A difficult moment?' Sorrel's voice was flaring dangerously. 'This *is* my own house. Where's Kenny?'

'In the den. But I wouldn't go in if I were you.'

'Why?' she rapped out. 'Do you need tickets?'

Sorrel was nearer the truth than she knew. As she flung open the door of Kenny's den she suddenly understood the whirring noise. It came from a cinema projector. A freshly painted white wall was being used as a cinema screen. The silent moving picture, projected onto it, was of a naked man with a ginger crew cut, towering over a girl wearing a cheap necklace and nothing else.

'Home-made from the look of it.' Mickey spoke interestedly from behind her.

The film was indeed home-made. Sorrel did not recognize the man but the girl was one of the extras from *Angel Dwellings*. A third nude flickered onto the screen.

'Oh dear,' murmured Mickey.

The third naked figure was more familiar. It was Kenny Shorrocks.

The speed with which those shambling sportsmen cleared the room was living proof of how they'd gained their original reputations. Suddenly it was all car doors slamming and people rushing back, apologetically, to retrieve jackets.

Kenny could be heard stumbling up and down on the gravel outside, imploring people to come back, and assuring them that Sorrel was a good sport really.

The 'good sport' had collapsed into an armchair whilst Mickey, no slouch in these matters, switched off the projector and dropped the two reels of film into his flight bag.

'Evidence,' he said. 'We might be glad of it one day.'

Kenny staggered back into the room.

'They've all gone.' He sounded indignant. 'I just hope you're satisfied. And where's my fucking film?'

'Somebody took it.' Mickey's tones were as clipped and assured as they would have been in a dressing room after an opening night.

'I'm Mickey Grimshaw. I quite enjoyed your performance, what I was allowed to see of it. If I have a criticism to make, it was that you lacked a certain vivacity. *Inert*, that's the word I'm looking for.'

'Is he being funny?' asked Kenny in wonder. He had plainly

never met a Mick before. 'Who's got that film? It cost me a bleeding fortune.'

'Did you pay for that filth with my money?' Sorrel was out of the armchair and spoiling for trouble.

'Have you ever heard the like?' Kenny appealed to Mickey. 'I put a roof over her head and this is how she talks to me.'

'The whole thing is the most ghastly mess.' Mickey spoke soothingly. 'But never mind, Kenneth, it's soon going to be sorted out.'

'By who?' Kenny had found somebody's half-empty glass and was taking a swig.

'By me.' Mick was at his most airily infuriating.

'Just who the fuck do you think you are?' Kenny grabbed Mick by the front of the collar of his check shirt.

Sorrel let out half a scream, but only half. The speed with which her husband had been flung through the air was something she had not expected.

'I'll tell you who I am, I'm your wife's best friend.' Mick dusted an imaginary speck from the front of his jeans. 'Last year I spent a thousand dollars on self-defence lessons and I never waste money.'

'You'd no right to do that,' whimpered Kenny from the carpet. 'I've had bad legs.'

'Tough. I just hope they can get out of bed and down here by ten o'clock tomorrow morning. That's when you and I, Mr Bollocks, are due to have a straight talk.'

13

Sorrel always found morning September sunshine to be one of Nature's most glorious freaks. Coming as it did at the dying end of the year, by all the rules it should have been a fading and wistful thing. Yet it wasn't. For Sorrel it always seemed to blaze with hope. She had often tried to explain this to herself and never succeeded.

As she came down the stairs she was just content that this was so and relieved to hear that Mickey's and Kenny's voices – already coming from the direction of the veranda – did not appear to be raised in argument.

Ray Fossett was at the bottom of the stairs watering the giant cactus.

'Go easy on that water, they're born in deserts,' warned Sorrel. 'And what's wrong with your face?' Was it jealousy or mortal indignation which was making Ray look so cross?

'You never told me that Mickey Grimshaw was a Macho-Mary.'

So that was it. 'He's changed,' said Sorrel. 'They're different in San Francisco.'

'Who does she think she is? Coming here and sending the boss flying! I've had to go out for Ellerman's Rub. Different? I know that type. She's just an old book in a new jacket.'

Sorrel tried to keep her temper. 'Ray, I have to tell you that if you carry on calling Mick "she" the chances are he'll sock you too.'

'Just let her try,' said Ray darkly. 'I don't like to see a real man caught off his guard by a queen. I'm funny like that.'

Sorrel marvelled at the self-hatred buried within this statement. Suddenly Ray was rating Kenny a real man. Not for the first time she found herself wondering whether the former female impersonator was a little in love with the ex-footballer.

'How's your mother?' She thought she'd try a different

tack. One glance at his face was enough to know that it was the wrong one.

'Death's door? It turned out to be Valium withdrawal. That stuff is the curse of the council estates. Strikes me you'll need more than a pill before you go out there.' The rumble of male voices had become more heated. 'Miss Grimshaw's laying down the law like Portia in *The Merchant of Venice*.'

Sorrel walked through the arch, onto the veranda, to hear Mickey saying, 'A clean breast of things, that's the only way out of this mess. The tax authorities aren't fools. They keep an eye on personal appearances. They check the newspapers. I want a list of the lot of them and I want the genuine sums. We can get copy statements of all Sorrel's *Angel Dwellings* earnings. There's simply no need to swindle.'

'Swindle? That's a dangerous word.' Having registered Sorrel's arrival, Kenny was immediately trying to sound important. 'I could probably sue you for that word. And what if I refuse to give you this list?'

'I'm doing *The Russell Harty Show* while I'm over here,' smiled Mickey. 'I shall lead the conversation round to taxes and explain that I never renounced my British citizenship. That means I pay twice over – here and in the States. I will then become very indignant about people, in British show-business, who perpetrate tax swindles. And I shall name names.'

'Right out loud?' gasped Sorrel. 'On television? They'd edit it out.'

'They'd have a job. The show isn't pre-recorded.'

Kenny reached for his cigarettes. 'The thing is, boss . . .' He paused to light one.

Ho-ho, thought Sorrel. So now Mickey's *boss*!

'The thing is, we've got a bit of a cash-flow problem.'

Mickey nodded, then asked, 'You presumably own this house? That's one asset you could liquidate, instantly.'

'Sell Bellaire?' gasped Kenny.

Sorrel was irresistibly reminded of Scarlett O'Hara speaking about Tara.

'You also seem to have a fleet of cars.'

'Yes,' interrupted Sorrel, 'and whose is that custard-coloured Rolls on the front drive? Somebody must have left it behind, last night.'

'They didn't, it's mine. You switched on the illuminations so I went out and cheered myself up with a new car. Well, not new, secondhand.'

Sorrel resisted the impulse to hit him. She had to remind herself that he would only enjoy it. Instead she asked, 'And what did you use to pay for it?'

'I've got it on appro.'

'That one's easy.' Mick made a note on a pad. 'It goes back.'

'Now just a minute . . .' Kenny's voice was rising.

Mick's stayed deadly level: 'I think I'll get a suit from Tommy Nutter for *The Russell Harty Show*. I hope you always remember to keep receipts, Sorrel?'

'There you are!' Kenny seized hold of this. 'Hear what the man's saying? How many times have I said the same thing? P'raps now you'll listen to me. Go on, boss, I'm listening.'

Sorrel saw, quite clearly, that Mickey had won the day. It began to dawn on her that Kenny, like herself, had been waiting for a big hand to come down, out of the sky, and scoop them out of all the mess. Mickey Grimshaw might be everything that Kenny disliked and mocked but he was the nearest thing to that big hand which was ever likely to arrive at Bellaire.

'I'll see my accountant on Monday morning,' said Mickey. 'Don't look so frightened, Sorrel. He won't bite you. He's even got a sense of humour.'

Suddenly she felt unaccountably lighter. Something was going to be done about her waking fears. For the first time that morning she actually felt she had a right to this September sunshine.

There was an elaborately stagey knock at the glass door.

'I don't care if it *is* the bailiffs now,' grinned Kenny. 'Come in.'

It was Ray Fossett.

'Can I tempt anybody to morning coffee?' he asked. 'That's if a San Francisco clone doesn't mind accepting a fairy cake from a drag queen who was once in *Soldiers in Skirts*.'

459

'You weren't?' Mick was visibly thrilled. 'Those shows were amazing. I really loved them.'

'There you are then, daughter,' said Ray Fossett smugly.

'But I thought it was all meant to be macho, these days?' Sorrel found herself completely at sea.

'But what you didn't know is that real drag queens are our great heroes,' Mickey explained impatiently. 'Without them we'd have nothing. They were the ones who turned on the police at Stonewall.'

Sorrel knew both these gay men well yet, sometimes, she felt she didn't know them at all. It was as though you were only allowed to see just so much. Each had different definitions of the limits. She had once read *The Trials of Oscar Wilde* and the phrase 'feasting with panthers' sprang to mind. Much about her boys was wary and untamed yet they had both proved themselves to be entirely reliable. Unless you counted Ray Fossett serving drinks, in a lace apron, at a porno party. They'd be good in a war, she thought. Was Stonewall a war?

'She's wondering what Stonewall was' – Ray Fossett was being irritatingly knowing – 'and she doesn't like to ask. It was a night in New York when the queens got sick of being hassled by the police. A night of blood and feathers.'

Mick overrode this with 'It was the beginning of everything.'

'Or the end,' Ray interjected, 'depending on how you look at it. I can do without Gay Liberation. I preferred things when poofs were mysterious, like the Masons.'

'I could've been a Mason.' Kenny Shorrocks never liked to be left out of a conversation for too long. 'Come to that, I could've been a homo too. But I wouldn't have been the queer sort.'

'Is there another breed we've not been told about?' asked Ray interestedly.

'I'd have been the same kind as Eeek,' explained Kenny. 'He believes you should be allowed to marry your best mate. All the women would be kept in a compound. When you fancied one, he thinks you should just be able to go up the road and take your pick.'

'And this is the man I've kept fed and watered, for years?'

cried Sorrel. 'Enough's enough! God knows, I'm more scared of accountants than I am of the dentist, but self-preservation has to start somewhere. Thanks for your offer, Mickey. The nearest phone's in the next room. Please start dismantling this mess immediately.'

Like all actresses, Sorrel Starkey had to be sure she was wearing the right clothes before she felt capable of playing a scene properly. For the visit, with Mickey, to his accountants, she chose something appropriate for a courtroom drama – a navy blue suit with white gloves and a white Jackie Kennedy pill-box hat.

Kenny had distanced himself from the whole unravelment, simply giving Mickey carte blanche to gather together every scrap of information necessary. For two weeks Mick had lived in a flurry of bank statements and had smoothed out a whole heap of scrumpled, and previously discarded, receipts.

'Bellaire? You ought to have renamed it The Shambles!' His investigations had revealed a great deal about the Shorrockses' chaotic lifestyle and he had already carried many piles of paper, on their behalf, to his accountant's offices at the back of John Dalton Street.

Today was Sorrel's first visit and she was viewing it as apprehensively as she would have done an audition. What's more, she didn't feel right for the part. Mick had become so slick and American that she had expected the accountant's office to resemble a small version of ICI. The reality proved to be up a polished oak staircase which creaked at every tread.

'It's straight out of Dickens,' she said. 'Are you sure they understand theatre people? Look at that fire extinguisher, it could have come out of the ark.'

'Mr Pym is as modern as tomorrow.' Mickey pressed a white china bell-button on a door marked *Lang, Pym & Pettinger (Chartered Accountants) Established 1889.*

'It all looks frighteningly respectable.' The truth was that Sorrel was very much ashamed of the financial mess which she had allowed to accumulate around her.

'Pretend it's an abortionist's,' said Mickey, who understood her apprehensions.

'I've never had an abortion in my life!'

At just that moment, the door was opened by a woman in a blouse and skirt who looked as though she had never owed a farthing to anybody. The actress immediately felt over-dressed for the occasion.

'Good afternoon, Mr Grimshaw.'

Sorrel was impressed. Mick wasn't 'Mr' in the way you earned for yourself, in the theatre. He was real 'Mr Grimshaw' like proper grown-ups. She was feeling about ten herself. As the woman led them to Pym's office, memories began to stir of a beetle-browed mathematics master who had never been able to make Sorrel understand trigonometry.

She was too much on edge to take in more than the fact that the office was comfortable enough, in a roll-top desk and leather armchair kind of way. She hardly dared look at the man who knew the full extent of her financial iniquities.

The first things she registered were kind eyes and a very good-quality, foulard silk tie. Bald and reassuringly plump, Mr Pym did not look like a man who would get easily agitated. Real life, the free world outside, intruded onto his desk in the shape of a framed photograph of a jolly-looking woman holding onto a struggling Cairn terrier.

The sight of a dog inspired Sorrel to tell the truth and shame the devil: 'I have to be quite honest –' it came out too posh and too quickly – 'I want to turn round and skedaddle.'

Mr Pym smiled. 'My wife and I are great fans of your show,' he said graciously.

It was a nice smile but Sorrel just wished he'd cut the cackle and start the blood-letting.

'I have been doing quite a lot of talking to the Inspector of Taxes,' he began. He must have noticed that Sorrel had gone white at this because he added, 'Do sit down.'

She was glad to oblige. Mr Pym was talking about her waking bogeyman as though the Inspector was just any old human being.

'He appreciates the fact that you have been so forthcoming. To be honest, I think he is quite bucked at the prospect of closing both yours and your husband's files.'

This hopeful opening had a strange effect upon Sorrel. It

462

relaxed her tensions and freed her to view the proposals outlined by Mr Pym as the plot of a play. Every possible asset must be liquidized. Bellaire would have to go. Likewise the cars, Kenny's boat, the paintings, silver, furs and all of Sorrel's jewellery.

'They can't take Spud, can they?' This had been her one great secret fear. Her dog was famous enough to be valuable to somebody launching an advertising campaign. If they were planning on taking Spud, she and the dog would be on the night ferry for Dublin quicker than you could say 'broken contract'.

'I don't think there'll be any question of that. Spud should swell your future earnings.'

'And I'll buy Magda's paintings from you,' said Miek. 'That way we'll keep them in the family.'

This was another relief. Sorrel had gone to a lot of trouble to track down these pictures. They were the only material possessions she really cared about. Let everything else go, let it all go. Gander had always said, 'What money can make, money can mend.'

They couldn't take her 'family'. Spud and Mick and Gander weren't going to be put up for auction. The rest was nothing.

'And will this get us out of our mess?'

'I understand that Mr Shorrocks would like to acquire the tenancy of a public house?'

'He thought it might give us a roof over our heads and provide some income.' Sorrel felt quite proud of this statement. It was suitable dialogue for the place and made her sound less of a dope.

Mick spoke up again: 'Provided it's in the right place, a pub's not such a bad idea. Ray Fossett understands bar-cellar work. If they fill the place with signed photographs,' he explained to the accountant, 'the public should turn up out of curiosity. Their fame will get people over the doorstep, the rest will be up to Kenny.'

'I think a cup of tea is called for.' Mr Pym moved across to the marble fireplace and bent down to switch on an electric kettle. For the first time, Sorrel felt carefree enough to look around and she noticed a tray with Crown Derby cups and saucers on it together with an old oak biscuit barrel.

Mr Pym straightened up. 'Whilst the kettle is boiling,' he said, 'I want to ask you a very serious question. Lang, Pym and Pettinger are an old-established firm with a reputation to consider. I need your positive assurance that neither you, nor your husband, has concealed any asset or income from us.'

'I've been through everything with a fine-tooth comb,' said Mick. 'They haven't.'

'Miss Starkey?' Mr Pym's questioning look was stern.

'No, nothing. Nothing at all,' warbled Sorrel gaily. 'But I've just had an idea. I know where there's some money which would help pay off the debts. I've never collected my profits from the hardware shop.'

'The hardware shop?' Mr Pym's reproachful tones were reminiscent of Edith Evans as Lady Bracknell. 'No mention has been made, to the Inspector of Taxes, of any hardware shop.'

Sorrel discarded her new-found belief in the Inspector as Father Christmas. She felt back in the dock again. Both Mickey and Mr Pym were gazing at her as though she was the accused.

'What shop's this?' asked Mick.

'I inherited it. It was the same time as *Angel Dwellings* started so it just slipped into the background. You'd have to ask my mother. Only I'd rather you didn't,' she added hastily.

'I fear we must.' Mr Pym switched off the kettle peremptorily. It hadn't boiled but he switched it off anyway.

'Mrs Starkey will have to be sent for,' announced Mickey importantly.

Mick was the last person Sorrel had expected to turn into the public executioner, but he was already demanding Gladys's phone number at the shop.

They had run out of small talk. The solemn bell of the Town Hall clock was shuddering out four o'clock. As Sorrel gazed through Mr Pym's window, even her thoughts had deteriorated to the level of: This office has an excellent window cleaner.

A bigger thought intruded: It's only a little hardware shop.

Why are they making me feel as though I've perpetrated a City scandal?

The respectable female clerk put her head around the door. 'Mrs Starkey's arrived,' she said and then, averting her eyes from the men, she mouthed silently at Sorrel, 'She's using the toilet.'

'She would be,' replied Sorrel. 'Inspecting toilets is her favourite hobby.'

'Don't you be so cheeky.' Gladys was through the door and bristling. 'And *you* can take the grin off your face –' this was to Mickey – 'I'm no keener than the next person on being summoned to town in my second-best coat. What's so urgent? I've had to put the Closed sign up. God know's what the Esso Blue man will think! What are you staring at, Sheila?'

'That perm. It's so corrugated.'

'I have them done to last.' Gladys sniffed dangerously.

'Could we get down to business?' The accountant extended his hand to Gladys. 'I am Eric Pym.'

She shook it ferociously. 'The sooner the better. Time's money to me.'

'I understand your daughter is joint owner of a retail hardware outlet.'

Gladys's mouth tightened and her eyes swung accusingly to her daughter. 'Have you been using that shop to try and get credit?'

'It's nothing like that,' interjected Mr Pym hastily. Sorrel could see that he was not experienced in arbitrating in passionate family dramas.

'Anyway,' announced Gladys, 'it's not her shop. She's got nothing to do with it. Not any more.'

Sorrel was astounded. The last person on earth she would have expected to swindle her was her own mother.

'Half of it was certainly left to me. I saw a copy of Gran'ma Starkey's will.'

'And don't you ever read anything you sign?' Gladys, whose tones were scathing, now addressed the room at large. 'She's in a dream. She lives in a world of her own. I've had to put up with this since she was a babe in arms. I sometimes think there's a vital part missing.'

Gladys rounded back on her daughter. 'It was bad enough when you spent your life in a daze but now it's got more serious. I don't say you're drunk all the time, it's more deceitful than that. You pass for normal but the truth is you've reached the stage where you're permanently pickled in that vodka. You remind me of expensive bottled fruit!'

Gladys now began to address her daughter over-patiently, as though Sorrel had suddenly gone deaf. 'What did I get you to sign?'

'I don't remember. I'm always signing things.'

'Kids? You do your best to protect them and you end up hauled into town like a wanted woman.'

Mr Pym attempted to explain: 'Your daughter has tax problems . . .'

'Precisely. And I tried to save her from herself. Why should that girl pay tax, on her profits from the shop, at a film star's rate?'

'I've never been a film star.'

'No, but you've been a fool. I don't know how you manage to remember your lines. You signed everything back to me. I pay tax on it at the lower rate. You get the lot on my death.'

Sorrel was bewildered. 'But you said my profits from the shop were "in the doings under the thingy". Those were your exact words.'

Gladys's eyes went up to heaven. 'Sheila Starkey, your tongue will get you hung. I was talking about *little presents*. The law does allow a mother to give her daughter little presents. It's within limits, it's legal.'

'Did this money ever change hands?' asked Mr Pym.

'No,' snapped Gladys. 'And she's not getting it now. I've changed my mind. I'm not working every hour that God sends to forward more money to Whitehall. And you needn't go looking for it, Sheila. I moved it when the men came to mend the leak.'

'At what point did Sorrel sign this document?' asked Mickey.

'Right at the beginning. It took forever to go through probate. Once we got it she was already making a fortune.

466

Where's your money gone?' she demanded of her daughter. 'What have you done with it all?'

'In a word, Kenny.'

'Yes, and I bet you helped him too. Even before she started Sunday school she was taking a knife to her money box.' Without pausing Gladys put her face close up to Mr Pym's and demanded: 'Are we in the clear?'

He treated her to a huge beam. 'I think the time has come to make a nice cup of tea.'

'I'm thinking of having a party,' said Mickey to Gladys, who was opening her handbag. 'Would you like to come?'

'I can just imagine your sort of party,' snorted Gladys. 'I'm not interested in drugs.' She took a Valium tablet from her purse and swallowed it.

'What sort of party is it going to be?' asked Sorrel.

'A good one, in my suite at The Midland. I'm going to throw a lot of unexpected elements together and see what happens. Do come, Mrs Starkey.' He was all innocence. 'I know my mother would love to see you. Sorrel, can you give me Mamie Hamilton-Gerrard's telephone number?'

'You'll be asking for June's next!'

'Why not?' smiled Mickey.

It was obvious to Sorrel that Mick had grown bored with the role of ministering angel. The little demon inside him was back in charge. In the last few weeks he had been so good that she could refuse him nothing.

'Yes, give me June's number while you're at it,' he demanded. 'I want this party to be really memorable.'

14

British Rail were slipshod custodians of The Midland. During the period of their stewardship, the establishment rolled so far downhill that it ceased to be a great hotel and merely remained a big one.

Mickey looked disparagingly around the public lounge. 'Orange and green,' he shuddered. 'And they have those big gold paper lampshades in every sleazy motel in Reno, Nevada.'

Sorrel's mind was running in a different direction: *'Wherever you like, whenever you like . . .'*

It had suddenly dawned on her that The Midland had both a back and a front entrance. That access to the upper floors was to be gained by both a lift and a staircase. Two people could arrive separately and leave separately. Two people could take two rooms and only use one.

She started guiltily. Ruby had chosen that moment to emerge through the revolving doors, from the street, and was heading towards them. She was in a spectacular sable coat and a less impressive headscarf.

'I'm just going upstairs, to Steiner's, to get my hair combed out for your party,' she explained. 'Jake's coming on from the office. What time's the official start?'

'Six o'clock.' Mick and Ruby had long been on kissing terms. 'Officially, I've asked people for drinks but the hotel are laying on a whole load of things to eat.'

'Very wise,' nodded Ruby. 'Manchester never says no to something approximating a good high tea. Ever since Nancy Mitford's book came out, the rest of England seems to think it's non-U to offer more than salted peanuts.'

Together they headed for the lift. The hairdressing salon was on the mezzanine. Sorrel and Mickey got out at the first floor.

'Time has stood still here.' Mick led the way along the red

carpets of a marble-lined corridor. 'Just wait till you see my suite.' His key went into the door. 'Behold! These rooms can't have changed since Dame Nellie Melba came to Manchester.'

Sorrel wandered around the suite, enchanted. Time had only added a veneer of nostalgia to the huge sitting room. With its rose-shaded lights and grey silk wallpaper and silver brocade upholstery, the whole thing was out of an old musical comedy. There was even a white grand piano, set between two windows, which looked out onto a narrow balcony. Somebody had filled gold wicker tubs, on legs, with copper beech leaves and white flowers. The only intimation of reality was the sight of a number thirty bus, for Chorltonville, grinding below them, past the side of the YMCA.

'Mick! It's exactly the kind of posh we dreamed about when we were little.' Sorrel reflected that there are few pleasures to compare with being on the inside when you've been on the outside, looking in.

Together, they began to inspect the food which had already been laid out on white-damask-covered tables. From caviar to meat balls the spread was lavish.

'And all tax deductible,' beamed Mickey happily.

Sorrel lifted up one of the tablecloths and peered: 'They're just plain trestles underneath.'

'So are we,' said Mick, and added fervently, 'Thank God I'm common!'

Porters now began to carry in silver ice buckets and crates of champagne. They were followed by an obsequious waiter who spoke in murmurs: 'If I might suggest, sir, the bath could be filled with ice and we could cool the bottles in there.'

'And I suggest you've not met many actors!' exclaimed Sorrel indignantly. 'Bathroom? Once they've had a couple they would be quite capable of tottering off into the night with bottles up their jumpers.'

'As Madam wishes' was the graceful reply. And he motioned the porters to stow the crates under the trestle tables. 'You're quite right,' he added in surprisingly human tones. 'It never does to pander to thieving bastards.'

'Who's actually coming?' Sorrel, who could never resist

free food, was already spoiling the design of the table by cutting into a pâté.

'Everybody.'

'Gander?'

'I sent her a card but I haven't had a reply.'

Suddenly there was laughter from the corridor outside. It had to be some of the cast of *Angel Dwellings*. Actors and actresses are good value at a party. They always enter laughing. Once these early arrivals had got a drink in their hand, the food seemed to draw them like a magnet.

'It's disgraceful I know,' said Nadine Taylor. 'I think it comes as a result of all those years on the breadline. Oh look, smoked salmon!'

The room was filling rapidly. It was like *Mr Manchester's Diary* come to life. Sheelah Wilson who ran the biggest model agency in the town entered looking imperishable, in black and pearls, clashed cheekbones with Diggory Mallet, accepted a glass of champagne and began to regale her immediate neighbours with a story of a Sunday luncheon party where she had served a pork and bean cassoulet to her distinguished guests.

'How they farted!' she cried with delight. Manchester parties tend to be more rip-roaring than London ones.

Across the room, Sorrel caught a glimpse of Harold Riley, the painter.

'I prefer his work to Lowry's,' said Mickey. 'It exactly matches my own romantic view of this merchant city. And here's Miss Romance in person.'

Mamie Hamilton-Gerrard, in a Cilla Black wig and a gauze frock, had fluttered into the room with Mother.

'I'm worried about you, Sorrel.' Mother was all concern. 'You look awful tonight. Are you sickening for something?' Mamie was startling Mickey with some unexpected baby-talk.

'Aren't ooh going to take ickle Mamie back to Hollywood? I's good as Shirley Temple.'

So that's what Mamie was like at private parties. Sorrel had heard but she'd never seen it before.

'She doesn't know it,' Mick came up and whispered to Sorrel, 'but in a minute she's going to sing.'

'I shall boo.'

'No you won't. You'll mean to boo but the wicked old bag will weave her spell and you'll be cheering with the rest. She never fails.'

And that was exactly what happened. Mamie began by pleading that nobody wanted to hear 'ickle me'. But, in next to no time, Mother was at the grand piano and Mamie sang.

She took a trite little song and turned it into distilled fun and excitement. It so exactly matched the mood of the party that Sorrel wanted to go up and put her arms around such instinctive talent. She knew it would be no use. Attempt to embrace Mamie and you would find the same kind of unyielding ironing board as Gladys Starkey. Beryl Grimshaw had got Sorrel's mother pinned up against the white marble fireplace. Sorrel moved across to join them.

'I think Mickey's going to surprise us all,' cooed Beryl. 'I've certainly not given up hope of wedding bells. I think he's got a little sweetheart tucked away in San Francisco. Whenever I suggest a trip over there he says, "No. Meet me in New York instead." I suspect a love nest. I sometimes think I might just drop in and surprise them.'

'I shouldn't do that.' Gladys spoke firmly. 'You're a big woman and the shock might kill you. Don't look now, Sorrel, but trouble's just walked in.'

Sorrel did look. She turned round to see June Gee and Martyn framed in the doorway. They were in deep evening dress which made them look as though they were trying to suggest that they were going on somewhere more important afterwards.

Two hands went over Sorrel's eyes and she smelled French cologne and rich cigar smoke.

'Jake Shapiro,' she exclaimed delightedly. The hug he gave her was so warm and generous that she couldn't help thinking that Barney had been made out of Jake's body. Well, his and Ruby's. She felt a twinge of that awful guilt again.

From out of the corner of her eye Sorrel could see that June was circulating slowly. Her mauve kaftan was voluminous enough to create a wide space around her but sometimes she paused and seemed to be handing something pink to selected people.

'What's she doing, Jake? What's she handing out? I daren't look. We're not speaking.'

A man's voice behind her said, 'Which is very silly. Come on, Sorrel, we've all got a living to earn.' It was Martyn Gee.

Dinner jackets, thought the actress, did nothing for body-builders.

'You've surely no quarrel with me, Sorrel?'

'You both piss in the same pot,' she replied reasonably.

'Sheila Starkey, where will people think you were brought up?' Gladys plainly did not consider her daughter's reply to be at all reasonable. 'June, come here! I want you. Now just make it up, the pair of you. Here and now. This is meant to be a party, not a blood feud.'

Sorrel felt caught on the hop. 'All I can say is she'll have to apologize for that awful article.'

June seized the opportunity with both hands. The big eyes went so 'sincere' that Sorrel got ready to wince.

'Sweetie . . .' June's voice was dripping with self-reproach. 'However did we let it happen? *Us!*'

'You tell me. You wrote it.'

'Yes, but the naughty sub-editor cut it to shreds and changed the meaning.'

'What are those cards you're handing out?'

This reminded June to rake the room with her eyes. Sheelah Wilson's husband was within arm's length so June's gloved hand immediately shot out and thrust a pink card in his direction.

'Eight o'clock, Ernest,' she said. 'Eats afterwards. Bring Sheelah.'

The card never reached him, Sorrel had grabbed it.

DEATH? DON'T MAKE ME SMILE
a lecture-demonstration
by
JUNE GEE
Free Trade Hall Manchester
Friday October 25th
N.B. Not a film. See the glamorous psychic
sensation in person

The deckle-edged card was properly, even elaborately, printed. Somebody had used a cheap rubber stamp to add: *ADMIT TWO: CELEBRITY ENCLOSURE.*

'But that's tonight,' gasped Sorrel in near disbelief.

'And you are invited.' June could have been reassuring one of her own children.

'Look what Martyn's just given me.' Mickey was also holding an invitation.

June seized this moment to pass among the guests, handing out more cards. It was like watching a flutter of pink doves, but the invitations only seemed to land in famous hands.

'Mick, she's grabbing your guests. She's all set to clear your party.'

'Beats switching the lights up at the end. They were only asked till eight. Oh look, she's trying to suck a kiss off the man from the *Evening News*.'

'You never asked reporters?'

'Of course I did. I owe them a lot. So do you if you pause and think about it.'

It now became obvious that June wasn't just passing out invitations. She was also managing to build a tense atmosphere. Mabel, the wardrobe mistress, and the two girls from makeup, were looking definitely disgruntled.

Sorrel pushed her way through the crowd, grabbed three cards off June and handed them to these good friends. Ruby Shapiro was amongst the privileged but she was looking distinctly puzzled.

Absentmindedly fingering the card, to test its quality, Ruby said, 'Of course this sort of thing's against my religion. Not that we're anything like as frum as we used to be. My trouble is, I'm my mother's daughter but I've spent a lot of time in Paris.'

Jake winked conspiratorially at Sorrel. If Barney was going to age as well as his father had done, there should be boundless mileage left in him yet. Men stayed attractive much longer than women. Sorrel risked a good hard look at herself in a mirror on the wall behind Jake. She always looked first at her own defects. She could do with a mite less flesh on her cheekbones. Oh well, it could be worse. But if she was going to turn herself into a glamorous mistress, it had better be sooner rather than later. She longed to ask after Barney but she didn't have to.

'Barney was meant to be here.' Jake was peering around the room.

'Mandy will have thrown another of her temperaments.' This came from Ruby. 'That pair waste more theatre tickets than they use. She doesn't deserve him. I'd like to smack her. If she lost the tin opener he'd starve to death. And now she's discovered frozen dinners.'

Ruby finished the champagne in her glass. 'And mean? The house is like a fridge. She has the central heating permanently turned to dim. All she cares about is diamonds. Mind you, she buys well, I'll give her that. She understands investment. The best thing Barney could do would be to open a charge account for her at De Beers. And then he could march off and take a mistress.'

'What?' Sorrel could not believe she had heard aright.

'She doesn't mean it,' murmured Jake comfortably.

'Who doesn't? I most certainly do.' Ruby swapped her empty glass for a full one, from a passing tray, and nudged Sorrel to do the same. 'Barney needs love in his life.'

And she looked Sorrel straight in the eye.

'Three glasses of champagne, Ruby?' Jake spoke equably. 'That's the first time I've ever known you take three.'

'Perhaps I'm going to drink a private toast,' she replied, and moved across the room to join Ray Fossett who was talking frocks with Doris Dintenfass.

Kenny Shorrocks was not present. Cocktail parties made him uncomfortable. As he now viewed Mick as a friend, he had insisted upon sending Irish Dez and Eeek to act as bouncers. Mickey had not seen any real need for this but he had allowed it because Eeek made him laugh and the idea of an Al Capone touch, at his farewell party, had appealed to him.

The bouncers, stationed on the door, had plainly fallen down on their job because into the room came a woman who looked (there was no other word for it) poor.

Sorrel nudged Mickey. 'Who's that?'

'Looks like a fan who's managed to dodge her way in.'

The woman advancing towards them might have been a careworn sixty or she could have been seventy. The dyed red hair was white at the parting. Her coat had been to the cleaner's once too often. Lisle stockings led down to canvas shoes with a hole cut in one of them to allow for a bunion. Yet there was something brave about her. She had plainly taken a deep breath and was determined to talk to Sorrel.

'Be kind,' warned Mickey.

'I don't need telling.'

Ignoring the stares she was getting from guests, the woman came right up to them. There was something familiar about the wise eyes. For the most part, you only saw eyes as concerned as that on dogs.

'Sheila? You don't know me. Well you do, both of you, but it was years ago. I phoned your house and they said you'd be here. I didn't want you to just find it in the paper. I've just come off the bus from Cleveleys. I'm Mrs Gander's sister. I'm sorry to have to tell you that she passed away this afternoon.'

Now the woman was crying and so was Sorrel. As he put his arms around the pair of them, tears were beginning to well in Mick's eyes too.

'It's all right,' sobbed Gander's sister. 'Everything's going to be OK. We're bringing her home.'

Sorrel was shaking harder than she had known it was possible to shake. Gander gone. It couldn't be true. She was filled with terrible guilt. Sorrel had known it was likely to happen but she had only seen her friend once, since the illuminations.

'I'm glad the pair of you managed to take her to Fleetwood.' Gander's sister blew her nose. 'It was the last time she got out.' She began to dry her eyes. They were Gander's eyes, that's why they had been familiar, and Sorrel started crying again.

'We all need a stiff drink.' Mick was looking around for a waitress.

'Not for me.' The woman was already moving towards the door. 'Strong drink's no friend of mine. I'll be in touch about the arrangements. But we're definitely bringing her home.'

Sorrel and Mick saw her to the corridor and then to the lift. As the doors closed Mick said, 'Do you know who that was?'

'Gander's sister.' Sorrel wasn't making sense. She felt as though her ultimate safety net had been ripped from under her. Gander had always been the place to run when there was nowhere else to go.

'That was "Our poor Edie",' said Mick. 'You've just been talking to the original of Lettie Bly.'

Gander's funeral was at Pendleton church. The arrangements had been left in the hands of her sister. Edie was used to sparse, so Gander got the same. She didn't even get 'All Things Bright and Beautiful'. There were no hymns, the organ was being mended.

What broke Sorrel's heart was that Edie had insisted upon taking her own cheap wreath off the top of Gander's coffin and had proudly replaced it with Mickey's and Sorrel's floral tribute from Fabian's of King Street.

Somehow Edie's wreath got left behind, at St Thomas's, when the cortege set off for the final committal at Weaste cemetery. As the car pulled away from the church, Sorrel waved through the window at old Mrs Tatton who had started one of her gasping attacks during the service and had decided not to come on to Weaste.

In the car, there were just the three of them. Unless you counted the young curate, sitting next to the driver, in the front. He had referred to Gander as 'Lilian' throughout the service and the woman he described in his sermon had nothing to do with warm reality. Sorrel suspected it was a standard speech into which he had inserted lines like 'Born in this parish and educated at St Thomas's school'.

The car followed the hearse downhill to Weaste. The coffin was in nasty pale wood with chrome handles.

'I wish I'd brought Spud,' said Sorrel. 'Gander loved him and he'd make it look more of a crowd. It's not fair. She did everything for everybody and there was nobody there.'

Edie just smiled and said, 'Yes, but just think who'll be waiting to meet her on the other side. It'll be a big day in heaven. There'll be tramps and kids who always called her

Auntie and about two hundred women she lent "a pound to be going on with". I bet some of the biggest rogues in Paradise will turn out for your Auntie Gander.'

Sorrel had never seen a body buried before. Although she knew there would be a hole in the ground, she wasn't prepared for the smell of disturbed earth and the straining noise of a coffin being lowered on braid straps. At first they got the box in a bit crooked and it stuck.

'Don't hurt her,' she said involuntarily. And who did they think they were kidding with that awful artificial grass around the edges of the hole? Edie handed her some earth.

'I'm not doing it.' Sorrel pushed Edie's hand away so violently that the earth fell on the coffin anyway. Then she couldn't bring herself to leave. 'If we go, they'll fill it in and she'll just be in the cold ground.'

'That's life, love.' Edie wiped her eyes. 'By hell she was a good 'un! She's not on her own. Dick Gander's right underneath.'

'Room for one more down there, Mrs.' A gravedigger, smoking a Woodbine, had emerged from behind some sooty elderberry bushes.

'Very kind of you I'm sure,' said Edie, 'but I'm being burned. Mickey, make her come. She can't hang around like this, she'll get her own death of cold.'

'Bye, Gander,' gulped Mickey. 'And thank you.'

All three of them were blowing their noses as they picked their way to the main path. As they headed towards the cemetery gates, Sorrel suddenly remembered the day in Rookswood Avenue, during the war, when Gander had managed to get hold of some little pickling onions. Peeling them, they'd cried till they laughed. She would never be able to forget that awful hole in the ground, but life had to go on and good memories were beginning to creep back. Should they have come so quickly? It seemed almost awful.

'Let's get rid of that morbid black car and walk to a pub,' suggested Mickey.

The one they found had only just opened its doors and smelled strongly of years of old ale mixed with this morning's fresh disinfectant. It was Lanry, a brand much favoured by Gander, and this nearly set Sorrel off again.

'Vodka?' asked Mick hastily. 'What's yours, Edie?'

'Just a bitter lemon, but I wouldn't mind one of those ham rolls out of the glass case. If that's not being cheeky,' she added hastily. 'Our Lily'd be pleased to think that we buried her with ham.'

It was only now that Sorrel noticed the small diamond of black cloth carefully stitched, as mourning, to Edie's fawn sleeve.

'Lil's left me the bungalow,' Edie went on. 'And half the money. You get the rest, Sheila. I think you'll be startled. She certainly wasn't without. There was a letter with the will. She particularly wanted you to have that little Chinaman, with his head on a spring. And the rainbow bottle from the bathroom. Pity they've never had you on *This Is Your Life*. Lil always said she wanted to walk on and give Eammon Andrews a sniff from that bottle.'

Gander hadn't quite gone. Something of her was left behind in Edie.

From the counter, Mick held up a bottle of bitter lemon, with an obscure label, questioningly.

Edie nodded her assent.

'Don't you drink any more?' asked Sorrel.

'At one time they couldn't make one big enough or strong enough for me. That's over, thank God.'

'How did you do it?'

'I'm not telling you. Before it would be worth anything you'd really have to *need* to know. When you do, I'll be there. I'll be in Cleveleys. You know the address. You'll be as welcome as you always were. Both of you.'

Mick had joined them with glasses and a roll on a plate.

Edie bit into the roll. 'Whoever made this cob,' she said, 'was offering no consideration to people wearing false teeth.' She chewed and swallowed. 'If we're going to be friends, Sheila, I've got to tell you something. You may be a very good actress but I can't stand Lettie Bly. The poor boozy cow is such a tragic loser.'

And Edie smiled a secret smile which Sorrel was in no position to question.

15

The Ringway Aerodrome of Sorrel's childhood, an RAF control tower and some sheds in a field had turned into Manchester Airport. Sorrel stood watching as Mickey checked in his baggage for San Francisco.

The Duke of Edinburgh had officially opened this new terminal but the public had not been allowed in for months. Sorrel looked apprehensively upwards. There had been worries about the safety of the huge modern Italian chandeliers. These great globs of glass looked like bunches of grapes which had mutated peculiarly. If the wires had rusted once, could they do it again?

For safety's sake, Sorrel moved a bit to the left. She wasn't feeling at all secure, and why were airports allowed to play 'I'm Leaving on a Jet Plane' over the Tannoy? The fact that Mickey was going was bad enough. She didn't need it setting to music.

'That's done.' Mick was stowing his passport and tickets into an inner pocket of his leather jacket. 'I have to clear customs at LA.'

'Mr Grimshaw?' It was a handsome man in a dark uniform. 'If you would like to come this way for the VIP lounge . . .'

'Where did I put my baggage chits?' Mick was suddenly seized by that pocket-patting panic which attacks people at airports.

Sorrel tried to be helpful: 'If they were green, you had them in your hand a moment ago.'

Mick's hand went to a side pocket of his jacket and a small brown glass bottle flew through the air and landed with a crash that smashed it.

Zzz . . . the fumes which arose from the floor had a faint echo of something erotic. Yet they also smelled of dirty socks and household bleach.

'Everybody stand back,' Mick called out authoritatively. 'I'm afraid I've dropped a sexual stimulant.'

'Oh look, it's Sorrel Starkey,' said somebody interestedly. Then they went 'Phew!'

The fumes were having the most horrendous effect upon Sorrel. A bright flash of light, in front of her eyes, was changing from green to yellow and she could hear her own heart beating so loudly that it sounded like a giant walking around in her head.

'Christ! Somebody's dropped some poppers.' This came from one of a pair of flight stewards, with moustaches, who were grinning knowledgeably.

The man who had been attempting to lead Mickey to the VIP lounge turned into a hero. Grabbing a janitor in a brown overall, he said, 'Sand over this, fast. And then proceed as for vomit. I'll give you a moment to get your breath back, sir,' he added smoothly, to Mickey.

'Are you smuggling drugs?' asked Sorrel indignantly.

'It isn't a prohibited substance. A friend of mine wanted to try the English kind. I had to search Earl's Court for it and now it's smashed.' Mick looked around worriedly. 'I just hope nobody's got the wrong kind of bad heart. It could kill them.'

'And you take this stuff for *pleasure*?' It was all beyond Sorrel.

'You don't take poppers, you sniff them. Sorrel, you're into areas you wouldn't understand. Before I go, I've got to say two things to you. You're never going to win with Kenny. He's got a slave complex. His thinking is so convoluted that, if you ever got ahead of him, you would have changed into a devious person yourself. You deserve some happiness. Grab it.'

Sorrel's heart was nearly back to normal but she had started to develop a headache. 'I need fresh air. Is that it? Have you done?'

'Not quite. How much use have you got for Eeek?'

'Less than none.'

'I'm glad of that. He might be coming out to California. Just on a visit.'

Was she hearing right or was it the effects of the fumes?

'Eeek? Mick, there's nobody as anti-gay as Eeek.'

'He had me kidded too, for a while.'

The man from the VIP suite reappeared, looking anxious.

'You can't have Mr Grimshaw for a moment.' Sorrel held up an imperious hand. 'I'm trying to save him from himself. Why Eeek?' she demanded. 'He's got a nice enough nature but why not somebody with a bit of wit and style?'

'I can provide all of that myself. Too much sometimes. I love you, Sorrel. I'll call you as soon as I get home.'

For a moment they clung together and then he moved off with the airport official. As he turned to wave, Sorrel found herself stabbed by one word. Home. Mickey had called San Francisco 'home' and it struck her as disloyal to Manchester.

'Aren't you going to wave him off from the observation platform, Lettie?' It was the man with the brush and the sand.

Sorrel shook her head. 'Where do I find a cab?'

'One level down. You've struck a bad time. The morning plane from London's just coming through.'

On the gloomy covered lower level there was a strong smell of petrol and exhaust fumes and Sorrel was forced to join a queue for taxis. The number of Indians in Manchester seemed to have grown enormously in the last couple of years.

As she opened her copy of *The Stage*, to check last week's television ratings, a low voice behind her said, 'How about sharing a cab into Manchester?'

She turned. 'Barney! Where did you spring from?'

'Zürich. My flight was delayed for hours. Want some duty-free cologne?' He was already fishing in a Marlborough carrier bag.

Sorrel hesitated. 'Who did you really buy it for?'

'My secretary.'

'Then I'll have it. No, that's not fair. She probably doesn't get much.' But Sorrel didn't hand it back. She just stood gazing at him in uncomplicated pleasure.

The Indian family in front of them began to argue violently in some foreign language.

'I bet my great-grandparents looked as alien as that when they first arrived,' smiled Barney. 'The Indians are taking over Cheetham Hill. Irish immigrants had it before the Jews. Manchester's always been a wonderfully hospitable city.'

Sorrel didn't want a lecture in social science. She wanted

482

something more physical. 'Nobody's got to get hurt,' she said, 'but I'm formulating a plan.'

Barney seemed to find this statement amusing, which annoyed her.

'Do you want to have an affair with me, Barney Shapiro, or don't you?'

'Shh.' He nodded warningly towards the Indians who were now arguing incomprehensibly over a pair of yellow-looking golden earrings.

'They can't understand a word. Oh Barney, just looking at you makes me hungry for you. I was going to ring you on your direct line. My plan's a good plan but first we've got to sell Bellaire. After that, Thursday nights are going to be rapture night. You will be OK for Thursdays?' she asked anxiously.

'Very OK.'

'It's going to be wonderful. Just you, me and a great big double bed.'

The father of the Indian family smiled sweetly at Sorrel and said in a broad Oldham accent, 'We all watch *Angel Dwellings* in Werneth.'

'What d'you mean, no mothers have miscarried?' Mamie Hamilton-Gerrard was snarling this into the telephone as Sorrel pushed open the green room door. 'You promised me that injection and my appointment is today.'

So the stories were true. Mamie was going to that doctor who injected people with human placenta.

It was the latest thing on offer for those who sought eternal youth. Sorrel wished she hadn't overheard this revealing bit of conversation. One way or another, Mamie would make her pay for it. The veteran star was not alone in her quest for rejuvenation. One of the women in another soap opera was said to have taken three weeks off and gone to Switzerland for a course of injections of extract of sheep's entrails. Three thousand pounds had been the rumoured price.

Sorrel did not go in for any of these fads. She had even given up the slimming pills. The most she took these days was a Yeast-Vite tablet; that and a swig from her guilty secret. The flat bottle was back in her handbag. A quarter-bottle of

Smirnoff vodka. This morning, when they stopped the car –
for Ray to nip into the off-licence – he had emerged with a
larger size.

'All they'd got,' he said. 'Good job you've got a clutch bag
today.'

Sorrel found this bigger bottle strangely unnerving. Her
usual one was an attempt at disciplined rations. A larger size
meant that double the amount would be temptingly available.
It wouldn't stow into the normal compartment in her bag and
she was scared it would clank against something. Vodka,
mouthwash, Amplex; her handbag was weighed down with
bottled goods.

Why did she do it? It was a question she sometimes forced
herself to consider but it never seemed to throw back the
same answer. She needed something to calm her down – that
one always came back. But every day it rang with a different
echo. Worries about selling Bellaire. Worries about the
pressures of the show. Worries about being shackled to
Kenny Shorrocks. On a bad day she would even find herself
surrounded by revived worries from her childhood.

Last Tuesday she had relived the whole horror of failing
the RADA entrance examination. One glance at Nadine
Taylor, who had passed it, had been enough to conjure up
these bad memories. Sorrel had used this as an excuse to slip
to the cloakroom and take a swig from the neck of the bottle.
And she had *hated* herself for doing it.

This degrading behaviour would have to stop. Once the
house was sold, once they were in the pub, once she was safely
in Barney's arms . . .

The green room door was burst open and Nancy Varndell
flew into the room. She was followed by the two black kids
who were comparing travel brochures. In long-running
serials, travel equals escape.

Nancy, eyes shining, headed straight for Sorrel and tugged
her into a corner.

'Can you keep a secret? Graham's popped the question.
Last night, in the Film Exchange.'

The Film Exchange was a club in Quay Street, much
favoured by television people. Graham was a civilian who

owned a brush factory. Nancy had expected everybody else to get as excited as herself when his firm went over to nylon bristles.

'We had scampi meunière and Graham thought they were a bit off-colour so, while the waiter took them back, he proposed marriage.'

After gazing surreptitiously around the room, Nancy fished down her dress and produced a spectacular sapphire engagement ring, hanging on a gold chain.

'We were waiting on the doorstep of Ollivant and Botsford, this morning, before they'd even raised the iron shutters.'

'It's beautiful.' Sorrel was marvelling at such a gloriously uncomplicated life. 'Why the secrecy?'

Nancy stuffed the ring below her neckline. 'I don't want it all over the papers before I've told my mother.' She looked warily around the room. 'You never know who the *mole* might be.'

All soap operas have a mole: somebody privy to secrets who makes a second living by selling newsworthy tips to the press.

'Graham had to be sure I wanted children. Me? I want about six. When I've told my mum, I suppose I'll have to tell him.' Nancy was nodding balefully in the direction of Bernard Conroy the producer, who had come into the room with his secretary and was now engaged in animated conversation with Mamie Hamilton-Gerrard.

'Mamie, they should bottle you and sell you as a tonic!' he was exclaiming.

Sorrel wondered why Mamie was suddenly giving her a look of such malevolent satisfaction. What fortuitous bit of evil had suddenly entered that jealous mind?

'We'll be starting a family as soon as possible,' chirped Nancy. 'Wedding, house and kids; in that order.'

'What about your career?'

'Acting's just something I happen to be able to do. And where would a career get me?' Nancy lowered her voice. 'God forbid that I should end up like Mamie!'

No, thought Sorrel, but I might.

'Mamie's wonderful at real life on the screen,' continued Nancy confidently, 'but she's no good at living. It's as though all the good things in her are saved for the performance.'

Sorrel felt bound to agree. But it had all been so easy for young Nancy. She had walked straight out of acting school into *Angel Dwellings*. Now, it seemed, she was heading for a life like something off one of June's rosier greetings cards. Sorrel did not begrudge the child one iota of happiness, but the clear-running simplicity of Nancy Varndell's life made her own seem the more chaotic. Sorrel hadn't had her second drink yet. Before they ran the first scene she decided she would just slip to the cloakroom and ration herself to one slug of vodka and a quick squirt of Gold Spot.

Sorrel moved back towards her handbag. Mamie moved faster. Accidentally on purpose, Mamie kicked the bag flying across the room. The clasp hit the skirting board. The bottle flew out and smashed on the floor. This was ten times worse than Ringway. A pool of liquid spread across the floor and whoever invented the theory that vodka didn't smell, was wrong.

'Whose bag is that?' asked Bernard Conroy.

'Not mine.' Mamie smiled prettily. 'My tiny shoe seems to have tipped out somebody's secret.'

'Whose is it? I want an answer.'

Yes, thought Sorrel, and I want a drink. What the hell do I do now?

'It's yours, Sorrel, isn't it?'

'Yes. Well, it was.'

'See me after rehearsal. Five o'clock in my office.'

He's just a jumped-up schoolmaster, thought Sorrel. And he's one of the sadistic kind who used to take pleasure in making you wait for your punishment.

The morning seemed endless. Sorrel only had a few scenes in the episodes so she had a lot of time to sit and think. She was not comfortable with her own thoughts. Anger was mixed with panic. Overall, there was fear that the nameless something – which was always coming to get her – was getting closer. She needed a drink.

In the Marshall Arms, at lunchtime, she had two large vodkas. There was no pleasure in them. It had been a long time since there had been any pleasure in alcohol. The careful, therapeutic dose was merely ingested to calm her shaking.

486

The afternoon was made worse by the fact that Mamie was, noticeably, refusing to rehearse closer than two feet from Lettie Bly. They finished early so Sorrel was forced to hang around.

Five o'clock finally came. Bernard Conroy had a new secretary in his outer office. This one was not in love with him.

'I've never worked for anybody like the man,' she said. 'He keeps tinned prunes in his desk drawer.'

Sorrel filed this away. She wasn't a child of the blitz for nothing. Everything has its uses in wartime, and this was definitely war.

'Tell her she can come in.'

Considering Conroy had to look straight past Sorrel, to call this out to his secretary, the actress considered that he had got a cheek. He had also had his desk moved nearer to the window, which left her with a long walk. It was like a Gestapo film. She was not offered a chair.

Conroy signed two letters, very slowly, and then gazed coldly at Sorrel through the lenses of his spectacles. Just as she was about to say '*Ja, mein General?*' he spoke.

'You do realize what you're doing to Mamie, don't you? You're shortening her life.'

'Me? What have I done to her?'

'You've rocked the boat, Sorrel. You've made waves. That good little soul is far too grand a trouper to complain . . .'

Sorrel interrupted him. 'She's as devious as a bag of snakes.'

'I didn't hear that.'

'I'll repeat it. No, I'll improve it. Mamie Hamilton-Gerrard took over where Adolf Hitler left off.'

'Jealousy is a most disfiguring emotion.' Bernard Conroy burped surreptitiously.

'And senna pods are more effective than prune juice,' said Sorrel, and immediately hoped that this wouldn't get the poor secretary into trouble.

'Vodka.' Conroy was gazing unblinkingly.

Sorrel decided to stare him out: 'What about vodka?'

'It's got to stop.' He blinked. 'Vodka and bad publicity and personal appearances to the detriment of your performance.'

'Do I ever forget a line? I might stumble occasionally, anybody can do that, but I don't need ten takes on a single shot. Can you say the same for your beloved Ghost of the Music Halls?'

'She says you unnerve her.'

'She would, wouldn't she; I thought she never complained?'

'She didn't. I caught her crying at lunchtime.' Bernard Conroy looked pained at the memory.

'What you caught was another nail intended for my coffin. If you want tears, I'll give you tears; here, now. We're actresses. It's our job. Tears? Watch!'

To the count of three they began to roll down Sorrel's cheeks. They had nothing to do with real life, this was merely a technical accomplishment.

'You're very hard, Sorrel,' sighed Bernard Conroy.

The tears turned to real ones, fuelled by genuine emotion. 'Hard' was unfair.

Conroy's face went back to concrete. 'They may have cheered you in Blackpool but you're not a big star to me. You're just a jobbing-actress. I've given you one warning about drinking during rehearsals. This is your second. My patience is wearing dangerously thin. Turn up the worse for wear just one more time and I'll fire you.'

16

Kenny Shorrocks now decided that the one thing he wanted in life was a pub called the Nun's Prayer. If it wasn't a white elephant, it was certainly a near relation to one. Solidly built and set on a corner, at the back of Deansgate, it had been erected in that mid-Victorian era when breweries poured back small fortunes into pubs and spared no expense on grandiose fixtures and fittings. The Nun's Prayer had two bars plus a select room, a snug and, halfway up a flight of stairs, a smoking-concert room. It also boasted eleven regular customers.

The landlord was a depressed old blob who moved in slow motion. He reminded Sorrel of someone walking under water.

'Our trouble is,' he enunciated bronchially, 'we haven't got a gimmick.'

'No, but we have.' Kenny was all confidence.

Sorrel could have kicked him. There was something called 'outgoings' to be purchased and the last thing they wanted to do was bump up the price of the tenancy. How did anybody arrive at a value on all this mahogany and the ancient cast-iron tables, set in varnished fretwork alcoves? Sorrel was a novice in these matters. Would the stained-glass windows, decorated with portraits of forgotten Manchester heroes, have to be valued too? She decided to concentrate on the eleven customers.

'Trade seems slack.'

'A couple more lads, from the printworks, used to roll in around this time. But the bosses went and put them on two till ten.' A woollen vest with rubber buttons was poking through the landlord's open-necked shirt and a jar of pickled eggs, behind the counter, looked as though they hadn't been opened since the abdication.

Yet the place had definite possibilities. In Sorrel's mind's eye, the woodwork was already gleaming, fires were burning in the elaborately tiled grates and she was trying to decide how to hang a hundred framed photographs of all their famous friends.

'*Where stage meets sport.*' She could already see it in the Northern gossip columns. She might even encourage June to invent a ghost.

'You've got my phone number.' Kenny was gazing critically at the sediment in his pint of bitter. 'If you get a better offer than mine, give me a ring at Mere.'

Bellaire was the problem. It remained stubbornly unsold. For all Kenny's high-flown talk of an offer, he needed cash from the house to buy his way into the pub.

Viewing the Shorrockses' house was rapidly turning into Cheshire's latest leisure pursuit. On Saturdays and Sundays the estate agent was all but resident on the premises. Most of the alleged would-be purchasers simply came for a good gawp, and were not above a little petty pilfering. Sorrel soon learned to lock away small, portable items. There were some genuinely intending purchasers who brought cheque books. One man arrived with a small suitcase, tantalizingly full of cash. It seemed as though the richer these people were, the more insulting would be their offer.

'That's how they got rich in the first place,' fumed Kenny. 'I'm pinning my hopes on the Sowerbutts.'

Dave and Jennifer Sowerbutts were a young couple who had got lucky and won the pools. That was how Sorrel first met the pair. She had presented them with their cheque at the London Hilton. They were a Manchester couple, from Gorton, and she had found herself sharing a first-class compartment with them, on the train back to the North.

The Sowerbutts might have scooped a record-breaking dividend but they didn't quite belong to themselves. The pools company had provided them with a dour financial adviser.

He was dead set against their purchasing Bellaire.

'You see, Sorrel,' said Jennifer Sowerbutts, who was thrilled to be on social terms with the leading lady of *Angel Dwellings*, to say nothing of her having the star wriggling on a pin, 'you see we have to be very careful that nobody takes advantage of us. I'm in the same position as an heiress.'

It was Jennifer who had filled in the winning line. A statuesque girl with blonde hair rinsed pink, small eyes and thick ankles, she had already embraced petty snobbery with rapture.

'I don't want to take Dave too far out of his class.' Jennifer straightened her Rolex watch for the third time that afternoon. The pools company had given it to her for waiving the 'No Publicity' cross on her coupon.

'Dave's never lived in more than rented property. Between ourselves, Sorrel, they're council house people.' If Jennifer overdid the use of the name Sorrel, this was nothing to the besotted way her husband trotted out Kenny's.

'Kenny, Kenny, Kenny . . .' It was like a roar from the terraces. Dave was a handsome, good-natured lad but every time Sorrel saw him he seemed to have put on weight. She sometimes wondered whether Jennifer was trying to wipe out her council house husband with the frying pan.

'Good bit of timber, this,' he would bawl, as he slammed a meaty hand at the frame of a door. Dave was in the building trade but Jennifer ('Please, not Jenny') was looking around for something else for him.

'I can see a future for us in a high-class china shop,' she said self-importantly.

Dave gave the Medieval-Moderne fireplace a resounding smack and roared, 'Built to last this, built as solidly as a brick shit-house!'

The Sowerbutts never questioned the price. Their financial adviser tried some haggling but Dave and Jennifer were just children in a toffee shop. And they couldn't make up their minds. They wavered, they hesitated, they brought her father to have a look and he proved to be more interested in the inside of The Swan at Bucklow Hill. Jennifer's mother approached Bellaire like the Holy Sepulchre. She even changed into house slippers to look around. One Sunday afternoon the Sowerbutts hired a mini-coach and brought a whole party of friends. For days afterwards, empty Harp lager cans kept turning up in unexpected places.

491

Other potential customers rose up and vanished but the Sowerbutts kept coming back like the Cheshire rain. With every visit they got more chummy. When they invited Sorrel and Kenny to a night out, at the dog-track, the actress began to wonder whether the pools winners were after a desirable residence or a deep and abiding friendship.

'We're selling one thing and they're after quite another.' If she sounded disgruntled, it was understandable. She had just lost ten pounds she couldn't afford, on a greyhound called San Francisco Mick.

'No, they want the house.' Kenny liked the Sowerbutts. 'That clever-clogs who's teaching them how to handle cash is the stumbling block. Couldn't you just take him upstairs and let him slip you a length?'

Several times the matter was almost settled and then – like the demon king in a pantomime – up would pop the pools representative, to throw yet another blanket of caution around the enterprise.

By this time, Sorrel was privy to some of the couple's most intimate secrets. For all his building-site vitality, Dave had a low sperm count and Jennifer was desperate to conceive.

'At least I can go to private doctors now,' she confided to Sorrel. 'Don't tell Dave but I'm going to have my fortune told again on Wednesday.'

Later that week, the landlord of the Nun's Prayer rang Bellaire. 'I've had an offer that's just a bit better than yours and he's prepared to close the deal immediately. What shall I do?' Sorrel handed the phone to Kenny who said, 'Give me till Friday and I'll top him by an extra thousand quid, in pound notes.' Kenny replaced the receiver. 'How about appealing to the general public? How about saying we've served them faithfully for donkey's years and now we're broke?'

'Have you no pride?' raged Sorrel. 'You've bled me dry and now you're after poor people's ha'pennies. You can count me out of that one!'

As she marched through the veranda, and into the garden, everything seemed to be turning into money. Those weren't ornamental shrubs in the flower beds, they were just pound signs. That wasn't a swimming pool, it was a price tag. Kenny had turned her into his own money box, only now it was empty. He could pick her up and try to rattle her but there wasn't a farthing left. Everything had gone into Bellaire and nobody wanted to buy it.

'Don't cry, sweetheart.' It was Ray Fossett. 'You're wanted on the phone. It's Mrs June.'

'Tell her I'm out.'

'She tricked me into saying you're in. Don't leave me with egg on my face. Just have a word with her. It might give us a good giggle afterwards.'

As they walked across the lawn, Ray let out a dramatic sigh. 'He'll never raise the cash by Friday. Bang go my chances of being Manchester's first drag barmaid.'

'Cut the camp, Ray, I'm not in the mood.' Sorrel stalked back into the house and picked up the hall telephone. 'Yes?'

At the other end of the line June was singing 'With a Little Help from My Friends'.

'You're singing flat, June. You always did. That's why Mickey would never let you be in our concerts.'

'You owe me, Sorrel Starkey.'

June said this in a voice of such deadly certainty that Sorrel's blood ran cold. The last hands she wanted to fall into were June Gee's.

'How come? In what way?'

'I've sold Bellaire.' June now began to sing 'On a Wonderday Day Like Today' and Sorrel felt herself in no position to criticize.

'Who've you sold it to?'

'The magazine made me see this pools winner woman. Poor soul, she's yearning for motherhood and her husband fires blanks. My guide actually showed me these listless little spermatozoa trying to fight their way to an egg.'

'Get to the point.'

'Is your house a bit like that open-air school for tubercular children? Is it cream with some big round windows?'

Sorrel knew for a fact that June had driven past Bellaire on a Sunday spying expedition but she merely replied, 'You could say that.'

493

'I'll be very startled if she isn't with you, cheque in hand, by six o'clock. Don't take a penny less than the asking price. Bellaire is where Jennifer is going to conceive.'

'Oh my God . . .' Sorrel had to sit down.

'All part of the service,' cooed June. 'I just want you to remember one thing –' her voice became inflexible – 'you owe me.' June now treated Sorrel to one of her famous bell-like laughs. 'Don't worry, sweetie, I may not come and collect my pound of flesh for years.'

At five forty-five, as predicted, the Sowerbutts arrived with their cheque book. If Sorrel was plagued by thoughts that she was taking part in a rewritten version of *Faust*, she pushed them to one side.

Jennifer Sowerbutts was a changed woman, one who glowed with confidence and expectation. As she laboriously wrote out the cheque she told Sorrel, 'I've had a most unusual afternoon with one of the most gifted women of our time. It was like a Nativity play. June Gee was the Angel of the Lord and I was a humble version of the Virgin Mary. Bellaire's where it's going to happen. I feel like asking you whether Dave and me could nip upstairs, for a naughty, straight away.'

'Please feel free.' Sorrel reached for the cheque. 'Any room you like. All the sheets were changed this morning. You've missed out the date on this.'

Jennifer filled it in and Sorrel let out a sigh of relief. The eerie thoughts refused to go away. If June Monk had such a large hand in this predicted conception, would the Sowerbutts' infant be like Rosemary's Baby?

Sorrel's sympathies with Jennifer's gynaecological problems were genuine. She had strong but suppressed maternal instincts of her own. The only children she had ever wanted were Barney's children. That being impossible she had always put a brave face on the matter by saying that, given a choice, she would prefer a litter of puppies. Only sometimes she just wanted a baby, any baby, her own baby. On these occasions she would fish the card of birth pills from the bathroom rubbish bin and remind herself that a child who got the worst characteristics of herself and Kenny Shorrocks could end up as the next World Dictator. Thoughts like this had not arisen for some time. These days, drab attempts at sex, with Kenny, were just a memory. Jennifer Sowerbutts' cheque would be her passport to renewed rapture with Barney.

The pools winners bought the house and some of the larger furniture but they were not interested in all the period trimmings of Bellaire. Jennifer was downright patronizing about the Clarice Cliffe pottery and Lalique glass and the bronze and ivory statuettes of picture-hat ladies being led by straining borzoi hounds.

'Box it all up and pack it away,' urged Ruby. 'It can only appreciate in value. It's the real thing and nobody's going to manufacture any more.'

On the morning of the move, the Sowerbutts' van arrived before their own had left. Sorrel stood out on the gravel looking at Bellaire for the last time.

'Whatever possessed you to buy it, Kenny?' she asked, not unpleasantly. 'You don't even like the country.'

'It reminded me of the swimming baths at New Brighton. When we were kids, that was the only place me and Eeek were ever happy.' Kenny looked around puzzled. 'Where is Eeek?'

'He didn't finish the last of the crates till two o'clock this morning' was Sorrel's evasive answer. Sooner or later, she would have to give Kenny the letter in her handbag.

The Sowerbutts themselves now rolled up in their new Volvo. They were dressed identically, in jeans and cowboy shirts, which looked as though they had just come out of the cellophane packets. Sorrel found herself wondering whether these outfits had been bought especially for the removal.

'We left everything to the men,' said Jennifer. 'We've been looking at flock wallpaper in Altrincham. Dave's set his heart on some he once saw in an Indian restaurant.'

For the first time, Sorrel felt a sense of loss. She had put a lot of herself into Bellaire and now it was going to be papered over.

The Sowerbutts' removal men were already carrying a purple and yellow tweed sofa from the van. A boy followed with a spindly plastic standard lamp which could have come off the set of *Angel Dwellings*. Was it a cherished wedding present from their former existence? There was something so pale green and sad about this stick of furniture that Sorrel wanted to cry. Jennifer was watching Sorrel closely.

'I feel awful,' she said. 'You'll just be in rooms over a grotty pub and we'll have all this.'

'Save your pity.' Sorrel picked up a heavy potted azalea she had been going to leave behind. 'Bricks and mortar change nothing. You'll still be yourselves when you walk through that door. And I'll still be me at the Nun's Prayer.'

'Hey lads . . .' she called out to their own removal men. 'Will you give me a lift to town?' With Bellaire behind her the only way was up.

Everybody, it seemed, had turned out to help. Even as the van swung round the corner of Nunnery Street Ray Fossett, who had gone on ahead, emerged from the front door of the Nun's Prayer with arms outstretched.

'Welcome Mine Hostess!' he called out as Sorrel handed him down the azalea. 'You've no shortage of volunteers. It's like Dunkirk in there. I'll stop out here with the handsome removal men. Mrs Shapiro's checking the inventory with the brewery rep. Your mother's got enough water on the boil for a confinement. And old Edie's fighting her for a pan to make some chicken broth. She's just landed in from Blackpool with an old hen.'

As Sorrel and Ray fastened back the main swing doors, to allow the furniture through, Gladys Starkey appeared, with her hair tied up in a duster, carrying a can of Brasso.

'God knows why the sanitary inspector didn't have Mr Harrap locked up. He must have been the muckiest landlord in Manchester.'

'Never mind, he's gone now,' said Sorrel, soothingly.

'Gone? Come with me.' Gladys led the way into the saloon bar where Mr Harrap was sitting unhappily, on a bar stool, supping rum. He had a greasy trilby on the back of his head and, today, his vest was poking through the revers of an ancient melton overcoat. If he looked like a nautical version of Rip Van Winkle – just awakened from the twenty years' sleep – this was because he had an African grey parrot in a big brass cage at his feet, and a small monkey on his shoulder.

'Good morning, monkey.' Sorrel had often thought she might like one. The little animal seemed to know this because it leapt straight through the air, landed on her shoulder and placed its arms, delicately, around Sorrel's neck.

'Nelson is not included on the inventory. I'm not parting with the livestock.' Mr Harrap, who'd plainly had a few, began to cry. Edie now appeared, looking fierce, with a potato peeler and a carrot.

'Pull yourself together, George Harrap,' she said sternly. 'I'm surprised at you. You, who once threw out five Polish airmen, single-handed!' Edie, as was only to be expected, knew a great deal of Manchester pub lore. 'George was known as a hard man,' she explained. 'They used to come from miles around, spoiling for trouble, fancying their chances.'

Kenny, who had followed the van by car, walked into the pub carrying a pile of his own tasselled England caps. 'These can go behind the bar for luck,' he said, piling them on the counter.

'I had luck once,' sniffed George Harrap, 'but it ran out on me. I want to give you a bit of advice, Kenny. Never hit anybody on licensed premises. When you get them to the front door, just fling them at that iron lamp post. I might have had the reputation but that iron post was the *real* hard man.'

'Isn't it time you were off, George?' asked Kenny, not unkindly.

'I'm in no rush. Anyway, where am I going? Did you know that you can only move a quality parrot just so often, in a lifetime? Swinton, that's where we're going.' He made it sound slightly worse than the Valley of the Shadow of Death.

'There's some very nice parts to Swinton.' Gladys was bridling with pride of postal address. The monkey chose that moment to leap from Sorrel's shoulder onto her mother's.

'Get it off me!' screamed Gladys. 'And get that dirty old man out of here. I've been through three bottles of disinfectant already.'

'I've let meself go, it's a fact.' George removed the chattering monkey, reproachfully. 'I only went to pieces after

497

the wife died. Golden days, golden days! Anyway, you can't chuck me out. It's opening time. I'm your first customer. I think I'll have a change. I'll have a pint of mixed.'

Ray Fossett being still outside, Edie was the only person who knew how to pull one. Sorrel noticed that Gander's sister's hair had been dyed again, right up to the parting.

George Harrap took the drink and held his glass critically to the light. 'By heaven, Kenny,' he said, 'your beer's cloudy!'

Kenny and Sorrel had wanted to close the pub, for a month, to redecorate. The brewery, wary of trouble with the licensing authorities, had insisted that at least one bar should remain open. Kenny picked up a sign from behind the counter. It read *You Can Get A Drink Today Lads But Come And Have A Real BALL with KENNY SHORROCKS At The Grand Re-Opening* (*Watch Press For Details*).

'This should already be on the door. Where the hell's Eeek?'

Sorrel suddenly felt uncomfortable. 'I've got a letter for you.'

'I don't want a letter. I want Eeek.'

'You can't have him, Kenny. I'm no wiser than you are. It's all supposed to be in this note.'

Eeek had borrowed one of Sorrel's best envelopes. Kenny ripped it open and pulled out a sheet of cheap, lined paper. It didn't take him long to read the letter.

'Judas fucking Iscariot! D'you know what he's done? He's done a bunk. Just when I needed him, he's gone and hopped it. I can't believe it. Why? He was like a brother; he was like more than a brother. *Why?* Whatever it was, we could've sorted it out.'

'May I see it or is it private?'

'Private? It's a fucking mind-bender!' Kenny thrust the letter at Sorrel. 'See if an educated brain can make something of it. I certainly can't.'

The painstaking handwriting did not look as though it had been used much since Eeek learned it at school.

Dear Ken

Well this is it. It is better if we go our separate ways. There is things about me you do not know. You would go spare. Don't know if you gave me the red track-suit for keeps so have packed it (clean) with the rest of your kit. We had some good laughs Ken didn't we?

Good luck
Graham

Sorrel couldn't have sworn to it but she thought she detected a tear-stain on one corner of the page.

'I bet it's those rapes in Moss Side.' Kenny looked solemn. 'He sometimes vanished on Thursdays. I'd have stood by him. I'd have spoken up for him in court.'

Sorrel suspected that she knew better but, for once, she managed to keep her mouth shut.

Ruby Shapiro now marched into the bar with the brewery representative. 'I've double-checked everything, Kenny,' she said. 'We've crossed off what's missing. Mr Telfer's insisting that you do the final check but you should be able to put your signature to these pages inside twenty minutes.'

'I had friends once,' said George Harrap. 'We used to keep the jollifications going till all hours. Bag of crisps for the monkey, if you please, barmaid.'

Ruby motioned Sorrel into a corner. 'There's stuff up in those attics you wouldn't believe! Amazing Victorian junk. Boxes and crates of the stuff. It doesn't appear on any list so it strikes me it's yours.'

'I'll just ask.' Sorrel moved back to the counter. 'Mr Harrap?'

'No, I won't have another, for the moment, thank you.'

'What about all the stuff in the attics?'

He looked uncomfortable. 'I thought I'd be gone before you found it.'

'Don't you want it?'

'What would I want with it? O'Malley's had no use for it either. It was all there, thick with dust, when I took over.' George Harrap went back to his glass.

'But you'll want it,' Ruby whispered excitedly to Sorrel. 'You'll be thrilled. The far attic's like Aladdin's cave and half the treasures are theatrical. Come with me.'

As they passed through the door marked *Private* Sorrel could hear Spud barking in the distance; he must have smelled the monkey. Walking Spud was not going to be a problem. There were public gardens at the back of Deansgate. And he was earning enough money in his own right for a taxi driver, who was an ardent fan of the show, to be paid to take the dog for longer runs in Platt Fields. As they climbed the creaking stairs, Sorrel was forcing herself to be cheerful lest the vast areas of brown-painted Anaglypta walls, and the worn linoleum, reach out to depress her.

'There was a smell of antique boiled cabbage too,' said Ruby sympathetically, 'but your mother frightened it away with open windows and boiling water and air freshener. There's a single-minded streak in Gladys which is quite remarkable. She must have been scrubbing since dawn.'

Through an open door, Sorrel saw some of the sitting room furniture from Bellaire. The chic white leather looked strangely at variance with bare floorboards and the faded Edwardian grape-patterned wallpaper.

'Kenny's welcome to that floor.' They continued their climb. 'I'm going to make myself a huge studio bed-sitting room on the top floor. Does Jake snore?'

'He sometimes makes a little popping noise.'

'That's not pig-honking like Kenny. That's just nice and companionable.' Through a landing window Sorrel caught a glimpse of one of the towers of The Midland. Her heart rejoiced, but it would hardly do to ask whether Barney made popping noises too.

'The best treasure trove's in that far room at the end.' Ruby pointed and led the way.

The real treasure trove's going to be in The Midland, thought Sorrel, happily, as she followed Ruby through a brown door.

It was just like the dusty prop room, under the stage, at Salford Hippodrome, even to the big brass bedstead. There were drop-end sofas and folding screens and Berlin wool-work pictures and stuffed birds under glass domes and enough blue and white china, decorated with pheasants, for a banquet.

'But look at this.' Ruby tugged a box from under a marble-topped washstand. 'These posters must have gone up, behind the bar, every week for years. And somebody's taken them down and kept them. Look!'

Ruby held up a long, narrow playbill headed *Prince's Theatre Manchester.* The production advertised was Grace Warner in *A Royal Divorce.*

'It's seventy years old.' Ruby couldn't have been prouder if she'd printed it herself. 'Look at the prices; fauteuil stalls, half a crown. And there are dozens of them. They'll look wonderful downstairs on the walls. But that's not all . . .' One attic led into another. Ruby switched on a light, snatched up an old peg bag and used it as a duster.

A hundred pairs of eyes stared back at Sorrel through the glass of a huge brown frame, containing dozens of sepia photographs of forgotten stars from the turn of the century.

'Now look at the book!' exclaimed Ruby.

It was a thick, dark red, leather-bound volume with the word *Visitors,* lettered in gold, on the cover. Sorrel opened it at random and the first signature which leapt out from the page was *Marie Lloyd.* The legendary music-hall comedienne had added a date in 1902 and an address in Brixton. In the Comments column, Marie had written: 'The nicest thing about the landlady is her sister Mabel.'

'This pub was once theatrical lodgings,' breathed Sorrel in amazement. She couldn't understand why her eyes were filling with tears. Yet, when she thought about it, she did understand. They were tears of belonging. She had climbed an unprepossessing staircase and, at the top of it, she had found her own kind. It was as good and as unexpected as a surprise party.

'You have to make it work, Sorrel.' Ruby said this and left the room abruptly.

Make what work? Through a murky window Sorrel was afforded another view of the newly cleaned Midland Hotel gleaming in the sunlight.

Mr Harrap had got no nearer to Swinton. He was still flat out in one of the alcoves, in the saloon bar, with the trilby rising up and down on his chest.

'It's nearly opening time again.' Edie had been a tower of strength all day. 'Nudge him, Sorrel.'

'I don't like to.'

'This trade will soon toughen you up.' Edie shook Mr Harrap by the melton shoulder. 'Come on, George. The liquid farewells are over. Let's be having you!'

Mr Harrap stirred, murmured, 'Yes, let's be having your glasses,' and went back into his coma.

Gladys Starkey, dressed for off, now emerged from the living quarters. She was pulling on a pair of gloves over hands that were red and wrinkled from nine hours in hot water.

'You've been a brick, Mother.'

'I couldn't have people saying a daughter of mine was living in filth. What are you going to do with that man? If he stops there much longer you'll soon be having to dust him.'

The saloon bar already looked a different place. The mirrors were a tribute to Windowlene and there was a strong smell of Mansion Polish. Gladys grabbed a spoon from a pint pot of newly washed cutlery on the counter. Standing well back, she gave Mr Harrap a nasty poke with it. Nothing happened.

'You should never have let it get to this.' She made it sound as though Sorrel had poured beer into the man through a funnel. Handing her daughter the spoon, Gladys added, 'Wash that again, in very hot water, before you let anybody eat with it.'

'I could hardly have sent him out drunk in charge of a monkey,' retorted Sorrel indignantly. The friendly little animal was sitting up on a stool, eating a banana.

'And it's not very sensible to keep feeding that creature. How do they go to the toilet?'

'Same way as you and me, I suppose. You're obsessed with toilets, Mother. Your initials should really have been W.C.'

Gladys treated her daughter to a withering look. 'You're certainly *coarse* enough for pub life. Goodbye, Edie. Don't let them take advantage of you.' Gladys headed for the door.

'Fasten it back, would you?' Edie called after her. 'It's half past five. We should be selling beer.'

The trade at lunchtime had been surprisingly brisk. People

had called in to wish Sorrel and Kenny good luck and the telegraph boy and the florists' vans had brought greetings from friends further afield. Nelson, the monkey, had now finished his banana and was delicately extracting an arum lily from a floral tribute sent by June.

'Put that back,' said Sorrel severely. Amazingly, he obeyed and then started looking around for something else to do. The parrot stirred warily in its brass cage.

'I should have put my mother in a taxi.'

'I doubt it would have suited her.' Edie, who was pulling draught beer through the pipes, followed this with a shout of 'Ray! The bitter's going off. Can you do me another barrel? No, Sorrel, you'll never please your mother. But that doesn't stop her loving you to death.'

Sorrel could not have been more amazed if Edie had announced that Gladys Starkey had once been on the game.

'I know a lot about love.' Edie emptied the slops into a white-enamelled jug. 'You do, when you've gone short of it. You've never said anything about my feet. New shoes. I've had me bunions done. The solicitor advanced me some money. That inheritance is making a lot of dreams come true.'

'I don't suppose you'd consider working for us full time?'

'Nothing doing. I've frittered away too many years in public houses. I hate the places.'

'But you still came today.' Sorrel gave her a hug. 'Thank you, Edie.'

'I came because our Lil would have wanted me to. Oh my God! That monkey's got one of Kenny's caps. Come here, you little bugger!'

'He'll come to me,' laughed Sorrel. 'Nelson, come on, I'll show you how to wear it. There you are. Oh dear, it's too big.'

The embroidered blue velvet cap, with its gold tassel, came right down over the monkey's eyes. Chattering furiously, he snatched it from his head and ran along the counter with it in his hand. As Sorrel started to give chase, Nelson dropped to the ground, darted through the open door and disappeared down Nunnery Street.

Edie was nearer the door. 'You man the bar,' she called,

lifting the mahogany flap and breaking into a run. 'These new feet of mine are like a fairy's.'

As Edie disappeared into the black night, the parrot let out a loud screech followed by, 'Gentlemen in overalls will kindly use the vault!'

Mr Harrap stirred again and muttered, 'Rule of the house.'

Sorrel could hear the clank of bottles coming nearer. It was Kenny, sweating through with a crate of pale ales.

'I've been thinking about Eeek,' he panted. 'They've never solved that girl's murder in Baguley.' Kenny looked around with satisfaction. 'This bar's looking more ship-shape.' Suddenly he noticed something: 'I'm a cap short. Some thieving bastard's already gone and half-inched one of my England caps.'

'Yes,' was the best Sorrel could manage. 'Could you just keep an eye on things for a minute?' She had decided to follow Edie. But Sorrel had not got halfway to the door before Edie returned, empty-handed.

'Not a sign. He's disappeared into the thin air. Could be down an alley or up a drainpipe or anywhere.'

'This is a bloody madhouse!' stormed Kenny. 'No Eeek, cap gone missing . . .'

'Order please! I will have order!' yelled the parrot.

Kenny grabbed Mr Harrap by the shoulder and shook for England. 'Wake up,' he said roughly. 'You've got to go.'

An elegant woman in white walked in from the street. It was a full theatrical entrance. Perched on her red curls, at a jaunty angle, was the missing cap. In her arms she carried both Nelson and a large bunch of roses.

Thrusting the flowers at Sorrel this vision said, 'I just came to wish you luck.' It was Pat Phoenix, the actress who played Elsie Tanner in *Coronation Street*.

Mr Harrap gazed at her in disbelief: 'It's nothing but stars. I think they must have started walking out of the television set.'

'He won't go,' said Sorrel, helplessly, to Pat. 'It's the old landlord.'

'He'll come with me,' said the older actress, 'I've got a taxi waiting outside.'

'Nay Elsie,' protested Mr Harrap. 'I'm past that sort of thing.'

'It's not on offer,' she replied easily. 'Where's he going with his menagerie?'

'Swinton.' Sorrel sniffed the flowers. 'These are beautiful, Pat, thank you.'

'Whoops a buttercup!' *Coronation Street*'s biggest star heaved the old drunk to his feet. 'I'll drop him off. And you –' she said firmly to Sorrel – 'don't you go giving all the profits away.'

Mr Harrap looked sadly around the saloon bar. 'The best years of my life . . .' he began.

But Pat interrupted him with 'I know, love, I know. The best years of *all* our lives. Come on, there's a good lad.'

As Sorrel and Kenny and Edie waved the cab away from the front door, Gander's sister said, 'That woman's a bloody object lesson. I know for a fact she lives in the opposite direction. Guess what? You can finally be said to have taken possession of the Nun's Prayer.'

17

The coin dropped. Sorrel was in a public telephone box. 'Can you speak, Barney, or are you surrounded?'

'I can speak.'

She glanced nervously through the rain-spattered window. Nobody in Albert Square was taking any notice of her. They were just skirting puddles, and late stragglers were scurrying towards office buildings.

'I've never spoken to anybody on a direct line before.'

'It's only a telephone.'

'If you're going to be lofty with me, I'm not going to find it very easy to be brazen.'

'I love you, Sorrel. I long for you to be brazen. You promised us a great big double bed. When can we be brazen together?'

Sorrel found this such heady stuff that she had to steady herself against the shelf above the directories. 'Can your secretary hear this?' she asked sternly.

'This is my direct line, Sorrel. To answer it, I step into a small sound-proof chamber and a panel slides shut. It's never serviced by the GPO. My repairman comes from another planet.' Barney stopped sounding like the Man in Black. 'My secretary most certainly cannot hear me.'

'Good, because she'd be startled. I want you to book a single room, at The Midland, for next Thursday night. Get there by six thirty and wait for the phone to ring.'

'This all sounds most intriguing. Will I be blindfolded?'

'Will you be there?' Sorrel's voice began to rise with impatience and excitement.

'Next Thursday, six thirty. It's a date.'

The line went dead. Somebody had obviously seen fit to cut them off. Sorrel didn't care. All that needed saying had been said. The words she particularly cherished were 'It's a date'.

She was a girl going on a date. In her head, she began to sing her special childhood Blackpool song, 'I'm Going to See You Today'. Only there were six days to wait. As she emerged from the box and put up her umbrella, Sorrel began to plan to draw a little calendar on the back of her script. She could cross off each succeeding day. Friday, Saturday . . .

A taxi, crossing the top of Mulberry Street, just missed her and this brought everyday reality back into sharp focus.

They had been in the pub for exactly a fortnight. With a cash register of his own, Kenny had ceased badgering Sorrel for money, so she could be sure of being able to pay her bill at The Midland. The pub was having a most salutary effect upon Kenny. It had given him something to do. Suddenly he was somebody of consequence again. Somebody in his own right. There was a new gleam to Kenny Shorrocks. He arose early and shaved immediately, and clothes had started going to the dry cleaner's again. This was the closest Sorrel had ever seen him to happy.

Kenny did not seem to mind that she had made a separate life for herself on the top floor. The biggest attic was now painted white and furnished with a rose-coloured carpet and a lot of the refurbished Victoriana from the dump room. It looked like poshed-up theatrical digs from the turn of the century. It sounded like bedlam. Solid brick and timber masked the noise, from the pub beneath, into something muffled and bearable. The great intrusion came from lorries, trundling over the setts in the street below, on their way to the printworks. Sorrel seized upon the fact that it went on all through the night, and wrought an opportunity.

'Do those bouncing trailers drive you mad too, Kenny?' she had asked.

'Not me. This head hits the pillow and dies.'

'I wish I could say the same. I can cope with it most of the time, but Thursdays are awful. I lie there thinking about camera-day on Friday. The more I worry about not sleeping, the wider awake I seem to get. I'm starting to look awful in close-ups; big black bags under the eyes. I was three quarters of an hour in the makeup chair last week. I think I might go and get a bit of peace, at a hotel, on Thursday nights.'

'Why not? I could use those nights to have a few of the lads round, after time. I never like to with you upstairs.'

It was settled. For the first time in her life Sorrel Starkey had used a lie to strike a bargain. Heaven only knew what Kenny was planning. Sorrel could imagine, but she didn't care.

'Sorrel?' Kenny looked awkward. 'You wouldn't walk out on me for more than Thursdays, would you? Since Eeek went, you're my best mate.'

She could tell that he hadn't enjoyed asking this. 'I'll stay just as long as you keep your nose clean. Drag me through the tabloids again and I'll be off like a shot.'

Sorrel had her fingers crossed, for luck, as she said this. Discreet as they were, her own plans could land her in the newspapers, without any help from Kenny. She had not entered into this marriage to become a working man's 'mate' but that role was infinitely more comfortable than being his wife. Who, she wondered idly, was wielding Kenny's bedroom cane, these days? Perhaps that was what he wanted Thursdays for.

Sorrel was a woman in love. And for the first time in many years it was all right to be in love. It was permitted, it was even encouraged. Barney wanted her as much as she wanted him and, soon, they could celebrate their love together.

Those six days seemed to take for ever to go down. Every night, as the Town Hall clock struck twelve, Sorrel would religiously cross off one of the squares she had drawn on the back of her script. Suddenly, every love song, every late-night Ingrid Bergman movie, seemed to have been written especially for her. One morning, on *Housewives' Choice* they played 'Too Young' and the years rolled back to an ecstatic point where she remembered that first night, under the stage at Salford Hippodrome.

Sorrel was in the middle of getting dressed. With sudden resolution she took her clothes off again, faced a long cheval mirror, and tried to see her own body through someone else's eyes. Someone else's? This was a moment of real truth. She tried to see herself through Barney's eyes.

508

'I was seventeen,' she said to her reflection. The face which stared back at her was ageless. She knew its defects but they were the same ones that had always been there. The neck was still taut enough. If there were ring marks around it, they were very fine ones. She did a quick calculation. And then wished she hadn't. It was well over twenty years since he'd seen her naked. Her bust would definitely not pass the pencil test. Whose did, over the age of twenty? That apart, if she was working in America, she could still have posed for *Playboy* magazine. Her eyes went lower.

'Oh my God!' She said it aloud. Would she be able to find a hairdresser prepared to dye her pubes to match her topknot? The matter had never even entered her head before her honeymoon, but Barney wasn't Kenny Shorrocks. Barney deserved the best.

Sorrel started to laugh. Better leave them alone, she thought. Dye might taste. She had suddenly remembered Barney's freewheeling abandon in bed, that eager tongue . . .

And in that moment another problem vanished. With Kenny Shorrocks she had always suffered from something she privately described to herself as 'dry juices'.

'Mmm,' said Sorrel in appreciative anticipation. Dry juices were not going to be a problem with Barney Shapiro.

The young porter carried Sorrel's bag into Room 307 and then opened the bathroom door for her inspection.

'Fine.' She handed him a ten-shilling note. Too much but a stingy reputation soon spreads.

The porter hesitated. 'We're not supposed to ask, but would it be all right if I had your autograph?'

Sorrel signed. It was a real album. Perry Como was on the opposite page. Her eyes were already seeking out the telephone.

The porter still seemed inclined to linger: 'We had the Beverley Sisters last week. Billy Wright was with them.'

'I shall be alone.' Sorrel spoke almost too sharply. She had asked for a quiet room because Kenny had been listening when she telephoned. The double bed was supposed to be for extra comfort. The room was certainly almost uncannily

509

silent but she had not expected to look out onto white, glazed-brick walls, dotted with a lot more hotel windows, opposite to her own.

'Would you like the curtains drawn?' asked the porter.

'Please.' Sorrel immediately wondered whether this made her sound as though she was about to get up to something. Would he never go?

'You look younger than you do on television,' he said – and she wished she'd given him a pound.

As the door closed with a discreetly expensive click, Sorrel had a tentative bounce on the edge of the bed. Soft but not too soft, which would be all to the good. She only had to pick up the telephone and the operator would connect her with Barney. It was a big thought. Sorrel decided to savour the moment. Besides, there was a tricky process to be organized.

Vodka. Since the row with Bernard Conroy, Sorrel had been rationing herself severely. She had reduced her intake, but half past six still meant a strong slug. Opening her case, Sorrel produced a silver hip flask which she had come upon in the back attic. Next to it she had packed a bottle of Listerine.

This controlled drinking did not fill her with the same guilt as the compulsive swilling had done. She saw it as medicinal. It was a decisive step along the route to the day when she would stop drinking altogether. The only trouble was that one slug cried out for its brother. It set up an itch for more. Well, it couldn't have more. Drink went with unhappiness, and that was over. Sorrel's hand reached for the telephone.

'Operator. I believe you have a Mr Shapiro staying in the hotel? Would you please connect me with him.' There was a pause followed by a ringing tone. Sorrel's stomach actually lurched with excitement.

'Bonsoir.'

It sounded like Charles Boyer. Could this be right? Sorrel hadn't used any French for years. 'Monsieur Shapiro? Est il là?'

'You wish to speak to the great secret lover?' laughed Barney. 'This stud is at your service.'

Sorrel looked at her registration card. 'I'm in Room 307,' she said. 'And I'm all yours.'

*

'What's this called in Yiddish?' They were lying naked on top of Sorrel's bed.

'That's my schmuck. Only at the moment, it's just a shmickeler.'

'I bet I could soon turn it into a schmuck again.' Sorrel stretched luxuriously. In the past hour she had forgotten time and flown through space and got lost with her love. 'And what's this called?'

'I understand it's known as your shmooey. But it's not a word I would recommend you to use in polite society.'

'Who cares about polite society? We're here. We're safe. And do you know the best part? Sooner or later we can just curl up and go to sleep next to one another.'

'When do we eat?'

'Barney!' She slapped his shoulder. It was wonderfully hard and firm. His whole body had become more precisely defined since she last saw it. Men! It wasn't fair.

He began to draw her outline, his finger against her skin. As it rode lightly over a nipple, which caused her to murmur, he said, 'It's not so much where we eat as how we eat. We can hardly ring for room service.'

'I thought of packing some pies. But they were pork.'

'You'd be surprised at what I eat nowadays.'

Frozen dinners and things out of tins, Sorrel had already heard this from Ruby. She didn't want to talk about that. It belonged to a world with a wife in it. 'Tell me about when you were little.'

'What d'you want to know?'

'Everything.' Sorrel had only ever had snatches of Barney, trailers, now she wanted the whole picture.

He eased himself closer, relaxed as a cat. 'All my childhood memories are full of Zillah.'

'Your nurse?'

'My sister.'

'Your *sister*?' Sorrel sat bolt upright.

'Where did you shoot to? Come back, I'm missing you.'

Sorrel did not need two invitations. 'I'd completely forgotten about her. Why does she never get mentioned?'

'She married out. What's more she married a German. That counts for as good as dead in our family. They practically sat shivah for her.'

'And you've never seen her since?'

'I see her, they don't. She's in New York. The husband died. He left her one rich lady.' Barney started to laugh. 'Zillah's had everything done to herself that can be done. The nose has been altered, her face has been lifted, she's even had her stomach lifted. She swears it's left her with pubic hair running sideways.'

'You're kidding!' But she could tell he wasn't. 'Sideways?'

'Yep. May I inspect yours?' Barney slid down and began to blow like a furrier.

'Don't do that if you want dinner.'

'What's dinner? Mmm . . .'

As Sorrel arched her back, she thought of a tomcat lapping milk, only the saucer of milk was turning into a pool and the ripples were spreading wider and wider and wider . . . Everything gradually started to judder. It was like *Star Trek*. Beam me up, Scotty, she thought and the voice, inside her own head, sounded frenzied with absolute completion.

They managed with sandwiches from room service. Barney hid in the bathroom whilst they were delivered.

That same week Sorrel had to give two big press interviews. In both of them, she made a point of saying that she always ate enough for two people. And she emphasized this with comical stories against herself. Both statements appeared in print. Thereafter, the catering arrangements, in her Thursday hotel bedroom, became easier. Sorrel would order a gargantuan amount of food for one person and it would be wheeled in, inside a heated trolley, before Barney arrived. They would often talk about venturing to a restaurant but – on the one occasion they tried it – the pair of them nearly walked slap into Doris Dintenfass coming out of a casino, with her husband, in Chinatown.

'I think Ruby knows anyway,' Sorrel said to Barney as they scurried back to the safety of The Midland.

'Yes, but she wouldn't want it spelling out. I know my mother.'

Sorrel soon learned what it meant to be a mistress. She discovered the pain of not having first call on the most important man in her life. Even Thursdays were not hers by right. Jewish men will protect a marriage above all else. On the odd occasion when Barney had to forgo a rendezvous, for a family engagement, Sorrel was left feeling like a failed shoplifter. She didn't cancel the room because these nights also represented Kenny's grasp on freedom. And a bargain was a bargain.

According to Ray Fossett, Thursday nights at the Nun's Prayer were about as wild as Rome at its height. It was all after-hours boozing and spin the bottle, for wife-swapping, on a spectacular scale. A wife, it seemed, was not an absolute necessity. Any willing woman was sufficient passport to these orgies.

'It beats any of the films he had hidden at Bellaire,' Ray assured her. 'They go in for Swedish videos too. Limbs on the floor and limbs on the screen, you can't tell where one ends and the other starts. And they're at it till daybreak. God knows what the milkman makes of the noises.'

'How do they find the energy?' Sorrel was more fascinated than critical.

'Pep pills, purple hearts. A chemist called Jepson brings a big bottle of them.'

'Has he got a blue-black chin and a sinister moustache?'

'Yes, and two more growing out of his ears. You've got to give the poor sod marks for trying. He's a sexual antique.'

'He's my stepfather!' Sorrel was past caring. Kenny, now making a marked success of the pub, was much easier to live with. So long as these revels took place in his private quarters, they would not endanger the licence. She had only laid down one stricture. She got Ray Fossett to warn Kenny that he was not to try and rope in any of her own colleagues.

The Thursday evenings when Barney failed to materialize were the worst part of this new regime. Sorrel had begun to hate his wife with a silent passion that verged on the pathological. Let Barney appear in a new tie and she had to will herself not to ask whether Mandy had chosen it. The thrill of invisibility had worn off. Week in, week out, the pair of them were stuck in one room. This went on for many months. On the odd Thursdays she found herself forced into an evening of her own company, Sorrel could never sleep. She would lie there tossing and turning, full of frustration and unresolved anger.

Mickey often got the brunt of this. As hopes of sleep ebbed away, she would place a call from the hotel room, to California, and talk for hours. Money was less of a problem these days. Mr Pym had seen to that. And her share of the funds from Gander's estate was on deposit in her bank.

'Miss Starkey? They're just getting the party in San Francisco. Please hold the line.'

There was a pause and then somebody at the other end said, 'Hello.' It wasn't Mickey's voice but it was a startlingly familiar one.

'Eeek?'

'It's not me,' he replied. He sounded terrified.

Mickey must have picked up an extension. 'Of course it's you. Put the phone down, Eeek.'

There was a click then Sorrel asked, fascinated, 'Is he living there? Are you two an item?'

'How your mind runs on sex. It must be that second career of yours. We're most certainly not an item. I just thought that, if he came to San Francisco, he'd have a chance to see that all gay men are not necessarily like Ray Fossett.'

'Were they once an item?' Sorrel was even more fascinated.

'No,' snorted Mickey. 'Poor Eeek was in an iron closet. He thought that if he ever came out, he'd have to wear eye shadow, and adopt a girl's name, like our friend Miss Fossett. San Francisco's broadening those horizons.'

'I wish you'd broaden mine for me. Barney had to stay at home again and I've got my period.'

'Are the two events conjoined?'

Bull's-eye as usual. 'I can't help wondering.'

'The trouble with that relationship of yours is that sex is too high on the menu. It's almost the whole meal. You need to put some romance back into it.' Mickey began to extemporize: 'Moonlight and mystery and strolls by the river.'

'We sometimes sneak out for a walk, down by the Rochdale Canal.' Sorrel was gnawing at a cold lamb chop.

'The Rochdale Canal!' exploded Mickey. 'I'm talking about fountains and violins and champagne – only not too much champagne in your case. I'm talking about Vienna. The pair of you can surely wangle a weekend away together. Whatever happened to imagination?'

'We play fantasy games all the time.' Sorrel was indignant. 'We choose houses from *Lancashire Life* and furnish them and decide who we'll invite to dinner . . .'

'And get nowhere. It's pathetic. Eeek . . .' he called out. 'Put that chest expander down, you'll deform yourself.' In explanation to Sorrel, Mickey added, 'He's pumped up like Steve Reeves these days. Now hear me, Sorrel, and hear me well. You're not the only one who bends my ear with international calls. Barney rings too. I'm safe. I keep my gob shut. I'm half the world away. That doesn't alter the fact that my primary loyalty is to you. He's thinking of leaving her.'

Sorrel swallowed a piece of lamb in astonishment and it went down the wrong way.

Ignoring her strangulated choking noises, Mick continued: 'We've never had this conversation but – if you'll take my advice – you'll get him to Vienna and prove that you're a whole person. Seduce him at a different level. It isn't enough to be a good lay.'

'Can Eeek hear all of this?' asked Sorrel in horror.

'If he goes running to Kenny Shorrocks you have my full permission to tell your husband that his Eeek has got a Costa Rican boyfriend who's hung like a horse. *Ouch!* That hurt. Sorrel, do you want to marry him?' Mick was at his most businesslike.

'I just want to be with him. Yes, of course I want to marry him. I've always wanted to marry him.'

'Then don't send out any signals that it's what you're after. Just show him the real you again. Do it in Vienna. One of my favourite places on earth is the Hotel Sacher. It's on Philharmonikerstrasse just by the Opera. Barney's practically a millionaire these days, make him take a suite.'

'Mick, that script just got you an Oscar.' The world was no longer blurred and colourless. Sorrel felt in sharp focus again and life was full of technicoloured possibilities.

'But Sorrel, don't dream about it. Make it happen. Desire, belief and anticipation, I taught you the technique in Cornucopia Mews. I'm going but Eeek wants a word with you.'

Eeek's Liverpool voice already had Californian overtones: 'Listen to him, Sorrel,' he urged her solemnly, 'I did. If I can make things happen so can you. Will you do something for me? Choose your moment and tell Kenny why I vanished.'

18

'You could meet me in Zürich,' said Barney. 'From there we could fly on to Vienna.'

It had all been almost too simple. Christmas was coming and Sorrel was due for a week away from the show. Contractually, it had to be taken before the end of the year. Barney was going to Switzerland on business and could extend his trip. All Kenny asked was 'Why Vienna?'

'Because Mick thought it might do me good.'

That was good enough for Kenny. Mick was the man who had eased their passage into the Nun's Prayer. In Kenny's eyes, the scriptwriter could do no wrong.

'Yes, you go. You enjoy yourself. You deserve a break. I was going to throw a big party at Christmas so I'll grab the chance and have it early, while you're away.'

Sorrel's passport was in order, she didn't need any jabs for Austria, flights were available and the Hotel Sacher had written back saying that they would be happy to accommodate Mr Shapiro and travelling companion in one of their best suites. All Sorrel needed was some new luggage so she lashed out on a set fit for a real adventuress.

Sorrel carried the cream and fawn flight bag, with its Vuitton logo, across the concourse of the International Arrivals terminal at Zürich. Something felt wrong, unusual. And then she realized what it was. It wasn't *wrong*, it was very right. For once there were no eyes staring. Her famous face didn't mean a thing in Switzerland.

Barney was already waiting by the Hertz desk. Not that they were planning on hiring a car, it had just seemed a sensible place to meet. If he had met her off the flight from Manchester, somebody could have spotted them. Oh, it was a very good place to meet. She doubted there was a more handsome and distinguished-looking man in the whole of

Europe. As they fell into one another's arms Sorrel thought, Move over King Edward and Mrs Simpson!

Barney held her out at arm's length and looked her up and down. 'How long have you owned a sable coat?'

'It's full length on your mother. Thank God the sleeves are enormous!' As Sorrel pushed them, luxuriantly, back she was quick to add, 'Ruby only knows I'm staying at the Hotel Sacher, she doesn't know who with.'

'You think?' For once Barney sounded ironically Jewish. He looked years younger than he did in Manchester and much more relaxed. 'A holiday air' is a tangible thing and Barney was glowing with it.

They soon found the International Transfer desk, there was no delay on their flight and they couldn't have said 'I love you' more than half a dozen times before they were up in the air and eating first venison, and then strawberries marinated in champagne.

'Can you get all this first class back, off the business?' asked Sorrel anxiously.

'No. You're my own wonderful, expensive luxury.' The plane banked steeply and Barney peered down towards the ground. 'Munich must be somewhere to the left.'

Sorrel was thrilled. 'You mean Germany's just below us?'

'There used to be a lot of Shapiros in Munich.' He looked sad. 'I doubt there's one left there today.'

Customs clearance at Vienna took no time at all. *Flughafen Wien* it said on the wall. Sorrel had never realized that Vienna's real name was Wien.

'Only it's pronounced Veen,' explained Barney. 'I did four years of German at one of those expensive schools they sent me to. Jake nearly went mad but it was part of the curriculum.'

'They stopped German at my high school just as soon as the war started,' swanked Sorrel virtuously. But she had already sensed that a small cloud was beginning to gather. 'Anyway, Vienna's not Germany. It's Austria.'

'Hitler came from Linz.' The night air was cold and Barney hailed a taxi.

At first they drove through that kind of dark international nowhere which surrounds all airports. Suddenly, by the side of the road, Sorrel saw light pouring from an old inn with a sloping shingled roof and wooden shutters and a sign, in foreign-looking script, which read *Gasthof Schreyvogel*.

'We're abroad,' she exclaimed in a voice of near disbelief. 'Ever since Ringway it's been like being inside a plastic pea-shooter, but now we're really abroad.' As the taxi got nearer to the city centre Sorrel kept letting out gasps of delighted astonishment.

'Look! All those beautiful colour-washed buildings and that monument like flames with flowers growing around them. Some of the people are straight out of *Hansel and Gretel*. Quick, or you'll miss that old man in a cloak – his hat's got a paintbrush stuck up the back. Oh I do see why Mick raves about this place. It's elegant and comical in the same breath. I love it already. It's like a children's Christmas annual. It all looks so friendly and jolly.'

'Oh yes,' replied Barney quietly. 'They're known for being very gemütlich in Wien.'

The car was slowing down by an illuminated sidewalk cafe. Now it stopped.

'Sacher,' announced the driver and got out.

'This surely can't be it?' Sorrel's opinion of Mick was shaken. 'It's just a cafe.'

'It's the right place, the hotel was started by the Emperor's pastry-cook.' Barney had been reading a guidebook on the flight.

'It doesn't look very posh to me,' said Sorrel. 'We put commercial travellers in better places than this in Manchester.'

That was before she got inside.

Sorrel's training for posh had begun with Rookswood Avenue yearnings. Even as they were bowed through the doors, and the luggage began to vanish noiselessly, she recognized distilled luxury in the true grand manner. Everything was on a small scale and discreetly subdued except for the crystal chandeliers. They were a glittering, tinkling operetta in themselves.

The concierge, behind his polished desk, in a severely tailored uniform with crossed golden keys embroidered on the lapels, was saying in French, 'Yes your Highness,' to a girl who couldn't have been more than nineteen – wearing a simple white dress that couldn't have cost less than two thousand pounds. Sorrel thanked God for Ruby's Russian sables, even if the skins of little dead animals did prick her conscience.

The concierge's assistant was addressing an exotically dishevelled old woman, in English, but calling her 'Gräfin'.

'Countess,' translated Barney quietly.

'That's not a countess,' exclaimed Sorrel. 'It's Lady Boswell!'

Hearing her name, the old fortune-teller, whom Sorrel had last seen in Ed Shotter's Attaché Club, turned and peered.

'Sorrel!' she yelled. 'Just the person. I've been meaning to write to you. I want a signed picture to put outside my booth. I'm going back to Llandudno next season.'

'Lady Boswell, Mr Shapiro,' murmured Sorrel, like somebody out of a play by Oscar Wilde.

'Known her for ever.' Lady Boswell called this over to the desk. 'She's a big star. *Vedette*,' she yelled, as though they were deaf as well as foreign. Turning back to Sorrel she confided, 'The Viennese always love it when you throw in a bit of French. It was the language of the court. A bit of parlez-vous works wonders round here.'

The fact that these new arrivals were known to this dazzling old rag-bag had a dynamic effect upon the reception desk and Barney was soon filling in arrival forms and handing over passports.

How continental would they be about two surnames? wondered Sorrel silently.

'I love the old Sacher,' laughed Lady Boswell happily. 'Used to come here with the baronet before I got the band of gold out of him.' She gave Sorrel a knowing wink. Were the aigrettes the same ones she had worn in her hair at the night club? Lady Boswell's long black panne-velvet evening coat was spattered with black jet and trimmed with monkey fur. She reeked wonderfully of a scent Sorrel recognized as My Sin.

'Just off to see *Die Fledermaus*,' she said. 'No man, don't need one. You do. Oh dear; well, you'll just have to keep following the lorry. And Sorrel, take more water with it.'

Strangely enough Sorrel did not resent this. One mystic word from June and she would have felt like slapping her. Lady Boswell was different. The gypsy had never told her much but she'd never told her wrong.

Lady Boswell called over to Barney, 'Goodnight, dear. Not many of your race left in Old Vienna. Us Zigeuners are a bit thin on the ground too. The only thing we can do is forgive and forget.' And then she added: 'I suppose.'

The concierge looked politely blank-faced but his tailoring suddenly struck Sorrel as military.

It was the manager who took them upstairs in the lift. They emerged onto a corridor which proved to Sorrel, more than any science lesson had ever managed, that there really was such a thing as infinity. More little chandeliers were hung in a row all along the ceiling. At either end of the corridor was a mirrored wall which made the chandeliers go on for ever and ever.

'Amen,' said Sorrel; for so did the reflections of herself and Barney. She took his arm lovingly as the manager threw open a pair of double doors.

The suite was all white, with more glittering crystal overhead. Every carved surface was highlighted with gilt. And all the lavish drapes and covers were crusted with gros-point embroidery.

Sorrel wandered around entranced. 'God bless you, Mickey Grimshaw,' she said. 'It's magic.'

After reminding them that the hotel's Blue Bar was world famous and their restaurant unrivalled in the whole city, the friendly manager shook hands and departed. Barney pulled back an embroidered curtain. He was looking across the road at a huge stern-looking building. 'That must be the Opera,' he said quietly; too quietly.

'What's wrong?'

There was silence for a moment and then Barney replied: 'I don't belong to the forgiving religion. And I can hear the ghosts of Nazi jackboots.'

*

521

They slept late and Vienna was a new city in the morning. It had snowed during the night, which was a very good excuse to get back into bed and make love again. Afterwards, Sorrel had the bathroom first. There was a telephone in there and she decided to ring Lady Boswell from the soap bubbles.

'Good morning. How was *Die Fledermaus*?'

'I got it wrong, dear. Turned out to be *The Merry Widow*. What a size! You could have lived off the woman for a fortnight. Seen the snow?'

'That's why I'm ringing you. Where can I buy some fur boots?'

'First things first. You're worried I'll be indiscreet. Well I won't. Boots? Try the Kärntnerstrasse. It's their version of Bond Street. But Sorrel, *haggle*.'

'In Bond Street?' Sorrel was unconvinced.

'They all haggle here, dear. Tell 'em you're famous. They swank too. Like me to come with you?'

'No. I'll be OK. Have dinner with us one evening?' It was wonderful to be part of a pair and to be able to extend invitations. Sorrel hadn't wanted company this morning because she needed more than snow-boots.

Vodka. For some reason the duty-free had not come round on the second plane so her morning slug had only consisted of the one little miniature bottle she had managed to carry off the flight. Freed from the strictures of Manchester, Sorrel had even hoped that she would not need this.

As the hall porter pointed out the direction of the Kärntnerstrasse, she was already feeling the familiar shakes and panics. It was no use, she needed that steadying drink and she needed it fast.

'Is the bar, by any chance, open?'

'But of course.' This seemed to be the hotel's favourite English expression. 'It's back through the lobby.'

There was little daylight in the bar and Sorrel could not decide whether this made her feel more or less guilty. 'A large vodka, please. Straight, no ice.'

Ice only took the edge off the reviving kick. Only she hadn't had it yet. Why wouldn't the barman move away? Sorrel did not want him to see her hand shaking as she raised the glass.

He went to put the bottle back and she downed the drink in one gulp. Dare she ask for another, immediately?

The urbane barman noted Sorrel's empty glass.

'Same again, madam?' he smiled.

There would have been criticism in the smile in England. Here there was none. Sorrel had another and then one more. She decided against charging it to the room and the bill came as a bit of a shock. So did the cold air when she emerged into the street.

Why was she reeling? It had to be admitted that this vodka had tasted stronger than it did in England. Still, just three vodkas weren't going to . . . Sorrel jumped back on the pavement. A car, coming in the wrong direction, had just missed her. Only it wasn't the wrong direction. It was the right one. They drove on the left or was it the right? Sorrel was feeling something she hadn't felt for years. She was feeling tiddly.

It is a strange fact that bodies which have grown used to being fuelled by alcohol resent change. Introduce a new brand of spirit, ingest it at a different hour, and the whole metabolism becomes unnerved.

A bit pissed, in court shoes, in five inches of snow. This is bonny! thought Sorrel. She thanked God that Barney was still up in the suite, surrounded by his maps and guidebooks. She was plainly going to have to be very careful about drinking in Vienna.

The shoe shop was blandly international enough to be a disappointment. The excellent goods on offer were almost the same as she would have found in King Street, in Manchester. Sorrel got them to pack up her own shoes and decided to have a clomp down Kärntnerstrasse in the new boots. The dress shops were nothing special. Everything looked expensive but just missed being chic. What did it matter? There was a wonderful smell of freshly roasted coffee beans and the wicked fur shops would have thrilled Catherine of Russia. What's more, Sorrel had been too hasty about the clothes. The modern versions of traditional outfits were sensational.

No. Full-length dirndls with black velvet waist-clinchers

might look all right here. Get them back to Manchester, and people could think she was preparing to be the next Mamie Hamilton-Gerrard. Dismissing thoughts of foreign fancy dress, Sorrel wandered into a little gift shop which seemed to be full of model hedgehogs, in everything from porcelain to plastic.

What, Sorrel wondered, was their significance?

'They are Mecchi,' explained the woman behind the counter. 'Lucky hedgehogs.'

Spud loved hedgehogs. He always regarded them as his friends. 'Do you have one, for a dog, in rubber? And what's that?'

The woman picked up a comical painted wooden carving of a man with a copper coin sticking out of his bottom. 'It is a harmless vulgarity.'

'But what's it meant to be?'

'We give them to people,' replied the woman evasively, 'at New Year.'

'Why?'

The woman cleared her throat. 'It is to wish them a little man who will come into their lives and shit money for the next twelve months.'

'Do you have a female version?' Just the present for Kenny Shorrocks!

'No ladies,' replied the woman firmly.

'We have them in England,' said Sorrel. 'In fact my husband thinks he married one.'

The three strong drinks had not only taken the safety brake off her tongue, they were now crying out for their brothers. That vodka *must* have been stronger than at home. Morning craving, on this scale, was unusual. Would one more drink lead to chaos? Would that one cry out for its sister so that Sorrel would soon need the whole family swimming around inside her?

She walked quickly out of the shop, sprayed her mouth with breath-freshener and reminded herself that all she had ever wanted from life was sitting looking at a guidebook in the Hotel Sacher.

Food was the next problem. Although Barney no longer

kept to a Kosher diet he drew the line at pork. Neither of them wanted chicken and Sorrel refused to sit at the same table as anybody eating veal. She regarded it as too cruel. They weren't all that hungry anyway. In the end the inspired proprietor of the side-street cafe produced a platter of salami garnished with design-conscious salads.

'Definitely not pig,' he announced.

The food was good but very salty. Sorrel gulped down a lot of unaccustomed white wine from a glass dispenser, in a stand made of iron vine leaves, on the table. Normally she found wine a nuisance. It blurred her edges without hitting the spot.

At the end of the meal the waiter came up and said, 'Good salami, Hungarian salami, donkey salami.'

Donkey? Sweet animals like those on Blackpool sands? It was as bad as eating old friends. Sorrel felt close to tears – though quelling her desire for sleep was rapidly becoming a bigger concern.

'Barney, could we go back to the hotel?'

'I thought we were going to the Kunsthistorisches Museum?'

Even the name made her feel more weary. 'You go. I need to sleep. I don't know what's wrong with me. I'm all out of flunkey.' Did her speech, she wondered, sound as slurred to him as it did inside her own head?

Barney, all concern, put a hand to her forehead. 'You're a bit clammy. D'you want to stop at a chemist's and get something?'

'I'll be all right when I've had some sleep.' And then she burst into tears. 'That poor donkey,' she sobbed. 'It's my punishment for wearing a fur coat.'

The next few days were a tightrope walk. Sorrel had love in her heart and a bottle in her bag. She didn't want the alcohol yet she had to have it. To herself, she acknowledged that her drinking was a problem; which is a very different thing from acknowledging an actual drink problem. Alcohol was a nuisance, it spoiled things, it got in the way. For years it had been her crutch and now she wanted to walk without it. Only she couldn't. The idea of the bottle, hidden in the drawer of the Vuitton suitcase, seemed to take on a life of its own. It even had a voice.

'I've got German cousins here,' the bottle said, when Barney took Sorrel to the Vienna Woods. The cousins were fiery spirits called Schnapps. Imbibed at an open-air bar, they went straight to Sorrel's head and made her argumentative; she could hear her own voice making trouble when all she really wanted was to love and be loved.

The fairground in Vienna is called the Prater. The most spectacular attraction is the Big Wheel. It seemed to rise up almost as high as Blackpool Tower and each carriage was the size of a single-decker tram. The ride is slow, the views are spectacular. When their carriage got to the top, the wheel seemed to stick. The pause was perhaps ninety seconds –just long enough for the voice of the bottle to take over.

'You're sweating, Sorrel. I could stop that. You've got this weird fear you can't put a name to. I could blank that out too. I'm not a bottle, Sorrel, I'm your albatross. I'm your real lover and I'll never let you go.'

These jangling thoughts were running through Sorrel's head at breakneck speed. She turned and clung to Barney. 'Help me,' she said. 'Just help me.'

'What's the matter, little heart?'

The wheel started again.

'I don't like heights.'

Barney took her in his arms. The ground began to come towards them again. The hotel was up the road. The bottle was in the bag. The midair halts, which allowed each carriage that had reached the ground to disgorge passengers, were protracted agony. But each one brought Sorrel closer to her bottle. And the chance to cast light in dark places was gone.

This punctuated descent gave her time to realize just how unlike other people she had become. Barney never drank much but, on holiday, he would suggest beer at lunchtime and drinks and wine in the evening. Sorrel was powerless to refuse this additional alcohol yet it threw her into chaos. One sip over her usual ration meant that she would not be able to guarantee her subsequent behaviour. She would hear herself laughing too much, tears arrived too easily. Once, she had even become downright abusive and called Barney 'a failed art student'.

This holiday, which had been meant to bring them closer together, was turning into a nightmare. But Sorrel was awake and the only way she could bear her situation was by increasing the bottled anaesthetic she had come to loathe.

One afternoon they went to the Palace of Schönbrunn. Sorrel had once been in a production of *L'Aiglon*, the play about the Emperor Napoleon's son, the poor little King of Rome. The boy had spent some years at Schönbrunn. The Austrians preferred to speak of him as the Duc von Reichstadt and they spoke with inherited love. During the Second World War, when the Germans insisted upon returning his long-dead corpse to the French, the Viennese kept his heart. Schönbrunn, they claimed, was the only place where the frail youth had ever been happy.

Happy? Sorrel found his palace of a playground one of the most melancholy places she had ever visited: lavishly beautiful and unbearably sad. As the guide droned on, in English, about a baroque building decorated in the rococo manner, the group of tourists passed under painted ceilings, through a ballroom lined with mirrors and into a panelled parlour, dominated by an elaborate porcelain stove. A hidden door, in the wall, led into a small picture gallery.

There was a white marble death mask of the unhappy duke under a glass cover. But what really caught Sorrel's attention was an insignificant portrait, high up on the wall, of a woman without crown or decorations. There was something curiously familiar about the sitter.

'Who's that?' she asked the guide.

'The Duc's governess, his one true friend.'

Thank God he had a Gander in his life, thought Sorrel. The governess's eyes were Gander's eyes. They looked down at her as though they knew everything, but they were not gazing in judgement. Gander had always said if you'd got to run it was better to run forwards.

'Barney,' said Sorrel, 'I've got to stop drinking.'

For the first time in forty-eight hours the look he gave her was unguarded. 'Thank God, it's finally out in the open.'

'I've been hiding things from you.'

'You haven't. You were even beginning to taste.' Barney wasn't sparing her. 'And there's no deodorant on earth can stop it coming out of your pores.'

Sorrel started to cry. 'You mean I stink?'

'No. Don't cry. It's just a strange, haunted, sweetish smell.'

Relief and horror were now mixed into Sorrel's tears. 'What about you? You used to smell of new bread. It was my favourite thing about you. That's gone. It's vanished.'

'You're talking about the scent of Youth.' Barney looked more like a beautiful sad clown than ever.

'I spent my youth waiting for you,' sobbed Sorrel. 'And while I was waiting I got into the habit of drinking.'

'We'll make it better,' he said. 'We can do it. Together, there's nothing we can't do.'

There and then, in front of a dozen assorted international sightseers, Barney put his arms around Sorrel and held her close. 'Thank God we can finally talk about it,' he said. 'I've felt so locked out.'

The theory of stopping boozing was one thing. Now Sorrel was living with the reality. She had not had a drink for twenty hours and her mind and her body were throwing out jagged protests.

Panic! She lay twisting on the hotel bed, in a pool of sweat, yet she was freezing cold. Sorrel was so aware of all her own muscles that she felt like a living anatomical diagram; except that the muscles in the diagram would not be jerking, involuntarily.

'More water?' asked Barney from his chair across the room.

'It would only make me throw up again.' He looked so calm and safe as he sat there, reading an expensive book about the Hapsburgs, that Sorrel wanted his arms around her again.

'Just come and hold me close, Barney. The fear's the worst. One drink and it would stop. But I don't want it – only I do. Just hold me.'

He sat on the edge of the bed and rocked her like a baby. 'Shh,' he said, 'you're safe.'

528

It was like being held up, when she was little, to see the lights of Manchester. Sorrel started to weep. 'I don't mean to be bad . . .'

'You're not bad. You just got stuck in a trap. We're getting you out of it.'

Sorrel had not slept much during the night. Now she dozed off. It wasn't real sleep. It was like hovering beneath the surface. The fears took on triangular shapes and used their points to prick her back into consciousness. When she opened her eyes the ormolu clock, on the mantelpiece, showed that only five minutes had passed. Time felt elongated and a band was playing in the distance.

'Could you eat anything yet?'

Sorrel shook her head. The music was 'The Gold and Silver Waltz'. It was all waltzes in Vienna. But when you looked down a courtyard, to see where the violins were coming from, it was not unusual to find an old bullet scar in the masonry. Viennese operettas were just tinselled fake. Orson Welles was the one who had got it right in *The Third Man*. Why had the music changed to zithers, and would it never stop? Even a polka would make a change. As if on cue, the rhythm changed to polka-time. Or a march? The music changed again. Was this a real band or was it inside her own head?

Sorrel decided to find out: 'That music's very loud, isn't it?'

Barney looked puzzled. 'What music?'

She was, she was hearing things. Sorrel struggled to her feet in an even bigger panic. 'I'm going to the bathroom.' After padding unsteadily across the room she pushed open the white rococo-panelled door.

Sitting in the bath, staring up at her, was the biggest spider she had ever seen.

'Barney! Come quickly, look at this!'

'At what?'

It had vanished. Suddenly two more appeared. One moment they weren't there and the next they were. It was as though they had just flashed into being. They weren't quite as large as the first one and they were moving. As they travelled across the white porcelain, fine orange antennae began to project from their black heads.

529

'Don't say you can't see those!' she screamed. Grabbing a heavy tumbler Sorrel imprisoned them within the glass. 'There! They're horrible but we'll have to let them out of the window. I'm not killing them.'

Barney looked frightened.

'What's the matter, Barney? They're only spiders.'

'There's nothing there.'

'There is,' insisted Sorrel. 'And I don't know why you can't hear the band. Good heavens! Now it's playing the theme music from *Angel Dwellings*.'

'Keep calm.' Barney reached for the bathroom telephone. 'Operator? This is Mr Shapiro. I need a doctor and I need one fast. And operator? Try and get me a Jewish doctor.'

It was the first thing Sorrel had found funny in days. Only, suddenly, it was too funny to be bearable. Time was now like strands of sticky toffee and the next quarter of an hour seemed endless. Barney persuaded Sorrel to climb back on the bed but the music was deafening and she was watching a spider's web growing, menacingly, across the corner of a window.

'You *must* be able to see it,' she kept insisting. 'It's you that's funny, not me.'

Clambering to her feet again, she staggered across the room. Her legs were dreadfully weak but the web seemed to be made of strong fuse wire. Three of the curious insects were weaving at a furious pace.

'A dew drop's got in from outside, Barney. Don't tell me you can't see that?'

Barney held her close. 'It's real for you but it's just in your head.'

'You promise?'

'I promise.'

Sorrel took a deep breath. 'Then I need a drink to get rid of it.'

'You don't. You need a doctor.'

'Don't be so fucking smug with me. I need a drink.'

There was a knock at the door and Barney leapt across the room to open it.

'Mr Shapiro? I am Doctor Plesch.'

530

'Thank God you speak English!' Barney held open the door.

For a moment Sorrel thought that Jake Shapiro had walked in off the streets of Vienna. But, as he got closer, she realized that Dr Plesch was older and more lined. It was the reassuring air he brought with him that was most like Jake. Barney was already explaining their predicament.

'. . . and now she's seeing spiders.'

'Would you be so good as to wait in the sitting room, Mr Shapiro? Come and sit down, Mrs Shapiro.'

'I'm not Mrs Shapiro,' said Sorrel and thought: Not yet. Would that ever happen now? She felt so weak that she began to weep, helplessly.

The doctor indicated the communicating doors with his head and Barney left the room.

'Tell me,' said the doctor. 'It's time you told somebody so why not me?'

Out it all came. And there was relief in the telling. Sorrel spared herself nothing. In ten minutes she unearthed years of hidden bottles and furtive deceits.

'Must I multiply the amounts you have told me by two?' asked the doctor. 'It is often the case with people like yourself.'

Sorrel was indignant. 'I may drink too much but I'm very truthful.'

'Then you are fortunate. Love of truth is often the first thing to fly out of the window.' He slipped a thermometer under her tongue.

'So-be-so,' he said. Or something which sounded like that. Then he took her blood pressure.

'Up,' he announced. 'But that was only to be expected. Have you been noticing any glittering coloured lights?'

'No, but there's a spider running across your forehead.' Sorrel needed somebody else to tell her that they were not real.

'There is no spider. There is a delusion running through your mind but we can do something about that.'

It was all as impersonal as chromium plate. Sorrel needed some reassurance that Dr Plesch knew that she too was a human being. 'You're Jewish, aren't you?' Were you here during the bad times?'

The doctor nodded. 'Hidden in Steiermark, near the Tauern Pass. They were not all bad people. Somebody died so I can help you today. Let me go and talk to Mr Shapiro. You do want to stop drinking?'

'I must. It's wrecking everything. It's as though I'm a car and drink is the petrol. I don't want it but I have to have it. Yes, of course I want to stop. I've got to.'

Nodding politely, the doctor left the room. For the second time in her life Sorrel decided to listen at the door. The last time had been at Gander's on the night of the illuminations. That overheard conversation had been about booze too.

She didn't use the same door Dr Plesch had gone through. She went out into the small hallway and listened from there.

'Medical science has little to offer such unfortunates.' This was the doctor talking.

'Psychiatry?' ventured Barney.

'Freud always said he could do nothing. Jung maintained that the only recoveries he ever saw came about as a result of some significant spiritual change. There are, of course, the more recent American self-help groups but these are outside my province. I'm writing you a prescription for sedatives. These will see her through the worst of the withdrawals. What you have been witnessing is known as delirium tremens. The lady is an alcoholic.'

Sorrel wanted to fling the door open and protest. The diagnosis was so damning. No, better to stay here and listen. She might learn more.

'Ration the sedatives. Two immediately and then one three times a day. We don't want her exchanging one bad habit for another. That's another of their tricks.'

Their tricks? They? I'm me, thought Sorrel. She didn't want to be part of some mysterious, trick-ridden They.

'If she shows any signs of going into a fit, call me immediately.'

Fits? Now he was talking rubbish. She'd never had a fit in her life.

'And the future?' asked Barney.

'Doubtful. If that sounds depressing, all I can add is that I may be a doctor but I believe in miracles. I'm alive and practising in Vienna again. That's a miracle.'

'Your account?'

'It's not often I get to see the inside of the Hotel Sacher, Mr Shapiro. Forget it. It was nothing.'

Nothing? Just a Jewish favour given and received. The word *Alcoholic* was flashing on and off, in Sorrel's mind, like a neon sign. Dr Plesch had stated boldly something that other people had only ever dared whisper. *Alcoholic . . . Alcoholic.* The neon sign had now transferred itself, from Sorrel's brain, onto the white wall opposite her. How could something, in such a vivid shade of shocking-pink neon, be dismissed as nothing?

Alcohol takes seventy-two hours to quit the human body. The sedatives made Sorrel feel less like a caged tiger and damped down her craving for booze. It was as though they hit the same spot but came in from a different angle.

By the third day reality had replaced the last of the hallucinations. That was the morning that Dr Plesch, unbidden, chose to call.

'Today we reduce the pills to two,' he announced. 'Tomorrow you get one. On Friday you survive on your own resources.'

As Barney handed her the last tablet Sorrel felt apprehensive. The effects would wear off but the frightened, aching place inside herself would still be there.

'I'll put the rest down the loo.' Barney began to head for the bathroom.

Sorrel headed him off. 'No,' she said. 'I don't need them but I need to know they're there.'

Barney looked dubious. 'I'd rather get rid of the things.'

'I have to be trusted with *something*, Barney,' pleaded Sorrel. 'Trust me with these.' She took the pills from him, put them in her handbag and let out a deep sigh. 'I feel like chewed string.'

'The whites of your eyes are clear for the first time in months. I can suddenly see the girl on the doorstep at Magda Schiffer's again.'

He had been so good. The strangest thing about the drying-out process had been Sorrel's burning need for closeness, for physical intimacy. The need for strong arms around her. She had craved the reassurance of lovemaking on a gargantuan scale and he had served her unfailing banquets.

Sorrel moved across to the window and looked out, again, at the Opera House. That facade which had grown so familiar, too familiar, in the last few days. 'I'm scared of life without an anaesthetic.' She was finally coming out with the truth. 'It's too abroad and foreign here. If I've got to find my feet, I'd rather do it in Manchester.' The snow on the pavements was turning to slush. 'Please don't think I'm hallucinating. I'm not. But I'm beginning to hear the ghosts of Nazi jackboots too.'

'Home?' asked Barney.

'Please. D'you think there's any way we could get flights today?'

Barney looked concerned. 'Will you be OK if we part in Zürich?'

'Part?' Wrenching herself from alcohol had left Sorrel highly insecure. What kind of parting did he have in mind?

Barney reassured her with 'Only until next Thursday, at The Midland. I still have a day's business to finish off in Switzerland.'

A greyness, like the sky outside, began to descend upon Sorrel. One hotel bedroom back to another. And this was the trip that had begun so full of hope for a future that might, some day, be out in the open. No mention whatsoever had been made of Barney leaving his wife. Mick had been so sure that this was on the wind. Sorrel felt as though she had failed an audition. In many ways this trip had been like her whole career. She was an actress who had never made the West End. Instead, she had just twinkled dimly in a twice-weekly television serial.

Dr Plesch could probably have told her that self-pity, of this kind, was one of the less attractive characteristics of the alcoholic personality. But Dr Plesch wasn't there. On his last visit his parting words had been: 'Remember this, Sorrel, whether you drink or whether you don't you will always be an alcoholic. It is simply an illness. But one drink will always be one too many and ninety-nine will never be enough.'

19

The taxi from the airport smelled of stale fish and chips. It was raining, it was dark, it was December. But Sorrel was back in Manchester and that was always a welcome embrace in itself. The bright orange street lights of Deansgate faded as the cab began its bounce over the wet paving setts of gloomy Nunnery Street.

Nobody was expecting her. It was after closing time and the pub was in darkness. Or was the light inside simply obscured by the heavy, lined curtains? Sorrel paid off the driver who was piling luggage, obligingly, on the top step.

As she slid her key into the door she said to him, 'Could you just give me a hand with it, into the corridor inside? Sorry to have to ask you.'

'Pleasure to be of assistance. Town's dead on a Thursday night. What's that funny smell? It's catching me breath.' The man was gasping. 'I'm a bit asthmatic.'

Sorrel thrust another pound note into his hand and pushed him out into the night. 'Drains,' she said. 'We're getting them fixed.'

Was Dr Plesch right? Was her love of truth beginning to fly out of the window? The rank odour was most certainly not drains. She had last encountered it, at Ringway, with Mickey. Poppers, that's what the smell was.

Opening the door again, she called guiltily after the driver, 'Breathe in deeply! Get plenty of fresh air in your lungs.' If the poor soul had asthma she didn't want to find herself up on a manslaughter charge.

Should she fasten all the locks or not? The pub was not quite silent. Sorrel had gradually become aware of distant chirrupings and murmuring and now she caught a muffled moan which was neither of pleasure nor pain but sounded somewhere in between. On the floor above, somebody turned up Shirley Bassey singing 'Love for Sale' and, just as quickly,

536

turned it off again. The snatch of song was enough to remind Sorrel that Thursday night was party night at the Nun's Prayer.

The bare light bulbs, on the pub corridor, seemed a whole world away from the Hotel Sacher. Now Sorrel was really listening properly. There was something furtive about the murmurs and sighs; it was as though the party was spread thinly over the whole house and laughter had been forbidden.

Sorrel began to move deeper into the building, where she noticed a wisp of a beige brassiere hanging from the knob of the newel post. As she climbed the stairs, the acrid smell of sexual stimulant was getting stronger. With her head buzzing, she had to skirt the contents of a full ashtray which somebody had kicked over on the landing. The only light, up here, came from the kitchen door – which was ajar.

From out in the shadows, Sorrel saw two middle-aged women, pressed against the sink, in a passionate embrace. Would real lesbians have allowed that man to watch them? Suddenly realizing what he was doing with the hand, inside his trouser pocket, Sorrel moved hastily along the landing.

She felt more foolish than shocked. She had suddenly realized that in the midst of all this sleaze, she was still wearing her best hat. It was a white Garbo felt with a brim that drooped over one eye. Talk about being unsuitably dressed! Somewhere in the distance a woman screamed and a man shouted, 'You can grope anybody. That's the rules tonight.'

Sorrel was beginning to be frightened. She decided to clamber up the stairs to the safety of her own attic. On the top landing window sill, somebody had abandoned the outer packaging of a Polaroid film and some photographs. They seemed to be of limbs rather than faces. Whoever would want to take a picture of a bare bottom with the marks of knicker elastic across it?

Sorrel opened her own attic door. Safety? What madness had given her that idea? The only illumination came from the flames of a coal fire which had been banked up like the foothills of hell.

Naked, on the floor, lay Kenny Shorrocks. Straddling him, in torn cami-knickers, was June Gee. One breast had escaped its silken moorings and was bouncing grotesquely, up and down, as she rode Kenny like a horse. Kenny's hair was long these days and June was using it as reins.

'Yes . . .' screamed June, away in a world of her own. 'Yes, yes, *yes!*'

It was only as the flames leaped in accompaniment that Sorrel realized that Kenny was blindfolded. He couldn't see what was happening. It was being forced upon him. Trust June Gee to have found a way of coping with Kenny Shorrocks's conscience!

'Why not come in?' There was a hand on her shoulder. 'The water's lovely and warm.'

The hand belonged to Martyn Gee. Somebody must have rubbed all of those bare muscles with baby oil. His black G-string underpants were straight off an advertisement for male underwear in the cheaper advertising pages of the Sunday tabloids.

'Loosen up, Sorrel,' he said. 'At least you can have a drink.' From behind one of his over-exercised thighs Martyn produced a bottle of Smirnoff vodka.

It would be so easy. One drink and she could leave them to their world and retreat into one of her own. Martyn had already unscrewed the cap and now he was reaching for a thin, half-pint glass.

It was the size of the glass which suddenly reminded Sorrel of some words of Edie's: '*They don't make one big enough or strong enough for me.*'

'No,' she said. And the decision made her feel curiously blessed. 'No, I don't want one.'

What Kenny Shorrocks did with his body was his own business. Sorrel had asked him to keep her friends out of his orgies but she had never counted June as a friend. Sorrel was annoyed that he had made free with her own bedroom – extremely annoyed – but it could be cleaned, it could be disinfected. She certainly wasn't going to sleep at the Nun's Prayer tonight. There was cheap evil on the air. You could almost taste it. Some hotel would have to have her.

Compared with the recent horrors of withdrawal, none of these things were problems. They were just annoyances, and the biggest irritant was the fact that June had a starring role. If Sorrel knew the clairvoyant, and she did, June would insist upon having a dreadful, sexually liberated inquest.

'We must talk this whole thing through.' June, who had now got her breath back, heaved the wayward bosom back into its thin silk cover.

'If you came for your pound of flesh,' replied Sorrel, 'I'm sorry my husband was only able to serve you with about three ounces. I'm afraid it's all he's got.'

There was one thing to be said for being sober, it certainly helped you to find a good exit line. But where was she going? Oh dear, Sorrel supposed it would have to be The Midland. No, she wasn't having that forced upon her. The Midland was sacred territory.

'Love the hat!' called June, mockingly, as Sorrel went down the stairs to God knows where.

The next morning, in a single room in an anonymous commercial hotel near Manchester University, Sorrel climbed back into the clothes she had first put on in Vienna. By now they were so far past their original freshness that she was beginning to feel as though she was playing Blanche Dubois in a long tour of *A Streetcar Named Desire*.

It was the kind of hotel that had asked no questions but demanded payment in advance. As she walked out into the cold sunlight and up Oxford Road she remembered the excitements that this thoroughfare had offered to a stage-struck child. Two variety agents had once had offices here. One was supposed to have discovered Gracie Fields. The other called his premises Pantomime House. Carrol Arden, *Stylist to the Stars*, still had a salon at All Saints' with a signed picture of Sophie Tucker in the window. Sorrel averted her eyes from the register office where she had been fool enough to marry Kenny Shorrocks and noticed that Smiths, the theatrical costumiers, had vanished.

Further up the road, just before the railway arch, Hulme's windows still boasted a dusty display of greasepaint and rhinestone tiaras and multicoloured ostrich feathers under glass domes. A young girl was looking through the window at the framed photograph of General Tom Thumb, the Victorian midget entertainer. Sorrel had always been startled by the fact that he had a full set of white whiskers. What had happened to the framed invitation from Sir Henry Irving?

The child must have registered Sorrel's reflection in the window because she now turned to stare at the actress in the flesh.

'Aren't you Sorrel Starkey?' The suppressed excitement in the question could have belonged to Sorrel's young self.

Automatically, the world-weary professional pulled Ruby's sable coat over the creased dress beneath. 'Guilty,' she replied.

'I always stop and look in this window for luck.' The child's words were tumbling over one another with excitement. 'I want to go on the stage but my mother won't let me. Just looking in this shop window helps.'

'I used to think it helped me too.' Sorrel found herself surprised at overtired thoughts that were turning into words. 'I used to think the stage was all that mattered. I was wrong. If you've any sense you'll stay out here in the daylight, and be happy.'

'That's awful.' The child had a face made for the stage, with wide eyes and a generous mouth. 'You sound just like my mother.' The dark red hair belonged on a Pre-Raphaelite painting in the City Art Gallery. 'Whenever I mention the theatre she throws back her head and sings "On with the motley with their paint and their powder". I don't care. I'm going to be famous. Nothing's going to stop me.'

'Then God help you!' said Sorrel, meaning it, and carried on in the direction of the Nun's Prayer.

Suddenly she remembered the intensity of being twelve years old with nothing but burning ambition for company. And the chances were that the redhead didn't even have a Mickey Grimshaw to aid and abet her dreams. Sorrel felt deeply mean. Perhaps she should turn back and offer the child some more comfortable words. As she half turned, meaning to retrace her steps, the little girl was already following her. Did the small train-case contain a pair of tap shoes? Sorrel felt like weeping.

540

The girl went bright red: 'I wasn't really following you. I just wanted to see where you were going.'

'Home.' It would be too cruel to add that she didn't really know where 'home' was. Sorrel had to offer better than that: 'Have you had any stage experience yet?'

'No. I passed the audition for the children's chorus of The Palace panto but she wouldn't let me do it. She said it was common. I really want to be a straight actress, like you.'

'Then let me give you a piece of advice.' Sorrel wished she sounded a bit less like an adjudicator at a drama festival. 'It's advice that was given to me by a very famous old actress called Lily Bear. Whenever you walk on the stage and speak your first line, always hit a higher note than the last person who was talking. That way the audience will think you're exciting and interesting and you'll make them sit up. What's your name?'

The child pulled a comical face. 'Carmen Kinsella. We're Irish and my mother likes opera. I've every intention of changing it,' she added hastily.

'Leave well alone,' advised Sorrel. 'Carmen Kinsella will look very good on the bills. That's the posters,' she explained 'And now I've really got to go.'

'Can I just say something?' asked Carmen Kinsella.

'What?'

'Thank you. Not just for being nice today but thank you for Lettie Bly. Sometimes, when she's talking, you make it so real that I feel you're doing it just for me.'

A tiny wave of that golden glow, which comes from a responsive audience, swept over the actress. '*Doing it just for me.*' It was almost exactly Mickey's definition of a real star. And to think that, only moments before, she had been so untrue to a profession that could hand her warmth like this. God forbid that Lily Bear should ever get to hear of her temporary defection. She would probably have Sorrel's name read out at the top of St Martin's Lane!

Sorrel had not been expecting winged feet to take her back to the Nun's Prayer but now they did. The pub smelled reassuringly of buckets of disinfectant. Daylight had cut Kenny Shorrocks down to size. He was just a man with a hangover, sipping steaming tea from a thick mug and pulling up the collar of a polo-necked jersey to hide a love-bite the shape of Brazil.

'You came back a night early' was all he had to say for himself. Under the circumstances, if there was any known reply to this, Sorrel was unable to lay hands on it.

June had sent a large sheaf of arum lilies with a packet of Christian Dior tights pushed inside. As though, at the last moment, she had considered the flowers to be not quite adequate.

Sorrel marched up to the attic, turned on the bath, hung up Ruby's fur coat and put all the rest of her clothes into the dirty linen box. She never wanted to see them again. She emptied enough Mary Chess bath-essence under the tap to make the room smell like a Catholic church and climbed into the bath. Water would heal, water would cleanse. For the first time in days Sorrel felt comfortable inside her own skin.

Rehearsals began again on Monday morning. Returning to *Angel Dwellings* always felt like stepping back into 1947. That was the year in which Mickey had originally chosen to set the show. Ever since, fictional television-time had stood still.

Genuine clothes of the period were getting harder and harder to find, and the next day started with an argument. Mabel, the wardrobe mistress, had managed to get her hands on a little fur-fabric jigger-jacket. It could have been designed for Lettie Bly. That was not how Mamie Hamilton-Gerrard chose to view the garment.

'Red Biddy's got to go to a wedding this week.' Mamie was already fingering the mock leopardskin covetously. 'This would be just the thing.'

Mabel looked helplessly at Sorrel. It didn't do to oppose Mamie in anything. The echoes of her tantrums could ricochet around the rehearsal room for weeks.

Sorrel was made of sterner stuff. Wresting the jacket from Mamie, she put it on and buttoned it up to the neck. 'Lettie can get hundreds of episodes of wear out of this. It would be a sin to waste the coat on just one wedding sequence.'

'She's already got more clothes than Danny La Rue,' wailed Mamie.

'If we're talking pantomime, Mamie . . .' retorted Mabel with renewed spirit, 'you'd run the risk of looking like Mother Goose in this.'

Mamie's boot-button eyes went shiny black. 'Lettie Bly can get hundreds of episodes out of it, can she? That's only supposing Sorrel Starkey lasts that long.'

Mamie's mother rushed to place a worried hand on her daughter's forehead. 'Shh, baby, calm down,' and then she whispered, 'We mustn't quote privileged dinner-table conversations.'

This could only mean that they had been feeding Bernard Conroy's fat face again. Both of the Hamilton-Gerrards were skilled in evil. If they had meant to unnerve Sorrel they had succeeded. She wasn't going to let them force her to take a drink. The bottle was in her bag but that was only as insurance. It was like having a policy she didn't want to have to claim on. The penalty clauses were too great. Nevertheless, Sorrel's mind began to flash *bottle-cloakroom-unscrew*. No. She wouldn't give Mamie the satisfaction.

There had been much surprise, the previous day, when Sorrel had settled for tonic water at lunchtime. The surprise practically turned to applause when she stuck to this same non-alcoholic beverage after rehearsal. The bored cast of a long-running show love new crazes and Nadine Taylor and Alan Pomphret soon joined her on the wagon. This had given rise to a lot of good-natured ribbing from the others. But Sorrel was not alone at the centre of it and she was grateful for that.

Kenny Shorrocks, who had started to live with a drink in either fist, found this sudden move to temperance disturbing.

Gladys Starkey might have been expected to welcome the change but she did nothing of the kind: 'Trust you to stop just as Christmas is coming up,' Gladys grumbled down the telephone. 'You'll be nothing but a death's head at the feast.'

Sorrel was feeling well enough to find this amusing but rehearsals, that week, were no joke. Mamie was out to get her. A clear head had sharpened Sorrel's intuitions to a point where she could almost *feel* Mamie Hamilton-Gerrard vibrating with the need for revenge.

It came on the Wednesday. Sorrel's ability to learn lines was the envy of all of *Angel Dwellings*. She was always what they called DLP, meaning dead letter perfect. Not this week. In the days when Mickey wrote the scripts he had studied his actresses. Having been an actor himself he knew better than to hand them tongue-twisting dialogue. The succeeding generation of writers were skilled in many things but not this.

One of this week's pair of episodes had been written by a writer who was besotted with the character of Lettie Bly. Consequently, he had given her great reams of unmanageable dialogue. It looked fine on paper, but getting your tongue around it was impossible. Sorrel decided to complain to the director.

Mamie interrupted her complaints with: 'It's all a matter of technique, darling. Try saying "Red leather, yellow leather, red leather, yellow leather" over and over again. It will make your tongue more flexible.'

'My tongue is quite flexible enough,' replied Sorrel dangerously. 'I simply cannot say these lines. You try. Go on, let's hear you!'

'Oh no, dear. You get to keep your own lines just like you got to keep my coat.'

My coat? Sorrel allowed Mamie the luxury of the last word and persevered with the tongue-twister: 'Properly speaking poliomyelitis is not a plague.' It was easy enough to say it out of context but not, at full speed, in the middle of a long speech full of similar traps.

Bernard Conroy had recently issued a firm directive about not changing dialogue. That week's programme director was new and too inexperienced to dare to think of going against this memorandum.

'The funny thing is that *pissed* I'd probably be able to manage it easily.' Sorrel confided this to Nadine Taylor.

Nadine, all sympathy, comforted her with the assurance that, once Conroy heard the speech on camera, he would be bound to let her change it.

Sorrel wished she could believe her. The line began to haunt everything. She spent so long going over it that the words lost all meaning. Her dreams, that week, were nightmares of pushing her way through a forest of capital P's whilst Mamie Hamilton-Gerard intoned the line perfectly, like some self-satisfied running commentary, from an echo chamber.

A small thing like this is enough to throw a whole performance. *Angel Dwellings* always moved from the rehearsal room into the studios on Thursdays, for the first of their two camera-days. And still they wouldn't let her alter a word. Sorrel seriously thought of ringing Mickey in San Francisco and asking him to intervene. But Mickey's name carried less weight than it had done in the early days and she knew that the pair of them were already seen as too friendly.

'Properly speaking poliomyelitis . . .' Her lips had turned to blubber yet again and this was the seventh attempt to get the shot into the can.

Mamie, also in the scene, made a great show of raising her eyes to heaven. Just as a microphone swung over her head she saw fit to ask: 'Why not try a shot of vodka, Sorrel? It may be highly unprofessional but it generally sees you through.'

It was so exactly what Sorrel was thinking herself that her temper snapped. 'I don't need seeing through. I need some proper dialogue like Mickey used to write.'

'Well your precious Miss Mickey's gone and abandoned you, hasn't he?'

'How dare you call him that?' yelled Sorrel. 'Where the fuck d'you think you'd be today if it wasn't for Mickey Grimshaw? I'll tell you where you'd be – in the retirement home with the rest of the music-hall has-beens.'

'I am a *star*!' screamed Mamie.

'So you keep telling us. A real star wouldn't have to.' Sorrel was beyond scoring points. What came tumbling out was the simple truth: 'Nobody admires you as much as I do. I always have. All my life I only ever wanted to be your friend.'

'I would rather be friends with a pig.' Mamie used the last word to reach a high note of triumph.

Sorrel topped her with: 'Pigs are nice. You're not. My one fear in life is that I might end up like you. The only smiles you've got are for sale. And sometimes you overact.'

That did it. Mamie all but swooned into Alan Pomphret's arms murmuring, 'Get the nurse. Where's Mother?'

Black-clad Mother had run from her standard position, in the shadows, behind the camera. Her old claws scratched deep into Sorrel's face.

'You shan't attack the baby!' she cried. 'You shan't. I'll kill you first.'

'If you do, I'll die smelling bad breath,' snorted Sorrel, caring nothing for the fact that blood was dripping onto her fake-fur jacket.

Nadine and one of the black girls pulled a sobbing Mrs Hamilton-Gerrard off Sorrel as both Bernard Conroy and the director panted down the iron staircase from the control room.

'You will apologize,' shouted Bernard Conroy.

It took a moment for it to dawn on Sorrel that Conroy was shouting at her. 'Apologize? I need stitches. Anyway who says I've got to apologize? You? Why don't you go back to community hymn-singing where you belong? You couldn't produce pussy!'

Pushing Sorrel aside, the producer bent over Mamie who was giving a remarkable performance of somebody struck by lightning.

'Sweetheart,' he said, 'she'd no right to say those things. No right whatsoever. Of course you're a star. Has somebody gone for Sister Blakeney? What you need is a nice little lie-down in your dressing room.'

'No.' Mamie threw Sorrel a malevolent flash of a glance before turning herself back into the oldest actress on earth. 'No, Sorrel has spoken no more than the truth, though she could have picked her words more kindly. I am a has-been. There would be no point in my going on. Not today, not any day. This has been a real eye-opener . . .' Mamie's voice was beginning to tail away but somehow she managed to add, 'I didn't realize I'd outstayed my welcome.'

She invested this statement with such defeated sincerity that, for a moment, even Sorrel was kidded.

Bernard Conroy had tears in his eyes. Sadly, Mabel from wardrobe took Red Biddy's coat from the back of a chair, picked up her handbag from the table and began to carry them away.

'Where the hell d'you think you're going with those?' called Mamie. 'Oh my God!' she cried abruptly. 'What's the significance of a stabbing pain in your left arm?'

For once she had lost her audience. They were still upset but the real panic was over.

'All right everybody,' called out Conroy. 'We're going to break until tomorrow morning at nine o'clock. And you –' he added in an aside to Sorrel – 'you can see me after the recording finishes tomorrow.' Once a schoolmaster always a schoolmaster.

As it was a Thursday, Sorrel could pack up her troubles and take them to The Midland where Barney would soon be waiting to meet her. It wasn't easy to bring down the curtain on the events of the day and turn herself into a textile merchant's secret. The curtain refused to stay down. Every time it rose, inside her head, it seemed to jerk more angrily. And, each time, it revealed Mamie Hamilton-Gerrard upstage centre, in a hissing white limelight, breathing hatred.

An acid test of a great star is whether the performance remains etched on the audience's mind after the show is over. By these standards Mamie ranked with the immortals. What's more, at a distance, those accusing old eyes in that pained face were managing to fill Sorrel with delayed guilt.

It was just a performance, she tried telling herself. The show's never over with Mamie. But what a performance. It had to be based on some sort of truth. Perhaps she does have a heart. Maybe I've really wounded her.

By the time she got to The Midland, Sorrel was seriously considering asking the French Restaurant to send round a lobster dinner, for two, to the Hamilton-Gerrards. But would it stay warm all the way to their cold house in Stockport?

These over-generous thoughts were driven from her head by a scene taking place on the carpeted corridor outside the hotel's cocktail bar. Sorrel was carrying her key towards the lift when she noticed one of the hall porters barring the way of a smartly dressed woman in white.

'I know who you are –' the porter was glancing around as

though he didn't want anyone else to hear – 'and I know what you are. We don't let women of your sort ply their trade in here.'

The woman didn't look a prostitute. 'I'm just meeting a friend.' There was something familiar about the voice which was neither Manchester nor Irish. She had a wonderful figure, a lively intelligent face and a great cloud of blue-black hair with an unashamed streak of white at one side.

'Either you go quietly or I get the house detective,' announced the porter.

It was. It was Monica Dolan, the little girl from Rookswood Avenue who had always said she was going to be a nun. Either that or a whore.

Sorrel acted quickly. Tapping the porter on the arm she said, 'There must be some mistake. This lady's waiting for me.'

With ill-concealed fury Monica Dolan snapped, 'Jesus, Mary and Joseph! Trust you to go and wreck everything, Sheila Starkey. The last thing on earth I needed was help from the biggest piss-artist in Manchester!'

The only reply Sorrel could think of was 'I've stopped.'

'Well your reputation's certainly not died down.' There was no placating Monica. 'Just bugger off quickly and quietly. All the man wants is a five-pound note.'

Dazed, Sorrel headed for the lift. Gander had always said, 'Be sure your sins will find you out,' but Sorrel had genuinely believed that, apart from the cast of *Angel Dwellings*, nobody knew she drank too much. For all of Monica's fury, she still looked as attractive, and as much fun, as she had been in their childhood. It would have been nice to have just chatted.

Sorrel didn't care two figs that Monica seemed to have achieved the less reputable of her childhood ambitions. It seemed that the other woman was more judgemental. Just being Sorrel Starkey had been enough to get herself rejected by a hooker. No. That was unfair on Monica. Just being Sorrel Starkey 'piss-artist' had caused the trouble.

Yet again the words *I thought nobody knew* rang round Sorrel's head. The lift doors opened at the third floor. What on earth did Barney think he was doing, pacing up and down the corridor like that?

'Hello.' Sorrel smiled for the first time that day. 'You look like an expectant father.'

The words seemed to stun him. Glancing at the numbered tag on her key he said, 'I assumed they'd put you in 307 again. Why pretend? I didn't assume, I asked downstairs.'

'That was a bit indiscreet.'

'Let's talk in your room.'

There was a preoccupied air of 'touch me not' about him. 'Barney? What's the matter?'

'In your room,' he said nervously. 'We don't want a scene out here on the corridor.'

Totally at a loss – they had parted the best of friends in Zürich – Sorrel began to struggle with the key. She had no mechanical aptitudes so The Midland's locks had always been a mystery to her. Barney took the key and in one neat movement opened the door.

'What's up?' she asked, as always going Northern when worried. 'Don't tell me Mandy's found out?'

'She certainly found *something* out. Sit down.'

Considering she always paid her own hotel bill, Sorrel decided that Barney was being just a bit too high-handed. 'I'll sit down when I feel like sitting down.'

'Suit yourself. Mandy's pregnant.'

It couldn't be possible. 'Who's the father?'

'I am.'

'You can't be.' But his white face told the whole story.

'I can and I am.'

It was the worst moment of Sorrel's life. She didn't know whether to smack Barney or weep. She felt like a rag doll with all the sawdust knocked out. 'But how? How can it be possible? You said you'd stopped all that ages ago.'

'I said we'd stopped making love. I didn't say she'd stopped looking at the calendar and taking her temperature . . .' His voiced tailed off.

Sorrel's rose. 'And you oblige her with a quick poke?'

'Put like that, yes. She *is* my wife, you know. And Jake needs grandchildren.'

'Jake?' Sorrel could hardly believe her ears. Yet when she thought about it, for even a moment, she could. It was all that stuff about Abraham-and-his-seed-for-ever all over again. 'Your father's got everybody nicely kidded. People think of him as a purring old tomcat when he's still as dangerous as they make them. What Jake wants Jake gets. The old bastard casts a very long shadow. His money makes sure of that.'

Barney wasn't having this. 'He worked hard for what he's got. So did his father. Jake just wants to be sure that there'll be more Shapiros. It wasn't making love, Sorrel. It was just duty. No way did I see it as making love.'

Sorrel was furiously unconvinced: 'You can't do your duty without an erection. Don't tell me you got that by thinking about your father!'

Barney spread his hands helplessly. 'You know me. It doesn't take much.'

'That's very flattering. But, of course, my feelings are nothing. I'm just what I always was – the shiksa.'

'You're everything.' Barney tried to put his arms around her.

'But you still had to knock a baby together.' Sorrel pushed him away.

'And don't ask me to try and understand. I've wasted my whole life trying to understand you. Just who does Jacob Shapiro think he is? God the Father? I'll tell you who he is. He's just a Yiddisher pirate who came to this town and took and took and took. What if he did give a few lousy pictures to the art gallery? That was the least we could expect in return.'

'They were quite good pictures actually.'

Barney was trying to sound reasonable and this drove Sorrel to wilder flights of fury: 'Everything everybody says about you lot is right. You're here but you don't mix in. You're just out for yourselves.' She meant none of this yet she couldn't stop. 'You've got your own country now. We've given you your promised land. Why don't you all just go and live in it?'

What demon was taking over? Dear God, it would be 'gas chambers' next.

'Stop me, Barney,' she sobbed. 'Please stop me.'

'I've no right,' he said sadly. 'And that's the trouble. You and I have got ourselves into a situation that has no rights to it.'

Sorrel stumbled into the bathroom, turned on the tap and began to splash her face with cold water. There was nothing to be gained by looking like a weeping wife. 'I don't know where all that anti-semitic stuff came from,' she called out. 'If you asked me I'd be Mrs Shapiro tomorrow.'

'That's where it came from.' He was still standing in the middle of the bedroom looking serious and businesslike. 'The damage has to end here.'

For a moment Sorrel's hopes rose and then common sense blocked them with thoughts of an unborn Shapiro.

For once, Barney looked his age as he said, 'It has to end.'

Sorrel had been wasting cold water. There was no controlling the tears that began to fall as she sobbed, 'I bet I could have given you babies. We have them in our family like shelling peas . . .'

'Tell me honestly –' Barney was looking around – 'aren't you sick to death of hotel bedrooms?'

'It was the best I could think of. Suggest something better and I'll go along with it.'

Barney shook his head. 'It's thieving. I can never think of it as adultery with you. But what we've been doing was just petty pilfering. You deserve better.'

'Offer me better.' But Sorrel knew that it was no use. The honourable Jewishness that had been one of Barney's main attractions was still the stumbling block that stood between them. It was true that bright romance had been tarnished by months of being confined in a British Transport hotel. Vienna hardly counted. It had been more like a necessary stay in a nursing home than a celebration of love.

Yes, in her heart of hearts, she had begun to tire of meals on dinner wagons and 'Kindly vacate your room by mid-day'. But that had been when she was in a position to criticize the situation. Now – as it was being wrested from her – love in the Midland Hotel suddenly seemed the most precious thing on earth.

This silence was appalling. Something, anything, had to be

551

said to break it. 'I never pinched,' she announced defiantly. 'I only protected what was mine in the first place.'

Sorrel was seized by panic. Already she was talking in the past tense. In one sentence she had lifted an iron gate on all the flooding horrors of loneliness and pain. Something of this must have shown in her face because Barney's arms were immediately around her and, this time, she did not push him away.

'I know,' he said, 'I do know.'

Sorrel tried to erase the shaking from her voice. 'I always hated that bloody song on *Housewives' Choice* and now it's thrumming round and round in my brain.'

'What song?'

She shook her head. Then, what the hell, it would have to be said sooner or later: "Walk Away, Please Go". Matt Monro sings it. He used to be a bus conductor. And *don't* laugh at me. It all began with you laughing at me, on that doorstep, outside Magda's.'

'I was loving you, not laughing. I do love you. You know that?'

'Yes.' She held him for a moment, wondering whether it was for the rest of a lifetime, then gently pushed him away.

'I'm going to start talking.' She said it quietly. 'I just want you to head for the door and walk out. There's not one word we could add that will help us. I'll just talk till you're gone.

'Get moving, Barney.' She turned and stared at a cream-painted wall. She had never liked cream paintwork. It was part of her lonely green and cream childhood. Sorrel forced herself to carry on talking: 'You needn't worry that I'll stop being friends with Ruby. I won't. She's been too good to me for that. And all that anti-semitic stuff was just nonsense I'd stored up for some great fury. Well I've had my fury now, and much good it's done me. I hope your Jewish baby's beautiful. I hope he has your black hair and your blue eyes and I hope you've learned a bit and you let him marry who he wants . . .'

The tears began to fall again. When she'd finished rubbing them away Barney was gone. From her handbag Sorrel took out the detested flat bottle. She didn't want the alcohol but now she had to have it.

The contents of the bottle were soon consumed. She needed more and there was nothing to stop her going to get it. She was free to go anywhere. But Sorrel didn't want to leave the place that had once spelled happiness. Barney's had been the last hand to touch the door handle and she didn't want any new reality. Just for a while she wanted to leave things as they had been. She walked over to the telephone.

'Room service? Would you send me up a bottle of vodka.'

The disinterested voice at the other end announced that they only sent miniatures up to the floors. Sorrel slammed down the receiver, lifted it up again and had herself connected to the Nun's Prayer. The phone rang for a long time before Ray Fossett answered it.

'Ray? I'm thinking of coming home.' For the second time in a week the word sounded singularly inappropriate. 'Is he planning one of his parties?'

'Well it *is* Thursday. I've got a hotpot on to keep their peckers up. And a skinhead's already delivered the video.'

'You make me feel very welcome,' muttered Sorrel. 'I'm at The Midland. Bring me up a bottle of vodka.'

'Should you?' Ray Fossett sounded concerned but this soon vanished as he added, 'Actually, the skinhead was quite dolly.'

'I don't care if he looked like Alain Delon,' snapped Sorrel. 'Get that vodka up here fast. I'm in 307.'

As she paced up and down the room, anger began to replace emotional pain. Wild plans began to formulate in her mind. Why should she be left to bear all of this alone whilst Barney went back to a life of cosy domesticity in Southport? 'Petty thieving' were the words that rankled. If anybody had done any pinching it was Barney's precious Mandy. Sorrel had a good mind to ring Southport and put her in the picture. Only the woman might miscarry as a result and Sorrel didn't want that on her conscience.

She needed to talk to somebody. She tried to place a call to Mickey but all she got was Eeek's recorded voice announcing that Mickey was in LA at a script conference and that he wouldn't be back until Tuesday. Eeek then invited callers to leave a message.

Sorrel waited impatiently for the answering machine's high-pitched bleep to cue her to speak, then she bawled: 'Eeek was always a silly sod, Mickey. If you want burglars, why don't you just put an advertisement in your front window?' With this she slammed down the receiver.

There was nobody she could talk to, nobody she could tell. Nobody except Mickey knew – these were the secretive lengths to which she had gone, to protect Barney Shapiro. And what had he done for her?

He had loved her. And that had been more than enough. Sorrel threw herself onto the big, empty double bed. She wondered whether anybody had ever died on the mattress? The tears broke through again and, this time, the sobs were the clenching kind that really hurt. As she gave way to this awful grief Sorrel lost all sense of time and place. She was only brought back to the surface by first a gentle tap on the door and then a more insistent bang.

When Sorrel stumbled across to open it she found herself confronted by a large red-headed woman who looked like an overblown version of Pat Phoenix, the actress.

'I've brought the vodka.' This was announced in a throaty voice with a slight hiss to it. 'I managed to convince the downstairs reception that I was your personal maid.'

The big hands were the giveaway. Only now did Sorrel realize that it was Ray Fossett in full drag. She had heard a lot about his years as a female impersonator but this was the first time she had actually seen him dressed as a woman. The beige, mink-marmot stole looked like something at a posh whist drive. 'And that's my good blue Gina Fratini you're stretching,' she cried indignantly.

'You told me to give it away.'

'I didn't expect you to sling it on your own back. Where's my vodka?'

'They'd no idea, downstairs, that I was Arthur not Martha.' Ray was very pleased with himself. 'I've got your hooch in this chaste Kendal's carrier bag. I often drag up for Thursday nights. I'm quite a feature.'

Sorrel pulled the bottle from out of the carrier. 'Does the transformation stretch all the way to underwear?' she asked, fascinated in spite of herself. Ray had been right to keep this dressing-up a secret. Sorrel was surprised to find that she was just a bit shocked.

'Women's underwear? Certainly not!' Ray was sternly indignant. 'What d'you take me for, a kinky transvestite? Now then, what's the problem? Tell your sister.' He had already found her a glass.

What could she say that would cause the least damage? 'I loved somebody. He's gone.' Even that bald statement left Sorrel feeling that she was putting Barney at risk. Yet why shouldn't she? Because, that's why. Just *because*. 'Do you want a drink too?' she asked Ray.

'No dear. I should be opening pickled cabbage. Are you really annoyed about the dress? It let out beautifully.'

'No, I'm not annoyed.' People had to take their pleasures where they could find them.

'I'm glad. Now I feel free to admit that not a lot's found its way to Oxfam. When I got up and mimed to "Big Spender", your Blackpool illuminations frock never looked lovelier. All men are bastards, Sorrel. You should know that by now. I certainly do.'

'Mine wasn't a bastard.' That past tense again. She began to cry.

Ray moved in and held her close.

'Your bust's hurting me, Ray. What in God's name is it made of?' Sorrel began to laugh dangerously wildly. It had suddenly struck her that she always seemed to get the cut-price version of everything. Even in this dark hour of need, her sole comforter was an artificial lady.

But he was her friend. She had chosen him. The last thing Sorrel wanted Ray to feel was that she was laughing at him. 'That blue dress looks better on you than it ever did on me,' she said, meaning it.

'I've got the height to carry it. Listen dear, I must go. Somebody's got to set the scene. Don't get too maudlin-drunk, no man's worth it.' Ray headed for the door. Where on earth did he manage to get court shoes in that size?

'Oh God, you've noticed the bats,' he groaned, looking down at his feet. 'I'm afraid I'm a girl who was always cursed with big bats.'

'Watch out for the house detective' was the best reply Sorrel could come up with.

'You'd do better to warn the house detective against me!' With a lurid wink Ray was through the door and gone.

Now Barney wasn't the last person to have touched the handle. Sorrel had another drink whilst she thought about this. And then another. And then one she hardly noticed, followed by a drink she managed to knock over.

Alcohol wasn't hitting the right place. Instead of calming her down it was acting as a stimulant. Where would Barney be now? Halfway down that soulless East Lancashire Road on his way to Southport. Would his wife be expecting him or would his arrival be an unexpected surprise? They had made a baby and they'd made it in the standard way. All the talk of thermometers on earth couldn't alter that. Sorrel's thoughts were whirling as she imagined Barney making skilful, tender love to that spangled doll she had seen outside the synagogue. Only the doll had turned into a lumpy woman who needed diamonds to draw attention away from a double chin.

And Barney had preferred *that* to her.

No, 'preferred' was the wrong word. And if there was a right one it could only be in Hebrew. Sorrel wished she'd asked Ray to bring some bottles of tonic water too. What the hell! Why kid herself? Tonic would only weaken the effect and Sorrel needed to drink to the point of oblivion.

It wouldn't come. More tears came but not oblivion. When the tears were over she saw that there were just a couple of inches of vodka left in the bottle. She wanted sleep. She needed *out*. What use was that amount of vodka going to be to a mind that was racing like the speedway at Belle Vue?

And then Sorrel remembered the sedatives. The ones from Vienna. Which handbag had she brought? Yes, her good Gucci – they should still be inside the zipper compartment. As she pulled them out, Sorrel remembered that these were the pills that Barney had minded so conscientiously. Black, engraved German words stared up at her from the label. The directions were written in violet ink. Such a pretty colour. Sorrel remembered the care and concern Barney had lavished upon her in the Hotel Sacher.

Yes, well he'd lavished care and concern elsewhere; there was an unborn child to prove it. How could you fight that? And, once it came into the world, what chance would she stand then? Then? It was all over *now*. Sorrel swallowed two of the pills with a mouthful of vodka and then washed down a couple more.

Ten frenzied, pacing minutes later nothing had happened. Sorrel took three more tablets. At this point she began to feel a bit blurred around the edges. She took this as a cue to cease her pacing and lie down. She began to remember a song she had once been obliged to sing in an advanced Shakespearean production at Liverpool.

> Sleep O sleep come kiss me now
> Be my only lover
> With thy lips upon my brow
> Every trouble's over . . .

What was the next verse? The song had always been interrupted by somebody shouting out: 'The strings my lord are false'. The strings were false all right and the last thought she could manage to hold onto was: What difference does a thermometer make. . . ? He was still unfaithful to me.

20

Sorrel was a hundred fathoms under water and plodding along the seabed in lead diver's boots. She needed to make more water. She needed to go to the lavatory. But some constraint from another section of her life was preventing her.

Surely, under water, the voices she could hear talking should have been bubbling? Or did under-water voices only bubble in cartoons? Who did they belong to? Were they coming to *get* her? Sorrel felt a jellyfish sting her sharply on her cheek.

'Come on, love.'

How could Ray Fossett be here – at the bottom of the sea –when he was scared to death of water? That's why he'd never learned to swim. Another stinging slap: 'Come on, sweetheart, we want you back in the land of the living.'

Sorrel opened her eyes to winter sunlight. She wasn't down among the dead men, she was in the Midland Hotel. Ray Fossett was dressed as a man. Why that should seem odd she couldn't remember. Thinking was like trying to pull reluctant strands of seaweed off a rock. Who was the man with a pale face and long black hair parted in the middle? Jangling a large bunch of keys, he was dressed in a black jacket and striped trousers.

'Would you mind stopping that?' Sorrel managed to ask weakly. 'It's going right through my head.'

The man plainly felt that some explanation was called for: 'I'm one of the trainee hotel executives, Miss Starkey, and it's been a big honour to be of assistance.'

'Trainee hotel executive,' scoffed Ray Fossett. 'That's not what they call her at some of the lowest dives in Manchester. She usually answers to Miss Morticia. Still, we'd have been lost without her pass-key. You should thank your God, Sorrel Starkey, that there's more than one form of freemasonry in this town!'

Sorrel tried to rise to her feet but the legs she had swung

over the side of the bed were distinctly wobbly. 'I need to go to the loo,' she said.

'I should bloody well think you do,' exclaimed Ray Fossett. 'You've been asleep since Thursday. Grab her other arm, Morticia. We'll have to swing her over to the toilet between us. Come on, whoops-a-daisy . . . Right, you're on the seat. We'll leave you to it. If you're anything like me, I can't go with a strange queen watching.'

Would he never shut up?

'Are you in a fit state to pull your own trolleys down?' called Ray through the closed door.

'What day is it?' she called back.

'Saturday.'

Saturday? That brought her to with a start. Sorrel's mind began to whirl. What had happened to Friday? And Friday was camera-day. How on earth would they have been able to record all Lettie's big scenes without her? It wouldn't have been possible. She broke into a cold sweat.

'Are you OK?' called Ray through the door.

'Why didn't you wake me up?' Sorrel was now on her feet, washing her hands. She splashed cold water on her face and drank some more from a thick glass tumbler. The hand that held the tumbler was shaking alarmingly. She called out again: 'How could you let me sleep through camera-day?'

'Let you?' The bathroom door was flung open by Ray Fossett. 'Don't use that tone with us, lady. Nice thanks for concealing a suicide attempt! The pair of us spent all yesterday walking you up and down. But I don't suppose you remember that?'

Sorrel suddenly registered the fact that Spud the dog had come into the bathroom and was gazing at her with worried eyes that were full of love.

'Oh Spud,' she said, kneeling down and putting her arms around him. Under these jangling circumstances, affection was the one thing guaranteed to remove what little wind there was in Sorrel's sails.

'We did our best.' Ray's friend with the keys was also beginning to show signs of indignation. 'We even smuggled Bolton Joan up the back stairs.'

'Who's she?' asked Sorrel in wonder. 'And what made you think I needed an audience?'

'She's a he,' retaliated Ray Fossett. 'Bolton Joan is one of the finest physicians south of Chorley. Does the word *stomach-pump* bring back any memories? Why did you do it? Why didn't you tell me you were going to do away with yourself?'

'I didn't. I wasn't.' Still crouched on the floor with Spud, Sorrel found these thoughts too big for her aching brain. 'All I wanted was a good sleep.'

'Foreign tablets,' snorted Ray. 'The doctor said if you'd taken just one more there would have been another star in the heavens on Thursday night.'

Sorrel was still hugging Spud for comfort. As always, when he needed a bath, he smelled like Owbridge's Lung Tonic. But it was a familiar smell. It was safe.

'What about camera-day?' Sorrel forced herself to ask this. 'How did they cope?'

'They didn't.' Ray produced a letter from an inner pocket. 'I feel just like one of those mothers who gets worried stiff because their child's gone missing and then want to tan the arse off them when they turn up.' He handed Sorrel the letter. 'Read this. It's from the studio. Bernard Conroy brought it round to the pub himself.'

The sound of tearing paper – as she ripped open the envelope – was almost more than Sorrel's head could bear.

'You've got more reporters waiting downstairs than we had for the Beatles,' said Ray's friend the trainee.

Dear Sorrel,

On Thursday you started a fist fight in the studio. Today you have neither shown up for taping nor seen fit to send us any explanation.

Enough is enough. A formal letter listing your various breaches of contract will be sent to you next week. Consider yourself fired.

Yours sincerely
Bernard Conroy

Ray Fossett gave Sorrel no time to think about the letter. 'It's the push, isn't it? I can't say I'm surprised. It was like

Muldoon's picnic at the Nun's Prayer yesterday. First the stage manager arrived looking for you like a bloodhound, then the floor manager, then Conroy bustled in. The scriptwriters got drunk, arguing how to rejig the episodes without you. The cast are all blazing. They're being made to work right through the weekend, so you can just imagine!'

Sorrel could imagine only too well. She opened her mouth to speak but there was no stopping Ray Fossett. 'Don't get me wrong, dear, I said nothing. Not even when somebody from the legal department arrived with a sinister black briefcase. But it's only fair to tell you that your name's mud in this town.'

'And there are more reporters downstairs than we had for the Beatles,' repeated the man called Morticia with something very close to satisfaction. 'You might, at least, have rung the Samaritans.' This was said in tones of funereal reproach.

'When all I wanted was a good sleep?' Sorrel's temper had risen and now it was close to snapping. God but she needed a drink! Only drink was the trouble. One way or another, drink had led to nine tenths of all this mess.

As if reading her mind, or perhaps it was from long experience of the actress, Ray Fossett announced primly: 'And you needn't think the answer's in a bottle, Sorrel, because it isn't. I don't know what's happened to gratitude, Morticia, but there's certainly none going spare round here.'

Sorrel felt like Cinderella with the Ugly Sisters. 'Thank you for your help.' Why did she sound as though she was opening a garden party? 'I'll never forget it.'

Spud followed Sorrel as she headed into the bedroom and grabbed her coat.

'Thinking of sneaking out the back way?' sneered Ray. 'It won't wash. The Sunday papers have got lookouts posted.'

Sorrel forced a brush through her hair. 'I never sneaked out the back way in my life.' Only it wasn't true. She had once sneaked down the back fire escape, from Barney's bedroom, at the dead of night. Barney; why did she have to start thinking about him again, now? It had set her head whirling back into the same state that had led to vodka and Viennese sedatives. Barney was Manchester. *Angel Dwellings* was Manchester. Manchester was the monster. She had to get away.

Flight, that's what was called for. Sorrel began to cram the few things she had brought with her into the overnight bag. A train; she would head for the station and take a train.

'I'm going away, Ray,' she announced. 'You can come with me if you want. There won't be as much money as before but we'll make out somehow.' Sorrel reached for Spud's lead and clicked it into place.

Ray looked awkward. 'I'm not quite a free agent. You see Kenny stamps my insurance card and that means a lot to me. And though I say it myself, the Nun's Prayer would be in a mess without me. I've got a whole life these days, Sorrel . . .' His voice tailed off. He couldn't look her in the eye.

'Keep your whole life.' Sorrel's matter-of-fact tones disguised hurt feelings. 'I'm off to find a proper life for myself. Come on, Spud, let's see if we can make you Lord Mayor of London.'

It was Spud who led the way to the lift. If ever a dog had natural star quality it was this white border collie with the black patch over one eye. Sorrel didn't bother looking back and the lift doors opened mercifully quickly.

There were already a couple of passengers on the downwards descent. They looked the kind of middle-aged people who spend a weekend in a hotel whilst doing their Christmas shopping. Everything about them was orderly. They were dressed in the sort of casual clothes you can get, by mail order, from *The Observer*. Sorrel had often wondered whether they would be as safely respectable as the photographs in the advertisements. They were. Next to them, she felt like something that should have been put out – by the side of the dustbins – at the back door of a theatrical costumier's.

'Excuse me –' the woman had an Edinburgh accent – 'aren't you Lettie Bly?'

At least there would be no need for any more of that torture. 'Haven't you heard?' asked Sorrel. 'She *died* yesterday.'

As the lift doors opened at the ground floor, there was a loud cry of 'There she is' and photographers' flashlights began to explode.

'And this is the funeral,' added Sorrel sweetly, to the bemused couple, as the whole of the Northern press corps, together with Fleet Street reinforcements, leapt towards them.

'Sorry to ruin your weekend,' she said to a man from the *Daily Mail* who wouldn't, normally, have been working on a Saturday.

'It's a big story, Sorrel.' At least he had the grace to look apologetic. 'Did you overdose? Could you just give me a line?'

He was drowned with a chorus of 'This way, Sorrel', 'Could you just look over here?', 'What about a brave smile?'

Just what did they think a smile would look like on a face that had received no real attention since Thursday? It would look awful. And that, of course, was what they wanted. Questions were being shouted at her from all sides. The only thing to do was throw her head back – so the shadows underneath her eyes wouldn't show in the photographs – and force her way through the crowd, to the reception desk.

'I stayed a little longer than intended,' she said to the girl behind the counter. And twenty reporters wrote her words down in twenty shorthand notebooks.

The receptionist looked embarrassed to the point of panic. 'Your account's not ready, Miss Starkey. I'll just have to slip and check with the manager.'

'Stay where you are.' Sorrel opened her handbag. 'I'll leave a signed blank cheque.' No response. 'I presume that will do?'

'It's all a bit unusual.' The girl was plainly thrown by the fact that reporters were writing down her every word.

Sorrel finished signing the cheque, slammed it on the counter, announced, 'I never claimed to be usual', and headed for the front door.

Spud chose that moment to turn quickly and inflict a severe nip on the calf of an old enemy, from the *Daily Mirror*, who let out a little cry of pain. Mentally, Sorrel promised Spud a pound of best fillet steak.

The first taxi driver, recognizing Sorrel, pulled his cab off the rank and reached back, with his hand, to open the passenger door.

'London Road Station.' As Sorrel and Spud clambered inside she registered the fact that her pursuers were piling into the rest of the taxis.

'London Road's called Piccadilly these days,' grunted the driver. 'You're living in the past.'

What was so wrong with that? Manchester was highlighted by pale December sunshine. Sorrel stopped hating the place but she still had to go. If the newly cleaned City Art Gallery looked like a pale golden Greek temple, then – somewhere behind it – Shapiro House must be gleaming in similar triumph. Magda Schiffer had always maintained that the cotton money earned in one building had bought pictures for the other.

Those same pictures Sorrel had screamed about on Thursday. Sorrel refused to think about that and remembered Magda telling her to take what she wanted. '*Take what you want, take it . . . and pay for it.*' Well, Sorrel had taken the lot. Fame, love . . . and now the taxi meter, ticking its way to the station, was just a fraction of the high price she had paid in return.

As the cab passed Lewis's department store, Sorrel thought back to going there with Gander to see Father Christmas. There were half-crown presents in his grotto and she had received a book called *Myth Stories of Greece and Rome*. It had been too old for her at the time but Gander had said to remember there was a war on and that Sorrel would be glad of it, by and by.

The book had eventually become a favourite. In fact it was still on her shelves at the Nun's Prayer. It was the book with the story of Pandora's Box in it.

Sorrel remembered Gander reminding her of this on the night she switched on Blackpool illuminations. Something about Pandora opening the box and letting out all the troubles of the world.

'Like mucky dusters,' had been Gander's description. Sorrel glanced, over her shoulder, through the smoked-glass rear window of the taxi. Her own cab was being followed by a line of others. Even as she looked, one of the taxis overtook them and a photographer's flash bulb lit up the interior of her own.

The mucky dusters are certainly in full pursuit, she thought. What was the end of the story? Something about a scrumpled-up piece of silk at the bottom of the box. And that was meant to be Hope.

'We'll cling onto Hope,' she said to Spud. 'We're not beaten yet. We'll be back. They've not seen the last of us. None of them. We'll go away and we'll *make* it right.'

BOOK THREE

A WHOLE WOMAN

1

Sorrel and Spud were on the train for London and so was most of the press contingent. She couldn't stay locked in the lavatory, with her dog, for ever. Oh for the days of individual first-class compartments when you could bolt the door from inside! Since electrification, all the seats in all the carriages were either side of a central aisle. Still, modernization had put a buffet-bar on the train and its shutter generally went up about five minutes out of Manchester.

Sorrel's need to avoid the reporters was overridden by her desire for a drink. Cautiously, she opened the lavatory door and, spying that the coast was clear, began to tug Spud across the bouncing, swaying bit between two compartments.

'You owe me, Sorrel Starkey.' A determined woman was blocking her way.

It was dark in this swaying area and the feeling of being on a cake-walk at a fairground always seemed to unnerve Spud. 'Could you just let me through?' asked Sorrel. 'I wouldn't want my dog to be sick on your shoes.'

As the woman stepped back into the light, Sorrel saw that it was Libby Taylor, the journalist who had stage-managed her honeymoon at Portmeirion.

'You owe me,' Libby Taylor repeated.

They were now standing on a firmer floor but Sorrel didn't feel particularly safe. She looked down from the window of the train, as it sped past the rooftops of terraced houses beneath the embankment, and remembered that Libby Taylor had kept stum about the finer details of that unsavoury honeymoon.

'What do you want?' she asked.

Libby, with her usual uncanny ability to turn herself from a monkey-headed fiend into a human being, smiled easily. 'I want your story and I want it exclusively. But I need a quick decision. Forty thousand pounds, Sorrel, that's what I'm empowered to offer you. All you have to do is get off the train with me at Stockport.'

'Forty thousand?' gasped Sorrel. She had, of course, heard of such spectacular offers but she had never quite believed in them. 'What on earth would you want for that?'

'The lot.' They were getting nearer to Stockport so Libby was speaking urgently. 'We'd want the full dope on the suicide bid, the truth about the row with Mamie plus all the dirt you've got on Kenny Shorrocks.'

'I couldn't do it to him.'

'He wouldn't think twice about doing it to you. I've got a car waiting in the station yard. We'll drive you off into Cheshire and hide you away.'

'I loathe Cheshire.'

'We'll take you anywhere you want. Here, have a drink.' Libby produced a miniature bottle of vodka. 'You must be needing one.'

She was speaking no less than the truth. But much as Sorrel wanted that drink she could imagine the strings attached to it. Strings? Chains more like. Once her story had been sensationalized in a Sunday paper she would have to live with the consequences for the rest of her life.

Libby unscrewed the cap of the little bottle and a faint, unbelievably desirable whiff of vodka reached Sorrel's nostrils. 'I need that story,' said Libby. 'And I need it this afternoon.'

'You can't have it.' The train was already on the high viaduct above Stockport and now it began to slow down, as it pulled into the station.

'Is that your last word on the subject?'

'I'm sorry, Libby, it has to be. I'm not telling it to you and I'm not telling it to anybody. There isn't enough money on earth for that.'

The train pulled to a halt. Libby thrust the open bottle at Sorrel. 'You can have this anyway, you poor cow. Must dash. If one canary won't sing I'll have to get to work on the other.'

Libby had already got the door open and now she descended to the platform, slammed it shut, and broke into a loping run. More than ever she looked as though she had been begotten up a tree. Not caring who was watching, Sorrel slurped back the vodka from the neck of the little bottle and began to lead Spud to the bar.

Bar? It was more like a dull corner of the Press Club. Sorrel's actual arrival was the cue for an outbreak of noisy, false bonhomie and the offer of a lot of drinks.

'I'll buy my own,' she announced firmly. 'And there's no point in asking me any questions because I'm not answering them. And don't tread on the dog.'

At this a ticket collector she hadn't noticed turned round and said, 'That dog will have to go in the guard's van.'

'Not if he's got a first-class ticket,' protested Sorrel. 'And he has.'

'That's only at my jurisdiction,' said the little Hitler self-importantly. He even looked like Hitler. 'And I'm saying he's got to go in the guard's van.'

'May I have a couple of miniature vodkas?' Sorrel was addressing the girl behind the counter.

'I'm only doing my job.' The ticket collector was not enjoying the glares and rumblings coming from the press. 'Can I see your tickets, madam?'

Sorrel produced them. As purchasing them in Manchester had left her unpleasantly on view, it seemed a bit much that she was not going to be allowed to use the things properly. If Spud was going in the guard's van, so was she. Paranoia had begun to set in. Spud was a famous dog and this lot were so hungry for a story that one of them might try kidnapping him, in the hope of making her talk. If they were hungry she was thirsty, and she handed over a pound to pay for her miniatures.

'The guard's van's up at the head of the train.' The collector returned her tickets.

'Sieg Heil!' She straightened her arm in a Fascist salute and thought: All that money to sit on other people's cases. No, it was too much. Sorrel suddenly saw red. 'You are failing in your duty, Adolf! These gentlemen are pestering me and I wish to complain.' Her voice was getting grander and grander. 'If I submit myself to the indignities of your luggage van, I want your solemn assurance that they will not be permitted to enter.'

571

'You'll have to take that up with the guard.'

'And now you're blocking my way.' Sorrel's icy tones would have cleared a passage through a crowded rehearsal room. The ticket collector stood aside and allowed her to sweep past him. Sorrel now tried to beat the train to London by hurrying Spud down the aisle which divided seated, gawping passengers.

British Rail might have modernized everything else, but the guard's van looked like something that might have been used to transport Jews across Europe. Go away, Barney! she thought. I'm in too big a mess to dare think about you. There were even bars on the windows.

The guard himself looked as though he could have been left behind from the days of the London, Midland and Scottish Railway. He even wore the old-fashioned, thick, black flannel uniform and he appeared to have removed his bottom teeth for comfort.

'Well if it isn't Lettie and Spud! By God, you look rough, Lettie. Been overdoing things on the dock road again?'

Was the man confusing fiction with fact? Nobody would ever believe Sorrel when she told them that there were people who did.

'You've certainly made headlines this morning.'

He was brighter than she'd given him credit for. He was also doing his best to be helpful. 'Fancy an Aspro?' The painkilling tablets he now produced, from a waistcoat pocket, were sealed inside a long tape of grubby paper. 'We can even run to a brew of tea.'

Spud licked the man's hand, which always meant that somebody was OK, so Sorrel said, 'At the moment, I'm more worried about reporters getting in here.'

'When I've got the rulebook and a sledgehammer?' Her new friend actually produced this sinister item from behind its rusty, metal clasp. At that moment the door from the corridor slid back and the officious ticket collector bustled in and joined them.

'While you're here,' he said to Sorrel, 'I'll just have your autograph. It's not for me. I don't watch it.'

Sorrel had taken enough: 'Then why should I give you my autograph?'

'Because I'm the public. We made you and we can break you.'

Sorrel signed.

'You mean you came just as you were?' asked Shelagh Starkey incredulously. 'Without so much as going back to the pub to pack a suitcase?'

It was strange to hear the voice of common sense on this most nonsensical of days. And it was good to be back in Shelagh's little house in Bedman's Row. Nothing had changed since Sorrel first found it – down the alley off St Martin's Lane – all those years ago. Close friendship had matured between the namesakes but the house had stayed like something out of a pantomime with its beamed ceilings and twisting staircase.

There were more framed theatrical playbills on the walls than ever. As Shelagh had got older she had come into her own as a distinguished character actress. She always framed a poster from each show she was in and hung it, on a top corridor, until the production was no more than a theatrical memory. That's when the poster got moved downstairs.

'Those poor reporters are still outside,' she announced as she came back from peering round the net curtains in the hall window. 'It's turned dreadfully cold. D'you think I should take them out some soup?'

'Soup? Only if I can put poison in it first.' Sorrel never failed to find it startling that Shelagh, the bishop's daughter, put being a Christian before anything else. 'The way they chased me from Euston was just like a hunting print with Gordon Square instead of fields and taxi cabs for horses. Never try and convince me again that the fox enjoys it!'

'You're not a fox,' pointed out Shelagh reasonably. 'Sorrel, what are your plans?'

'I just had to get away. If it's not convenient . . .'

'When you've always been told to consider this house as your second home? Of course it's convenient. Stay as long as you like. You can stay for ever as far as I'm concerned. Look, I've got a matinée at five o' clock; I think I'll ring Lily Bear and ask her to come round and keep you company. She's bored to death at the moment and somebody will have to walk Spud. You can't go out yet. Not with that lot outside. If you won't eat anything now, what do you want for supper?'

'Eggs, an omelette, any old thing.' Sorrel broached a nervous question. 'May I have a drink?'

'Yes dear, but replace what you take. I won't accept that you have to have it and I wish you'd get help.' Having said her say Shelagh changed the subject firmly with 'It wouldn't surprise me, once the reporters have gone, if Lily didn't suggest going out.'

'They'll never go.' Sorrel was beginning to give way to gloom again.

'Rubbish. The first editions are on the street by half past eight. You're not their sole concern, Sorrel. It's Saturday. I expect they'll all be very eager to get back to their families.'

Sorrel had once been shocked to see, in a photographer's window, a family wedding group featuring a well-known Northern reporter as father of the bride. He had actually looked human. It had taken this photograph to convince Sorrel that the press were not a race apart who spent their time on other people's doorsteps.

At that moment, one of the pack outside suddenly decided to ring Shelagh's bell again. As Sorrel moved upstairs to get her drink she could hear the safety chain going back and, after a mumble-laden pause, her friend saying: 'I'm afraid not. I don't want to be mean but there's a perfectly good public one in Leicester Square.'

Too right! thought Sorrel, remembering the journalist she had once let in, for just the same purpose, at Bellaire. On the way down from the bathroom he had managed to pinch a framed photograph of herself in a bikini. The next place she saw it was in the pages of his newspaper. Sorrel had two drinks instead of just the one she'd been planning and began to feel almost human.

Lily Bear arrived an hour later dressed to the nines and determined to view the whole situation as an adventure: 'It's when they're *not* on the doorstep you have to worry,' she decreed. 'The little darlings dogged everything I did, during the war, and that's what made me nice and famous. I've every reason to be very grateful to the press. If you'd any sense, Sorrel, you would paint your face, invite them in, and hold a press conference. Just give them a bit of something to print, refuse to add anything more, and they'll head back to their editors like lambs. Is that the best outfit you've got with you?' Lily Bear was already at a mirror attacking her own hair with a comb.

'She's got a wardrobe full of London clothes upstairs.' Shelagh was plainly seeing the sense of Lily's argument and both actresses now prevailed upon the visitor from Manchester to face the reporters.

Sorrel went higher up the house to change. When you own a white border collie, wearing black is difficult – white hairs seem to attach themselves from the very air. For this reason, Sorrel had always kept smart, dark clothes for London.

'Downstairs!' she commanded Spud who had followed her. 'Mother's dressing for the scaffold.'

For once he refused to obey her. Rubbing against the skirt of the black silk suit she was taking from a hanger, he managed to shed one white hair onto it. Sorrel hadn't the heart to stop him. One of Spud's great delights in life was christening new clothes.

'We're in this together,' she told him. 'I'll talk to them and if that doesn't work you have my full permission to go for their throats. No, Spud, I didn't mean that,' she added hastily – the performing animal had grown uncannily good at taking stage direction. What would she say to them? That was the problem.

Lily Bear came clacking up the winding stairs on black patent high heels. 'We must write the script,' she announced importantly. 'But first I'm going to spray you with Mitsouko. It's imperative we kid them that you're a star. The trouble with those soap operas is that they hand people something precious close to stardom but it's not quite the real thing. Take these so-called stars away from the series that brought them into prominence and they wither and fade like a Christmas balloon. Mind you, Arthur Lowe did all right after *Coronation Street*.'

Sorrel now found herself engulfed in exotic spray from an

atomizer. Lily Bear didn't even pause for breath. 'We must take this situation and use it. We must make you blossom into a real name in your own right. At least you left the show with a bang. That should keep your name nice and hot for a couple of months.'

'But I don't want to be a freak attraction.'

'*Want* doesn't come into it. A freak attraction is what you are. Be grateful for it and you can turn this whole mess to your own advantage.'

Ten minutes later – looking like a West End leading lady heading for a cocktail party – Sorrel descended the stairs. Behind her, Lily Bear was still picking white bits off Sorrel's silk suit, like a proud mother. 'Just say what we agreed, and no more. Shelagh, have you put the drinks out in the dining room?'

'Just as you said, whisky and gin.'

'Well done, but take those nuts away. This isn't a dainty social occasion. A drink will warm them up but that dining room of yours should keep things strictly formal. Effortless superiority, that's what we're aiming to show them.' Lily Bear, heading for the door, glanced back over her shoulder. 'Stop muttering to yourself, Sorrel. You know your lines perfectly. We'll be all right just so long as you stick to the agreed script.'

With this Lily flung open the door and began to sparkle at the assembled reporters as though she was still entertaining the troops at E1 Alamein. 'Boys!' she exclaimed. 'Step right in. It's opening time and Sorrel's buying.'

As the reporters filed into the dining room Sorrel tried to see it through their eyes. Whatever must they be making of the eighteenth-century ancestors on the walls and the silver pheasants on the Sheraton sideboard? As Shelagh Starkey poured drinks into old crystal, Lily Bear drew the dark red velvet curtains against the twilight. It was all a far cry from *Angel Dwellings*. Not for the first time, Sorrel thanked God for Lily Bear's strong sense of theatre.

'Gentlemen – ' Lily had changed her style of address to match the room – 'Miss Starkey has a few words to say.'

Sorrel cleared her throat and went into the prepared

speech. Old Lil had been adamant that it must be delivered in standard English with no wry Lettie Bly additions. 'I am sorry to have kept you hanging round, especially as I know that some of you must have deadlines to meet. I have been more than a little upset today and needed time to get my thoughts together.

'The facts of the matter are these: the studio has decided to terminate my contract and that is something you can only discuss with them.' The next part worried her but Kenny Shorrocks could hardly be said to have attempted to come to any kind of rescue. 'I have decided to leave my husband and seek a divorce. You will appreciate that I cannot say any more about this until I have consulted solicitors.' They seemed a reasonable enough audience so she now added Lily Bear's final line: 'I am prepared to answer general questions but not intrusive ones.'

The loudest voice to arise from the immediate babble came from a craggy man in a British-warm overcoat. 'Did you try to kill yourself, Sorrel?'

If that wasn't intrusive, she'd like to know what was! Nevertheless she answered: 'No. I overestimated the number of tablets I would need to get a good night's sleep.'

'Do you use tablets habitually?' This was from the only woman present.

'No. That's why I overslept.'

Sorrel's mildly indignant answer managed to raise something like good-natured laughter through which somebody asked, 'Did you know that Kenny Shorrocks has sold his version of the story to one of the Sundays?'

Sorrel's startled face must have given them the answer because another man called out, 'Your friend Libby Taylor's got him holed up in a room at The Imperial in Blackpool.'

'Well I hope she knows what she's doing because Kenny Shorrocks would screw the crack of doom. And please feel free to quote that.'

A babble of indecipherable questions now arose. Sorrel had sounded dangerously like Lettie Bly, which was exactly what they wanted.

Lily Bear assumed a pained face and held up a hand for

silence. 'That's it, boys,' she announced. 'You're not getting any more. The girl is distracted. She doesn't know what she's saying. Sorry, but that's got to be the end.' Abandoning distinction she added, 'On yer bikes!'

Sorrel failed to respond to more shouted questions. The man in the British-warm asked Shelagh, 'Are you her auntie?' There were repeated demands for 'Just one last picture' and, as the final flash bulb exploded in front of the portrait of Bishop Starkey in the cathedral close, the press allowed themselves to be charmed out of the room and shepherded into the night by Lily Bear.

'I must get to the theatre.' Shelagh began pulling on her raincoat. 'That last comment of yours was a bit unguarded, Sorrel.'

'I was thrown by that man saying Kenny's sold his story. What story? I suppose we'll just have to wait for the first editions of the Sunday papers.'

2

As Sorrel and Lily Bear scurried through the gaudy, electric-light horror of Leicester Square, crowds were pouring into one cinema and out of another. Sean Connery seemed to be on everywhere. The newsvendor on Coventry Street was still selling the *Evening Standard*. The headline on the placard outside his tarpaulin shack was *JEREMY THORPE – NEW REVELATIONS*.

'And that's another poor soul they built up to knock down,' observed Lily Bear. 'When are you expecting the Sundays?' she asked the man.

'Any minute, doll. They're late.'

'Of course Jeremy Thorpe won't get the chance to do another show to save his face,' Lily Bear continued helpfully.

An accordionist in the doorway of the Café de Paris spotted Sorrel and immediately broke into the theme music from *Angel Dwellings*. She turned back, fiddled in her handbag and flung a shilling into his cap on the pavement. 'Oh dear,' she sighed. 'It must look as though I'm already glad to pay for a bit of recognition.'

Rain had started to fall. The shining black pavement was now ribboned with reflected neon light as Sorrel and Lil hurried to shelter under the canopy of the London Pavilion. This was where Sorrel had first met Mucky Matt. The film showing was *The Return of the Pink Panther* and a new generation of young provincials were gazing across at Eros' statue. They'd had time to be born and grow up in the years since Sorrel ran away from home. She put up her coat collar and tried not to think where those years had got her.

A van paused for a moment. From inside, somebody threw down a thick wad of newspapers partially covered in brown paper and tied with coarse string. A news-seller dived forward, slashed the string with a knife, pulled back the wrapping and revealed the headline *SORREL LOVED HER*

GIN AND NOOKIE. It was accompanied by an old photograph of herself and Kenny toasting one another at Portmeirion.

'I've not drunk gin in years,' she exclaimed indignantly. She could already make out the words 'Kenny Shorrocks reveals all . . .'

Lily Bear, in the middle of paying for the paper, turned round and said, 'I suppose gin was shorter than vodka for the headline.'

Sorrel seized the paper from Lily. 'Let's get in a doorhole and read it.'

'We are distinguished actresses, dear, not drug addicts. We'll read it at The Ritz.'

'Full story – centre pages,' read Sorrel aloud and began to tear open the paper.

'What time do the others arrive?' Lily asked the man as she took her change.

'It varies.'

'The porter can send out a boy. That's my paper, Sorrel, and you're not looking at it until we're sitting down comfortably.' Lily took it from her just as she'd found the appropriate pages. 'I don't want you collapsing on the edge of Soho. The rain's slackening, the lights are on green. We'll cut along past Swan and Edgar and hurry down Piccadilly.'

'Can't I just have a peek?' asked Sorrel, panting behind. 'Every photograph seemed to be of me with a glass in my hand.'

'Well, they would be. I love The Ritz.' Lily had folded the newspaper up again and now it was tucked under her arm. 'Especially The Palmery. All that pink and gold and the white statues and water tinkling from that fountain thing.'

Sorrel thought of snatching but judged that Lily Bear would be good at snatching back.

The older actress trotted on and continued blithely with her conversation: 'Did you know that, in the twenties, Monsieur Ritz asked Lady Mendl to redesign the ground floor? She simply walked across to one of the writing desks, took a piece of paper and wrote on it: "Change nothing. My fee is one hundred pounds." She maintained that if he didn't pay for her advice he wouldn't value it. Jewish of course. She was Elsie de Wolfe in those days. Contain your impatience, Sorrel, we'll be there soon enough.'

The Ritz Hotel was as warm and embracing as Lily had promised. And only now, as they settled in pink velvet armchairs beside the indoor fountain, did Lily allow Sorrel to take the newspaper. It wasn't long before Sorrel wished she hadn't. A blush, the like of which she'd forgotten she was capable of, began to burn her face as she read the article.

'The bastard! That bloody limping bastard. I had to have gin by the bed, did I? I could tell a different story. Do you know what he wanted by the bed? Only a horsewhip, that's all!'

'One of that kind, was he?' replied Lily interestedly. 'Waiter! We are in need of attention.'

'Good evening, Miss Bear, always a pleasure,' he said in an Italian accent.

'You know Miss Starkey of course?'

The blush had not yet subsided and, for a mad moment, Sorrel contemplated sitting on the newspaper to hide it.

'I'm always working when your show's on – ' the waiter was addressing her – 'but my wife must be your biggest admirer in Streatham.'

Sorrel watched his eyes slide covertly towards the terrible press photograph of herself and Spud reeling through The Midland. The caption read 'Drunk in Charge of a Famous Dog'.

'A very dry martini,' demanded Lily Bear suavely. 'And I think Miss Starkey could do with a large vodka on the rocks.'

As the waiter moved away Sorrel said, 'I'll never dare order a drink in public again.'

'Good,' observed Lily Bear. 'Only I wish I could believe it. Now then, I've not got my spectacles so you'll just have to tell me what the little darling's got to say for himself.'

Sorrel rattled the pages open again in fury. 'According to this, he was just a poor little working-class footballer who was dazzled by a beautiful actress. Beauty, at least, he does grant me. The rest is filth. I'm supposed to have worn him out with my sexual demands – which is a laugh. It gets worse than that.

He says I would never send Spud out of the bedroom. No mention of separate bedrooms of course. He wouldn't want Manchester knowing that. He's even dragged my mother into it . . .' Sorrel ran a finger down the columns then read aloud: ' "My mother-in-law is an officer's widow and Sorrel's antics are a great embarrassment to a lady of her class." '

'How does he get round all the headlines he's made himself?'

'That's the best bit. Listen: "I admit I've been a bit of a lad but ours was an open marriage. Sorrel was free to sleep with who she wanted. Other people have said she was too close to coloured members of the cast. But I'm not prejudiced in that way." Well all I can say is, thank you Libby Schneider!'

'Schneider? I thought you said her name was Taylor.'

'She changed it.'

'Ah.' Lily nodded significantly. 'Jewish.'

'I won't have a word said against them,' retorted Sorrel sturdily.

'Won't you, dear?' Lil's old eyes smiled uncritically. 'I guessed you'd only been telling me half a story. Oh well, never mind, all this sensational nonsense will be round fish and chips on Monday. And here come the drinks. Waiter, would you get somebody to ring The Caprice and order a table for two, in my name, for nine fifteen?'

'Nine fifteen? But of course, madame.'

Sorrel had to make a conscious effort to stop her mouth from falling open. The Caprice was only the smartest theatrical restaurant in town. 'You're mad, Lil,' she said in wonder. 'The Caprice is all seeing and being seen. I feel like crawling away into a hole.'

'Not if I've anything to do with it. Why d'you think I made you have that bath? Why did I spend hours on your hair? You're going to march in there with your head held high and show the world you're still a going proposition. These things are sent to test us. Not to infuriate us, just to see what we're made of. You'd better do as you're told, Sorrel. I'm not in the habit of backing duds. Cheers!'

Sorrel had been thinking of the way the waiter had said 'But of course, madame' with the same internationally assured air as the concierge at the Hotel Sacher. 'Lily, you're not really anti-semitic, are you?'

'I'm against nothing but closed minds. What I always say about Jews is "Let them into your career but not into your heart." It only leads to trouble. I know. I've been there.'

For a moment Sorrel was tempted to blurt out the whole story. But perhaps Lily Bear had secrets that she too wanted to keep, for the far-away look vanished from her eyes and she said quickly, 'Look how the chair-back covers are still held in place by hatpins. I expect we've got Lady Mendl to thank for that too.'

'I'm just not sure about The Caprice, Lil . . .'

'You've no choice in the matter. And, what's more, you're paying. That way you'll appreciate the chance I'm giving you. Porter! The very man, could you send somebody out to get all the Sunday papers except this one.'

Lily Bear's name got them a good table at the restaurant. It was like being inside a padded-silk chocolate box with china hands, for light fittings, holding fans. For a moment The Caprice was only half full but Sorrel knew, once the curtains of West End theatres rang down, that the place would soon be spattered with as many celebrities as featured in the rest of the Sunday papers. The journalists' descriptions of her flight across England were reasonably accurate. She was disappointed that only one of them had dared quote her reference to Kenny and the crack of doom. Lily Bear was described as 'veteran comedienne' and all Sorrel could do about the appalling photographs of herself was sit back and laugh at them.

'I look like my own mother at a funeral. And I wouldn't care but that wicked camera-hog of a Spud has come out marvellously in all of them.'

'Spud's wonderful,' said Lily Bear with pride. 'When I took him down to the Embankment Gardens, to do his duty, he kept giving his paw to all his fans. I felt like John Gielgud's mother. Oh look, there *is* John Gielgud.' Lily smiled graciously and inclined her head. A lot of that went on at The Caprice. Table-hopping too – people would rise and cross and speak. The less famous had to do the walking.

583

Lily Bear was eating partridge, and a grilled Dover sole was putting new life into Sorrel. 'I'll sue,' she vowed, 'I'll sue Kenny, and Libby Taylor too.'

'I shouldn't, dear. You'll take a year off your life and the only people who make real money out of these things are the lawyers.' Lily was gazing critically at Sorrel. 'You're beginning to look human again,' she announced. 'In fact you look wonderful. What we need now is a good agent to push you.'

Lily Bear pulled a partridge bone out of her mouth. 'Are you OK for money, Sorrel? I could easily pay for this dinner.'

'I'm fine. My accountant made me save and I was left some money. Quite a lot; you can have two puddings if you like.'

A few tables away, a man rose to his feet and flashed a beaming smile in their direction. 'Eddie Bolitho,' murmured Lily. 'Not an agent. He's in provincial management, puts on plays.' The man was now moving towards them. 'I'd rate him the last resort rather than the first. Eddie!' She cried out his name as though this chance meeting was the greatest possible pleasure. 'I don't believe you know Sorrel Starkey. She's Queen of the Tabloids this weekend.'

'Never did Di Dors any harm.' The man was in his sixties. He looked like one of those silver-haired male models on advertisements for iron tablets. There was nothing wrong with his clothes but they were not as band-box fresh as the other diners'. And eagle-eyed Sorrel noticed that his cufflinks didn't match. One was gold and one was tin.

'Doing anything?' Bolitho asked Lily Bear.

'Nothing until the spring. I'm going to Stratford again. The roles aren't settled yet but I'm hoping for Juliet's nurse.'

'You've got so grand,' he sighed. 'How would you feel about a nice, short, number-one tour? I'm talking February, March. We've got a little farce that would just suit Miss Starkey and there's a cracking comedy role in it for you.'

'What little farce?' asked Lily almost too pointedly.

'A new one,' he replied evasively. He turned to greet Jessie Matthews who was being ushered to the next table with a woman who might have been her sister. 'Jessie!' he exclaimed in a way that would have got bricks thrown at him in

Manchester. 'I adored your bit of nonsense on television last week. . .'

Whilst this was going on Sorrel was startled to receive a brisk kick on the shin from Lily Bear who was shooting her a warning glance worthy of Gladys Starkey.

Eddie Bolitho now transferred his attentions back to their table. 'A good tour's what you need to let the dust settle.' This was addressed to Sorrel.

'She'd want to see a script,' Lily announced firmly. 'You can send it care of me.'

'Still in Evelyn Gardens?' he asked politely.

'I bought the lease,' Lily smiled. 'Be warned, Eddie, I'm an expensive woman nowadays. We're both expensive women.'

'I'll get a script round to you on Monday. Make sure she lets you see it quickly, Miss Starkey.' With a polite nod he returned to a table of foreign-looking women.

Lily Bear was watching them closely. 'Nobody we know,' she announced. 'Perhaps they're providing his money these days. Still, it proves one thing, Eddie Bolitho's nobody's fool and he obviously sees you as box office. The world's your oyster, Sorrel! I think I'll make an appointment for you to meet my agent next week. Now there's a man who always makes me wish I was twenty years younger. You'll love Hilary. He's class on toast.'

The pudding they settled for was made of hot spun sugar with ice cream inside it. Lily only allowed Sorrel to have one liqueur with her coffee. The bill paid, they rose and made their way to the door. One waiter helped Sorrel into her coat, another was assisting a big blonde woman out of hers.

The woman said, 'I'd better have that brooch off the lapel. I'll keep it with me. They're real aquamarines.'

It was June Gee with Martyn in attendance. He was the only man in the restaurant in a dinner jacket.

'Hello, Sorrel,' gushed June. 'The Caprice, I ask you! Haven't we both got on?'

Sorrel couldn't fail to notice the folded Sunday papers under Martyn's arm. June's eyes followed this glance: 'Oh, *those*,' she said. 'Those will be round fish and chips on Monday – won't they, Miss Bear?'

'My very words! How does she do it?' Lily Bear asked nobody in particular. 'I think our taxi's waiting, Sorrel.'

As they stepped out into Arlington Street Lily said, 'I dislike very few people but I can't stand that woman. I wouldn't care but she seems to be everywhere these days. She'd get where Vaseline wouldn't!'

'I've finished with her.' Sorrel began to climb into the cab.

'Sweetie,' June's voice called down to Sorrel from the top of the restaurant steps, 'I'll be in touch. Old friends are still the best.'

Sorrel did not reply and Lily Bear, who knew how to bring down the curtain on any scene, closed the cab door with an emphatic bang. But Sorrel was no longer convinced that she had seen the last of June Gee.

It wasn't like an agent's office at all. Hilary Bates's premises were not up some scuffed staircase on the Charing Cross Road. He did his deals from a pretty mews cottage at the back of Berkeley Square. The ground floor was the reception area with two white sofas and a frighteningly smart black girl at the switchboard. The flower arrangement on her counter could only have come from Constance Spry and the pictures on the walls were by David Hockney.

This will do me very nicely, thought Sorrel as she thanked God for having nudged her into wearing her new red coat. Just let Hilary Bates like me, she prayed as white doors opened to reveal a small lift. I had too many years of linoleum corridors and glass doors marked *Inquiries*.

There was another Hockney in the office above. It was a drawing of a naked youth on a bed. But Hilary Bates definitely wasn't gay. He was an engaging boy-man in a dark suit and an Old Etonian tie. He looked so scrubbed and innocent that Sorrel could not imagine his knowledge of the theatre earning him so much as the price of a haircut. And his dark hair was very well cut.

'Good morning,' he said with an amused smile.

Good teeth, she noticed, and not capped. The agents whom Sorrel had previously encountered would never have dreamed of getting to their feet. Nor would they have smelled of Trumper's Essence of Limes.

'We have more than one friend in common,' announced young Mr Bates confidently. 'I was on the telephone to Mickey Grimshaw yesterday in LA. My wife is more than half in love with Mick. I get a bit bored with cries of "What a waste!"'

'How is he?'

'Up to the eyes in the pilot episode of his new serial. They keep changing the title. He wanted one of my clients for it but American Equity are being tricky.'

He's smart as paint, thought Sorrel, and curiously sexy. He's one of those fortunate people who manage to make you feel more attractive than you thought you were. But she only wanted to be accepted as a client. Her self-esteem was still at a low ebb.

As coffee was brought in by a stern middle-aged secretary who looked as though she had a job keeping him in order, Hilary Bates proceeded to make Sorrel feel better about herself: 'I'm a great admirer of your work. I first saw you when I was still a schoolboy and I went to stay with my aunt in Perthshire.'

He emphasizes the youthful bit, thought Sorrel. He knows he looks too young so he's turned it into part of his act. Aloud she said, 'A producer once told me that actresses should be on the lookout for bright little boys sitting in the audience. He says we're forever doing auditions for work we'll get ten years hence.' Oh dear, was she talking too much already?

'You were doing *Mrs Warren's Profession*,' he remembered. 'God knows what possessed my aunt to take me to see that. But I knew – even then – that you were going to mature into something important. I'm going to come right out into the open. I'd love to represent you but I'm stuck with a problem of loyalty. I only have a very short list of clients and you're very similar in type to somebody who took the risk and came with me, when I started up on my own.'

Before Sorrel could ask 'Then why the hell drag me across the West End?' he added, 'Lily wanted me to meet you and Mick practically ordered me to represent you. But I just don't

587

know. Oh God! She's brought those squashed-flies biscuits in again. It's a battle of wills. She knows I can't stand them.' Hilary Bates looked thoughtful. 'The trouble is you're a few years younger than my established client and I don't want ructions on my hands.'

'At least it's got me out of the house' was Sorrel's weak response. 'Who's the other client?'

Hilary Bates was sure enough of himself to keep silent and hide behind an open smile.

Who wouldn't be confident? thought Sorrel. Sitting behind a desk that could have belonged to Richard Brinsley Sheridan with his feet on an original Aztec rug. Suddenly she noticed another painting, one of a woman. 'I love that picture,' she said, to break the silence.

Hilary Bates was all eagerness. 'It's Hockney's favourite model, Celia Birtwell. Would you believe that she comes from somewhere called Irlams o'th' Height?'

'Me too!' exclaimed Sorrel. 'Now you mention it, I think I used to see her on the bus for Swinton. She always got off at the milk bar.'

The milk bar and the 57 bus were hardly raising the tone of the proceedings but they seemed to be acting on Hilary Bates as a stimulant. 'That's fascinating. It's almost too much of a coincidence. Perhaps it's meant. And Mickey was very insistent too.

'Oh dear,' he sighed, 'I just don't know. Would you very much mind if I slept on it?'

The look he gave Sorrel suggested he wouldn't mind going to bed for quite another purpose. Strangely enough, she didn't object to this. It was all in the abstract and anyway it made her feel more valuable.

'And Sorrel,' he added, 'watch out for Eddie Bolitho. He's already been on to me about Lil's availability. Some thoughts of getting up a tatty tour for the pair of you together. The last thing you want to do, at this moment, is disappear off into the provinces. What you really need is some prestige exposure. I'll call you tomorrow.'

The next day Lily Bear appeared at Shelagh's carrying a

slightly battered script of a play. The green front cover was blank and the title page, inside, had been carefully cut out.

'One farce from Eddie Bolitho.' She slapped it down on the dining room table. 'Well, Sorrel, it's not Shakespeare but it's not bad of its kind. We could probably do something with it. You can't move outside for Christmas shoppers. Hilary's dead set against my doing this piece but he hasn't seen the letter I've just had from those little sweethearts at the Inland Revenue.'

Hilary Bates himself chose just that moment to telephone. 'Sorrel? First of all I've got to give you Mickey's love. They're going to be spending Christmas in Reno, looking for locations. I've also been thinking about the talk we had yesterday . . .'

Sorrel held her breath and thought: Please don't send me back to Charing Cross Road.

'I'm sorry but I'm afraid somebody else will have to take advantage of this opportunity.'

After suggesting that it would be pleasant to meet again, when Mick was next in England, the theatrical agent added, 'Sorrel, I cannot say this too firmly: Beware of Eddie Bolitho. And please say that to Lil too. I love the old girl to death but she's overfond of the sniff of a quick pound note.'

When Sorrel delivered the message – not sparing Lily any details – the old actress snorted, 'Well of course he's right but that little smarty-boots can be a bit *too* Eton and Oxford at times. He seems to forget that actors are just rogues and vagabonds. Who says we're doing the play anyway? We're only thinking about it.'

Lily was distinctly huffy for the rest of her visit, which did not last long.

Eddie Bolitho's play was still, as it were, on a back burner. The two actresses had neither accepted nor refused his offer. Close examination of the script rang bells in Sorrel's head. It wasn't a new farce at all. Sorrel had appeared in the piece years before, in weekly rep, when it had been entitled *Bed, Breakfast and How's Your Father?*

She could have wished that the plot did not call for the

leading lady to get significantly drunk in the third act. Lily Bear was not over-thrilled at being offered the role of a Blackpool landlady.

'All put your plates out for pudding . . .' Spectacles on the end of nose, Lily was trying out a bit of script for size. She pulled a face and removed her glasses. 'I suppose there's a laugh to be got out of it. Anyway, we have until after Christmas to make up our minds. Somehow I can't see myself doing it.'

The contrary streak in Sorrel seized upon this dubious statement and made her want to do the play more than anything else on earth. But she didn't mention this aloud. If Lily agreed to go on the tour she would be doing Sorrel a favour. And Sorrel Starkey wasn't down to begging. Her sole reason for giving the play serious consideration was the fact that somebody actually *wanted* her.

Lil was right. It could wait. In the meantime Sorrel decided to try to like Christmas 1978. There would be no point in buying spectacular presents for Shelagh and Lily. They wouldn't be offering anything grandiose in return and would only be embarrassed. Instead, Sorrel decided to splash out on a really good Christmas tree. She got up early one morning and crossed from the end of Bedman's Row into Covent Garden. The market wholesalers only sold to shopkeepers but they had been calling out 'Hello' to Sorrel since she was seventeen so she was fairly confident that they would let her buy a tree.

Buy a tree? Sorrel could hardly believe her eyes. The old cast-iron and glass market halls were filled with boutiques and galleries and bookshops. The only remnant of the fruit and vegetable market was a framed engraving of the interior of the Floral Hall marked 'Rare' and priced at twenty-seven pounds.

Sorrel decided to try Soho. Here she was in for another shock. Whoever had allowed the developers to pull down the handsome Old Fire-Iron building? The former residential theatrical club had been replaced by an office block that was exactly how Sorrel imagined Frankfurt.

Whatever would old Bertha, the former warden of The Fire-Iron, have made of all these sex shops and porno-cinemas? As nobody else was averting their eyes Sorrel gazed frankly into one of the window displays and wondered what you were meant to do with a double-headed vibrator.

They still sold Christmas trees in Berwick Market. Sorrel bought a good tall one for four pounds. The trees were propped up against a shop which had once been an Italian grocer's and now boasted a sign on the door which read: *Adults only. Persons passing beyond this point may find material displayed inside which they could consider indecent. Please do not enter if you are easily offended.*

The door swung open and a shabby middle-aged man came out with a mop and bucket. 'Hey, you!' he called out roughly to Sorrel and she thought she detected a Lancashire accent. 'I recognize you from off the telly. Does the 38 bus still go from Manchester to Little Hulton?'

'I think so,' she replied. It was years since Sorrel had been on a bus.

'I still miss the place,' he said, and turning his back on her he began to mop the step. His words sent Sorrel back to Bedman's Row feeling homesick.

'I got one with roots,' she explained to Shelagh. 'It's less cruel than those poor sawn-off things and I thought that Lil could put it in her bit of garden afterwards. Now I'll have to go out again and get some trimmings.'

'Hold your horses.' Shelagh was already searching happily for a bucket for the tree. 'Let's go down into the cellar. There are boxes of decorations down there that can't have been opened for fifty years.' The bucket found, Shelagh slid back a door in the hall panelling, felt inside and switched on a light. 'Watch yourself,' she warned. 'These are the worst stairs in the whole house.'

'Won't the decorations have rotted to bits?' asked Sorrel.

'Not down here. Feel, it's bone dry. My uncle always claimed that these cellars went back to William and Mary. I daren't get anybody to date them or they'd probably try and stop me knocking in nails.' Shelagh was leading the way towards an assortment of dusty cedar-wood chests and enamelled military trunks. One was marked *Loyal Flags & Bunting* in childish, white-painted lettering.

'There's the chap we're looking for.' Shelagh pulled down a small tin trunk. 'Never take one of these into a theatre, Sorrel. It always means a death.' She undid the hasp, pulled back the lid and removed a layer of ancient tissue paper.

'You *made* them!' exclaimed Sorrel in delight as she lifted out an angel with muslin skirts and silver wings.

'Of course we made them. We were still at the vicarage then. There was plenty of breeding but precious little hard cash. Those wings are made of Leete's silver paper. Penny a sheet and it's never gone black.'

'And look at these stars.' Sorrel's delight in small things had never abandoned her. 'I'm almost scared to touch them. Coloured glitter dust and it's stayed stuck for all these years.'

Shelagh pulled the top off a box covered in rainbow-shaded paper. 'I'm afraid these Santas are looking a bit bedraggled. I remember my brother and I sitting sewing them together. Just imagine, he ended up a Brigadier-General.'

'And such neat little stitches. I'll wash them.' Sorrel spoke urgently. 'I can easily make new cotton-wool beards.' She was remembering how Gladys Starkey had never allowed her to use the good scissors nor make anything for Christmas that would cause a mess. 'We'll make it just like it used to be when you were little. It'll be even better because all this tinsel's gone a wonderful shade of gold. What're these?'

'Tin holders for the candles. There should still be some boxes of candles right down at the bottom. I didn't know I remembered that. You do me good, Sorrel.'

The tree set the tone for that whole Christmas. Shelagh baked with goodwill and Lily Bear procured a brace of pheasant from an old admirer in the country. The pheasant were taken down to the cellar to hang and cobweb-covered bottles of port and brandy were brought up. Sorrel even made paper chains for the sitting room because modern decorations didn't seem right with the tree from Christmas past.

No gift, they decided, must cost more than three pounds. This wasn't meanness but a product of the happier side of

Sorrel's imagination. For days her thoughts had mouldered in gloom and now she set out to conjure up the Christmas spirit.

Lily Bear came to stay for the holidays and brought enough clothes for a winter cruise. Shelagh Starkey, who was a regular church-goer, insisted upon the other two actresses accompanying her to church, for the midnight service, on Christmas Eve.

St Mary Magdalene's was at the end of a courtyard, under an archway, off Shepherd Market in Mayfair. It was spectacularly high Anglican; incense, puzzling bells, everybody crossing themselves – Sorrel found it hard to believe that she was in the Church of England at all. In some ways it reminded her of the Catholic church she'd gone to with Judy when they lived at the Old Fire-Iron. But St Patrick's in Soho Square had always seemed grateful for immigrants' ha'pennies whereas St Mary Magdalene's plainly saw itself as God's own branch of Fortnum and Mason. The church wardens even wore morning coats and striped trousers, and a lot of the congregation were in evening dress.

St Mary Magdalene's weren't content with one priest at the altar. They had three. As the priests went through the ritual intricacies of a High Mass, in their cloth of gold vestments, Sorrel wondered what was missing. Humility? She pushed that thought aside and gazed instead at the banks of candles at the shrines around the church. Not one of them was lit. That's what was wrong. Not even the candles on the High Altar.

'*Gloria in Excelsis Deo. . .*'

The words rang round the church from a choir hidden in the organ loft. Within moments, acolytes dripping with Brussels lace were holding lighted wax tapers to the biggest candles. And a cassocked verger and soft-footed sidesmen performed the same duties at all the shrines. A huge brass chandelier came down from the ceiling on a chain and was only raised back when all its candles were ablaze. Throughout all this the choir were trying to outdo angels.

'Out of darkness into light eh?' muttered Lily Bear appreciatively. 'Good as panto in the old days at Drury Lane.

Sorrel, I can't just give you a mean little three-quid present. Let's do that play.'

3

Rehearsals for the play had not been easy. They had taken place in a hired room on Great Newport Street, in London, where Lily Bear turned from a friend into a fiendishly active stranger with a quick eye for the main chance.

'I make no excuse for myself,' Lily had said, after emerging victoriously from a battle over a wig she wanted replacing. 'I'm not a good rehearser, I never have been. We've got two cheapskate weeks to get this thing right and it simply isn't long enough.' All of this had been to Sorrel. Lily had then called across to the producer: 'Either I pull the kipper from up my jumper or it doesn't come on the stage with me.' She had not stayed a star by merely twinkling prettily.

Eddie Bolitho was saving money by directing the play himself. Sorrel had been horrified to discover that the supporting cast seemed to have been recruited from Esther Mooney's waiting room. Two young girls, in particular, were about as experienced as Sorrel had been when Miss Mooney sent her to join the repertory company at Salford Hippodrome.

'Of course he's paying them in brass washers.' Lily Bear loosened her mink coat and adjusted a floppy black velvet artist's hat. 'Oh well, at least we're getting proper salaries and first-class travel.'

It was Sunday and they were on the train for Liverpool where the play was due to open the following night.

'Tickets please.'

Sorrel had not been looking forward to this moment and now it was upon her: 'I'm afraid I was only supplied with a second-class ticket so could I pay the difference?' She opened her wallet quickly and tugged out some notes.

'I can't be hearing aright.' Lily's face, under the Rembrandt hat, was a study in disbelief. 'You're starring. Surely first-class travel was in the contract?'

'No. I'm not very hot on contracts.'

'Hilary did mine. Not, it has to be admitted, with the best of goodwill. Please God he doesn't take it into his head to come up and see this travesty. The man's trying to give you your change, Sorrel. Get a receipt and claim it back off the income tax.'

Laboriously, the ticket collector began to make out a slip and Sorrel wondered whether his was the last indelible pencil left on earth.

'Of course the great days of touring are over.' Lily Bear was wearing her 'remembering' face. 'My dear, if you were in a musical comedy, the company had its own train. Crewe Station on a Sunday was as theatrical as Charing Cross Road. And the Variety people! Once they got into the big money it went straight onto their backs. Everything was for show. The wives were some of the most fantastic sights I've ever seen. I'll never forget Kitty McShane swaying out of the station buffet, at Crewe, in the biggest picture hat on earth – and every solid inch of it covered in ermine tails. It's all very different these days.' She glared pointedly at the yellow and white satin track-suit Sorrel had decided to wear for comfort.

'Take no notice of me,' Lily continued, 'I'll be my usual self once this bloody show has opened. It's got me rattled. Why don't we know the title? Why was it just called "a farce" in the contracts? No dress rehearsals until tomorrow and goodness only knows what the scenery's going to look like!'

After a lot of licking at the lead, the ticket collector had finished his painstaking work with the pencil stub. 'Last seats for lunch,' he announced. 'The restaurant car's two coaches up.'

There was something about the sight of a silver soup tureen being carried down a swaying dining car which always, inexplicably, raised Sorrel's spirits – her vision of heaven included dining cars. She wasn't expecting much of the food itself so she wasn't disappointed. For once, as the view through the window changed from the Midlands to the North, Lily Bear didn't seem to be counting Sorrel's drinks. They were, after all, about to go into battle.

Their heavier items of luggage had gone ahead in the care

of the company manager so they only had light suitcases to carry off the train at Liverpool Lime Street.

'I always think that Liverpool is a wonderfully raffish city.' Lunch had restored Lily Bear's enthusiasm. 'It's almost possible to believe that there are still pirates here. Did you know it was a great centre for the slave trade? Oh my God!'

Lily was looking at a poster for the city's Royal Court Theatre. She only needed spectacles for close reading and now she read aloud: 'Sorrel Starkey in *The Gin and Nookie Scandal* – so that's his title!'

'Gin and Nookie?' gasped Sorrel. 'It's straight out of those awful headlines. He can't be allowed to get away with it.'

'He already has. Those posters will have been up since Friday.'

'And why is my name the only one above the title?' Sorrel could hardly believe what she was seeing. She had never realized that star billing could look so lonely. 'Why is your name at the bottom?'

'That's Hilary's doing. He said that, if I insisted upon doing this play, bottom-top billing would give me all of the fun and none of the responsibility.'

'But I don't want responsibility.'

'Well I'm afraid you've got it.' Sorrel had never heard Lily Bear sound so serious. 'In our business everything comes at a price.'

The Monday morning papers carried brief references to the fact that Sorrel Starkey was attempting a comeback in a stage play. Just when a bit of publicity would have done her no harm, Sorrel was mildly humiliated to discover that her name had slipped in prominence. She now rated about an inch of newsprint towards the middle of the paper.

'You can't expect more in a preliminary announcement.' Lily Bear was standing next to Sorrel, in the wings, hoping for the dress rehearsal to begin. 'But fall on your bum tonight and you'll be back on the front page quicker than you can say *The Gin and Nookie Scandal*. Well, well, well . . . so that's where he got the set from.'

Lily Bear was indicating the faded words *September Tide*

painted on the back of one of the pieces of canvas scenery. 'Poor old Gertie Lawrence made her return to London in *September Tide* after the war. This little lot must have been mouldering in storage ever since. I bet it's hired. He'll just have got somebody to turn round with a paint pot to change a Cornish cottage into a Blackpool boarding house.

'When in hell's name are we going to begin?' She asked this of a passing assistant stage manager.

'Mr Bolitho's still scouring Scotland Road for a three-piece suite and the dinner gong.'

'I did warn you, Sorrel.' News of the producer's dubious whereabouts seemed to have injected Lily Bear with guilt. 'I never said he was Binkie Beaumont.'

This was a reference to the most elegant theatrical manager in London. His less successful provincial counterpart now hove into view bearing a plaster plaque of Anne Hathaway's cottage. He was followed by two stagehands carrying a bright orange cut-moquette sofa. 'Isn't it wonderfully common?' enthused Eddie Bolitho. For the purpose of rehearsal he was dressed as 'one of the lads' in cheap jeans and an artificial leather flying jacket.

'I wouldn't care,' murmured Lily Bear reproachfully to Sorrel, 'but this is a Howard and Wyndham theatre. They're used to the best and we've landed them with this.'

Now it was Sorrel's turn to feel guilty. Lily was only here out of loyalty. And the producer seemed more interested in positioning that hackneyed turquoise and yellow portrait of a Chinese lady than he was in starting the all-important dress rehearsal.

'I don't care how many years he's been in the business. He's still a bloody amateur.' Lily Bear owned no greater insult.

Theatrical superstition has it that a bad dress rehearsal leads to a good first night. On the strength of that afternoon's run-through of *The Gin and Nookie Scandal*, the sparse audience which braved the February snow, and made its way into the theatre at seven o'clock, should have been treated to a night to remember. And, in its own way, it was.

Sorrel had been allotted the number-one dressing room,

nearest the stage. It was the first time in her life that she had ever been given this honour and she couldn't help feeling she was there under false pretences. Half the biggest stars in England must have looked into the mirror, and the reflection she saw – staring back at herself – was that of a soap actress on the skids. She put a bit more white greasepaint in the corners of her eye makeup and took a reinforcement gulp of vodka from the silver hip flask. It was the first time Sorrel had ever done this in a dressing room in a theatre, but needs must when the devil drives. And the devil wasn't just driving this production, he seemed to have sent his personal representative to present and produce *The Gin and Nookie Scandal*. At the end of the dress rehearsal Eddie Bolitho had said: 'Well I can't pretend it's really ready. Let's just hope they won't notice.'

The glare Lily Bear handed him brought the word 'sacrilege' to mind. The theatre was Lily's only real religion.

The curtain had already gone up. Sorrel's first entrance did not come until just before the end of Act One. Over the Tannoy, on the dressing room wall, she could hear the action onstage and uncomfortable February coughing from the audience. When Lily Bear failed to get an expected laugh Sorrel managed to make it feel her own fault. How could she have brought old Lil down to this? And what would the actress say if she knew about the silver hip flask? The theatre wasn't like television with its lunchtime boozing opportunities. Drinking before the final curtain came down was one of the biggest sins in Lily Bear's book. In the past Sorrel had been equally critical of people who did it.

She forced herself to look in the morror again and what she saw, this time, was self-hatred and fear. Not stage fright – a rush of that would have been understandable and almost welcome. She could have used it to hype herself up for the coming performance. No, this was a feeling of impending doom. It was nothing new. These days she woke up with it every morning. Tonight, it had followed her into a theatre and the usual antidote of vodka was failing to drive it away.

The Tannoy crackled and, registering that Lily must be making her exit, Sorrel got up and went across to the sink to clean her teeth. Before she'd even had time to sit down and renew her lipstick Lily was knocking at the dressing room door.

'Well they've not much sense of humour, dear, and I think I smell nurses!' This was her way of saying that the audience was papered with complimentary tickets. 'I managed to drag one big laugh out of them but Esther Mooney's protégée went and trod on it. I was under the illusion I was popular in this town. Mind you, when I compare this so-called farce with some of the beautiful shows I've done in this very theatre. . .'

'I'm sorry, Lil. It's my fault.'

'Why? Don't tell me you're the income tax collector in disguise? I got myself into this and I knew precisely what I was doing. You need to save your reputation. I need cash. Don't use me as an excuse for moping. Just get out there and try to wring some laughs from them.'

The loudest laugh of the evening now reached them over the loudspeaker. It had followed a horrendous sound of splintering wood.

'She's managed to smash the banisters!' Lily stubbed out her cigarette in rage. 'I'm not kidding, that girl can't find her way from one side of the stage to the other. It's enough to drive a proper actress to drink.' Her voice suddenly became deadly serious. 'Watch yourself, Sorrel. Keep the whites of your eyes clear. You're going to need your wits about you tonight.'

As Sorrel made her first entrance she received a thin but gratifying round of applause. She could have done without the audible murmurs of 'Lettie Bly' from the audience. Hastily, she reminded herself that it was Lettie who had handed her star billing. Lily was right, this carried responsibility with it and Sorrel brought everything she knew to the task of convincing the audience that they wanted to be entertained.

Farce is a deceptive form of theatre. It looks very slap-happy but relies on split-second timing. The actress Lily Bear had complained about was a dizzy young girl called Imogen Lake, all bouncing cleavage and jutting bottom. In rehearsal she had given a performance that was just about adequate.

Faced with an audience, her inexperience was as much on view as her bust. Sorrel only had to begin to get a laugh for Imogen to kill it stone dead by barging in with the next line.

Farce also relies on the actors behaving as though the extraordinary circumstances which surround them are perfectly natural. That's what makes it funny. Miss Lake had so little understanding of this technique that Sorrel would not have been surprised to find the girl winking at the audience. This inept performance threw everything off balance and the first act failed to register at all.

Sorrel came off the stage and went straight to Lily's dressing room. The old actress was taking a rest on the sofa with her feet up. 'Weekly rep in Torquay, dear, that's what she'd done. And that's before you even ask. Her mother was once an assistant to The Great Watson, the illusionist. That's why she smiles so much. It's in the blood.'

'I would like to saw her in half.' Sorrel slammed off into her own dressing room, took an angry slug of vodka, and changed for the second act.

This went better. Most of her scenes were with Lily Bear and the pair of them managed to make bricks without straw. They didn't add or subtract anything from the script, they merely used talent and experience to give the play a gloss it didn't deserve.

Sorrel had another sly drink to celebrate this. One act to go – and this contained her most testing scene. The character she played had to get rip-roaring drunk whilst attempting to make a parcel of a large rocking horse. It involved Sorrel climbing under and over the wooden toy and even demanded a very 'Yoiks-tally-ho!' scene in the saddle, complete with a gin bottle in her hand. By a supreme effort of will, Sorrel had managed to push aside thoughts that the public might confuse these antics with her own recently reported behaviour. The result was five comic minutes that should have been as good as anything she had ever done on stage.

The scene started well. The audience was loving it. Then, suddenly, every laugh seemed to be followed by a mysterious smaller one. As the scene progressed, the audience seemed to be getting irritated. Sorrel felt she was losing them and she

601

couldn't understand why. That was when she noticed something.

Down by the footlights, in a red dress which left nothing to the imagination, little Miss Imogen Lake (who should have been standing stock-still) had chosen to imitate Sorrel's every move. No wonder the audience were confused. They didn't know which way to look!

Sorrel kept control of her temper – just – but she never managed to regain that magnetic hold she'd had on the audience. Instead of rising to a comic crescendo, the play limped to a close. The final curtain fell to polite applause but no more.

As it was raised again, to reveal the cast lined up and bowing, somebody shouted from the stalls: 'We expected to see Lettie Bly.'

This hit Sorrel like a bucket of cold water. They had been a dull little audience but in no way abusive. Somebody else, from the same section of the theatre, now took up the cry: 'Yes! We wanted Lettie.'

'Well you can fuck off home because she's not here!' Sorrel's temper had finally snapped. Down came the curtain.

Unbelievably, it went straight back up again. 'That's torn it,' breathed Lily – out of the corner of her mouth – as she swept a polished smile across the stalls and up to the two tiers above. For a small audience they were managing to make a remarkable uproar and, for the first time in her career, Sorrel heard real booing. The curtain descended again and this time it stayed down.

Lily Bear looked at Sorrel with undisguised pity. 'Oh my dear.' She laid a hand on Sorrel's arm as though there had been a death. 'You made the mistake of answering them back. You used the one word guaranteed to alienate your audience. And they never, ever forgive it. I can safely promise you one thing. Your name will be all over the front pages again tomorrow morning.'

If Sorrel broke one theatrical rule that night, Eddie Bolitho broke another. Minutes after the curtain fell he barged into her dressing room without knocking. Bolitho couldn't have chosen a worse moment. Sorrel was gazing disconsolately at the empty hip flask.

'Are you totally mad?' he shouted at her.

'Yes, and bad too *and* dangerous to know.' Sorrel wasn't joking. The full enormity of what she had done on the stage had finally dawned upon her.

'I've never seen an audience so inflamed,' ranted Eddie Bolitho. 'A woman near me actually pulled a fire extinguisher off the wall.'

'You can't blame me for that. She must have been looking for an excuse to do it. She was probably sizing it up all night.'

'I *can* blame you. She wanted to throw it at the stage. And I'm being blamed for bringing you into this theatre.'

Sorrel, feeling curiously detached, noticed that the collar of his shirt was beginning to fray. He was already second rate and she'd managed to turn him into something worse. For a moment she actually felt sorry for Eddie Bolitho.

Without invitation he sat down. 'The front-of-house manager's already sent for a doctor.'

'Don't tell me there were casualties?'

'He's the injured party. He's in the foyer besieged by furious patrons. The doctor's going to examine you.'

'Is he?' Anyone who knew Sorrel better would have been warned by her tones. 'All I can say is I hope they've sent for a big one. Nobody's going to get me to take my clothes off against my will.'

'He's simply going to ascertain whether you are drunk.'

'But you promised them a drunk, Eddie. You even put it on the posters.'

'I would advise you not to leave this theatre.' Eddie was on his feet and heading for the door.

Sorrel barred his way. 'I'm not sure I'm going to let you leave this dressing room. Not until I've told you what I think of you. You advertise me like a gin bottle then leave me to answer for the consequences. Do you know why they expected to see Lettie Bly? Because you put her name in bigger letters than mine, outside the theatre.'

'I mistook you for a classy attraction.' For all his bold words Eddie looked scared.

'Did you? I recognized you as cheap the moment I clapped eyes on you.'

'Lily Bear should have warned me.' Bolitho looked as though he regretted these words the moment they were out of his mouth. And he did right, for Sorrel grabbed for her hairbrush and used it to whang him one.

'You leave Lily out of this,' she stormed; and then she hit him again. Somebody else seemed to be doing it, not herself. It was like the night when she had found herself hurling anti-semitic remarks at Barney. Something had taken over.

Seeing her hesitate in thought, Bolitho snatched the opportunity to get the door open. 'Violence will be reported to the Provincial Theatre Council too,' he shouted, over his shoulder, as he retreated down the echoing corridor.

Sorrel half expected Lily Bear to come in from next door to ask about the noise but she didn't. This made her feel as though she'd been sent half-way to Coventry. It wasn't a comfortable feeling. There was a bottle of champagne behind the dressing table frill – Sorrel had thought there might be visitors from *Angel Dwellings* and had planned to give them a proper first-night drink. She had intended to be comically wry about the play but she had intended to do it in style.

Nobody came. It was symptomatic of Sorrel's situation that the bottle was hidden. Other people would simply have had it waiting, with glasses, on the dressing table. With sudden decision she got it out anyway, ripped off the wires and began to thumb up the cork. It popped and she poured. There is something peculiarly accusing about champagne drunk in wanton loneliness. The bottle, with its gold foil and pretty red paper seal, seemed to be saying to her: 'I'm designed for parties but you couldn't wait. You don't want me but you've got to have me.'

If that doctor's expecting a drunk, thought Sorrel grimly, I'll do my best to give him one. She had only stopped drinking in Vienna because it got in the way of her love for Barney. How near was Southport to Liverpool? Ten miles, fifteen? Sorrel had another drink to take away the pain.

The doctor arrived. He was shown in by a worried theatre manager who quickly disappeared.

Sorrel went straight into battle with 'Blood or urine? You can have either.'

He took the wind out of her sails by being kind: 'Why don't you just sit down and let's talk?' He was a youngish but fatherly man with sympathetic eyes. He reminded Sorrel of Colonel Prothero who had brought the news of her father's death.

'May I sit down, too?' he asked.

'Would you like a drink?'

He shook his head. 'I'm driving.' There was a pause whilst he looked at her uncritically, then he asked, 'Would you say that you were fit to drive?'

'I don't know how. I never learned.'

Another silence. Why didn't he accuse her of something or get high and mighty? She could cope with that. 'I never learned a lot of things.' Sorrel was surprised to hear this come out of herself but it was no less than the truth. Why didn't he get on with it? 'Please feel free to draw a chalk line on the dressing room floor if that's what you usually do.'

'I'd rather you just answered a few questions. How much did you have to drink before and during the show?'

'That much!' Sorrel picked up and slammed down the silver hip flask. 'Vodka. It takes over a quarter and under half a bottle.' How well she knew this.

'Would you say you were drunk?'

Sorrel never told less than the truth and anyway she had decided that she liked the man. 'Not drunk but not sober. I'm never quite sober. If I let myself get too near the surface I hurt.'

The doctor seemed to understand this statement. 'You need help, Sorrel. And it would make my task easier if I took you up on that offer of a blood sample. OK? You have the right to call another doctor of your own choice. I'm sorry to have to tell you that the manager sees this as a serious business. The Provincial Theatre Council will be convening to discuss your case within seventy-two hours. Would you roll up your sleeve? A blood sample should soon tell us the whole story.'

The whole story? Sorrel didn't know whether to laugh or

605

cry. Would a blood sample tell the doctor about a loveless childhood and Barney and the years with Kenny Shorrocks and the fights with Mamie Hamilton-Gerrard?

'If that blood can speak – ' she watched as he drew it from her arm – 'it will simply tell you that I only ever wanted to belong.'

The doctor removed the hypodermic. 'You've got yourself into a pretty pickle, haven't you?'

'Yes, but I'll get myself out of it. Everything's a mess but I'll make it work again.' Sorrel believed that. She had to. Still clinging onto Hope she reminded herself that she was born under the sign of Cancer the Crab. The odds might seem against her but crabs are very tenacious. And suddenly she knew something else. In her heart of hearts she hadn't even let go of Barney Shapiro.

Quickly, she refilled her glass with champagne and raised it in a toast: 'I give you the future,' she said.

'Not with that in your hand.' The concern in the doctor's eyes was genuine and he suddenly sounded much more Northern as he added: 'There'll be no future for you till you get shut of the bottle.'

4

'Operator, when this call's over would you please ring me back and advise duration and charge?' Sorrel did not want to bump up Shelagh Starkey's telephone bill. The long American ringing tones ceased as somebody picked up the receiver at the other end. 'Mick? Have you been reading the English papers?'

'Yes.' Even that much sounded frosty.

'Well, they exaggerated. I got a bit pissed and there was this meeting and now I'm not allowed to work in any provincial theatre for twelve months. I can work in the West End,' she added. It came out too brightly.

'You are your own worst enemy.' He sounded more chromium-plated American than usual and very far away. 'Do you think that anybody in their right mind is going to think of employing you? I wouldn't.'

'Well it just so happens, Mr Clever, that I've been offered employment.'

'Where? In a sideshow in Blackpool?'

It was a bit too near the truth for comfort. 'No.'

'Where?'

Sorrel hesitated. 'A friend of Ray Fossett's has arranged a little tour for me.'

'When you can't work in theatres?'

'There's nothing to stop me working in gay night clubs. They're springing up everywhere. Diana Dors does it.'

'Diana Dors has got something to offer. She can sing and dance. When Lola Montez fell on bad times she went round exhibiting her diamonds. What are you proposing to show them – your bruises? Or shall you just fall over?'

Sorrel was getting annoyed. 'I'm going to do a little monologue to music and then I'll take part in question and answer sessions. It's not actually a monologue, it rhymes. It's called "I'm the Girl Who Just Can't Refuse".'

'You're as bad as that man Bolitho. You're selling them your own tragedy. You don't need gay night clubs. What you need is Alcoholics Anonymous.'

Mickey was still quacking into thin air as Sorrel replaced the receiver. Too many people had tried to offer the same solution. Alcoholics Anonymous, she knew, preached total abstinence. Sorrel could not see why, when she was feeling most lame, her friends expected her to walk without a crutch.

She now became preoccupied with preparations for her cabaret tour. At least it wasn't booked by an agent up one of those dreaded staircases. Lawrie and Andy were two boys from Glasgow whose office was in the maisonette flat they shared in Earl's Court; their agency was called Annie Lawrie's. For the most part they booked drag acts and male strippers. The two partners were more stage-struck than truly theatrical but they went to great lengths to get Sorrel's act together.

The look of things seemed to be enormously important to them and Sorrel soon found herself being draped in solid silver sequining by a man who had once worked for Shirley Bassey's dressmaker. Glasgow-Andy, a tattoo artist on the side, had designed the dress. Lawrie, who was both agent and drag performer, got together some musicians who had once worked for Dorothy Squires and they recorded Sorrel's backing tape. These highly professional musicians were not at all impressed by Sorrel's rhyming monologue. In the end the pianist persuaded her to substitute an old cabaret number: 'It's Illegal, It's Immoral and It Makes You Fat'. What's more, they didn't just record the accompaniment, they talked her into putting her whole singing performance onto a tape cassette.

'Some of the clubs you'll be working in will have very naff sound systems,' explained the pianist. 'At least the DJs will know how to drop in a tape. You'll find you're safer just opening and shutting your mouth and miming to it.'

By the time those boys had finished with her tape Sorrel sounded like a cross between Marlene Dietrich and Eartha Kitt. But they lavished casual affection upon her and for the first time in months she was actually enjoying herself. Three different hairstyles were tried before the boys were satisfied. When she needed silver shoes somebody rushed to Oxford Street; she was forever refusing offers of the loan of rhinestone stage jewellery. Lettie Bly, the great outsider, had always been something of a gay icon. Sorrel Starkey was reaping the benefits.

When the tour opened, at a club in Birmingham, a whole gang of lively new acquaintances followed Sorrel up the motorway for the fun of a night out. Officially, she was accompanied by a road manager cum driver named Niall Peters. A former free-style wrestler with peroxided hair, Niall was built like a colossus and sounded like Kathleen Harrison from *Mrs Thursday*. His devotion to Lettie Bly came second only to his passion for Grace Jones.

As Niall put his hefty knee into Sorrel's back and hooked her into the corselette, which went under the sequins, he said, 'The place is packed. I doubt whether Judy Garland would have rated a bigger turn-out.'

Sorrel's stomach lurched under the whalebone. 'This thing's so tight I'm scared I'll faint in it.'

'Don't for God's sake do that, darling. Half those Black Country queens are only here to see whether you pass out.' He must have noticed the alarm in her eyes because he added, 'You've nothing to worry about, Sorrel. They're all on your side. They came because they love you.'

The tape began with a fanfare of trumpets – pinched from a record of the band of the Grenadier Guards – and then mixed into the *Angel Dwellings* theme. As Sorrel, all red hair and silver sequins, walked quietly into the spotlight, the place erupted into the sort of reception she had dreamed about as a child when she'd stood in front of the bedroom mirror and said to her own reflection: 'Ladies and Gentlemen, for my next song I would like to sing . . .'

They were still yelling and shouting as she went into her opening number and she was glad that her singing was pre-recorded because she would have had difficulty in concealing the emotion she was feeling. It wouldn't have gone with 'It's Illegal, It's Immoral and It Makes You Fat'. There was as much applause again at the end of the number. As Sorrel turned the switch on her hand microphone she could see that men were actually standing up on tables, at the back, to get a better view of her.

'If I fall over,' she ad-libbed into the microphone, 'it's the corset not the booze.'

They were hers. Somebody rushed on with an opened champagne bottle and a glass. From the other side, as prearranged, another boy darted out with a high stool. Sorrel sat down with a happy smile which was offering grateful love right back to her audience.

'Now it's your turn,' she announced. 'Ask me anything, anything you like.'

The first questioner was already planted at the front but there was really no need for him. *Angel Dwellings* was their passion, Lettie Bly their friend. Sorrel simply sat there and behaved as though she was talking to Mickey. He might disapprove of this venture but even he couldn't have denied that she'd got Lettie's boys eating out of the palm of her hand. It went on for twenty-five minutes. Another burst of 'Tenement Symphony' was Sorrel's cue to sweep out of the spotlight and into the part of the evening she was dreading.

Niall Peters had the pictures ready. Glossy photographs and a shaming saucer full of loose change. Over the loudspeakers the disc jockey announced: 'The legendary Sorrel Starkey has consented to sign photographs at seventy-five pence a throw. It's handbag time, boys, and the right change would be appreciated.'

Handbag time? Sorrel had never seen so many moustaches in her life! And chequered shirtsleeves, rolled up to reveal beefy muscles. Times had changed but the eyes were the same over-aware eyes Sorrel remembered from Cornucopia Mews. Even as their hands doled out cash – in exchange for a moment of her time – those eyes were flickering beyond her in search of the next sexual conquest. Sorrel consoled herself that it was no worse than being at a theatrical party where all eyes lusted towards the powerful. And anyway, she cleared a hundred and seventy-three pounds and twenty-five pence on glossy ten-by-eight reproductions.

She signed them all 'Love from Sorrel Starkey' and every time she wrote it she meant it.

The whole of that tour was punctuated by hi-energy music. That and the old Abba hit 'Dancing Queen'. Most of her dates were in discotheques. The questions from the audience were almost boringly similar. Only in one area did they differ from the stock questions she had been parrying, with stock answers, for years. That area was Kenny Shorrocks. In his time as a footballer Kenny had been much photographed, half naked, draped in Page Three Girls. Sorrel was surprised to find that gay men of over thirty still regarded him as a dream-figure of potent sexual nostalgia.

The curiosity always started coyly, but ended in the same bold question: 'Sorrel, how well was Kenny hung?'

'Well, boys, that's for me to know and you to wonder.' She would nod to the disc jockey who would immediately punch up her closing music. It made for a good exit.

The press left Sorrel alone. For all the interest they took in her tour of gay venues she might just as well have been appearing on the sub-continent. She was in a world of its own and it was suiting her very nicely. The only exception was a Sunday paper which tried to make something of the fact that Sorrel Starkey was appearing in establishments 'where sex-drugs are readily available'. After years of the Nun's Prayer Sorrel was way beyond getting het up about poppers. The thing she found puzzling about the discos was the ever-present smattering of men in stylized black leather. Some of them even went as far as Nazi forage caps and had sinister sets of handcuffs attached to their belts.

'S and M,' explained Niall Peters. 'Half of them are just dress-ups but the harder cases are really into pain.'

Niall knew how to keep his mouth shut and when Sorrel told him about Kenny's similar tastes his sole reaction was 'What a wasted opportunity! I don't mean the sex part – but a real slave can come in very handy. You could have put him to work doing anything for you and he'd have been thrilled to bits. Orders, dear, they love obeying orders.'

Another song which haunted Sorrel's foray across England was the old Connie Francis recording of 'Where the Boys Are'. And wherever the boys were, Sorrel went. She soon learned that there was a whole discreet network of gay hotels and guest houses at all points of the compass; and she was served scrambled eggs for breakfast in a dozen different fancy ways. She even had them accompanied by a radish, carved into the shape of a water lily. She was 'Mother' and her boys were out to please her.

On one point, Sorrel had remained adamant; she had refused to appear in Manchester. But Niall kept telling her: 'You don't know what you're missing. There's a whole huge scene there. It's England's San Francisco. You can have had no idea of what was going on behind closed doors.'

Sorrel had become a prime attraction in a specialized market, and Manchester venues were falling over one another to secure her services. The biggest offer of all finally won them.

Sorrel had never noticed the dull front door marked *Heroes*, on Ridgefield, fifty yards from the Salmon sisters' shop in King Street. When she thought hard about it she remembered having to skirt dustbins in the daytime. At night, the door opened into a high-tech reception area which led down into one of the best discos Sorrel had ever worked in. With its black paintwork and silver industrial rigging, the boys had put mauve satin neckties a long way behind them. Sorrel walked down the stairs to find them dancing frenziedly – under a revolving lighting system – in outfits that were either butch government-surplus or well-washed reinterpretations of clothes for the building site. Ray Fossett was the exception. He was swanning around in a Courtelle safari suit which he had managed to make look halfway to drag. Sorrel might privately consider that he had defected to Kenny's side but Ray was behaving as though he had personally invented her. At the far end of the club, men in black leather, beer cans in hand, lingered morosely in a white vaulted cellar-bar under the very pavements of Deansgate. Sorrel suddenly realized that she could tunnel straight across to The Kardomah. Only nowadays The Kardomah was just the basement of an office block.

The boys of Manchester welcomed her back like exiled royalty. The show she gave that night had a polish and a sheen which was way beyond anything she had known how to offer in Birmingham. When the inevitable question came, 'How was Kenny hung?' Sorrel decided to give them an answer to remember: 'Ever seen a little electric light switch? Then you've seen Kenny Shorrocks!'

It was at this moment that she noticed two men who were writing down everything she was saying. They didn't look like reporters and they didn't look like Heroes customers. That night she cleared over three hundred pounds on signed photographs.

The letter arrived, by hand, the next morning. As Sorrel was staying at a private hotel in the suburb of Whalley Range she was astonished that the solicitor's messenger had managed to find her.

Dear Miss Starkey,
We are writing to you on behalf of our client Mr Kenneth Shorrocks. This letter is to inform you that our client is no longer prepared to allow you to use his name for your own financial gain. On the strength of your performance at Heroes Club last night we have advised him that he could confidently proceed against you in an action for slander.

If these performances do not cease forthwith Mr Shorrocks will seek damages with all the weight the law allows.

'And then they're mine sincerely. Can he? Can he do me for slander? I've only told the truth. I've a good mind to make him get it out in court!'

The boys produced a lawyer. 'It's really only an informal communication,' he judged. 'And not a very good one of its kind. If any more questions about Kenny come up from the audience I would advise you to dodge them.'

Sorrel tried this. She even tried reading the lawyer's letter to her audience. It didn't work. The Sorrel they loved was the girl who was prepared to tell everything. Gay audiences are notoriously fickle and the actress's novelty value began to diminish. The tour limped to a close, in a half-deserted ballroom in New Brighton. This left Sorrel with a sequined frock that was beginning to come unravelled and two thousand unsold photographs of herself.

'But I had a ball,' she told Shelagh Starkey back in London. 'And my hair was never so well done in all its life!'

Sorrel had meant to bring back a present for Shelagh, from her travels, but nothing suitable had caught her eye in the provinces. Instead, she decided to go down to Portobello Road and see what she could find in the antique market. It was still too cold to study the clutter on the outdoor stalls so Sorrel wandered into one of the covered arcades where more expensive antiques were laid out, on trestle tables, in makeshift hardboard booths.

Sitting behind one of the tables, minding a vast collection of pot dogs, was a woman Sorrel thought she recognized. She couldn't put a name to the face. She didn't want to stare and, anyway, her attention had been caught by a Victorian Staffordshire version of Spud.

'How much?' she asked.

'Forty-five. It's not one of those new ones, from the Isle of Man, cast in the old moulds. It's genuine. I know the house it came from.'

As the woman spoke, Sorrel realized where they'd met before. It had been at a film and television awards ceremony about ten years earlier. The woman had once been one of J. Arthur Rank's film stars and here she was flogging pot dogs and giving every sign of thoroughly enjoying herself.

'I'm sorry.' Sorrel smiled guiltily. 'I didn't recognize you at first.'

'How are the mighty fallen, eh? It's all a bit different from going up to get an award at The Dorchester. I got it for the only television I ever did. Actress of the Year and then sweet nothing ever since.'

Try as she might, Sorrel couldn't remember the woman's name. Patricia Roc? No, it wasn't her. 'Do you get recognized a lot down here?'

'I pass unnoticed.' The former film star spoke with serene satisfaction.

'Would I?' asked Sorrel urgently. A plan, whole and complete, had fallen into place in her mind. 'I'll take this dog. Would I pass unnoticed?'

'There are all sorts down here.' The woman began to wrap

the ornament in newspaper. 'The only thing people are interested in is a bargain. You've got one with this because I need to take the rent by lunchtime.'

Sorrel had got more than a bargain – as she walked out of the arcade she began to study Portobello Road with new interest. The whole sloping street was full of life: vegetable barrows mixed up with junk stalls and people hurrying out of cafes, slopping tea onto the paving stones and calling out to friends.

It was a purposeful place and Sorrel Starkey needed a purpose. Now she'd found this energy on the Portobello air she wanted more of it. Inside some of the closed shops there was shadowy mystery; she craved that as well. There was too little mystery in Sorrel's life. She had explored everything she had ever wanted to know about – things like love and success and being posh – right down to the bare bones. Portobello was like coming across the attics in the Nun's Prayer or opening the tin trunk in Shelagh Starkey's cellar. It was things she didn't know about. There was hidden magic here.

The sign on the window of one of the shops, converted into a rabbit warren of an antique arcade, read *Stalls to Let – Apply Miss Newton at the Military Uniform Stall, Inside.*

'This is a bloody big van.' Niall Peters had his meaty hands on the driving wheel of the hired vehicle.

'Bellaire was a bloody big house,' replied Sorrel. They were heading up the Finchley Road towards the motorway for the North. 'I wish Spud had a safety belt.' The dog was sitting bolt upright, on the bench-seat, between them. Suddenly he let out a loud bark. He must have caught a whiff of Indian restaurant. Spud had led a haphazard life and takeaways were among his chief delights.

'Not till we get to Manchester.' Sorrel exchanged a hug for an affectionate lick.

'Are you really going to strip Kenny Shorrocks bare?'

'He can keep the big furniture but I'm taking everything else. There's enough thirties stuff to sink a small ocean-going liner. There's everything from dinner services to gilt and ivory crinoline ladies. I was never one for doing things by halves.'

Niall Peters looked pained. 'I still can't see you selling your past – behind a stall – in the Portobello Road.'

'It won't be me,' Sorrel pointed out reasonably, 'I'll just be a woman in a woolly bob-hat. The stall's rented, this van's eating up petrol, the last thing I need is a negative attitude.'

Sorrel broke into a quick chorus of 'I'm Gonna Accentuate the Positive' and they whiled away the journey to Manchester by singing selections from American musicals. For a big man Niall could do a remarkable imitation of Liza Minnelli. The sight of Lancashire turned Sorrel into Gracie Fields. The sun was shining as they reached the outskirts of Manchester and she even attempted George Formby.

The van turned into Nunnery Street. 'Trust me to have sung myself hoarse just when I might have to shout.' Sorrel stopped laughing and primed herself to meet her husband. Surprise was a vital element in this exercise. She had given him no warning of her impending arrival.

'Where do I park?' asked Niall.

'Outside that tatty betting shop.' Even as she was saying this Kenny emerged through the bookmaker's doors, in shirtsleeves, clutching a wad of five-pound notes.

Sorrel wound down the window. 'You're going to get mugged!' she called out. Opening the door she jumped down to the ground with Spud leaping ahead of her.

'Hi, Spud.' Kenny stuffed the notes in his back pocket and attempted to stroke the dog. Spud backed away from him.

'That's a bit hurtful.' The eyes Kenny turned on Sorrel were full of that familiar, little-boy, reproach. 'You've even managed to turn my own dog against me.'

'*Your* dog? After what you said about him in the newspapers it's a miracle he doesn't savage you.' Sorrel was well used to Kenny's diversionary tactics. Her arrival had thrown him – she could tell that by the way he was rubbing his chin to see whether he'd shaved properly. 'I've come for my things.'

'What things?'

'Things I paid for. I've come to take them away.'

'You and whose army?' asked Kenny. Niall Peters now appeared round the front of the van and Kenny sneered. 'Oh I see, it's strong-arm stuff, is it?'

'Aren't straight men beautiful when they're roused?' asked Niall. More than ever, he sounded like Kathleen Harrison.

'Not another one!' snorted Kenny. 'I don't know where you manage to find them.'

'She found me in the wrestling ring, dear. And I was in the winning corner. Want your face putting in?'

'Look, Sorrel,' gulped Kenny. 'We're civilized people . . .'

'No we're not and we never have been; more's the pity. I earned all that stuff upstairs by presenting prizes in stinking bingo halls and opening fridge-freezer shops. And you put me there. As much of my money went into this pub as yours, but you're welcome to it. All I want is the stuff I used to collect and the Victorian junk I rescued from the far attics.'

'I don't know about that.' Kenny attempted to smile at passers-by who were beginning to stare. He only succeeded in looking shifty. 'I'd have to think about it.'

'You've got thirty seconds, starting now. Either give me what I want or I'll land you with the juiciest divorce Manchester's ever known. I could take you to the cleaners, Kenny. I could cop for half of everything. But I don't think you're capable of starting again. And I am.' Sorrel thought of throwing in a dramatic reference to her own ability to scrub floors if necessary and then thought better of it. Instead she said to Niall Peters, 'My address book's on the dashboard. Would you get it for me? I want to look up Libby Taylor's number.'

'Don't bother,' interjected Kenny hastily. 'We needn't drag the press into this.'

'Why not? Aren't they meant to be big mates of yours? You even proposed to me in the tabloids. It was their wedding, not ours. I do want a divorce, Kenny, but all I'm asking for is what I can carry away today.'

'It's a bloody big van.' Kenny spoke ruefully.

'It was a bloody expensive experience!'

Kenny's eyes filled with easy tears. 'Given even half a chance I would have been your slave, Sorrel.'

'Told you so.' This came from Niall Peters in a pleased voice.

Kenny didn't seem to hear it. 'You were my great lady. I'd

have done anything for you. Anything at all. You'd only have to have said the word.'

Sorrel was suddenly struck by a wicked idea. If Niall was right, and slaves enjoyed being ordered around, she could put Kenny to immediate use. 'Come on, let's go in. I've got a box of red stickers in my pocket. I'm going to slap them on everything that's mine. And you, Kenny Shorrocks, are going to pack everything up so that it gets back to London without breaking. And that's an order. Understood?'

The look of drooling devotion she got in return gave Sorrel the shudders and she did not feel very proud of herself. Pausing only to have one quick vodka – and even then affixing red stickers to the framed play-bills in the public bar – Sorrel began to plunder the Nun's Prayer. If the gummed paper circles made the first floor look as though it had been attacked by measles, they turned the attic into a surrealist version of an epidemic.

Ray Fossett, who hadn't been given the big hello he expected, panted up the stairs behind her and began criticizing in aggrieved tones: 'If you don't mind my saying, you're taking all the character out of the place.'

'Watch yourself, Fossett!' Sorrel was in no mood for weak limbs. 'Just watch yourself or I might start grabbing frocks back as well.'

Her own resolution and strength of purpose were surprising her. As she gazed out of the attic window resolution misted into nothingness. The spring sunlight was shining on the towers of the Midland Hotel. What did *things* matter compared with lost love? She knew that if she wept she'd be lost; besides, she had another job to do in Manchester. It would involve finding a taxi that was prepared to take her and a dog.

The best vet Sorrel had ever known was in Altrincham. He had looked after Spud when they lived at Bellaire. Today she planned to take the dog back to see Mr Garner. Spud had developed an intermittent limp and only the best advice was good enough.

'It's arthritis.' Mr Garner lifted Spud down from the table. 'Good boy. It's the curse of border collies. We can certainly do something about it but I'd like to be able to keep an eye on him. Would you consider leaving Spud here, for a few days? What he really needs is a country holiday. The best thing I can suggest is that I do what I can for him and then we reintroduce him to longer romps.'

Sorrel hesitated. Spud was a big part of her frail belonging and the idea of being parted from him was not easy.

'I'm not talking about kennels.' Plain, sandy Mr Garner seemed to understand owners as well as he did their dogs. 'I know of a farm where they even give them their own armchairs.'

Sorrel looked down at Spud. He chose this moment to wag his tail.

'OK,' she said, after a moment's tortured indecision. 'Let me write down my number and address in London. If anything goes wrong, call me and I'll be on the first train. And you,' she said sternly to Spud, 'just you remember you're an actor. Actors have to be brave. It goes with the territory.'

It was only after she'd rushed outside that Sorrel realized she hadn't paid for the consultation. She'd left at speed because Spud hated to see her upset. Mr Garner would send a bill. As Sorrel climbed back into the waiting cab, she made a determined effort to pull herself together. Not that it wasn't leaving one of her best friends behind, because it was. But she was blowed if some taxi driver was going to be able to go around saying that Sorrel Starkey was back in Manchester in a flood of tears.

'They're like one of the family aren't they?' Sorrel had forgotten how nice Manchester taxi drivers could be. 'From the very minute you give them a name.'

That did it. The tears rolled. She remembered the way Spud had seemed to recognize her at their first meeting in the pet shop in Tib Street. The other side of her mind was full of thoughts of sunlight on The Midland roof. Were there new lovers being happy underneath it? Spud and Barney had never met. Why this should strike her as infinitely sad she didn't know; but it did. The road from Altrincham to Manchester was hauntedly familiar. It had once led her backwards and forwards from dreadful Bellaire. As they passed through Stretford, Sorrel was looking into cars going in the opposite direction. She half expected to see the Sowerbutts but she didn't and all she could wonder was what evil Bellaire had managed to do to the poor pools winners.

Outside the Nun's Prayer the doors of the hired van were hanging open. It was now crammed to the ceiling with cardboard boxes and readily portable items of furniture. As Sorrel paid off the taxi, she saw Kenny Shorrocks hesitate with a flowered chamber pot and then put it, for safe keeping, onto the floor, by the front seat. Niall Peters came down the pub steps empty-handed and closed the van doors.

'That's it then,' said Kenny to Sorrel.

'Yes, that's it. Are you sure we've got everything, Niall?'

'Everything. I double-checked.'

Sorrel did not want to go back into the Nun's Prayer. 'Say goodbye to Ray Fossett for me.' This was to Kenny. 'I've got all I want. I won't ask for more in court. You've got my word for that.'

'Would you just tell me something?' Kenny looked awkward but hopeful. 'It's just that I've got a feeling about something. You know where Eeek is, don't you?'

Sorrel began to climb into the van. 'Oscar Wilde was right,' she said over her shoulder. 'He maintained that people who disappear generally turn up in San Francisco. Eeek's with Mickey.'

Kenny looked absolutely gob-smacked. 'You're joking!'

'I'm in too much of a hurry to joke. Goodbye, Kenny.'

The full enormity of what Sorrel had told him must now have dawned on Kenny because he blurted out, 'But I shared a bed with him. Not once, dozens of times. I left myself wide open. He could have got at me when I was asleep.'

'I think you would have felt something.' Sorrel spoke thoughtfully. 'But if you're all that worried you can always go to the clinic for a check-up. After all, it's where you sent me!'

As she wound up the window Sorrel hoped that these would be the last words she would ever be obliged to address to her husband. The van swung into Deansgate, the flowered chamber pot began to roll around the floor and Sorrel started to laugh. 'Guess what, Niall? We've left the poor sod without so much as a pot to piss in!'

5

One of Shelagh Starkey's cellars now became Sorrel's stockroom. Sorrel insisted upon paying rent for it: 'After all, I'm in business now. Like the cards?'

> Sorrel Starkey
> Bygones and Bric-a-brac
> Stall 27
> Attwood Arcade
> Portobello Road W11

The arcade had once been a double-fronted gents' outfitters. A faded sign above the front of the shop still read *Percival Attwood – High-Class Ready-Mades & Hosiery*. It surprised Sorrel that nobody had seen fit to rip down the sign and sell it on one of the stalls inside. You could get anything in the Attwood Arcade from a papier-mâché carnival head to a china thimble. The converted shop smelled of mothballs and old hymn books. Most of the stalls specialized and Sorrel was aiming at the growing demand for 1930s artefacts. She felt no sentimentality about putting a price on the huge Bretby vases, decorated with a design of storks, which had once graced the inglenooks of Bellaire. She would be only too happy to see the back of the polka-dot Susie Cooper dinner service. One of the gravy boats was missing; Kenny had thrown it at the dining room wall, in the middle of a row about garlic.

The plunder from the attics of the Nun's Prayer was not for sale. She viewed it as a gift which the pub had handed to her from its theatrical past. And Sorrel Starkey never gave away presents. Besides, there was the future – one day she would have a home of her own again and she planned to decorate it around this unique collection of Manchester theatricalia. That and a set of particularly good pans were the only things she intended to rescue from her marriage. This dream of a little house was like a wistful Yeats poem and she didn't dare think about it too hard lest she should see Barney Shapiro coming in from the garden. There was no denying that he was in the dream, albeit at the far edge. He was still in all of Sorrel's daydreams. She wasn't the kind to lock out one of her own.

Shopkeeping was in Sorrel's blood and she thoroughly enjoyed being down on the market. She was fascinated to discover that almost all of her sales were made to other dealers. Portobello sold to proper antique shops who sold to grander versions of themselves who did business with America. As the Susie Cooper dinner service was finally packed up and carried away Sorrel found herself wondering how many years it would be before gravy was poured onto those plates again?

There was a side of the actress which viewed her appearances at Portobello as a character performance. True to her declaration to Niall Peters, Sorrel's hair was scraped under a woolly bob-hat. She barely bothered with makeup, and track-suits were much more convenient than draughty skirts. The other dealers in the arcade viewed her stock with approval. It didn't clash with anybody else's merchandise and they could be trusted to mind her stall whenever she nipped over the road, to the pub, for a quick one. Somebody would always find her a cardboard box or help date a puzzling item. It was all as neighbourly as the North of England.

The boy on the next stall dealt in the ephemera of pop music. He wrote songs himself and always refused to sell a pair of wire-framed glasses which, he claimed, had been stolen from John Lennon's bedside – in Hamburg – by a mutual girlfriend. There was even a Marchioness in the arcade. She had her own ermine-trimmed coronet, from the last Coronation, perched up above her booth. She was quite prepared to part with it at the right price. One Friday the coronet went to an American and, by Saturday morning, another was in its place.

It didn't take long for Sorrel to discover that it was only

worth setting out her stall for the last three days of the trading week. She was soon buying to replenish her stock. If an auction or a tempting jumble sale clashed with a trading day, she had no hesitation in leaving her stall in the hands of the custodian of John Lennon's stolen spectacles.

Christian German was a rivetingly good-looking young man. Tall and lean with green eyes, he had a lion's mane of blond hair. The fact that his clean but tattered denim clothes always looked as though they'd been flung on impatiently, heightened rather than detracted from his beauty. He barely bothered to fasten shirt buttons and there was often a disturbing amount of pale golden body on view.

Sorrel only enjoyed looking at him. Her interest never went any further than that. But he pleased the eye and made the day more decorative. He also filled the air with the smell of cannabis. Christian viewed the local police with complete indifference and was forever rolling joints, in brown liquorice cigarette-papers, on top of his counter. He always did it on a Creole cookery book which had once belonged to Billie Holliday. 'I'll just make me another little Billie,' he would murmur. Eventually he persuaded Sorrel to try one but it did nothing for her.

Early one Saturday morning, a figure from Sorrel's past walked into the arcade. It was Mucky Matt the Piccadilly procurer. The passing years had plainly treated him generously for he was covered in Italian casual clothes and his watch was a genuine Cartier. Not that you could judge Portobello customers by what they wore.

'Good morning, Sorrel,' he said casually. 'Have you by any chance got any thirties Spode?'

'No.'

'Pity.'

And that was that. It was the full extent of his interest. No commercial sexual proposition, nothing – he just moved on down the arcade. She could have been just anybody. It left Sorrel feeling her age.

Christian German didn't make things any better when, later on that morning, after exhaling a cloud of spent marijuana smoke, he eyed Sorrel kindly and said, 'You know what? If you just had your face lifted, I bet I wouldn't half fancy you.'

Is there something in astrology? This was the kind of day that left Sorrel wondering because she had not just one but two more visitors from her past.

The first was June who spent too much, in a patronizing way, and made Sorrel feel bad about the fact that Spud was still kennelled at the farm. The second arrival was Ruby Shapiro, dressed perfectly for the occasion, as usual, in a cream linen boiler suit.

'If the mountain won't come to Mahomet. . .'

'Ruby, your waist! How've you lost all that weight? It's wonderful.'

'We've just spent a fortnight at Tring. I never want to see raw celery again. I don't believe you've ever met my daughter, Zillah.'

The last time Sorrel had heard about Zillah, she'd been in bed with Barney. She found herself looking into his eyes again but they were in an unlined female face. If that was a face lift, Sorrel decided she wouldn't mind settling for one. It was no use, she had to ask: 'How's Barney?'

'They lost the baby.' Ruby quickly picked up a Loetz glass plate. 'How much?'

'Have it.' All that pain and disruption and there wasn't even a new life to justify it.

'Business is business, Sorrel. I'll pay for it but you can give me a discount.'

'Have it for love.' Sorrel was preoccupied with her own thoughts.

'That I cannot refuse. Have dinner with us at the hotel tonight. We're at The Connaught.'

'I can't. I'm going to the theatre.' It was the truth. No baby. No Barney and no baby. Did Ruby know the plate was Austrian?

'Well, don't be a stranger, Sorrel.' Ruby put it in her calf shoulder-bag. 'I'm going North tomorrow. You know where we live. We miss you. All of us miss you.'

'I'm sorry about the baby.'

'I'm sorry too.' Ruby looked straight into Sorrel's eyes.

'More sorry than I dare tell you.' Her gaze swivelled to her daughter. 'Zillah! Stop staring at that beautiful young man on the next stall. I'm not kidding, you young people go out and meet trouble halfway.' But she said it affectionately and her affections still included Sorrel Starkey.

'I'm getting much more modern, Sorrel. This daughter of mine has come back from New York with a lot of new ideas. She's trying to make me change my thinking.'

The elegant Zillah treated Sorrel to a worldly-wise Shapiro wink. And as mother and daughter hurried off, in the direction of Notting Hill Gate, Sorrel was left wondering what to make of this. It had been almost as though she was being flagged signals.

Shelagh might have allowed Sorrel to rent one cellar for her boxes of stock but that was the only money which changed hands; unless you count the fact that Sorrel scrupulously refilled the decanters she emptied and brought home fresh produce, from Portobello, for their dinner table. From the time of her first visit to Bedman's Row, Sorrel had been so dazzled by Lily Bear that she had failed to assimilate the sterling qualities of Shelagh Starkey.

Lily's glamorous dazzle had taken a long time to die down but the aborted production of *The Gin and Nookie Scandal* had left the old star a little wary of Sorrel. The show had simply played one week in Liverpool, with an understudy in Sorrel's role, and then closed. There had been no open quarrel with Lily but these days she tended to call when she knew Sorrel would be out. This gave Sorrel a chance to appreciate Shelagh in her own right. She finally saw her for what she was – a thoroughly good woman. But that didn't mean a boring one.

'I loathed church as a child,' Shelagh would say. 'Of course we had to sit at the front and learn the catechism and the gospel for every single Sunday. We were dreadfully Protestant in my father's parishes. I think that's why, when I came to London, I took to St Mary Mag's in such a big way. People may call it "The Sunday Opera" but it's better than pitch-pine pews and unloving charity.'

St Mary Magdalene's had once been a highly aristocratic church but the great houses of Mayfair had, for the most part, been converted into office blocks; these days it attracted a clever congregation. Talent had replaced blue blood and the rush-seated chairs were filled with magazine editors and doctors and university dons. They came from all over London to enjoy St Mary Mag's exotic brand of the Anglican faith. Though a Church of England vicar, Father Medlicott prided himself on being just a little bit more Catholic than the Pope.

Sorrel often wondered whether the Archbishop of Canterbury knew that one of his churches kept a saint's jawbone in a gilt receptacle and thought nothing of processing a relic of the true cross, around the church, in a small picture frame studded with real diamonds. 'Rome may have given up services in Latin,' the vicar would smile sweetly, 'but at St Mary Mag's we still believe it to be the language of heaven.'

Anglo-Catholicism being full of its own brand of teasing humour, Sorrel never quite knew what to take seriously. A boy from *Vogue* even tried telling her that, on Palm Sunday, portly old Father Medlicott would be led round the church on a donkey. She started going to church to please Shelagh and stayed because it proved to be as spectacular as anything she'd ever seen on a stage. She often felt that one of the Borgias would have quite enjoyed it.

But cut through the incense and the lace and you got to an undeniable core of solid faith. Sorrel felt she belonged to nothing and nobody, yet this congregation saw itself as part of a meaningful whole. It was just like the real Catholic church near the Old Fire-Iron. St Mary Magdalene's worshippers believed that one consecrated communion wafer left in the gilded, curtained box on the altar meant God was present. He was there.

Sorrel took all of this with a pinch of salt. And yet . . . once she had found herself alone in the church, with just the winking sanctuary lamp for company, when she suddenly realized that there was an extra silence superimposed on top of the ordinary silence. And in that quiet was peace. That's what really drew Sorrel Starkey back to St Mary Mag's.

In worldly Mayfair she found herself confronted by thoughts of infinity and eternity. Outwardly, she was still scathing about the church: 'All those "Hail Marys"! Do they think the poor woman's deaf? Why don't they just say it once and trust she's got it? She's meant to be Jewish. I know Jewish women. They're sharp, they're quick. If Our Lady's anything like Ruby Shapiro she won't be at all struck on all that repetition.'

Unlike many Protestants, Sorrel had no difficulty in calling the Virgin Mary 'Our Lady'. Much in her previous experience, the Dolans, the Catholic residential club, had prepared her for the ways of the Mayfair church. 'But the Dolans didn't go to a cocktail party in the crypt after High Mass,' she said accusingly to Shelagh, 'and they were very down on the idea of gays. Sometimes I look round that congregation and it's like one of the audiences on my night-club tour. I've even seen black leather at Benediction.'

'They managed to get there, that's the point.' Shelagh Starkey put a china funnel into a pie dish and added red wine to a steak and kidney mixture.

'I only go because London's so dull on a Sunday.' Sorrel felt the need to defend her position. 'Nobody managed to get me confirmed when I was little and they won't now, so they'd better not try.'

'That's entirely between yourself and the Almighty. Would you mind pounding me some mushrooms and garlic into a paste?'

Whenever Sorrel looked around St Mary Mag's she marvelled at the prices some of their holy tat would fetch on Portobello. Her mind was becoming a dealer's mind and it was all she could do, when visiting people's houses, to stop herself from upending their vases to look for the manufacturer's back-stamp. She was also becoming fake-conscious. Sorrel now realized that when she bought the Staffordshire collie, for Shelagh, she had been sold a pup. What's more, every time she looked at this dog, on top of the sitting room desk, her conscience pricked her. Spud was still up in Cheshire.

Just as Sorrel decided to bring him back to London,

Shelagh got a part in a new play which was going to be tried out on tour. It didn't seem fair to bring the dog from the freedom of a farmyard to an empty London house, and Sorrel didn't like the idea of him skulking miserably underneath her stall, so off went another monthly cheque for his northern upkeep. And then – four weeks later – another one. And so it went on; the situation was very far from satisfactory.

June Gee, of all people, brought matters to a head. She came down to Portobello Road to ask Sorrel whether she'd heard the latest about Mickey. Rumour had it that he was about to descend upon London. June had given a private sitting to a Hollywood columnist who had sworn that this was the case. 'It's all very secret but he's supposed to be looking for English actresses. He must have said something, on the phone, to you. . . ?'

'We've rather let our phone calls slide.' The balder truth was that, since their conversation about Sorrel exhibiting herself in night clubs, Mickey had left her severely alone.

'You've let everything slide.' A cottage-shaped teapot slipped from June's pudgy paws and smashed on the floorboards of the Attwood Arcade. 'Don't worry, I'll pay for that. Or else I'll buy something expensive to make up for it. Yes, you've let everything go. People are saying you're behaving disgracefully towards your doggie. He's as good as dumped . . .' June refused to allow Sorrel to interrupt. 'I know about these things. A friend of mine is in constant contact with dogs on the Other Side. Every time you leave a dog they think of it as your death. Not that there *is* any death,' she added hastily as she began to tinkle a china spoon, irritatingly, inside an orange basket-work jam-pot. 'It wouldn't be fair to bring him back to London. Not after months of freedom. Why don't you just write to that farm and ask them to find him a good home?'

'Because he's my friend.'

'A real friend would give him the freedom to start a new life. I think I'll buy that Lalique cocktail set off you.'

'You won't. It's not for sale.' It was, but not to June Gee. Sorrel too had principles about things going to good homes.

June looked miffed and changed the subject: 'How much

would you charge to have oral sex with Idi Amin? It's my new game. I'm asking everybody.'

'Nothing. I just wouldn't do it.'

'The trouble with you is that you're too high-principled. Except when it comes to that dear little doggie!' Giving the Lalique cocktail set a hurt glare, June marched off in a huff, leaving Sorrel to sweep up the pieces of teapot.

She also left Sorrel feeling less comfortable than she had found her. June was everything that was awful but, when it came to Spud's welfare, she had a point. The idea of never seeing him again was dreadful, but what kind of life had she to offer him? If June was right, and every major parting was a death for dogs, then Spud must already be through his mourning and out the other side.

Sorrel's grief was about to begin. That night, after much fevered thinking, she sat down and wrote a letter to the owner of the kennelling farm.

> . . . and he particularly likes children so please try for a home with a family. They don't need to be rich people. I will willingly pay them. Just be sure that they are kind. Spud is getting on and I want him to have a happy old age. I don't want him putting to sleep.

Tears hit the page as Sorrel steeled herself to finish the letter. For years she had been messy in her own dealings with herself but Spud deserved upright treatment. He was going to be allowed to run free, into a new life. But he had *chosen* her . . . she'd always thought that. It was no use. He needed fresh air and fields. Sorrel sealed the letter and before her resolution could fail her, she ran and posted it in Covent Garden.

Sorrel Starkey had made some big mistakes in the past but this was a massive one. If she had done the right thing, why did she feel so conscience-stricken? And she missed Spud. He wasn't going to come back. It hurt. Twice that week she got as far as dialling the kennel number and both times she forced herself to put down the receiver.

The very morning Sorrel decided to go up to Cheshire and get him, the letter arrived: '. . . gone this afternoon to a good home with a prosperous family who are suitably conscious of the fact that he was once a very famous animal'.

So that was that; except it wasn't. More wretched than she would have believed possible, Sorrel decided to take her misery to the silence of St Mary Magdalene's. She lit a candle for Spud's safety and happiness and had a long, hard think. With Spud gone she was truly on her own. Perhaps the time had come to try to belong to something bigger.

Sorrel walked out of the church and stood hesitantly at the clergy-house door. Her mother would have been shocked by the empty gin bottles beside the priests' dustbin. Sorrel rang the bell marked *Fr Medlicott*.

The head which peered down from an upstairs window was balding and ringed with tight old auburn curls. The pink face was surmounted by a pair of twinkling, gold-rimmed spectacles: 'Hello? Yes? Ah my dear . . .' The celibate priest always sounded like a neutered old tomcat until he added the word 'child'. 'Ah my dear child. I thought you were the third beggar of the morning. Hang on, I'll throw down the keys.'

The clergy-house smelled strongly of roasting meat and faintly of leaking gas. Father Medlicott's study was on the first floor. The furniture looked as though a lot of old ladies had each left him one good piece. There were a few items of sacred, baroque carving and, on his writing desk, a framed photograph of two 1920s women under a parasol. Sorrel mentally christened this 'Mummy and Auntie in a cornfield'.

'Once the Angelus has rung we can allow ourselves a glass of sherry,' beamed Father Medlicott.

As if the angels had heard him, a bell in the church tower went ting-ting-ting three times and then carried on chiming for a few more strokes. Throughout all this the old priest muttered devoutly but indecipherably, then crossed himself and let out a breath of air like a man who had been under water.

'I didn't mutter because I don't know the words,' explained Sorrel. 'I thought it would be dishonest to just go mumble-mumble-mumble.'

'Very dishonest.' Father Medlicott reached for the Amontillado bottle and two glasses. 'What can I do for you?'

'I think I'd like to be confirmed.'

'You want me to instruct you in the Faith?'

'I've done some terrible things.' Sorrel felt it only fair to warn him.

'Your first confession will take care of those.'

Sorrel had not bargained for this. 'Won't that general confession prayer, in the middle of the service, do?'

'Not at St Mary Magdalene's.' Father Medlicott was all High Church reproach. 'Why do you want to be confirmed?'

'I need a friend. I thought it might as well be God.'

Gerald Medlicott looked as though he was about to be seized by an apoplexy. 'And yet there is a certain directness in what you're saying,' he managed after a moment.

Sorrel thought she'd better try harder. For once she abandoned truth and said what she hoped would please: 'If I get married again I'd like it to be in church with the full performance. When my divorce comes through,' she added brightly.

For a moment Sorrel wondered whether Father Medlicott was going to pour her sherry back into the bottle, but he handed it to her and said, 'The purpose of instruction in the Faith is to prepare the candidate to receive Holy Communion. Divorced persons can't do that. Not at St Mary Magdalene's.'

'You can keep your poxy sherry.' Sorrel Starkey actually tried to hand back a drink. 'If God won't have me, how do I go about joining the devil's lot?'

The priest paled. 'Don't even mention the Evil One as a joke. I mean that.'

'Who was joking?' Sorrel was furious. It had taken courage to come up here and now it seemed that she was even forbidden the Kingdom of Heaven.

'Drink your drink, enjoy it, and let us think. Things aren't as bad as you assume.' There was a likeable, practical side to Father Medlicott. 'I can take this up with the Bishop. Each case is viewed on its own merits. Would I be right in presuming you were the innocent party?'

'We haven't decided yet.' Sorrel definitely felt more cheerful. 'Which do you think would be the best?'

Now the priest did choke on his sherry. It went all down the regulation thirty-nine buttons of his cassock. Many were the jokes made about these buttons. They were said to represent the 39 Articles of Faith, the rules of the Church of England – of which a good few were totally disregarded at St Mary Mag's. Divorce, it seemed, was an altogether more serious business.

'Catholic teaching is very firm on this subject.' The priest was back in control of the situation.

'But you're meant to be a Protestant!'

Father Medlicott could not have looked more affronted if Sorrel had accused him of being illegitimate. Nevertheless, that good old soul tried again: 'Let's put aside all the rules and regulations for the moment. They're man-made, they're just there to keep us on the right rails. I've not been a priest for all these years without learning some simple truths. If you take one step towards God, he will take two towards you.'

'It's just that I feel so left out of things when everybody else goes up to the communion rail. Just me, on the chairs, like a lonely plum.' Sorrel was finally telling her inner truth. 'I have to belong to *something* . . .'

'I know. It must be awful. We must see what can be done. In the meantime just keep coming to Mass. And in the autumn be sure you come on the parish pilgrimage to Walsingham.'

'What's Walsingham?'

Father Medlicott refilled her glass. 'A place where miracles happen. It's only going to be eleven pounds for the whole weekend.'

'Eleven quid for a miracle! Can you put me down for two?' Sorrel wasn't quite joking.

'Oh my dear.' He forgot 'child' and looked quite shocked. 'Do be careful! God might give you both. And then you'd have to handle them.'

It was all, suddenly, reminiscent of the conversation with Magda Schiffer in Albert Square: '*Take what you want, take it and pay for it.*' Sorrel made up her mind, there and then, to be very careful what she asked for in Walsingham. 'Is it wrong to hope?' she asked. 'I'm only asking because I got it from a pagan story.'

'Wrong? It's Christian virtue. "Now abideth these three, faith, hope and charity." Being interpreted, charity means love.'

'I love like anything. Just as much as I hope. I'm afraid it's all very muddled.'

'You take your muddle to Our Lady of Walsingham. I can promise you she has many satisfied clients.'

'Is it a doll at Walsingham? I mean is it one of those carved idols?'

'They're only aids to prayer. We Anglo-Catholics believe Our Lady to be a *living* doll!' The priest smiled at his own daring joke. 'I've loved our conversation, Sorrel, but now I must ask you to excuse me. I've got some young men from Saatchi and Saatchi coming to luncheon.'

Sorrel's glass was empty again so she was glad of the excuse to leave. On her way through Shepherd Market she stopped off at The Grapes and bought herself another dock of sherry. Mentally she raised it to the Virgin Mary in heaven. Here's to a miracle, she thought and then wondered if this was sacrilege in a pub. Oh well, if God knew everything he'd know she drank too much. He would also know that, for all her bravado with Father Medlicott, she was in desperate need of just *something*, anything . . . there had to be more to life than this.

The telegram read: 'You have just got time to sober up. I hit London on Friday. Love Mick.' As far as Sorrel could make out from the symbols at the top of the GPO form, it had been sent from New York. Her excitement was mixed with alarm. Mick's very telegram seemed to crackle with energy and her own was at a low ebb. What's more the red was growing out of Sorrel's hair and she shuddered to think what he would have to say about her woollen balaclava.

There was no question of getting sober. These days Sorrel was never reeling, she was just permanently topped up. She viewed this state as a return to controlled drinking. It wasn't satisfactory but she wasn't an embarrassment. Clothes – they would be the problem. She had bought nothing new for two years and Mick was more critical than a fashion editor.

Money was not a worry. The stall was doing well and Mr Pym, the Manchester accountant, had made sure that her investments were kept moving profitably. There was even money coming in from overseas repeats of *Angel Dwellings*. The uncharitable had been heard to say that poverty was the one thing which might have taken the glass out of Sorrel Starkey's hand.

She had three days to turn herself back into the actress Mick remembered. Sorrel had never given up hope of work in the theatre. It just hadn't come. As she emerged from the hairdresser's on Dover Street and picked her way towards the Bond Street branch of Rive Gauche – they had promised to try to obtain a cream alpaca suit in her size – she found herself wondering which of the Mayfair hotels Mick would allow to cosset him this trip.

In the event he turned out to be hiding somewhere mysterious in South Kensington. 'Miss Starkey? This is Blakes Hotel. Mr Grimshaw will be collecting you, with a car, on Sunday morning at eleven thirty. Would you please dress for a smart lunch in the country.'

The cream alpaca would do very nicely. When she looked up Mick's hotel in the phone book it turned out to be in dismal old Roland Gardens. This conjured up visions of the play *Separate Tables* with lonely spinsters living out their declining years in a genteel boarding house.

As Mickey sprang through the front door at Bedman's Row like a jack-in-the-box released, Sorrel asked, 'Why are you staying so far out? Have you fallen on bad times?'

'When I'm at Blakes? Honestly, Sorrel, you're hopelessly out of touch. Only the very rich and famous disappear into Blakes' bosom. I just passed Andy Warhol's business manager, on my corridor, looking for Bianca Jagger. What sort of stones have you been hiding under since showbusiness gave you up?'

It was all very humbling but Sorrel was reassured to see that the car, parked at the back of Bedman's Row, was from good old Daimler Hire and that the chauffeur was one of their special breed of friendly uncles.

'So now it's Tonbridge, sir?' he inquired of Mickey.

Sorrel was horrified. 'Tonbridge? Do think twice, Mick. We might run into June Gee. She's got a house there.'

'That's where we're going to lunch. She must subscribe to Celebrity Services. They send out lists of who's staying where. They're worse than private detectives. June certainly knows where Blakes stands in the scheme of things. She sent me enough flowers for a first night. Lilies!'

'It's always lilies and it's always awful. No. I'm not going.'

'Now come on, Little Nell. Put your old curiosity shop behind you. Not that I don't want to hear all about it. We've got an hour to catch up. June particularly asked me to bring you. She says she's got a friend of yours there. Somebody from Manchester.'

It's a punishment, thought Sorrel. This is what comes of skipping Mass for a joyride. For the first time in her life she felt uncomfortable in Mick's company. She was unable to feed him the latest West End theatrical gossip – she didn't know any. She knew even less about current television scandals. It struck her as odd that he still seemed to view *Angel Dwellings* as important. To Sorrel it was just something she'd once done. The fact that Diggory Mallet was supposed to have tried to get up to something untoward, with a cinema usherette, in the dark, was of only marginal interest to her.

'How's Eeek?' she tried eventually.

'Sex mad. I sometimes think he's forever catching up on all those lost years in Manchester. The most I ever see of him is his back – disappearing into bathhouses.'

Perhaps serious conversation might be better: 'Did you ever find real love, Mick?'

'No, but I found my city and that's been enough.'

Sorrel half expected him to repeat the old suggestion that she might like to visit him in San Francisco, but it didn't come. Not that she would have gone anyway. Screw him! No, that wasn't fair. He was still her Mick. She still loved him more than a brother but now there was a barrier between them. Looking out of the car window she noticed that the pubs were beginning to open.

Mick still didn't miss a trick: 'We'd better stop for a drink for you.'

So that was it. Drink had taken everything else away and now it was even managing to distance Mick. The pub they went into was full of people called Guy and Sholto and Jennifer. They all seemed to know one another and to fit into a Sunday morning where Sorrel had no place. Admittedly Sundays were always the worst day of the week but was she forever doomed to be on the outside looking in?

The Daimler purred on through Kent and into Tonbridge. June's house was outside the town in a commuter-money hamlet on a hillside.

'Would you believe the house is called Twin-Ordinances?' asked Mick in mock wonder.

The chauffeur slid back the dividing glass partition and said over his shoulder, 'I think this must be it.' He swung the car into a drive lined with copper-beech hedging. A hundred yards on they came to a fork with a fake country signpost. One arrow was marked *Healing Sanctuary*, the other said *Residence – Strictly Private*.

'There you are. She doesn't want visitors,' said Sorrel hopefully.

'She wants us.' Mick was all wicked anticipation. 'She's wanted us since we were eight.'

'Mr Grimshaw?' The chauffeur was at his most respectful. 'I don't normally ask but would you mind taking my album in and getting Mrs Gee's signature for me?'

Mick took the album and gasped at the house which now came into view. 'Jesus! It's the size of a health farm.'

'Don't say Jesus,' said Sorrel automatically but she could understand why Mick had cried out. The sprawling mock-Tudor residence even had its own stable block with a tin heart on the weathervane.

'How in God's name has she done it?' asked Mickey. 'Mind you – ' he closed the glass partition – 'those psychic sittings of hers must have presented her with years of opportunities for blackmail.'

The car slid to a halt. As the chauffeur bounded round to open the door and Sorrel put her feet down on the gravel, she recalled that Mickey never said a word he didn't mean. Had blackmail bought the Volvo and the Bentley or did they

637

belong to other lunch guests? These thoughts were dispersed by the sight of two young people emerging from some speckled laurel bushes.

'The twins,' breathed Mickey. 'Through puberty and out the other side. God help the world!'

Perhaps seventeen, they were both startlingly blonde in phosphorescent nylon track-suits. Junelle was her mother all over again and Jason had his father's muscular build. But Martyn Gee's eyes had always reminded Sorrel of a friendly golden retriever. Jason's were eerie. They could have belonged to a mad greyhound.

'You're Sorrel Starkey,' he said arrogantly. 'We always had to tell people that you were our godmother.'

'Mummy always meant you to deflower Jason.' Junelle's voice, like that of her twin, had been coated by an expensive school. 'June wanted you to have Jason's sacred virginity. But he got next door's au pair preggers, when he was thirteen.'

'I'm very open-minded about sex though.' Jason was giving Mick a look that was exactly how Sorrel imagined rent-boys.

'Watch yourself!' She murmured this, involuntarily, to Mick.

'Now I'm sure I was right about blackmail.' Mickey said it perfectly audibly. 'From the look in his eye, that boy's obviously got it in his genes.'

'Jason's got plenty in his jeans,' sniggered Junelle and Sorrel wished she'd had two preparatory drinks at the pub instead of just the one.

Somewhere inside the house a dog barked excitedly. Strange that an animal should bring the only human touch to this seedy moment. The dog barked again and it wasn't just any bark. It was one which Sorrel and half the television viewers in England should have recognized anywhere. The bark belonged to Spud.

6

The white front door, studded with black wooden pegs, creaked open and June stood on the top step in fluttering pink chiffon. 'Welcome to Twin-Ordinances.' Her trill turned into a scream as the white border collie with a black patch over one eye knocked her sideways and flung himself at Sorrel.

'My love. My good love. . .' Sorrel tried to hold onto Spud but he was doing all of his tricks for her, one after another, in ecstatic succession.

'What's that animal doing here?' demanded Mickey like somebody out of a melodrama.

'He's been dognapped,' cried Sorrel. 'That's what he's doing here. June Gee's nothing but a fucking dognapper.'

'Not the *f* word,' pleaded June. 'It's the one thing I don't allow in front of the kiddies. Do come in.' She was still trying to be very high society. 'Martyn's got a pitcher of margaritas ready.'

'You know what you can do with your margaritas *and* the jug . . .' Sorrel's fury knew no bounds. 'You schemed this dog out of me. You even flung in psychic mumbo-jumbo. No wonder they drummed you out of the mediums' union. He was mine and you had to have him. Everything I've ever had you've always wanted. And this dog means far more to me than Kenny Shorrocks did!'

'But she didn't want the dog, Mick,' said June sweetly. 'She'd had enough.'

Sorrel advanced on June. 'You all but hypnotized me into writing to that farm in Cheshire. You came down to Portobello twice. You went on and on about it.'

'Well, you did write.' June was still being charmingly reasonable.

'And I've regretted it every moment since. It's all right, Spud. You're safe. I've got you back.'

'Nope,' said June. 'You haven't got him back at all. I

adopted that animal for a purpose. He's coming on my next lecture tour with me. The audiences will love it. What a lot of fuss. It's not even a thoroughbred. You're not having him back, Sorrel, and that's that.'

Sorrel thought quickly. Bending down, she whispered an old cue into Spud's ear: 'Enemy.' All the hair stood up on his backbone and, looking at June, he pulled back a lip to reveal one white fang. The growl was the more menacing for being so low.

June backed away. 'I've never seen him do that before.'

'The next thing I tell him to do is – ' Sorrel spelled it out – 'K-I-L-L. I daren't say it aloud or he'd do it.' The fact of the matter was that Spud would only have lunged into a stage attack, but June wouldn't know this. 'You're always saying, "There is no death." Want to put it to the test?'

'Oh, keep your dog.' June threw up her hands impatiently. 'But do hurry up inside or the veal will spoil.'

'I never eat veal.'

'Well you can have an omelette . . .'

Before Sorrel could say that an omelette would choke her, Mick took charge: 'You stole that dog, June. Sorrel's right, you've always wanted everything she's got, and I've a terrible feeling that includes me. Well you're not getting me. Taking Spud was taking happiness. I've called Sorrel every kind of fool on earth but she's got a good heart. Yours is bad.' Now he turned equally seriously to Sorrel. 'And if you are ever weak-willed enough to speak to this cow again I'm through with you.'

June wasn't letting it go at that: 'How dare you call me a cow, you screaming queer! I'm Sorrel's oldest friend. I love her. You've always been jealous of the fact that I knew her first.'

'It is impossible to be jealous of fat, phoney nothing.'

Having delivered this considered judgement Mickey swept Sorrel and Spud towards the waiting Daimler. 'I'm sorry I didn't get you Mrs Gee's autograph,' he said to the chauffeur, 'but we've just discovered that she is a common thief.'

'Common?' screeched June. '*Woman's Own* called me a great lady. And I'll trouble you to bleeding-well remember it!'

Giving the haughty imitation of Noël Coward and Gertrude Lawrence that they had been rehearsing since they were seventeen, Mick and Sorrel climbed into the car with Spud. As he sank back onto the beige felt upholstery, Mick said, 'I hadn't intended opening that drinks cabinet, but give me a scotch and fix yourself a vodka. Her face! She looked like a boiled beetroot.'

As the car ate up the drive and Sorrel busied herself fixing drinks Mick started to laugh uproariously and Spud chose this moment to remember him as an old friend. The brief drama had turned the half-American back into the Mick of Sorrel's childhood. She was as glad to have him back as she was to catch a whiff of Spud's familiar smell of Owbridge's Lung Tonic.

'Mick? Have I ever told you why I was always made to call June Monk my best friend? It was during the war. Mr Monk was in the paint trade and my mother was always hoping to get black-market Walpamur out of him. She never did.'

Mickey stopped laughing. 'The person I'm sorry for is poor old Martyn. He paid a terrible price for getting his hands up her blouse. Did you notice that her tits are beginning to sag? And what are we meant to do about lunch? Where are we?'

'Kent.'

'We'll go to Rochester,' announced Mick. 'I've always wanted to walk where Dickens trod. Perhaps we can find the pub in *Pickwick Papers*.'

They got there too late. Lunch had finished at two o'clock. The only place they could find open was a Wimpy Bar. The chauffeur, perfectly correctly, carried his cheeseburger to a separate table. But this made Sorrel feel sad: 'And there's something very melancholy about Rochester too.' She was gazing through the window to be sure that Spud was safe in the car. 'All those mudflats and that neatened-up ruin of a castle.'

'It isn't Rochester, it's you.' Mickey was squirting ketchup from the red plastic tomato. 'Buxton was also supposed to be melancholy *and* Mere. It's not the places, it's the state of your head. I long for you to see San Francisco, but I know you'd only view it through a gauze of misery. Come when you're well.'

'I'm not ill.'

'That's not what we'd say in California. We're very tough on substance-abusers there. You certainly made a hit with Hilary Bates. He might not have taken you on as a client but he keeps going on at me to have you camera-tested for the new show.'

New show? Perhaps all the hair dyeing and new clothes had been for a good purpose.

Mick – ahead of her – looked as though he wished he'd kept his mouth shut. 'I daren't risk it, Sorrel. Don't look at me like a female version of Spud, I daren't. They're tremendously disciplined in the States. For all I called June a fat nothing she's certainly got the reins of her own life firmly between those chubby paws. She's an amazing creature, really – all star quality and no talent to go with it.'

'Star quality, June?' Sorrel felt so betrayed she could have squirted the tomato ketchup at him.

'Immense star quality. Always has had. Look how she's got us talking about her now.'

'And I'm finished.' It was neither a statement nor a question. It came somewhere in between.

Mick refused to be drawn. 'I'm beyond giving you stage directions. Look what a mess you made of Vienna.'

For the first time Sorrel dared speak aloud about Ruby's visit to Portobello. She described it in detail to Mickey and ended by saying, 'So if she's finally accepted Zillah back, after the mixed marriage, and she says she's coming around to modern American thinking, I just wondered whether she was trying to tell me something . . .'

'Like what? Don't answer that. You place me in a very difficult position, Sorrel. Barney's my best friend. Not like you're my best friend, that's something else, always has been. But he stays up late at night, just mooching around that freezing cold house. And that's when he rings me. I know what Ruby doesn't. He won't leave Mandy now because the gynaecologist discovered something nasty. It's not bad enough to kill her,' he added hastily.

'That's a terrible thing to say. I'll have to go to confession.'

'Why will you have to go to confession when I said it?' But

as usual he had got inside the pleats of Sorrel's mind and she was forced to carry on listening as he continued: 'You've let everything get into such a mess. Everything; it would take a miracle to sort you out.'

'Funny you should say that because I'm going shopping for one.' And now she did it. Before he could come up with any awkward questions Sorrel picked up the red plastic tomato and squirted it at him. She scored a bull's-eye – right on the nose.

'Have a paper napkin, Mick, and listen to me. Do you know who my favourite character in Dickens is? Mr Micawber. He always said that something would turn up. And eventually it did. I always thought Mr Micawber must have been the happiest person ever because he valued it when he got it. Well, you're looking at Mrs Micawber. I'll get it and I'll value it. God how I'll value it!'

Not many charabanc outings start from Mayfair and even fewer begin with the motor-coach being blessed with holy water. Old Father Ninian came downstairs, from the top attic of the presbytery, to do it. He was said to be 'practically a saint' and owned one of the largest collections of toy soldiers in England.

'How I envy you all,' he beamed innocently from under his black biretta. Shoving a shilling into Father Medlicott's hand he murmured, 'Light a candle for me in the Holy House at Walsingham and give Our Lady my love.'

They were all behaving as though they were going to call upon the Mother of God. Sorrel had not stopped finding this a bit eerie. The parishioners of St Mary Mag's rarely took their prayers directly to the Almighty. Instead, they implored the Virgin Mary and the saints to put in a good word for them. It was like having friends in high places.

Father Medlicott was on the seat in front of Sorrel and Shelagh and – as the coach sped through North London – he turned round and announced: 'I'm not talking to myself. I'm saying a "Hail Mary" for every church we pass. Oh look, there's Wembley Stadium. Would you say that counted? After all, Billy Graham was there!' Father Medlicott let out a giggle and began to compare themselves with the Canterbury pilgrims. Sorrel perked up at this and half expected the passengers to break into bawdy stories. Benign old Lady Rose, sucking humbugs across the aisle, was said to have once known the King of Spain in the kind of way that leads to the confessional.

Just before they got to Cambridge, the parish priest called out to the driver: 'I say! I think we might be glad to stop at a pub.'

Slowing down, the driver called back in a mildly scandalized voice: 'I thought this was meant to be a church outing?'

'We are not Methodists,' intoned Father Medlicott.

A drink enlivened everybody to an extent where Admiral McKechnie's widow spoke to Sorrel for the very first time and offered her the loan of a Walsingham guidebook. As the coach bowled along towards Ely, where they planned to open their picnic hampers, Sorrel turned the pages and found out more about 'England's Nazareth'. That was another way of saying Walsingham. It was all so obscure; what on earth had she let herself in for?

Shelagh Starkey had never believed in ramming religious history down her lodger's throat so it took this book to tell Sorrel that, just before the Norman Conquest, a woman called the Lady Richeldis had a series of visions of the Virgin Mary. Richeldis believed that she was shown the wooden building where Christ was born. She was told to take very precise note of the measurements and to build just such another at Walsingham.

Sorrel yawned but read on because the McKechnie woman was giving her encouraging smiles from across the aisle and she didn't want to hurt her feelings. A wooden statue of the Virgin and Child was placed in this Holy House and a whole cult grew up around it. When beseeching prayers were offered, miracles started to happen. And routes from all over England began to converge on the small Norfolk village. The earliest pilgrims just lit gifts of wax tapers but soon the simple wooden statue wore a golden crown, ablaze with jewels, and kings came to worship at Walsingham.

It was all a bit too like school for Sorrel. Suddenly she remembered Mickey learning the Causes of the Reformation to get shut of his grammar school and into RADA. The book had got to the Reformation too. When the Protestants came to power it seemed that they had considered the statue of Our Lady of Walsingham to be such a potently Catholic force that they had taken the carved image to London, where it was publicly burned.

'Noël Coward was right when he said that Norfolk was very flat' – Shelagh interrupted Sorrel's reading – 'but he neglected to mention how huge the skies always seem. How far have you got with that learned tome?'

'She's just gone up in flames.'

'Nothing much happened after that for centuries. Not until Father Hope Patten came to Norfolk. He belonged to our end of the Church of England.' Shelagh nudged Father Medlicott who was just beginning to nod off on the seat in front. The Bishop's daughter believed in making parsons work for their living. 'Tell Sorrel about Alfred Hope Patten.'

'He wasn't *easy*.' Father Medlicott could have been discussing a difficult actress. 'But he had immense vision and courage. He went to Walsingham as vicar and put another wooden statue in the parish church. It was all highly illegal. His bishop nearly went barmy. But it soon became obvious that the supernatural was in charge again. And the Church is meant to be about miracles.'

'Don't I remember them trying to make him take it out?' asked Shelagh.

'They tried. In the end he got permission to move it to another place. But I don't think the Bishop expected him to process it through the village to a brand-new Holy House. The Protestants practically threw bricks. It was all most invigorating! Of course, nowadays, Walsingham is just like a tasteful, holy version of Pontin's.'

In her brief time at St Mary Mag's, Sorrel had managed to grasp some understanding of the wide differences between the opposing ends of the Church of England. Whatever would the stern Protestants have made of this Mayfair coachload who were now singing lustily as they followed the

645

same route into Walsingham that Henry VIII was said to have travelled on his knees? Their praises of Mary could not have been found in *Hymns Ancient and Modern*. But the words would have been familiar to anybody in Dublin:

> 'She is mighty to deliver
> Call her, trust her lovingly
> When the tempest rages round thee
> She will calm the troubled sea . . .'

Will she calm *my* troubled sea? wondered Sorrel miserably. Now they'd got to a bit about 'peace and blessings to restore'. She needed all of that too. She needed a miracle. But how were you meant to go about getting one? Perhaps the instructions would be in the seventy-five-pence handbooks which were now being passed around.

Sorrel's first sight of Walsingham left her wondering whether Walt Disney knew about the village. It was all twisting and winding, with russet brickwork and half-timbered houses overhanging the main street.

'The Roman Catholics are back here too,' explained Shelagh, 'and the Greek Orthodox have converted the old railway station into their church. Onion domes, icons, the lot!' The coach was slowing down. 'Our shrine's behind this tall wall. Those windows up there are the hospice where we're staying. The food is unbelievably bad so I've packed enough for the five thousand.'

As they climbed down from the bus they were greeted by a tiny nun with a list. She seemed almost too old to be doing the job. As she went ahead of them – through a huge wooden door in the wall – Sorrel was reminded of a flickering candle flame. Even one glance had been enough to see that Sister Angela burned very brightly.

The hospice was all clomping footsteps on bare boards. The rooms had nameplates on the doors – they were called after the various titles of the Virgin Mary. Sorrel was glad they were not in *Star of the Morning* because it had been the name of the seamen's hostel in *Angel Dwellings* and she wanted to forget that. She and Shelagh were in *Mother Inviolate* which struck Sorrel as almost gynaecological.

'Wear good praying clothes,' advised Shelagh, who was already changing into a pair of stretch slacks. 'There's rather a lot of kneeling.'

It was all kneeling. One service followed hot on the bells of another. The shrine chapel was like a russet brick, tile-roofed Spanish mission. Inside it was so full of holy dark and incense that Sorrel had difficulty in picking out details. But it wasn't like Norfolk, it was more like a saint's day abroad.

'Go back quietly on your own,' suggested Shelagh, as they lined up to process around the gardens, at twilight, carrying lighted candles inside waxed paper boxes. They were walking behind the statue which was borne aloft under more flares. Electric bells, like an ice-cream van in a big way, rang out from the tower and everybody was singing an interminable hymn about the history of the place.

Sorrel was quite shocked to see one of the boys from Saatchi and Saatchi sneak out a hand to fondle the bottom of a girl called Daisy Bouverie. Oh well, if God knew how much fluff there was in your pocket, the chances were that he also knew that the boy from the advertising agency was a bottom man. Had he forgotten that Sorrel needed a miracle? And how were you meant to go about getting one? Everything here was so wrapped up in gilded flummery that it seemed too simple a question to dare to ask.

That evening, after Benediction, the party from St Mary Mag's took themselves to a pub called the Oxford Stores. The place was nothing special but Father Medlicott got very convivial and a few drinks had a startling effect upon his curate. Sorrel had always thought of this young man, with his hank of black hair hanging into one eye, as a sallow drink of water; but a drop of gin began to oil some indiscreet stories out of him. They were mostly about a politician called Tom Driberg. As this High Church MP wasn't there to defend himself, Sorrel found it unfair and not her idea of Christian. She was used to that kind of spiteful gossip, done better, in the theatre. She didn't want to stay and listen to it here. They might believe in the mysteries of Walsingham but they had a funny way of showing it.

'I'm going to get some fresh air,' she said to Shelagh, who

nodded understandingly. In fact, Sorrel went straight to another pub she had spied along the way and charged herself up with a couple more stiff vodkas. As she walked back towards the hospice, she looked into some holy antique shops. To Sorrel's experienced eye, the prices in one shop seemed a bit opportunistic. And in another she was frankly shocked to see a communion chalice marked *Reduced to Clear*.

The only way back into the hospice seemed to be through a small wooden door set into the big one. Once she had creaked her way inside Sorrel decided to have a wander round the grounds.

Three full-sized crucifixes stood blackly against the moonlight and she passed beyond them and made her way towards an artificial cave which would have been just the thing for an outdoor production of *Aladdin*.

'Are you looking for something?' It was Sister Angela, the nun like a candle flame.

'I'm looking for a miracle.' Moonlight had revived Sorrel's need.

'Why don't you go and ask Our Lady? She's never been known to send anybody away empty-handed. Just go into the Holy House and talk to her like you would your own mother.'

'I can't talk to my own mother.' There was just enough of Gander in the nun to turn Sorrel back into a child.

'Go anyway. Take her your needs. She's probably expecting you.'

This awful ease with the supernatural was nothing like June Gee's. Here again Sorrel was reminded of Gander who always sang hymns as though she meant them. And this poor old nun shouldn't have to be guiding people round at this ungodly hour . . . More to please Sister Angela than anything else she descended the steps into the shrine chapel. There was nobody there except for the silence upon the silence. Sorrel didn't even have to look for the winking light upon the altar. She could *feel* that it would be there. God was in his box.

The inner shaft of the tower opened out into the centre of the tiny church and windows, at the top of it, let in moonlight like a lantern. The smell of incense was now mingled with the odour of spent wax. There were enough altars for a continental cathedral and Sorrel let out a sigh of pleasure at the sight of shimmering models of ships, in silver, hanging from the ceiling. She moved across to look at two ornate tombs. One had a painted carving of a dead bishop on top of it. The other represented Alfred Hope Patten on his deathbed. It was an ascetic face but Sorrel liked the look of him. She would have betted anything that, like herself, he wasn't a quitter.

If she was going to talk to statues she might as well begin here: 'Walsingham *is* magic,' she said, 'there's something extra here. I knew it the minute I got off the bus. It's just that people got in the way. I'm going to the Holy House. Wish me luck.'

The Holy House, at the back of the church, was like a building within a building. The guidebook had said that it was made from stones brought from ruined abbeys and monasteries. Sorrel stepped through the doorway. She had already crowded into this little shrine with the other pilgrims but now there was just herself and a hundred flickering candles and the wooden statue, on the altar, of the woman with the baby in her arms. Somebody had dressed her up in a garment like a brocade cape.

'They covered me in spangles,' said Sorrel, 'and those came a bit unravelled too. I'm in a mess . . .' It all began to come out. Some of it was words aloud and some was just in her head; but it all came out.

'I wanted to be famous and I wanted to be loved and I got both and I was awful at it. Being famous doesn't matter any more – honestly. I just want to go back to being part of the human race. And I know I drink too much but I can't stop and I can't see any way out of it. Help me. Please help me.

'I've not told you the biggest thing . . .' Sorrel decided to sweep through all the Church's strictures about adultery. This was between herself and the Star of the Sea. 'I want Barney. Please, if you're there, would you ask God if I can have Barney Shapiro back?'

As Sorrel wiped her eyes and blew her nose she noticed some big night-lights, inside glass shades, standing in niches in the wall. One was labelled *Sorrel Starkey*. She went right up and it was still there, in black Magic Marker on a white label. How on earth had that got here?

As she made her way back into the grounds she walked slap into Shelagh Starkey, coming out of a lighted French window, from the hospice sitting room.

'Are you OK, Sorrel? I was just coming to look for you.'

'Who puts those glass night-light things in the Holy House?'

'I think people send money to the shrine offices to get it done.'

'Did you send for one for me?'

'No.'

'Somebody did.'

Shelagh smiled. 'The great thing about having been famous is that you must have more friends than you've ever met. Do come inside. Father Medlicott's had one over the eight and now he wants to play charades.'

7

Nothing happened. Sorrel had not expected trumpets to sound or angels to sing but she'd expected *something*. Waiting weeks turned into months, anticipation gave way to frustration, and Sorrel took it out on St Mary Mag's. She stopped going.

She had never told anybody the full extent of the hopes she had invested in the Norfolk shrine so when she started referring to Walsingham as 'that sacred swizz' Shelagh became puzzled and a little hurt. And Sorrel couldn't bring herself to offer an explanation.

Father Medlicott demanded one. One frosty January morning Sorrel was hurrying across Shepherd Market to deliver a Shelley jug to an antique shop owner, who had commissioned her to find it, to make up a pair. To her annoyance the shop was not yet open. The pharmacy opposite was, and Father Medlicott stepped out of its doorway wearing a long black cloak. He had already opened the box containing a preparation for haemorrhoids and was busy reading the printed sheet of directions. Sorrel's red ski-hat must have bobbed into his line of vision for he now gave her the benefit of a reproachful gaze.

'I had thought of calling upon you,' he said. 'We've missed you. I expect God has too. Where have you been?'

'Licking my wounds. I asked for a miracle and I didn't get one.'

'Sorrel, Sorrel, Sorrel . . .' He sounded just like her old headmistress, except Miss Bolt would have said 'Sheila'. For all the difference it made, Sorrel might still have been twelve because the priest went on: 'Whatever are we going to do with you?'

'Forget me like I've forgotten St Mary Mag's. If I got what I asked for at Walsingham it would be different.'

'My dear child, Our Lady is not a vending machine. You

'don't just put in your fifty-pence piece and expect a favour to come out at the other end.' Sorrel would have betted anything that he was about to assume a holy expression and he obliged her. 'You can rest assured that the Blessed Virgin will have taken your needs to God.'

'He's certainly in no rush to do anything about them. It's no use, Father, I'm a lost cause.'

'I refuse to believe it.' He retorted this so firmly that his indignant breath left a little cloud on the cold morning. 'God moves in tides and seasons. It's the Evil One who deals in easy, instant solutions.'

Sorrel resisted the temptation to say that turning water into wine was a pretty snappy conjuring trick – the last thing she wanted to provoke was a sermon. With some relief she noticed that the absent antique shop owner was now putting her key into the door of her premises.

'I must go,' said Sorrel. 'I hope your bottom soon gets better, Father Medlicott.' Suddenly realizing that this friendly Northern candour could be taken for rude, she decided to soften it with some helpful advice: 'That stuff the chemist's sold you is as big a swizz as Walsingham. Go back and ask for Preparation H. Mamie Hamilton-Gerrard swears there's no finer remedy for a touch of the Farmer Giles.' Only at this late date did Sorrel realize that both Mamie and Bernard Conroy the producer were martyrs to complaints of this nature. Perhaps that's what had drawn them together in the first place.

Father Medlicott was not prepared to let her go as easily as that. 'What if I said we needed you?'

'I wouldn't believe it. And I'll tell you something else. If Jesus Christ came back today, I bet you wouldn't let him receive Holy Communion either. He's another who wouldn't be conventional enough for the Church of England. Good morning, Father.' Sorrel turned on her heel, walked into the antique shop and sold the woman the jug for nineteen pounds, cash.

Underneath Sorrel's selection of woollen hats, the red dye was beginning to grow out of her hair again. A shade which the charitable would have called 'ash blonde' began to appear at the roots. This time Sorrel let it go on appearing. It grew quickly, at the rate of about an inch a month. Red hair belonged to Lettie Bly and each succeeding inch took Sorrel further away from that auburn albatross.

There would be no point in pretending that her life had become any more cheerful. In later years, when these testing times were over, Sorrel would look back on the early 1980s and marvel that she had ever got through them. It was like viewing life through a mucky window or living with permanent jaundice. On the nights when even alcohol would not put her restless mind to sleep, Sorrel learned that the sky is truly at its blackest before the break of dawn.

One thing prospered – her stall. These days Sorrel was known on the market as the Deco Lady. Christian German was always suggesting she put it above the stall. His stoned, teasing humour did much to help her through these months and years.

'Deco Lady,' he would say, 'do get your face lifted. It's the only thing that's stopping us being Dante and Beatrice, Romeo and Juliet, Sonny and Cher. Considering all you've done to it, the body's still smashing. But the face tells too many unhappy stories.'

'You're a cheeky sod,' she would protest, but this didn't stop her liking him. Christian was a kind-hearted soul, always willing to take Spud to Holland Park, in his jeep, and give him a run. The dog was almost as well known a Portobello character as the Deco Lady. Every morning, at precisely twelve o'clock, he would walk halfway down the block to his own butcher's. Spud had reached this arrangement independently. Sorrel had given up trying to pay the man.

'There goes Spud,' people would say as though God was in his heaven and all was right with the world. These same people were always waiting hopefully for the American dealers to arrive. 'When the Americans come . . .' was their permanent cry. But when they came they were reluctant to part with their dollars. The days when they had shipped away container-loads, of any and every kind of antique, were coming to an end. Sorrel always did well out of them because Art Deco was becoming all the rage in the States. She dealt regularly with buyers from the West Coast and New York and the Lalique cocktail set finally found its way into the hands of a private collector from Chicago.

Miss Newton, at the military uniform stall, owned the only telephone in the arcade. The message marked 'Urgent' was from Shelagh. It asked Sorrel to ring an unfamiliar Manchester number. Taking a pile of loose silver from the cash box, Sorrel cut through the crowds to a public telephone booth.

It wasn't a voice which answered at the other end, it was a series of asthmatic wheezes. Sorrel was certain that these must belong to Mrs Tatton, her mother's neighbour in Rookswood Avenue, one of the few people left who still addressed her as Sheila.

'I don't want to panic you, Sheila, but your mother's in a bad way. It was a stroke. They kept her in for a bit but now she's home and it's pitiful. I think you ought to come.'

'How bad is she?' Sorrel was already annoyed with herself for not adjusting easily to the idea of being a dutiful daughter. But Gladys had never been a loving mother. 'How bad?'

'Bad. There's no other word for it. Her speech has gone, she's dragging one leg and the hand on that side doesn't seem to work properly. She shouldn't be on her own. She keeps dropping things.'

Sorrel suddenly remembered that Gladys – on the morning they had moved into the Nun's Prayer – had risen at dawn to scrub her way through the whole day. And that was enough. 'I'll come. I'll get a train tonight.'

'If you've not got a key, I'll have to let you in,' wheezed Mrs Tatton. 'She can't manage the front door.'

Sorrel pushed aside the glowing thought that Barney might also be in Manchester and repeated: 'I'll get a train tonight.'

At Euston Station she came down firmly against first-class travel. Fame had been the only thing which had caused her to buy a seat in compartments where people didn't want to talk – and fame was a thing of the past. Or so she thought. If the ticket collector proved to be difficult about Spud, the pair of them could travel in the guard's van. The train was half empty but a beery-looking Manchester businessman elected to settle himself down in the seat opposite to her.

'First a day in London,' he grumbled, 'and now no dining car. I hate that London. They've got port wine you can see through. It's Lettie Bly, isn't it? I must say you've let yourself go, Lettie!' With this he closed his eyes, presumably to sleep off the effects of the inferior port.

Let herself go? It was as though she was already back in Manchester. Whilst retaining her own Northern candour, Sorrel had forgotten how devastating it was to be on the receiving end. Once she was sure the man was asleep she changed seats.

Spud was the one who was almost recognized on the journey from Piccadilly Station to Rookswood Avenue: 'Isn't he like that dog who used to be on *Angel Dwellings*?' The taxi driver asked this without giving ash-blonde Sorrel a second glance.

She got the cab to stop at Mrs Tatton's. The light was on in her mother's house but the curtains were drawn.

'You're a good girl,' said Mrs Tatton. 'I've only just told her you're coming.'

'How did she react?' Sorrel noted that glaring overhead lights were still the fashion on the Ravensdale Estate.

'She just made noises.' The neighbour looked nervous. 'She can't really manage much more than noises. They should never have let her out. She understands everything,' added Mrs Tatton hastily, 'doesn't miss a trick.'

Never did, thought Sorrel and wished she could feel more warmly disposed towards the situation that had been thrust upon her.

'Have you got a key?'

Sorrel shook her head. Gladys had never allowed her to take one away on the grounds that she would be bound to lose it.

'I'll let you in.' Mrs Tatton bent down and pushed a barbed cat back into the through room. 'Let's go,' she wheezed, as though she had been watching a lot of American films on television.

At first glance the Gladys Starkey who sat in an armchair looking into a fire that was laid but not lit, looked unchanged. But that was only at first glance. As Gladys turned her head

Sorrel saw that she was not quite so well groomed as usual and one eye and the right side of her mouth were pulled down, like half of the mask of tragedy.

'I tried doing her hair but I couldn't get it to her satisfaction,' apologized Mrs Tatton. 'You know how particular she is.'

Yes, and she's not deaf either, thought Sorrel. I can tell that by the look on her face.

'Hello, Mother,' she said and steeled herself to give the crooked mouth a kiss. Normally when they did manage a kiss, it was only on one cheek, but Sorrel didn't want Gladys to think that she found her affliction distasteful.

The look which Gladys gave her daughter was hard to read. Fury mixed with something that, in anybody else, could have been taken for affection. Her mouth opened awkwardly and she said, 'I can't . . .'

'Can't what?' asked Sorrel. She was actually thinking of herself as 'Sheila' again. The house was as much like a stand at a pre-war Ideal Homes exhibition as ever. 'What can't you?'

'Take no notice of that,' whispered Mrs Tatton, 'she says it all the time. "I can't" is about all she can say.'

'I can't . . .' There it went again.

Mrs Tatton seemed able to ignore it. 'I got some boiled ham in for you, Sheila, just in case you landed in peckish. It's in your mother's fridge with some English tomatoes. You'll find my own bottle of salad cream on the top. I'll leave you to it. Ta-ta, Mrs Starkey,' she called out over-brightly as she handed Sorrel the spare key and left.

Gladys immediately gave Sorrel a look which said as plainly as any words: 'Don't lose that key', and her daughter moved into the kitchen to put the kettle on.

'We'll manage,' Sorrel said as she went. 'If there's one thing I'm good at coping with it's emergencies.'

Gladys's daughter was less good at monotony and routine. On Tuesdays and Thursdays the ambulance came to take Gladys off to physiotherapy. It wasn't a true ambulance, more a bus, full of disconsolate faces gazing down on other people's crazy-paving and crocuses. It always managed to block the avenue and provoke honking. Everybody in Rookswood

Avenue, except the Starkeys, seemed to have a car these days. They were mostly new people. And they weren't in and out of one another's houses as they had been in Sorrel's childhood.

On Mondays the speech therapist came to call. Deborah was a mousy girl with pink-rimmed glasses, much given to Laura Ashley prints. She described herself as 'into drama' and was presently rehearsing for an amateur production of *Oh What a Lovely War!*

Deborah would encourage Gladys to suck used postage stamps onto the end of a drinking straw and transfer them to the other side of the table. There, Gladys was meant to drop the stamps, one by one, until she had made a little paper pile. Throughout this process, Deborah would expect Sorrel to listen to an endless account of her amateur experiences. She regarded Alan Ayckbourn, the playwright, as second only to Shakespeare. And 'I'm like Beryl Reid. I'm a great believer in building a part from the feet upwards' was a typical sample of Deborah's conversation.

As showbusiness had treated Sorrel like a punchbag, she had little in common with this woman who viewed the theatre as an enthralling toy. The professional actress almost envied the speech therapist. For Deborah, the mysteries of the theatre were still wondrously intact. When the speech therapist switched on her portable tape recorder Sorrel generally fled the room. The words Gladys tried to form always turned into mangled, strangulated sounds.

'It's all there,' Deborah would say, 'we've simply got to get her powers of communication organized. Stimulation, that's the thing! Have you such a thing as a family photograph album?'

Though the question was addressed to Sorrel, Gladys's eyes immediately shot towards the top drawer of the bureau. It was amazing how much she could convey with those old green eyes and nods and shakes and tosses of the head. It sometimes seemed to Sorrel that Gladys could even communicate inflections.

But the only real words that came out were always the same: 'I can't . . . I can't.'

Sorrel had heard these so often that they had turned into a

657

vocal version of the Chinese water torture. 'I can't . . . I can't.' Sometimes she felt like screaming, 'Change the record!' It wasn't that Gladys was not trying; she was. It was as though the needle was stuck in a groove. 'I can't . . . I can't.'

Sorrel handed the speech therapist the photograph album and the girl opened it at random. 'What a handsome man! My goodness me, I bet he caused some hearts to flutter in his time.'

It was a picture of Norman Jepson in his wedding blazer. The look of loathing which Gladys directed towards the photograph left Sorrel wondering whether her mother actually needed words.

'Patients often respond wonderfully well to happy memories from the past,' beamed Deborah.

Gladys transferred her black look from the album to the speech therapist and Sorrel went into the hall to get her raincoat and Spud's lead. When she came back into the through room, to fasten the lead onto his collar, Gladys flashed a look which said: 'And just you come home sober.'

Spud led the way down the path. These days there were people on the Ravensdale Estate who spoke of him as 'Sorrel Starkey's guide dog'. She was all right going out but on the way back from the pub she sometimes needed a bit of nudging. Pub? Pubs more like! They never went down to Irlams o'th' Height because most of the village had disappeared under a road of almost motorway proportions. Instead, they always trudged up the hill towards Swinton. Sorrel never really took in the names of the public houses. She thought of them in terms of 'The one where you have to mind the step' and 'The bleak one with the dated jukebox'.

She never had more than two drinks, in any one pub, in the mistaken belief that this would cause less comment. It was well known locally that Sorrel Starkey always had two drinks in each of five pubs and that she'd been barred from a sixth for shouting at a man who addressed her as Lettie Bly.

'A large vodka and may I have some ten-pence pieces for the jukebox?' After the first drink, which just about leavened her into a semblance of a human being, Sorrel always needed to buy noise to drown out her own unhappy thoughts.

'There's a man been in, looking for you.' The barmaid pushed an empty glass up against the vodka optic. 'He's on the phone at the moment.'

Sorrel did not react. Things had reached a stage where she did her best to avoid human contact. Her opinion of herself was at an all-time low level. Moving across to the jukebox she dropped in a coin and pressed *17B*. It was Leo Sayer singing 'I'm a One Man Band'. Sorrel took a deep swig and as the melancholy music filled the empty pub she walked back to the bar.

'Could I trouble you for the same again please?' Advanced drunks are frequently painfully polite. There is suppressed apology in their every request. Sorrel took the drink to a far table and sat down with Spud at her feet. She had forgotten to bring her library book; that was another good way of cutting off the world.

A young man came through the door from the public bar. He was jingling a handful of loose change. Sorrel noticed the barmaid give him a covert nod in her own direction.

'Miss Starkey?'

Oh God, not a reporter's notebook! He looked too young and innocent for that.

'I wonder if I could just ask you a few questions?' He pulled up a stool and sat down next to her. 'I'm on the local paper but I feed stories to several of the nationals. Have you ever seen the *Where Are They Now* column?'

Sorrel had indeed seen this obscenity which delighted in recounting how former stars of the London Palladium were reduced to doing bread-rounds. She decided to say nothing – absolutely nothing.

'The thing is, we've heard your divorce is coming up so there might be quite a nice bit of public interest in you again.'

Sorrel treated him to a look she had borrowed from her mother.

'What are you doing these days, Miss Starkey?'

For the first time Sorrel had some true understanding of the strength of Gladys's position. Being scathing with a glance was a thoroughly satisfying process.

The boy went red. 'I'm only trying to do my job,' he

stammered. 'Were you never young? Did you never want a chance?'

Me oh my, thought Sorrel, you'll do all right! You're barely out of the egg but you already know how to turn on the manipulative tricks. Aloud she still said nothing.

'Can I buy you a drink?'

'No.' It was the only word she was prepared to utter. If anybody had brought her to this moment it was herself. But the tabloid press had certainly had a good meal off her downfall. She owed them nothing. She was beginning to feel sorry for the young reporter. How on earth was he going to manage a dignified exit?

She needn't have worried. He just got up and walked over to the counter. 'Is this Sorrel's local?' he asked the barmaid.

'Poor cow, they're *all* her locals.' The woman didn't even bother to lower her voice. 'I sometimes think she's drunk herself onto another planet.'

Already anticipating Sorrel's next move, Spud got to his feet and began to lead her towards the door. Her audience of two watched her go. What did they know? Where had they been? Only these days she wished she'd never been anywhere. She wished she'd just been content to be an ordinary person like the ones going past on the 38 bus. They had every right to be in this early spring sunlight which had nothing to do with Sorrel Starkey and only made her feel guilty.

'*They're all her locals.*' The woman's words rang round her head. Sorrel's minor deception had failed. Nobody was kidded. Well, if they wanted a piss-artist, she would show them one! Spud was already leading her towards the next port of call and the look in the dog's clever eyes was apprehensive.

Sorrel got home later than usual that day. There had already been a row in the bank; the cashier had maintained that he couldn't decipher her signature.

'Ask anybody,' she had shouted. 'They'll soon tell you I'm the poor cow who drank herself onto another planet.' A mother with small children started complaining about bad language. In the end, they cashed Sorrel's cheque just to get her out of the place.

Sorrel's own mother had 'You're late' written all over her face.

'Why can't you talk to me?' screamed Sorrel. 'It's months since I've talked to anybody. You don't know what it's like. I'm dying inside. Say something to me. You could if you tried. Say anything, anything at all just so long as it isn't *I can't*.'

Gladys looked right into Sorrel, opened her twisted mouth and said clearly and distastefully: 'You're drunk.'

Gladys's powers of movement kept pace with the continued improvement in her speech. Sorrel was so relieved to hear her mother talking again that, for the first time in decades, she actually listened to what Gladys was saying. An altogether warmer woman seemed to have emerged from the other side of the stroke – which wasn't to say that Gladys's powers of criticism were in any way impaired.

'That Samantha's lad-mad!' She was talking about the young assistant who had held the fort, at the hardware shop, during her illness. 'She's chucked the boy from the Indian takeaway in favour of the new paraffin man. The only thing to do is look on the bright side; at least we'll be sure of regular deliveries!' Even in her absence, Gladys's business was prospering. Sorrel's stall on Portobello seemed to be going through difficult times. Christian German, who was minding the stall, kept ringing up to urge Sorrel to look for new stock in the North. Sorrel's days were ruled by pub opening hours. Though she was forever planning to head off on a buying expedition, it was always 'tomorrow'. She was also going to stop drinking – and that was tomorrow too.

Much as Gladys's health had improved, she still wasn't well enough to leave. Sorrel knew that Christian had managed to shift all her smaller stock and she rang the woman dealer near Father Medlicott's church in Shepherd Market, asking her to take the more valuable items and sell them on commission.

It was the end of an era. And another legend's days were numbered. As Gladys's legs got better Spud's grew worse. Sometimes, on their way back from the pub, he would simply have to sit down on the pavement and wait for the use to come back into them. Each time he did this he seemed to get to his feet a little more hesitantly. Sometimes, in the night, Sorrel would hear him crying out in his sleep.

'It's no good.' Gladys was rubbing the dog's back legs. 'You'll have to take him to the vet. Spud must be the oldest border collie on earth. I've never heard of one living as long as this before. I think he just keeps alive to look after you.'

Sorrel dreaded to think what the vet might suggest but she couldn't bear to see Spud in pain, so she rang Mr Garner and made an appointment. As usual, they went to Altrincham by taxi. Spud had difficulty in getting into the car and Sorrel was obliged to carry him at the other end.

'Put him on the table.' Mr Garner looked serious. 'Well then, Spud, let's have a look at you.' As the vet began to manipulate his limbs Spud cried out in pain.

'Don't hurt him,' pleaded Sorrel.

'I'm afraid each passing day must be hurting him a bit more.'

'What can you do?'

'Not a lot. He's had a remarkable innings.' This was followed by silence. The vet was plainly leaving the next move to Sorrel.

For the first time she admitted to herself just how lacklustre her dog's coat had become. And Spud had always taken such a dandy's pride in his appearance. 'If he was your dog, what would you do?'

The vet looked relieved. 'If he was mine, I'd be looking towards putting him down. And I'd do it within the next few days.'

'Do it now.' Sorrel had been rehearsing this dreadful possibility since Stretford. 'But I'll have to be with him. If I got to that door I'd only change my mind.'

'I'm afraid I was prepared for this.' The vet removed a paper towel from an enamelled kidney bowl and lifted up a hypodermic. 'I've already got everything ready. I promise you he won't feel a thing. It will all be over in a moment. Just hold him steady.'

Sorrel held Spud tight. She could feel his heart beating underneath his skinny ribs. He chose that moment to give her a look of trusting love. And then Spud's light went out. Sorrel even felt his heart stop. One minute there was life. The next there was unlife.

Blinded by tears she gave Spud's dear, tatty old coat a last stroke and sobbed, 'You won't let him go to a glue factory, will you?'

'You can collect his ashes.' The vet offered her his own clean handkerchief.

'I wouldn't know where to scatter them. He's lived in so many funny places.'

Sorrel did not say goodbye to the animal on the table. That was just a dead dog who looked like Spud. Making for the door, she held it open, as if to allow the real Spud to come with her. She did the same outside with the door of the taxi. If June Gee was right – and there was anything in Spiritualism – Sorrel had to be sure that Spud knew that he was still wanted.

Spud's death was worse than any bereavement Sorrel had ever known. For forty-eight hours she made no pretence of drawing a sober breath and even Gladys seemed to understand.

On the third morning, Sorrel dragged herself up to Swinton to look for a birthday card for Shelagh Starkey. Every window display in the new concrete shopping precinct seemed to feature Easter chicks and pastel bunnies. They reappeared again in the best card shop, where birthdays seemed to have been shoved into a far corner. Sorrel blinked her way back into the sunlight and caught sight of an establishment she always thought of as 'the fifty-pence shop'. It sold nothing but bankruptcy stock and ends of lines at bargain prices. A Day-Glo sign on their window proclaimed *Greetings Cards – Special Offers*.

Sorrel picked her way past displays of plastic toys and floor-to-ceiling shelves of bubble bath-essence in primary colours. Finally she found the cards. They were in an open wire tray. Some of them were halfway to good and she even debated sending Shelagh a musical card which played 'Happy Birthday to You'. But the tune was like demented pixies hammering on her overhung brain. As she hastily closed the card and put it down, her attention was caught by another.

After all these years ... it couldn't be possible! The photograph on the front was of herself and Spud. Engraved across it, in gold letters, were the words *Old Friends Are Best*. It was one of the cards June and Martyn had produced in the early days of *Angel Dwellings*. Sorrel looked young and hopeful in the picture and Spud still had an obstinate tuft of puppy hair on the top of his head. She couldn't just leave him in a wire tray for anybody to maul over, so Sorrel took the card to the check-out and bought herself and Spud for five pence.

Descending the concrete steps, she walked across the road to the post office and addressed the envelope to Mickey in San Francisco. Crossing out June's awful verse ('Through thick and thin, we'll lend a pin ...') she wrote instead: 'Spud died on Monday at four o'clock.' As she waited in the queue for the sealed card to be weighed for airmail, Sorrel reflected that this gesture was the nearest thing to a funeral service that Spud would ever have. She desperately wanted a drink but hated the idea of her dog's living memorial being a lonely, drunken woman lurching from one Swinton pub to another. He deserved better than that.

Nobody was looking so she kissed the card before she posted it and then marched straight into a public call box and rang her mother: 'I've got to go somewhere,' she said. 'It's somewhere important. Expect me when you see me. I can't explain ... Bye.'

Streets of terraced houses and the back of a rugby ground led to the bleak top road where Sorrel hailed a bus for Bolton. When she got there she transferred to a train.

Train? It was more like a charabanc on railway lines. In Sorrel's youth, children had arrived at Blackpool in style. During the daytime Sorrel knew she was grown-up and accepted that she had entered middle age. But at night she had this recurring dream that she was still at school and absolutely unable to learn the one lesson which would finally release her. At night she was still a child.

Sorrel looked through the train window for the cut-out figures of two men carrying a ladder which had always marked the three-quarter point of the journey to the coast. In the 1940s, to have said 'to the coast' would have sounded as though you were trying to talk like Betty Grable. But this was 1982. Now Sorrel got her first glimpse, on the far horizon, of the tower. Not that there was anybody to give her sixpence for spotting it. When the train finally stopped at Blackpool North, she could hardly believe her eyes. The beautiful, dark, mysterious station of her memories had been pulled down and replaced by something in life-size Lego. What's more, it didn't seem to be in the right place. It was too far back from the road.

It only took one step outside the station for Sorrel to be reassured. Blackpool still smelled of spun sugar and vinegar and pubs at opening time. In her childhood, the smell of beer had been one of the great mysteries of life. In those days pubs either had frosted-glass windows or thick lace curtains. She and Mickey had often taken young delight in going round in a revolving door to catch a glimpse of the mysteries which lay inside. Well now she knew. Sorrel knew altogether too much about pubs and she was in urgent need of one at the moment.

A concrete underpass brought her out at the top of Talbot Road. Here again the shops were full of Easter eggs. Didn't the Church have a name for the day before Good Friday? Yes and it was the day the Queen gave out little bags of money to the deserving poor. Today was Maundy Thursday. The road led downhill to Talbot Square where Sorrel had switched on the illuminations. Even on that night she had been overly conscious of the red neon sign which said *Yates's Wine Lodge*. What use was there in remembering that she had held Spud up to be cheered by the crowds? Sorrel pushed open the door of the wine lodge. Yates's sold draught champagne. Though a pretty idea it would not touch the aching spot. They also sold something called Famous Australian White Wine. It was said to be fortified with brandy and touched the spot so well that it frightened Sorrel. People addicted to this dreamy syrup waited, shivering in doorways, for the wine lodges to open. There were Yates's all over the North. Marble and mahogany temples to Bacchus. The one in Liverpool still boasted a

Victorian sign which read *Drink Makes a Good Servant But a Poor Master.*

Too bloody true! thought Sorrel as she ordered a Famous Australian White Wine. She had it the traditional way, hot with sugar. She had meant to ration herself to two of these potions but finished up having five, on an empty stomach. Feeling halfway to chloroformed, Sorrel staggered across the road and onto a tram on the promenade.

'Fares please.'

'Cleveleys.' Through the tram window Sorrel looked back, over her shoulder, and saw the view of the North Pier which she and Mickey had kept turning round to look at, on the day when they first went through a stage door. The tram reached Gynn Square. In the old days she would have got off to wind her way up the hill to Mr Tuffin's boarding house.

'The old days'. It was the first time Sorrel had ever caught herself thinking like that. She supposed she must be getting old. The tram continued to swish along the rails for Cleveleys. She got off at Anchorsholme which was just a brick tram shelter, on a man-made clifftop, in the middle of nowhere. There were no boats on the grey Irish Sea.

Crossing to the top of the road which led to Gander's old bungalow, Sorrel wondered whether to have one last drink. But there was nowhere to have it. Not true, there was a hotel on a far promontory. There would always be a hotel on the horizon – that was half the trouble. Sorrel continued down the road, opened a wrought-iron gate, walked up the path and knocked on Gander's sister's door.

Nobody answered. There was another door, set in a trellis, at the side of the house and Sorrel rattled it open. Edie looked up, startled. She was down on her knees with a trowel, putting in spring bedding plants. 'What a nice little surprise. You're as welcome as the flowers in May.' It sounded so like Gander that Sorrel started to cry. Edie immediately got to her feet and warm arms went around Sorrel.

'Phew!' snorted Edie. 'No need to ask where you've been. You've been in Yates's and you've been on their white blobs. My God, Sorrel, hot blobs for breakfast! That *is* the end of the road.'

'I hope so,' sobbed Sorrel. 'Oh I do hope so. I've come because you always promised to tell me how to stop drinking. Tell me now. Please . . . I need to stop. It's taken everything.'

8

'Alcoholics Anonymous?' Sorrel was refusing to believe what Edie was trying to tell her. 'That's the same solution everybody offers.'

'But I'm not everybody. I'm different.' This new Edie was a woman with authority. 'I know it works. I know from experience.'

It was not what Sorrel had been expecting. 'You could have told me that ten years ago.'

'You wouldn't have listened. I had to wait until you were desperate before there was any chance of you hearing me.'

There was precious little chance of her listening to the words Alcoholics Anonymous! Sorrel felt like screaming. Instead she shouted: 'I've come all this way on a bus and a train and a tram because you promised me you'd tell me how to stop drinking . . .'

'And I've told you.' Edie remained serene. 'What were you expecting? Some granny-witch trick? Did you think I'd go in the back garden and pick you some secret herbs? There *are* no secret herbs, Sorrel. Do what I did. Go to AA. It works.'

Edie's manner was so inexorable that Sorrel made the mistake of trying to put the older woman in her place: 'Don't think I'm swanking, Edie, but I happen to be quite well known . . .'

'And don't think I'm swanking, Sorrel, but there are people ten times as well known as you in the fellowship.'

'What's the fellowship?'

'AA. Alcoholics Anonymous.' Edie seemed able to lob that organization in from any angle.

'Who are these famous people?'

'Well I know of a Dick and a Buzz but they don't have surnames. I don't have one either. When I go to meetings I'm just Edie, an ex-drunk. I'm happy, Sorrel. Are you?'

'Do I look happy?' Sorrel gazed into Gander's old Chinese

lacquer mirror and saw herself as she really was – a bag-lady who happened to have a roof over her head. Next to her own reflection she noticed Edie looking around the room, puzzled.

'Sorrel, why haven't you brought Spud to see me?'

'He's dead.' Tears of unhappiness and frustration and panic began to fall. Alcoholics Anonymous – the idea was so final. It was like some dreadful footballer's life story serialized in a Sunday newspaper. She had no clear picture of how AA worked but men in white coats certainly came into her blurred thoughts on the subject.

Edie poked the fire. 'I'm sorry about Spud. But at least he was one job you saw right through to the end. I used to cry a lot –' this new Edie spoke dispassionately – 'I cried nearly every day. I was all but addicted to jukeboxes. I had to have the music dreamy and sad. One for my baby and ninety-eight more for the road!'

Sorrel stopped sobbing and stammered, 'You too?'

'Me and a million others. But that was yesterday. We got sick and tired of waking up, every morning, scared to death of getting out of bed.'

Sorrel was astounded. 'I thought that was only me.'

Edie laughed gently. 'We all thought it was "only me". And we all hated ourselves. There was no need. If I can do it, any bugger can. You're here. You've asked. That means you're certainly in with a chance.'

'Am I?' asked Sorrel hopefully. But black thoughts swam in and seized the hope. 'No. You've no idea of some of the things I've done.'

'Listen, I've heard people admit to murder in an AA meeting. And then they found out they weren't the only one in the room.'

Sorrel immediately resented the idea of something which thought it had all the answers. 'I think I'll go to a doctor. Privately, not on the National Health.'

'He'll take your money, that's for sure. There's doctors out there who've made millions out of us. But when he's finished he'll tell you that he's only a specialist and you'll need to go to the experts.'

'Who are they?' asked Sorrel eagerly. 'I'll cut out the middle man and go straight to the experts.'

'The experts are AA.'

It was worse than a game of chess.

'A lot of people are going to be very sorry about Spud,' said Edie. 'I would have expected it to have been in the papers. You must feel very on your own without him. But there's no need. I've already told you the answer.'

Sorrel suddenly remembered that she didn't want Spud's memorial to be a lonely woman lurching from drink to drink. 'Are you really happy?'

'Yes. And I didn't believe it was possible. I didn't think it was in me.'

'It's not in me.' Sorrel meant this.

'How will you know till you give it a try?'

'How do I do that?'

Edie pointed to the telephone. 'Ring AA.'

If it was 'game, set and match' in tennis, what was it in chess? 'Checkmate', that was it. Sorrel had reached checkmate. 'Will you ring them for me?'

'No.' Edie was at her most firm. 'You have to do this for yourself. I'm even going to force meself to charge you for the phone call. That way you'll value it.'

Just like Lady Mendl and Monsieur Ritz, thought Sorrel. Not that there was anything luxurious about ringing an organization for reformed drunkards. The number Edie gave her was a Manchester one. The woman who answered the telephone only asked Sorrel one question: 'Do you want to stop drinking?'

'Yes.' Edie had gone out of the room and Sorrel couldn't leave it at that. Suddenly she found herself pouring out more troubles and fears than she had ever dared examine. In Gander's old house she was shaking out all her mucky dusters and clinging desperately to the idea of 'Hope at the bottom of the box'.

The woman listened sympathetically enough but after commenting briefly on what Sorrel had said, she began to talk about herself. It was downright eerie. As this stranger gave the actress an account of her own drinking days, she could have been talking about Sorrel's own experiences. The setting, the details, were different but the core of the story was exactly the same.

'I had this lonely place, that hurt, inside me,' the stranger said, 'and drink seemed to fill it up. But that was at first . . .' As the story unfolded, even some of the details were the same. Bottles in her handbag, always getting drunk when she really wanted to be at her best, never having more than two drinks in one pub. It took a lot to impress Sorrel Starkey and she was impressed.

'How do I find out more?'

'Come to a meeting in Manchester tonight.' The woman gave her the time and the place and said she would look out for Sorrel. 'By the way, try not to have another drink. Just until you've heard what we've got to offer, just for today.'

At the very moment when Sorrel felt she was finally being understood this came as a serious stumbling block. 'If I don't have a drink, by half past seven my hands will be all shaky.'

The woman just laughed. 'Don't worry. Everybody there will know what you're going through. Nobody will be in any position to criticize. They've all had the shakes themselves. You're coming to the most expensive club in the world but we all pay our dues before we get there.'

Edie came back into the room with a mug of coffee just as Sorrel was replacing the receiver. 'Well?' she asked.

'If you thought white blobs for breakfast were the end of the road, I think this is. A meeting in a church hall!'

'Don't be so daft. The room's only hired. You're not at the end of the road. You're at the beginning.'

She might have been feeling beaten and battered but Sorrel Starkey was still an actress: 'Edie?' she asked. 'What should I wear? I don't want to look out of place. I thought perhaps a felt hat?'

'Wear what you want. I'd say it was impossible to turn up in the wrong thing. The first two members who ever spoke to me were a binman and a lady mayoress.' Edie smiled with real love. 'I almost envy you. Getting sober's like being made brand new. You're in with a chance of a whole new life.'

The most reassuring thing Sorrel saw at that first AA meeting was a cardboard sign, on the table, which said *Who You See Here, What You Hear Here – Leave Here*. The people ranged round this table, in a church hall beyond the university, all looked human and ordinary but strangely assorted. It could have been a meeting of a dramatic society. And, in its own way, it was.

Alcoholics Anonymous was founded by problem drinkers for problem drinkers. Sorrel was amazed to discover that there were no bosses and no rules. Instead, their suggested programme of recovery involved making twelve carefully defined steps towards a new life.

But at that initial meeting, it was simply put to the newcomer that it was the first drink that did the damage. If Sorrel avoided the first one there was no way she could have the second. She was only asked to consider the idea of doing this on a daily basis.

From the word go, a woman called Peg took Sorrel under her wing. 'For Gawd's sake,' roared Peg in tones of South London, 'I wouldn't dream of telling you I'll be sober next week. I'm an alky, love, I couldn't handle an idea as big as that. I'm just doing it for today.'

Peg was big and jolly and fifty-something, in charity-shop clothes. She had such fine fly-away hair that Sorrel longed to tell her about Linco-Beer shampoo. Sorrel had always believed in fair swaps and the woman seemed anxious to give away every bit of information she owned on the subject of keeping sober.

'The only way you hold onto sobriety is by giving it away,' bawled Peg. For all her noisiness she had hurt grey eyes. 'I'm passing the bloody message, dear, aint I?'

All of this had been before the meeting. It now began properly. Somebody read something from a book and Sorrel gave him no marks for performance.

'I think I'll have to go,' she whispered to Peg. 'It's my hands. They won't stop shaking.'

'Sit on them,' advised her new friend. 'The interesting part comes next.'

This interesting part was a woman who said she was going

to share her 'experience, strength and hope' with them. Sorrel immediately thought that the speaker had cribbed this line from Dame Edna Everage. An astonishing quarter of an hour later Sorrel was sold enough on AA to have decided that Dame Edna must have pinched the line from them. Pinched it and cheapened it.

This 'sharing' had simply consisted of the woman recounting what it had been like when she was drinking, how she had found AA, and what her life was like today. The speaker recounted events and emotions which exactly paralleled Sorrel's experiences. The sort of things she had hidden as dark secrets were held up to the light and scrutinized for what they really were – the symptoms of a killer disease.

When the woman had finished everybody was encouraged to say a few words. When it came to Sorrel's turn she was too moved to speak. The others seemed to understand. It was extraordinary. For the first time in her life, in a dusty church hall, back or beyond of nowhere, Sorrel Starkey finally felt she belonged.

The speaker announced that they were going to say a prayer but Sorrel was reassured to hear that this was to 'God as you understand him or don't understand him'. And an empty pint pot was passed around with the injunction: 'Please remember we are self-supporting by our own contributions.'

The one thing she didn't appreciate about the proceedings was the tea made with sterilized milk. Nobody seemed in a hurry to leave and Peg went off and found Sorrel a duplicated list of Manchester meetings. She was astonished to find that, some nights, there were nearly a dozen, in different parts of the city.

'Keep coming back,' advised Peg. 'What you need is ninety meetings in ninety days.'

This seemed such an enormous commitment that Sorrel felt bound to reply, 'I'm not sure that I could find all that time.'

'You found time to sit in pubs, didn't you?' Peg was one jump ahead of her. They all were. 'If you feel like picking up a drink,' warned Peg, 'don't. Pick up the phone and talk about it instead. Write down my number. Call me any time, day or night. There's no need to start bloody crying. Somebody once gave me their number when I was in need. I'm only paying back. One day you'll be able to do it for somebody else.'

It was all built along lines which Sorrel understood. But if anybody had told her that, night after night, she would find her way to AA meetings in Sunday schools, in mental hospitals, in a Jesuit presbytery and a Quaker meeting house – she would not have believed them. But she did keep going back because these people had something she wanted.

'They've got a special look in their eyes.' She was trying to explain it to Gladys.

'I expect their eyes are startled to find they're no longer bloodshot!' But Sorrel could tell that Gladys was pleased. And one day her mother even shoved twenty pounds into her hand and said, 'For God's sake go and get your hair done. But don't have it dyed red again. That went with the woman who drank.'

Ninety meetings in ninety days; one of her favourite ones was in Bolton Town Hall where recovering alcoholics sat under portraits of deceased aldermen. Riding home on the top deck of the bus from Bolton, she looked down on another illuminated Town Hall – glittering through the rain – perhaps five miles away, amidst the lights of Manchester. As the bus bounced along, Sorrel suddenly found herself filled with an extraordinary feeling. It was so good it was like her very first drink of alcohol – that magic feeling she had been trying to find again ever since. But she hadn't had a drink. What could it be?

The fact of the matter was that Sorrel was simply experiencing a sense of well-being. It had been so long since she'd had one that she didn't even recognize it.

Some members of the fellowship tried to warn Sorrel that she was going through a honeymoon period but Big Peg brushed this aside with 'All I can say is I must have been on my honeymoon for five years. And it's getting better every day.'

Sorrel simply felt as though she was a dry sponge who had been put back into the water. Every new idea she heard at meetings flooded in and made her the more buoyant. She was afloat again and – miraculously – despite all she had done to herself in the past, she was still whole.

Then she hit a rock. One of the suggested steps involved handing your life and your will over to a power greater than yourself. 'It's no good,' she said to Peg, 'I tried that once. I went to Walsingham and look where it got me!'

'Some people might say it got you here,' was Peg's dry answer. This was enough for Sorrel to feel that she'd come out of the waterweeds and was back in the stream. She even took two buses to St Benedict's, Ardwick, which was Manchester's equivalent of St Mary Mag's. Not to a service. It was just that Sorrel had heard that there was a statue of Our Lady of Walsingham there so she went and lit a candle to say thank you.

As she held the wick to one that was already aflame she said, 'If it was you who did it then I'm very grateful.' She even managed one 'Hail Mary' for old times' sake. Sorrel did this on her knees because she wanted to be in the proper position for praying, to say what she had really come to ask. Now she risked it: 'You won't forget about Barney Shapiro, will you? Thank you. Yours sincerely Sorrel Starkey. Amen.'

The stained glass of St Benedict's windows was the colour of nicotine on a smoker's forefinger. It was like being inside a perpetual thunderstorm and the big, heart-shaped black iron candlestands reminded Sorrel of the Spanish Inquisition. All in all she was glad to get out into the sunlight where a gang of kids were kicking a half-collapsed football around an open space between concrete tower blocks.

The Manchester of L. S. Lowry's paintings had all but gone and Sorrel had been so anaesthetized by drink that she had failed to hear the bulldozers or register the changing skyline. Soon after she got sober she had decided to go and look for the old Hadassiah restaurant which she had last known in its incarnation as the Cromford Club. The place had played a big enough part in Sorrel's life for her to wonder what was going on there today.

It had gone. The whole of that side of Market Street, all the old shops and alleyways and dark passages opening into curious little courtyards, had vanished. They had been replaced by a huge yellow-tiled, covered shopping precinct. Only other AA members could believe that Sorrel Starkey had been so drunk that the Arndale Centre had been built without her even noticing.

But she was stone cold sober today and outside St Benedict the half-deflated football, banging against concrete, was too defeated a sound for a clear crisp morning. Sorrel decided to cut through the new corporation housing development and pay a visit to Belle Vue Zoo and Pleasure Gardens on the other side of Hyde Road. Her duty done in church, she now planned to treat herself to an adventure. She had never been on Belle Vue's most famous fairground ride – an antique roller-coaster called The Bobs – and she planned to rectify that omission. So what if she was well over forty? Sorrel Starkey was learning to live in *the now*.

Too late! The now did not include The Bobs. All that was left of the ride was a few wooden uprights. The main exits of the pleasure gardens lay wide open, the turnstiles had vanished, mechanical diggers were ploughing up the tree-lined boulevard which had once led to the tiger house and the Elizabethan Suite. Wimpeys the builders had already raised a sign on the site of the Mappin Terraces announcing their intention of building an architect-designed housing estate.

Sprawling in the distance, like the most that had ever been managed in wood and asbestos, lay the great ramshackle bulk of the King's Hall. A brave red, white and blue banner was stretched across its front announcing *The Last Belle Vue Circus*.

Would that also be over? Sorrel decided to get closer and find out.

As she picked her way over recently dug clods of earth, she noticed that they were already sprouting white clover and that cabbage butterflies were hovering above the pale flowers. And now she spotted some gaudy circus caravans grouped round the battered building which, in the past, had held everything from wartime Hallé concerts to free-style wrestling. As a child, Sorrel had once seen a poster for this wrestling which had just featured two nearly naked men and the words *Belle Vue*. The infant Sorrel had read and understood it phonetically – belly view. Though it had made perfect sense it had seemed a bit 'rude' for The Height.

A middle-aged dwarf came down the steps of one of the caravans. He wasn't a midget. He was the kind with an over-large head and chubby hands like June Gee's and short, bowed legs. But behind his National Health, wire-framed glasses, he had a sweet smile. 'There used to be a little steam train where you're standing.' Sorrel was surprised to hear that he had a German-sounding accent.

'I know.' If he was a circus clown perhaps she should mention that she too was in showbusiness. It was so long since she had worked that Sorrel thought better of it and said instead, 'I remember that train quite clearly. And the poor old camel with the wooden saddle; he cost sixpence a ride.'

'All gone,' the clown said gravely. 'Just vanished as though the children didn't matter. Do you remember the firework displays over the lake? They always played the Grand March from *Aida* when the elephants came on.'

'Oh yes, and people dancing foxtrots, in the open air, on a real ballroom floor. It's awful,' sighed Sorrel. 'Terrible. But at least we'll remember it and we've still got tomorrow.' And if that sounded like a sentiment by June Gee she didn't care. She meant it. Alcoholics Anonymous might be teaching Sorrel Starkey to live in today but she was beginning to do it with a view to tomorrow.

The circus box office was in another of the caravans and she bought two good seats for the following Friday. Her mother would put up a show of grumbling then climb into her second-best coat (Sorrel could already hear her saying 'You never know who's sat on those seats before') and then Gladys would thoroughly enjoy herself.

It was as though the stroke had finally given Gladys Starkey a licence to glow. She was turning into something surprisingly close to an entertaining companion. But, recently, there had been repeated comments about being seen out with a daughter who looked like an unmade bed.

The time had come for Sorrel to buy some new clothes. From Belle Vue she took a bus into the city centre and made

677

her way towards King Street. The Salmon sisters were no longer in business. 'The Bond Street of the North' which had once been full of nothing but Manchester fashion merchants had now been taken over by branches of nationwide chains. Rita Salmon would have viewed the sight of Sorrel in a washed-out black track-suit as a challenge. Sorrel stared through a shop window. Would the confident teenage assistant, on the other side of the glass, have inherited Rita's attitude? Sorrel wasn't sure her own new-found confidence was up to this test.

'And all the clothes are so juvenile,' said a familiar voice behind her. It was Ruby Shapiro.

'Don't look at me!' Sorrel felt even more of a mess than before. 'I know I look terrible.'

'I am looking. And I'm liking what I see. Clothes, they can be fixed. Your skin looks ten years younger and your eyes! Where did you get that serene look from?'

This question was better than getting a part in a new show. Night after night Sorrel had gone to meetings, just working on herself and hoping for that enviable AA look in the eyes. And now, without any fishing for compliments, Ruby Shapiro had announced that it was finally here. Sorrel flung her arms around her old friend. 'Where do I get the clothes to match it? You've always told me what to wear. Tell me again.'

'Let's go and think about it in Kendal's. Let's go and have some coffee.'

Kendal's ground floor seemed to have fewer carpets but more perfume counters than ever and still smelled like Sorrel's idea of Araby.

'May I?' A woman in a white overall, whose makeup looked as though it had been done by numbers, bore down on Ruby with a scent spray.

'No you may not. In furs? Are you mad? They'd stink for a month.'

Sorrel had already noticed that Ruby's sables – the ones she'd borrowed for the trip to Vienna – had been reworked into one of the new broad-shouldered coats with a chinchilla collar. Catching her staring at these shoulders Ruby said, 'Elegant, isn't it? But murder for getting through doors. Sometimes I have to walk into a room sideways.'

678

The express lift began its upward purr and as the doors opened, at the top floor, an old woman carrying a mop and bucket across the marble concourse cried out in delight, 'It's Sorrel Starkey! D'you remember me, Sorrel? I mopped up after you the day you got engaged to that bad bastard and knocked over the meat and tater pie.'

Oh but life tasted good again! Ruby and Sorrel moved across to a table and sat down. As the Jewess slackened her impressive furs she looked almost guilty and embarrassed. It was obvious that Ruby was debating saying something important so Sorrel kept silent.

Finally it came out: 'I was wrong, Sorrel, and now I know it. There should have been no need for that shabby fandango with Kenny Shorrocks. I blame myself for that. Don't interrupt . . . this is going to be a speech.

'I should have let you marry Barney. You're a good girl. You've faced up to your problems and we'll soon have you looking a million dollars. Your mother needed you and you didn't think about yourself. You did your duty. You came home. You may not be Jewish but you've got a Jewish heart. I should have forgotten tradition. You're the wife my son should have had.'

Moved as she was by Ruby's words, for the first time in her life Sorrel resisted the temptation to ask after Barney. In an AA meeting she had heard someone say that the woman who does not learn by her mistakes is condemned to repeat them. If Barney ever wanted to see her again – fine. But this time Barney Shapiro was the one who would have to make the running.

Fascinated outsiders were forever trying to get Sorrel to define alcoholism. 'It's when drink costs you more than money' was the best she could manage.

At the end of ninety drink-free days she cut down her meetings to two a week. But nothing was allowed to interfere with these. Sorrel saw them as her lifeline. She had learned so much in this strange selection of rooms that sometimes she was left thinking that there was more than people in them. She began to understand why magicians, traditionally, sat in circles. There were occasions, as a meeting progressed, when a power would build up on the air which was so strong that Sorrel felt they could have lit an electric light bulb with it.

She witnessed miracles. She watched shambling wrecks turn back into whole people. She heard things spoken which seemed to be beamed directly to her needs. Some of the speakers infuriated her. But Sorrel discovered that, like it or not, these were generally the ones she needed to listen to the most. One night a woman who seemed to have been grinding on for twenty minutes suddenly said, 'For forty years I blamed my mother for not being the woman I would have chosen. I expected the poor woman to give away more warmth than she'd got.'

It exactly described and explained Sorrel's own relationship with Gladys Starkey. She began to listen more closely as the woman went on to say, 'When I was a newcomer, an old member told me, "If everybody in this room could put all their troubles in a pile, in front of them, and we could all go round and pick a new set – the chances are we'd go straight back to our own."'

Sorrel Starkey was finally learning that she was uniquely qualified to be herself.

Even when the meetings ended, members tended to stick together for the rest of the evening: 'Sorrel, I know a woman who says she knows you . . .' Big Peg and her protégée were sitting drinking coffee in the Greek's on Oxford Street in Manchester. Posh it wasn't, the cafe was next door to an amusement arcade. But poshness had lost its hold over Sorrel. These days she saw it as having been one of her early, minor addictions.

'What's the woman called?' There had been many such addictions. Applause was one of them. If they weren't harmful there was no necessity to give them up. And renewed health and vitality were prodding Sorrel to do something about returning to the stage: 'Peg, you'll turn that coffee into syrup if you put any more sugar into it. Who is this woman?'

'She's called Dee. She lives in Moss Side. She's married to a West Indian.'

'I don't know any Dee.'

'Is your mother's name Gladys?'

'Yes.'

'Well then, Dee knows you.'

Half of the population of Manchester claimed to know Sorrel Starkey. She wasn't much interested. She was thinking about something else: 'I used to call myself Mrs Micawber. I used to say something would turn up. I never thought it would be AA.'

'Dee knows your friend June Monk too. Mrs Micawber? Know what they call me in Moss Side? Mrs Fagin! Nothing was ever too hot or too heavy for me. Not that I ever nicked things myself but I seem to have been born with this talent for shifting stuff.'

'And has AA changed all that?' Even as she said it, Sorrel realized that she must sound a sanctimonious prig.

'No it sodding-well hasn't. But I am trying to give up the swearing. Know anybody who wants to buy some duvet covers with a picture of Elvis on the front? OK, Sorrel, I know AA members are meant to be honest about everything but at least, these days, I'm an honest fence. Dee knows Mickey Grimshaw too.'

'How? Describe her. What's she like?'

'She's a white lady who tries to pretend she's black.'

'With makeup?' Sorrel was intrigued. 'Or does she just sing "Ol' Man River" a lot?'

'Dee's a real case. She tries to talk in Jamaican dialect. But even I can tell she gets it wrong. And on Sundays she dresses up to the nines, with a white picture hat and gloves, and goes off to that Hallelujah church with the real black women.'

'Come on.' Sorrel got to her feet.

'Where are we going?'

'Where d'you think we're going? To meet her, of course! I want to know who this mysterious woman is.'

They took a bus to Moss Side, a Manchester district which had been demolished in the cause of progress and rebuilt in housing department concrete. Friendly brick terraced houses had given way to nightmare walkways, in tower blocks, in the sky. Drugs, girls, sawn-off shotguns, curry patties, West Indian chicken – you could get them all in The Moss. There were still respectable hearts left there but they beat a little fearfully these days.

It was nine forty-five, on a dark night, when the bus let them off by the huge silvered metal vats of the Harp Lager building. 'This street's known as the front line,' Peg announced cheerfully. Sorrel was suddenly feeling apprehensive and she tried not to stare too hard at the handsome black youths lingering in the doorways of crumbling old brick buildings left over from a happier past.

What were they waiting for? As cars slowed down – without actually stopping – the young men would dart out and engage the drivers in short, hushed conversations. The talk was punctuated by constant glances to the left and right; then something was handed over, and cash came back through the wound-down window. The street light caught the gleam of metal foil and Sorrel thought immediately of Christian German. What she was witnessing was the takeaway drugs trade.

'It didn't worry me when it was just a bit of smoke.' Peg led the way across the main road. 'But now they're selling wraps of stinking skag as well. That's heroin on your side of town.' A police car came roaring up the road and missed them by inches. 'Some of the poor bastards are only out there dealing to feed their own habit. They're in a trap. Half of The Moss is in one kind of trap or another. The place is built on huge traffic islands with roads round them. Come the revolution, they'll be able to lock us off like sewer rats.'

Sorrel had never heard Peg sound so bitter. Neither had she seen so many discarded beer cans and old chip papers on a grass verge. Didn't the council send anybody round to clean up? She was relieved to see that their route was leading away from the ominous tower blocks and towards a crescent of semi-detached council houses. Some looked dog-rough whilst others were almost defiantly well tended. Discarded mattresses in one garden, clipped privet hedges round the next.

'She lives in one of these.'

Through an uncurtained window, Sorrel saw a large framed portrait of the Emperor Haile Selassie, painted in oils on a ground of black velvet. An equally black man with Rastafarian dreadlocks was gazing out at her. There seemed to be criticism in his look. 'It's not this one, is it?' she asked nervously.

'No. And you're quite safe. For once Lettie Bly will come in handy. Lettie was always regarded as a bit of a heroine round here.' Peg continued to march round the curve of the crescent. 'They know you hit a bad patch. They read the papers. That bastard Shorrocks might get a bit of stick round here but you'll be all right. People can say what they like about The Moss but we're not short on compassion. It's this one.'

The house was one of the well-tended kind. Peg pushed open the garden gate and banged on a black front door.

'Me coming,' yelled a woman's voice. 'Hold your noise, me heard you!'

The door opened and there stood a fatter, older but unmistakable Delia Dolan from Rookswood Avenue.

'You always said you'd marry a black man!' Sorrel was hugging her in delight.

'Me did, girl, me did.' Delia led the way across a hall and into a living room that would have been tidy enough even for Gladys Starkey. A grave negro, with white just beginning to show in his hair, was sitting beside the artificial logs of an electric fire reading *the Manchester Evening News*. And a half-caste teenaged boy and girl looked up from doing their homework at either side of the dining table. It was all as ordered as a tableau.

'This am me man,' said Delia proudly. 'This am Carlton Carstairs.'

He rose to his feet and shook Sorrel's hand gravely. 'I've heard a lot about you.' In contrast with his wife, his accent was almost standard English. Had he been an actor Sorrel would have described him as having tremendous presence. 'These are our younger children –' the voice was deep enough for the Royal Shakespeare Company – 'Ella and Otis.' Carlton Carstairs flashed a slow smile. 'My wife has always been an admirer of the great entertainers.'

'Brown girl,' said Delia to her daughter, 'put the kettle on. Or perhaps Auntie Sheila would prefer a droppa rum?'

683

'I don't drink any more.' Peg had obviously preserved her anonymity, which was AA's way of saying that she hadn't mentioned Sorrel was a member of the fellowship. 'I've not had a drink for nearly a year,' she added proudly.

'Very wrong,' snapped Delia. '"Take a little wine for thy stomach's sake," that's what the good book says.' She looked very stern and searching. 'Have you found the Lord Jesus Christ as your personal saviour, Sheila?'

Oh dear. But the husband proved to be altogether more relaxed than Delia. And what made the Manchester-Irish woman feel she had to talk like a nigger minstrel troupe? But, when she thought about it, Sorrel knew without being told. It was like shiksas who managed to land Jewish husbands and became more Hebrew than the Israelites. All this 'Don't gimme rice' talk was just Delia Dolan's way of clutching at some belonging.

Sorrel decided to change the angle of the conversation. 'How's Monica?'

This was plainly a mistake because Delia flared up with: 'She lives round the corner at sixty-six Bulmer Close. Sixty-six am two thirds of the devil's number. One morning that whore's going to wake up with the whole lot branded on her forehead.' Delia made a disapproving sucking noise with her upper lip against her teeth. The only time Sorrel had ever seen this before was on a Channel Four documentary about problems in Jamaica.

After that they didn't stay long. When they got outside Peg said, 'I gather the other sister's more your cup of tea?'

'I'd love to see her again,' admitted Sorrel, 'but I don't know whether she'd want to see me. I buggered something up for her, one night in The Midland. Actually I was only trying to be helpful.'

'Part of the programme is making amends.' Peg often startled Sorrel by the speed with which she could flip in and out of AA jargon. 'She's only round the bloody corner. Why don't you go and give it a whirl?'

'I'll go on my own, if you don't mind.' She wasn't sure how much Peg knew about Monica Dolan.

Sorrel should have known better: 'They call her the Queen

of the Moss,' grinned Peg, 'but she advertises herself as
Mistress de Kink. Better get your apology in fast or she might
get the cane out.'

9

This council house door had a spyhole in it. And the sound of
bolts being withdrawn and chains rattling back was almost as
ferocious as the barking of dogs from within. The door
opened. Monica Dolan now had two white streaks in her
great tumbling mane of black hair.

'You're not a punter.' Her voice was still as passionately
accusing as it had been in their childhood. 'You do realize that
this is a knocking shop?'

'Do I look worried?' Sorrel hoped she sounded less
nervous than she felt.

Two American pit bull terriers tore out from behind the
flimsy black skirts of Monica's outrageous nylon negligée.
They were brindle-coloured and looked ready for trouble.

'Meet the Kray twins,' said Monica. But Sorrel had already
bent down and was receiving a lot of licks and tail wagging.

'They've never done that in their lives before.' Monica was
openly astonished. 'You must have a bit of St Francis of Assisi
about you. Come in.'

The chandeliers in both the hall and the living room were
nineteenth-century French crystal. 'Did you know that those
are real?' asked Sorrel. 'They were originally designed for
candles. They're worth a bomb.'

'I don't buy rubbish. Everything's antique except for the
bed upstairs. That gets replaced quite often.'

Sorrel tried not to stare as Monica added a pair of knickers
to her professional ensemble. Instead, she looked around the
room. It was not at all what she would have expected. The
dove-grey walls were covered in a collection of framed,
embroidered samplers and the armchairs were real Regency,
button-studded in rose velvet. Where had Monica managed
to find that gambling table and those wonderful black
papier-mâché chairs, inlaid with mother-of-pearl?

But it was a human room. The shelves of books didn't look

as though they were just there for show and a battered teddybear sat on a shelf, underneath something which had once belonged to Monica's mother. It was a gaudy holy engraving, circled with the inscription *I Will Bless The Houses In Which The Picture Of My Sacred Heart Shall be Exposed And Honoured.*

Monica adjusted the waistband of her knickers. 'Sorry,' she said, 'I was dressed for work.'

'This room is absolutely beautiful.' Sorrel was still looking round with pleasure. 'I've always wanted white velvet curtains. Do they spend one week with you and two at the cleaner's?'

'They wash,' said Monica shortly. 'In my line of business everything has to be washable.'

'Oh, stop being so on the defensive.' Sorrel considered she had taken enough of it. 'And before we go any further I'm sorry if I said too much in front of that hall porter in The Midland.'

'I'm the one who should be sorry. I was a bit of a bitch that night. Do you want a drink? Oh no, I forgot, you've stopped.'

'How the hell do you know that?'

'Nothing goes on in this town that I don't get to hear of,' smiled Monica. 'And just you remember it. Shall I put the kettle on?'

'Could I go to the lav?' asked Sorrel. 'Everything was so correct at Delia's that I didn't dare to ask.'

'Upstairs on your right. So you've been to see that headcase, have you?' she called after Sorrel who was climbing a staircase covered in a prettily sprigged French paper that couldn't have cost a penny less than twenty pounds a roll. 'I wonder our Delia doesn't just black up and have done with it!'

Sorrel opened what she took to be the bathroom door, got one of the biggest shocks of a lifetime, closed the door hastily and found another. Never in her whole life had she been so relieved to see an unremarkable bathroom suite.

As she sat on the lavatory her thoughts were spinning: I must remember that I wasn't invited here. I just barged in. I'm sure I saw what I thought I saw, in that boxroom, but I must try to be very cool about it. I'll be judged by my reactions and I want to be friends with Monica again. She likes dogs and nice things and she was always my favourite girl in Rookswood Avenue.

Coming down the stairs, she decided to hum casually and was horrified to find that the tune which came out was 'Love for Sale'.

Indignation seemed to have seeped back into Monica: 'I don't want you to think I'm hustling on the rates. This isn't a council house any more, I bought it off them. The bloody council moved me here in the first place. I was compulsorily purchased out of Beresford Street. Sit down. Now that was a good house for whoring. Beresford Street had a cellar – the clients used to line up to be shoved down there. Want a Penguin biscuit? Don't give any to the dogs. Ronnie's got an enzyme deficiency and I don't believe in giving one what the other can't have.'

'Monica?' Sorrel was picking her inflections as carefully as her words. 'Should there be a man, tied up with a clothes-line, in your boxroom?'

'No there bloody shouldn't,' raged Monica. 'I'd clean forgotten him. The bastard only paid for two hours. You make the coffee. I'll just undo his knots and see him off the premises.'

The moment Monica strode out of the room the two pit bull terriers' one ambition in life seemed to be to get a taste of Sorrel's Penguin biscuit. 'No,' she said firmly and decided to find out which one was which. A specialist in domination would presumably have her dogs very well trained.

'Ronnie, sit!' A muscular little rump dropped obligingly to the rose-pink carpet. 'Now you, Reggie.' They might have looked like fugitives from a chain gang but they were every bit as keen as Spud on being scratched behind the ears. Sorrel still wasn't sure whether Monica was pleased to see her but she had certainly made two new friends here.

What were those mysterious noises overhead? No, it was better not to wonder. Quite quickly they turned into creaks on the stairs and sounds from the bolts and chains on the front door. Monica marched back into the room on her stilettos, waving a twenty-pound note in either hand.

'He's a regular client so he gets to pay afterwards. Always comes here on the way home from his Masonic lodge. People think of whoring as one long round of sex, but it isn't; not my kind. My job is simply taking money off men – the best way I can. I could see clients every hour on the hour if I wanted to. Know how long it is since I had what you would call sex?'

Sorrel was fascinated. 'No, tell me.'

'I couldn't. It's been so long that I've forgotten.' The phone rang.

'Hello . . .' Monica flipped open a large desk diary. 'I can fit you in tomorrow night at five past nine.' Her voice was suddenly severe and totally devoid of real emotion. She sounded as correct as somebody who had learned English as a second language. 'Not nine o'clock and not ten past. Repeat what time I said . . . And now apologize for troubling me . . . OK. But a moment early or a moment late and you will be very severely punished.'

As Monica replaced the receiver she said to Sorrel, 'That threat will probably do far more for him than anything that will really happen. It's all in their heads. I'm not making excuses for myself, I don't have to. But it's only an act. I don't get off on it.'

'I had a husband who was into all of that.' Sorrel suddenly remembered that she had been left in charge of the kettle and went into the kitchen.

'I know. He used to buy time here. Why have you come to see me?'

The programme of Alcoholics Anonymous had, if anything, reinforced Sorrel's basic honesty. 'Ten minutes ago I couldn't have told you. I just came on a whim. You were near. But now I suddenly realize I'm missing something. I'm the only woman I know who hasn't got a girlfriend who dates back to her childhood. Have you got one?'

'An actress couldn't be friends with a hooker, Sorrel.'

'Why not?' Even five minutes of Monica had been refreshing if startling. 'There's nothing to choose between us. I thought of that when I was listening to you on the telephone. We both sell illusions. And I'm not even working.'

'Don't bother with that awful instant coffee.' Monica spoke

with sudden decision. 'I'll put some real beans from Kendal's into the grinder. Isn't it funny how people can talk ninety to the dozen about sex but they're too shy to talk about friendship? I'm really glad you came. You can buy a fuck at the park gates but where can you buy a friend? I hope it wasn't your money Kenny Shorrocks spent here.' Monica placed the top on the coffee grinder and pressed the button. 'I read about the divorce.'

'It was the non-event of the year. I didn't even have to appear.'

The top suddenly flew off the grinder and both Monica and Sorrel found themselves covered in fine brown powder. 'Jesus, Mary and Joseph,' bawled Monica. 'This is what comes of trying to do things in style.'

But the faint embarrassment of friendship proffered and accepted had vanished and the pair of them were soon cleaning up the kitchen and grinding a second effort. As the coffee began to splutter into the filter machine, and the house was filled with that hopeful smell, the two women started to reminisce about Rookswood Avenue. They remembered June Monk misinforming them about the facts of life and Mickey bossing them into doing concerts on top of an old air-raid shelter. And they remembered all of their early ambitions.

'I blame that bloody Reverend Mother,' declared Monica. 'If ever a girl had a vocation it was me. I should have been a nun. That's been the nightmare of this job. Once a Catholic, always a Catholic. I still go to Mass but I've never taken Our Lord's body into my mouth since I've been on the game.' Monica had flung off the negligée and was climbing into clean slacks and a jersey which had been airing on a clothes-maiden. 'From what I've read, you've not had an easy time of things either.'

'No, but I wouldn't have missed it.' And Sorrel suddenly knew the reason why. 'It brought me to who I am today. Where did you get that jersey?'

'Out of a catalogue. There's no fun in shopping on your own.'

'We'll go shopping together.' Sorrel was suddenly, joyfully, reminded of her favourite line from *Uncle Vanya*: 'We shall sing and dance and be as sisters . . .' But she didn't say it aloud.

Monica interrupted these thoughts with: 'Do you miss all that fame?'

'No. I pass unnoticed and it suits me very well. Just occasionally I still get recognized. A funny thing happened in The Height Co-op yesterday. I was reaching for a can of tuna when a man rushed up to me with a camera and snatched a picture. Wham-bam-flash! He didn't even have a shopping trolley.'

'Could he have been from the newspapers?' Monica was removing her scarlet lipstick with Johnson's baby lotion and cotton wool.

'No. You develop an instinct for them and the bell didn't go off in my head. This was just some man, in an anorak, with an expensive camera.'

'The press have been here.' Monica pulled a distasteful face. 'I was supposed to have been entertaining a vice cop, for free. As if!' A troubled look passed across her face. 'Being friends with me could bring you problems, Sorrel.'

'Who cares?' Sorrel was back on the floor with the Kray twins. 'It's all settled. Ronnie and Reggie were practically waiting for me to arrive.'

'Are you a size twelve?' asked Monica.

'Yes. Why?'

'Here.' Monica pulled a beautifully ironed black linen dress off the clothes-maiden. 'Have this. It's a good one but it looks too tarty on me.'

Despite her recovery from alcoholism Sorrel was still left with one hangover from her drinking days. She did not surface easily in the mornings. She always woke up feeling as though her brain was beside her on the pillow. It took two cups of coffee for it to slot back into place. Rude awakenings were anathema to her and this particular morning had begun with a bang.

'Come on, Sheila.' Gladys was rattling back the curtains like a machine gun. 'It's about a pound a minute from America and he's already had to wait while I came upstairs.'

691

Sorrel was still halfway between dreams and reality. 'Who has?'

'Mickey. I let you sleep in this morning. He says it's the middle of the night in San Francisco.'

'What's he doing up then?' Sorrel was struggling into her dressing gown.

'Ask him, not me. Come on, Sheila, quick's the word and sharp's the action!'

Sorrel crawled down the stairs and lifted the receiver. There was still no chair by the telephone so she had to sit on the bottom step. 'Mick? What are you doing up at this ungodly hour?'

'I just got back from San Francisco General. A friend of mine's sick. A whole lot of guys are sick in the city these days.'

Sorrel came to with a start that echoed round her head to the accompaniment of the word AIDS. 'Are you OK, Mick?' she asked anxiously.

'I'm fine but you're not. I'm just looking at a photograph of you with a can of fish in your hand.'

'What photograph?'

'One I paid somebody to snatch. Your poor old face! It's just like a map of the world.'

Sorrel was all indignation: 'Was it you who made that awful man sneak up on me in The Height Co-op? If you wanted a picture that much, I'd have sent you one.'

'Yes and it would have been retouched to glory. I needed to see the terrible truth. Now shut up before you start, and listen. I'm very proud of the way you've handled your drink problem and I want to give you a present. You're going to have a face lift.'

'Plastic surgery? On yer bike!' The letterbox rattled open and two bills landed on the mat. Sorrel's head simply wasn't together enough to cope with Mick in full spate.

But there was no stopping him: 'The new face is just part of a long-term plan I've got for us. I've found out the name of the best man for the job in England but you'll have to go and see your own doctor first. I'm putting it all in a letter.'

'Save yourself the postage.' Now the postman was talking to the milkman who was rattling bottles up the path. 'And get to bed.'

'Are you at the bottom of your stairs?' asked Mickey. 'Go straight into the through room and have a look at yourself in the mirror over the fireplace. I'll hold on.'

'You've more money than sense.'

'I'm trying to give you a present. Just go and do it.'

'No.'

'Yes. And if you ring off, I'll ring your mother and make her make you do it.'

He would too. 'You're a pig, but hang on.'

Sorrel stumbled wearily into the living room and looked in the mirror. Every picture tells a story and the face which gazed back at her spoke of years of misery. Mickey knew her too well. He must have realized that, first thing in the morning, she would do anything for a quiet life. Ruby had not lied when she said the eyes were looking good, and her skin was certainly in better condition than it had been for years. But the mirror showed her that there was too much of that skin. This was Mick at his most cruel. The steps which led her back to the telephone were angry ones.

'You bastard!'

'I bet you don't look how you feel inside.' He was totally unrepentant. 'All I'm offering to do is make you match. It's time you were acting again. You don't look bad enough to play real character parts – you just look dreary. The eyes are more amazing than ever but all the rest wants hauling up.'

Gladys came down the stairs and brushed past Sorrel. 'Does that lad realize how much this call must be costing him?'

'He's mad,' said Sorrel, replacing the receiver.

There would be no chance of going back to sleep now so she drifted into the kitchen and began to make coffee. From time to time, her eyes strayed thoughtfully to another reflection of herself, in the glass of the kitchen cabinet.

A quarter of an hour later the telephone rang once more. 'It's me again. Have you been at the mirror pulling your jowls back and seeing what could be done?'

This was so exactly what Sorrel had been doing that she could have flung the phone through the hall window. 'I haven't got jowls,' she said loftily.

'You have on my picture. Is Doctor Moult still your doctor?'

'Don't you go writing to Doctor Moult,' warned Sorrel, who was now in full possession of her faculties.

'I'll put a note for him inside the one to you.' Mick suddenly began to sound about ten. 'D'you think you might go along with the idea? I'll pay. All I'm trying to do is keep a promise. I want to turn you into a real star.'

Sorrel relented. 'Can I think about it, over Christmas?'

'Course you can. I'm going to Santa Barbara. Where will you be spending it? I like to know, then I can imagine you.'

'I'm spending Christmas in a whorehouse.'

'That's a better exit line than any I ever wrote for you.' And this time it was Mick who replaced the receiver without giving her a chance to explain or say goodbye. Their loving battle to infuriate one another had now been going on for forty years.

Christmas had already led to a lot of discussion in Rookswood Avenue. Gladys generally spent it with somebody called Phyllis Bentley who dated back to her years in Kendal's dress department. 'Phyllis was good enough to have me when nobody else was interested so nowadays I feel almost obliged. She asked you too but I don't think you'd like it. Last year was her first Christmas without Sid and it was a bit morbid. She even laid a place for him. God knows what she'd have done if he'd materialized while she was carrying in the gravy! How would it be if all three of us went and had the set lunch at The Wendover in Monton?'

'You, me and Phyllis Bentley in paper hats? No, I'll go to Monica's.' She had been seeing a lot of Monica lately.

Gladys might have changed but not completely and she looked a little dubious as she said, 'It's your own life and I don't suppose you can catch anything off the knives and forks. But Sheila, promise me again that you won't go sitting on Monica's toilet.'

All of these Christmas discussions had taken place days ago. Now Sorrel had something else on her mind: 'Mother? What would you say if I told you I was thinking of having a face lift?'

In the old days Gladys could have been guaranteed to talk

about flying in the face of nature. Since the stroke her reactions were likely to be more stimulating and unpredictable. She gave Sorrel's features as hard a look as any that Sorrel had given the mirror and said, 'Make sure you don't end up looking startled. If you're getting one, get a good one. It's not something you can leave in the cloakroom.'

Opposition would have caused Sorrel to ring Mickey for a positive discussion. Now she was left feeling dubious. As she watched television she would gaze at faces she knew to have had benefit of surgery. There were no two ways about it, some of them looked distinctly Chinese. Oh well, she had the whole holiday to think about it. In the meantime there were cards to be written and presents to be bought. Gladys was almost impossible to buy for: 'What would you like for Christmas, Mother?'

'Surprise me!'

This startled Sorrel. In the past Gladys had practically given written notice of what she expected. 'Surprise you? You've certainly changed.'

'No, Sorrel, you've changed.' But it was the first time Gladys had ever called her Sorrel. 'I think you'd better buy me a good, tight perm.' Gladys hadn't changed all that much.

The Corn Exchange in Manchester had been turned into an antiques market and Sorrel found a Victorian plate, with lacy china edges, engraved with a view of the North Pier at Blackpool. This could go off, last-minute airmail, to Mickey.

On the very next stall she happened on a carved wooden copy of the statue at Walsingham. Though it might seem an odd gift to take to a knocking shop, Sorrel knew that it would be exactly to Monica's taste. It only cost seven pounds so she walked across to King Street and ordered some flowers to be sent to Moss Side on Christmas Eve. Monica had already refused to accept anything towards the food so Sorrel bought her a bottle of pink champagne instead.

It would have taken another alcoholic to understand that the idea of buying drink, for somebody who could cope with it, gave Sorrel a wonderfully luxurious feeling. She didn't drink herself, but it was the season of goodwill and Sorrel Starkey had rejoined the human race.

As she got on the bus for home, Sorrel pulled back the newspaper from around the statue and found herself struck by a sudden, dazzling thought. Things had started to happen that they'd asked for in the hymn. The one they'd sung on the way into Walsingham.

You did restore my blessings, she thought as she looked at the statue. One by one they're starting to come back.

The radio taxis were charging double fare over the holiday period and the driver was going at about seventy miles an hour. You could tell it was Christmas morning because the streets were dotted with proud fathers taking children, on new bikes, to see their grandmas. The most spectacular bicycles of all were in The Moss, and the most lavish Christmas trees. There was a ribboned wreath of artificially frosted fir branches around the spyhole in Monica's front door. When Sorrel pressed the bell, the Kray twins' very barking seemed to announce that this was no ordinary lunchtime.

Monica opened the door. She was wearing a white dress, a gold paper crown and a huge black eye.

Sorrel nearly dropped the bottle of pink champagne in shocked horror: 'What the hell happened to you?'

'I got a bad punter. I had to go to Midnight Mass in dark glasses. Plenty of old punters there too. The dark glasses saved them from having to look me in the eye.'

'How on earth are you going to cook in white?' Sorrel had settled for a patterned blue and black suit which wouldn't show the splashes and could be sent to the cleaner's.

'It's as good as done.' The whore was a tremendous homemaker. 'I've only got to make the gravy.'

Monica's tree was a real one, decorated with artificial Granny Smith apples and red ribbon bows. It only looked a bit like Kendal's Christmas windows. There were more bows and fir branches around the collection of framed samplers but the best thing was the smell on the air. The turkey came out of the oven and it had been cooked in a way Sorrel had never seen before. Monica had roasted it in muslin soaked with butter. It was something of an experiment. But once they peeled back this outer covering, the bird was revealed in shades of taut, gleaming gold. The two dogs were in ecstasies of excitement.

'I'm afraid they're not having any,' said Monica, 'or Ronnie would be at the vet's by five o'clock. I got them their own treat, they're having tripe.' She had already popped the champagne cork and found Sorrel some iced Perrier. 'I won't unwrap my proper present yet. I'll put it with yours, under the tree, until after the Queen's speech.'

Since she stopped drinking Sorrel's appetite had come back in a big way. They began with black caviar in savoury pastry cases, shaped like mince pies but without the lids. The turkey was all the better for tiny pork sausages and roasted smoky bacon and a sage and chestnut stuffing. Not for the first time Sorrel wondered why Brussels sprouts seemed entirely appropriate on Christmas Day and bloody terrible for the rest of the year.

Mindful of Sorrel's recovery, Monica had even contrived a perfectly acceptable plum pudding without alcohol. They were real people having a real Christmas. As they sprawled, gorged on food, in front of the television set, Sorrel was not even critical of the Queen's performance. Just as Her Majesty reached a line about 'Our Commonwealth cousins under more burning skies' somebody rang the doorbell and woke up the dogs who began to bark warningly.

'Who the hell. . . ?' Monica got to her feet and went out into the hall. Sorrel lost interest in the Queen and watched casually as her friend opened the front door to reveal a shabby, middle-aged man, standing on the doorstep. He was holding a small zipper-bag.

'Good afternoon. Are you open for business?' he asked nervously.

Monica, who was still wearing her gold paper crown, snapped, 'Do I look as though I'm open for business? It's Christmas Day. Where's your fucking sense of occasion?' She slammed the door and came back into the room. She was plainly rattled. 'God alone knows what the Queen would say if she knew that had happened.'

'You never know what's happening when you're on

television. When I was in *Angel Dwellings*, the police once managed to fix the exact time of a murder because Lettie Bly was singing "The Rose of Tralee" at the very moment the witness heard the screams. Monica, d'you think I should have my face lifted?' Sorrel sighed. 'The trouble is they all look so obvious afterwards.'

'That's the ones you know about.'

'Show me one I don't know about.'

'You're looking at it. I'd have been finished on the game ten years ago if I hadn't gone in for a bit of nip and tuck.'

'You're having me on. Where are the scars?'

'Behind my ears.' Monica pulled back her long hair impatiently 'Look! If anybody gets to see them you just say you had a mastoid operation as a child. There's a fine white line on my scalp too. Only my hairdresser knows about that.'

Sorrel was suddenly embarrassed. 'When I brought the subject up, I swear I'd no idea. I'd never have guessed.'

'You weren't meant to guess. This is a good one. Norris Blatt did it.'

'Norris Blatt is the man Mickey wants me to go to!'

'Then go. He knows how to charge and he's too conscious of the fact that he's a bit of a character but there's nobody else, in London, to touch him. Let's open the presents.'

There were two for Sorrel. The first one she unwrapped contained a picture of Spud, worked in petit-point embroidery, in a gold heart-shaped Regency frame.

Monica had been watching carefully for Sorrel's reaction and now she looked pleased. 'I did it myself, between punters. I even refused to allow one of my transvestites to put a few stitches into the background. And I could have charged him good money for the privilege!' Monica's professional tones turned to joy as she pulled back the scarlet tissue paper from around the Walsingham statue. 'Oh Sorrel, it's beautiful! She's exactly the same size as my Infant of Prague. The same person could have done them both.'

Pleasure had suddenly filled Monica with energy. 'Come upstairs, you'll see.' Still unwrapping her second parcel, Sorrel panted behind Monica, as she led the way to the first floor.

'The other statue's in my bedroom.'

Sorrel had now got the Christmas paper off the second gift and had discovered a sealed envelope inside. She had never been in Monica's bedroom before. Sitting down on the bed (and imagining Gladys's face if she could see her) she opened the envelope. It was full of twenty-pound notes.

Monica lifted down a carved figure from a shelf. 'This is the statue. Don't worry, I keep his face turned to the wall during business hours. Look! They are – they're exactly the same height. You couldn't have given me anything I'd like more.'

'But what's this?' Sorrel held out a fistful of banknotes.

'The money Kenny Shorrocks spent here.' Monica was all casual impatience. 'I checked the exact amount in my old appointment books. I bet you anything he used your cash. We can't have that standing between us.'

'I can't take it.'

'You've got it. And don't think you can get cross with me. When it comes to putting people in their places, I'm a professional. Want to see the tricks of the trade?' Before Sorrel could answer Monica flung open the door of a large fitted wardrobe.

The smell of air-freshener gave way to the faint but unmistakable odour of poppers. Perhaps they'd spilled onto the strange black leather garments hanging inside. The contents of the wardrobe were eerie to the point of evil. No colour – everything was black. Long leather cloaks and cruel black satin, corsets and patent-leather thigh-boots with six-inch heels and yard-long zip fasteners. Monica was rooting amongst the dead-looking wigs, in the kind of overhead cupboard normally reserved for spare blankets. As she pulled down some ropes, covered in black velvet, two plaited leather stock whips rattled to the ground.

'It's no use, I don't like it.' Sorrel was quite frank. 'And I hope you don't do all this and then sleep on the same bed.'

Monica began to attack her hair with a brush. 'The wooden stocks and the chains and all the really heavy stuff's next door. You don't have to tell me, I know. I've got to get out of this pig-swill.' She was examining her black eye in the mirror

699

inside the wardrobe door. 'I can suddenly see the whole set-up through your eyes and it gives me the creeps. It took a long time to come this far down the road.'

There was nothing to be gained by being judgemental. Instead Sorrel decided to be practical: 'What would you do instead?'

'Would you believe I haven't even got a National Insurance card? I can hardly trot off to the labour exchange. There's a massage parlour coming up for sale, off Portland Street. It's not Rookswood Avenue's idea of respectability but it's a hell of a lot safer than this specialist stuff. I've had enough of sitting here wondering whether the last man to make an appointment on the phone could be the next Ripper.'

'Did your mother ever know the whole story? You've no idea how much I envied you because of your father. I always thought Eddie Tarmacadam was a lovely man.' Through the window, across the garden, in a house down below, Sorrel was watching a blindfolded black child, in a pretty organdie party frock. She was chasing other children, and a laughing man and woman, around a room hung with paper garlands.

'I'm sorry to disillusion you, Sorrel, but Eddie Tarmacadam was the first. It was my own father who taught me that men will pay you to keep your mouth shut.'

Now the little girl had got hold of the man's legs and he swept her joyfully into the air. 'She wants to watch out,' said Monica bitterly, 'daddies can be dangerous. One way and another my father set me on the right road to this bedroom.'

'Are you making your punters pay for what he did to you?'

'Spare me the amateur psychology, Sorrel! I came to this side of town because they'd have me. There was a time when nobody loved The Moss like I did. These days, it's getting full of dangerous skag-heads and all I know is I've got to get out.'

Whilst Monica was talking Sorrel had been counting the money from the envelope. It came to eight hundred pounds. 'Can you afford to buy the place off Portland Street?'

'I'm about five thousand short. I can hardly go to a bank and say I'm planning on opening a massage parlour with a typed menu of extra services! I'll tell you one thing. I won't be offering anything like this.' Monica gave the wardrobe door a savage enough kick to make Sorrel realize that her friend must be stunningly effective at her job.

Monica had never had a chance and now she needed one. 'Take this cash back,' suggested Sorrel. 'That would be eight hundred towards it.'

'No way. That's yours. I'll find the money somewhere.' She bent down and picked up a folded letter which had fallen to the floor. 'I bet you've never seen one of these?'

'What is it?'

'A testimonial from a slave. I charged him fifty quid for the pleasure of writing it.'

Sorrel hoped that Monica wouldn't hand it to her. She didn't want to touch it.

As if sensing this Monica unfolded the sheet of paper and began to read aloud: ' "This is a testimonial to Mistress de Kink from her humble slave John. I wish to have the honour of stating that the Mistress is most wonderfully cruel and gifted in all aspects of corporal punishment . . ."'

The derision in Monica's voice now gave way to real sadness as she said, 'Oh yes, the whip and the cane and the cat o' nine tails – the Mistress has had her revenge with the lot. Know what, Sorrel? I once had a client who took twenty-five lashes without a murmur. When he got down in the hall, Ronnie went for his ankle. Didn't so much as break the punter's skin but the silly sod screamed blue murder for a tetanus injection and an ambulance.'

Monica suddenly looked remarkably like the young girl who had wanted nothing more than to be a nun. 'It's funny but it's awful. I've got to get out.'

It might not have seemed like Christmas any more but the slave's testimonial had given Sorrel Starkey the beginnings of a good idea.

Some Harley Street consultants keep reassuring framed photographs of wives and children on their desks. Norris Blatt had film stars. Under the surgical circumstances, Sorrel would have expected more reticence from these international names. But the lavishly inscribed photographs all bore

701

witness to the fact that these stars were delighted to have drunk at Mr Blatt's fountain of youth.

Norris Blatt's desk was fake Georgian but the London surgeon surprised Sorrel by being genuine Manchester. In fact he was almost too genuine. Sorrel surmised that he must have come South with a slight Lancashire accent and, finding he couldn't erase it, had gone to the other extreme and emphasized it. There was hardly anybody left in Manchester who still began their sentences with 'Nay, bloody 'ell-fire'.

Sorrel knew that surgeons were styled Mister rather than Doctor because their profession was descended from surgeon-barbers. With his florid face and theatrical tailoring Norris Blatt could easily have played Sweeney Todd.

'Admirin' the beauty chorus?' he barked genially. 'There's everything there from thread veins to a full sex change. Did you know I've done four cabinet ministers? Not that you can get the politicos to part with so much as a bloody snapshot!'

Humming the song 'It's Hush-Hush', Mr Blatt turned an Anglepoise lamp full in Sorrel's face, walked around his desk, and began to examine the flesh around her jaw. The way he kneaded and plucked reminded Sorrel of Ruby Shapiro choosing chicken.

'Doctor Moult's given you a clean bill of health,' he announced. 'Wonderfully regenerative organ, the liver!' With this he got out a huge magnifying glass and his own eye looked enormous as he examined the skin around Sorrel's. He was so close that she could smell his Wright's Coal Tar Soap and this reassured her far more than the striped shirt or the thick silk tie. As if reading her mind he asked, 'Flashy bugger, aren't I? As a matter of fact I'm just a clever scholarship lad from Collyhurst.'

'I didn't think there was anything but a dog's home at Collyhurst.'

'You're a cheeky mare,' he laughed. 'But your skin's stood up to the saloon bar punishment. I was expecting a corned-beef nose. Ready to have your photo taken?'

As Sorrel had been instructed to attend the consultation without makeup, the idea of a photo session filled her with alarm. Mr Blatt seemed to sense this: 'They'll be vicious,' he

702

said, 'but nobody gets to see them except for you and me. Bet you've never seen a Polaroid camera as big as this before?'

Sorrel hadn't, and as flashes exploded and life-sized faces began to emerge from the camera, she wondered why Kenny Shorrocks and his Thursday night friends had never got hold of such an advanced item. Perhaps they had. She neither knew nor cared. She was suddenly very nervous.

''Ave a humbug,' said Mr Blatt, producing a paper bag from his pocket. 'Just a minute. Open your mouth first. Oh good, you have got your own teeth.'

'If I hadn't, couldn't you have done it?'

'Me? I can do any bloody thing I set me mind to. Now let's have a look at these.' The pictures were indeed brutal. And Sorrel suddenly realized how carefully she must have been angling her head towards the mirror in recent years. That familiar reflection was one she could just about live with. These pictures looked like *Keep Death off the Road* gone flabby.

'I've known women faint at what I can reveal with this camera.' Norris Blatt took hold of one of the prints, placed a sheet of clear plastic over the top, and began to draw on it with a Chinagraph pencil. The man might seem everything that was brash and vulgar but his hands told a different story. They were wonderfully clean and fine. As the fingers moved certainly over the plastic surface, they were so confident Sorrel wondered whether women had ever fallen in love with him – just for his hands.

'That's where the jawline should be –' his pencil made a black mark – 'but your skin's got too big for your face. And you're not a puppy, you're not going to grow into it. I could tighten the jaw and give you an eye job but Mr Grimshaw wrote suggesting something more radical. Having examined you, I'm inclined to agree with him.'

'Mr Grimshaw can piss up his leg and slide down the steam.' Two could play the Northern game!

'Nay, bloody 'ell-fire, he's only paying!'

'Yes, but I'm going to pass my good luck on to somebody else,' said Sorrel enigmatically. 'If I have the whole lot done, how long will it last?'

'Seven years. Not to the exact month but thereabouts.'

'And how many times can you do it?'

'Three. But I'll be very surprised if you want the third one.'

Sorrel picked up one of the photographs and looked at the full horror. 'I've never done anything by halves. These photos prove that. I'll have the full thing. How soon could you manage it?'

'I could probably lift up that phone and get you a bed tomorrow. Anything else while we're at it? Tits, arses . . . I do the lot.'

Sorrel reassumed her grandest standard English. 'I plan to take my tits and my arse to a gymnasium, thank you.'

'Well, give the surgery time to settle down.' He was irrepressible. 'I wouldn't want anything to snap.'

Sorrel was horrified. 'It won't, will it?'

'Course it won't. Just don't come the Lady Muck on me. I can't stand people thinking they're better than I am.'

'Oh, I don't think that.' Sorrel spoke eagerly. 'I think you're just like that man who used to be round the Manchester markets, slapping linoleum and saying, "It won't break, it won't tear." Do you remember him?'

'Him and Barmy Mick who used to throw fly-catchers to the crowd and Second-Hand Mary the human rag-bag . . . Don't worry, Sorrel. There's a beautiful woman somewhere underneath all that mess and it's my job to find her.'

'How much is this going to cost Mickey?'

'I've come a long way from Collyhurst. He won't get much change out of five thousand.'

'I'd have expected you to say "Five thou",' laughed Sorrel.

'I'm a creature of surprises,' replied the unperturbed surgeon.

'I plan to give somebody a surprise. Do you have anywhere I can put my makeup on? I'm going straight off to the bank to get the big surprise rolling.'

They didn't even recognize Sorrel at her London bank. These days she was just a name and a Manchester address on their computer. There were a few questions, and some whispered consultations behind the counter, before they were prepared to hand over five thousand pounds from her deposit account. She had asked for hundred-pound notes but it transpired that these existed only in Scotland. The largest English denomination was fifties. Even so, the wad she pushed into her handbag was a bulky one.

Registered post? No, you had to put the sender's name and address on those blue and white envelopes and that wouldn't do at all. She walked from Piccadilly into Shepherd Market and bought a thick brown envelope and a small spiral notebook at the stationer's. 'You couldn't sell me such a thing as a leaky ballpoint pen?' she asked hopefully.

'No,' said the woman behind the counter without showing much interest, 'but it just so happens I've got one in the waste-paper basket. Mind your gloves.' They were used to all sorts in Shepherd Market. As Sorrel walked back into the street she looked at the girls, soliciting on the pavements. But she was more interested in the punters. Taking a deep breath Sorrel marched straight up to a timid-looking man, in a cheap copy of a Burberry raincoat, and said, 'Would you come and have a cup of coffee with me, please?'

'No offence, duck – ' the voice was Nottingham – 'but I'm looking for something a bit younger.'

'I'm sure you are.' Sorrel nevertheless steered him into one of the iron chairs round an outdoor table in front of a cafe. 'This will only take a minute.'

'Is it a survey?' The man's eyes were glued to Sorrel's notebook and pen. 'I wouldn't want you to think that I make a regular habit of hanging round places like this. You could say it was curiosity that brought me here.'

'Of course you could. Two cappuccinos, please.' This was to the waitress who had appeared from inside. 'Now don't take flight,' she said to the man, 'I just want to borrow your handwriting.'

He looked at her as though she was mad. 'I'm signing nothing.'

'Oh no,' explained Sorrel reasonably, 'you won't have to sign it. It's anonymous.'

'That's all right then.' The man sounded distinctly relieved.

Before he had a chance to think further Sorrel pushed across the open notebook, handed him the leaking pen and said, 'Just put "From a grateful punter". And then would you mind writing the envelope? I'll dictate the address to you.'

As the pen made wonderfully suitable splodges, Sorrel reflected that this was like Method acting translated into real life. The finished product was readable but exactly the kind of mess she had been hoping for. 'Thank you so much. I do hope you find what you're looking for,' she added brightly.

'I think I'll just make my way to the station,' was his gloomy reply. 'You've put me off my stroke. It doesn't take much. Weren't you once Sorrel Starkey?'

'Yes, and I've every intention of being her again. Good morning.'

Sorrel sailed under the market arch, in the direction of Curzon Street, where she had an idea there was a post box. Now that she'd seen Norris Blatt's photographs she realized that the face lift was a professional necessity. Mick would read rejection into any attempt to refuse to allow him to settle Blatt's account. Five thousand pounds for nothing might be viewed as a stroke of good fortune. But Sorrel knew one thing about good luck. If it was ever to come back to her door again, then this favour had to be kept moving.

She dived into a doorway which opened onto a tiled corridor into an office block. After looking round to see that nobody was watching, Sorrel wrapped the wad of fifty-pound notes around the fake message from 'the punter' and stuffed the lot into the stout brown envelope addressed to Monica Dolan.

Sorrel didn't waste so much as a moment on the moral arguments involved in helping to finance a massage parlour. Instead she handed them over to a power greater than herself. 'You know everything so you must know why I can't register this,' she half thought and half murmured. 'But if it's meant to get there please see that it does. And if it falls into somebody else's hands then I just hope they need it.'

There was no denying that the Alcoholics Anonymous programme of recovery provided the answer for every possible eventuality. These days Sorrel's God had nothing to do with church or sermons or the Pope being fanned with ostrich feathers in old newsreels. Her God was simply that benign force which kept her sober. The power she had chosen as being greater than herself was called Love.

The only unusual thing about the otherwise unremarkable hospital room was the mirror above the wash basin. It wasn't there. In its place was a slightly darker square of pink paint and four Rawlplugs. It had taken Elizabeth, the pretty blonde nurse whom Sorrel saw the most, to explain. When patients were undergoing facial surgery Mr Blatt always had the mirrors removed.

'You look a bit like *The Return of the Mummy's Curse*,' said Elizabeth. But Sorrel already knew that much. Peeking into a forbidden powder compact she had been confronted by two bloodshot eyes gazing out from a head swathed in bandages.

Now the Floor Sister bustled into the room bearing a pair of white cotton gloves. 'I think we'd better have these on today, Miss Starkey.' She was Scottish and plump in tailored navy blue and a tall, old-fashioned nursing cap which looked like frozen lace knickers.

'What do I need gloves for?' asked Sorrel.

'To stop you scratching.'

'I don't itch.'

'You will.' Sister McFee spoke with deepest satisfaction. 'And especially behind the ears.' She moved across the room and adjusted the blind about a quarter of an inch.

'She's doing everything by the book,' Nurse Elizabeth explained when Sister had gone. 'Mr Blatt's due any minute and the old bag's got the raving hots for him.'

'Do these gloves mean I'm any nearer to getting the bandages off?'

'The front drainage tubes might come out today. And that's a definite stage nearer.'

The waiting days seemed endless. Some perverse working-class streak in Sorrel kept making her wish she was out of the alleged luxury of this private room and in some jolly public ward, with gran'mas covering themselves in talcum powder, before the visitors arrived. The view from her window was of a red-brick wall divided into sections by black drainpipes. Inside her bandages, inside this room, she felt as though she was in a cocoon inside another stuffy cocoon. The unreality was broken by Shelagh Starkey who brought home-made chicken soup which Sister allowed Sorrel to drink through a glass straw. Lily Bear also turned up, on a pouring wet afternoon, with all the latest West End gossip.

'D'you remember an actress called Miranda Cottle? She's just had her face done.'

Lil's tones had been enough to raise dark suspicions. 'What went wrong?'

'I shouldn't have mentioned it.'

'Well you did.' The rain was battering against the window pane.

'Poor Miranda,' sighed Lily. 'They say she's not been across her own doorstep for a month. Her bottom eyelid hangs open and it keeps leaking tears. Well, you did ask, Sorrel.'

'Now I wish I hadn't.'

'The silly girl had it done on the cheap. If Mick plans to turn you into a real leading lady, then I think you've been very wise. Mind you, every line and wrinkle in this old face of mine is money in the bank. They're what gets me the work.

'I've come to give you a piece of advice, Sorrel.' Lily leaned over and pinched some grapes which Ruby had ordered to be sent in. 'Don't turn into one of those woman who has plastic surgery and then never stops talking about it. They're bores. Neither must you make too much of a secret of it. When you do your next press interview, add a few years to your age. That way, instead of not being bad for forty whatever-it-is, you'll be regarded as sensational for fifty-five.'

Having delivered this advice, Lily picked up her umbrella and stomped off to beat the rush-hour traffic. It had been good of her to turn out in such remorseless rain. It was even leaking from the down-spout on the over-familiar brick wall opposite the window. Elizabeth chose this moment to carry in a funereal arrangement of flowers. The message, on the card she handed to Sorrel, said that they had come from Mickey.

'Just look at those awful purple bows,' moaned Sorrel. 'D'you think they do flowers especially gloomily for nursing homes? Take no notice of me. It's the weather. I just wish this bloody rain would stop.'

'Me too.' Elizabeth held up the flowers for Sorrel to sniff. 'I'm going to Birmingham for the weekend.'

Sorrel sneezed.

'Oh God – ' Elizabeth was all contrition – 'don't say you're allergic to pollen.'

'I'm just allergic to this place.'

'I'm with you there.' The nurse placed the arrangement on the walnut shadow-veneer dressing table. 'In Birmingham, I'm supposed to be going to meet a man with a name beginning with an M. He could be wearing a diver's wristwatch. He's supposed to be going to change everything.'

Sorrel was at a loss to understand. 'Have you been reading your horoscope in the papers?'

'No, but we had this fortune-teller in a fortnight ago and she told me. You might have heard of her, actually. She's quite well known. She's called Mrs Gee.'

'June?' It was the first interesting thing in days. 'What the hell was June having done?'

'We're not supposed to tell.' Elizabeth relented: 'As a matter of fact she's been in a lot. You name it and June Gee's had it done. This time it was her bust. And she had something done downstairs.'

'What's downstairs?' Sorrel was thinking geographically.

'I suppose she's got the same downstairs as you, me or any other woman. Only now it's been tightened. I think I can hear Sister. Don't for God's sake tell her I told you.'

Sister McFee came through the door with her 'orders from the top' face on. She was carrying a steel surgical tray with a towel over it and Sorrel was irresistibly reminded of the day Mr Garner put down Spud.

Sister uncovered the tray and produced a pair of surgical scissors. 'Mr Blatt was coming in himself today to take off the bandages but he's been called to the burns unit. A man of his brilliance doesn't just do vanity work.'

'Watch it,' warned Sorrel. 'My bit of vanity's paying your

709

wages.' Immediately she'd said this she regretted it because Sister McFee began to advance upon her with the scissors.

'Is this it?' asked Sorrel nervously.

'This is it.' The nursing sister had already cut through some basic tie and now she started to unwind the yards of gauze. 'Nurse, slip to the office for the big hand-mirror.' Layer after layer of bandages and padding was removed and discarded. All Sister said throughout the process was: 'Mr Blatt's hoping to look in and check your stitches at about six thirty.'

And, at the mention of his name, Sorrel could have sworn that she heard Sister's heart miss a beat. Elizabeth now returned with the mirror and Sorrel grabbed for it. 'Quick, let me see!'

Sister intercepted this move and laid the looking glass flat on the bed. 'Now keep still or it will fall and smash. And we don't want seven years' bad luck, do we?'

'What does it look like?' Sorrel appealed to Elizabeth who was standing where the patient couldn't see her.

'Nurse is not paid to have an opinion on a surgeon's work.' Sister McFee poured some lotion onto cotton wool and started to clean Sorrel's skin. After a while she said, 'There, that's the best I can do for the money. Hand Miss Starkey the mirror.'

Sorrel took the mirror from Elizabeth, took a deep breath, and looked at herself . . . the scream she let out must have been audible on the Marylebone Road.

'Let me explain . . .' Sister McFee was still being entirely reasonable.

Altogether too reasonable for Sorrel. 'You can explain in the High Court,' she stormed as she grabbed the telephone and began dialling 0101 for America. Mickey Grimshaw also had some explaining to do.

10

'May God forgive you for I never will.' As Sorrel's rage mounted so did her voice. 'Mick? I've finished up looking like a fucking nineteen-year-old. Return to showbusiness? What in? *Anne of Green Gables?*'

'Just calm down.' For once Mickey sounded every year of his age and more. 'They *all* look like that to begin with. Surely Norris Blatt explained?'

'He's not here.' Sorrel felt marginally reassured – but only marginally.

'Well I'm here, I know, and they do. In a month's time the whole thing will have settled down to a point where you will simply look as though you've had about a year's good sleep.'

'Then why have you never had it done yourself?'

'Because I'm a man and I don't fancy the idea of having to shave behind my ears. Can we just leave the whole thing at that, Sorrel?' She could almost have believed that he was pleading. 'I've got bigger things than face lifts on my mind.'

'What's wrong?' There was only silence. 'Are you still there?'

'Yes. I'm here . . . just about.' He sounded close to tears. 'Eeek died this morning. Remember how big and gleaming and strapping he used to be? Well, at the end, I doubt he weighed seventy-five pounds.'

Sorrel forgot all about herself: 'What did he die of? Was it AIDS?'

'How boldly you say the word. We don't. We talk about "the virus". And I'll tell you something else that nobody cares to say aloud – San Francisco is turning into the world's biggest ghost town. You should see my address book. I've only got two Y's left. All the rest are crossed out and marked RIP. Rest in peace . . . I'm finally praying to that God of yours – the one I don't believe in.'

Sorrel snatched into the air for words of comfort and found none she could apply to Mick's situation.

'Tell me something, Sorrel, do you really believe there's going to be a Day of Judgement? Because if there is, I've every intention of breaking the whole thing up. I won't be answering God's questions. I'll be the one demanding answers.'

'You mustn't talk like that . . .'

'Why not?' He was wild with anger. 'Go on, if you know, tell me.'

'Because this life is just a blink in Eternity.'

'Jesus!' It was distilled derision. 'And that comes from a woman who, not two minutes ago, was in a panic about a face lift. Last week I needed a photographer in a hurry. I called three of the best guys in the city and d'you know where they were?'

'In the hospital?'

'In the graveyard, Sorrel. Down among the dead men. The handsome, the talented . . . this virus is taking the cream of the crop.'

'Will Eeek have a funeral?'

'Oh yes, you allow us that much.' It was as though he was trying to turn her into the enemy. 'And before you ask, I'm fine, thank you. Though God alone knows why – I certainly did everything possible to qualify. Would you do something for me?'

'Anything.' And she meant it.

'Kick Kenny Shorrocks in the balls. Eeek kept asking for him. I even offered to fly Kenny over but he wouldn't come. It's bloody ironical really, Eeek was beginning to do very well with that little air-conditioning business. Your ex-husband stands to inherit everything. Kenny might never have known it but he was the one person Eeek really loved.'

'Would you send some flowers in my name?' asked Sorrel. 'He was always lovely with Spud.' She started to cry.

Mickey suddenly sounded much more considerate. 'I promise you there's no need to worry about your face.'

'Oh that!' She brushed it aside impatiently with: 'That can take care of itself. What can I do for *you*? Kenny apart, there surely must be something?'

'Just be there for me. And stand by for action. I'll be over soon. First we'll revive your career and then I'm going to turn you into an international name. Onwards and upwards – that's what I always say. Did I tell you that poor Barney was here, on business, during all of the hospital drama? He was wonderful with Eeek. He thought nothing of sitting in that public ward, for hours, just talking to him about Manchester.'

Under the circumstances Sorrel hardly liked to ask but she did anyway: 'Does Barney ever mention me?'

'Only every hour on the hour. There's still a light for you in that window. Good morning.'

'Satisfied?' asked Norris Blatt.

'More than satisfied.' It was a fortnight later and Sorrel was visiting him in his consulting room. 'You're a genius.'

'Now tell me something I don't know.'

'OK, I like you.'

'I know that.' Mr. Blatt was getting out his camera again 'Stands to sense we should like one another. We're both impudent.'

'But you overdo the broad Manchester bit.'

'Strictly between ourselves, Miss Starkey – ' the voice had changed completely – 'I can sound like the Middle Temple and The Athenaeum rolled into one.' He grinned and reverted to his more usual style: 'But t'other bugger's what's earned me the money. I've made it very easy for people to imitate me. It's what you might call buried advertising.'

This time Sorrel had no reason to flinch when he turned the Anglepoise lamp full on her face and said, 'We'll do a couple of shots for the file and I suppose we'd better let Mr Grimshaw see what he's getting for his money.'

Sorrel suddenly had an idea: 'Would you mind doing just one extra?'

'No sooner said than done.' The first flash went off. 'Who's it for? Your best beau?'

'No. Just for somebody I haven't seen for ages. Somebody who was always saying that I ought to get it done.'

'Keep still. So you've no complaints?'

'Just one slight worry. My right cheek still hasn't got quite as much feeling in it as it used to have.'

'They're coming out nicely. I'll do just one more. The sensation might return but, if it doesn't, you'll just have to get them to kiss you on the other side. Everything comes at a price.'

'Don't I know it.' Sorrel could not have said this more seriously. She looked across the desk and began to study the face on the photographs. It simply looked alert and glad to be alive and wonderfully well. She was suddenly reminded of Nina Simone singing 'Now We Are One – My Soul and I'. Those might not have been the exact words but that's how Sorrel felt.

Blatt was looking at the pictures too: 'There are two things I won't do. I refuse to be a party to harsh cosmetic work and I won't put tits on Chinamen.'

'You've invented that second part.'

'Not a bit of it. They come to London from somewhere called Boogy Street in Singapore. I'm told it's nothing but fake hermaphrodites but there's none of my handiwork there. If you want a print take that middle one.'

Sorrel took the photograph, gave it another moment to dry and then wrote across the top: 'I've had it all hauled up! Fancy me now? Love, Sorrel.'

'I suppose you'll want an envelope too? Here.'

'Thanks.' Sorrel addressed this to Christian German at the Attwood Arcade.

'We'll post it,' sighed Blatt. 'Once you've restored their beauty they expect you to be a bloody universal provider. I suppose you'll be going shopping for new frocks next?' He nodded his head wisely. 'It generally takes 'em that way.'

'Only one frock,' laughed Sorrel. 'But it's got to be a knock-'em-dead ball gown. I'm under orders. Mickey Grimshaw's coming back to England to take me somewhere special. Only he won't say where.'

By the mid-1980s Wilmslow had become to Manchester what Beverly Hills is to downtown Los Angeles. The shops in this expensive outlying suburb were the nearest thing Manchester had to Rodeo Drive.

714

'Did you know that Wilmslow even has its own credit card?' asked Ruby Shapiro, hands on the steering wheel. She might have been recently widowed but Ruby's mourning did not extend to her new sports car. It was a scarlet one, an Alfa Romeo. 'Mind you, I've heard that some of them are so strapped for cash that they even use the card at the fish and chip shop. That's not to say there isn't a lot of old merchant-money in Wilmslow. There is. Pots of it.'

'How could you have encouraged me to spend all that on just one dress?' groaned Sorrel from the passenger seat.

'But what a dress! In such a dress you could tell Imelda Marcos to go take a powder.' Without so much as pausing for breath Ruby continued: 'I've changed my will, Sorrel. You get the diamonds. I don't see why you shouldn't borrow the Wartski necklace to go to the ball. There are earrings to match. We'd have to tell the insurance people.'

'But why?'

'Because they're only covered for me.'

Was Ruby being obtuse on purpose? With some embarrassment Sorrel asked, 'Why have you suddenly decided that I should have them? They must be worth a fortune.'

'I'm leaving them to you because Barney's wife asked me, once too often, whether she could try them on.'

'What about Zillah? I'm not being ungrateful but she is your daughter.'

'That one's got more than she knows what to do with,' snorted Ruby. 'That Kraut of hers must have trotted off to the jeweller's every time they had a cross word.'

The car had already passed through Irlams o'th' Height. As Ruby swung into Ravensdale Estate, Sorrel reflected that this was un unlikely place to be discussing diamonds from Wartski. At one time, the Mayfair jeweller had maintained a branch in Llandudno. This explains why many rich, older Northern women own important pieces by the master craftsman. And one day, it seemed that Sorrel was going to inherit some too. The very idea was just too high-flown for Rookswood Avenue, where the roar of Ruby's sports car was already causing people to rush to their front windows.

Gladys appeared first at her window, and then on the front

doorstep, with a damp chamois leather in her hand. As the car came to a halt she called out, 'It would almost pay you to open your own petrol station, Ruby.'

Ruby already had her window wound down. 'You like?'

Manchester has great contempt for 'ten-bob toffs' but demonstrations of real wealth are regarded as reflecting credit on the whole city. And the Shapiros were well known for being good to their employees. All of this allowed Gladys to be genuinely complimentary. 'It's a bobby-dazzler. That red's a bit testing. You'll have to watch that you don't wear pink with it.'

'Your mother was born with natural chic!' Ruby was getting out of the car. 'You should have come with us to Wilmslow. The dress they're altering is sensational.'

Two children, a boy and a girl – Sorrel didn't know their names – were giggling at Ruby. 'Your mother was born with natural chic,' mimicked the boy.

Ruby, not one bit abashed, advanced upon him. 'Have you no respect for a woman of seventy-nine years of age?'

'Seventy-nine?' The boy was amazed. 'Do the police know you're driving that thing?'

'I imagine they must.' Ruby won him with a smile. 'They certainly follow me enough.'

'I'm eighty,' Gladys announced proudly. It was almost like a swanking competition. 'What's the dress like?'

'She has to go back for a fitting.'

Gladys led the other women away from the children and said in lowered tones, 'There's a man coming back here. I just couldn't get shut of him. I didn't know the fellow from Adam but he insisted on calling me Gladys. That's what made me think he must be a reporter. They do that,' she added kindly, for Ruby's benefit. Stars' mothers have their own ways of countering Alfa Romeos.

'If he gives you any trouble,' advised Ruby, 'call Monty Klein.'

Sorrel laughed. 'If I'm going back into the business, I can hardly call a lawyer every time a reporter hoves into view.'

'When she goes back on the stage – ' Gladys squeezed the water out of her window leather – 'I'm selling up and going

716

into a nursing home. She can do what she likes with her own life. But I'm not up to fame – not a second time around.'

A Vauxhall Cavalier, coming round the corner of the avenue, prompted Ruby to say, 'I'd better get moving. I seem to be blocking everything.'

'It's only that man who came before.' Gladys was giving the coachwork on the bonnet an admiring rub with her chamois leather.

'Watch yourself with him,' advised Ruby as she climbed into the car. 'I'd stay myself but I've promised to push poor Doris Dintenfass round Manley Park lake.'

The man getting out of the Vauxhall must have been in his late forties. He had a greying ginger crew cut and a good beige double-breasted suit only spoiled by tired lapels. The top button of his shirt was undone, above the knot of a paisley tie, and he was carrying a brown leather document case. Sorrel had to give her mother full marks for perspicacity. This was almost certainly a member of the press.

'Sorrel, isn't it? I couldn't be sure. You're looking so young.'

'Just a minute,' Gladys interrupted him grandly. 'Surely you can see we're waving goodbye to this Alfa.'

The man was already bending and peering inside the car. Yes, he's definitely reporter, thought Sorrel. And this one is not from a local rag.

'Anybody I should know?' he asked.

Gladys dropped the car a curtsy that could have been meant for the Duchess of Gloucester. 'They don't like you saying.'

Sorrel darted her mother a warning glance. As far as she knew, she had nothing to fear from the press. But years in their hands had left her wary. 'What can I do for you?' She was anxious to get things out into the open.

'Have you had your face lifted?'

There was such a thing as too out in the open. 'No comment.'

'OK. Answer me something else. Have you got a toy boy?'

It was Gladys who stepped in and replied, 'You want your mouth washing out with soap.'

The man ran his fingers through the ginger crew cut. Sorrel's heart suddenly sang. She knew him.

The reporter opened his document case and produced a black and white photocopy of the picture she had sent to Christian German. ' "I've had it all hauled up," ' he read aloud. ' "Fancy me now?" Could we have your comments on that?'

'I think you'd better come into the house.' She was tempted to add: 'Said the spider to the fly.' It was a rare moment. Not only did she know the man – she had something on him!

'Into the house? Are you mad?' Gladys was gazing incredulously at her daughter.

'Never more sane. But too many curtains are twitching.'

'Well as long as you think you know what you're doing . . .' Gladys led the way up the path. 'I just hope those children aren't running off to their mothers with this story,' she muttered to Sorrel.

'They didn't hear. They were only interested in the sports car. Do come in.' Sorrel attempted to imitate June Gee at her worst and succeeded. 'We're simple folk. You'll have to take us as you find us.'

The reporter seemed to be under the impression that things were going his way. 'Are you aware that the young man you sent this to is a heroin addict?'

'No I didn't know that.' The idea left Sorrel genuinely stricken. 'Poor Christian.' But there would be time for sympathy later. For the moment she had a situation to save. 'What is your name?'

'Perry Snape. I ghosted Nadine Taylor's life story.'

'Well, Perry, just let me get my thoughts together. Perhaps Mother would put on the kettle?'

'And perhaps Mother wouldn't.' Gladys flashed her daughter a look which said: 'If you think I'm missing out on any of this, then you're very much mistaken.'

'Let us sit down.' Sorrel was spacing out her words like royalty. 'Where do you live, Perry?'

'Timperley.'

'Fancy that! I think Susie Mathis has a house there.'

Anxious to be seen as a neighbour of Manchester's best-known radio personality, the reporter replied, 'Yes. We're just up the road from Susie. On the other side, a bit towards Altrincham.'

'We?'

'My wife and I.'

'What colour's your front door?' asked Sorrel in altogether more plebeian tones.

'Blue,' he answered in a puzzled voice. 'Why?'

'Got you!' Sorrel was practically dancing with delight. 'So Mrs Snape lives in a house with a blue front door, just up the road from Susie's. Your wife sounds like a woman who shouldn't be too difficult to find.'

'Why should you want to?' He still seemed more puzzled than worried.

'I hope I don't have to. The ginger crew cut was the clue.' She felt straight out of a play by Agatha Christie. 'You see, Mr Snape, I've seen you before. Not in the flesh – though it has to be admitted that you had no clothes on.'

'Sorrel!' exclaimed a scandalized Gladys. 'No clothes on?'

'He was in a film Kenny had at Bellaire. Kenny was in the film too. So was one of the girl extras from *Angel Dwellings*.'

'I think I will go and put that kettle on.' But Gladys didn't move. She was gazing at Mr Perry Snape as though he was Dr Crippen in The Chamber of Horrors: 'No clothes! He doesn't look the type.'

'He's the type all right. Mind you, he didn't have the beer belly in those days.'

'Anybody could come up with a story like that.' But Snape's nerve was plainly going. 'Prove it! Go on, prove it.'

'All it would take is one telephone call to California. A friend of mine's still got that film. He's never been able to bring himself to part with it. He says it's one of the funniest things he's ever seen.'

The reporter's face, which had turned white, was now going red. 'It's not funny if you've got married since. It's not funny if you've changed your whole way of life . . .'

'So people are allowed to change?' Sorrel looked again at the picture of herself. 'I'm glad to hear that.'

'This is blackmail,' he spluttered.

'I know,' smiled Sorrel serenely, 'and I'm loving it. Is that document case, by any chance, recording everything we're saying?'

His hand slammed wildly onto the combination lock and the briefcase emitted a protesting microphone whine. 'No,' he said.

'I've been caught that way before. You can't kid one who's kidded thousands.' Sorrel was beyond caring about the legalities of the situation. 'Get one thing straight. There is no toy boy.'

'Answer me something – ' Gladys had interrupted them – 'is this lad Jewish?'

'Not that I know of.'

'Then there's nothing in it. You can take a mother's word for that. Just what d'you think your poor wife would say if she happened to go somewhere where this film was shown?'

'My wife doesn't go to places like that.'

There was no stopping Gladys. 'And you're prepared to break that poor woman's heart?'

Perry Snape looked desperate. 'What d'you want me to do?'

Sorrel opened her mouth to speak but Gladys waved her aside. 'I want you to listen to your conscience, Mr Snape. You march in here, armed with information off a drug addict. Is it any wonder we start talking about an eye for an eye and a tooth for a tooth? Have you got daughters, Perry?'

'One.' He actually swayed and steadied himself on the sideboard.

'Then you will understand why I would think nothing of getting my coat on and going to Timperley. You're not dealing with Sorrel Starkey. You're dealing with her mother. And I'd kill for my child.'

This strange demonstration of love, coming after all these years, was too much for Sorrel and tears she could hardly explain began to roll down her face.

'Don't cry,' pleaded Perry Snape. 'I can't bear to see a woman cry. I mean to say, this signed photo is obviously a fake . . .'

'Not good enough,' snapped Gladys. 'Your boss isn't going to swallow that.'

'Christian German's got a heavy heroin habit.' The reporter looked shamefaced. 'We would have had to be very sure of our ground before we dared to run the story.'

Gladys put her own face very near to his. 'But you still came here and crucified us?'

'It's my job.' He said it quietly and miserably. 'I was good at English at school. It's just my job. There'll be no story. I can guarantee that.' Without pausing he added, 'Limping Shorrocks swore that film was destroyed.'

'Well it isn't.' Sorrel was already shepherding him towards the door.

'Will you get it back for me?' He sounded much younger than the man who had marched so confidently up the garden path.

'No. I've got to trust you, so you'll just have to trust me. When I go to America, I might see if I can get it burned.'

'Are you going to America soon?' He was turning back into just any reporter.

'One day. After I've re-established my career over here.' And Sorrel could now have been any actress giving an interview.

'Will you be going to the *Angel Dwellings* silver jubilee? I hear they're having a full-scale formal ball.'

So that's why Mick had instructed her to buy a ball dress. Now it was Sorrel's turn to feel nervous.

721

11

In the last years of her drinking Sorrel had stopped wearing a watch. She hadn't needed one. It was never later than she thought. Once she got sober, this melancholy, inbuilt clock stopped ticking in her brain and the days began to speed by on wings. The change reminded her of the transition from endless, early childhood to fast-moving *Children's Hour* days. She needed a wristwatch again and she needed a diary. And it seemed next to no time before her appointments culminated in Mickey's arrival in England.

The Midland was closed for rebuilding so Mick was spending the *Angel Dwellings* Silver Jubilee week at The Portland. This new hotel, built behind the stone facade of one of the magnificent old Manchester cotton warehouses, was comfortable and friendly and made a real effort to accommodate showbusiness people. But it wasn't The Midland. It didn't have a place in Mickey and Sorrel's past or in their special affections.

On the morning of the grey winter's day of the jubilee ball, the pair of them set out on a sentimental journey. They hired a cab to take them down to the dock road which had inspired the television serial. Sorrel never had any reason to go down into that part of Salford so she was as startled as Mickey by the changes. All the tenements and terraced houses and pubs and port authority buildings had vanished. In their place was a housing development, like a dolls' village, built around a basin of the Ship Canal.

'What in God's name is that?' gasped Mickey.

'That, sir, is Salford Quays,' replied the taxi driver without much pride. 'It hasn't got a heart. It's got a steakhouse instead.'

Mickey and Sorrel climbed out into the cold and viewed the transformation. The Toytown houses were surrounded by anonymous apartment blocks whose only concession to the past came in names like The Merchant's House and in marine suggestions on the top of some fussy weathervanes. But seagulls had still followed the course of the canal on its forty-mile inland journey. An old woman was ripping a Mother's Pride loaf apart and throwing it to the birds. She had a nicotine-stained, blonde beehive hairstyle, a grubby raincoat, no stockings and toasted legs.

'I fed them when I lived round 'ere,' she bawled defiantly, 'and you won't stop me now.'

'I wouldn't dream of it.' Mickey moved nearer to her and Sorrel followed.

'What do you make of all this?' he asked the woman politely.

'They're not houses, they're just bloody money boxes.' The gulls seemed to know her. One was even sitting on top of her head and she reached up and gave him a crust. 'Where's the kids? Where's the dogs? You bloody yuppies have gone and ruined everything.'

'I'm not a yuppie. I'm much too old for that.' Mickey was attempting to warm her up with his charm.

'Don't come the phoney American accent with me,' snapped the old blonde. 'I can hear a Manchester-Yank a mile off. I remember the real McCoy. Nylons, Hershey Bars, chewing gum . . . I got the lot, over the road, in The Salisbury.'

Sorrel thought she'd give the woman a treat: 'This is Mickey Grimshaw. He invented *Angel Dwellings*.'

It was not a treat. 'So you're to blame, are you?' she demanded fiercely. 'Well I blame you for all of this.'

'Me?' Mickey's voice actually squeaked in surprised indignation. 'What have I got to do with it?'

'You held us up to ridicule on the television.' The woman scrumpled up the bread wrapper and stuffed it into a torn pocket. 'You made us out to be a bad lot so they shifted us to Little Hulton and built this. Yes, you're to blame and I hope you're satisfied.' In typical, contrary Salford fashion she added: 'But we miss you, Lettie. You was all the women who ever waited for a man to dock.' With a curt nod to the actress she walked away.

Mickey watched her go with more undisguised affection than Sorrel had seen in his eyes for years. 'You'll never win with them,' he said. 'That's why I've always loved them. It was worth coming just for her.

'Wait there for us,' he called out to the driver. 'We're going to explore.'

The Cannon cinema complex looked unlikely to offer them more to look at than film stills. And the Copthorne Hotel was just a waterside version of the one Mickey was already staying in. They headed towards the houses. They had been experts at nosying through windows since their childhood. But there wasn't a lot to see. 'Unless you count framed limited editions of lithographs and Habitat sofas.' Mickey sounded rueful. 'I suppose this is the well-designed world we used to dream about in The Kardomah. I've got exactly the same cream linen curtains in San Francisco. Hang on, I'll show you something with a bit more fire.'

He fished inside his overcoat pocket and produced a flat, dark red leather jewel-case. 'I had dinner with Ruby last night. She says she wishes you well to wear them.' Mick opened the case and revealed the Wartski diamonds. Even on this sunless day, the necklace and earrings seemed to reach out and grab light and return it in shimmers of amazing depth and magnificence. 'They make rhinestones look pretty pathetic, don't they?'

'For God's sake put them away.' Sorrel was immediately looking around for muggers.

'They're insured for two hundred thousand smackers. Mamie Hamilton-Gerrard will go green.'

'Please put them away,' begged Sorrel. 'I thought Ruby had forgotten.'

Mick tucked the case back in his pocket. 'She wouldn't tell me about your dress.'

'I won't either. You'll just have to wait. It's cold. Let's go back.' Arm in arm they walked away from the canal bank. 'Does Mamie know I'm coming tonight?'

'Yes.'

It was too short an answer and Sorrel immediately started to read meanings into it. 'Yes what?'

'She cut up a bit rough. But I said that if you couldn't come, I wouldn't go either. That fixed them.'

Sorrel let go of his arm. 'In other words I'm not wanted?'

'Sorrel, your contribution to *Angel Dwellings* was enormous. You've got to be there.'

'I'm not going where I'm not wanted. Have you got a ten-pence piece? I'd better cancel my appointment at the hairdresser's.'

Mickey stopped walking. 'You have to be there tonight. It's all part of my long-term plan. Everybody who matters will be there and you're in dire need of a job. In two years' time I plan to do a great big show in the States. American Equity will never let me use you if you haven't established your name again. Mamie's going to announce her retirement tonight . . .'

'Then it's her night and she can get on with it.'

'Bollocks! The night belongs to all of us. I've not come all this way to be thwarted by a bit of silly pride. Ever since I can remember, I've been trying to teach you that ours is not a nice business. Accept that, and it's perfectly possible to be happy in it.'

'I only ever wanted her to like me.' Sorrel was at her most stubborn.

'Well she doesn't. Why should she? You're every bit as talented an actress as she is and you're much younger. Every time the poor cow claps eyes on you she must be reminded of her own diminishing returns. I thought that precious AA of yours was very hot on the serenity prayer?'

That was the trouble with Mick, thought Sorrel. He was full of bits of idle information which he could turn to his own advantage. The prayer in question went: 'Grant me the serenity to accept the things I cannot change and the courage to change the things I can . . .'

'OK, you've got me,' sighed Sorrel. She was blowed if she was going to let him accuse her of being a coward. 'I'll go. I'll even try to be nice to Mamie, though God knows how she'll be with me.'

'Just promise me one thing, Sorrel.' Mickey spoke gravely. 'She's eighty-seven years old. Promise me you won't strike the first blow. If she starts anything, stand beautifully still and I'll pull her off you.'

Two skinheads suddenly materialized from behind a glass and steel warehouse. As they spotted Mickey, one yelled out, 'Poof!'

'Do you still have to put up with that?' asked Sorrel in wonder.

'I've got so used to it, I'd almost miss it.' Nevertheless, he began to hurry Sorrel towards the waiting taxi.

The skinheads followed. 'Poof!'

'Faggot!'

Inside the safety of the cab Mickey slammed the door and pulled the jewel-case from his inner pocket. As the engine started, and the taxi began to move, he flipped open the lid and flashed the Wartski diamonds in the skinheads' startled faces.

'Losers!' he yelled back. And he yelled it in triumph.

When a ball was first mentioned, Sorrel had entertained visions of herself with bare shoulders and a deep cleavage. It was Ruby who had said, 'Leave the Naked Look to girls with newer sets of equipment. Settle for distinction.'

Ruby must already have had the diamonds in mind when she encouraged Sorrel to buy the dress with its high-necked black velvet bodice, long tight sleeves and a bare back. The huge skirt was in layer upon layer of white organza. This was dotted at random with black beauty spots, velvet circles, varying in size from a sixpence to a side plate.

Once she was in the dress, Sorrel walked towards the mirror. This was a trick she'd learned, long ago, from Lily Bear. The moving reflection was exactly what people would see as she came towards them. Did it really need the diamonds?

And then she added them. The amazing blue-white stones threw out their multiplications of sparkle and turned her into a woman who seemed ageless and imperishable.

'It's the first time I've ever seen you looking my idea of famous.' Gladys had come quietly into the room. 'Did you hear the car? Mick's here. White dinner jacket, bit common, this isn't the South of France.' Gladys began to fasten the safety catch on the necklace. 'Would you believe that he wants me to babysit for him? He's brought his mother! I'm not being mean, Sorrel, but that's a new three-piece suite downstairs and I fear for the springs of my settee.'

'Nip down and tell him to come into the hall. I want him to get the full effect as I come down the stairs.'

'Did you remember to scrawp those new shoes on gravel?' asked Gladys as she went. 'You don't want to go breaking your neck.'

Sorrel had already done that but she had forgotten scent. She dabbed Moment Suprême on her neck and wrists and, hitching up her dress, behind her knees. As she straightened her skirts she said to herself in the glass: 'Well, love, that's just about as far as you can go.' The diamonds blazed back at her. 'In fact it's just about as far as anybody could go!' if only Barney could have seen her looking like this.

The boxed-in staircases of Rookswood Avenue were not really designed for big entrances. In the little hall below, most of the space was being taken by Beryl Grimshaw. She had seized a commanding position and crammed Mickey and Gladys against the hallrobe.

As Sorrel came into view, Mickey's mother began a slow handclap and called out: 'Three cheers for Mr Danny La Rue!'

Sorrel refused to be niggled by this reference to the female impersonator, so Beryl tried again: 'I can see now why my beautiful evening gown, from Evans, wasn't considered good enough.'

Mickey was wearing an expression Sorrel hadn't seen since the day he left for RADA. The day when Beryl pursued the train with his teddy-bear. 'Nobody's mother will be there,' he muttered angrily.

'I'm not nobody's mother. I'm the author's mother. They should all be very grateful to me. If I hadn't had you, none of them would be working today. I bet Mamie's mother's going.'

'She'd have a job,' retorted her son. 'She's been in Southern Cemetery for years.'

'And it's been in the papers, they're limited for space at that

727

ball,' added Gladys. 'You stop with me, Beryl. I've got a whole two-pound box of Terry's All Gold.'

Mickey opened the front door and helped Sorrel down the steps. 'Mind that good frock on the privets,' warned Gladys. Everything and nothing had changed.

The skirt was so big that Sorrel had to sit on her own in the back which meant that Mickey, next to the driver, had to talk to her over his shoulder.

'Twenty-five years of *Angel Dwellings*. You must be feeling proud,' she said to him.

'Why? Everybody keeps on saying that. I did it. It was good. It took off. So what? I had the talent – the crime would have been if I hadn't done it.'

There was no pleasing him. There never had been. Even two miles from Manchester they could see that the studio buildings were floodlit. Rockets had started to go up into the night sky. Without the man who had been more than a brother, this would never have happened. Sorrel was remembering the little boy, with the odd eyes, she had first met in Mr Tuffin's boarding house. The child who'd said, 'Want to see a puppet show?' As Mick turned round again she gave him a look of great love and then let out such a terrible scream that the driver swerved and braked.

'Mick! Your poor eyes. Was the operation very painful?' The eyes were no longer odd. Both were green.

'Contact lenses,' he explained airily. 'I can also have two blue ones if I want. There's nothing wrong with my eyesight. It's purely cosmetic.'

'Then do take them out,' she begged. 'The real thing always makes you look wicked and special. I don't want to arrive with a stranger. God knows, I'm nervous enough as it is!'

Times had changed and so had the management. Sorrel didn't really know any of the people standing shaking hands on the receiving line. There was one exception: a floor manager she remembered rushing around in headphones now seemed to be a member of the board. His wife, next to him on the welcoming committee, had clapped eyes on the Wartski diamonds and was now giving her own narrow sapphire bracelet a dissatisfied glance. Sorrel felt so guilty that she had to suppress a terrible urge to admit she was in borrowed sparklers.

The smell of champagne, in the close confines of the foyer, was disturbing; Sorrel was glad when Mick found her some orange juice and they could move out into the grounds to watch the firework display. The last of the rocket sticks came down with a clatter and the first of the set-pieces began to illuminate and burn. Loudspeakers blared out *'Tenement Symphony'* as a life-sized model of the *Angel Dwellings* building began to appear before them, outlined in giant sparklers and Catherine-wheels.

'Still not so much as a tear of emotion?' She was teasing Mick.

'No, but you'll be broken up in a minute. I know what comes next.'

The tenement faded away and all attention turned to a fifty-foot doorway. With pyrotechnic crackles and hisses, two figures began to take shape. They were Lettie Bly and Spud as they had first appeared in episode one. They'd even got Spud's piece of string. Out in the street, huge crowds of the public were watching all this from behind iron railings. And now, at the sight of the woman with the dog, they began to whistle and stamp and cheer. Sorrel Starkey was still theirs. They had not forgotten her.

'Now you know why I told you to wear waterproof mascara,' said Mick in tones of deep satisfaction. But his blue and green eyes were suspiciously bright for one who made such a point of not being impressed.

Inside the main building, the iron doors between the two biggest television studios had been rolled back into the walls. The whole area had been transformed into one vast ballroom. It was ringed round with those black velvet curtains, covered in tiny electric stars, that you see twinkling in television variety shows. But it didn't stop at that. The designer had suspended huge blue and silver gauze clouds from the ceiling. And there were gilded angels flying between them. The dance band were on the deck of a white paddle-boat which stood in the middle of the ballroom floor.

'All those decisions!' Mick was looking round the crowd.

'What decisions?' Sorrel was waving to Nadine Taylor and her husband who were already carrying plates of split lobster away from the buffet. Years of success had plainly not diminished their actors' appetites.

'All that deciding what to wear and where to have their hair done and who to bring as a partner – and they think it *matters*.'

'What does matter?'

His answer surprised her: 'Being kind. Gander was right. You've just got to do your best and hope for the best. As I came into this transformation scene I had the weirdest experience. I stopped seeing people. It was as though the place was filled with huge balloons. All puffed up with their own self-importance.'

Did this, Sorrel wondered, include herself? 'Pity there wasn't a mirror. I bet your own balloon wouldn't have been a tiddler.'

'Probably the biggest!' he grinned. 'Let's go and grab some food. Gander also said: "Lobsters is lobsters." My God! Cop a load of that. Mamie's excelled herself. That outfit must have been stuffed in a prop basket since the last tour of *Chu Chin Chow*.'

The veteran actress was wearing a spangled harem outfit with Arab pantaloon trousers and a gauze cape. She looked a hundred disguised as seventeen. There were even two artificial beauty spots. On her head was a tight cap of pale pink nylon curls. And on her arm was Bernard Conroy.

'Don't worry about him,' hissed Mick. 'He's been given the golden handshake. There's a set of teeth that have definitely been drawn.'

Yet these were the same two people who had once made Sorrel's life hell. As they came bobbing towards her, like the marionettes at Fleetwood, a wave of compassion swept through her. It was just an old rag-queen accompanied by a fierce set of dentures. There was nothing left to fear.

Untrue.

'Sorrel? It is you, isn't it?' Mamie was peering over-elaborately. 'Yes. The plastic surgeon's left just enough for me to recognize. Well, this is it. This is my last night. I'm going home at twelve. Come to my dressing room at five minutes to midnight. And Sorrel – come alone.'

It was enough to wreck the former Lettie Bly's whole evening. What could the old crone want? What's more, the encounter had left Mickey annoyed with Sorrel.

'I thought you'd joined the grown-ups. You never will until you learn to say *No*. Whatever Mamie wanted could have been said there and then, on the spot. God preserve me from actresses! The wicked old cow's covered herself in spangled veils and she has to go and give a mysterious performance to match. Midnight with Mamie? Perhaps we should ring Monica Dolan. She might know somebody who could lend you a revolver.'

His flights of fantasy were only interrupted by the arrival of a tall, angular man with a crooked smile. 'Miss Starkey? May I have this dance?' As he led Sorrel onto the floor he said, 'Mickey never introduces anybody . . .'

But Mickey had already darted across the polished surface and now he murmured into Sorrel's ear, 'You're in the arms of the new executive producer. He's said to be into older women.'

'I heard that,' laughed the man.

'You were meant to.' The departing Mick plainly liked him.

Sorrel was busy trying to remember the intricacies of a slow foxtrot. In her head she was saying to herself: Promenade through and step, lock, step. This limited conversation. Mamie, she noticed, was now sitting on a little gold chair, pulling Morecambe prawns apart viciously, and watching her every move.

'I'm Donald Ronson.'

'If you want to talk, we'd better go and sit down,' said Sorrel. 'I'm a terrible ballroom dancer.'

'Me too,' he laughed. 'Come on. Not there . . . a bit further along.'

So he was also wary of Mamie. As Sorrel sat down she noticed her own ankles and burst out laughing. The ladder she had sprung in one of her silk stockings was broad enough for Lettie Bly at her most abandoned.

'Is that enough to ruin your whole evening?' asked Donald Ronson teasingly.

'It would take more than that. I've been too far and done too much to be thrown by a silk stocking.' Sorrel wondered whether to simply take them off. Donald Ronson was too young for her to be in awe of him. Besides, he had that enviable gift of immediate intimacy.

'This is all so much better than I was expecting.' He stopped looking around the floor and turned to Sorrel. 'But you're the best bit. You will come back to us, won't you?'

Back to what? Lunch? Drinks in the Film Exchange? No, that had closed. Surely not into the show? No. That just wasn't possible.

But it seemed that it was: 'You left a big gap in *Angel Dwellings*. Nobody's ever managed to fill it. Once Mamie goes, we'll be very low on the original characters. The whole show is bedded in nostalgia. We really need a bit of that Starkey magic around the place again.' He looked puzzled. 'Hasn't Mick said anything to you?'

Was all of this part of Mick's long-term plan? Sorrel decided to look enigmatic and the actress inside her said: Shake your head slowly so the diamonds will flash and your price will go up. But did she *want* to go back into *Angel Dwellings*?

Yes, of course she did. Quickly, she asked, 'Would I have to dye my hair red again?' An older, wiser Sorrel knew that, if she was to return, Lettie Bly must – somehow – be left behind at the end of the working day.

'You could have a wig.'

'And the wig could stay on a block at the studio.'

He seemed to understand. 'Was she that much of an albatross?'

'It was just that I didn't know how to handle it.' But Sorrel also knew television companies. Bargain offers didn't stay on a friendly basis for long. She had to strike whilst she was still in a seller's market: 'You wouldn't want to find a replacement for Spud, would you?'

'Mick came up with the idea of your inheriting Red Biddy's parrot.'

Sorrel thought of mentioning that she was already quite friendly with two pit bull terriers but immediately had visions of headlines like *MASSAGE PARLOUR PUPS*. No, that wouldn't do. She'd be better sticking with the parrot. Sorrel Starkey, the professional, was back in business.

Mamie didn't make a farewell speech. Instead, she sang her goodbyes. Alone in a spotlight, in the middle of the floor, the bizarre outfit simply looked theatrical and no longer ridiculous.

'You were my hope
You held me up
You were my life
I gave you love . . .'

She wasn't just saying goodbye to the people here. Sorrel could sense that this song was for all of the audiences that Mamie had ever entertained. The voice was older and thinner but the talent Mamie held out – for their final inspection – was miraculously intact and gleaming. It managed to remind that packed ballroom of long-gone pantomimes and forgotten West End successes and of milestones in broadcasting and of twenty-five years as Red Biddy . . .

As the spotlight reduced, until just her face was illuminated, Mamie had convinced everybody there that all she'd ever had was a lifetime of audiences. And that those audiences had been enough.

Through the thunderous applause Sorrel whispered to Mickey, 'If only that same woman would be waiting for me in her dressing room!'

The studio had grown in size in the years since Sorrel had been away. It took several minutes to find her way to the dressing corridor. She looked on the call sheet pinned to the notice board. Mamie was still in number one.

Sorrel knocked.

'Come in.'

Mamie was sitting at the mirror taking a swig from a quarter-sized bottle of brandy. That was something new. Sorrel opened her mouth to say something complimentary about the performance but Mamie was in first.

733

'This won't take long. You needn't sit down. I've not got much conscience but I want Mother to rest comfortably in her grave.' Mamie gave Sorrel a long, cold look. 'So they're having you back.' It wasn't a question; Mamie had always owned a keen ear for jungle drums. 'You're finally going to land up on the top step of the tenement. Well all I can say is, you're welcome to it. You'll find out what I've been going through for the last twenty-five years. How the others will hate you! You have to hold onto that top step like grim death.'

Mamie took another thoughtful swig. 'It won't take you long to learn why I didn't have much time for you. But we should never have made that doll.'

'What doll?'

'It had red hair.'

'I don't understand.' But Sorrel did understand the way Mamie was holding onto the bottle. She'd been there herself.

'It was a doll that Mother knitted. We christened it Miss Starkey. We used to pour gin on it. Then we changed to vodka. That's when you changed to vodka.' Her voice was as dispassionate as somebody discussing the price of fish. 'We used to stick gramophone needles into its heart.'

'But that's terrible . . .'

'It's over. It's gone. I burned it the day of Mother's funeral.'

She had to ask. 'When was that?'

'Three years ago. She was buried on Maundy Thursday.'

Sorrel suddenly had a vision of herself three years ago, in Blackpool. Going down to have her very last drink at Yates's Wine Lodge. And trying to remember the name the Church had for the day when the Queen gave out little bags of money. Her whole new life had started on that Maundy Thursday.

'So now you know,' said Mamie in dismissive tones.

'I know something else. I know about the way you're drinking. I've done it.' Sorrel was amazed to find that her prime emotion was pity.

'Oh *that*,' rapped Mamie impatiently. 'That's gone on for years. Until today I always did it at home. Now there's no need.' She kissed the flat bottle. 'This is my only friend and I loathe it.'

734

'But you don't have to.' Sorrel was all crusading urgency. 'You could do what I did. You could go to AA.'

'You must be joking! AA is for the little people. I am a star.'

'But . . .'

'I have handed you every opportunity to make a clean exit, Sorrel.' Mamie's voice was rising dangerously. 'Just do as you're told. Scram!'

'Let me have one last look at you,' begged Sorrel.

'Why?'

'Because I need to look at you hard. I need to remember. You're everything I don't want to become. Goodbye, Mamie. If you want forgiveness, I forgive you.'

'I just want my dead mother to stop throwing her old pans around my kitchen,' raged Mamie. 'I'm sick of her haunting me. That's the only reason I told you. Get out! The number-one dressing room's still mine for tonight.'

12

For the first time in her life, Sorrel was seeing the floorboards of the house in Rookswood Avenue. She must have been in London when her mother went over to fitted carpets. Now these carpets, and even the underfelt, were rolled up, ready to follow the furniture which had already gone to the auctioneer's. Gladys, in a coat and hat and gloves, was sitting on top of a pile of suitcases. She seemed to have got smaller and looked like an elderly evacuee.

Sorrel had been back in *Angel Dwellings* for two and a half years. She was, if anything, more famous than ever. True to her word, Gladys was finally going to live in a nursing home.

'There's still time to change your mind.'

'And lose a month's deposit?' Her mother was outraged. 'Phyllis Bentley and I will be very comfortable at Mount Erskine. We're only going to use it as a base. You won't know us – we'll be gadding off everywhere. Who'd have thought the shop would have brought all that money? I'm told that Mr Jalal is open every hour that Allah sends.'

The shop had been bought by a Pakistani who had blithely changed its trading purpose and was now selling mixed groceries. He was said to have moved his huge family into living quarters which had not been occupied since Sorrel's grandmother died.

'As soon as I saw they'd got Shanks toilets at Mount Erskine, I knew it was for me.' Gladys looked round the through room. 'I never did get round to taking down the picture rails. I put it off for twenty years.'

'They're back in fashion.'

'Nice for the new people.'

It seemed to Sorrel that Nature had got the lighting wrong. Bright spring sunshine did not go with the end of an era. Gladys looked at her watch. 'In two minutes, Arthur Bentley will be late.'

'I could have got you a taxi.'

'When Phyllis has got a son? And please don't think you're coming to settle me in. I'm not a little girl.'

Sorrel, who had never cared a toss for what people thought, wondered whether they were saying that she had put her mother in a home. 'You'll be able to come and stay with me as often as you like.'

'Have you found a cleaner yet?'

'No.'

'Then you've some hopes of seeing me there! I know you, it'll be books everywhere. You're your father all over again.' Gladys looked round the room. Stripped bare, it had developed an echo. 'This house was meant to be just a stepping stone. Some stepping stone, I've been here for fifty-four years! We used to come up and watch them building it. I remember your father stepping over a piece of string, between two wooden pegs, and saying, "There you are, Gladys, there's your kitchenette." '

A black car was coming up the avenue. Gladys straightened her hat. 'That's Arthur now. I could wish it wasn't an old Cortina. They're bound to judge you by what you arrive in.' She had already got off her suitcases. 'You could do me a favour and carry the two big ones to the gate. I don't like to trouble him. He's got a built-up shoe.'

Sorrel took hold of her mother's best Antler luggage and Gladys picked up her old patent-leather hatbox. 'This is nearly an antique,' she said. 'Like me.' Looking towards the spot where the winged armchair had always been, she said to somebody who wasn't there: 'Come on, love. You're coming with me.'

We're so alike, thought Sorrel. And it's only in the last couple of years I've started to realize it.

Back straight, head held high, Gladys sailed down the path and handed her hatbox to the grey middle-aged man who was already holding open the gate.

'This is a very sad morning,' he said.

'Don't be so daft, Arthur,' snorted Gladys. 'Me and your mother are all set to be the naughtiest girls at Mount Erskine. And Sorrel, watch out that front door doesn't slam on you. I

737

won't be inside to let you in. Hey you!' She was calling out to the boy who had been so fascinated by Ruby's car. 'Don't you know better than to go kicking a tin can around? It means there's going to be a death. That's a merry thought to leave on, isn't it?' she asked brightly as she gave Sorrel a quick kiss, climbed into the car and sat bolt upright, staring ahead, until Arthur Bentley closed the car boot and limped round to the driver's seat.

Gladys wound down her window. 'I'll ring you tonight at Fallowmeadow Road,' she called out to Sorrel. She had arrived here as a bride. And now she was being driven away, for the last time, by nobody more special than the son of a woman she'd once worked with.

In the house the telephone was ringing so Sorrel stopped waving and hurried up the path to answer it.

'British Telecom have been.' It was Monica Dolan. 'Your line's installed at Fallowmeadow Road. I'm there now.'

'She's gone.' It didn't seem enough to mark such a significant passing.

'If the men have come and read your mother's meters, I'll drive up and collect you.'

'No, there's nothing left to carry. You wait there for Ruby. She's bringing my sitting room curtains. I'll get a cab.'

'You'd be just as quick walking.'

Sorrel slammed the door for the last time and posted the keys through the letterbox. Her thoughts were full of people from her childhood –Tattons and Ganders and Dolans and Monks. All gone; and now the last of the Starkeys was following them. As she swung round the corner of the avenue, she turned back for a final glance. Not a single house was painted green and cream.

Walking down Ravensway, she remembered it without the built-on garages and annexes and extensions. She remembered the days when every house had been scrupulously careful to look no different from the next. And now they all ate chilli con carne, and argued over the rival merits of Chinese restaurants and of holidays in Canada and Corfu.

The house she had bought for herself was in that section of Irlams o'th' Height which had not been affected by the road development. It was near to Light Oaks Park. These days it was perfectly possible to sit on the grass by the duck pond. The Clean Air Act had seen to that.

The houses in Fallowmeadow Road were, in their own way, predecessors of Ravensdale Estate. Bigger and older, they had been built for shopkeepers and senior clerks in the cotton trade. Most of the Edwardian red-brick villas were semi-detached. Sorrel's was more like Mr Tuffin's boarding house at Blackpool, even to the stained-glass window in the front door. It was in a short terrace, up on a bank, with a flower bed to the side of the steps from the road.

Sorrel opened the front door and looked around the sizeable hall. It was nearly a room in its own right, which was one of the reasons which had decided her on the house. That and the grey Connemara marble fireplace in the sitting room. The hall was already beginning to look like her own. Yesterday evening she had filled it with her collection of framed Manchester theatrical trivia. Everything from Marie Lloyd with a bunch of cherries in her teeth to the poster for *A Royal Divorce*. It all looked better here than it had ever done at the Nun's Prayer.

A door banged somewhere in the empty house and this was followed by the sound of footsteps on bare boards.

'Is that you, Monica?'

Monica Dolan appeared at the top of the staircase carrying Sorrel's last remaining painting by Magda Schiffer. Mickey still had the rest of them, in America. 'This just fell down. The cord broke but the glass didn't smash.'

'What it really needs is old-fashioned picture wire. Ruby might just have some. I'll call her.'

Monica began to descend the stairs. 'The men installed four jack plugs. The phone they brought is in the morning room. I've just rung La Voluptua. I left ten pence by the side.' La Voluptua was the name of Monica's massage parlour.

Sorrel was highly critical of the new telephone the engineers had left behind. It weighed little more than a plastic shoehorn. What satisfaction would there be in slamming that down on Mickey Grimshaw? As she punched up Ruby's number, she was wondering whether it was still possible to get really heavy phones, with dials?

'This is Juniper House.' The voice on the recorded message was male and unfamiliar. 'Due to the sudden death of Mrs Ruby Shapiro, all calls are being referred to Miss Robinson in the personnel department at Shapiro House. The number to ring is . . .'

Sorrel replaced the receiver unsteadily. She felt distinctly swimmy. For only the second time in her life, she was close to fainting. Everything was going in and out. Monica must have seen this because she grabbed hold of Sorrel and sat her down on a kitchen chair.

'I only saw her on Tuesday morning. Ruby's dead. What's today? I can't think straight . . .'

'Thursday.'

'She was meant to be coming round with my curtains. Oh God, that sounds awful . . .'

'No it doesn't. What you need is a brandy.'

Sorrel shook her head. 'I can't have it.'

'Surely just a medicinal dose wouldn't do any harm?'

Sorrel's mouth actually watered. In her mind she was *tasting* the brandy. But she couldn't have it. It would still have been the first drink and it would still have done the damage. 'Put the kettle on. I'll have coffee instead.' Once again she rang Juniper House and this time she made a note of Miss Robinson's number.

'I bet that's the undertaker's voice, Monica. There should be some coffee mugs in that cardboard box labelled Black and White whisky.' The idea of that brandy was still haunting the edges of her mind. AA were right when they said that alcohol was very patient. Well it could stay patient! She would ring Miss Robinson instead.

At least this wasn't another recording '. . . the funeral took place this morning and the family are now sitting shivah.' Miss Robinson plainly wasn't Jewish for when she said 'sitting shivah' she sounded as though she wished to appear to be just trying the words for size.

'Already buried?' asked Sorrel, in near disbelief.

'They don't believe in hanging about.' Then the girl went back to being formal. 'Are you a family friend?'

'Yes.'

740

'They will be receiving friends, at home, during the seven days.'

Sorrel suddenly remembered on old engraving which Edie had at Blackpool. It was called *What Is a Home Without a Mother?* Ruby was dead and she was buried and she wouldn't be at Juniper House like she'd always been. Sorrel began to shake so hard that all she could do was put down the telephone.

'Put your head between your knees.' Monica was at her fiercest.

'I don't want to put my head between my knees. I want to do something.' In every bereavement Sorrel had ever known, death had always filled her with this fierce, almost chemical, energy. It was as though the very life force was asserting itself against the inevitability of all our deaths. 'Did the engineers leave phone books?'

'Hall table. Stay where you are. I'll get them. What do you want me to look up?'

'The Jewish Museum. It probably comes under Manchester. Give me the book . . .'

The man at the other end of the line had a voice of great kindness so Sorrel had no hesitation in pouring out her problems: 'The thing is I don't know what you're meant to do,' she explained, 'and I don't want to go doing the wrong thing.' This relentless energy had left her chewing her bottom lip like she had done when she was on the slimming tablets.

'The family will be saying prayers for a week. It is customary to call and offer them a small gift.'

'Flowers?'

'No. Perhaps a cake.'

'Any special sort of cake?'

'How about a *nice* cake?'

All the time they had been talking the man's voice had seemed to contain extra question marks. The same had been true of Ruby. It was the first thing Sorrel had ever noticed about her. But outside the synagogue, on the day of that dreadful wedding, Ruby had vowed: 'I'll be a good friend to you – the best.' And this had never been less than true. Suddenly near to tears, Sorrel had difficulty in asking, 'Does the cake have to be Kosher?'

741

'Oh yes.'

It was only after she had rung off that Sorrel realized she'd forgotten to ask whether she should turn up in mourning.

'You can't really go wrong in a black suit,' advised Monica. 'Jewish women live and die in them. Sorry, that was an unfortunate choice of expression.'

'Everything's still in trunks and boxes.' Too much had happened on one day and Sorrel was suddenly feeling close to tears again.

'Leave it to me. I'll sort you out. I've already unpacked the steam iron.'

'You are good.'

'Five thousand pounds in cash in a brown envelope,' replied Monica, watching Sorrel closely.

Sorrel knew she had to turn in the performance of a lifetime and hoped she could accomplish it in one puzzled word: 'What?'

'Nothing, just checking.' Monica was totally deceived. 'Somebody cast their bread upon the water and sent me five thousand quid.'

But I never expected it to come back in *diamonds*, thought Sorrel. It had suddenly dawned upon her that she was now an heiress.

These days Monica lived in a service flat at Rusholme. This didn't stop her dropping Sorrel off on quite the other side of town. Tobias, the Kosher bakers, were already closed.

'Leave me here anyway.' Sorrel climbed out of the Mini. 'I'll walk up to Deli King and get a cake there.'

With the passing years Broughton seemed to have got even more noticeably Jewish. There were definitely more of the bearded men in black hats and long black raincoats. There had always been little boys in prayer caps, held on with hair-grips. But had they always had tight twists of Orthodox ringlets, dancing in front of their ears? Not for the first time, Sorrel caught herself thinking that the 1980s hit song 'I Am What I Am' had different meanings in different parts of the city. Everything, everywhere, was more proclaimed.

You needed sharp elbows in Deli King and some of the

customers should have been barred from using a supermarket trolley, for life. It was early evening so most of the cakes left on display looked a bit plain and worthy. Sorrel was already feeling an interloper but the woman buying bagels, at her side, had a kind face so she risked asking, 'Which cake would you take to a family sitting shivah?'

'None. They'll be snowed under with cakes. Take wine instead. That keeps.'

The label on the hock bottle proclaimed it to be produce of Israel and strictly Kosher. 'Could I have a carrier?' Sorrel asked the girl at the check-out. She didn't really want to be seen wandering around Broughton Park with a bottle in her hand. Word might get round that she'd gone back on the booze.

It took her only five minutes to walk to Juniper House. Broughton Park was still as much another country as it had been in Sorrel's childhood. One of the Shapiros' neighbours even had ruched blinds made of shocking-pink suede. Sorrel had expected the curtains at Juniper House to be closed but they weren't. Everything looked as usual. Even Ruby's red car was standing in the side drive. The door was opened by the housekeeper, who wasn't Jewish.

'Come in, Miss Starkey.'

Bereft of stage directions, Sorrel pulled the wine out of the carrier and thrust it at the elderly woman.

'No. You're meant to give that to Mrs Zillah. The ladies are all in the big drawing room. Mr Barney and the other men are through in the dining room, saying prayers. It goes on for seven days.' Emily, the housekeeper, nodded significantly towards Ruby's huge Empire mirrors on the hall walls. They were all covered with dark dust sheets: 'That's something else they do. Can I say something?'

'Of course.'

'She did love you. "Good as any daughter," she used to say to me, "Good as any daughter." ' The housekeeper blew her nose. 'She was a good 'un herself.'

'The best.' And the tears Sorrel had vowed to control threatened to flow.

'Aunt Gilda's here from Solihull' – Emily lowered her

voice – 'and don't we know it!' Opening the drawing room door she announced Sorrel with no more formality than 'It's Miss Starkey.'

'Am I glad to see you.' Zillah got to her feet from an armchair. She wasn't in black, she was in a grey flannel suit. The other two women weren't in mourning either. One was Doris Dintenfass in her wheelchair. The other was an antique stranger.

'I've not got the words,' said Sorrel. 'I'm just so sorry. So very sorry.'

'They kept trying to phone you,' explained Zillah, 'but your mother's line was always engaged.'

'She's gone into the nursing home. The last few days have all been arrangements.' Did Zillah know that she'd ripped her lapel? This hardly seemed the moment to mention it.

But Zillah had seen where Sorrel was looking. 'We do that,' she explained. 'It's the modern version of rending your garments. Have you met Aunt Gilda?'

The antique opened her disapproving mouth and said, 'I'm Mrs Kaye to the shiksa.'

Sorrel hadn't heard that awful word for twenty years. Aunt Gilda looked for all the world like Jacob Shapiro in drag. This effect was heightened by the fact that she was wearing a sheitel. The traditional wig looked more like coconut fibre than human hair. Mrs Kaye continued to glare at Sorrel. 'Why doesn't she just take the diamonds and get out?'

'Gilda, enough!'

'Just give them to her and tell her to go.'

'It's not as easy as that. Monty Klein has to see to everything.' Zillah turned to Sorrel: 'He's the executor.'

Sorrel had taken against Mrs Kaye on sight but she felt honour-bound to say, 'Look, if it's going to cause family trouble, I'd rather not have them.'

'No.' Zillah was as firm as Barney at his firmest. 'They're yours, Sorrel. Ruby was absolutely definite about that.'

'Isn't it enough that my sister-in-law dropped dead collecting that yenta's curtains?' Aunt Gilda's mouth snapped shut and turned into the full Shapiro rat-trap.

Zillah immediately showed the family in a better light:

'That's the last way I wanted Sorrel to find out. Honestly, Gilda . . .'

'Honestly Gilda nothing! Those diamonds were bought with Shapiro money. By rights they should be going to Barnet's wife. They should be going to Amanda.'

'Well that's not what the will says.' Zillah flashed Sorrel a warning look. 'Take no notice. Gilda's just upset.'

'Hello, Sorrel,' said Doris Dintenfass, helpfully, from her chair. 'Love the little suit. Wallis Shops?'

'Hello, love. How're you doing?'

'I'm missing Ruby terribly.'

'Me too.' Ruby would have sorted out Aunt Gilda in seconds.

'And did she know the value of that Matisse?' Gilda was off again. 'What good will it do in the City Art Gallery?'

'It will save on death duties,' sighed Zillah wearily.

Sorrel looked at the painting of the open shutters with the two swans on a cobalt-blue river. Swans – how long was it since she had last thought of herself and Barney as that? How young and sentimental and foolish they had been. Yet she had never stopped loving him, not even for one second. The whole of this conversation had been accompanied by a low murmur of male voices from the next room. Barney was only the other side of a wooden door yet – for all the good it would do her – he might just as well be a million miles away.

'I'm sorry there had to be such a lot of fuss over a necklace and a pair of earrings,' said Sorrel helplessly.

'Necklace and earrings?' screeched Gilda. 'And bracelets? And rings? And the Boucheron pendant Jacob brought back from Paris? For a woman who's managed to scheme her way into a cool half million, you're very casual.'

'Half a million?' gasped Sorrel in something close to horror.

'See the eyes light up, Zillah? See the greedy shiksa's eyes?'

'Don't use that word,' stormed her niece. 'And show some respect for Ruby's wishes. This is our friend.'

Sorrel's arms went impulsively around Zillah. 'Your mother once said to me: "The only stylish way out of this mess is to go." And that's what I'm going to do now.'

'You're our friend,' repeated Zillah stubbornly. 'They're yours and you're going to get them.'

But Sorrel didn't really care about the inheritance. Money, she could earn. All she wanted was a man in the next room who was praying to the God of Abraham and of Isaac and of Joseph. Half a million pounds had changed nothing.

Deaths always come in three. Sorrel had arranged her house removal to coincide with a week's holiday from *Angel Dwellings*. When she returned to rehearsals Nadine Taylor greeted her with 'Get your black out. Diggory Mallet's passed away. He died at Denville Hall but they're bringing the body back to Manchester for the funeral.' Denville Hall was the actors' retirement home, in the South of England. But Diggory, like all the principals in the show, had been genuinely Northern.

'One goes and one arrives,' continued Nadine. 'We've got a new girl. She can't be twenty and she's already managed to infuriate just about everybody.'

'Is she the one playing my niece? Until I opened the script, I didn't even know that Lettie had got a niece.'

'They established the character while you were away.' Nadine pulled a face. 'Fay Bly. Red hair and a bust like puddings boiling over.'

Sorrel looked round the rehearsal room. 'So where is she?'

'Being photographed, outside, in a bathing suit. She's only been here a week and she's already made *The Sun* and *The Star*. I think she must be obliging somebody in the publicity office.' All of this was most unlike the equable Nadine. Usually she just got on with her job and refused to become involved in back-biting.

'What's she called?'

'Carmen Kinsella.'

'And what's more, it's my own name.' The reality had walked into the rehearsal room on white, beauty-queen high heels. She was buttoning a white cotton dress over a green satin bikini. The legs seemed to go on for ever. And could all that dark red hair be her own? This vision walked up to Sorrel and said, in a voice of throbbing urgency: 'You changed my life.'

'Did I?' Sorrel was startled. And, oh dear, it was a bit early in the morning for all this dramatic intensity.

'You told me not to change my name.'

'When?'

'I was just a kid in tap shoes.' The delivery was purest 1940s Hollywood. 'It was outside that theatrical costumier's on Oxford Road. It's a pizza place now.' She invested this last line with a sadness worthy of the Moscow Arts Theatre.

Did this go on all the time? Sorrel was always suspicious of young performers who couldn't stop acting off the stage. It generally meant that there would be nothing left for the show. But this was not the case with Miss Kinsella. Rehearsals began with a read-through and her work was sure and honest, with a brand of burning sincerity that reminded Sorrel of old videotapes of herself, in early episodes.

Carmen Kinsella . . . it was all coming back. Sorrel remembered returning from Vienna and being forced to spend the night in that tatty hotel beyond the university. She'd met the child on her walk back to the Nun's Prayer.

'You taught me a great lesson,' insisted Carmen. 'You took trouble with me. It's like a sacred trust. One day I'll take trouble with somebody else. I've got to. Sorrel, *Angel Dwellings* is my great opportunity. If you ever notice me getting big-headed, you would tell me, wouldn't you?'

'No.'

'Why not?' Carmen Kinsella was startled into sounding downright ordinary.

'Because I once asked a wardrobe woman to do the same for me. And when she did, I nearly bit her head off. Come on, they're going to run our kitchen scene.'

It began with Sorrel, alone with the parrot. She was supposed to have inherited it from Red Biddy. Carmen made her entrance on such a lively note that Sorrel was left wondering whether the viewers would notice that she and the bird were still there.

'Carmen? Is it really necessary to come slamming in on such a high note?'

'But you told me to do it. All those years ago you said: "Always enter on a higher note than the last person who was speaking." You said it would make people sit up and take notice of me.'

'Yes, but I didn't intend you to wipe me, and a red and green parrot, right off the screen.'

'I'll try and remember.'

'You'd better.' And Sorrel instantly decided to keep a close watch on a fault in herself. Addressing the child, she'd heard Mamie Hamilton-Gerrard's voice coming from within her own.

Diggory Mallet's funeral was the cause of much discussion. They all wanted to go but it was on Friday afternoon and the management said they would have to work on Saturday, to make up the lost time. Sorrel had known Diggory Mallet all her life without realizing that he had a Swinton connection. At some time his family had bought a plot in Swinton cemetery and there was one space left.

The funeral took place at the parish church. Everybody got themselves up in black but Carmen Kinsella's outfit was the talk of the cast. There was far more material in her huge lace mantilla than there was in her black velvet mini-dress. The vicar was forced to wait whilst she posed for the photographers outside the church.

The service was brief. The committal was grim. Earth thudded on the old actor's coffin and it was with some relief that everybody filed out of the graveyard and took over a pub called The Forrester's.

'Well that makes two deaths for me.' Sorrel accepted a glass of Coca-Cola from Alan Pomphret. 'I wonder who's going to be the third? Where's Nadine?'

'Gone off to see whether she can get an early *Evening News*. She's got herself very worked up because nobody remembered to put Diggory's death in the announcements. She wants to see if it's in today's.'

'What difference will it make? Poor Diggory, I've known him since *Children's Hour*. He once told me I'd never make a real actress until I lost my virtue.' Nadine came through the door clutching a newspaper. 'Is it in?' asked Sorrel. 'Alan's got you a gin and tonic.'

'Give me a minute, I'm just going to look.' Nadine began to rustle through the pages at the back of the paper.

'Wasn't Mick in *Children's Hour* too?' asked Alan Pomphret.

'Yes.' Sorrel resisted the temptation to add that Mickey was in the middle of writing something new for America. She was ready for a gamble. If the offer of international stardom came she would grab it with both hands. She had no intention of staying in *Angel Dwellings* until it was time for her own funeral.

'Did you actually know Diggory Mallet?' Reporters had followed them into the pub and one was now questioning Carmen Kinsella.

Carmen pulled a string of black rosary beads through her fingers. 'He changed my life.'

'Just who does she think she is?' muttered Nadine.

'I'll tell you who she is.' Sorrel did not say this unpleasantly. 'She's the next generation, knocking at the door. And she's bound to win through – that's how the world goes on.'

'Sorrel?' Nadine, who had found the deaths column, looked up from the newspaper. 'You know the Shapiros, don't you?'

'Yes. Why?' Not Barney. Please God, don't let Barney be dead.

'Which one's Amanda?' Nadine began to read from the paper: ' "Suddenly at home in Southport." The burial took place yesterday.'

13

When Ruby died Sorrel had written Barney a short letter of condolence which came straight from the heart. The words had almost written themselves. His wife's death meant that Sorrel had to unscrew her fountain pen again. And this time she was left chewing the end. What could she say? Every line she wrote seemed to be loaded with double meanings. Her sentiments either looked insincere or else heavy with invitation. After ripping up five separate attempts, she decided to call Mickey for professional writer's advice.

'Well you certainly can't say you're sorry. It would be a black lie. How do you really feel about it? It's me. Be truthful.'

Sorrel hesitated before she replied. 'I thought he would have got in touch.'

'With the woman hardly cold in her grave? It wouldn't be decent.'

'I've thought that too.'

'You do realize you've woken me up? You plainly haven't got a letter in you. Leave it for the moment. Time will sort the whole thing out.'

But time was something she hadn't got on her side. 'I'm not getting any younger, Mick.'

He was having none of this. 'Actresses of your age should go down on bended knees, every night, and thank God for Joan Collins. She's taken the last milestone of sex appeal and moved it fifteen years up the road. Are you still going to the gym?'

'Yes.'

'Good. Sooner or later I'm going to want you in splendid nick for the new show.'

'What if I said I wanted real life?'

'I should have thought you'd had quite enough of that! Goodnight.'

But she did want real life, though it couldn't be denied that two and a half years of *Angel Dwellings* had left her hungry for change, for new professional opportunities. Sorrel's social life would have surprised her television audiences. Mostly she just went home from the studio, fell into the bath, made herself a light supper and read her way through the evening.

At weekends she would cook. All her recipes reminded her of friends. Gander's pea soup and Shelagh Starkey's pheasant in port wine, and lamb in a brownstone pot à la mode de Ruby Shapiro. Gladys would never come for Sunday lunch because it was the best meal of the week at the nursing home and she was determined to get her money's worth out of Mount Erskine. But Monica would turn up, and Nadine and her husband, and even Carmen Kinsella.

It had not taken Sorrel long to discover that Carmen was just a child in need of a lot of affection. Even a little attention was repaid with doglike devotion and she was always willing to arrive early and peel potatoes and enthuse over Sorrel's latest junk-shop finds.

'I love the bamboo umbrella stand.'

'When we were children, Mickey Grimshaw and I used to stay in the same holiday boarding house. Somehow my house has ended up looking very like it. They had a duplicate of that umbrella stand in their hall. Look, I've even managed to find the same kind of varnished paper sunshade to go in it. I do wish Mick would hurry up and come for a visit. I want him to see it all.'

The spare bedroom had been decorated with Mick very much in mind. All the old children's books were up there and Sorrel had even put Pollock's toy theatres between them; just like they'd had in their youth, in Cornucopia Mews.

But it looked as though the first guest was going to be somebody quite different. Zillah turned up one Sunday morning with a man friend waiting in a car outside and arms full of dresses on hangers.

'Could I ask you to mind these for me? I'm off to Brazil. And when I come back, could you bear to have me for a couple of nights? Barney's inherited Juniper and goodness only knows what he's going to do with it. I'll have to come

751

back to England to talk to Monty Klein.' The man in the car outside tooted impatiently.

'I'm coming, Lionel!' she shouted. Then Zillah murmured to Sorrel: 'Lionel's divine, dear. And so in love with me. Where was I? Oh that brother of mine . . . he seems to have forgotten how to carry on a sensible conversation.'

'D'you mean he's gone wild?' asked a perturbed Sorrel.

'Just the opposite. All turned in on himself. It's tragic. By the way, Monty Klein wants to talk to you too. Would you ring him? Must dash. I should be at Ringway already. I'll bring you back a Carmen Miranda hat!'

Some people might have objected to having been turned into a left-luggage office and prospective lodging-house keeper – all in one breathless swoop. Not Sorrel. She knew that this was Zillah's way of staying friends. And that made her happy. It took away the last lingering doubts about having been paid off in diamonds.

When Sorrel telephoned Monty Klein he seemed anxious to set up a meeting. 'It needn't be in the office,' the solicitor said. 'We could have a drink. How about Henry's Bar behind Kendal's?'

This wine bar was up some imposing marble steps. Hadn't these swing doors once led into the offices of a shipping company? The open-plan conversion took up the whole of the ground floor. It was all fake marbling and stencil-work. Sorrel settled herself down in the kind of basket chair which, at one time, had only been seen in cinema cafes. The place was full of people carrying portable telephones. She tried to decide which of the men by the bar was Monty Klein. Oh well, the fame of her own face would guarantee his finding her.

'We haven't met since you put ham sandwiches on a Seder plate.' He had come up from behind. The young man who had looked like Woody Allen before anybody had heard of Woody Allen was now middle-aged and bald.

'What will you have to drink?' he asked. 'I have to get it from the counter.'

'Perrier.' Asking for mineral water, these days, provoked no comment. Half the town was on it.

As the Shapiros' solicitor, in black jacket and striped

trousers, walked up to the counter, Sorrel remembered that she had once forged a Chanukah card in his name. He wasn't just their solicitor, he was Barney's oldest friend. Was this meeting strictly business or had he come as some kind of ambassador? His bottom had got a lot bigger, she certainly noticed that.

Monty returned from the counter with their drinks. 'Barney asked me to arrange this chat.'

Sorrel's hopes rose.

'It's about the will.'

They fell again. 'Doesn't it have to go through probate?' She didn't really care if it had to go through Portsmouth!

'Yes. It looks as though there could be some horse-trading over art bequests to institutions, so I want to be seen to be doing everything by the letter.'

He smiled at Sorrel and said, 'You needn't worry about your jewels. They're in the safe deposit. When you do get them – and you will – you might consider selling one of the lesser pieces to buy some insurance for the rest.'

This was about as interesting as talking about fax machines. That's what they were discussing loudly at the next table – whether the Mitsubishi was better than the Nashua. Sorrel supposed she'd better make some comment on the insurance suggestions. 'A man called Pym looks after me and money. I'll get him to call you. Can we cut the cackle, Monty? How's Barney?'

How many times, under how many different sets of circumstances, had she been forced into asking people this? Well, this is the last time, she thought. The humiliation ends here. Only she had to repeat 'How is he?' to get Monty going.

'Ruby's death knocked him sideways. Amanda's, coming straight on top, nearly finished him off.'

Sorrel hesitated before she asked her next question. But it concerned a possibility which had been haunting her for weeks: 'Amanda didn't do anything stupid, did she? Ruby always told me how keen she was to get her hands on those diamonds.'

'Relax,' said Monty. 'It was pernicious anaemia. There was a long history of it. Anything else?'

For as long as she'd known him, Sorrel had protected Barney and kept secrets. Now there was no need. 'How much, in recent years, has he told you about me?'

'Enough. Without being indiscreet, I'm not just Ruby's executor, I'm Barney's joint-executor too.'

Sorrel was rapidly losing patience: 'Must you reduce everything to pounds, shillings and pence?' Now she became reckless. 'I'm talking about *love*.'

'You'll wish you hadn't,' warned Klein.

'Why?'

'I've been friends with Barney since we were six.'

'So what do you know that I won't like?'

'It's all the fault of that Hamilton-Gerrard woman.' Monty looked around to be sure that nobody was listening. 'Barney says they wouldn't have you back in *Angel Dwellings* until she'd gone. He refuses to do the same thing to you in real life. He says it would be too shoddy.'

'That's for me to decide.'

'You can't decide about something that's not on offer. He won't do it to you, Sorrel.'

Suddenly the piped background music, and the cash-conscious chatter from the next table, started to get to Sorrel: 'Money isn't everything!' she yelled at them. 'And that comes from a woman who's known what it is to share one pair of silk stockings. So put that in your Mitsubishi and fax it to Japan.' It was quite true about the stockings – she'd shared them with Judy Weatherall at the Old Fire-Iron.

'Do calm down,' begged Monty Klein, who had aged more conventionally than Sorrel.

'Why? I'm trying to talk to you about the only man I've ever loved.'

Monty shook his head sadly. 'You'll never get him to make the first move.'

'Well, I'm not doing it.' Sorrel got to her feet. 'Not this time. I'm the one who's always had to make the running. I've been such a decent little chap that it's a miracle I haven't sprouted a moustache. It's Barney's turn to be the man. And you can tell him that with my compliments.'

One of the young men at the next table looked at Sorrel in

fascinated wonder. 'You are something else,' he said with admiration. 'Any time, lady! Any time at all.'

There was a long queue of people waiting on the St Ann's Square taxi rank. Everybody in front of Sorrel seemed to be Jewish. Even when she finally reached the head of the queue, the taxi drivers were doing their infuriating trick of cruising slowly down the line of passengers and calling out: 'Anybody for South Manchester? Anybody for Didsbury?'

'I've a good mind to report you to the hackney office,' Sorrel called back in fury.

'Oh shut up, Lettie, and get in. Irlams o'th' Height?'

Fame had its compensations. People found it hard to believe that Sorrel had never learned to drive. First she hadn't been able to afford it and then she became too committed to the bottle. More recently, when she had inquired about lessons, Sorrel had been told she that would need one for every year of her life. And she couldn't imagine herself cooped up with a driving instructor for that number of hours.

The good years are passing, Barney, she thought, as the cab got stuck in traffic on Brindle Heath. Then it suddenly shot forward. Was this an omen? Sorrel was back to seeing signs and portents in the very cracks of the paving stones.

The little garden, in front of her house at Fallowmeadow Road, was looking the proverbial picture. The last of the wallflowers were throwing out waves of evening scent and her foxgloves and delphiniums were already beginning to spike. Tucked between their roots, in pockets of earth, Sorrel had hidden nasturtium seeds so as to be sure of an autumn blaze. If only life could be planned as easily as a garden!

Her cleaner must have gone before the second post arrived because the mail was still lying on the mat. The top one was an Equity ballot paper. She could tell that just from the envelope. The letter with the American stamp looked much more promising. Like many people who write for money, Mickey Grimshaw only put pen to paper when it really mattered. In truth, he'd put fingers to word-processor but there was a nice juicy amount of typescript on the page.

Dear Miss Diamonds,

This isn't going to be easy to write. I've just had Barney on the telephone. It seems I've done you a grave disservice.

He never stops watching you on the television and is much daunted by your restored beauty. He feels he has nothing to offer 'such an amazing woman'. His words, not mine.

As a matter of fact, last time I saw him getting out of the shower, he struck me as a million dollars' worth of mature man-meat. Those years on the squash court haven't half kept him trim. I'd rate him way above Clint Eastwood. Before you start licking your lips, Barney's absolutely convinced he wouldn't stand a chance with you. He won't even try. God knows what that awful Mandy must have done to his self-esteem. I would say that the ball was in your court.

Oh no it isn't, thought Sorrel grimly. Not after the message I've just sent with Monty Klein. The ball's in Barney's court. She went back to the letter.

Why not cut your losses and look to a future without him? I hope this has not caused you to rip up the page because I have hot news. The first block of scripts is drafted. The pilot episode is gleaming. You won't have to camera-test because I can show them tapes of recent episodes of *Angel Dwellings*. I can't absolutely promise they'll have you. I'm still battling with American Equity about your star status. Even if the television company agree to your doing the pilot, it would still be a gamble. In the States, shows don't get off the ground as easily as they do in the UK. And casts can be changed at the last minute.

We've always gambled in the past. It would mean your leaving Angel Dungeons to take a chance. You're not without money. You could have the diamonds copied in paste and sell the real thing.

Anyway, leave it with me. I'll write more when I know more. Probably around the end of the year. Telephonic communication will continue as usual.

Lots of love
Michael Clever-Balls

It was exactly what she had been calling him in her own mind! America . . . after all these years. Was that what she wanted? No. She wanted what she had always wanted. But did Barney want her? He certainly seemed to have different excuses for different people. Or did he just let each of them see so much? Why didn't he bring the whole problem to her?

Because he was Barney. And that meant upright and honourable and clean-cut – and she could cheerfully have kicked him! But that would involve confronting him. And this time he was the one who was going to have to find her. Perhaps Mick was right. Perhaps the answer did lie in America.

Sorrel turned on the radio. Connie Francis was singing a modern disco-version of 'Where the Boys Are'. There were certainly plenty of the boys in California. A sign? Enough of that. Most AA meetings have a notice on the wall which says *Let Go and Let God*. You simply ask the Power greater than yourself to take your troubles on board. And after that, if you carry on worrying, you've done away with the request.

Sorrel offered up a quick prayer to her own idea of God: Just show me what to do and give me the strength to do it. And then she sat down and ate a whole packet of chocolate digestive biscuits for a bit of uncomplicated comfort.

Somebody along the terrace was burning leaves. If she was going to cut some hydrangea heads, for drying, the time was now. The Canterbury bells were heavy with seeds and the orange and golden nasturtiums were doing what Sorrel had meant them to do. They were proclaiming the fact that autumn had come to Fallowmeadow Road. Sorrel, secateurs in hand, looked around her little garden. Those dog daisies were hardly the thing to cut and take to Gladys. She would have to get the taxi to stop at a florist's.

The brochure for Mount Erskine described it as 'a queen amongst residential homes' and went on to talk about 'this commodious, converted private residence' and 'complete freedom with full eventide care'. If Sorrel had been asked to describe it she would have said that Mount Erskine was a big, ugly old house with a lot of new fire escapes. It was outside

Urmston, it was set in a dank shrubbery, and they knew how to charge. Still it was Glady's choice and Gladys's money.

Whenever Sorrel went to visit her mother, there was much talk of Matron and Mr Waddilove. They were the joint proprietors of Mount Erskine. The establishment was almost a soap opera in itself. Mr Waddilove had once been married to Matron but wasn't any more. But he and his former wife and the new Mrs Waddilove all lived on the premises and looked after the residents.

'It's a very modern arrangement,' said Gladys, who would once have been appalled, 'but we reap the benefits. There aren't many of these places that have shopping trips to Boulogne.'

Whenever Sorrel went to see her mother she didn't have to say much. She was just expected to thrust her flowers forward and listen to the monologue.

'I've had a terrible shock, Sheila, terrible. But I'll come to that in a minute. Last night we went to see *West Side Story* done by the amateurs. Guess who was Maria? That speech therapist who used to come to Rookswood Avenue – Deborah. Quite good but somebody should have told her to take off her glasses.'

'What's the shock you've had?'

Gladys ignored this question. 'The shock' was obviously being saved for the grand finale. And to think that Sorrel had once wondered from where she inherited her sense of theatre.

'Any new boyfriends?' asked Gladys.

'Honestly, Mother!'

'Well I have. Or I could have. Mr McGregor invited me out for morning coffee. I didn't go. His teeth click and he didn't have a friend for Phyllis.' For a moment Gladys looked her age and mildly bewildered. 'Sometimes I forget whether I've told you things or not. Did I tell you that Ruby Shapiro and I had a serious conversation before she died?'

'No.' Sorrel was looking in one of the fitted cupboards for a vase for the spray chrysanthemums which Gladys still liked so much.

'We came to the conclusion that we should never have

758

stood in your way. We were both big enough to admit that we should have let you marry Barney.'

Had Gladys spent all these years thinking that she had been a major impediment to happiness? Had she given herself the same importance in the drama as Ruby and Jacob Shapiro? The odd thing about this sudden realization was that it filled Sorrel with startled guilt. The truth was that her own mother's wishes in the matter had never been studied for a moment.

'So if he asks you now, I think you should accept him.'

Guilt turned to fury: 'Chance would be a fine thing.'

'Don't take that tone of voice with me. Show some respect. These walls are no more than partitions. You can even hear the gentleman in the next room piddling in the commode.'

'Mother!'

'And don't be so narrow-minded. You're my daughter, you once lived inside me. We should be able to discuss these things. Now for the surprise! Who's the last person on earth I would want living here?'

Sorrel thought for a minute. 'Norman Jepson. Don't tell me my stepfather's moved in?'

'Him? He's another Mr Waddilove. Last time I heard, he was living with a mother and daughter on that road past the margarine works. No, just nip down the corridor, count three doors along, and knock. And don't think you're taking her any of my flowers because you're not.'

'Who?'

'You'll see.'

Sorrel went out into the corridor and did as she was bidden. One door, two, three . . . she knocked.

'Come in.'

The voice was familiar but Sorrel couldn't place it. She opened the door.

Sitting up in bed was a wadded, pink satin mountain. Beryl Grimshaw was attacking a small boiled egg with a spoon.

'Hello, Sorrel. I bet you're wondering what I'm doing here. It didn't seem fair that one mummy should have what the other wasn't getting.'

Mick had never said a word.

'I think your mother's a bit put out because I get extra attention. That's the power of the dollar for you. I'm the only woman here whose account is settled by the Bank of America. D'you think you'll like Hollywood?'

Hollywood? Yes, if the American job ever materialized, Sorrel supposed the bulk of the work would be shot in Los Angeles. It was a big thought for Urmston. 'I don't know that I'm ever going to get there.'

'You will. Mickey always gets his own way. I once thought that you and he would make me some grandchildren,' sighed Beryl, 'but he's not as other men.'

So she's finally accepted it, thought Sorrel.

'No. Mickey's had other passions. He's always been wedded to his work.'

When Sorrel got back to her mother's room Gladys was agog for reaction.

'What's this special consideration she says she gets?' asked her daughter.

'They've put her on a diet,' snorted Gladys. 'She'll never stay the course. You need moral fibre to survive at Mount Erskine. Quick, Sheila, listen! Mr Prentice is piddling in his pot. They're beautiful quality commodes. They're Royal Worcester.'

Sorrel didn't ring for a cab because it made for a delayed exit. Instead, she picked one up outside Urmston station and it dropped her off in Portland Street in the city centre.

Monica's massage parlour, La Voluptua, was at the back of this main street, on the second floor of an office block. The actress never went there during business hours because Monica worried that the press might get hold of the story of Sorrel Starkey visiting questionable premises. As at Moss Side there was a spyhole. When Sorrel pressed the bell Monica opened the door herself. These days she simply ran the place and staff coped with the customers.

'We can't go yet,' she said, 'Andrea's still doing a punter, in the back.'

The premises had once been the offices of a middle man in cotton. There was a main reception area with a desk and telephones and sofas for waiting. The rest of the place was divided into cubicles with pastel-shaded doors. Everything else was grey and white. If it hadn't been for the framed poster of a topless Samantha Fox, you could have been at the dentist's.

Sorrel walked over to the window and looked down on all the neon signs of Chinatown. The scarlet and gold arch was illuminated and the big car park, with its multicoloured brick mural of an oriental galleon, already looked packed. 'Busy tonight,' commented Sorrel. 'There must be hundreds of Chinese restaurants in Manchester and once there was only the Ping Hong.'

'Two Ping Hongs,' Monica corrected her. 'Where shall we go to eat? I just want to kick off my shoes and forget my diet and gorge myself on steaming sieves of dim sum.'

Sorrel wandered back to the desk. 'How about the Woo Sang?' It was at that moment that she noticed the envelope addressed to Myra Hindley at Cookham Wood Prison.

No other name in Manchester provokes stronger female emotions. One of the victims of the moors murderers had been picked up not three hundred yards from La Voluptua. 'Monica, why on earth are you writing to her?'

'You weren't meant to see that.'

'Well I'm sorry but I did.'

Monica looked embarrassed. 'It's just that I read an article that said she wanted to be a nun. And that a German convent was prepared to have her. I thought if they'd have her, they might have me too. I wondered if she'd send me the address.'

'You still want to be a nun? You'd need to want something pretty badly to be writing to Myra Hindley.'

Now it was Monica's turn to look out of the window. 'It's never really left me alone. If that's what's meant by a vocation then I've got one.'

'Surely you wouldn't have to go all the way to Germany?'

'Desperate situations call for desperate remedies. I had to get out of The Moss and now I've got to get away from here. I've never lost my conscience. I tell myself that the girls are better off working for me than they would be outside, pounding the pavements, on Bloom Street. The fact of the matter is, I'm providing them with the occasion of Sin.'

761

How many years was it since Sorrel had heard that expression? It must have been at the Old Fire-Iron. 'Are the clients here the same as in The Moss?'

'Clients are clients. The girls might just as well be Kleenex. That doesn't make the men any less. It just makes them men. Andrea's finishing one off now. He's decent, handsome, considerate enough to have had a shower before he came. All he'll want is a massage and a hand-job. And then he'll want out – fast. It means no more to them than having their noses blown. I'd just like half an hour to be able to explain it to their wives. Men have these needs that drive them silly and hustlers like taking cash off them. It's as simple as that.'

The pale blue door of the middle cubicle opened and a girl emerged wearing a short white nylon overall. She was followed by a man, already dressed for the street but still straightening his tie.

It was Barney Shapiro.

He took one horrified look at Sorrel and said, 'This has to be the worst moment of my life.'

'Or the best.' She was surprised at her own calm. 'Men have their needs. I've just been learning that.' Part of her threatened to get very angry (How could he?) but something was also telling her that, when you hand your problems over to a Power greater than yourself, you get back what you need; not what you want.

And she needed Barney Shapiro. Even here, in this sanitized version of a whorehouse, she loved him every bit as much as she had done in that illogical first moment on Magda Schiffer's doorstep.

Barney had always been such a closely guarded secret that Monica was at a loss to understand what was going on. 'Look,' she said, 'if you'd rather forget about the dim sum, Sorrel . . .'

'You don't know who this is, do you?' Sorrel pointed at Barney. 'This is the only man I've ever loved.'

'And I've always loved you.' The silver hair, next to the suntan, didn't look old – it looked sensational.

'Well bless you, my children,' laughed Monica. 'It may be bad for business but don't let me stand in your way. Come on, Mr Punter, the least you can do is ask the lady out to dinner.'

Barney looked as though he didn't know what to say next, but he managed: 'Have you eaten. . . ?'

'No.' Sorrel took his hand, led him to the door and began to walk down the staircase into Chinatown.

At the bottom of the stairs a man was resting two brimming plastic carrier bags on one of the outside steps. It looked as though he had been to one of the Chinese cash and carry establishments. The noises of the street were already floating up to meet Sorrel and Barney.

Barney cocked an ear. 'That sounds remarkably like Barry Manilow singing in Chinese.'

'That is Barry Manilow singing in Chinese. It's "Somewhere Down the Road".'

'Hello, Sorrel,' said the man with the plastic carriers. He seemed to have neglected to put in his bottom teeth. 'Itsh coming on rain. Town's dead.' There is always some negative soul waiting to tell you that Manchester is dead.

Could it be? Sorrel looked more closely. It was, it was Kenny Shorrocks. Barney put his arm around her protectively as she said, 'No, Kenny, you're wrong. The car parks are full and look how the lights are blazing through the drizzle. Town's more alive tonight than it's been for years.'

14

The people who nodded approvingly at Sorrel Starkey and her distinguished escort would have been much startled if they could have heard the words she was singing to him as they walked along the promenade:

'Dear old Blackpool, always just the same
Oh Granny's bum
Is wet with rum
She sat in it, for shame.

It was a song from her childhood, it came from the very best pantomime she ever saw. Six weeks had passed since their reunion at La Voluptua. In that time they had become something new. They had become good friends. All passion was far from spent but Sorrel had been Barney's mistress in the past and it would have been all too easy to fall into that role again. Resuming where they had left off would have been like taking part in a number-two tour of an old hit. And Sorrel wanted a brand-new production. For the moment, friendship was doing her very nicely, thank you.

In the past they had spent so long hidden in hotel bedrooms that she had forgotten what fun he could be when released to the sunlight. And if people thought they were too old to go out and play – tough! He was as fond as she was of joke presents and outings on a whim. That's what had brought them to Blackpool on this early winter's afternoon. But zzz . . . there was no denying that the old magnetism was still there. He must have been feeling it too because he suddenly tightened his hold on her arm and said, 'Why do we have to dash back? I could easily get you back to Manchester, in time for the hairdresser, in the morning.'

The Silver Cloud was in the corporation car park behind the tower. It was still much too early for dinner. They were supposed to be going to the new Wheeler's Restaurant in The Imperial.

'But Wheeler's is a London or a Brighton thing,' said Sorrel suddenly. 'It makes me feel disloyal to Robert's Oyster Bar. Tell you what, I'll settle for the posh place if you'll let me have a saucer of prawns, at Robert's, first.'

The oyster bar hadn't changed since her childhood. There were still trays of seafood on marble slabs and the man in the white coat carried your selection to tables between oak partitions with leaded lights.

Barney's attitude to prawns hadn't changed either: 'If you don't mind I'll just watch.'

'That's nearly as bad as people who say, "I'll just have one of your chips." '

'Yes, the least he could do is have a cup of tea,' said a croaking woman's voice. Lady Boswell was spearing winkles, from a saucer, with her own hatpin.

'Yes, still alive,' she said happily. 'Know how old I am? For years I've lied like a gas meter about me age but I'm ninety-four. Life's wonderful, isn't it?'

'Yes,' replied Sorrel, and she meant it. 'I suppose I've still got to keep following the lorry?'

Lady Boswell narrowed those old eyes which still glittered as darkly as her spatterings of jet. 'Follow it? I'd say your nose was right up against the tailboard. You lucky girl!'

It was nice to be thought of as a girl again, even if it was by somebody of ninety-four.

'My best years were my fifties,' observed Lady Boswell. 'Oh how the little baronet and I made hay!'

'Would you ever think of coming to stay with me, in Manchester, for a few days?' asked Sorrel impulsively. 'A postcard would always find me at the studios.' Did that sound like half an invitation? Pehaps she ought to give her the address.

Lady Boswell was ahead of her. 'Don't bother with the address. You'll soon be moving, in a big way. I'll find you, Sorrel. Will I have to go over water to do it? That's the question.'

'Isn't it settled?'

'Not yet.' Lady Boswell gave one of Barney's biceps an appreciative squeeze, treated Sorrel to a wicked wink, and sailed towards the door and the gathering dusk.

She left a thoughtful actress behind her. 'I've never believed a single word June Gee told me but that old woman's been telling me the truth since I was ten. Fancy a blow along the pier?'

The North Pier no longer charged a penny. It was free. The planks under their feet looked more haphazardly mended than they had done in Sorrel's childhood. But the gulls were still crying around the Moorish domes of the wind shelters. And the noises were the same – waves rolling and distant trams ploughing their way between Fleetwood and Starr's Gate. Out of season, Blackpool didn't smell of beer and vinegar. It smelled of the sea.

'See that building, Barney?' They were approaching the deserted shadowy bulk of the Pier Pavilion. 'The most magical thing in my life happened to me just here. Up those steps. That's where Mickey and I went through our very first stage door. I smelled greasepaint for the first time. It was the most alluring smell on earth and nobody uses it any more.'

'Sorrel, will you marry me?'

Somewhere out at sea a distant ship's siren sounded warningly.

Could she be hearing Barney properly? 'Lady Boswell says I might have to go over water.'

'We'll go anywhere you like.' His voice was as urgent as it had been at the very beginning. All those years and years ago.

'Will we, Barney? Oh please. Yes please.' Barney Shapiro had finally made the first move.

The very next morning Mickey turned up in Manchester. Sorrel was standing on King Street talking to Bryan Mosley from *Coronation Street* when he came thundering down the new tiled walkway. Mick was exploding with plans to change her life. His dream of starring Sorrel in an American television series had turned into a tangible reality. She suddenly found herself being told about scripts and asked to consider dates.

Barney might have said he would 'go anywhere' – but for how long? Mick was talking in terms of a twelve-month contract with options on a second and a third year. 'Have you signed next year's *Angel Dwellings* contract?' he asked anxiously.

'Yes.' Might this save her?

'Never mind. These things can be bought back. They do it all the time in LA.'

'I just thought you'd arrived for the birthday party,' she said helplessly. It was three years to the day since the jubilee ball and *Angel Dwellings* was having its twenty-eighth birthday.

Mick was not best pleased: 'You might show a bit more enthusiasm. I could have had my pick of a dozen American names, but I fought for you.'

He had always fought for her. Always. Where would she have been without that first audition piece which he'd written when they were twelve? When nobody else wanted Sorrel, Mick had handed her the freedom of Cornucopia Mews. He had made her famous. He had even bought her a new face. He was her friend. Weighing that in the scales, against the word 'lover', was like having two globes, rotating in different directions, inside her head.

Mickey had been watching her face. He knew every shade of expression so well that all he had to say was 'Tell me.'

'Barney's asked me to marry him.'

'And Barney's no music-carrier.'

His quick mind had grasped the situation in one fell swoop. Many husbands of famous wives are content to make hotel reservations and answer the telephone and act as chauffeur and be written off in the accountant's books as 'manager'. Barney Shapiro was rich in his own right but his wealth depended on his running a business from Manchester. There could be no changing that. It was something that Shapiros had been doing for a hundred years.

Mick was still watching her closely: 'I'm going to come right out into the open and say that I really need you for this part. I only wrote it because you said you were hungry for new opportunities.'

'I was.' Sorrel hadn't realized until now that she was shredding a paper handkerchief into bits.

767

'I need a decision by midnight – British time. But you're the one who's going to have to make it, Sorrel. Nobody's going to be able to say I stood in the way of your happiness. All I've done is kept my promise to you.'

It had not taken Sorrel all these years to realize that she had been gifted with two prime relationships in her life. There had been Barney to dream about and Mick who had made things happen. But two prime relationships in one life is a contradiction in terms. And now she was being called upon to settle the matter.

'Did you say that I've got until midnight?'

'Yup. Is Barney wearing a white tuxedo to the party, or a black one? It would be better if we matched. After all, you're going to have one of us on either arm.'

These days The Midland was known as the Holiday Inn Crowne Plaza Midland Manchester. The entrance steps were now wider and once Sorrel and her two escorts in black dinner jackets got inside, they found that the interior had been transformed beyond recognition.

'I'm always wary of Sorrel in red,' said Barney. 'You never know what she might do.' He had no idea of the significance of his words. They had left behind the *Angel Dwellings* party which was still limping to a close at the studios. It was a quarter to twelve and Sorrel had kept her quandary to herself.

'All this is much grander than Holiday Inns in the States.' Mick was looking round the pillared entrance hall where more steps led up to a raised, carpeted tier with tables set around a white grand piano.

'It's supposed to be much more like it was at the turn of the century. Evening, Bruno.' Barney shook hands with the head waiter. 'At least you're still here. May we have some coffee?'

'But of course.'

Sorrel was no nearer a decision than she had been since Mick had arrived and revealed his disruptive plans. Mickey was still looking around. 'I like it,' he said. 'It's all much more airy. The only things I don't like are those plastic vines, hanging from the ceiling. I'd like to let a little monkey loose in them.'

You would, thought Sorrel. You've already let a monkey loose in my mind. What do I *do*? Silently she prayed her standard prayer: Show me what to do and give me the strength to do it.

The pianist was tinkling 'These Foolish Things'. But sweet, foolish things reminded Sorrel of both men. She remembered Mick buying a Christmas tree in fogbound Strutton Ground and Barney walking her across the bridge into Salford and pointing out the Flat-Iron Market where the Shapiro empire had begun.

Suddenly the pianist was being rivalled by singing which could only be described as raucous. It was coming from the Trafford Room, once the most discreet restaurant in Manchester. Unaccompanied, a woman was bawling 'I Want the Last Waltz With You'. It sounded like a pub near the docks in the old days.

A waiter came across to Sorrel and said, 'I apologize, Miss Starkey. This isn't like us at all. It's a party booking.'

A group of women in cocktail dresses which looked straight from the pages of Grattan's catalogue emerged from the Trafford Room. They were also wearing paper hats and bearing plastic carriers labelled *Holiday Inn*. Three of them disappeared into the ladies' cloakroom but one, in peacock blue, had spotted Sorrel. Drink emboldened, she grabbed a friend and advanced upon the table.

'I told you it wasn't too posh for us, Noreen,' said the one in peacock. 'Look! Lettie Bly's here. We won't sit down, Lettie, but could I just say something? Time and again, when I've been fed up, I've said: "Well, never mind, I'll switch on the telly and see how Lettie's doing." The poor cow's not had a lot of luck, has she?'

The woman had such sympathetic eyes that Sorrel found herself realizing that there had been not two but three great influences in her life. The third great love had always been the audience.

'No, not a lot of luck,' repeated the woman's friend who was in bronze Lurex.

'But I have.' And Sorrel meant this. 'The real me has. So much . . . you can have no idea how much. This gentleman

769

wants to take me to Hollywood and this one wants to marry me.'

'Would you just be living in sin in Hollywood?' asked the one in bronze.

'No. I'd be in a serial.' She didn't dare look at Barney.

'But the other offer's real life?' The woman with kind eyes transferred her attention to Barney. 'Are you the one who wants to marry her? Stand up, let's have a look at you.'

Barney got to his feet. It had suddenly dawned upon Sorrel that the audience was taking it upon itself to make the decision for her.

'You are a Manchester lad, aren't you?'

'Oh yes. Fourth generation.'

'And will you be good to 'er?'

'I promise.'

The woman turned back to Sorrel: 'I can't see that there's any argument. Sorry, love' – she threw this at Mickey – 'Hollywood can't have her. We have to look after our own in this town. Well, congratulations! We won't stop.' And smiling happily they headed back towards the cloakrooms.

'I think I ought to get them some champagne.' Barney, equally full of smiles, was following them.

Sorrel turned to Mick: 'You're sure you don't mind?'

He spread his hands wide. 'Fly free, little heart.'

'I love you, Mick.'

'But you love Barney and Manchester more.' Though he sounded rueful the blue and green eyes were smiling.

'Mick, you're part of my Manchester. You always have been. You're part of my belonging. But I'm happy. I'm finally happy and I never thought it would be possible. Let somebody else have Hollywood.'

And anybody who loves Leicester or Leipzig or Antwerp or Pittsburgh Pennsylvania will understand why Sorrel Starkey was thinking that there is a great deal to be said for being contentedly provincial.